Praise

★"A must for romance readers."
—*Booklist*, starred review

★"An irresistible tribute to classic screwball-comedy romances that
captures the 'delicious whirling, twirling, buzzing' of falling in love."
—*Kirkus Reviews*, starred review

"A sexier, modern version of *You've Got Mail*
and *The Shop Around the Corner*, this will hit
rom-com fans right in the sweet spot."
—*BCCB*

"A strong addition to romance collections."
—*SLJ*

"Sympathetic characters and plenty of drama."
—*Publishers Weekly*

Praise for *Starry Eyes*

★"A sweet and surprisingly substantial friends-to-more romance."
—*Kirkus Reviews*, starred review

"Vivid plots and endearing characters make
this novel impossible to put down."
—*SLJ*

"A layered adventure–love story that's as much about the families we
have and the families we make ourselves as it is about romance."
—*Booklist*

Hate to Love you

Also by Jenn Bennett

Alex, Approximately

Starry Eyes

Serious Moonlight

The Lady Rogue

Chasing Lucky

Hate to Love you

Jenn Bennett

Includes *Alex, Approximately* and *Starry Eyes*

SIMON & SCHUSTER BFYR

NEW YORK   LONDON   TORONTO   SYDNEY   NEW DELHI

SIMON & SCHUSTER BFYR

An imprint of Simon & Schuster Children's Publishing Division
1230 Avenue of the Americas, New York, New York 10020

Alex, Approximately text © 2017 by Jenn Bennett
Starry Eyes text © 2018 by Jenn Bennett
Cover illustration © 2021 by Emmy Smith
Cover design by Laura Eckes © 2021 by Simon & Schuster, Inc.

SIMON & SCHUSTER BOOKS FOR YOUNG READERS
and related marks are trademarks of Simon & Schuster, Inc.
For information about special discounts for bulk purchases, please contact
Simon & Schuster Special Sales at 1-866-506-1949 or business@simonandschuster.com.
The Simon & Schuster Speakers Bureau can bring authors to your live event. For more information or to book an event, contact the Simon & Schuster Speakers Bureau at 1-866-248-3049 or visit our website at www.simonspeakers.com.
Interior design by Hilary Zarycky
The text for this book was set in Adobe Garamond Pro.
Manufactured in the United States of America
2 4 6 8 10 9 7 5 3 1
Library of Congress Control Number 2020937642
ISBN 9781534477391
ISBN 9781481478793 (*Alex Approximately* ebook)
ISBN 9781481478823 (*Starry Eyes* ebook)
These titles were previously published individually.

Contents

Alex,
Approximately

For the evaders, avoiders, dodgers, and side-steppers.
You probably have a good reason for hiding.
May you work through it and find your inner lion.

LUMIÈRE FILM FANATICS COMMUNITY
PRIVATE MESSAGES>ALEX>ARCHIVED

@alex: They just announced the summer schedule for free films on the beach to kick off the annual film festival. Guess which Hitchcock they're showing? North by Northwest!

@mink: Seriously?! Hate you. But I already saw NxNW on the big screen last year, so . . .

@alex: Doesn't count. Beach movies are cooler. It's like a drive-in without the car exhaust. And who doesn't want to watch a chase sequence across Mount Rushmore while you dip your toes in the sand? Here's an idea. Tell your dad you want to visit him in June and we can go see it together.

@mink: Not a beach girl, remember?

@alex: You've never been to a real one. East Coast beaches are trash beaches.

@mink: ALL beaches are trash beaches. *peeks at film festival schedule* Besides, if I WERE going to visit my dad, I'd rather come the final week of the festival and see all those Georges Méliès films they're showing . . . INDOORS. As in: sand free.

@alex: --------> THIS IS ME FREAKING OUT. (Are you serious?! Please be serious. We could actually meet in real life?)

@mink: I don't know.

@alex: If you're serious, then come and see North by Northwest with me. Outside on the beach, as nature intended.

@mink: Films shouldn't be seen outdoors, but okay. If I come, we'll meet at North by Northwest on the beach.

@alex: It's a date!

@mink: Whoa, hold your horses. I said *if* I fly out to California to visit my dad. I'm just dreaming. It will probably never happen. . . .

"I don't think I caught your name."
—Cary Grant, *North by Northwest* (1959)

I

He could be any one of these people.

After all, I don't know what Alex looks like. I don't even know his real name. I mean, we've been talking online for months now, so I know things that matter. He's smart and sweet and funny, and we've both just finished our junior year. We share the same obsession—old movies. We both like being alone.

If these were the only things we had in common, I wouldn't be freaking out right now. But Alex lives in the same town as my dad, and that makes things . . . complicated.

Because now that I'm descending a Central California airport escalator in Alex's general vicinity, watching strangers drift in the opposite direction, endless possibilities duke it out inside my head. Is Alex short? Tall? Does he chew too loud or have some irritating catchphrase? Does he pick his nose in public? Has he had his arms replaced with bionic tentacles? (Note to self: not a deal breaker.)

So, yeah. Meeting real-life Alex could be great, but it could also be one big awkward disappointment. Which is why I'm not really sure if I want to know anything more about him.

Look, I don't do confrontation well. Or ever, really. What I'm doing now, moving across the country one week after my seventeenth birthday to live with my dad, is not an act of bravery. It's a masterpiece of avoidance. My name is Bailey Rydell, and I'm a habitual evader.

When my mom traded my dad for Nate Catlin of Catlin Law LLC—I swear to all things holy, that's how he introduces himself—I didn't choose to live with her instead of Dad because of all the things she promised: new clothes, a car of my own, a trip to Europe. Heady stuff, sure, but none of it mattered. (Or even happened. Just saying.) I only stayed with her because I was embarrassed for my dad, and the thought of having to deal with him while he faced his new postdump life was too much for me to handle. Not because I don't care about him either. Just the opposite, actually.

But a lot changes in a year, and now that Mom and Nate are fighting constantly, it's time for me to exit the picture. That's the thing about being an evader. You have to be flexible and know when to bail before it all gets weird. Better for everyone, really. I'm a giver.

My plane landed half an hour ago, but I'm taking a circuitous route to what I hope is the backside of baggage claim, where my dad is supposed to pick me up. The key to avoiding uncomfortable situations is a preemptive strike: make sure you see them first. And before you accuse me of being a coward, think again. It's not easy being this screwed up. It takes planning and sharp reflexes. A devious mind. My mom says I'd make a great pickpocket, because I can disappear faster than you can say, *Where's my wallet?* The Artful Dodger, right here.

And right there is my father. Artful Dodger, senior. Like I said, it's been a year since I've seen him, and the dark-headed man standing under a slanted beam of early afternoon sunlight is different than I remember. In better shape, sure, but that's no surprise. I've cheered on his new gym-crafted body every week as he showed off his arms during our Sunday-night video calls. And the darker hair wasn't new either; God knows I've teased him about dyeing away the gray in an attempt to slice off the last few years of his forties.

But as I stealthily scope him out while hiding behind a sunny CALIFORNIA DREAMERS! sign, I realize that the one thing I didn't expect was for my dad to be so . . . happy.

Maybe this wouldn't be too painful, after all. Deep breath.

A grin splits his face when I duck out of my hiding spot.

"Mink," he says, calling me by my silly adolescent nickname.

I don't really mind, because he's the only one who calls me that in real life, and everyone else in baggage claim is too busy greeting their own familial strangers to pay any attention to us. Before I can avoid it, he reels me in and hugs me so hard my ribs crack.

We both tear up a little. I swallow the constriction in my throat and force myself to calm down.

"Jesus, Bailey." He looks me over shyly. "You're practically grown."

"You can introduce me as your sister if it makes you look younger in front of your geekazoid sci-fi friends," I joke in an attempt to diffuse the awkwardness, poking the robot on his *Forbidden Planet* T-shirt.

"Never. You're my greatest achievement."

Ugh. I'm embarrassed that I'm so easily wooed by this, and I can't think of a witty comeback. I end up sighing a couple of times.

His fingers tremble as he tucks bleached platinum-blond strands of my long Lana Turner pin-curl waves behind my ear. "I'm so glad you're here. You are staying, right? You didn't change your mind on the flight?"

"If you think I'm going to willingly walk back into that MMA fight they call a marriage, you don't know me at all."

He does a terrible job at hiding his giddy triumph, and I can't help but smile back. He hugs me again, but it's okay now. The worst part of our uncomfortable meet-and-greet is over.

"Let's collect your stuff. Everyone on your flight has already claimed theirs, so it shouldn't be too hard to find," he says, gesturing with a knowing dart of his eyes toward the luggage carousels, one brow cocked.

Oops. Should've known. Can't dodge a dodger.

Having grown up on the East Coast, I'd never been farther

west than a single school trip to Chicago, so it's strange to step into bright sunlight and look up at such a big, überblue sky. It seems flatter out here without all the dense mid-Atlantic treetops blocking out the skyline—so flat, I can see mountain foothills girding the entire Silicon Valley horizon. I'd flown into San Jose, the nearest airport and actual big city, so we have a forty-five-minute drive to my dad's new house on the coast. Not a hardship, especially when I see we'll be cruising in a glossy blue muscle car with the sunroof wide open.

My father is a CPA. He used to drive the most boring car in the world. California has changed that, I suppose. What else has changed?

"Is this your midlife-crisis car?" I ask when he opens the trunk to stow my luggage.

He chuckles. It totally is. "Get in," he says, checking the screen on his phone. "And please text your mother that you didn't die in a fiery plane crash so she'll stop bugging me."

"Aye, aye, Captain Pete."

"Goofball."

"Weirdo."

He nudges me with his shoulder, and I nudge back, and just like that, we're falling back into our old routine. Thank God. His new (old) car smells like the stuff that neat freaks spray on leather, and there's no accounting paperwork stuffed in the floorboards, so I'm getting the posh treatment. As he revs up the crazy-loud engine, I turn on my phone for the first time since I've landed.

Texts from Mom: four. I answer her in the most bare-bones way possible while we leave the airport parking garage. I'm finally coming down from the shock of what I've done—holy crap, I just moved across the country. I remind myself that it's not a big deal. After all, I already switched schools a few months ago, thanks to Nate LLC and Mom moving us from New Jersey to Washington, DC, which basically means I didn't have a notable friend investment in DC to leave behind. And I haven't really dated anyone since my dad left, so no boyfriend investment either. But when I check the nonemergency notifications on my phone, I see a reply on the film app from Alex and get nervous all over again about being in the same town.

@alex: Is it wrong to hate someone who used to be your best friend? Please talk me down from planning his funeral. Again.

I send a quick reply—

@mink: You should just leave town and make new friends. Less blood to clean up.

If I look past any reservations I may have, I can admit it's pretty thrilling to think that Alex has no idea I'm even here. Then again, he's never really known exactly where I've been. He thinks I still live in New Jersey, because I never bothered to change my profile online when we moved to DC.

When Alex first asked me to come out here and see *North by Northwest* with him, I wasn't sure what to think. It's not exactly the kind of movie you ask a girl out to see when you're trying to win her heart—not *most* girls, anyway. Considered one of Alfred Hitchcock's greatest films, it stars Cary Grant and Eva Marie Saint, and it's a thriller about mistaken identity. It starts in New York and ends up out West, as Cary Grant is pursued to Mount Rushmore in one of the most iconic scenes in movie history. But now every time I think about seeing it, I picture myself as the seductive Eva Marie Saint and Alex as Cary Grant, and we're falling madly in love, despite the fact that we barely know each other. And sure, I know that's a fantasy, and reality could be so much weirder, which is why I have a plan: secretly track down Alex before *North by Northwest* plays at the summer film festival.

I didn't say it was a good plan. Or an easy plan. But it's better than an awkward meet-up with someone who looks great on paper, but in real life, may crush my dreams. So I'm doing this the Artful Dodger way—from a safe distance, where neither of us can get hurt. I have a lot of experience with bad strangers. It's best this way, trust me.

"Is that him?" Dad asks.

I quickly pocket my phone. "Who?"

"What's-his-face. Your film-buff soul mate."

I've barely told Dad anything about Alex. I mean, he knows Alex lives in this area and even jokingly dangled this fact as bait to come out here when I finally decided I couldn't handle living with Mom and Nate anymore.

"He's contemplating murder," I tell Dad. "So I'll probably meet him in a dark alley tonight and jump into his unmarked van. That should be fine, right?"

An undercurrent of tension twitches between us, just for a second. He knows I'm only teasing, that I would never take that kind of risk, not after what happened to our family four years ago. But that's in the past, and Dad and I are all about the future now. Nothing but sunshine and palm trees ahead.

He snorts. "If he's got a van, don't expect to be able to track it down." Crap. Does he know I've entertained that idea? "Everyone's got vans where we're headed."

"Creepy molester vans?"

"More like hippie vans. You'll see. Coronado Cove is different."

And he shows me why after we turn off the interstate—sorry, the "freeway," as Dad informs me they're called out here. Once the location of a historical California mission, Coronado Cove is now a bustling tourist town between San Francisco and Big Sur. Twenty thousand residents, and twice as many tourists. They come for three things: the redwood forest, the private nude beach, and the surfing.

Oh, yes: I said redwood forest.

They come for one other thing, and I'd be seeing that up close and personal soon enough, which makes my stomach hurt to think about. So I don't. Not right now. Because the town is even prettier than it was in the photos Dad sent. Hilly, cypress-lined streets. Spanish-style stucco buildings with terra-cotta tile roofs. Smoky purple mountains in the distance. And then we hit Gold Avenue, a two-lane twisting road that hugs the curving coast, and I finally see it: the Pacific Ocean.

Alex was right. East Coast beaches are trash beaches. This . . . is stunning.

"It's so blue," I say, realizing how dumb I sound but unable to think of a better description of the bright aquamarine water breaking toward the sand. I can even smell it from the car. It's salty and clean, and unlike the beach back home, which has that iodine, boiled-metal stench, it doesn't make me want to roll up the window.

"I told you, didn't I? It's paradise out here," Dad says. "Everything is going to be better now. I promise, Mink."

I turn to him and smile, wanting to believe he might be right. And then his head whips toward the windshield and we screech to a stop.

My seat belt feels like a metal rod slapping across my chest as I jerk forward and brace my hands on the dash. Brief pain shoots through my mouth and I taste copper. The high-pitched squeal that comes out of me, I realize, is entirely too loud and dramatic; apart from my biting my own tongue, no one's hurt, not even the car.

"You okay?" Dad asks.

More embarrassed than anything else, I nod before turning my attention to the cause of our near wreck: two teen boys in the middle of the street. They both look like walking advertisements for coconut tanning oil—tousled sun-lightened hair, board shorts, and lean muscles. One dark, one light. But the towheaded one is mad as hell and pounds the hood of the car with his fists.

"Watch where you're going, dickwad," he shouts, pointing to a colorful hand-painted wooden sign of a line of surfers marching their boards through an Abbey Road–looking crosswalk. The top says: WELCOME TO CORONADO COVE. The bottom reads: BE KIND—GIVE SURFERS RIGHT-OF-WAY.

Umm, yeah, no. The sign is nowhere near official, and even if it were, there's no real crosswalk on the street and this white-haired shirtless dude doesn't have a board. But no way am I saying that, because (A) I just screamed like a 1950s housewife, and (B) I don't do confrontation. Especially not with a boy who looks like he's just inhaled a pipeful of something cooked up in a dirty trailer.

His brown-haired buddy has the decency to be wearing a shirt while jaywalking. On top of that, he's ridiculously good-looking (ten points) and trying to pull his jerky friend out of the road (twenty points). And as he does, I get a quick view of a nasty, jagged line of dark-pink scars that curves from the sleeve of his weathered T-shirt down to a bright red watch on his wrist, like someone had to Frankenstein his arm back together a long time ago; maybe this isn't his first time dragging his friend out of the road. He looks as embarrassed as I feel, sitting here with all these cars honking behind us, and while he wrestles his friend back, he holds up a hand to my dad and says, "Sorry, man."

Dad politely waves and waits until they're both clear before cautiously stepping on the gas again. *Go faster, for the love of slugs.* I press my sore tongue against the inside of my teeth, testing the spot where I bit it. And as the drugged-out blond dude continues to scream at us, the boy with the scarred arm stares at me, wind blowing his wild, sun-streaked curls to one side. For a second, I hold my breath and stare back at him, and then he slides out of my view.

Red and blue lights briefly flash in the oncoming lane. Great. Is this kind of thing considered an accident here? Apparently not, because the police car crawls past us. I turn around in my seat to see a female cop with dark purple shades stick her arm out the window and point a warning at the two boys.

"Surfers," Dad says under his breath like it's the filthiest swear-word in the world. And as the cop and the boys disappear behind us along the golden stretch of sand, I can't help but worry that Dad might have exaggerated about paradise.

LUMIÈRE FILM FANATICS COMMUNITY
PRIVATE MESSAGES>ALEX>ARCHIVED

@alex: Busy tonight?

@mink: Just homework.

@alex: Wanna do a watch-along of The Big Lebowski? You can stream it.

@mink: *blink* Who is this? Did some random frat boy take over your account?

@alex: It's a GOOD MOVIE. It's classic Coen Brothers, and you loved O Brother, Where Art Thou?. Come on . . . it'll be fun. Don't be a movie snob.

@mink: I'm not a movie snob. I'm a FILM snob.

@alex: And yet I still like you. . . . Don't leave me hanging here, all bored and lonely, while I'm waiting for you to get up the courage to beg your parents for plane tickets to fly out to California so that you can watch North by Northwest on the beach with a lovable fellow film geek. I'm giving you puppy eyes right now.

@mink: Gee, drop hints, much?

@alex: You noticed? *grin* Come on. Watch it with me. I have to work late tonight.

@mink: You watch movies at work?

@alex: When it's not busy. Believe me, I'm still doing a better job than my coworker, a.k.a. the human blunt. I don't think he's ever NOT been high at work.

@mink: Oh, you deviant Californians. *shakes head*

@alex: Do we have a date? You can do your homework while we watch. I'll even help. What other excuses do you have? Let me shoot them down now: you can wash your hair during the opening credits, we can hit play after you eat dinner, and if your boyfriend doesn't like the idea of you watching a movie with someone online, he's an idiot, and you should break up with him, pronto. Now, what do you say?

@mink: Well, you're in luck, if you pick another movie. My hair is clean, I usually eat dinner around eight, and I'm currently single. Not that it matters.

@alex: Huh. Me too. Not that it matters. . . .

2

I'd seen my dad's new digs during our video chats, but it was strange to experience in person. Tucked away on a quiet, shady street that bordered a redwood forest, it was more cabin than house, with a stone fireplace downstairs and two small bedrooms upstairs. It used to be a vacation rental, so luckily I had my own bathroom.

The coolest part about the house was the screened-in back porch, which not only had a hammock, but was also built around a redwood tree that grew in the middle of it, straight through the roof. However, it was what sat outside that porch in the driveway that jangled my nerves every time I looked at it: a bright turquoise, vintage Vespa scooter with a leopard-print seat.

Scooter.

Mine.

Me on a scooter.

Whaaa?

Its small engine and tiny whitewall tires could only get up to forty mph, but its 1960s bones had been fully restored.

"It's your getaway vehicle," Dad had said proudly when he brought me out back to show it to me the first time. "I knew you had to have something to get to work this summer. And you can drive yourself to school in the fall. You don't even need a special license."

"It's crazy," I'd told him. And gorgeous. But crazy. I worried I'd stand out.

"There are hundreds of these things in town," he argued. "It was either this or a van, but since you won't need to haul around surfboards, I thought this was better."

"It's very Artful Dodger," I admitted.

"You can pretend you're Audrey Hepburn in *Roman Holiday*."

God, he really knew how to sell me. I'd seen that movie a dozen times, and he knew it. "I do like the retro leopard-print seat."

And matching helmet. I therefore christened the scooter Baby, as a nod to one of my all-time favorite films, *Bringing Up Baby*—a 1930s screwball comedy starring Cary Grant and Katharine Hepburn as a mismatched pair who become entangled by a pet leopard, Baby. Once I'd decided on the name, I committed. No going back now. It was mine. Dad taught me how to use it—I rode it up and down his street a million times after dinner—and I would eventually find the nerve to ride it around town, come hell or high water or drugged-out jaywalking surfers.

Dad apologizes for having to work the next day, but I don't mind. I spend the day unpacking and driving my scooter around between jet-lagged naps on the porch hammock. I message Alex a few times, but keeping up the illusion of what I'm doing with my summer is a lot harder than I thought it would be. Maybe it will be easier once I've gotten my sea legs here.

After my day of rest and a night with Dad playing The Settlers of Catan, our favorite board game, I'm forced to put my new-found independence to the test. Finding a summer job was one of my misgivings about coming out here, but Dad pulled some strings. That sounded fine enough when I was back in DC. Now that I'm here, I'm sort of regretting that I agreed to it. Too late to back out, though. "The summer tourist season waits for no one," my father cheerfully tells me when I complain.

Dad wakes me up super early when he goes to work, but I accidentally fall back asleep. When I wake again, I'm running late, so I get dressed in a tizzy and rush out the door. One thing I didn't expect when I moved out here is all the morning coastal fog. It clings to the redwoods like a lacy gray blanket, keeping things cool until midmorning, when the sun burns it away. Sure, the fog has a certain quiet allure, but now that I have to navigate a scooter through my dad's wooded neighborhood, where it's occasionally hanging low and reaching through branches like fingers, it's not my favorite thing in the world.

Armed with a map and a knot in my stomach the size of Russia, I face the fog and drive Baby into town. Dad already showed me the way in his car, but I still repeat the directions in my head over and over at every stop sign. It isn't even nine a.m. yet, so most of the streets are clear until I get to the dreaded Gold Avenue. Where I'm going is only a few blocks down this curvy, traffic-clogged road, but I have to drive past the boardwalk (Ferris wheel, loud music, miniature golf), watch out for tourists crossing the road to get to the beach after blimping out at the Pancake Shack for breakfast—which smells a-m-a-z-i-n-g, by the way—and OH MY GOD, where did all these skaters come from?

Just when I'm about to die of some kind of stress-related brain strain, I see the cliffs rising up along the coast at the end of the boardwalk and a sign: THE CAVERN PALACE.

My summer job.

I slow Baby with a squeeze of the hand brakes and turn into the employee driveway. To the right is the main road that leads up the cliff to the guest parking lot, which is empty today. "The Cave," as Dad tells me the locals call it, is closed for training and some sort of outdoor fumigation, which I can smell from here, because it stinks to high heaven. Tomorrow is the official start of the summer tourist season, so today is orientation for new seasonal employees. This includes me.

Dad did some accounting work for the Cave, and he knows the general manager. That's how he got me the job. Otherwise, I doubt they would have been impressed with my limited résumé, which includes exactly one summer of babysitting and several months of after-school law paperwork filing in New Jersey.

But that's all in the past. Because even though I'm so nervous I could upchuck all over Baby's pretty 1960s speedometer right now, I'm actually sort of excited to work here. I like museums. A lot.

This is what I've learned about the Cave online: Vivian and Jay Davenport got rich during the first world war when they came down from San Francisco to purchase this property for a beach getaway and found thirteen million dollars in gold coins hidden inside a cave in the cliffs. The eccentric couple used their found fortune to build a hundred-room sprawling mansion on the beach, right over the entrance to the cave, and filled it with exotic antiques, curios, and oddities collected on trips around the world. They threw crazy booze-filled parties in the 1920s and '30s, inviting rich people from San Francisco to mingle with Hollywood starlets. In the early 1950s, everything ended in tragedy when Vivian shot and killed Jay before committing suicide. After the mansion sat vacant for twenty years, their kids decided they could put the house to better use by opening it up to the public as a tourist attraction.

Okay, so, yeah, the house is definitely kooky and weird, and half of the so-called collection isn't real, but there's supposedly some Golden Age Hollywood memorabilia housed inside. And, hey, working here has got to be way better than filing court documents.

A row of hedges hides the employee lot tucked behind one of the mansion's wings. I manage to park Baby in a space near another scooter without wrecking anything—go me!—and then pop the center stand and run a chain lock through the back tire to secure it. My helmet squeezes inside the bin under the locking seat; I'm good to go.

I didn't know what was considered an appropriate outfit for orientation, so I'm wearing a vintage 1950s sundress with a light cardigan over it. My Lana Turner pin curls seem to have survived the ride, and my makeup's still good. However, when I see a couple of other people walking in a side door wearing flip-flops and shorts, I feel completely overdressed. But it's too late now, so I follow them inside.

This looks to be a back hallway with offices and a break room. A bored woman sits behind a podium inside the door. The people I followed inside are nowhere to be seen, but another girl is stopped at the podium.

"Name?" the bored woman asks.

The girl is petite, about my age, with dark brown skin and cropped black hair. She's also overdressed like me, so I feel a little better. "Grace Achebe," she says in the tiniest, high-pitched voice I've ever heard in my life. She's got a strong English accent. Her tone is so soft, the woman behind the podium makes her repeat her name. Twice.

She finally gets checked off the list and handed a file folder of new-hire paperwork before being instructed to enter the break room. I get the same treatment when it's my turn. Looks to be twenty or more people filling out paperwork already. Since there aren't any empty tables, I sit at Grace's.

She whispers, "You haven't worked here before either?"

"No. I'm new," I say, and then add, "in town."

She glances at my file. "Oh. We're the same age. Brightsea or Oakdale? Or private?"

It takes me a second to realize what she means. "I'll start at Brightsea in the fall."

"Twins," she says with a big smile, pointing to the education line on her application. After another new hire passes by, she shares more information about this place. "They hire, like, twenty-five people every summer. I've heard it's boring but easy. Better than cleaning up pink cotton candy puke at the boardwalk."

Can't argue with that. I've already filled out the main application online, but they've given us a handbook and a bunch of other weird forms to sign. Confidentiality agreements. Random drug-testing permission. Pledges not to use the museum Wi-Fi to view weird porn. Warnings about stealing uniforms.

Grace is as befuddled as I am.

"Competing business?" she murmurs, looking at something we have to sign, promising not to take a similar job within sixty miles of Coronado Cove for three months after ending employment here. "What do they consider a similar job? Is this even legal?"

"Probably not," I whisper back, thinking of Nate LLC constantly spouting off legal advice to my mom, like she wasn't a lawyer herself.

"We-e-ell, this is not legally my signature," she says in her pretty English accent, making a vague, wavy scribble on the form as she waggles her brows at me. "And if they don't give me enough hours, I am heading straight to the nearest cave mansion within sixty miles."

I don't mean to laugh so loud, and everyone looks up, so I quickly quash the giggles and we both finish our paperwork. After we hand it in, we're both assigned a locker and given the ugliest vests I've ever seen in my life. They're the color of rotting jack-o'-lanterns. We don't have to wear them for orientation, but we do have to wear HELLO, MY NAME IS . . . stickers. And when everyone is done slapping them onto their chests, we're herded down the employee hall, through a steel door (with a sign reminding us to smile), and into the main lobby.

It's huge, and our footfalls bounce around the rock walls as we all crane our necks, looking around. The entrance to the cave is at the back of the lobby, and all the stalagmites and -tites are lit with orange lights, which only ups the creep factor. We're led across the expansive lobby past a circular information desk, a gift shop that looks like it was transported from 1890s London, and a sunken lounge area filled with couches that might have been stolen from the set of *The Brady Bunch* . . . all of which are the exact color of our ugly vests. I'm sensing a theme.

"Good morning, seasonal new hires," a middle-aged man says. He, too, is wearing a pumpkin vest with a tie that has the Cavern Palace art deco logo printed all over it. I wonder if that's mandated for the male employees, or if he bought it from the gift shop with his employee discount. "I'm Mr. Cavadini, the museum floor supervisor. Though all of you will be assigned team supervisors, those supervisors report to me. I'm the one who makes the schedules, and the person who approves your time cards. So you may think of me as the person you most want to impress for the next three months."

He says this with all the excitement of a funeral director and manages to frown the entire time he's speaking, but that might be because his dark blond hairline seems unnaturally low—like his forehead is half the size it should be.

"What a woeful twat," Grace says in her tiny voice near my shoulder.

Wow. Sweet little Grace has a filthy mouth. But she's not wrong. And as Mr. Cavadini begins lecturing us on the Cave's history and how it attracts half a million visitors every year, I find myself looking around the lobby and scoping out the places I could be assigned—information desk, guided tours, lost and found, gift shop . . . I wonder which position would allow me to deal with as few disgruntled guests as possible. On my application, I checked off the boxes for "behind-the-scenes" and "working alone" preferences.

Café tables sit around an open balcony on the second floor, and I'm seriously hoping I don't get stuck working in food service. Then again, if I worked in the café, I would get to stare at not only a life-size reproduction of a pirate ship suspended from the ceiling, but also a skeletal sea monster attacking said ship. File that in the "not genuine" part of the Davenports' collection of oddities.

Movement catches my eyes. On a set of floating slate-rock stairs that curve around the pirate ship, two museum security guards in generic black uniforms are descending. I squint, not believing my eyes. How small is this town, anyway? Because one of those guards is the dark-haired dude from yesterday who was pulling his drugged-up friend off the road. Yep, that's definitely him: the hot surfer boy with the Frankenstein scars on his arm.

My panic meter twitches.

"And now," Mr. Cavadini says, "you'll split up into two teams and tour the museum with a member of our security. This side, please follow our senior security officer, Jerry Pangborn, who has worked for Cavern Palace since it opened to the public forty years ago."

He points the left side of the group toward a frail wisp of an old man whose white hair sticks up like he just exploded a beaker of chemicals in a science lab. He's super friendly and sweet, and though he probably couldn't stop a ten-year-old ruffian from stealing a piece of candy out of the gift shop, he eagerly steers his team of recruits to the left side of the lobby, toward a large archway marked VIVIAN'S WING.

Mr. Cavadini motions the surfer boy forward toward our group. "And this is Porter Roth. He's worked with us for the last year or so. Some of you might have heard of his family," he says in a bone-dry, unimpressed voice that makes me think he doesn't think too highly of them. "His grandfather was surfing legend Bill 'Pennywise' Roth."

A little *o-oh* ripples through the crowd as Mr. Cavadini hushes us with one hand and grumpily tells us all to meet him back here in two hours for our scheduling assignments. One side of my brain is screaming, *Two hours?* And the other side is trying to remember if I've ever heard of this Pennywise Roth guy. Is he a real celebrity, or just some local who once got fifteen minutes of fame? Because the sign on that Pancake Shack down the road proclaims its almond pancakes to be world-famous, but come on.

Mr. Cavadini heads back to employee hall, leaving us alone with Porter, who takes his sweet time strolling around the group to look us over. He's got a stack of printouts that he's rolled up into a tube, which he whaps against his leg as he walks. And I didn't notice it yesterday, but he's got a little light brown facial scruff going on—the kind of scruff that pretends to be bad-boy and sexy and rebellious, but is too well groomed to be casual. Then he's got all these wild, loose curls of sun-streaked brown hair, which might be fine for Surfer Boy, but seem way too long and irreverent for Security Guard.

He's getting closer, and the evader in me is not happy about this situation. I try to be cool and hide behind Grace. But she's easily half a foot shorter than me—and I'm only five five—so I instead just find myself staring over her cropped hair directly into Porter's face.

He stops right in front of us and briefly holds the rolled-up papers to his eye like a telescope.

"Well, all right," he says with a lazy California drawl and grins slowly. "Guess I lucked out and got the good-looking group. Hello, Gracie."

"Hey, Porter," Grace answers with a coy smile.

Okay, so they know each other. I wonder if Porter's the person who told her this job was "boring but easy." I don't know why I even care. I guess I'm mostly concerned that he'll remember me from the car yesterday. Fingers crossed that he didn't hear that cowardly squeal I belted out.

"Who's ready for a private tour?" he asks.

No one answers.

"Don't everyone speak up at once." He peels one of the papers off his rolled-up tube—I see EMPLOYEE MAP at the top of the sheet—and hands it to me while glancing down at my legs. Is he checking me out? I'm not sure how I feel about that. Now I wish I'd worn pants.

When I try to accept the map, he hangs on to it, and I'm forced to snatch it out of his fingers. The corner rips off. *Juvenile, much?* I give him a dirty look, but he just smiles and leans closer. "Now, now," he says. "You aren't going to scream like you did yesterday, are you?"

LUMIÈRE FILM FANATICS COMMUNITY
PRIVATE MESSAGES>ALEX>ARCHIVED

@alex: Do you ever feel like a fraud?

@mink: What do you mean?

@alex: Like you're expected to act like one person at school, and another person in front of your family, and someone else around your friends. I get so tired of living up to other people's expectations, and sometimes I try to remember who the real me is, and I don't even know.

@mink: That happens to me every day. I don't deal with people very well.

@alex: You don't? That surprises me.

@mink: I'm not shy or anything. It's just that . . . okay, this is going to sound weird, but I don't like being put on the spot. Because if someone is talking to me, talk talk talk, it's all fine until they ask me my opinion, like "What do you think about chocolate chip cookies?" And I hate CCCs.

@alex: You do?

@mink: Not everyone likes them, you know. (I like sugar cookies, just in case you were wondering.) ANYWAY, if someone asks me, when I'm put on the spot, I blank out and try to read their face to see what they expect me to say, and I just say that. Which means I end up saying I like CCCs, when I really don't. And then I feel like a fraud, and I think, why did I just do that?

@alex: I DO THAT ALL THE TIME. But it's even worse, because after it's all over, I'm not even sure whether I like chocolate chip cookies or not.

@mink: Well, do you?

@alex: I love them. I'm a fan of all cookies except oatmeal.

@mink: See? That was easy. If you ever need to figure out who you really are, just ask me. I'll be your reality check. No pressure or expectations.

@alex: Deal. For you, I will be my 100 percent real, oatmeal-hating self.

3

Porter hands out the rest of his maps while the other group's voices fade away. We then obediently follow him to the opposite side of the lobby, through the arch marked JAY'S WING, where we trade in the crisp, too-cold lobby air for musty, too-warm mansion air.

I feel like this is the part of the orientation I should be enjoying, but I'm so rattled by Porter recognizing me that I'm not paying attention to my surroundings. I want to hang back and get away from him, but there's only like fifteen of us, and Grace merrily drags me by the arm to the front of the group. Now we're walking right behind him—so close, he probably thinks we're devotees of his ass, which is pretty nice, to be honest.

"There are forty-two rooms in Jay's Wing, a.k.a. the world's biggest man cave," Porter says as he stops in the middle of a drawing room filled with all things trains. Train signs. Train tracks. Victorian first-class passenger train seats with stuffed velvet cushions. At the back of the room, there's even an old-fashioned ticket booth from London that looks to have been converted into a bar.

"Our beloved insane millionaire loved hunting, gambling, railroads, booze, and pirates," Porter said. "The pirates, especially. But who doesn't, really?"

Okay, so the boy's got a certain charm about him. I'm not immune to charm. And while he's talking, I realize he's got a low, gravelly voice that sounds like it belongs to a video game voice-over actor—easygoing and cocky at the same time. God, I bet he's so full of himself.

Why is he giving us this tour anyway? I thought security guards were supposed to stand around, waiting to yell at punks for putting their grimy hands on paintings.

When we head into the next area, I find out why.

"This is the slot-machine room," he says, walking backward as he talks. The room is filled with a maze of counters, at which you can sit and play one of a hundred different antique tabletop slot machines. Looks like the rarer ones are behind ropes.

Porter stops. "You might be asking yourself at this point, *Are all the rooms named after what's in them?* And the answer to that is yes. The museum owners are not creative—unless it comes to stretching out the workforce, in which case they are extremely creative. Take my job, for instance. Why pay a customer service manager to handle guest disputes when you can just send in your security team? You'll quickly find that the irrepressible Mr. Cadaver . . . sorry, Mr. Cavadini"—he gets a few snickers for that one—"likes everyone to be able to do every job, just in case you have to fill in for someone else. So don't get comfortable, because you, too, could be giving the next wave of new hires a tour in a couple of weeks. Better memorize that map I gave you, pronto."

Ugh. Great. I don't like the sound of this. Maybe it's not too late to apply for that cotton-candy-vomit-cleaner-upper job Grace was talking about earlier.

Over the next half hour or so, Porter breezily snarks us through the rooms in this wing. Rooms filled with: fake mummies (Mummy Room), weird Victorian medical equipment (Medical Equipment Room), and walls of aquariums (Aquarium Room). There's even a collection of sideshow oddities housed inside a gigantic circus tent. It's major sensory overload up in this place, and it's all blurring together, because there's no rhyme or reason to the mansion's lay-out, and it's all twisty turns and secret staircases and hidden rooms behind fireplaces. If I were a museum guest and had several hours to waste, I'd be thrilled. Total eye candy everywhere. But knowing I was supposed to memorize all this? Headache city.

At the end of the first floor, the maze opens up to a gigantic, dark room with a double-high ceiling. The walls are all fake rock, and a night sky rigged with LED stars twinkles above stuffed buf-falos and mountain lions, a glowing fake campfire, and a bunch of teepees—which several members of the male half of our group decide to explore, like they're five-year-old boys. It smells like musty leather and fur, so I opt to wait by the fake campfire with Grace.

Unfortunately, Porter joins us. And before I can slip away, he points to my name-tag sticker. "Were your parents obsessed with the circus when you were born, or did they have a thing for Irish cream whiskey?"

"Probably about as much as your parents liked wine."

He squints at me. "I think you mean beer."

"Whatever." Maybe I can duck into the teepee with the others. I pretend to be looking at something across the room in hopes that he'll ignore me and move on, a low-level evasive tactic, but one that usually works.

Not this time. Porter just continues talking. "And yes, my parents did name me after beer. It was between that and Ale, so . . ."

Grace playfully pushes Porter's arm and chastises him in her tiny, British voice. "Shut up, they did not. Don't listen to him, Bailey. And don't let him start with the name thing. He called me Grace 'Achoo' for half of junior high . . . until I tripped his ass in gym class."

"That's when I knew you were harboring a secret love for me, Gracie, so I felt sorry for you and gave you a break." He ducks away from her swat and grins, and I kind of hate that grin, because it's a really nice boyish smile, and I'd rather it wouldn't be.

Grace, however, is immune to its power. She just rolls her eyes. Then she volunteers more info about me. "Bailey's new. She'll be going to Brightsea with us in the fall."

"Oh?" Porter says, lifting a brow in my direction. "Where are you from?"

For a moment, I genuinely don't know how to answer. I'm not even sure why, but my brain is hung up on his question. I can't tell if he's asking what neighborhood my dad lives in. Maybe I should just say DC, because that's where I've been living with Mom and Nate—or even New Jersey, where I was born and raised. When I don't answer immediately, he doesn't seem to know what to do with me. He just stares expectantly, waiting for an answer, and that makes me choke up even worse.

"Probably Manhattan," he finally says, looking me over. "Just going by the way you're dressed, like you're headed to a *Mad Men* cocktail party. If you're going to stand there and make me guess, that's my guess."

Was that a slight? How was I supposed to know that the orientation dress code was going to be shorts and flip-flops? No one told me! "Um, no. Washington, DC. And I guess you're supposed to be part of some local famous family or something?"

"My granddad. Got a statue in town and everything," he says. "It's tough being legendary."

"I'll bet," I mumble, unable to keep the edge out of my voice.

He squints at me and sort of chuckles, as if he's not sure how to take that remark. We glare at each other for several long seconds, and suddenly I'm extremely uncomfortable. I'm also regretting I said anything to him. None of this is me. At all. I don't argue with strangers. Why is this guy getting under my skin and making me say this stuff? It's like he's provoking me on purpose. Maybe he does this with everyone. Well, not me, buddy. Find someone else to pick on. I will evade the crap out of you.

He starts to ask me something else, but Grace interrupts—

thank God. "So, which job here is the best?" she asks Porter. "And how do I get it?"

Snorting, he crosses his arms over his chest, and his jagged scars shine in the fake campfire light. Maybe Grace will tell me where Porter got the scars; I'm definitely not asking him.

"The best job is mine, and you can't have it. The next best is café, because you're above the main floor. The worst is ticketing. Believe me, you do not want that shit."

"Why?" I ask, self-preservation trumping my desire to avoid interaction with him. Because if there's a position here I need to avoid, I want to know about it.

Porter flicks a glance at me and then watches the males in our group emerge from the big teepee, one by one, laughing at some joke we missed. "Pangborn says every summer they hire more seasonals than they can afford, because they know at least five of them will quit the first two weeks, and those are always the ones running the ticket booth."

"Seems like information desk would be worse," Grace says.

"It's not, believe me. I've worked them all. Even now, I spend half my day at ticketing, fixing problems that have nothing to do with security. It sucks, big-time. Hey, don't touch that," he calls out over my shoulder toward a guy who's sticking his finger in a buffalo's nose. Porter shakes his head and grumbles under his breath, "That one won't last a week."

Everyone is done exploring this room, so Porter leads us out of the Wild West and through the rest of the wing, taking a path that snakes back around to the lobby—which is empty, because we've beaten Pangborn's group. While we wait for them, Porter corrals us all next to a panel in the wall near the lost and found and flips it open. Inside is a small cubby where a black phone hangs.

"I know what you're all thinking," he says. "This might look like an antique, but it isn't a museum display—shocker! See, a long time ago, people used telephones with cords. And even though you might find a few rare examples of technological advances in this museum, like the 1990s security cameras, or the junked printers in the ticket booth, the museum phone system is not one of them."

He picks up the receiver and points to three buttons on the side. "You can make outgoing calls on these, but unless it's an emergency, you'll probably get fired. The only reason you should ever use this fine antique is for intercomming. This green button, marked 'SECURITY,' will allow you to call me if there is some emergency you can't handle alone. Like this—" He presses the button, and a little radio on his sleeve beeps. "See? It's magic. O-o-o."

Then he points to the red button. "This one marked 'ALL' pages the entiiiire museuuuum," he says like he's yodeling across a canyon. "The only reason you'd do that is if you work in information and are telling everyone the museum is closing or on fire. Don't use it."

"What does the yellow button do?" I ask. I mean, I guess it's stupid to think I can avoid talking to the guy about work stuff, right? He has information I need. Maybe if I act professional, he'll do the same.

He points at me. "Good question, Baileys Irish Cream. The yellow button is a lobby-only intercom—see? *L-O-B-B-Y*. And it's mainly used by the information desk to page lazy dumdums who've lost their kids or wives." He hits the button and an unpleasant sound crackles from unseen speakers. He holds out the receiver to me. "Go on, say something, superstar."

I shake my head. Not happening. I don't like the spotlight. Now I'm regretting that I asked about the yellow button.

He tries to coax me into taking it with that laid-back voice of his, but his eyes are 100 percent challenge, like this is some sort of contest, and he's trying to see who'll break first. "Come on. Don't get shy on me now, glamour girl."

Again with the catty nicknames? What is his problem? Well, he can forget it. Now it's a matter of principle. I cross my arms over my chest. "No."

"It's just a little-bitty intercom," he says, wiggling the receiver in front of me.

I shove his hand away. Okay, maybe I kind of slap it away. But I've just about had it with him. I'm genuinely irritated.

And I'm not the only one. The easy-breezy manner leeches out of his face, and I can tell he's kind of pissed at me now too. I don't really care. He's not my boss, and I'm not doing it.

His jaw flexes to one side for a moment. Then he leans closer and says in a calm, condescending voice, "You sure you're cut out for this? Because speaking on the intercom is part of your job description."

"I . . ." I can't finish my thought. I'm angry and embarrassed, and I'm freezing up all over again like I did when he asked me where I was from. Part of me wants to cut and run, and another part of me wants to slug Porter in the stomach. But all I can do is stand there like a dying fish with my lips flopping open and closed.

It takes him all of five seconds to lose patience with me. I see the moment his eyes flick to the waiting crowd behind us—the moment he realizes he's supposed to be talking to them, not me—and something close to embarrassment crosses his face. Or maybe I imagined it, because it's gone a heartbeat later.

He holds the phone up to his mouth. "Testing," he says, and it echoes around the cavernous lobby. "My name is Bailey, and I'm from DC, where apparently mismatched shoes are the latest trend."

A few people chuckle as I glance down at my feet. And to my horror, he's right. I'm wearing the same style flats: one black, one navy. I have three pairs in three different colors, and because they're small and comfortable, I packed a pair in my carry-on. I was in such a frenzy to iron my dress this morning, I threw them on without looking before I walked out the door. WHAT IS WRONG WITH ME?

And, to top it all off, I now realize that Porter was never checking out my legs—he'd been staring at my shoes the entire time.

My cheeks catch fire. I want to melt into a puddle and slide under the tacky orange carpet. I can't look at him now, much less come up with a witty response. My mind has flipped on the auto-pilot switch and blanked out, and all I'm aware of is the sound of my own pulse throbbing in my ears. I'm so numb, I can't even manage to feel anything more than the smallest drop of relief when Pangborn shows up and swaps groups with Porter so we can tour the other wing.

I swear, if I never see that boy again, it'll be too soon. And if life is the least bit fair, I'll be assigned a job that's light-years away from him. I'll do anything. Clean toilets. Take out trash. I'll even make announcements on that stupid-ass phone. As long as it means I'll have little to no contact with Porter freaking Roth, I'll do it with a smile. Because one of his job requirements seems to be Getting a Laugh at Bailey's Expense, and I would rather get on a plane and fly back home to Mom and Nate if that's how things are going to be around here.

I think about Alex, and how much better I'd feel if I could go home and tell him about all this. He would definitely sympathize. And I need someone to vent to, because, really, could this day get any worse?

When the tour is over, and we get our schedule assignments from Mr. Cavadini, I find out the answer to that is: yes, oh hell yes, it sure enough can.

I stare at my printed schedule in disbelief. I've been assigned to ticketing.

LUMIÈRE FILM FANATICS COMMUNITY
PRIVATE MESSAGES>ALEX>NEW!

@mink: I started my summer job today. It was terrible. I hate it more than Dick Van Dyke's fake accent in Mary Poppins.

@alex: WHOA. That's a lot of hate, gov'ner! Are you still working with your mom like last summer? Or am I not supposed to ask? Is this a Forbidden Zone topic? I'm mentally checking the list and don't see it on there.

@mink: Not my mom. (It's on the list, but I'll give you a break this time. The list IS kinda long.)

@alex: You can shorten it any time you'd like. Say the word and I'll give you my e-mail. Or even my *gasp* real name!

@mink: o.O

@alex: All right, all right. Tell me about your terrible, no-good, really bad day. Does your boss suck?

@mink: Eh. Too soon to tell. I got stuck with the crap assignment and one of my coworkers is a colossal dickbag. He's going to make my life miserable. I can already tell.

@alex: Make him miserable right back. You are Mink! Hear you roar!

@mink: *cough* *sputter* *broken meow*

@alex: Chin up. You'll best this loser. Boys are dumb.

@mink: So true. How was your day, BTW?

@alex: Not bad. Now that summer's started, I'm back to the full-time, two-job routine. Usually I get all the dimwit coworkers at my main job, but maybe they sent them your way. Besides, I'm still holding out hope that my groovy friend Mink might get up the nerve to come visit her dad this summer and come see North by Northwest at the film festival with me. How can you resist Hitchcock? (And you call yourself a film snob. Prove it!)

"Whatever happened to chivalry? Does it only exist in '80s movies?"
—Emma Stone, *Easy A* (2010)

4

The rest of my training is a blur. I'm not even sure how I manage to find my way back to my dad's house. All I know is by the time Pete Rydell walks in from work, I'm armed and ready with a memorized list of calm, collected reasons as to why I can't work at the Cave . . . which quickly degenerates into me flat-out begging him to please-please-please let me quit. But he's not having it. Not even when I promise to apply to Pancake Shack and bring us home free pancakes every day for life. "It's just a ticket booth, Mink," he says, flabbergasted that I could be so bent out of shape about taking money from strangers. And when I try to justify my bitter dislike of Porter, one of his eyebrows is lifted by so much rising suspicion, it could inflate a hot air balloon. "The boy we almost hit on the crosswalk?"

"I know, right?" He remembers the drugged-out friend. He sees the light now.

Only, he doesn't. Things are now being said about how much

trouble he went through to pull strings to get this job, and how bad it would look for me to quit so early, and how living out here isn't cheap, especially on a single parent's salary—one that isn't a lawyer's salary, like Mom's—and that he'd like me to help pay for the insurance on the Vespa and my cell phone bill.

"This is good for you," he says in a softer voice, squeezing my shoulders. He's still in his CPA long sleeves and tie, not in one of his geeky 1980s sci-fi T-shirts, so he looks like more of a responsible adult at the moment. And I don't ever remember him being this decisive and firm. It's weird, and I'm not sure how I feel about it. It's making me a little emotional. "I know you don't believe me now, but you will. Sometimes you have to endure painful things to realize that you're a whole lot stronger than you think."

Ugh. He's so earnest. I know he's talking about what he went through in the divorce, and that makes me uncomfortable. I blow out the long, deep sigh of a girl defeated and duck out of his kind fatherly grip in one smooth movement, instantly feeling relief.

Once I have time to think things over rationally, I understand where he's coming from . . . in theory. If the point of me sticking it out at the Cave is because I need to be bringing in my own paycheck and showing him that I can be responsible, I'll just have to tough it out somehow. Figure out a way to see as little of Porter Roth as possible.

I might be an evader, but I suppose I'm no quitter. It's just a summer job anyway, right? That's what I tell myself.

Besides, I have other things to think about.

The next morning, I break out a map of Coronado Cove the second Dad's car has rumbled out of earshot. Time to do a little detective work. The Cave didn't schedule me for my first real shift until tomorrow, so at least I have one day of respite before I'm forced to start serving my jail term. I'd already messaged Alex, but he doesn't answer right away. I'm wondering if that's because he's at the day job. During the school year, he only works the day job after school, and every once in a while on the weekends. But now that it's summer, he said he's working there pretty much every morning, and clocking in at another job later.

My stomach goes haywire just thinking about it.

This is what I know about Alex's day job: I know that it's a family business, and that he hates it. I know that the business is on the beach, because he's said that he can see the waves from the window. I also know that there's a counter, so obviously it's a retail business. A retail shop on the boardwalk. That narrows it to. . . I dunno, about several hundred stores? But two details that may help me pin him down are ones that seemed unimportant when he first mentioned them. First: He complains that the scent of cinnamon constantly makes him hungry because a churro cart is nearby. Second: He feeds a stray beach cat that suns itself outside the shop and answers to the name Sam-I-Am.

Not a lot, but it's a start.

After studying the map, I strap on my scooter helmet and head down Gold Avenue toward the northern end of the boardwalk—opposite the Cavern Palace, a mile or so away. Sunshine's burning through the morning fog, the air smells like pancakes and ocean. The beach is already bustling with people. Locals and tourists, freaks and geeks. They throng the boardwalk like ants on a picnic. The water's too nippy for swimming, but that doesn't stop people from lining the sand with blankets and towels. Everyone's ready to worship the sun.

I've always disliked the beach, but as I find a place to park near the north end of the boardwalk and slather my vitamin-D-deficient legs and arms with mega-super-sensitive sunblock created for babies, the frail, and the elderly, I'm feeling slightly less hateful at the horde of bouncy string bikinis and tropical-patterned board shorts jostling past me, laughing and singing as they file toward the sand. There's not a soul here that I need to impress. No one to worry about accidentally bumping into. Coming out west is my do-over. A clean slate.

That was one reason I wanted to move out here. It wasn't just missing my dad, or Mom and Nate LLC fighting, or even the prospect of meeting Alex. In a strange way, the reason I don't know much about Alex, and vice versa, was one of my main incentives for moving.

Mom's a divorce lawyer. (Oh, the irony.) Four years ago, when I was fourteen, Mom took a case that ended up giving the wife full custody of the couple's daughter, a girl about my age. Turned out the jilted husband had a leak in the ol' brain pipe. Greg Grumbacher, hell-bent for revenge against my mother, found our address online. This was back when my folks were still together. There was . . . an incident.

He was put in prison for a very long time.

Anyway. It's a relief to have an entire country between me and old Greg.

So that's why our family doesn't do "public" online. No real names. No photos. No alma maters or job locations. No breezy status updates with geotags or posts with time stamps like, *Oh my gawd, Stacey! I'm sitting at my fav tea shop on 9th, and there's a girl wearing the cutest dress!* Because that's how messed-up people track you down and do bad things to you and people you care about.

I try not to be paranoid and let it ruin my life. And not everybody who wants to track somebody down is a sicko. Take, for instance, what I'm doing now, looking for Alex. I'm no Greg Grumbacher. The difference is intent. The difference is that Greg wanted to hurt us, and all I want to do is make sure that Alex is an actual human being my age, preferably of the male persuasion, and not some creep who's trying to harvest my eyeballs for weird, evil laboratory experiments. That's not stalking, it's scoping. It's protection for both of us, really—me and Alex. If we're meant to be, and he's the person I imagine him to be, then things will all work out fine. He'll be wonderful, and by the end of the summer, we'll be crazy in love, watching *North by Northwest* at the film festival on the beach, and I'll have my hands all over him. Which is what I spend a lot of my free time imagining myself doing to his virtual body, the lucky boy.

However, if my scoping turns up some bad intel and this relationship looks like it might have more fizzle than pop? Then I'll just disappear into the shadows, and nobody gets hurt.

See? I'm looking out for the two of us.

Shoulders loose, I slip on a pair of dark sunglasses and fall in step behind a herd of beach bunnies, using them as a shield until we hit the boardwalk, where they head straight to the beach and I go left.

The boardwalk area is just under half a mile long. A center promenade spills out onto a wide pedestrian pier, which is anchored by a Ferris wheel at its base and capped by a wire that ferries couples in aerial chairlifts to the cliffs above. And all of that is enveloped in midway games, looping roller coasters, hotels, restaurants, and bars. It's half this: laid-back California vibe, skaters, sidewalk art, comic book shops, organic tea, seagulls. And half this: bad 1980s music blasting through tinny speakers, schlocky Tilt-A-Whirls, bells dinging, kids crying, cheap T-shirt shops, overflowing trash cans.

Whatever my feelings about what this place is, I suspect it isn't going to be easy to find Alex. Those suspicions only grow stronger when I veer away from the Midway area and hit a stretch of retail shops near the promenade (maybe here?) and realize the scent that's been driving me crazy since yesterday isn't the Pancake Shack, it's freshly fried dough. And that's because there's an official Coronado Cove boardwalk churro cart every twenty or thirty feet down the promenade. Churros are like long Mexican doughnut sticks that have been fried and dipped in cinnamon or, as the sign tells me, strawberry sugar. They smell like God's footprints. I've never had a real churro, but halfway down the promenade, I make a decision to give up on everything: finding Alex, finding another job, the meaning of life. Just give me that sweet fried dough.

I plunk down some cash and take my booty to a shady bench. It is everything I hoped for and more. Where have you been all my life? It makes me feel better about my failed morning. As I'm licking the cinnamon sugar from my fingertips, I spy a fat orange tabby cat sunning on the sidewalk near the bench.

No. Could it be?

I glance across the promenade. Looks to be a vintage clothing store, a surf shop—Penny Boards, which may or may not be named after Porter's stupid grandfather—a medical marijuana dispensary, and a café of some sort. The cat stretches. I pull down my shades. Our eyes meet. Am I looking at Alex's stray cat?

"Here, kitty," I call sweetly. "Sam-I-Am? That wouldn't be your name, would it? Sweet boy?"

His listless gaze doesn't register my voice. For a moment, I wonder if he just died, then he rolls to one side, turning a cool shoulder to me with snotty feline aplomb.

"Was that your lunch?" a tiny English voice says.

My pulse jumps. I jerk my head up to find a friendly, familiar face staring down at me. Grace from work. She's dressed in shorts and a white spaghetti-strap top that says NOPE in sparkly gold rhinestones.

"It was the most delicious thing I've ever eaten in my life," I tell her. When she squints at me, I explain, "I'm from New Jersey. We only have boring old funnel cakes at the beach."

"I thought you were from DC."

I wave a hand, dismissive. "It's a long story. I only lived in DC for a few months. That's where my mom and her husband are. My dad went to college in California, at Cal Poly, and moved back west a year ago. A couple of months ago, I decided to move out here with him, and, well . . . here I am."

"My dad's a lab technician. He's from Nigeria," she says. "I've never been, but he left Nigeria and met my mum in London. We moved here when I was ten . . . so seven years ago? To tell you the truth, except for flying back and forth to England for Christmas, I've only ever been out of the state once, and that was just to Nevada."

"Eh. You aren't missing much," I joke.

She studies me for a moment, adjusting her purse higher on her shoulder. "You know, you don't really have a New Jersey accent, but you do sort of sound like you're from the East Coast."

"Well, you don't have a California accent, but you do sort of sound like a British Tinker Bell."

She snorts a little laugh.

I smile. "Anyway, this was my first churro, but it won't be my last. I'm planning to quit the museum and become a churro cart owner. So if you don't see me at ticketing tomorrow, give Mr. Cavadini my regards."

"No way," she squeaks, looking genuinely panicked. "Don't leave me in ticketing alone. Promise me you'll show up. Porter said three people already quit. We're the only people scheduled tomorrow afternoon."

Suddenly, my churro isn't sitting so well inside my stomach. "You and Porter sure are buddy-buddy." I don't mean to sound so grumbly about this, but I can't help it.

She shrugs. "We've been mates for years. He's not so bad. He'll tease you relentlessly until you push back. He's just testing your limits. Besides, he's been through a lot, so I guess I give him some slack."

"Like what? His world-famous grandfather won too many surfing trophies? It sure must be a drag, seeing statues of your family members around town."

Grace stares at me for a moment. "You don't know about what happened?"

I stare back. Obviously, I don't. "What?"

"You don't know about their family?" She's incredulous.

Now I'm feeling pretty stupid for not bothering to look up Porter's family on the Internet when I got home last night. Truth is, I was so mad at him, I didn't care. Still don't, really. "Kinda not into sports," I say apologetically, but honestly, I'm not even sure if surfing is considered a sport or a hobby or an art. People get on boards and ride waves, but is it an Olympic thing, or what? I'm clueless.

"His father was a pro surfer too," she tells me, sounding like she truly cannot believe I don't know this already. "The grand-father died, and then his father . . . It was all pretty horrible. You haven't noticed Porter's scars?"

I start to tell her that I did but was too busy being humiliated in front of my coworkers, but Grace is now distracted. Someone's calling her from a store down the promenade.

"Gotta go," she interrupts in her tiny voice. "Just please be there tomorrow."

"I will," I promise. Don't really have any other choice.

"By the way," she says, turning around and pointing at the orange tabby with a sly smile on her face. "That cat isn't answering you because he is a she."

My heart sinks. Wrong cat.

Well, it's only the beginning of summer, and I'm a patient girl. If I have to eat my way through every churro cart on the boardwalk, come hell or sunstroke, I will find Alex before *North by Northwest*.

LUMIÈRE FILM FANATICS COMMUNITY
PRIVATE MESSAGES>ALEX>NEW!

@mink: Guess what I got in the mail today? A brand-new copy of The Philadelphia Story.

@alex: Nice! Love that movie. We should watch that together sometime if I can find a copy.

@mink: Definitely. It's one of my favorite Cary Grant/Katharine Hepburn films!

@alex: Well, in other good news, since I know you LOVE gangster movies so much [insert sarcasm here], I just sent you a ton of God-father screens with Alex-ified captions, changing things up for you.

@mink: I'm looking at them right now. You think you're pretty funny, don't you?

@alex: Only if you do.

@mink: You made orange juice go up my nose.

@alex: That's all I ever wanted, Mink.

@mink: Your dreams may be closer to reality than you can possibly imagine. . . .

"You won't find anything cheap around here!"
—Lana Turner, *The Postman Always Rings Twice* (1946)

5

My first real shift at the Cave begins the next day at noon, and when I see the jammed parking lot, I nearly turn the Vespa around and head back to Dad's house. But Grace spots me before I can. She's waiting at the employee door, waving her arms, and now there's nothing I can do but march off to my doom. We clock in, stow our stuff in our assigned lockers, and don our orange vests.

Shit just got real.

Mr. Cavadini and his pointy blond vampire hairline greet us in the break room, clipboard in hand. "You are . . . ?"

"Bailey Rydell," I supply. It's been one day; he's already forgotten.

"Grace Achebe."

"What's that?" he says, leaning closer to hear her.

The irritation in her eyes is supreme. "ACH-E-BE," she spells out.

"Yes, yes," he mumbles, like he knew it all along. He hands

us plastic name tags. The sticker printed with my first name is stuck on crooked. It feels like a bad omen. "All right, ladies. Your supervisor on duty is Carol. She's tied up with a problem in the café right now. The morning shift at ticketing is ending in three minutes, so we need to hurry. Are you ready to get out there and make some magic happen?"

Grace and I both stare at him.

"Terrific," he says with no feeling, and then urges us out the door and into the employee corridor. "First thing you usually do is go to security"—he points down the hall toward the opposite direction—"to count out a fresh cash drawer, like we showed you in training. But today there's no time. You'll just have to trust that the supervisor on duty didn't steal anything or foul up the drawer count, because it comes out of your paycheck if they did. . . ."

I freeze in place. Grace speaks first. "Wait, what's that?"

"Come on, now," Mr. Cavadini says, pushing me forward. "Two minutes. Shake a leg. Security will meet you at the ticketing booth to get you set up and answer any questions. If you last a week, we'll consider assigning you a key to the booth. Otherwise, you'll have to knock to get inside, because it locks automatically. Good luck and don't forget to smile."

And with that, he guides us into the lobby and promptly abandons us.

The museum was empty during orientation. It's not now. Hundreds of voices bounce around the rocky cavern walls as patrons shuffle through the massive space, heading into the two wings.

The café upstairs is packed. People are eating sandwiches on the slate stairs, talking on cell phones beneath the floating pirate ship. So. Many. People.

But the only person I really see is standing against the ticket booths.

Porter Roth. Beautiful body. Head full of wild curls. Cocky smile.

My archnemesis.

His eyes meet mine. Then his gaze drops to my feet. He's checking to see if my shoes match. Even though I know they do, I check them again, and then want to take them off and bean them at his big, fat head.

But he doesn't say a word about it. He only says, "Ladies," and nods when we approach. Maybe this won't be as bad as last time. Balancing two covered cash tills in one hand, he raps on the ticketing booth's rear door four quick times before turning toward us. "Ready for the thrill of hot cash in your hands?"

The door to the booth swings open. For what seems like forever, Grace and I stand waiting while Porter enters the booth, swapping out the cash drawers, and two wide-eyed new hires spill out of ticketing, wiping away sweat like they've just been inside the devil's own boudoir and seen unspeakable, depraved acts that have scarred them for life.

Now I'm getting really nervous.

Porter's pissed. He's saying something obscene into the radio doohickey on his sleeve, and for a second, I wonder if he's telling off Mr. Cavadini, but then a shock of white hair comes bounding through the lobby and the other security guard—Mr. Pangborn—appears. He looks frazzled. And way too tired to be doing this job. "Sorry, sorry," he says, completely breathless.

Porter heaves a long sigh and shakes his head, less angry now, more weary. "Just escort them back to cash-out and watch them count their tills until Carol gets down from the café." He turns back toward us and whistles, tugging a thumb toward the booth. "You two, inside."

"Balls," Grace mumbles. "I don't remember how to run the ticketing program!"

"You'll do it in your sleep, Gracie," he assures her. For a second, he almost seems nice, and not the same boy who humiliated me in front of the entire staff. A mirage, I tell myself.

The booth is small. Really small. The booth smells. Really bad. There are two swivel stools, a counter that holds the computer screen, and a shelf beneath, on which the tickets print from ancient printers. The rear door is centered behind us, and there's barely room for a third person—much less Porter—to stand behind us and give directions. In front of us, it's just Plexiglas covered in smudged fingerprints separating us from a line of people wrapped around stanchions. So many people. They are not happy about the delay.

The dude standing at my window is mouthing, *Four*, and he's holding up four fingers, saying something nasty about me being an idiot female. That churro cart is looking better and better.

"Green means on, red means off," Porter's voice says near my face, a little too close. An unwanted shiver chases down my arm where his wild hair brushes my shoulder. It smells briny, like ocean water; I wonder if he's been surfing today. I wonder why I care. His arm reaches around my body and taps the counter, startling me.

"Right, yes," I say.

Dumbly, I glance down at the two-way intercom controls, marked OUTSIDE (to hear the customers) and INSIDE (so they can hear me). Green. Red. Got it.

"You'll pretty much want to keep the outside mic on all the time, but if you want to hang on to your sanity, you'll only engage the inside microphone on a need-to basis. Finger on the trigger," he advises.

They told us that in training. It's coming back to me now. Grace is freaking the hell out, so Porter has shifted over to her area. The jerk in front of my window is pressing four impatient fingers against the glass. I can't hold on any longer. I hit both green buttons and smile.

"Welcome to the Cavern Palace. Four adult tickets?"

The computer does all the work. I take the man's credit card, the tickets print, Mr. Jerkface goes through the turnstile with his jerky family. Next. This one's cash. I fumble a little with the change, but it's not too bad.

And so on.

At some point, Porter slips out and we're on our own, but it's okay. We can handle it.

I remembered how cold the Cavern lobby was during orientation, so I wore another cardigan. Ten customers into the line, and I now realize why they nickname the ticket booth the Hotbox. No air-con inside. We're trapped in a box made of glass from the waist up, with the sun beaming down on our faces, lighting us up like we're orchids in a freaking greenhouse.

I strip off the cardigan through my vest's gaping sleeve holes, but every few minutes, I have to swivel around to let someone inside the door—Carol, the shift supervisor, the guy from the information booth telling us to retake a season pass photo because the customer "hates" it, sweet old Mr. Pangborn delivering change for all the big spenders who want to pay with hundred-dollar bills. Every time I swivel around to open the ticket booth door, (A) I bust my kneecaps on the metal till, and (B) a blast of freezing cave air races over my clammy skin.

Then the door shuts, and the Hotbox reheats all over again.

It's torture. Like, this is how the military must break enemy combatants when they want to get information out of them. Where are the Geneva Conventions when you need them?

It gets worse when we have to start juggling other things like pointing out where the restrooms are, and handling complaints about ticket prices going up every year. Is this museum scary? How come we don't give senior discounts to fifty-year-olds anymore? The wind just blew my ticket away; give me a replacement.

It's a circus. I'm barely exaggerating. No wonder people quit the first day.

Not us. Grace and I have this. We're champs, fist-bumping each other under the counter. I handle the job the best way I know how. Avoid eye contact. Play dumb. Shrug. Evade the hard questions. Point them toward the information desk or the gift shop.

If we don't sweat away all our bodily fluid, we'll make it.

A couple of hours into our shift, things slow down considerably—as in, no one in line.

"Did we scare them all away?" Grace asks, wiping sweat from the back of her neck.

"Is it over?" I say, peering over the intercom to see around the stanchions. "Can we go home now?"

"I'm asking someone to bring us water. They said we could. It's too hot. Screw this." Grace uses the phone to page Carol, and she says she'll send someone. We wait.

A couple of minutes later, I hear four quick raps on the door and open it to find Porter. It's the first time we've seen him since the beginning of our jail sentence. He hands us plastic bottles of water from the café and gives me that slow, lazy smile of his that's entirely too sexy for a boy our age, and that makes me nervous all over again.

"You've both got that sweet Hotbox sheen. Looks better on the two of you than the last pair. By the way, one of them is . . ." He swipes his thumb across his throat, indicating that the kid quit, and not that he actually offed himself. I hope.

"Another one?" Grace murmurs.

He leans back against the door, one foot propped up, scrolling through his phone. The propped-up foot puts his knee in my space, mere centimeters from mine. It's like he's purposely trying to crowd me. "This job weeds out the weak, Gracie. They should flash their photos over the teepees in the fake starry sky in Jay's Wing."

"What time is it?"

He consults a fat red watch on his wrist with a funny digital screen and tells us the time. When I stare too long, he catches me looking and explains, "Surf watch. Swell direction, wave height, water temperature. Completely waterproof, unlike this stupid phone, which I've had to replace twice already this year."

I was actually staring at his Frankenstein scars, thinking about how Grace had started to tell me something tragic about his family yesterday on the boardwalk, but I'm relieved he thought I was looking at the watch.

"How did you get to be security guard, anyway?" I ask, cracking open my bottled water.

He spares a moment's glance from the screen and winks at me. Actually winks. Who does that? "Eighteen opens up all sorts of doors. You can vote, legally engage in any and all imaginative sexual activities with the consenting person of your choice, and—best of all—you can work full-time as a security guard at the Cavern Palace."

"Only one of those things I want to do and don't need any law to give me permission," Grace says sweetly from the other side of the booth.

I don't look at him. If he's trying to make me uncomfortable with all of that "imaginative sexual activities" talk, he can give himself a pat on the back, because it's working. But he's not going to see me sweat. Except for the fact that I've been sweating for the last two hours in the Hotbox.

"Taran's gone overseas for one week and you're already turning to me to satisfy your womanly needs?" he says.

"You wish," she retorts.

"Every day. What about you, Rydell?"

"No thanks," I say.

He puffs out a breath, acting wounded. "You leave a boyfriend wailing for you back east?"

I grunt noncommittally. Grace's stool creaks. I can feel both of them looking in my direction, and when I don't reply, Porter says, "I know what will fix this. Quiz time."

Grace groans. "Oh, no."

"O-oh, yes."

I risk a glance at his face, and he's grinning to himself, scrolling madly on his phone. "A quiz is the best way to get to know yourself and others," he says, like he's reading a copy from a magazine.

"He's obsessed with stupid quizzes," Grace explains. "He inflicts them on everyone at school. *Cosmo* quizzes are the worst."

"I think you mean the best," he corrects. "Here's a good one. 'Why Don't You Have a Boyfriend, Girlfriend? Take this quiz to find out why a super girl like you is still sitting home alone on Saturday night instead of pairing up with the boy of your dreams.'"

"Nope," Grace says.

"I'll just take this back, then," Porter says, attempting to snatch the water from Grace's hand. They wrestle for a second, laughing, and when she shrieks, spilling cold water on her orange Cave vest, I almost get Porter's elbow in my face. He holds the water over her head, out of reach.

"All right, you win," Grace says. "Do your damn quiz, already. Better than just sitting here, I suppose."

Porter hands her water back, settles against the door, and reads from the quiz. "'Your older sister takes you to a campus party while you're visiting her at college. Do you: (A) dance with her and her friends; (B) skinny-dip in the backyard pool; (C) grab a hottie and go make out in an empty bedroom upstairs; (D) sit alone on the couch, people-watching?'"

I don't bother answering. A young couple comes to my window, so I flip on the mics long enough to greet them and sell two tickets. When I'm done, Grace has chosen answer A.

"What about you, Rydell?" Porter asks. "I'm thinking you're answer B—secret exhibitionist. If you don't quit today, who knows. I might just look up on the monitors tomorrow and find you stripping by the Cleopatra Pool in Vivian's Wing."

I snort. "Is that what you've been imagining back in the security booth?"

"All afternoon."

"You're an ass."

He holds my gaze. "Scratch that. I think you're actually answer

C. You'd grab a 'hottie'"—he makes one-handed air quotes—"and go make out in an empty bedroom. Am I right?"

I don't answer.

He's not dissuaded. "Next question." He swipes the screen of his phone, but he's not looking at it; he's staring at me. Trying to intimidate me. Trying to see who'll blink first. "Did you leave DC because (A) you couldn't find any hotties to make out with? Or (B) your East Coast boyfriend is an ankle buster and you'd heard about legendary West Coast D, so you had to find out for yourself if the rumors were true?" he says with a smirk.

"Idiot," Grace mumbles, shaking her head.

I may not understand some of his phrasing, but I get the gist. I feel myself blushing. But I manage to recover quickly and get a jab in. "Why are you so interested in my love life?"

"I'm not. Why are you evading the question? You do that a lot, by the way."

"Do what?"

"Evade questions."

"What business is that of yours?" I say, secretly irritated that he's figured me out. And who is he anyway, my therapist? Well, I've got news for him, I've been to two of the best therapists money can buy in New Jersey, once with my mom and once on my own, and neither one of those so-called experts was able to keep me in the chair for longer than two sessions. They said I bottled up my feelings, and I was uncommunicative, and that evasion was a "maladaptive coping mechanism" to avoid dealing with a stressor, and that it was an unhealthy way to avoid panic attacks.

Says the man who wanted to charge my parents more than a college education for his expert advice. I'm coping just fine, thankyouverymuch. If people like this will just leave me alone . . .

Porter scoffs. "Seeing how this is your first day on the job, and may very well be your last, considering the turnover rate for this position? And seeing how I have seniority over you? I'd say, yeah, it's pretty much my business."

"Are you threatening me?" I ask.

He clicks off his phone and raises a brow. "Huh?"

"That sounded like a threat," I say.

"Whoa, you need to chill. That was not . . ." He can't even say it. He's flustered now, tucking his hair behind his ear. "Grace . . ."

Grace holds up a hand. "Leave me out of this mess. I have no idea what I'm even witnessing here. Both of you have lost the plot."

He makes a soft growling noise and turns back to me. "Look, I was just giving you a hard time—lighten up. But the fact is, I've been working here forever. You've been working here a few hours."

"But don't you already have me pegged? You know all about me, Mr. Famous Surfer Boy?"

He mockingly strokes his chin in thought. "Hmm . . . well, Little Miss Vogue," he says in that low, gravelly voice of his. The one I thought was all sexy and charming when he was giving us the tour. "Let me hazard a guess. You're some stuck-up East Coast sophisticate whose daddy got her this job where she's forced to have normal conversations with surf trash like me." He crosses his arms and smiles defiantly at me. "How'd I do?"

My mouth falls open. I'm so stunned, I feel as though I've had the wind knocked out of my chest. I try to untangle his words, but there's just so much there. If he's really just giving me a hard time, then why do I sense . . . so much bitterness?

How did he know my dad helped get me this job? Did someone in the office tell him? I mean, it's not like I'm some spoiled, incompetent rich kid with zero work experience and mega connections. My dad's just a CPA! But I'm not going to bother explaining that or anything else. Because right now, I'm halfway convinced a hole in my skull has blown right off and my brains are flowing out like molten lava. I think I might well and truly hate Porter Roth.

"You know nothing about me or my family. And you're a goddamn dickbag, you know that?" I say, so enraged that I don't even care that a family of four is walking up to my window. I should have. And I should have noticed that I left the green switch turned on from the last pair of tickets I sold. But the family's wide-eyed faces clue me in now.

They've heard every nasty word.

For one terrible moment, the booth spins around me. I apologize profusely, but the parents aren't happy. At all. Why should they be? Oh God, is the wife wearing a crucifix pendant? What if these people are fundamentalists? Are these kids homeschooled?

Did I just ruin them for life? Jesus fu—I mean, fiddlesticks. Are they going to ask to speak to Mr. Cavadini? Am I going to be fired? On my first day? What is my dad going to say?

If I was hot before, I'm not now. Icy dread sends an army of goose bumps over my skin. I point the scarred family to Grace's window and bolt out of my stool, shoving past Porter as I race out of the booth.

I don't even know where I'm going. I end up in the break room and then outside in the employee parking lot. For a second, I consider driving away on Baby, until I remember that I don't even have my purse; it's back in my locker.

I sit on the sidewalk. Cool down, get myself together. I have a thirty-minute break, after all, don't I? Thirty whole minutes to wallow in embarrassment over saying what I said in front of that family . . . thirty minutes to wonder how in the world I allowed Porter to provoke me into yet another argument. Thirty minutes to freak out over being fired on my first day. Me! The Artful Dodger. How did this happen?

This is all Porter's fault. He provoked me. Something about him just brings out the worst in me and makes me want to . . . lock horns. He thinks I'm a snob? He's not the first. Just because I'm quiet doesn't mean I'm aloof. Maybe I just want to be alone. Maybe I'm not good at conversation. We all can't be cool and gregarious and *Hey, bro, what up?* like he apparently is. Some of us aren't wired for that. That doesn't make me snotty. And why does he keep talking about the way I dress, for the love of God? I'm more casual today than I was on orientation. So sue me if I have style. I'm not changing myself to please him.

I'm not sure how much time passes, but I eventually head back into the break room. A few employees are milling about. I wait a few minutes, but no one comes to get me. I expect to be called into Mr. Cavadini's office, or at least for the shift supervisor to want to speak to me. When no one comes, I don't know what to do. I've still got several hours left on my shift, so I head back to the lobby, scanning for signs of an inquisition on the march. I bump into someone. I look up and see Mr. Cavadini, clipboard smashed against his chest, and my pulse triples.

"So sorry," I say, apologizing for what must be a record-breaking number of times in the last half hour. This is it. I'm done for. He's come to ax me.

"Please watch where you're going, Miss . . ." He pauses while his eyes dart toward my name tag. "Bailey."

"I . . ." Can't apologize again. I just can't. "Yes, sir."

"How's ticketing working out for you? Are you on a break?" His nose wrinkles. "You aren't quitting, are you?"

"No, sir."

He relaxes. Straightens his Cavern Palace tie. "Terrific. Back to your post," he says absently, focus returned to the clipboard as he shuffles away. "Don't forget to smile."

Like I could do that right now. I head to the ticketing booth in a daze, still unsure what I'll find there. I take a deep breath and knock on the door. It swings open. Porter is gone. A small line is forming on the other side of the glass, and Grace is handling it alone. Her shoulders relax when she sees me. She quickly switches off her mic.

"Hey," she whispers. "Are you okay?"

"Yeah. I'm not going to be fired?"

She stares at me like I've gone nuts then shakes her head. "Porter just apologized and let them in free of charge. People will forgive anything if you give them stuff for free. Don't quit! It's all good. And I need your help now, yeah?"

"Okay."

I close the door behind me and sit on my stool, waving the next person in line over to my window. I'm not sure how I feel. Relieved? Wiped out? Still humiliated and angry at Porter? I don't even know anymore.

Before I click on my mic, I look down and see a fresh bottle of water and three cookies sitting on a printed Cavern Palace napkin. One chocolate chip, one sugar, one oatmeal. A note in scraggly, boyish handwriting is inked on the napkin's corner, along with a drawing of a sad face. It says: *Sorry.*

LUMIÈRE FILM FANATICS COMMUNITY
PRIVATE MESSAGES>ALEX>NEW!

@alex: I need cheering up.

@mink: Me too. Want to watch Gold Diggers of 1933?

@alex: Blues Brothers?

@mink: Dr. Strangelove?

@alex: Young Frankenstein?

@mink: Young Frankenstein.

@alex: You're the best.

@mink: You're not so bad yourself. Tell me when you're ready to hit play.

"Sometimes you're better off not knowing."
—Jack Nicholson, *Chinatown* (1974)

6

I spend the next morning on the boardwalk. It's going much the same as my first morning on the boardwalk, which is to say that it's a bust. Despite zero signs of Alex, I've run into that stupid orange tabby again hanging around my favorite churro cart. I've now dubbed her Señor Don Gato (from my dad's and my favorite children's song, "Meow-meow-meow"). After all, she fooled me into thinking she was a "he" the first time around.

After pigging out and feeding churro crumbs to some bossy seagulls, I still have some time before I have to head over to the Cave for my afternoon shift. I'm not looking forward to facing Porter again. We didn't see each other after the cookies. Yeah, that was a nice attempt at making up for his dickery, but whatever. Maybe don't say anything you need to atone for in the first place.

Ugh. Just thinking about him makes me want to kick something. It also reminds me that I wanted to find a scarf to tie up my hair, so that it doesn't stick to the back of my neck when the sweating starts in the Hotbox. I throw away my crumpled churro paper in the trash can, say good-bye to sleepy Señor Don Gato, and head to a shop I spied during my previous Alex sleuthing—Déjà Vu. It's a small vintage clothing store with old mannequins in the window that have been pieced together from several different mannequin bodies—male, female, brown, pink, tall, small. When I go inside, a small bell over the door dings, a sound that's barely audible over the congo drums of the 1950s exotica music thumping over the speakers. The shop is dark, and it smells of a mix of musty old clothes and cheap detergent. Everything is jammed in tight, a browser's dream. There's only one other shopper in the store, and a bored college-aged girl with purple dreadlocks is running the register in the back.

I spot a rotating rack of old scarves near the counter. Bingo. Some of them smell funky, and a few are way too psychedelic for my taste, but there're dozens to choose from. Halfway through the rack, I find a gray-and-black striped one that won't clash too badly with my pumpkin vest at work. I pay the girl at the register. When she's ringing me up, the bell over the door rings. I glance over my shoulder to see two boys walking through the store. One is a burly Latino guy in a sleeveless T-shirt. The other is lanky and white blond, wearing shorts and no shirt at all. He walks with a limp, as if he's got an injured leg.

Crap. I know him. It's Porter's friend. The other guy from the crosswalk—the drugged-up one who slammed his fists on my dad's car. They both approach us.

"What up, *mamacita*?" he says in a lazy, raspy voice to the girl at the register as he sidles up to the counter next to me while she's getting my change out of the register. I glance up at his face. He's got high cheekbones and deep hollows beneath them, pock-marked by acne scars. His white-blond hair is a mess. Despite this, he might be more classically handsome than Porter. Almost model pretty. But he has a scarier vibe. Something's off-kilter.

"I told you not to bother me at work, Davy."

"Yeah, well, it's an emergency. I'm driving down to La Salva this afternoon. Need you to help a brother out."

"Not now."

He puts his hands on the counter and leans closer, blocking my view of their faces. I can still see her purple dreads draped over one bare shoulder. "Please," he begs.

"I thought you were chipping," she says in a hushed voice.

"I am, but you know how it goes. I just need a little." His soft tone matches hers, but I can still hear every word they're saying. I mean, hello. This conversation isn't private. Do they know that? "It's just for today."

"That's what you said last week," she argues.

"Julie, come on." He runs a hand down her arm, stroking a dreadlock with the tips of his fingers. "Julie, Julie, Julie."

She sighs. "I'll make a call and text you. Might be a couple of hours."

Satisfied, he turns back around and seems to notice me for the first time. "Hi there."

I don't reply, but I can feel him looking me over while I accept my change. I quickly shove it into my wallet, and then grab the bag with my scarf and head down the narrow aisle toward the door. I just want to get out of here, like, yesterday.

But I'm not fast enough. Footfalls dog my heels.

"Whatcha buyin'?" I feel a tug on my bag and turn around to see Davy pulling the scarf out. "Are you a cowgirl or a gang-banger?"

I snatch the scarf out of his hand. "Neither."

His companion snickers behind him.

"Whoa, now. Just curious," Davy says. "Haven't seen you around. What's your name?"

"I don't think so."

"O-oh, burn," the burly guy murmurs.

"Come on, cowgirl," Davy says. "Don't be that way."

I can't get through the door fast enough. Too fast. For the second time in twenty-four hours, I slam straight into another human being. The real Artful Dodger would be so disappointed in my slipshod getaway skills. My cheek smacks against a breast-bone made of steel. I jerk back, overcorrecting, and nearly lose my balance. Hands grip my forearms.

I'm staring at a Quiksilver Surfboards logo. I crack my jaw and raise my line of sight. Now I'm staring at the angry face of Porter Roth.

"For the love of rocks," I mumble.

The hard lines around his eyes soften when he sees me. Just

slightly. Then he looks above my head and gets pissed again. "What the hell do you think you're doing here?" He's not talking to me. That's when I realize he's not angry at me either; he's angry at the person standing behind me.

"Who are you, my mom?" Davy's raspy voice answers. "Relax, man. Ray and I were just grabbing something to eat then heading to Capo's place."

Porter's hands are still gripping my arms. I can't tell if he's holding me up or trying to keep me away from Davy. But standing so close, he smells strongly of coconut oil and wax—which smells pretty freaking good, frankly. And while I'm busy being intoxicated, he's still drilling Davy. "You mean to tell me that I didn't just see you walking out of Déjà Vu?"

I turn my head to see Davy backpedaling. "Julie asked us to come inside. It was nothing. We were just chatting about Capo's new dog. Get your panties unbunched."

Umm, he's lying. But there's enough testosterone flying through the air to start a war, no way am I tattling on Davy. And what do I care? Not my business. I just want to get out of here and go to work. And why is Porter still holding on to me? He seems to finally notice this too, and at the same time I shake him loose, he lets go of me and holds his hands back like I'm radioactive.

"And what are you doing here?" he asks me.

"Buying a scarf," I say, moving away from him. Why is he always in my personal space?

"You two know each other?" Davy asks, absently rubbing his

right leg. Looks like that's the injured one—the cause of the limp.

"We work together." Porter eyes Davy, and then my bag, like he doesn't believe either one of us. I'm insulted to be lumped in with this loser.

"Small world," Davy says, grinning. "You gonna tell me your name now, cowgirl?"

"Seems to me you're going to call me whatever you want, so what's the point?"

"Damn, girl." He hikes up his shorts. "Is she this mean to you at work?" he asks Porter.

Porter slides a glance down at me. I dare him with my eyes to say something smart. Go on, buddy. Show off. Tell him how you riled me up, acting like a pig, called me a snob, and I almost got myself fired. Make yourself look tough in front of your dirtbag friend.

But all he says is, "She's cool."

Huh.

Davy gives me another slow once-over and then snaps his fingers. "You should come to a bonfire. Saturday night at sunset, the Bone Garden."

I have no idea where that is, nor do I really care. Especially not after that dubious exchange I heard inside the shop.

Porter snorts. "Don't think I don't know that's where you first hooked up with Chloe."

"So?" Davy challenges. "Chloe's in LA now. Why you gotta bring up the past?"

"Why are you inviting her to the bonfire?" Porter jerks his thumb toward me.

Davy shrugs as his friend Ray urges him down the boardwalk, away from the vintage clothing shop. "It's a free country."

I'm not sure what that was all about, but I'm feeling pretty awkward being left alone with Porter. "I gotta get to work."

Midday sun lights up golden streaks on top of Porter's dark curls, and when he turns his head toward the ocean, the scruff on his face almost looks red. "Yeah, me too."

Crap. We're both working together again today? I forgot to check the schedule in my rush to get out of there after everything that happened yesterday. I'm not sure how much more of this strained togetherness I can handle. But he's looking at me sort of funny, scratching the back of his neck, like he wants to say something else. And now I remember the cookies he left me, and I'm wondering if he's remembering them too. Sure, as far as gestures go, it was okay. But for all I know, he could've stolen them from the café. I should have just thrown them in the trash, but I gave the chocolate chip one to Grace and ate the others.

Feeling uncomfortable, I mumble a good-bye and turn to leave. That chick from the shop, Julie, is standing outside, both arms and purple dreadlocks crossed over her chest, warily watching us. I avoid eye contact and keep walking.

"See you later, cowgirl," Davy calls in the distance somewhere behind me.

Let's hope not. As I pass the churro cart, I notice Porter heading in the same general direction, but his muscular legs carry him faster. Someone whistles, flagging him down. It's a middle-aged man, maybe my dad's age, with wavy, gray-brown hair, closely cropped. He's dressed in board shorts and a sleeveless T-shirt and looks like he could have been handsome when he was younger, but he's had some hard knocks. One of his arms is covered with faded tattoos; the other arm is missing—as in, completely gone.

I'm surprised to recognize Porter's eyes in the man's when I pass, then I glance at the puckering pink scars where the arm once was. Porter catches me staring. I quickly look away and keep going, face flaming.

I think this is probably Porter's dad and the "horrible" thing that Grace was talking about.

What in the world happened to that family?

LUMIÈRE FILM FANATICS COMMUNITY
PRIVATE MESSAGES>ALEX>ARCHIVED

@mink: What do you want to do after high school?

@alex: You mean, with my life?

@mink: I mean college. When I was younger, I used to think I wanted to go to film school. Be a director. But now I don't think I'd be so good at being in charge. I don't want that kind of pressure. Now I think I'd rather be behind the scenes, cataloging something.

@alex: Professional film hobbyist?

@mink: *blink* Is that a real job? Hopefully, it pays huge sums of cash.

@alex: Right there with you. My dad expects me to take over the family business, and I don't want to. Don't get me wrong: I like the family business. I enjoy it as a hobby. But I don't want the pressure of doing it full-time for money. What if I want to do other things, you know?

@mink: I hear ya. And I guess we have to start applying for colleges in the fall. Sort of scary. Too many schools. West Coast? East Coast? I don't know.

@alex: Enjoy your multitude of choices. Meanwhile, I'll be stuck at the local community college, working two jobs. My future is already mapped out for me.

@mink: That can't be true.

@alex: Some of us aren't so lucky, Mink.

7

My dad says the second day of something is always better than the first because you know what to expect, and he's right. The Hotbox is slightly more tolerable today. I sacrifice my long waves for an updo and tie the scarf pinup-style, which keeps the sweat from rolling down the back of my neck. Grace has taken preventative measures too, bringing in a battery-powered oscillating fan from home that she's mounted between our stations. Our biggest obstacle is juggling bathroom breaks, because we're drinking more water than horses after the Kentucky Derby.

Halfway through my shift, I get my thirty-minute break. Shucking my orange vest, I head upstairs to the café, where I find a lull in the line. The sugar cookie Porter gave me yesterday was pretty scrumptious, so I buy two and find an empty table in a private alcove under the pirate ship. I pull out my phone and look up what's been hounding me since I clocked in today.

Bill "Pennywise" Roth was a professional surfer who won a bunch of World Surf League championship titles and Triple Crowns in the 1980s. According to his online biography, he's continually ranked as one of the top surfers of all time. It looks like he died eight years ago. There's a photo of a life-size memorial statue out by the surfer's crosswalk, taken at sunset, with a bunch of flowers and surfboards propped up against it.

I start to read about how he grew up in a poor Jewish family and started surfing at the age of six, and how he fostered this entire multigenerational family of professional surfers: his son, Xander Roth, and his grandchildren—

Hold on. Porter has a younger sister, Lana, sixteen, and she's a state and nationally ranked surfer who'll be competing professionally for the first time this fall and predicted to join a yearlong world tour starting next January. But Porter won't? And what happened to his dad?

A shadow falls over my phone. I hit the power button, but not fast enough.

"Reading up on me?"

I grimace, squeezing my eyes shut for a moment. How did he find me up here? "Are you stalking me on the security cameras?"

"Every move," Porter says. Metal legs squeak against the slate floor as he spins another chair around backward and straddles it, legs spread, like he's riding a horse. He crosses his arms on the chair's back. "If you wanted to know something about my family, all you had to do was ask."

"I'm good, thanks." I start to gather up my stuff, but I'm only halfway through the first cookie, so it's pretty obvious that I just sat down.

"I saw you staring at my dad today." An accusation.

"I wasn't—"

"You were."

A tiny groan escapes my mouth. My shoulders fall. "I didn't know . . . I mean, Grace kind of mentioned something happened, but I didn't know what, exactly, so I was just . . ." *Just what? Digging my grave a little deeper?* "Curious," I finally finish.

"Okay," he says, nodding his head slowly. "So what do you already know?"

I turn my phone back on. "I got to here," I say, and point to the article.

He leans over the back of the chair and squints at the screen. "Ah. That's it? So you know who my grandfather was and how he died?"

"Didn't get to the death part," I say, hoping that doesn't sound as bad as I think it does.

He doesn't seem to take offense. "He was a big wave surfer. That means he had steel balls. Took stupid risks, even when he got too old to be doing it. In the winter, after big storms, the waves will crest really high north of the cove, up at Bone Garden. He took a big risk one morning after a storm when I was ten. I watched him from the cliffs. The wave ate him whole and spit him out onto the rocks. That's why they call it Bone Garden, by the way. He wasn't the first idiot to die there. Just the most famous one."

I don't even know what to say. A large family stops near our table to pose for a photo in front of the sea monster. We lean to get out of their shot, once, twice, three times. They're finally finished, and we're left alone again.

Uninterested in dredging up his grandfather again, I try to think of something else to talk about. My mind turns to what I thought I witnessed in the vintage clothing shop. "Was that your buddy or something? That Davy guy?"

Porter grunts. "We grew up together." He squints at me and says, "Was he bothering you?"

"Not successfully."

Porter's mouth twists at the corners. He chuckles softly. "Now, *that* I believe. He's not very bright. But he's pernicious. I do my best to keep my eye on him, but . . ." Porter trails off, like he was going to say more but thinks better about it and clams up. I notice his gaze flick over me, head to bare legs—not really in a lurid way. His eyes are tight, wary, and troubled, and there's something behind that dark emotion connected to Davy that I don't understand. I wonder if it has to do with that Chloe girl they were talking about.

Whatever it is, I decide not to pursue this any further. Another evasion tactic I've learned: Change the subject as many times as you need in order to avoid uncomfortable conversation.

"I see you have a sister who surfs."

"Yeah," he says, and he looks happy that I changed the subject too. "Lana's killing it. She's got crazy potential. People say she'll be way bigger than my pops—maybe even bigger than my granddad."

I wonder if this is a point of contention between them, if it hurts his boy pride. But he's digging his phone out from his pocket to show me photos. A girl on a board inside the tunnel of a giant, curling wave. I can't really make out much about her face, only that she's wearing a yellow-and-black wet suit like a second skin and looking like she's about to be swallowed by the ocean. Porter shows me others, some closer, some in which she looks impossibly upside down in the middle of the wave. The last one he shows me is the two of them together on the beach, both of them with curly hair drying in the sun, wet suits peeled down to their waists, brown skin gleaming. He's behind her, arms around her shoulders, and they're both grinning.

And right now, sitting across from me, there's nothing but pride on his face. He doesn't even try to hide it. His eyes are practically sparkling.

"She's pretty," I say.

"Looks like my mom. It's our Hapa genes." He glances up at me and explains, "Half Hawaiian. My grandparents were Polynesian and Chinese. My dad met my mom when he was my age, surfing the Pipeline on the North Shore. Here." He pulls up another photo of his mother. She's gorgeous. And she's standing on the boardwalk near my favorite churro cart, in front of a familiar shop: Penny Boards. Well. Guess that answers that; it was his family's shop, after all. Note to self: Pick another churro cart, already!

Feeling strangely shy, I glance at his face and then quickly look away.

"Is it weird having a younger sister who's going pro?" I ask, more out of nervousness than anything else.

Porter shrugs. "Not really. She'll be heading out on the Women's Championship Tour for the first time next year. It's kind of a big deal. She gets to travel all over the world."

"What about school?"

"My dad's going with her. He'll homeschool her during the tour. I'll stay and help my mom run the shop." Porter must see the look of doubt on my face because he blinks a few times and shakes his head. "Yeah, it's not ideal, but Lana doesn't want to wait until she's eighteen. Anything could happen, and she's on top of her game now. On the tour, she gets a small salary and a chance to win prize money. But the big thing is the exposure, because the real money is in the product endorsements. That's pretty much what we used to live off of until Dad lost his arm."

Sounds a little pageant mom–y, making the kid perform on stage for money, but I keep this opinion to myself. "You guys don't own the shop?" I say, nodding toward his phone.

"Sure, but what people don't understand is that the shop barely breaks even. The overhead is ridiculous; rent keeps going up. And now that my dad isn't surfing anymore . . . well, no one wants a one-armed man pimping hats."

Yikes. This conversation is heading into awkward waters. I turn away to find the sea monster's big eye judging me—*You had to be on your phone, looking this up at work, didn't you? Couldn't wait until you got home?*—so I turn back toward the table and pick at my half-eaten cookie.

"I knew one out of three had to be right."

"Mmm?" I swallow cookie while trying to look cool and nearly choke.

"You like sugar cookies. I didn't know which one. I was just hoping you weren't vegan or gluten-free or something."

I shake my head.

He breaks off a piece of my cookie and eats it, and I'm not sure how I feel about that. I don't know where his hands have been. We aren't friends. And just because his dad's missing an arm, doesn't mean I've forgiven him for being a grade-A assbag.

"You aren't going to ask me?" he says. "Or do you already know?"

"Know what?"

"How my dad lost his arm?"

I shake my head. "No, I don't already know. Are you going to tell me?" *Or should I just wait until you leave and look it up? That works for me, thanks, see you later,* hasta luego.

"Three years ago, I was fifteen, a year younger than Lana. I went down to Sweetheart Point to watch my dad surf for this charity thing. It wasn't a competition or anything. Mostly older surfers, a few big names. Out of nowhere . . ." He pauses for a second, lost in thought, eyes glazed. Then he blinks it away. "I see this big shape cut through the water, a few yards away. At first, I didn't know what it was. It heads straight for my dad and knocks him right off his board. Then I saw the white collar around its neck and the mouth open. Great white."

My mouth falls open. I shut it. "Shark?"

"A small male. They say it's like getting struck by lightning, but damned if it didn't happen. And let me just tell you—it wasn't like *Jaws*. Hundreds of people around me on the beach and no one screamed or ran. They all just stood there staring while this thousand-pound monster was dragging my dad through the water, and he was still leashed to his board by the ankle."

"Oh, my dear God," I murmur, stuffing half of the second cookie in my mouth. "Whaa haaappened next?" I say around a mouthful of sugar.

Porter takes the rest of the cookie, biting off a corner and chewing while shaking his head, still looking a little dazed. "It was like a dream. I didn't think. I just raced into the water. I didn't even know if my dad was still alive or whether I would be if I bumped into the shark. I swam as hard as I could. I found the board first and followed the leash to the body."

He pauses, swallowing. "I tasted blood in the water before I got to him."

"Jesus."

"The arm was already gone," Porter says quietly. "Skin flapping. Muscles hanging. It was a mess. And I was so scared I was going to make it worse, carrying him back to shore. He was heavy and unconscious, and nobody was coming to help. And then the shark doubled back and tried to get my arm too. I managed to hit him and scare him off. Took sixty-nine stiches to sew me back together."

He unfolds his left arm until it's extended in front of me, and rucks up the short sleeve of his security guard uniform. There, above the bright red surf watch, are his zigzagging pink scars, bared for my perusal. Looking at them feels pornographic. Like I'm doing something I shouldn't be doing, and any moment, someone will catch me . . . but at the same time, I can't make myself look away. All this golden skin, all these eggshell-glossy scars, a railroad track, crisscrossing miles of sculpted lean muscle. It's horrifying . . . and the most beautiful thing I've ever seen.

Seeing the scars reminds me of something else about myself. Something I can't tell him. But it tugs on a dark memory inside me that I don't want to think about, and a fluttering of unstable emotions threatens to break the surface.

I breathe deep to push those feelings back down, and when I do, there's that scent again, Porter's scent, the wax and the clean coconut. Not the suntan-lotion fake kind. What is this stuff? It's driving me nuts. I don't know if it's the lure of this wonderful smell, or his story about the shark, or my urge to contain my own unwanted memories, but before I know what I'm doing, my fingertips are reaching out to trace the jagged edge of one of the scars by his elbow.

His skin is warm. The scar is raised, a tough, unyielding line. I follow it around his elbow, into the soft, sensitive hollow where his arm bends.

All the golden hairs on his forearm are standing up.

He sucks in a quick breath. I don't think he meant to, but I heard it. And it's then that I know I crossed some kind of line. I snatch my hand back and try to think of something to say, to erase what I just did, but it just comes out as a garbled grunt. And that makes things even weirder between us.

"Break," I finally manage. "Gotta get back."

I'm so embarrassed, I stumble over my chair as I leave. The ensuing metallic grate of metal on slate echoes through the café, causing several museum guests to look up from their afternoon coffee. Who's artful now, Rydell? That never happens to me. I'm not clumsy. Ever, ever, ever. He's messing with my game. I can't even look at him anymore, because my face is on fire.

What is happening to me? I swear, every time I have any interaction whatsoever with Porter Roth, something always goes screwy. He's an electrical outlet, and I'm the stupid toddler, always trying to poke around and stick my finger inside.

Someone needs to slap a big DANGER! sign on that boy's back before I electrocute myself.

LUMIÈRE FILM FANATICS COMMUNITY
PRIVATE MESSAGES>ALEX>NEW!

@mink: Have you ever had a serious girlfriend?

@alex: Yes. I think. Sort of. What do you qualify as serious?

@mink: Hey, you're the one who said yes. I was just curious. How long and why did you break up?

@alex: Three months and the short story is she said I didn't want to have fun anymore.

@mink: Ouch. The long story?

@alex: Her idea of fun included hooking up with my best friend when I was out of town.

@mink: I don't know what to say. I'm sorry.

@alex: Don't be. I'd checked out. It wasn't all her fault. If you don't pay attention to things, they wander off. I learned my lesson. I'm vigilant now.

@mink: Vigilant with who?

@alex: I think you mean with WHOM.

@mink: :P

@alex: No one in particular. I'm just saying, I'm not the same person I used to be. I confessed; now your turn. Anyone you've been vigilant about in the past?

@mink: A couple of guys for a couple of weeks, nothing major. Now I pretty much look out for myself. It's a full-time job. You'd be surprised.

@alex: One day you might need some help.

"You see how picky I am about my shoes, and they only go on my feet."
—Alicia Silverstone, *Clueless* (1995)

8

I don't work with Porter for the next few shifts. Grace, either, which bums me out. The museum sticks me with some older lady, Michelle, who's in her twenties and has problems counting her cash fast enough. She's slowing down the line and it's driving me crazy. Crazy enough to march up to Mr. Cavadini's office, peer around the corner . . . and then just change my mind and clock out for the day instead of saying anything.

That's how I roll.

One morning, instead of roaming the boardwalk, Sherlocking my way from shop to shop, stuffing my face with churros, I spend it pummeling Dad in two rounds of miniature golf. He took a half day off from work to hang with me, which was pretty nice. He gave me the choice of either the golf or paddleboarding—and no way in heaven or hell was I dipping my toe in the ocean after hearing Porter's tale of terror on the high seas. Nuh-uh. I told Dad the whole story, and he was a little freaked himself. He said he'd seen Porter's dad outside the surf shop and knew the family were surfers, but just assumed the missing-arm incident had happened a long time ago. He had no idea how it went down, or that Porter had rescued him.

See. Only ten days in town, and I was already filling Dad in on choice gossip he hadn't heard, living here for an entire year. The man needs me, clearly.

My reward for spanking Dad's behind in putt-putt is that I get to pick our lunch location. Since we grabbed a light breakfast before our golf excursion, I call a breakfast do-over at the Pancake Shack. It's got a 1950s Americana diner vibe inside, and we grab stools at the counter, where a waitress in a pink uniform brings us glasses of iced tea while we wait for our pancake orders. My dreams have finally come true! Only, they haven't, because the Pancake Shack doesn't exactly live up to my expectations, not even their "world-famous" almond pancakes, which I give one thumb down.

When I voice my lukewarm grade, Dad sticks a fork in my order and samples a corner. "Tastes like Christmas."

"Like those almond cookies grandma used to make."

"The gross, crumbly ones," he agrees. "You should have ordered a Dutch Baby. Taste mine. It's terrific."

His is way better, but it's no churro.

"Still haven't found him, huh?" he asks, and I know he's talking about Alex. I told him the basic deal, that I'm gun-shy about confessing to Alex that I've moved out here, and that I'm trying to find him on my own. Dad and I are a lot alike in many (unfortunate) ways. He gets it. Mom wouldn't. Mom would have freaked her pants off if she knew Alex even existed in the first place, so there's that. But Mom didn't really pay much attention to anything going on in my life back in DC, so it wasn't like I went to any trouble to hide him. And now that I'm here, I notice that she still isn't all that concerned, as I have yet to receive any communication from her since the initial *Did Bailey arrive okay?* phone calls. Whatever. I try not to think about her lack of concern too much.

From my purse, I retrieve a tourist map of the boardwalk. It's just a cartoony one I picked up for free one morning. I'm using a marker to X out the shops that I've either surveyed or that don't fall into the parameters that Alex has unwittingly provided me— can't see the ocean from the window, not a shop with a counter, et cetera. "This is what's left to cover," I tell Dad, pointing the sections of the map I haven't hit yet.

Dad grins and chuckles, shaking his head. I try to snatch the map away, but he holds it against the diner counter, moving aside the cast-iron skillet that holds his half-eaten Dutch Baby. "No, no. Let me see this marvelous thing. You're thorough and precise, a chip off the ol' block."

"Ugh," I complain. "Weirdo."

"What? This is quality CPA blood running in your veins, right here," he says proudly, thumping the map like a dork. "Wait, how do you know he just wasn't working in one of these places on the day you went by? Or unloading a truck out in the alley?"

"I don't, but I figure I'll hit every shop twice." I show him my homemade legend on the corner of the map. Dots for even-day visits, squares for odd. Male symbol for a boy my age working there—but ruled out as a possibility for Alex upon initial assessment. Triangles for churro cart locations. And wavy lines for all three stray boardwalk cats I've found so far, including Señor Don Gato.

He puts his arm around my shoulder and kisses the side of my head. "With superior deductive skills like this, how could you not find him? And if he's not worth the hunt, you have nothing to be ashamed of."

"I knew I liked you."

"You kind of have to," he says with a grin.

I grin back.

Someone walks over to the counter, and Dad leans forward to look past me. His face goes all funny. He clears his throat. "Good morning, Sergeant Mendoza."

Waiting for a waitress to take her order is a tall, curvy Latina cop in a navy uniform. Wavy hair, brown woven through with strands of gray, is pulled tight into a thick ponytail at the base of her neck. A pair of dark purple sunglasses sits on her face. I recognize those: She's the cop who flashed her lights at Davy and Porter at the crosswalk, the first day I got into town.

"Morning, Pete," she says in a husky voice. One corner of her mouth curls at the corner. Just slightly. Then her face turns unreadable. I think she's peering down at me, but it's hard to tell, especially with the sunglasses on. "Dutch Baby?" she says.

"You know it," my dad answers, and laughs in an odd way.

I look between them. My dad clears his throat again. "Wanda, this is my daughter, Bailey. Bailey, this is Sergeant Wanda Mendoza of the Coronado Cove Police Department."

Like I couldn't figure that out. She smiles and sticks out her arm to offer me a firm handshake. Wow. Knuckle-cracking firm. I'm awake now. And I'm not sure, but I think she might be uncomfortable. Do cops get nervous? I didn't think that was possible.

"Heard a great deal about you, Bailey." She has? Who the heck is this and why hasn't Dad mentioned her? Are they friends?

"I do the sergeant's taxes," Dad explains, but it sounds like a lie, and both of them are looking in different places—him at the counter and her at the ceiling. When her head tilts back down, she taps her fingernails on the counter. I glance at the gun holstered to her hip. I don't like guns; they make me uncomfortable, so I guess we're even.

"I like your brows," she finally says. "Glamorous."

I'm caught off guard for a second. Then I'm pleased. "I do them myself," I tell her. Finally someone who appreciates the importance of a good arch. Plucking is painful.

"Impressive," she confirms. "So, how're you liking California?"

"It's a different planet." I realize that might not sound positive, so I add, "I like the redwoods and the churros."

That makes her smile. Almost. She lifts her chin toward my dad. "Have you taken her to the posole truck?"

"Not yet," he says. "She's never had posole. Have you?" he asks, giving me a questioning look.

"No clue what you're talking about."

She blows out a breath and shakes her head like Dad has let down his entire country. "I've got a messed-up schedule right now, but sometime in the next couple of weeks, we should take her."

We? Take her? They are a *we*?

"It will knock your socks off," Dad assures me while the cop places a to-go order with the waitress. He stands and fumbles with his wallet. "That reminds me . . . Bailey, give me a second. I need to talk to the sergeant about something." He hands me a wad of cash to pay for our check and then he walks with the cop down the counter, where they lean a little closer, but don't seem to be talking about anything all that important. That's when it all comes into focus.

Jeezy creezy. My dad's dating a cop.

She seems nice. Has a great handshake. Pretty hot. The same height as him. Hope she likes him as much as he likes her, because he's smiling like a doofus. Then I hear her quietly laughing at something he says, and see her push her purple glasses up to rest atop her head and that makes me feel better.

As I wait for the CPA–cop macking session to come to an end, I pack up my boardwalk map and look around the diner.

Without my dad's body blocking the view, I now notice the person who's been sitting on the stool adjacent to his. It's a boy about my age with sandy-blond hair. He's eating eggs and drinking coffee. When he moves his arm, I see two things: (A) He's wearing a red T-shirt screen-printed in black with Cary Grant's face, and (B) he's reading a guide to the summer film festival.

My heart picks up speed as my gaze flicks over him. He's eating slowly, engrossed in his reading, taking small bites of scrambled eggs. His well-fitting shorts reveal toned, tan legs. Worn sandals slap against the counter's metal footrest as his knee bounces. The orange-and-blue key chain sitting next to his plate is printed with a familiar logo that I've seen on the boardwalk: Killian's Whale Tours. That's not by definition a retail shop, but it is a storefront along the boardwalk that has a view of the ocean. One with a counter, and possibly a family-owned business. I mentally call up my map and place the shop about three stores away from a churro cart. No resident cat, but then again, cats are mobile.

Could it be . . . ?

My brain is telling me to slow down, but my heart is thinking, *Pennies from heaven!*

He's cute. But he's no Porter.

God, what's wrong with me? Who cares about stupid old Porter, anyway? I push him out of my mind and focus on what's in front of me, try to match it to the Alex I have in my mind. Could this guy be witty? Sensitive? He looks well-groomed. Are serial killers well-groomed?

This is harder than I thought it would be.

I pull myself together and remember that if it is Alex, he doesn't know who I am. To him, I'm just a girl sitting in a diner. I'm not Mink. Deep breath.

"Grant," I say.

He looks up from the brochure. "Excuse me?"

"Your shirt," I explain. "Cary Grant. *Only Angels Have Wings*, if I'm not mistaken." I'm not. I'm totally showing off. What a total geek I am, but I can't help myself.

His head drops. He smiles now, and he's got great teeth, a big, white smile. "Yes. You're the second person ever to recognize that, and I've been wearing this for almost a year." His voice isn't what I imagined. Sharper, somehow. But still good.

"I'm a huge Grant buff," I say. "*Bringing Up Baby, The Philadelphia Story, The Awful Truth, His Girl Friday*." I tick them off on my fingers, getting a little carried away and flushed in the cheeks. *Reel it back in, Rydell.* I clear my throat. "And *North by Northwest*, of course," I add, dangling that like the bait that it is.

"Everyone loves that," he agrees.

Huh. Can't tell if he's being droll or sarcastic. Then again, Alex has a superior sense of humor. Hard to tell.

He thinks for a moment, then says, "If I had to pick one, it would be *My Favorite Wife*."

"Seriously? I love that movie," I say. "Irene Dunne and Randolph Scott are brilliant."

"Adam and Eve," he agrees, smiling.

"I've seen it a hundred times."

"You know, Randolph Scott and Cary Grant were lovers."

I nod. "Probably. No one's ever proven it, but I don't doubt it. I think he probably liked men *and* women." I shrug. Who cares anyway? Cary Grant was sex on a stick. More important, he was charm on a stick. At least on the big screen. I don't really care what he did off the screen.

"Patrick, by the way," he says, and it takes me a second to realize he's introducing himself.

Patrick. Huh. Not Alex, but Patrick? Of course, we aren't using our real names online, so that means nothing. More important, does this feel right? I honestly can't tell, but my pulse is racing, so if that's any indication, maybe that's a yes? And he still doesn't know to connect the Me sitting here with the Online Me, so I guess it's okay to give out my real name now. Besides, my dad's a few feet away, not to mention a cop with a badass handshake.

"I'm Bailey," I say, then decide to add, "I'm new in town."

"Cool. Nice to meet another movie aficionado." He slides the film festival brochure toward me. "We have a summer film festival every year. This year's lineup is so-so. A few good things, like the Georges Méliès shorts and *North by Northwest*."

Heart. Pounding. So. Fast.

"I would love to see all of those," I squeak out in a voice higher than Grace's.

"Right?" he says, grabbing his keys and gesturing toward the festival brochure. "Keep that. It's hot off the presses. Anyway, gotta get back to work. I'm at the whale tours up on the board-walk—Killian's. Orange and blue, down by the big gold Ferris wheel. Can't miss it. If you ever want to have coffee and talk about Cary Grant, come by and see me."

"I might take you up on that offer." I hate coffee, but what-ever. It sounds so adult, so romantic. This is not a boy who'd get me fired or embarrass me in front of dozens of people. This boy is sophisticated. Whale watching! That sounds so much nicer than surfing.

He raises a hand, a triangle of toast clamped in his mouth, and jogs out the front door.

I'm reeling. Seriously, truly reeling.

"Who was that?" my dad murmurs over my shoulder, watch-ing Patrick get into what appears to be some sort of red Jeep.

"I'm not one hundred percent sure," I say. "But I think I'm getting warmer."

LUMIÈRE FILM FANATICS COMMUNITY
PRIVATE MESSAGES>ALEX>NEW!

@mink: Anything new in your life?

@alex: Like . . . ?

@mink: I don't know. Something happened recently that made me have a little more hope about the future.

@alex: Me too, actually, now that you mention it. Maybe. For your future hope . . . how far ahead are we talking? Tomorrow? Next week? (Next month?)

@mink: I'm a one-step-at-a-time kinda gal. So I guess I'll try tomorrow and see where that leads.

@alex: You definitely don't dive into anything, do you? (I was hinting.)

@mink: I really don't. (I know you were.)

@alex: Maybe sometimes you should. Take a chance. Do something crazy. (Are you going to ask your dad about the film festival?)

@mink: Is that what you would do? (Maybe I already have.)

@alex: With the right person? Yes. (When will you let me know?)

@mink: Interesting. (He's thinking about it. And so am I.)

"You're a good man, sister."
—Humphrey Bogart, *The Maltese Falcon* (1941)

9

I'm standing behind the Hotbox with Grace and Mr. Pangborn. He lost his key. We're holding our register tills, waiting for Porter to come back from the cash-out room and unlock the door. I'm not even sure if Porter's made it through the lobby yet, escorting the other ticketing agents we're supposed to be replacing. Heck, I don't even know if Porter knows we're locked out. I do know that it's a few minutes past noon and the line is pretty long. Freddy, the guy in charge of taking tickets at the turnstile, keeps peeping around the corner at us, the look on his face progressing from Antsy to Dismayed.

Mr. Pangborn sniffles and rubs his nose. "We'll give him another minute to make it to cash-out before I buzz him. No sense in making him panic. He's got to get the tills to the room first."

Grace and I look at each other, shrug, and both make *he's got a point* faces. What are we going to do? There's no one at the information desk right now. The lady who's supposed to be stationed there, who also has a key to ticketing, is outside in the parking lot, schmoozing with a tour party. Mr. Cavadini is on an extended lunch break with the shift supervisor. Besides, Mr. Pangborn doesn't like to bother him, and who am I to argue?

He leans back against the booth's door, a little breathless, and crosses one ankle over the other, revealing a pair of white-and-black striped socks. I sort of love them. And I sort of love Pangborn, even though his eyes are slits and he reeks of weed. Grace says she caught him vaping up in his car before work yesterday. He's got to be in his seventies. Let the guy have a few bad habits, I say.

"Next month will be my fortieth anniversary working at the museum," he muses in a soft voice. He's got a gentle way about him that makes you want to listen to what he has to say. I'm not sure why Porter gets so frustrated with him. He's just an old man. Have a heart.

Grace's lips pucker. "That's nuts."

"You must like it if you've stuck with it this long," I say.

"Eh, I like talking to people. And I don't have any college or training, so what else am I supposed to do? This is all I know." He scratches his head and his crazy white hair sticks up in different directions. "They tried to make me retire about ten years ago, but I didn't really have anything to do at home. I never married. I've got a dog, Daisy, but she gets tired of seeing me all day. So even though they didn't pay me, I just kept showing up for work."

"What?" Grace says, unable to hide her disbelief. "For how long?"

"Oh, about three months or so. Mr. Cavadini finally got sick of telling me to go home, so he officially rehired me and put me back on the schedule." He smiles, big and wide, lifting his shoulders. "And here I stand. It hasn't killed me yet. I think Porter should be in the cash-out room by now. Cover your ears, ladies. He's not going to be happy."

Grace knocks shoulders with me while Pangborn radios Porter. "Glad we're finally scheduled together again."

"Me too," I say, genuinely meaning it. "Team Grailey, taking care of business."

"Team Baice, dropping the hammer."

We both laugh until Freddy peeps around the turnstiles again and Grace makes a hissing sound at him. He leaves us alone now. "Got plans this weekend?" she asks me.

"I don't know. Why?"

"There's a bonfire on Saturday after work. Party on the beach."

I grip my till harder, thinking of Porter's friend Davy. "Is this the one at the Bone Garden?"

"Yeah. You've heard about it?"

"Only in passing."

"The core of it is a surfer crowd, but other people show up, too. They're usually every Saturday night in the summer. Sometimes they're boring, sometimes they're fun, but I thought it might be a good place to meet people from Brightsea, since you're new. I can introduce you."

The evader in me cowers, readying an excuse to turn her down, but the weird thing is, I think I want to go. Especially with Grace. So I say, "Sure, why not?" And before I know it, I'm telling her where my dad lives, and we're making plans for her to pick me up in her car. What do you know? I guess I'm a social butterfly. Must be all this fresh air and sunshine.

Or maybe it's just that I'm feeling more hopeful about life in general after finding out my dad has a new girlfriend. A kickass cop girlfriend. "We're just friends. Taking things slow," he assured me on the ride home yesterday. That was all he offered, so that's where we left it. As long as he's happy and there's no weirdness, I'm fine with it.

And speaking of fine, there's the other more important thing buzzing around in my brain: bumping into Patrick at the Pancake Shack. Patrick, and only Patrick, I remind myself for the millionth time, who may or may not be Alex. But I decided last night that I'm going to muster up the gumption to go talk to him again. I've been daydreaming about it off and on for hours. Epic sigh.

A rush of cool museum air blows across my arm, and my daydreaming is cut short when I have to step to the side to avoid the buffalo that is Porter, charging the ticketing booth.

"I'm going to rip out your large intestines, sew this key to the end of them, and then stuff them back inside your body."

Porter opens Pangborn's hand, shoves down a key, and closes the man's fingers on top of it. "Don't. Lose it. Again."

The older security guard smiles. "You're a good boy, Porter.

Thank you." Pangborn pats him on the shoulder, completely unfazed by Porter's bad attitude. He's a better man than most. "Come along, ladies. Freddy's got ants in his pants. Let's bust up this line and sell some tickets."

Team Grailey—I win the name game—kicks butt, per usual, and we do bust up that line, because we are the best. Our shift supervisor remarks on the good work we do, and when Mr. Cavadini drops by to check on us, for once, he even gets our names right. It's a good day, right up until about four p.m.

Museum foot traffic has slowed. My break's almost over and I'm nearly ready to power through my last couple of hours, but I've still got a few minutes, so I'm strolling through Vivian's Wing. I'm in the San Francisco Room, which has a Golden Gate Bridge that visitors walk beneath and a fake Chinatown street, where you can peer inside staged storefront windows that look like they did in the late 1800s. As I'm gazing at a Chinese tea shop, I notice two kids, maybe thirteen, fourteen years old, acting a little weird. They're standing a few yards from me, in the nearby 1940s San Francisco film noir display, eyeing a replica of the Maltese falcon, which is sitting on the desk of famous fictional detective Sam Spade—played by Humphrey Bogart on the big screen. One of them, a blond boy in a white polo shirt and Top-Siders, is experimentally touching the statue, while his friend, a drowsy kid with a backpack, keeps a lethargic lookout.

I can guess what they're planning. Morons. Don't they notice the security cameras? The backpack kid does see them, though, and he's inching around, blocking his Richie Rich friend with his body, looking up at the camera and judging the angle. I don't know what they hope to accomplish. Everything in the museum is glued, nailed, screwed, or locked down.

Only it's not.

Polo shirt touches the falcon, and it jiggles. Just a little. But enough.

They're going to rock it off its mounting. The jerks are planning a heist.

I glance around. Only a few museum guests in this room. I keep my head low and casually walk to the other end of the room, where I know from memorizing the stupid employee map that a call box is hidden in a wall panel. Making sure I'm not seen, I duck behind a potted palm, pop open the panel, and hit the button for security. Porter's voice booms over the old line.

"Talk to me." He's on his radio doohickey. I can tell by the click and static.

"It's Bailey," I whisper. "I'm in the San Francisco Room."

"That's a long way from ticketing, Rydell. And speak up. I can't hear you. Or are you trying to come on to me? Is this your sexy voice? I like it."

I groan and seriously consider hanging up. "Shut up and listen to me. I think some kids are trying to steal."

"I think you have the wrong number, sir."

"Porter!" I grind out. "They're stealing the Maltese falcon."

"Keep your pants on. I'm two rooms away. I'll be right there.

Don't take your eyes off them, but don't approach. They might be dangerous or something. I'm being serious right now, in case you can't tell."

The phone goes dead. After closing the panel, I casually step from behind the palm and pretend to be looking at some paintings while keeping an eye on the kids. They're still rocking the falcon statue. A couple is passing under the Golden Gate Bridge, and the two boys see them, so that halts their thieving for a moment. I disappear behind the potted palm again.

Come on, Porter. I know the falcon's not actual movie memorabilia, much like most of the rest of the stuff in this place; only two statues were used in the original film, and one was auctioned off for several million dollars. But it's the principle of the thing, and it makes me mad.

"Where are they now?" Porter's warm breath grazes the hair around my ear. My neck and shoulder involuntarily clamp together, and for some reason, he finds this amusing. "Ticklish, Rydell?" he whispers.

I ignore that comment and lower a palm branch to show him the boys, who are now rocking the statue again. "There. White polo shirt and backpack."

"Dirty little pigs," he mutters incredulously. "The falcon?"

I won't lie. A little thrill goes through me that Porter's as mad as I am. I like that we're on the same page about this. "What are we going to do?" I whisper.

"Rule number one in apprehending thieves and shoplifters

according to the Cavern Palace guidelines is that we absolutely do not make a scene. No chasing. No nasty blowups. Nothing that causes the other guests to feel uncomfortable, so that means we've got to smoke them out, nice and easy."

"I don't follow," I whisper.

Porter drops his head to speak in a lower voice. "We let them steal it."

"What?" My face is near his face, so close I can see all the golden flecks in his brown eyes. Did I know they were brown? I never noticed until now. "We can't do that."

"We can and we will. Then we'll follow them to the exit and bust their asses in the parking lot."

"Oh," I say, more than a little intrigued by this prospect.

"Now, they might split up. I've had this happen once before with a pair of Jay's cuff links last summer. Bastards got away with a thousand bucks' worth of gold while my ass got chewed out by Cadaver. So I might need some help. Will you?"

"Me? I don't know . . . My break's over."

"Bawk, bawk," he whispers back, cawing like a chicken. The tip of his nose touches mine, and we're so close, I can now see his chest lifting up and down . . . and the jumping pulse of a vein on his neck. Were his shoulders always this broad? Mother of Mary, he seems bigger up close. And instead of wanting to punch him in the stomach, which should be my normal Porter response, I'm starting to want something else that makes my breath come faster. My clothes suddenly feel too tight.

Oh.

God.

So what? He's attractive and has a certain damaged charm about him. It's just chemical attraction. Perfectly natural. Means nothing.

And because I'm on my break and it's cold in the museum, I'm wearing the cardigan, and that covers up the majority of the headlight problem that is now happening in my breast locale. Disaster averted. And the thought of it being a near miss is enough to throw a proverbial bucket of cold water onto the situation. God, this is ridiculous. It's just dumb old Porter. What am I afraid of? Nothing.

To prove it to myself, I move back and lift my head, meeting his gaze and his challenge. "Radio Grace and tell her I'll be late."

His smile could power a lighthouse. He quickly radios Pangborn and briefs him on the situation, giving the older guard a description of the boys and instructions to track them on the security monitors. But before he can notify Grace, our thieving boys are on the move.

The falcon is gone. I didn't see them take it. But the boys are huddled and the backpack's being swung from the shorter kid's shoulder. They're stashing the bird.

"Porter!" I whisper heatedly, tugging his sleeve.

"I see it," he says, keeping the palm frond bent to peer into the room. He radios Pangborn again, who saw it too.

"Got it all on tape," the old stoner confirms, his words coming from the tiny black box on Porter's shoulder. Apart from losing keys, this is probably more excitement than the two of them have had in months. "Go smoke 'em out, Porter. I'm watching from heaven."

Heaven. The security room. I wonder if Porter really does watch me from there, or if that's just him talking big.

The dopey-eyed kid zips up the backpack and slings it over his right shoulder, looks around, and then the two little robbers make their way beneath the bridge, strolling like it's Sunday and they didn't just commit a crime. The nerve!

"Time to follow," Porter says, nudging me out of our hiding place with a tap on my wrist. "We'll hang back at a safe distance, but not too far. There are a lot of exits, and they likely know that. Main entrance and gift shop are the fastest escape routes, but the easiest for us to track. Fire exits will set off alarms, but they could run and lose us—that's how the cuff-link bandits beat me last summer. And then there's the delivery door and the employee entrance."

"They're turning right," I say. "Heading toward the lobby."

"That kills three of the fire exits. Don't stare too hard. Just act like we're having a friendly chat. It's good that you're not wearing your vest. You look like you're asking me for help. Maybe you're just my girlfriend, visiting me for lunch."

I nearly choke. "Dream on."

"What? I'm not good enough for your champagne tastes?"

"Don't be ridiculous."

He snorts. "You prance around here, trying to look like a movie star in your expensive clothes, driving a Vespa, lawyer mom back in Washington, DC—"

His tone is light, almost teasing—not like our usual arguments—but it's what he's saying that surprises me. I stop in my tracks, but he pushes me forward. "Do you want to catch these guys? They're turning into the Egyptian Room. Might have just seen me too. We need to be careful."

We hang back for a second while Porter glances into the room. As he does, I say, "How did you know my mom's a lawyer?"

"Gracie told me."

Oh. "My clothes aren't expensive, they're vintage. I can't help it if your sense of style doesn't register anything higher than stoner chic and beach bum."

"Ooaf," he says, feigning offense. "You wound my tender sensibilities, Rydell."

"And my dad bought me the Vespa. It's restored. It's not like it's new or anything."

"That model's worth more than a new ride. Anyone who knows wheels knows that. The Cove's a collector's paradise for scooters. You need to keep that thing locked up at all times."

"I'm not an idiot," I tell him.

"Crap!"

"What?" I angle to see around him.

"Polo Shirt definitely spotted me. They're circling around to the main hallway." He radios Pangborn again. "You still see them?"

"Yeah, I got 'em on the overheads in the main corridor," Pangborn's voice says over the radio. "Looks like they're heading for the lobby."

The museum closes at six, and it's past four, so at this time of day, the main hallways on both wings begin to fill up with guests making their way back out to warm sun and fresh air. Our miscreant boys duck into the crowd and for a few seconds, we lose them in the flow. My pulse speeds as I bounce on the balls of my feet, trying to see over the heads of the slow-moving herd.

"Stop that," Porter says. "You're going to blow our cover. I can see them. They're hugging the south wall, so I don't think they'll break for the main gate or the gift shop."

"Employee hall?"

"Maybe. Or they could head straight to Jay's wing and try to use a fire exit there."

Porter's legs are longer than mine, and it's hard for me to keep up with him without doubling my pace. "I don't have champagne tastes. Just because I have style doesn't mean I'm a snob. And in case you haven't noticed, I'm not living with my mom anymore; I'm living with my dad. And I'm working this job, probably making a whole heck of a lot less money than you, Mr. I'm Eighteen; I Can Work Full-Time and All My Sexual Activity Is Legal.'"

"Unless it's with someone like you, then it would be illegal, because you're underage."

"Right." Before I can think of a wittier comeback, we're at the end of the corridor, and our suspects have taken a sharp right.

Porter was right: They aren't headed to the main gate or the gift shop. But they aren't going to Jay's wing or the employee hall either.

"What the . . . ," Porter murmurs. "The brats are going spelunking?"

Sure enough, the two boys stride through the back of the lobby, making a beeline to the gaping mouth of the cave. Why they'd head there, I don't understand. There's no exit inside, just a dark, looping path that ends up right back at the mouth of the cave. . . .

"Any cameras in there?" I ask.

"A few. The image quality isn't great," Porter admits.

"They're trying to lose us."

He thinks about this for a second and swears under his breath. We race to the mouth of the cave, where the boys have jogged down the stone steps and disappeared under the stalactites lit by creepy orange spotlights. Only problem is, the steps go two ways: left and right. The main route snakes through the cliffs, crisscrossing in the center like a pretzel where they open up into the center cavern. And the boys have split up.

"You go left," Porter tells me. "I'll go right. Whichever one of them you find, don't take your eyes off him."

"Meet you in the center." I take off down the stairs, cool air drafting up as I jog. It's dark and creepy down here, and the metal handrail that's been here since the museum opened has a clammy feel to it that gives me the heebie-jeebies, so I can't touch it. This makes running difficult, because caves are dark and damp, and the low lights around the walkway might be great for setting a mood, but they don't provide much in the way of illumination when you're chasing someone. Luckily, there aren't too many people lingering in the cave—and even fewer racing through it. I spot White Polo Shirt a few yards ahead, on another landing.

There isn't much to see in the cave, especially compared to the rest of the jam-packed museum, just a few info plaques with facts about caves in California and animals that live there, and the occasional bench for hot-blooded people to rest and enjoy the dark and gloomy view. I sail past a woman leaning against one of these benches and head around the pretzel turn toward the red-and-green glow of the main cavern.

Rocky walls lined with organically formed crevices and holes separate the cave into multiple chambers. It's a great place for hiding, and those little bastards know it. Several people mingle around the main plaque, marking the spot where Jay and Vivian found their pirate gold. A cheesy chest overflowing with carnival doubloons sits atop a flat rock. It's ridiculous. I'm embarrassed for everyone who has to gaze upon it, including myself.

But more than that, I'm embarrassed that I've lost the stupid kid I'm supposed to be trailing. I finally spot Porter, and he acknowledges me with a chin nod, but I can tell by the angle of his brow that he can't find the backpack kid either. How could this be? I glance around one more time, and out of the corner of my eye, I spot something: two white sneakers slipping through one of the larger hole formations in the rocky cave walls. Not Polo, but the backpack kid. Sneaky little monkey is doubling back up the stairs.

Porter's attention is elsewhere, and I'm not losing this kid again, so I take off after him. Up I go, back the way I came, twice as fast, pounding the stone steps.

The backpack kid tosses me a glance over his shoulder. He knows I'm chasing him, and he's not stopping. Too bad. Neither am I.

When he reaches the mouth of the cave, he hesitates long enough to spot his cohort, slamming up the steps on the other side. Then they're off, racing together through the lobby.

Porter said not to make a scene, but what about now? Do I just let these jerks get away? I quickly decide: No, I don't.

I book it as fast as I can go, giving chase. They nearly bowl over an entire family, who startle like ducks on a pond, jumping out of their way.

"Someone stop them!" I yell.

No one does.

I think about Porter surrounded by people that horrible day on the beach years ago, when no one would help him save his dad from the shark. If strangers won't help when someone is dying, they're definitely not going to stop two kids from running out of a museum.

Pulse swishing in my temples, I race around the information booth, pumping my arms, and watch them split up again. Polo is heading for the easy way out: the main exit, where there's (1) only a set of doors to go through, and (2) Hector, the laziest employee on staff.

But Backpack is headed for the ticketing booth and the connecting turnstiles. Freddy should be there, but no one's entering the museum, so he's instead chatting it up with Hector. The turnstiles are unmanned.

Like a pro hustler who's never paid a subway fare, Backpack hurdles over the turnstiles in one leap. Impressive. Or it would have been, had his backpack not slipped off his shoulder and the strap not caught on one of the turnstile arms. While he struggles to free it, I take the easier route and make for the wheelchair access gate.

I unhitch the latch.

He frees the strap.

I slip through the gate, and just as he's turning to run, I lurch forward and—

I jump on his back.

We hit the ground together. The air whooshes out of my lungs and my knee slams into tile. He cries out. I don't.

I freaking got him.

"Get off me, you crazy bitch!" He squirms below me, elbowing me in the ribs. I clamp my hand over his arm to hold it down. A breathless, evil laugh comes out of me in fits. I can't even say anything; I'm too winded.

"Oh no you don't," a triumphant male voice says nearby.

I twist to the side and spit hair out of my mouth. Porter is dragging Polo by the arm. He doesn't look half as winded as I feel. Stupid surfer genes. But now Freddy and Hector are coming—to gawk, I guess. And here's Grace, too; finally, someone with sense.

"What in the world is going on?" she asks.

"Watch him," Porter tells the three of them as he parks Polo on the ground. Then he pulls me off Backpack.

"She's crazy," the boy repeats. "I think she broke my leg."

"Whatever. She's got the strength of a tater tot," Porter says, pulling the boy to his feet, who protests and hobbles, but manages okay.

"Oww," he whines.

"Shut the hell up, you thieving-ass rat." Porter grabs the boy by his shirt, wrenches the backpack off his arm, tosses it to me. "Check it."

I unzip the pack. Nested in a wadded-up hoodie is the statue. I hold it up like a trophy.

The boy groans and tries to wriggle out of Porter's grip. "Nuh-uh," Porter says, urging him down next to Polo and pressing the button on his sleeve. "You and your punk-ass friend aren't going anywhere right now. We're going to sit tight while my buddy Mr. Pangborn makes a little phone call to our friends at the CCPD. Got that, Pangborn?" he asks into his radio.

"Got it," Pangborn's voice answers.

While the boys exchange panicked looks, a small crowd is forming. I brush off my skirt and notice that a small trail of blood runs from a nasty scrape on my knee. I don't even care. I'm still on an oh-so-sweet adrenaline high.

Porter grins, eyebrows high. "Damn, Bailey. You took him downtown. Full-on atomic drop body slam. I had no idea you had it in you."

Me neither, to be honest. "No one steals from Sam Spade and gets away with it," I say.

He holds his hand up, and I slap it, but instead of it being a simple high five, he laces his fingers between mine, squeezing. It's probably only for a second, but it feels longer. When he releases my hand, I'm a ball of chaos: fingers tingling from where his just were, mind trying to make sense of it. Is he just being friendly, or is this maybe some sort of surfer handshake?

Now he's crouching in front of me, inspecting my knee. "Ouch," he says. Gentle fingers prod the skin around my wound. "You busted that up pretty good."

"Yeah, stop poking it," I say, but I'm not mad.

"You okay?" he asks in a softer voice.

"It's fine."

He nods and stands, then gestures for the falcon, *gimme-gimme*. When I hand it over, he turns to the two punks.

"You know this thing is worthless, right? If you ding-dongs would've just hustled a little faster, I suspect all you'd get for it on eBay would be ten lousy dollars, and we'd just order a new one online the next day. But now you're going to start your teenage lives with criminal records."

"Screw you," Polo Shirt says. "My dad's a lawyer. A hundred bucks says he'll get you and the bitch fired."

Porter laughs and tugs a thumb in my direction as Mr. Cavadini rushes toward us through the gift-shop exit. "Nice try. Her mom's a lawyer too."

Uh, divorce lawyer living all the way across the country, but who cares? We both share a secret smile. Who knew that my archnemesis could make such a good partner? A crime-solving partner—that's all. No other kind of partner. I really need to wipe all those other thoughts out of my head, especially the confusing lusty thing that happened before we chased down these two kids. And the hand-holding. And the secret smiling.

Ugh.

Must rectify this tangled mess quickly, and I think I know how.

LUMIÈRE FILM FANATICS COMMUNITY
PRIVATE MESSAGES>ALEX>NEW!

@mink: I have a horoscope for you.

@alex: Do you? Lay it on me, because I've had a REALLY confusing day, and I need some guidance.

@mink: Okay, here it is: If life suddenly gives you a choice to say yes to a new experience, you should accept.

@alex: What if that experience might be a pain in the ass?

@mink: Why would you assume that?

@alex: Instinct. I've been burned before, remember?

@mink: Instinct is no match for reason.

@alex: At this point, I'm not even sure I've got either one of them on my side.

"Story of my life. I always get the fuzzy end of the lollipop."
—Marilyn Monroe, *Some Like It Hot* (1959)

IO

I'm doing this. I've got the day off, and I'm heading toward the Killian's Whale Tours booth. It's eerily gray and foggy this morning. So foggy, it's nearly noon and I still can't see much of the ocean. This is okay by me. Fewer tourists running around. It's like I have the boardwalk to myself.

So what if I've changed my mind twice? I'm really doing it this time. I mean, come on. It's Alex. At least, I *hope* it's Alex. And if it is, I'll know, because I know him. I should, shouldn't I? I've been talking to him online for months. We're practically soul mates. Okay, maybe that's a little much, but we're at least friends of some sort or another. We have a bond that stretches beyond our common interest.

Then there's the whole Porter situation. After the cops came and picked up the thieving kids yesterday—two run-of-the-mill officers, not my dad's Sergeant Mendoza—Porter was involved in paperwork to do with all that, so I didn't really see him again.

Which is good, because all these crazy feelings I was feeling about him . . . they were just a byproduct of adrenaline and elation over capturing those two boys.

Anyway, I'm not thinking about Porter Roth right now. I'm especially not thinking about his fingers twined through mine after the victory high five. That's banned from my brain. As if to underscore the matter, a low foghorn bellows offshore, making me jump. *Here be dragons, Rydell. Keep away, if you know what's good for you.*

I clear Porter from my head and continue walking. The orange and blue of the Killian logo appears. *We'll show you a whale of a good time!* Gee, if this really is Alex's family, I already see why he hates working here. Lame-o. The business is situated between two others, Shoreline Bicycle Rentals, and the booth that sells tickets to the Ferris wheel. I hover by the bike rental place until I spot Patrick's blond hair.

He's working. And it looks like he's alone.

I wait while he points someone down the boardwalk, giving them directions through the fog somewhere, then before I can lose my nerve again, I take three long strides and slow near the carved whale bench outside the ticketing window. A couple of seagulls scatter when I approach.

"Hi," I say. "Remember me?"

"From the Shack," he says. He's wearing an orange Windbreaker and white shorts. His sideburns are cropped shorter than they were in the diner, and the morning breeze is blowing blond hair across his eyes. "I never forget a film buff. But I do forget names. Remind me . . . ?"

I'm sort of crushed. "Bailey."

He snaps his fingers. "Bailey, that's right. Patrick," he says, extending his hand, and I pretend that I didn't remember his name either as I shake it.

Now I've got to play it cooler than I planned, so I say, "I was just taking a walk, seeing if there were any used-DVD stores on the boardwalk." I know there's one. I've already been inside it three times. "And then I saw you, and I thought, *Hey, maybe that guy would know*." Ugh. So awkward, but he doesn't seem to notice.

"Yeah, there's a little place called Video Ray-Gun, right in the middle of the promenade. Giant sci-fi ray gun outside. Hard to miss."

Crap. This is going to be harder than I thought. Didn't I give him a hint online last night? Unless this really isn't Alex . . .

"So, do you get a break here any time soon? Maybe you'd want to go browse some DVDs with me?" I hear myself saying. "You mentioned getting coffee sometime, but, you know . . ." My voice is getting smaller and smaller.

Come on. If this is really Alex, surely he'll remember me dropping the horoscope hint last night . . . won't he? I mean, he's always so attentive online. He remembers everything I say. Always gets my jokes, even remembers punch lines to gags from months back. But now he can't even remember my actual name? Maybe it really was a good idea that I didn't tell him I was moving out here, after all.

Hesitating, he leans over the counter and looks one way, then the other, peering into the fog. "All right. Yeah, sure. Why not. Business is slow. The current tour won't be back for a bit, so I guess I can take thirty. Hold on, let me close the gate and put up the sign."

I let out a long breath.

He jumps off his stool and reaches above his head to pull down a rolling metal shutter over the window, disappearing for a few seconds. When he reappears through a door on the side of the booth, he's got a GONE WHALING! BE BACK IN A FEW MINUTES sign, which he hangs on the shuttered window.

"Okay, Bailey. Let's go," he says with an inviting smile.

Feeling better, I fall into step with him, and we make our way to the promenade. He asks me polite questions—how long have I been in town? Where am I from? Oh, DC. Have I seen the president or toured the White House? Have I been to Dupont Circle?

By the time we get to the giant ray-gun sign, the only thing I've been able to ask him is how long he's lived in Coronado Cove (all his life), and where he goes to school—Berkshire Academy. The private school. This throws me for a loop. I never pegged Alex as a private-school kind of guy. I'm trying to figure this out as we step inside the shop.

Video Ray-Gun has one of those great dusty-musty smells that come with old stores, though most of their inventory doesn't date back more than a few years. They specialize in campy sci-fi movies, and because that's my dad's catnip, he's in love with this place. A few movie-related collectible posters and and toys grace the walls around the register, behind which hangs a TV where a *Godzilla* movie is playing. Two middle-aged long-haired men are paying more attention to the movie than to us when we walk past. Thank God, because I was just in here with Dad a couple of days ago, and I don't want them to recognize me.

The store is busier than I expected—not exactly the best place for a quiet, romantic get-to-know-you date, but what can I do now? It's all I have to work with. We stroll past oversize boxes of candy in retro theater packaging and a rack of upcoming Blu-ray DVDs available for preorder, and I try to pretend like I don't know where I'm going as Patrick leads me to the Film Classics section.

"They don't have a lot of stuff right now," he tells me, turning the corner around a bay of shelves. "I was just in here yesterday. But check this out." He grabs something off a shelf and hands it to me. "Boxed set of classic gangster films from the 1930s. It's a steal."

I accept the box and look at the back. "I'm not a huge fan of gangster movies."

"Are you kidding? *White Heat*? The 1932 version of *Scarface*? That was insanely violent for its time, really pushed the envelope."

"Yeaaah," I drawl, handing him the box back. "Not a big gun fan."

"Oh," he says, reshelving it. "One of those, huh?"

"Excuse me?"

He holds up both hands. "Hey, whatever you're into is fine. No argument from me. I just think film is film, and that you shouldn't paste your political views onto a piece of art."

Jeez. This isn't going well. I take a deep breath and pause for a moment. Maybe this is my fault? I don't really think so, but I strive to be the bigger person. "It's not that. I had a bad personal experience, so it's just . . . kind of a thing for me. Just not my cup of tea."

"Oh, God," he says, resting a sympathetic hand on my shoulder—just the tips of his fingers, actually. "I'm so sorry. I assumed. I'm being an ass. Forgive?"

"Forgotten," I say with a smile.

"Oh! What about *Breakfast at Tiffany's*? Everyone loves that."

Is he being serious? I mean, I love Audrey Hepburn, but I just can't watch Mickey Rooney playing a broadly caricatured Japanese man for goofs and giggles. No thanks. I tell him so. His argument isn't as strong for this one, but he's still disbelieving that I'm not singing its praises.

This is so weird. Our film mojo is off. Sure, we disagree online (all the time), but it's all good-natured. In person, it feels so . . . personal. We go through the classics section, shelf by shelf, but nothing seems to click with either one of us. It's like we're two completely different people, and the longer we're testing each other's tastes, the less we're liking each other. I'm starting to sweat in weird places and make awkward flirty jokes that don't land.

This is not going well.

The worst part is that he notices too.

"Sometimes they have more stuff in the back," he finally says after we haven't spoken in several long, excruciating seconds. "Let me go ask Henry if they've gotten anything new in. Be right back."

Great. Now I'm worried that he's giving me the slip. The first time I get up the nerve to ask a guy out on a date—a guy I've been fantasizing about for months—and it goes hellishly wrong. If he doesn't come back in one minute, I'm seriously considering sneaking out myself.

"*Breakfast at Tiffany's* is an overrated piece of fluff."

I freeze. No one's around. I glance down the aisle in both directions. Did I just imagine that? Or did someone overhear Patrick and me talking from before, and now I'm overhearing another conversation?

"It's not supposed to be a love story, you know. Which is the ironic thing in this particular situation, actually."

"Hello?" I whisper.

A DVD moves aside. I'm now staring at a pair of eyes. Someone's in the other aisle. I move another DVD and reveal more of the face through the wire shelving: scruffy jaw, slow grin, wild, sun-kissed curls. Porter. My hand clenches. "What the hell are you doing here?"

"It's my day off."

"And you're following me around?" I say, exasperated.

"No, you're following me around. I was in here when you paraded in with Patrick Killian on your arm."

I stand on tiptoes to peer over the top of the shelves. He raises his head to meet me and cocks both brows, a smug look on his face. My heart starts pounding, big-time. Why does he have this effect on me? Can't my body just be normal around him?

"How do you know him?" I whisper hotly, glancing around to make sure Patrick isn't listening. I don't spot him, so I guess he's either in back or has flown the coop.

Porter casually rests an arm on the top of the video rack. "I've known him since we were kids. He thinks he's a movie snob because his family is one of the local companies that sponsors the annual film festival. Big whoop."

Wait one stinking minute. Big warning bells ding in my head. I definitely think Alex would have mentioned if his family sponsored the festival. That's something you'd brag about to your film-geek friend, Forbidden Zone personal-detail restrictions aside. No way would he keep that from me. This is all wrong. But I don't think Porter is lying, because now I'm remembering when Patrick gave me the film festival brochure: "hot off the presses," he said. He got an early copy of it because his dad's a festival sponsor? It's still in my purse, and I'm fighting everything not to pull it out and scan the sponsor page for the Killian name.

Inside, I'm quietly panicking that Patrick isn't Alex, but all I can say to Porter is, "Oh, and you know better." It's a weak taunt, but my heart isn't into it.

"I know that you were right about *Breakfast at Tiffany's*," he responds. "Truman Capote's novella is about a gay man and a prostitute. Hollywood turned it into a romance. And don't get me started on Mickey Rooney. That was an embarrassing shambles. But…"

"But what?"

"I still think it's worth watching for Hepburn's performance. What? Don't look so shocked. It was my grandma's favorite movie. You don't know everything about me."

Apparently, I know nothing. *Who are you, Porter Roth?*

"And I'm not sure if you know everything about your date—"

"Jesus, do you have to talk so loud?" I whisper. "He's not my date." Not at this rate, anyway.

"Whatever he is, I'm telling you this because I hate to see you wasting all that primo flirt material on someone who doesn't appreciate it." He leans across the rack, beckoning me closer. "Patrick has a boyfriend in Guatemala."

My eye twitches. I blink. Stare at Porter.

Holy shitcakes . . . I think back to when I first met Patrick in the Pancake Shack, and him talking about Cary Grant and Randolph Scott being lovers. Patrick hesitating when I asked him to come here today. No wonder he was asking me about Dupont Circle; if I'd let him talk instead of running my nervous mouth, he'd probably have been seconds away from asking if I'd attended the annual Capital Pride festival there.

I don't say a word. I just slowly sink back down onto the flats of my feet, the top of Porter's face disappearing from my view. I straighten my skirt and turn, resigned, adding up my tally of humiliations for the morning. (1) My so-called date is a bust. (2) I'm a loser who can't tell straight from gay. (3) I'm no closer to finding Alex than I was weeks ago when I first came to town. (4) Porter witnessed the whole thing.

Patrick is striding toward me. "Nothing new in the storeroom," he says. His gaze darts to the second aisle, where Porter emerges from a section marked BLAXPLOITATION AND KUNG FU FLICKS. He's dressed in long gray board shorts and an unzipped army-green jacket with the words HOT STUFF embroidered next to a cartoon baby devil on a tattered breast pocket. His curly mop seems longer today; the bottom of his hair kisses the tops of his shoulders. His gaze connects with mine and sticks for a second, which does something funny to my pulse.

"Oh hey, Porter," Patrick says cheerfully. "How's Lana? Heard she was hitting the pro circuit."

"Indeed she is," Porter says, all lazy and casual. Still looking at me.

Patrick's eyes flit back and forth from Porter to me, like he's suspicious we've been talking behind his back. Great. Now I feel guilty on top of being humiliated. "Hey, Bailey, it's been fun, but my dad texted from the boat, so I probably should get back to work. Coffee sometime?"

He seems to mean it, surprisingly, and it hits me for the first time that, unlike me, he never thought this was a date. He just assumed we were two like-minded people hanging out. Does that make me an even bigger jerk if I walk away from this never wanting to see him again because he prefers another man's ham sandwich instead of my lady bits? I decide that yeah, it does. Add that to my never-ending list of major malfunctions.

"Coffee would be great. Or tea," I amend. "You want my phone number? Maybe we can catch some of the film festival together, or something."

"Sure," he says, smiling, and we head to the front of the store together, exchanging digits, before he waves good-bye, heads off into the fog, and leaves me standing outside with a tiny scrap of my dignity intact.

I should probably message Alex—just to feel things out, make sure he knows nothing about this fiasco. But at the same time, maybe I need to clear my head first. I wanted to find Alex so badly that I'd jumped to conclusions about Patrick and ignored good sense. That was a stupid mistake, but I don't want to beat myself up about it too much. I just . . .

I don't know what I want anymore, honestly.

"You okay?"

Porter stands next to me. The door to Video Ray-Gun swings shut behind us.

I let out a long sigh. "Yeah, I'm . . . just having a really bad day. It must be the fog."

"Can't be that," he says. "Foggy days are the best."

I wait for the punch line, but it never comes. He glances down at my knee; it's scabbed over from yesterday's takedown of the Maltese falcon thieves, but I was too vain to wear a Band-Aid today.

"I thought California was supposed to be sunny all the time," I tell him. "Foggy days are depressing."

"Naaa. They're kind of magical."

"Magical," I repeat dismally, not believing him.

"What, is magic too lowbrow for you?"

"Don't start with me today," I say, more weary than frustrated, but if he goes much further, I can't promise that won't change. "Do you enjoy picking fights with people?"

"Just you."

I search his face, unsure if he's teasing. "You fight with Pangborn all the time."

"Not true. He never fights back."

"So that's what you like?" I ask. "Someone who fights back?"

"Everyone enjoys a little witty repartee now and then."

Is that a compliment? I can't tell.

He shrugs one shoulder. "Maybe I do like someone who fights back. It's a mystery, even to me. I'm just a beach bum, remember? Who knows what goes on inside this simple brain of mine?"

Yikes. Awkward. Some part of me wonders if I should apologize for that, but then I remember all the craptastic things he's said to me.

A long moment stretches.

"Ever ridden a Ferris wheel in the fog?" he suddenly asks. "Oh! What about the aerial lifts?"

"Um, I don't do amusement park rides."

"Why?"

"They always break down and the seats are sticky."

Porter laughs. "Jesus, Bailey. What kind of busted rides do they have back in our nation's capital?" He shakes his head in mock disapproval and sighs. "Well, just because I feel sorry for your pitiful amusement park ride education, I suppose I'll take you on the Bees."

"What are the Bees?"

"The Bees. Buzzz." He tug-tug-tugs on my shirtsleeve, urging me toward him as he walks backward, smiling that lazy, sexy smile of his. "Those wires with the chairlifts that are painted like bumblebees? The ones that take people up to the redwoods on the cliffs above the beach? You board them next to the big golden wheel on the boardwalk with the shiny, shiny lights? Get to know your new town, Rydell. Come on."

II

"What's the matter?" Porter asks as we head down the boardwalk. Then it hits me: like the Ferris wheel, the ticket booth for the Bumblebee Lifts is next to the stupid whale tours window. I didn't think this through.

"Crap. I really don't want him to see me again," I say.

Porter is confused for a second. "Patrick? Why would he care?"

My answer is a long, sad sigh.

"All right, all right," he grumbles, but I don't think he's genuinely irritated. I'm more convinced he feels sorry for me, and that might be worse. "Go stand at the gate over there. I'll be right back."

I don't have the energy to argue. I drag my feet to the chairlift entrance and wait while a stooped, Filipino man—name tag: Reyes—with a raspy voice helps a few stragglers off one of the lifts. Other than one other touchy-feely college-aged couple, it doesn't look like anyone else is waiting to get on. I don't blame them.

Tendrils of fog cling to the swinging seats, which look much like ski lifts, painted yellow and black. The fat wires that carry the lifts over the boardwalk to the rocky cliffs rest on a series of T-shaped poles; one wire carries the ascending lifts, one wire holds the descenders. Big white lights sit atop each pole, but halfway up the line the fog is so thick that the lights just . . . disappear. I can't even see the cliffs today.

"Mornin'," the Bumblebees' operator says when I greet him.

"What do you do if something happens to one of the lifts?" I ask. "How can you see it?"

He follows my eyes, cranes his neck, and looks up into the fog. "I can't."

Not reassuring.

After what seems like an extraordinarily long time, Porter returns, breathless, with our tickets and a small, waxed bag. "Yo, how's it hanging, Mr. Reyes?" he says merrily to the operator.

"No food allowed on the Bees, Porter," the elderly man rasps.

Porter stuffs the bag inside his jacket and zips it halfway up. "We won't touch it until we get to the cliffs."

"All right," the man relents, smiling, and he extends an arm to escort us onto the next lift.

Before I can change my mind, we're boarding a swaying chair behind the groping college-aged couple. Each seat accommodates two people, snugly, and though we're covered by a plastic yellow-and-black striped bonnet above, it leaves our torsos exposed. This means (A) the coastal wind whips through the chairlift against our backs, and (B) we have a perfect view of the lovey-dovey couple ahead of us and their roaming hands. Terrific.

The operator pulls a handlebar down that locks us in around the waist. I sneak a glance at Porter. I didn't expect to be sitting so close to him. Our legs are almost touching, and I'm wearing a short skirt. I make myself smaller.

"Fifteen minutes up," the operator says as he walks alongside our slow-moving chair, "fifteen minutes back down, whenever you're ready to return. Enjoy yourselves."

And we're off. My stomach lurches a little, which is stupid, because we're not even off the ground yet; these Bees need more zippity-do-dah.

"You all right, there, Rydell?" Porter asks. "Not afraid of heights, are you?"

"Guess we'll find out," I say as my dragging toes leave the ground and we begin to take flight, ever-so-slowly.

"You'll love it," Porter assures me. "It'll be great when we hit the fog in a few minutes."

Once the lift operator ambles away to the gate, out of sight, Porter unzips his jacket a few inches and sticks his hand inside. A second later, he's pulling something out. It's cream colored and about half the size of a golf ball. I smell vanilla for one glorious second before he shoves the whole thing in his mouth.

His eyes close in pleasure as he chews. "Mmm. So good."

"What is that?" I ask.

"Illegal to eat on the Bees," he reminds me, slipping his phone out of his shorts pocket. "You sure you want to break the rules?"

I skipped breakfast. I was too nervous about meeting Patrick. What a dork. I still can't believe that all happened. It's like a bad dream that I can't shake. And now Porter's got warm vanilla wafting up from his jacket, right in my face.

"What the hell, Porter?" I whine. "It smells really good."

"Gracie did mention that you've got a mean sweet tooth when it comes to pastries." He's flipping through his phone, digging out another ball of whatever it is he's got. I think it's a vanilla mini muffin. I smell coconut, too. That might just be him, though.

"See if I tell her anything again," I complain, kicking my feet as we lift a little higher off the ground.

"Here we go," he says, finding something on his phone. "New quiz. Let's make a deal."

"NO QUIZZES."

"I'll be nice this time," he says. "Promise."

"Why should I believe you?"

"Because I've got a pocketful of moon muffins," he says with a slow smile.

I don't know the hell that is, but I really want one. My stomach growls.

"Wow, Rydell. You have a dragon living inside there, or what?"

My head lolls forward as I make little weepy noises. I finally give in. "Okay, but if you piss me off while we're stuck on this stupid flying bumblebee, just know that my nails are sharp, and

I will go for your eyes." I flash him my freshly painted ruby reds, filed to a vintage almond shape.

He whistles. "Pointy. That's one glam manicure. And here I was, thinking you were aloof. Sugar brings out the demon in you. Porter likey."

I get a little flustered, but not enough to stop wanting the muffins.

"So here's how this works. First"—he pulls out one of his prizes—"this is a moon muffin. Local Coronado Cove specialty. Fresh out of the oven over at Tony's Bakery right there." He points backward. "You think you like those sugar cookies at work? Well, you're going to love this."

He holds it in the tips of his fingers. I snatch it up, give the sniff test, and then tear it in two, ignoring him when he acts like this is a mistake. I taste it. Totally lovely. Spongy. Light. Dusted in vanilla sugar. "Yum," I tell him.

Porter makes a victory face. "Told you. Okay, quiz time. This one is for both of us. It's a . . . friendship quiz. We both have to give answers and see how we match up. To see if we'll make compatible friends or bitter enemies."

"Pfft," I say around a mouthful of moon muffin, brushing crumbs off my boobs. "Enemies. Quiz over; give me another muffin." I wiggle my fingers in his face.

He laughs and bats away my fingers. "No muffin until we answer the first question. Ready? Question one." He starts reading. "'When we fight, (A) it's like World War Three, and takes days for us to speak again; (B) we fight hard but make up fast; (C) we never fight.' What do you think? A, B, or C?"

God, what is it with him and quizzes? Grace wasn't wrong; he's obsessed. "Not C, that's for sure," I say. "But not A, either. I guess we're B. We fight hard, but we make up fast. But that's mainly because you bribe me with food. Keep that up, and we'll be okay."

"B it is." He holds out another muffin without looking up from his phone. I take it while he reads the next question. "'Our favorite way to spend our downtime is: (A) surrounded by friends at parties, the more the merrier; (B) always on the go, never staying still; (C) chilling alone.'"

"I'm guessing you'll say one of the first two things, but I'm more of a C kind of girl. Does that ruin our score?"

"Nope. I'm C too, actually."

Umm, okay. I'm not sure I believe that. Then again, it's his day off, and he's hanging out in a video store by himself, which isn't how I pictured him. "Oh, look!" I say, gazing down my side of the chairlift. "We're almost above the Ferris wheel now."

The boardwalk looks weird from here, just small bursts of color, and the tops of buildings. Cars rush by on my left, but who wants to look at the town? Unfortunately, I can't help but glance forward and catch the couple in front of us with their hands all over each other. I think there's more than kissing happening— wow. I quickly look away.

"These lifts sure are slow, aren't they?" I complain.

"I've taken naps on here," Porter says. "No lie. Next question.

'If one of us has a problem, we will: (A) keep it to ourselves; (B) immediately come to the other for advice; (C) drop hints and hope the other figures it out eventually.'"

"Put me down for selection A." Delicately, I dip my hand into Porter's gaping jacket until my fingertips hit the waxed-paper bag and find another muffin. It isn't until I'm pulling it out that I look at Porter's face and hesitate.

"No, please, go on," he says. "Do help yourself."

I give him a self-conscious grin. "Oops."

"You always go around sticking your hands down boys' clothes?" he asks.

"When they're full of baked goods."

"Tomorrow I'm coming to work with ten pounds of pastries in my pants," he mumbles to himself, making an *ooaff!* noise when I punch him lightly in the arm.

"Next question, for the love of vanilla," I beg. "How long is this quiz, anyway?"

"Back up—you chose A for the last one? I chose B," he says, and I struggle to remember what the question was. "That probably screws up our compatibility factor. Last one. 'The most important quality in a . . . uh, friendship is: (A) that we share the same interests; (B) that we like each other; (C) that we're always there for each other, no matter what.'"

I swallow the last of my muffin. "What kind of question is that? Shouldn't there be another option, like, (D) All of the above?"

"Well, there isn't. So you have to pick one."

"I refuse."

"You can't refuse."

"Think I just did, Hot Stuff."

He snorts at that. "But how will we know if we're compatible?" he moans. I can't tell if he's only teasing me, or if there's something more beneath the silliness.

"Gee, I don't know. Guess we'll have to actually be friends and find out for ourselves instead of taking a quiz."

He shuts his phone off dramatically and shoves it in his pocket. "No one appreciates the fine art of a good quiz anymore. Oh, here we go. Buckle your seat belt; it's about to get weird. Hope you're not scared of the dark, or anything. Feel free to stick your hand inside my jacket again if you need to."

Just in time, I turn my head forward as the lift enters the thick bank of fog that's rolling off the ocean. Porter was exaggerating. It's not pea-soup fog. We can still see each other. But the couple in front of us is a little hazier, and except for the occasional truck or tall building, the ground below, too. And it doesn't really have a scent, exactly, and it's not wet, either. But it feels different in my lungs.

"Why is it so foggy here in the summer?"

"You really want to know?"

I'm not sure how to answer that. "Uh, yes, I guess?"

"Well, you see . . . fog forms over the water because it's cold. And the Pacific stays cold here for two reasons. First, cold air from Alaska comes down along the California Current, and second, cold water comes up deep from the bottom ocean by something called upwelling, which has to do with wind blowing parallel with the coast and pushing the ocean surface southward. This stirs up the Pacific and brings up icy brine from the bottom of the ocean, which is so cold, it refrigerates the ocean air, condenses, and creates fog. Summer sun heats the air and makes it rise, and the fog gets sucked up."

I stare at him. I think my mouth is hanging open, I'm not sure.

He scratches his forehead and makes a growling noise, dismissing the whole speech. "I'm a weather nerd. It's because of surfing. In order to find the best waves, you have to know about tides, swells, storms . . . I guess I just picked up an interest in that stuff."

I glance at his fancy red surf watch peeking out from his jacket cuff with all its tide and weather calculations. Who knew he was such a smarty-pants? "I'm seriously impressed," I say, meaning it. "Guess you're the guy to sit next to if I need to cheat in biology."

"I aced AP Biology last year. I'm taking AP Environmental Science and AP Chem 2 this year."

"Yuck. I hate all the sciences. History and English, yes. No sciences."

"No sciences? Bailey, Bailey, Bailey. It appears we are opposite in every conceivable way."

"Yeah," I agree, smiling. I'm not sure why, but this makes me sort of giddy.

He laughs like I told a great joke, and then leans over the bar.

"So what do you think of our California fog now? Cool, right?" He cups his hand as if he can capture some of it.

Testing, I stretch my hands out too. "Yeah, it is. I like our fog. You were right."

We sit like that together, trying to catch the ocean in our hands, for the rest of the ascent.

At the end of the line, a waiting chairlift operator releases our bar and frees us. We made it to the top of the cliffs. Along with a tiny gift shop called the Honeypot—I really hate to break it to them, but bumblebees don't make honey—there's a small platform here lined by a railing and a few of those coin-operated telescopes that look out over the ocean. If it were a clear day, we'd be looking out over the Cavern Palace, but there's not much to see now, so only a few people are milling about. It's also breezy and chilly, especially for June.

I never knew California had such crazy weather. I ask Porter to tell me more about it. At first he thinks I'm making fun of him, but after not much prodding, we lean against the split-fence cedar railing, and while we polish off the last of the muffins, he tells me more about ocean currents and tides, redwood forests and ferns and ecosystems, and how the fog has been declining over the last few decades and scientists are trying to figure out why and how to stop it.

It's weird to hear him talk about all this, and like the scars on his arm, I'm trying to fit all his ragged pieces together: the security guard at work with the lewd mouth who made fun of my mismatched shoes; the surfer boy, struggling to pull his drugged-up friend Davy off the crosswalk; the brother whose eyes shine with pride when he talks about his sister's achievements; the guy who high-fived me when I took down the kid who stole the Maltese falcon statue . . . and the science geek standing in front of me now.

Maybe Walt Whitman was right. We all really do contradict ourselves and contain multitudes. How do we even figure out who we really are?

Porter finally seems to notice how much he's talking and his golden face gets ruddy. It's pretty adorable. "Okay, enough," he finally says. "What are you nerdy about?"

I hesitate, wanting to talk about classic film as passionately as he told me about ocean rain, but then I remember the incident with Patrick and my stomach feels a little queasy. I don't relish rehashing all that again. Maybe some other time.

"History," I tell him, which, though a compromise, is also true. "Confession time. I've been thinking lately that I sort of want to be a museum archivist."

He brightens, as if I've just reminded him of something. "Like, cataloging things?"

"Yeah, or I might want to be a curator. I'm not totally sure." Admitting it aloud makes me uncomfortable. I get a little squirmy and feel the need to flee the scene, but we're standing on a cliff, and there's nowhere to run. "Anyway, working at the Cave may not be a dream come true, but it's a start. You know, for my résumé. Eventually."

He squints at me, and I tell him a little more about my museum dream—which fits in with my Artful Dodger lifestyle: behind the scenes, low stress, geeking out over old things, preserving historically valuable pieces that most people find boring. As much as I love film, there's no way I'd ever want to be a director. I'm realizing that more and more. Put me in the shadows, baby. I'll happily plow through boxes of old files. "I like uncovering things that people have forgotten. Plus, I'm really good at organizing things."

Porter smiles softly. "I've noticed."

"You have?"

"Your cash drawer. Bills all facing the same way, creased corners straightened. Everything stacked and clipped together for the drop bag all perfect. Most people's drawers are a wreck, money turned every which way."

My cheeks warm. I'm surprised he's paid attention to details like that. "I like things neat and orderly." Stupid CPA blood.

"Orderly is good. Maybe you've got some science in you after all."

"Pah!" I exclaim. "Nice try, but no."

His eyes crease in the corners when he chuckles. "Guess you don't want to work in the Hotbox forever, though, huh?"

"God no," I say, pulling a sour face. "Not the Hotbox."

Just mentioning it by name makes us both thirsty, so we head inside the Honeypot and grab some drinks. By the time we're done with those, the sun's breaking through the fog—sucking it up, now that I learned that tidbit of science—and the warming midday air smells like my dad's backyard, of pine and redwood, clean and fresh. I breathe it in deeply. Definitely doesn't smell like this out east.

When we finally get back on the chairlifts, we're sitting closer. A lot closer. I feel Porter's arm and leg, warm against mine. His board shorts are longer than my skirt, his legs longer than my legs, but when the lift sways forward, our calves press together. I stare where our bodies are joined. For the tiniest of moments, I consider pulling away, making myself small again, like I did on the ride up. But—

I don't.

And he doesn't.

The bar comes down, trapping us together. Arm against arm. Leg against leg, flesh against flesh. My heart beats against my rib cage as if it's excitedly keeping time with a song. Every once in a while, I feel his eyes on my face, but I don't dare look back. We ride in silence the entire way down, watching the town get bigger and bigger.

A couple of yards before we hit the ground, he speaks up in a voice so quiet, I can barely hear him. "What I said the other day about you having champagne tastes?" He pauses for a moment. Mr. Reyes is smiling, waiting to unhitch our bar. "I just wanted you to know that I like the way you dress. I like your style. . . . I think it's sexy as hell."

LUMIÈRE FILM FANATICS COMMUNITY
PRIVATE MESSAGES>ALEX

NO NEW MESSAGES

"If what I think is happening is happening, it better not be."
—Meryl Streep, *Fantastic Mr. Fox* (2009)

12

I'm a mess. It's been eight hours since Porter and I parted at the Bees and I haven't been able to get his words out of my head. Sexy as hell.

Me!

He!

What?

He didn't say anything else, barely even looked at me when he told me he had to "skedaddle" because he promised to help his mom unload something at the surf shop that afternoon. I think I thanked him for the muffins and the chairlift ticket. I'm not even sure. I was so flustered. I might have told him I'd see him at work. Mr. Reyes asked me if I was okay, so I know I stood there too long, looking like a complete lunatic. Then I walked a half mile in the sand to the wrong parking lot and had to backtrack to get to Baby.

"That's all you're eating?" Dad asks from my left elbow.

I look down at my bowl. It's mostly full, but not because it's bad. It's really, really good, in fact. I'm sitting at a pink picnic table on the northern end of the cove, far from the madding crowd of the boardwalk. Wanda—sorry, Sergeant Mendoza—sits across the table. It's hard to think of her as a cop now, because she's dressed in jeans, and we're eating dinner with her on the beach in front of a pop-up food truck, the infamous posole truck. Also because Dad keeps calling her Wanda, and every time he says it, he smiles a little, only I don't think he knows he's doing it. I think they might be playing footsie under the table in the sand, but I'm too distracted to check.

Posole, it turns out, is this amazing Mexican slow-cooked stew made from dried corn, broth, chilies, and meat. They have red, green, and white posole for sale at the truck, and I'm having white, which is the pork kind, and the mildest. It's topped with sliced fresh radishes and cabbage, and there're plates of lime wedges at the tables. The sun is setting over the Pacific, so the sky is this crazy gold-and-orchid color, and the posole truck has these multicolored lights strung up over the tables, so it's all festive and fun. At least, it should be. But we can see a few surfers silhouetted in the dusky waves, and that's making me think of Porter, which freaks me out.

So no, I can't eat.

But I have to. I'm starving, and this is silly. I'm not going to be one of those girls who goes all woobly-woo over a boy and picks at her food. It's Porter Roth, for Pete's sake. We're practically archenemies. Look at our stupid compatibility quiz—didn't we fail that? Or did we? I can't remember now. All I remember is how cute and earnest he looked, talking about phytoplankton and ocean currents, and how the tiny hairs on his leg tickled when the chairlift rocked.

I feel feverish, just thinking about it again now, God help me.

But then, maybe he didn't even mean it. He might have only been teasing me. Was he only teasing me? A fresh wave of panic washes over my chest.

No, no, no. *This cannot be happening* is all I can think, my mind gleaming with terror.

I cannot like Porter Roth.

"Bailey?"

"Huh? No, I love it. Seriously. It's delicious," I answer my dad, trying to sound normal as I pick up my spoon. "I had a weird day, is all."

I push Porter out of my mind. Eat my soup. Concentrate on watching seagulls soaring around the shore. Then I hear my dad tell Wanda in a salacious voice, "She had a date today."

"O-oh," Wanda says, mouth curving into a smile.

"Dad, jeez."

"Well, you didn't tell me how it went. What was his name? Patrick?"

"If you must know, it went like this," I say, giving a thumbs-down sign and blowing a big, fat raspberry. "Turns out your daughter gets a failing grade in relationship chemistry, because, funny thing, but Patrick is gay."

Wanda makes a pained face. "And he didn't tell you before?"

"Not his fault," I say. "I guess I just made some wrong assumptions."

Dad grits his teeth and looks several shades of uncomfortable. He has no idea what to tell me. "Oh, honey. I'm . . . sorry?"

I shake my head. "Like you always say, never assume."

"Makes an ass out of 'me' and 'u,'" he finishes, quoting one of his favorite goofy word games. After a moment, he loosens up and drapes an arm around my back. "I'm truly sorry, kiddo. It wasn't meant to be, but don't let it get you down. This town is lousy with cute boys."

Wanda smiles to herself.

"Gee, Dad. I can't believe you just said that in front of your girlfriend," I say in a stage whisper, letting my head fall on his shoulder.

"Me either," he admits, rubbing my back. "Being a parent is weird."

Wanda wipes her mouth with a napkin, nodding her head. "So true. My baby is two years older than you, Bailey. And he's just gone through a crazy breakup."

"Wait, you have a son?"

She nods. "Been divorced for five years. He's nineteen. Went to a year of community college, and now he's taking summer classes at your dad's alma mater, Cal Poly. Electrical engineering. He's a smart kid."

As she's telling me more about her son, I dig into my stew,

wondering if I'll ever meet this guy. What if my dad remarries? Will I have a stepbrother? That's bizarre to think about. Then again, Wanda seems pretty cool, and the way she's talking about Anthony—that's her son—you'd think he was the most awesome guy on the planet. Besides, my dad's like me: He doesn't make rash decisions. I can't picture him rushing headlong into another marriage, not like Mom—who still hasn't called, just for the record. Not that I'm counting the days or anything, crying my eyes out for her like a ten-year-old kid who's been shipped off to summer camp and misses Mommy.

But still. One call? One e-mail?

If she thinks I'm calling first, she can think again. I'm not supposed to be the adult here.

When I'm done eating, I get up from the table and grab my phone out of my purse, which is stashed in the seat of Baby; I drove and met Dad and Wanda here. On my way back to the table, I notice that some of the distant surfers have stripped out of their wet suits. They've stuck their boards in the sand, propped them up like gravestones, and are trudging to the posole truck. My pulse leaps as I scan the three boys for Porter's face. I don't find it, but I do spot someone else limping across the beach: Davy.

Crud.

I don't really want to see him again, especially not while I'm with my dad. Unfortunately, no matter how low I duck as I sit back down next to my father, it's not low enough to escape his hazy gaze.

"Look who it is, little miss thing," he says in a rough voice. "Cowgirl. You work with Porter at the Cave."

I raise my hand a couple of inches off the table in a weak wave and lift my chin.

"Davy," he says, pointing at his chest, which is, as always, naked—even when the other two surfers are clothed. He's shivering. *Put a damn shirt on, dude.* "Porter's friend, remember?"

"Hey," I say, because it would be weird not to. But why did he have to mention Porter?

"Is that your Vespa?" he asks. "Sweet ride. Looks legit. Has it been restored?"

Wanda sits up straighter and speaks up before I can answer. "What are you doing out here, Mr. Truand?"

"Oh, hello, Officer Mendoza," Davy says, seemingly unfazed by her presence. "Didn't recognize you out of uniform."

"It's *Sergeant* Mendoza, and I can still arrest your ass, no matter what I'm wearing."

"I'll keep that in mind," he says, smiling like an insurance salesman.

Two older girls in bikini bottoms and T-shirts get up from a nearby table to throw away their trash, and Davy's friends start hitting on them in the worst way possible. All I hear is "ass for days" and "bury my face down there" and I want to either die or punch them all in the junk. The girls flip them off and after a short but brutal exchange, his friends give up and head to the posole truck like it's no big deal. Just another few minutes in their day.

Now that the circus is over, Davy seems to remember he was talking to me.

"So anyways, cowgirl, you're still invited. Remember?" He holds up a finger to his lips and winks at me. It takes me a second to realize that he's talking about the bonfire. I guess. Who really can tell when it comes to this idiot. I don't respond, and he doesn't notice. He and his buds are already distracted by the next thing—another car, this time full of more dudes. They race to go meet them. Thank God. I'm totally embarrassed to be on the same beach as these morons. They're bringing society down by several pegs, just breathing the same air as us.

"Go far, far away, please," I mutter.

"You know him?" Wanda asks, suddenly very concerned in a cop sort of way.

Now my dad's concerned too—in a father sort of way.

"No, no," I say, waving my hand. "He knows someone I work with."

"Porter Roth?" Dad says. "I thought he was a security guard, not a beach bum."

Guess that's where I picked up that phrase. "He is. I mean, he's not," I say. *Oh, crap.* I don't want my dad associating the two of them together. "Porter's not like Davy. I don't even know if they're really friends anymore. I ran into Davy on the boardwalk and he started calling me cowgirl because I was buying a scarf, and then he invited me to hang out, but that didn't mean I was going or anything—"

"Whoa," Dad says. "Slow down."

"Davy seems like such a dirtbag, ugh."

Wanda seems satisfied by my answer. "Stay away from him, Bailey. I mean that. He's trouble. Every time I bust him, he gets off on a technicality. But he's barely keeping his head above water. I'm talking serious narcotics—not weed or alcohol. He needs help, but his parents don't care enough to give it to him."

Jesus. I think about the vintage clothing store and that weird conversation I witnessed—how mad Porter was catching Davy coming out of the shop.

"But Porter isn't . . . ," I say, and wish I hadn't mentioned his name before I can even finish.

"Porter's okay," she says, and I hope she doesn't notice how relieved I am. "At least, I think he is. The Roth family's been through a lot, but they're good people. Still, you'd be better off staying away from that crowd. If Porter's hanging around with Davy, I'd advise you to steer clear and save yourself some grief." She says this last part more to Dad than me, and he gives her a little nod, like yeah, he understands. Message received.

Death by association. Porter Roth has now got a big red mark against him in my dad's book. I'm not sure what that means for me, because I don't even know what's going on between me and Porter. But if I did want something to be going on, hypothetically, does that mean it's impossible now?

I do know one thing: telling my dad about the bonfire is out of the question. Because chances that Wanda knows about this little

Saturday night hootenanny are pretty good, and he might ask her about it. Problem is, I really want to go now. Grace asked me, and I don't want to back out. Besides, Porter might be there . . .

But. (Why is there always a but?)

There's one person I haven't considered in any of this mess. Alex. Maybe I should ask his opinion. Or at least make an attempt to tell him what's going on. After all, he's probably just been carrying on, being his usual awesome self, while I've been spending the day wronging him left and right all over town, because I'm a horrible, horrible person. Doesn't he deserve a say-so in any of this?

LUMIÈRE FILM FANATICS COMMUNITY
PRIVATE MESSAGES>ALEX>NEW!

@alex: That horoscope prediction you gave me kind of came true in a weird way.

@mink: It did?

@alex: I followed your advice and it worked out. I took a risk and had one of the best days I've had in a long time. You were right. It's good to open yourself up to new things.

@mink: It's funny you say that, because I was going to ask your advice about whether or not I should do something. (This isn't about flying out there, by the way. Just so we're clear. Not saying it won't happen, but it's on hold for the moment.)

@alex: My advice is YES. Do it.

@mink: You don't even know what it is yet.

@alex: And I didn't know what your horoscope meant, but it worked out. Take a chance, Mink. You helped me; now I'm helping you. Whatever it is you're thinking about doing, my advice is to just do it. What's the worst that can happen?

"Nobody ever lies about being lonely."
—Montgomery Clift, *From Here to Eternity* (1953)

13

I don't work with Porter on my next shift. In fact, I'm not scheduled to work with him again until Saturday—not that I've obsessively checked the schedule. But the level of disappointment that hits me when I pick up my till and see Mr. Pangborn's white hair instead of Porter's tangle of curls is so crushing, I have to give myself a mental shake. Why am I getting so worked up over a boy? This isn't like me. At all.

"We're still on for tonight?" Grace says when Pangborn is escorting us to the Hotbox, merrily whistling what I think is a Paul Simon song. When I hesitate too long, she grabs my orange vest. "Don't you bail on me, Bailey Rydell."

"I'm not," I say, laughing as I push her away. "It's just complicated. I might need to fib a little to my dad about who we're hanging out with, so when you pick me up, don't mention any surfers."

She wrinkles up her face, and then gives me a *whatever* look. "Eight o'clock."

"Eight. I'll be ready, promise."

Pangborn does a little shuffling dance outside the ticketing booth door, one hand on his stomach, singing about some guy named Julio down by the school yard. "Yaa da-da-da-da!"

Grace grins. "That must be some fine chronic you got your hands on this morning."

"Nature's medicine, my dear," he corrects, making a quieting signal with his hand as he glances around—probably looking for Cavadini. "Never know who's listening around here."

A terrible thought crosses my mind. "You guys don't have sound on the security cameras, do you?" All the things Porter claims Grace tells him about me . . . what if he's been listening in on our conversations inside the Hotbox?

"Sound?" Pangborn chuckles. "We barely have sight. No, there's no sound."

Sweet baby Jesus. I sigh in relief.

"Why?" he asks.

"Uh . . . I just wondered if you guys were listening in while we gossiped in the Hotbox," I say, trying to cover up as best I can—and doing a crap job of it.

He chuckles. "No, nothing like that. We can't hear unless you call us, so gossip away. The system's old. Hasn't been upgraded in a decade, in fact. They're going to have to spend money soon. The offsite company that monitors the alarm system went out of business two weeks ago. Now if anything goes wrong in the middle of the night, all we can do is call the local police."

"Just call Bailey," Grace says. "She'll chase down criminals and jump them."

I bump her shoulder. "Shut it, Grace Achebe, or I'll start counting change as slow as Michelle."

"Noooo!" She waves her hand at Pangborn. "Hey, you gonna let us in any time soon? Not all of us have the luxury of your natural medication to make the day pass by faster."

The old security guard smiles goofily and knocks on the door, announcing, "Team Grailey reporting for duty, boys. Open up. I seem to have misplaced my key again. . . ."

After we're situated and on a roll, Grace turns off her mic and says, "Why were you asking Pangborn all that stuff about listening in on our gossip?"

"It's nothing, really," I say, but she's not letting it go. "I was just worried that Porter might be hearing our conversations."

"Why?"

"Because of some things he said a couple of days ago. It's nothing. Stupid, really. He knows I have a sweet tooth—"

"I told him that."

"Yeah, that's what he said."

"He's been asking about you lately. Quite a bit, in fact."

"He has?"

"Uh-huh." She glances at me from the corner of her eye.

"Like what about?"

She shrugs. "Just things. He's curious. That's his personality."

"Like a cat, huh?" So this is nothing out of the ordinary. She doesn't offer anything more, so I say, "Well, anyway. That's all there is. He was just teasing me with these muffin things on the Bees, and—"

I feel rather than see Grace's head swing in my direction. "WHAT DID YOU JUST SAY?"

"Oh my God, Grace. My ear holes. I didn't know you could be so loud." We still have a line, so I plaster a fake smile on my face and pass tickets through the tiny hole in the window. "That actually hurt my eardrums."

"But that's what you said, right? You said you were on the lifts with Porter? Why were you on the lifts with Porter?"

"It's a long story."

"We've got six hours."

I sigh. Between customers, I give her the short version of the story. I don't tell her about my ongoing hunt for Alex, because that seems too personal—I just tell her that I met Patrick and didn't realize I was barking up the wrong tree.

"Patrick Killian?"

I sigh. *How small is this town, anyway?*

"He should have told you," she says.

"I should have picked up on it."

Grace shakes her head. "I still say he should have made it clearer. No way both of you got signals crossed. Shame on him."

"I don't know about that," I say, but I appreciate her show of support.

She gives me the hurry-up signal.

I keep going with my story, leaving out most of the details, especially any details with secret feelings and legs touching. "He was just trying to cheer me up," I say, when I tell her about Porter and the Bees. "It was no big deal."

"Hmm," is all she says.

"What does that mean?"

"It means, that's all very interesting."

"Why?"

Four quick raps on the Hotbox door. I startle. Grace squeals. Four knocks only means one person. My nerves go crazy as Grace opens the door.

"Ladies," Porter says.

"Why, speak of the bloody devil," Grace says, giving me a smile that is so wicked, I can hardly believe it's on her sweet little face. I immediately regret I told her anything and try to signal back with my eyes: *IF YOU GIVE AWAY ANYTHING, I WILL STRANGLE YOU IN YOUR SLEEP.*

Porter glances at her, then me. I catch his gaze and try to look away, but it's like honey. I'm stuck. I can feel my insides melting and my heart trying to outrun a horde of zombies. I can't seem to inhale enough air. Stupid Hotbox. It's sweltering. I feel physically ill and fear I'm going to pass out.

"Hey," he says in a soft voice.

"Hey," I say back.

Somewhere in the distance, I hear a light tap-tap-tapping.

"Bailey." I really like it when he says my name. God, how silly is that?

"Yep," I answer.

"Customers."

Dammit. I manage not to say that aloud, but I do, however, spin around on my stool too fast and bang my skinned-up knee—which still hasn't completely healed—and yelp. The pain helps to break whatever crazy hoodoo spell Porter's got over me. Until something warm touches my hand.

I glance down. Porter's trying to hand me a folded-up tissue. My knee's bleeding again. I mutter, "Thanks," and press it against the newly opened scab while juggling the ticket window one-handed.

"You going to the bonfire tonight?" Porter says. He's talking to Grace, not me.

"Yep. I'm taking Bailey, if she doesn't lose her leg before the end of our shift. You never know in the Hotbox. It's a war zone in here. Better get out while you can."

"I'm getting, I'm getting," he says, pretending to be grumpy. Do I detect a jovial tone in his voice? Is he happy I'm going to the bonfire, or is that just my imagination? "Guess I'll see you both tonight, unless someone needs an ambulance first."

Grace shows up at my house promptly at eight. I've barely had enough time to change out of my work clothes into what I'm assuming is appropriate for a bonfire party on the beach, which for me means I'm dressed like Annette Funicello in one of the *Beach Party* movies from the 1960s: ruched red-and-white polka-dot top that fits me like a glove, scalloped white shorts, wedge espadrilles. When Grace sees what I'm wearing, she looks me over and says, "Cutest thing I've ever seen, truly, but you're going to freeze to death and then fall and break your neck. Ditch the shoes and find a proper jacket."

Crud. I trade the espadrilles for red sneakers. Meanwhile, my dad has fallen hard for Grace's charm and is trying to convince her to stay awhile and order pizza, play a game of The Settlers of Catan. She has no idea what that is, and he's doing a terrible job explaining. He's a long-winded talker when he's excited about stuff he likes, and I need to get us out the door, but now he's breaking out the ancient board game box. God help us all.

"Dad," I finally say. "We're meeting Grace's friends. No time for sheep trading."

He raises both hands in surrender. "Understood. You girls have fun. But, Grace, please bring her home at midnight. That's her curfew."

"It is?" I ask. We've never discussed such a thing.

"Does that work for you?" he asks. Now he's unsure too.

"Well, it doesn't work for me, Mr. Rydell," Grace says, "because that's my curfew too. So I'll have her home by a quarter of, because it takes me fifteen minutes to drive to my house from here. How's that, yeah?"

"Perfect!" Dad says, beaming. He's made the right parenting choice that syncs up with the choices of other normal parents. Life is good. And it's good for me, too, because now I can sneak out of here like some horrible juvenile delinquent daughter and go do something he wouldn't want me to do, while I've lied and told him we're going to the boardwalk. Before I lose my nerve, I grab a hoodie, tell him good-bye, and rush Grace out the door.

Grace drives a cute two-seater with a sunroof. All the way to the beach, she tries to give me the lowdown on who will be there and what the party could be like, but I'm still unprepared. The setting sun is turning the sky magenta as we pull off the road, well north of the cove, and park with a hundred other cars every which way alongside the highway, half in the scrabbly sand. Rocky cliffs rise up from the ocean, turning into mountainous coastal foothills in the distance. And the surf slams so hard here, it almost sounds like ominous music—only, there's that, too, pumped in from someone's car speakers. It echoes around a crescent-shaped bowl of jagged rock, a couple hundred yards or so below the road. And inside this crescent is a hollow sandy pit, where several dozen teens are congregated around a massive bonfire that throws wildly flickering light around the craggy walls.

The Bone Garden.

Grace and I make the downhill trek on a well-worn path through coastal grass. As we do, we're greeted by a motley array of scent and sound. Roasted marshmallows and skunky beer. Laughing and shouting and roughhousing. A boy crying in the shadows and another boy telling him he's sorry and please don't leave. *Me too, dude*, I think, because I'm having the same panic attack.

"Too late now," Grace says, sensing my need to flee. "It's a long walk back to civilization, anyway."

Like this calms me down?

Before I know it, we're leveling out, and she's seeing people she knows. And Grace knows everyone. She's hugging necks and waving at people. If there were any babies out here, she'd probably be kissing them. She's a natural-born politician, this girl. And she's introducing me to so many people, I can't keep up. Casey is a cheerleader. Sharonda is president of drama club. Ezgar was in juvie, but it wasn't his fault (I'm not sure what, but it wasn't). Anya is dating Casey, but no one's supposed to know that. And in the middle of all this, here's a surfer, there's a surfer, everywhere there's a surfer. Oh, a few skaters and bikers. One paddleboarder, because "that's where it's at," apparently.

There are just so many people. Most of them don't seem to be doing anything wrong, so as we wind through the crowd, I feel a smidge less guilty about lying to my dad tonight. Sure, I see a few people drinking beer and smoking, and I smell the same sweet scent that clings to Pangborn's clothes, so someone's passing around weed. But for such a big group, nothing crazy is going down. I mean, no sign of Davy and his bunch so far, fingers crossed. No sign of anyone else, either . . .

At some point during all this meeting and greeting, I lose Grace. I don't even know when it happens. One minute I'm listening to a confusing story about a fender bender involving an ice cream truck and an electrical pole, and the next thing I know,

I'm surrounded by people whose names I only half remember. I try not to panic. I just quietly slip away and pretend like I know where I'm going while I search for Grace's cropped hair, turning on my dazzling Artful Dodger charm: look casual and bored, but not too bored. Keep moving. That's the key to no one taking pity on you, the strange new girl. Because there are certain gregarious types who always will try to take you under their wing—the drama kids, for sure—and I can spot them circling like vultures. Must avoid.

But there's only so much pretend mingling you can do before people realize that you're just walking around doing nothing—not talking to anyone, not lining up at the keg that's sticking out from a pit in the sand, from which people are constantly pumping red plastic cups of nasty-smelling beer. So I finally make myself scarce and find an empty spot on a piece of driftwood in the shadows. The seating situation is a mishmash of rusting lawn chairs, wooden crates, flat rocks, and a couple of ratty blankets. It looks more haphazard than organized, like maybe some of this stuff just washed up on the beach earlier in the day, and I'm regretting I wore white shorts. It's probably cleaner sitting in the sand.

"Are you: (A) mad, (B) sad, or (C) lost?"

My stomach flips several times in quick succession.

Porter, or the silhouette of Porter, because he's standing in front of the bonfire, hands in the pockets of his jeans.

"C, lost," I tell him. "I had no idea Grace was so popular. She's also compact, so it's possible she's in the middle of one of these groups and I just don't see her. I was going to give her five more minutes to surface before I texted." I wasn't really, but I didn't want him to think I was going to sit here for hours alone.

"I think she was a fairy in a previous life. Everyone believes she's going to grant their wishes or something." He gestures at the empty space on my driftwood log. I gesture back, *Please, be my guest.* The fragile wood creaks with his weight. He mimics my pose, digging his heels into the sand, folded arms on bent knees. Firelight dances over the patchwork of his scars, etching shadowy patterns over his shirt. Our elbows are close but not touching.

I'm relieved he's not partaking in one of the various vices floating around. At least, he seems his normal sober self. No plastic cup in hand, no reek of smoke. Actually, he smells nice tonight, like soap. No coconut, though. I'm almost disappointed.

His head dips closer. "Are you sniffing me, Rydell?"

I rear back. "No."

"Yes, you were." He grins that slow grin of his.

"If you must know, I was just curious if you'd been drinking."

"Nah, I don't drink anymore." He stares into the bonfire, watching some idiots roasting marshmallows whose sticks catch on fire. "I remember being a kid and my parents hauling Lana and me over to my grandpa's house, and he'd have these wild parties on the patio. Surfers from everywhere came. I'm talking crazy stuff went down there. Drugs everywhere. Free-flowing booze. People getting naked in the pool. Famous musicians dropping by and playing in the living room."

"I can't imagine growing up like that." It seems weird. Foreign.

"Don't get me wrong. It wasn't like that in my house, or anything. My parents are the exact opposite. My pops, especially. I guess because he saw his dad partying all the time, he got sick of it. He's insanely competitive and everything is about surfing, so that means staying at the top of your game. No drugs, no drinking, staying in shape. Imagine an army drill sergeant and multiply that by fifty."

His dad and my dad couldn't be more different. I'm completely thankful for that and once again feel a pang of guilt for lying to him about being out here.

"As for my mom," he continues, "she's just trying to keep the shop afloat, because after everything that's happened, she'd rather have us all at home than on the water."

I can understand why. "Do you . . . plan on surfing professionally, like your sister?"

"That's a sore question, Rydell."

"Sorry, never mind."

He shakes his head. "No, it's cool. It's not that I can't do it, physically. I'm pretty good." He smiles a little, giving me a sideways glace, and then shrugs. "It's just that for a while, after the shark, I had The Fear. And you can't have The Fear. The ocean will eat you alive." He blows out a hard breath, lips vibrating, and cuts his hand through the air as if to say, *The end.* "But I eventually powered through that. Funny thing was, once I did, I wasn't sure if I cared about it anymore. I mean, I still like surfing. I hit the waves almost every morning. But I'm not sure if I want to compete anymore. I want to surf because I enjoy it—not because I have to, you know?"

"I know exactly what you mean." And I do, because he doesn't light up about surfing like he does when he's talking about ocean currents and weather patterns.

Someone hollers Porter's last name. He glances up and curses under his breath. A towheaded figure strides around the bonfire.

"Hey, cow patty."

Oh, terrific. It's Davy. I think he's loaded. Not like he was that time in the crosswalk, but he's definitely been drinking, because he stinks, and he's got that stuttering laugh that stoners have when they're high. He's also not limping, which makes me think he's not feeling much pain right now.

"What's going on over here? You two look awfully cozy."

"We're just sitting here, talking, man," Porter says, highly irritated. "Why don't you go see Amy and we'll catch up with you."

"Oh, you'd like that, wouldn't you?"

"What are you talking about, Davy?"

"Trying to get me back for my past sins? Because I invited her here"—he nods lazily toward me—"but looks like you're making a play for her, which isn't cool."

Um, what? Grace invited me, but no way am I getting in the middle of this.

"You're wasted," Porter says carefully, pointing an unwavering finger in Davy's direction, "so I'm going to give you five seconds to get out of my face."

I'm getting worried now. Porter is more than intimidating: He looks scary as hell. I've never really known many guys like this, more on the man side of the sliding masculinity scale. Not up close and personal, anyway.

Davy does something with his face that might be classified as a smile. "Hey, relax, man. It's cool. Forget it. Brotherhood over Bettys."

Gross. Am I the "Betty"? Porter's knuckles press against the side of my thigh—a warning. I guess he's got this.

"Besides, I've been planning something special for you. You know what today is, right? Anniversary of Pennywise's death, man. I'm giving him a salute. Check it out."

Davy marches off around the bonfire, calling out for somebody to bring him the "salute," whatever that means.

"Idiot," Porter mumbles. "It's next month, not today. He's such a waste of space."

I'm just relieved he's gone and that no one's punching anyone, but when I see Porter's brow lowering, I know it's not over. There's a loud noise, and sparks shoot in our direction. We sway backward as the crowd o-o-ohs! Someone's hauling more wood onto the bonfire on the other side. Several someones. Wooden crates, pieces of chairs, driftwood—all of it's being tossed into the sandy pit. The fire roars up like a beast. The partygoers gasp in delight. In no time, it's twice as tall as it once was.

Loud cheers fill the beach. Fire big. Fire strong. The horde is pleased.

Well, not everyone. Porter, for one. He's pulling me to my feet and cursing a string of obscenities near the top of my head. "Do they ever learn?"

"What's the matter?" I say, and it's then that I notice the fringes of the crowd beginning to unravel: here and there, several people are starting to pull away and head up the trail to the parked cars.

"It's the bonfire," Porter says. "When it's too high, everyone can see it from the road. People who live around here tolerate it until they can see it. Then they call the cops. It's like a goddamn Bat Signal. Morons!"

But it's not just that. Something else is happening across the bonfire from us. I get Porter's attention and point to where two boys are lifting Davy onto a large, flat rock on the edge of the beach. The surf crashes into the rock, spraying his legs with foam. He doesn't seem to care or notice. He's too busy holding something up in his hand that looks like a big stick, and when he shouts for everyone to shut up, the crowd quiets and listens.

"In honor of all our fallen brothers who've bashed their bones against these rocks in the garden of good and evil, tonight, on the anniverseary-rey," he stumbles, and then gets it right, "anniversary of Pennywise's death, I'm doing a military-style three-volley salute. Ready?"

What the hell is he talking about?

"Oh, God," Porter says.

Davy turns to face the wall of rocks, perches the stick on his shoulder, and then—

My world changes.

I'm . . .

Not on the beach.

I'm fourteen years old, and I'm standing in the living room of our old house in New Jersey. I just walked home from school. And there's broken glass and blood dripping on the expensive carpet. And my mom is screaming, but I can't hear anything at all.

Then the carpet turns back to sand and the crowd's roaring gleefully and everything's back to being okay. Only, it's not.

"Bailey!" Porter is shouting in my face, shaking me.

I swallow, but my throat is too dry.

"Bailey?"

I really am all right now. I am. It's okay. I'm mainly afraid I'm going to cry in front of him, and that would be humiliating. But it's too late, because I check my face and a few tears have already leaked out. I swipe them away and take a few breaths.

Boom!

The terrible memory flashes again, but I don't disappear this time. It just rattles me, hard. Maybe it wasn't Porter shaking me before. Maybe I'm just shaking.

"Jesus, what's the matter?" Porter says. He's pushed hair away from my forehead, trying to check if I'm running a fever.

"I'm okay," I finally say, moving his hand away. Not because I don't want his help, but I need to see what Davy's doing. He's reloading. Three-volley salute, he said, so there's still one more. I think he's got a shotgun. It's hard to tell from here.

I hate this. Hate being like this. It hasn't happened in a long time. And I wasn't prepared. If I know it's coming, I can brace myself. But this . . .

Davy puts the gun against his shoulder. Final one. I cover my ears with both hands. For a brief moment, I see Porter looking anguished and confused, then he pulls my head against his chest and wraps his arms around me. *Boom!* I jump against him, but he doesn't let go. And it helps. The explosion is muffled. I have a solid anchor, and I don't want to let go. It's embarrassing how hard I'm clinging to him now, but I don't even care, because he's safe and warm. It's just that he's prying me off him, trying to tell me something, and I really should be listening.

"We have to go, Bailey," he's telling me. "Now."

I see why.

Red and blue lights. The police are here.

"To repress one's feelings only makes them stronger."
—Michelle Yeoh, *Crouching Tiger, Hidden Dragon* (2000)

14

"I have to find Grace," I shout at him as we're racing across the sand.

It's total chaos, everyone scattering, half of them clogging the upward trail to the parked cars—but that's where the police lights are.

"Gracie knows how to take care of herself," Porter yells back. He's got my hand locked in his, and he's shouldering his way across the main path, heading toward the dark area of the beach, away from the bonfire. Away from the people. "She's been in this situation before, and she's got a million friends who can get her home."

That doesn't feel right to me. I try to tell him that, but it's so loud, I can't even hear my own voice. Now it's two cop cars—not one. And it strikes me just now: What if it's Wanda? Would she arrest me, even if I haven't been drinking? I picture Dad having to come pick me up from the police station and my stomach twists.

"CCPD," a booming male voice says over the squad car speaker. "Hands up where I can see them."

Holy crap. They're arresting someone. Hopefully it's Davy and his rock-blasting shotgun.

Porter gets us past the main herd of fleeing cattle. We jog around a boulder and he spots a secondary path through dry coastal brush that a couple of other partygoers are climbing. It's dark but serviceable. "Stay low," Porter tells me, and we head that way, sneaking through the dry grass. Just before we crest the hill, we have to stop and wait for a cop car with a high-beam spotlight to finish sweeping the area. When I'm half a second away from having a stroke, I get a text from Grace: *Where are you?* To which I reply: *Escaping with Porter. Are you safe?* She answers: *Yes, okay. Was worried I lost you. Tell P to go N on Gold to Cuangua Farm. Text me when you get home.*

I show Porter the texts. He nods, and when the coast is clear, we jog past a million parked cars until we get to what appears to be a sky-blue Volkswagen camper van—the kind from the 1960s and '70s that are long and surrounded with a ring of windows. Surfer vans, my dad calls them, because they're big enough to haul longboards on top. This one is covered with peeling surfing stickers on the back windows and has painted white fenders. Porter opens the passenger side and slips into the driver's seat from there, then beckons me in after him.

"Shit!" He's shoving the keys in the ignition as flashing lights head in our direction again. The engine protests and doesn't want to catch, and it's like a bad horror movie. "Come on, come on." And then—finally!—it rumbles to life, loud as you please. Wheels spin, kicking up sand, and then we're off, turning away from this nightmare, trundling as fast as a fifty-year-old bus can go, which isn't very fast at all, but who cares? The whole nasty scene is in Porter's rearview mirror.

I click on my seat belt and immediately melt into the seat. "Jesus."

"Are you okay?"

"I don't know."

"Do you want to talk about what happened back there?"

"No."

His brow furrows. "I'm sorry about all that . . . about Davy."

"Yeah. He's a complete dirtbag. No offense, but why are you friends with him?"

Fingers lift and fall on the steering wheel.

"We grew up surfing together. He used to be my best friend. His family life has gone down the toilet, so my dad took him under his wing for a while, trained him. My mom felt sorry for him. He practically lived at our house for a while. Then he got hurt surfing a few years ago. Has a leg full of metal and pins."

The limp.

"He's in a lot of pain, and it screwed up any chance he had of surfing seriously. Made him bitter and angry . . . changed him." Porter sighs heavily and scratches his neck. "Anyway, he started screwing up, and I told you about how my dad is. He wouldn't tolerate Davy's BS, so he stopped training him until he gets his act cleaned up. And on top of all that, Davy basically thinks I'm an idiot for not wanting to go pro, because he says I'm privileged and throwing it away. Also . . ."

Whatever he was going to say, he seems to think better of it and clams up. I wonder if it had to do with all the drunken smack talk Davy was spewing at the bonfire. About that girl they mentioned outside the vintage clothing shop, Chloe.

"Anyway, I'm sorry about all that," he says. "I'll go talk to him tomorrow when he's sobered up. No use seeing him tonight. It'll just turn into a fistfight. Always does. And who knows, maybe he got arrested this time. Might do him some good."

I don't know what to say to that. I can't imagine having a best friend you hate. That's messed up.

"It smells like you in here," I say after a long moment.

"It does?" The steering wheel on this van is enormous. I just noticed. Also, the seat is one giant thing that goes across the whole front of the van. And there're tiny rubber monsters stuck to the dash: an alien and a hydra and a Loch Ness Monster and a Godzilla. Wait, not an alien: a green shark. Huh. They're all sea creatures—all famous water monsters. What doesn't kill you . . .

"Coconut," I say. "You always smell coconut-y." Then, because it's dark in the van, and because I'm wiped out from all the panic and my guard is down, I add, "You always smell good."

"Sex Wax."

"What?" I sit up a little straighter.

He reaches down to the floorboard and tosses me what looks like a plastic-wrapped bar of soap. I hold it up to the window to see the label in the streetlight. "Mr. Zog's Sex Wax," I read.

"You rub it on the deck of your board," he explains. "For traction. You know, so you don't slip off while you're surfing." I sniff it. That's the stuff, all right.

"I bet your feet smell heavenly."

"You don't have a foot fetish thing, do you?" he asks, voice playful.

"I didn't before, but now? Who knows."

The tires of the van veer off the road onto the gravelly shoulder, and he cuts the wheel sharply to steer back onto the pavement. "Oops."

We chuckle, both embarrassed.

I toss the wax onto the floorboard. "Well, another mystery solved."

"Not a big one. Let's get back to yours." He turns down a small road on the edge of town. This must be the way Grace suggested. "I remember you mentioning something about not liking movies with guns in them when you were with Patrick in the video store."

Ugh. This again. I hug my stomach and look out the passenger window, but there's nothing but residential houses and it's dark outside. "God, you really did hear everything that morning, didn't you?"

"Pretty much. What happened? I mean, I did tell you about the whole shark incident, and I barely knew you then."

"Yeah, but you're all open and talkative. You probably tell everyone that story."

"I actually don't." His head turns toward me, and I see his eyes flick in my direction. "People at school know better than to ask me."

And I didn't.

"Look, I'm not going to force you to talk about something," he says. "I'm not a shrink. But if you want to, I'm a good listener. No judgment. Sometimes it's better to get it out. It festers and gets weird when you bottle it up. I don't know why, but it does. Just speaking from personal experience."

I don't say anything for a long while. We just ride in silence together through the dark streets, silhouettes of mountains rising on one side of the town, the ocean spreading out on the other. Then I tell him some of it. About my mom taking the Grumbacher divorce case when I was fourteen. About her winning it for the wife, about the custody she got for the wife's daughter.

And about Greg Grumbacher.

"He started harassing my mom online," I say. "That's how it started. He'd post nasty comments on her social media. When she didn't respond, he started stalking my dad, and then me. I didn't even know who he was. He just started showing up after school a lot, hanging outside where the parents carpool. I thought he was one of my friends' fathers, or something.

"We only lived two blocks from school," I continue, "so I usually walked home with a friend. One day when I walked home alone, he walked with me. Said he was my mom's coworker. And because he'd done all this detailed research online, he rattled off all this stuff about her, so it seemed like, yeah, he did know her. And I was too trusting. A stupid kid."

"I did stupid things when I was younger too," Porter says softly. "What happened?"

"I knew something was wrong by the time we'd gotten to the door, and I wasn't going to let him into the house, but it was too late. I was small and he was big. He overpowered me and pushed his way inside. . . ."

"Shit," Porter murmurs.

"My mom was home," I continue. "She'd forgotten some paperwork she'd needed for a case. It was just a lucky coincidence. If she hadn't have been there . . . I don't know. Everyone's still alive today, so that's a good thing. Still, when there's a crazy man waving a gun around in your house, threatening your mom—"

"Jesus Christ."

Deep breath. I check myself, making sure I'm not heading into shaky territory again, but I'm okay this time. "It was the sound that caught me by surprise at the bonfire. That's what does it to me in movies, too. Cars backfiring sometimes have the same effect. I don't like loud explosions. Sounds stupid to say it like that."

"Umm, not stupid. If that happened to me, I'd probably be the same way. Trust me, I've got hang-ups." He makes a broad sweeping gesture toward the collection of sharks and hydras on the van's dash.

I chuckle a little at that, touching one of the bouncy sharks' heads, and relax. "Yeah. So anyway. I guess a gunshot wound isn't the worst possible outcome. And the guy went to prison, obviously."

"God, Bailey. I don't know what to say."

I shrug. "Me either. But there you go."

"Is that why your parents divorced?"

I start to say no, then think about this for a minute. "The divorce happened over a year ago, but now that you mention it, things never were the same after the shooting. It put a strain on our family."

He nods thoughtfully. "Mom says misfortune either breaks people apart or brings them closer. God knows our family has seen enough of it to know."

"But your parents are still okay." I try not to make this a question, but I don't really know.

He smiles. "My parents will be one of those couples you see on the news who are ninety years old and have been together forever."

Must be nice. I want to say I thought that about my parents too, but now I wonder if I ever really did.

He asks me for directions to my dad's place and knows the neighborhood; he's lived here all his life, so that's no surprise. As the van climbs the last few winding redwood-lined streets, we're both quiet, and now I feel awkward about what I just told him. And there's something else, too: a nagging sense that in the midst of all this, I've forgotten something. A block away from home, I remember. Alarm floods my chest.

"Stop the van!"

"What?" he slams on the brakes. "What's wrong?"

I unclick my seat belt. "I . . . I'll just get out here. Thanks for the ride."

"What? I thought you said it's the next street?"

"It is, but—"

"But what?"

I shake my head. "I can walk the rest of the way."

The confusion behind Porter's eyes sparks and catches fire. Now he's insulted. "Are you kidding? You don't want your dad to see me, do you?"

"It's not personal."

"Like hell it's not. What, my camper van is too busted for Redwood Glen? Are all the BMWs and Mercedes going to chase me back down to the shore?"

"Don't be an idiot. There are no BMWs here."

He points to the driveway in front of us.

Okay, one BMW. But it's not like my dad drives a brand-new luxury vehicle, or that we live in one of these fancy houses—his place used to be a vacation rental. He's dating a cop, not a doctor; he watches sci-fi movies, not opera. Come to think of it, Grace's family is way better off than we are. But Porter is being stubborn, and it's closing in on midnight. I don't have time to argue with him about petty stuff like this.

"I have a curfew," I tell him impatiently.

"Fine." He leans across my lap and pops open the door handle. "Get out, then. I don't want to embarrass you."

Okay, now I'm mad. How did we go from me spilling my guts to fighting? I'm totally confused as to why his feelings are so hurt. Is he really this sensitive? So much for the stereotype that girls are the only ones who wear their feelings on their sleeves. I think about something Alex told me online once: Boys are dumb.

Irritated and a little hurt myself, I push open the heavy door and swing my legs outside. But before I jump out, all my tumbling feelings stick in my throat and I hesitate. This isn't how I wanted things to end tonight.

Maybe he's not the only one being dumb.

"The problem is," I say, half inside the van, half out, "that my dad is dating a cop, and the three of us were eating at the posole truck the other day, and Davy was there, and he made an ass out of himself in front of them . . ."

I rush to get the rest of it out before I lose my nerve. "And she told my dad that he's bad news, and that he's involved with a bunch of serious narcotic stuff—and after tonight, I really don't ever want to see him again, no offense. But during all of this, Davy brought up your name in front of them, so when he left, I was trying to defend you to my dad and Wanda, and she said your family is okay, but by then the damage was already done. Because my dad has blacklisted Davy, and I basically lied to go to the bonfire tonight, so he thinks I'm at the boardwalk with Grace."

Porter makes a low noise.

"Anyway, that's why," I say. "Thank you for rescuing me. And for listening."

I get out of the van and shut the door. It's old and ornery, so I have to do it again. Then I slog up the hill toward my dad's house. I don't get far before the van's headlights go out and the engine cuts off. Then I hear change and car keys jingling as Porter jogs to catch up.

Wary, I glance up at his face as he falls in step next to me.

"You shouldn't walk alone at night," he says. "I won't let your dad see me."

"Thanks," I say.

Three slow steps in tandem. "You could have just said that in the first place, you know."

"Sorry."

"Forgiven," he says, giving me a little smile. "Next time tell me the truth *before* I mouth off and say stupid stuff, not after. Saves me from looking like a jerk."

"I kind of like you being all hotheaded," I joke.

"Hot Stuff, remember?"

"I remember," I say, giving him a smile. "That's my house, there."

"Oh, the old McAffee place. That's got the tree going through the sunroom in the back."

"Yeah," I say, amazed.

"My parents know everyone in town," he explains.

Maybe now he believes me about not being fancy. I whisper for him to follow me to the far side of the house near the mailbox, where my dad won't see or hear us approaching if he's in the living room or his bedroom. His muscle car is parked in the driveway, so I know he's home, but I can't see a light on. I wonder if he's waiting up. It's the first night I've stayed out this late, so chances are good that he's still awake—especially since we made such a big deal out of the curfew. Now I'm feeling guilty again. Or maybe that's just all my nerves jingle-jangling because it's almost midnight and I'm standing in damp grass with a boy I'm not supposed to be seeing.

"So," Porter says, facing me.

"So . . . ," I repeat, swallowing hard as I glance around the dark street. A few golden lights glow in the windows of nearby houses, but there's no sound but the occasional passing of distant cars and a frog singing along with some crickets in the redwoods.

Porter shifts closer. I back up. *He's always in my personal space,* I think weakly.

"Why did you come to the bonfire tonight?" he asks in a low voice.

I fiddle with the zipper on my hoodie. "Grace invited me."

"You snuck out of the house because Grace invited you?"

He steps closer.

I step back—and my butt hits cedar. *Crap.* I've run into the mailbox post. I start to shimmy around it, but Porter's arm shoots out and blocks me. *Damn!* Ten points for surfer agility.

"Not this time," he says, trapping me with his hand on the mailbox. His head dips low. He speaks close to my ear. "Answer the question. Why did you come to the bonfire? Why sneak out at all? Why risk it?"

"Is this a quiz?" I ask, trying to sound mad, but I'm really just insanely nervous. I'm cornered—which I hate. And he's so close, his hair is tickling my cheek, and his breath is warm on my ear. I'm scared and intoxicated at the same time, worried that if either of us says another word, I might push him away.

That I might not.

I'm trying-trying-trying not to breathe so fast. But Porter shifts, and the hand that isn't trapping me falls to the side. His fingers dance over my hand, a gossamer touch, and he traces soft patterns on my open palm, Morse code taps, gently urging, send a thousand electric currents of signals up my nerves.

"Why?" he whispers against my cheek.

I whimper.

He knows he's won. But he asks one more time, this time against my ear. "Why?"

"Because I wanted to see you."

I can't even hear my own voice, but I know he does when a sigh gusts out of him, long and hard. His head drops to the crook of my neck and rests there. The fingers that were teasing me with their little tap-tap-tapping messages now curl around my fingers, loosely clasping. And the arm pinning me to the mailbox is now lifting away, and I feel his hand smooth down the length of my hair.

A tremor runs through me.

"Shh," he says softly against my neck. I nearly fall to pieces.

I don't know what we're doing. What he's planning to do. What I want him to do. But we're swaying and clinging to each other like the earth might crack open beneath our feet at any given moment, and I'm a little bit afraid that I really might be having a stroke, because I can hear the blood swishing around in my temples and my knees suddenly feel like they've gone rubbery and I might collapse.

Then he freezes against me.

"Whatwasthat?" he slurs, pulling all his wonderful warmth away.

Now I hear it. Windowpanes shaking. "Oh, God," I whisper. I'm going to have a heart attack. "It's the surround sound on the TV. My dad's probably watching some stupid sci-fi movie. It shakes the windows during the battle scenes." *Now come back here.*

Then we hear a slam. That was no TV. That's the door to the—

"Carport!" I whisper. "Other side of the house!"

"Crap!"

"That way!" I say, shoving him toward a bush.

Two quick strides, and he's hidden. I hear the squeal of the trash bin in the carport and exhale a sigh of relief; Dad can't see us from there. But that was close. Too close.

"Bailey?" Dad calls out. "Is that you?"

"Yeah, Dad," I call back. *Stupid curfew.* "I'm home. Coming around."

Movement catches my eye. I turn in time to see Porter sneaking across the street. He's pretty good, I must admit. No Artful Dodger, but still. When he gets to the other side, he turns to look at me one last time, and I swear I can see him smiling in the dark.

"Never trust a junkie."
—Chloe Webb, *Sid and Nancy* (1986)

15

Tiny arms hug me from behind. I'm engulfed by the scent of baby lotion. "I'm so, so sorry," Grace's elfin voice says into the middle of my back as she squeezes me. "Will you ever forgive me?"

It's the following day, and I'm standing in front of my locker in the break room at work. We texted last night after Porter sneaked away—and after my dad got over being amazed that he never heard Grace's car drive up, and why didn't she come inside? Ugh. Once you tell one lie, plan on telling about twenty more, because they pile up like yesterday's garbage.

"There's nothing to forgive," I tell her. I'm just relieved she didn't think I ditched her for Porter—or ask why I was with him. "But for Halloween, I'm dressing up like a tree and you're going as a sloth. I'll carry you around while you eat my leaves."

"You probably could," she says, releasing me and flopping back against the lockers, arms crossed. "You've got all that secret strength for taking down adolescent boys. Were you on the varsity wrestling team back in DC? Coronado Cove's got a Roller Derby team, you know. The Cavegirls."

I snort a laugh. "No, I didn't know that, but I'll keep it in mind for this fall."

"Look, I really am sorry for losing you at the bonfire. I didn't mean to. I don't even know how it happened. Freddy started talking to me and you just disappeared. Someone said you were talking to the twins—"

"I was. They introduced me to someone else. I don't know. I'm not great at being social," I admit. "Anyway, it all worked out."

She glances around the break room. Only a few people are there, and no one's paying attention to us. "So, yeah. Do tell. Porter took you home? And . . . ?"

"And what?" *Crap. So much for avoiding that subject.* I can feel my face getting hot, so I busy myself feeling around inside my locker for some nonexistent thing.

"I'm just saying, the two of you are spending an awful lot of time together and asking an awful lot of questions about each other—"

"I haven't asked any questions." *Have I?*

"And you're giving him an awful lot of looks that say *I'd like to jump on you with my mighty roller-derby strength.* And he's giving you looks that say *I'd like to surf your waves.*"

"You are nutty."

"Mmm-hmm. Let's see about that," she murmurs, and then calls out past my face in a chipper voice, "Afternoon, Porter baby."

"Hello, ladies."

My heart rate jumps to a five on the Richter scale. I attempt to look casual, stay cool as I turn to my right. But there he is, hand braced on my locker door, and whatever self-control I tried to muster just blows away like paper napkins on a windy day.

"You're still alive, so I guess everything went okay with your dad," he says.

"No problems whatsoever," I confirm.

"Good, good. Glad to hear it."

"Yeah." Is it just my imagination, or does he smell extra Sex Wax–y today? Did he do that on purpose? Is he trying to seduce me? Or am I just being sensitive? And—what the hell?—is the air-conditioning broken in the break room, because it suddenly feels like the Hotbox up in here. Note to self: Do not think the words "sex" and "wax" while he's standing in front of you. Ever, ever, ever.

"So, yeah," he says, sort of smiling to himself while he taps on the top of my locker. "I was just going to tell you, uh, both— tell you both," he clarifies, looking over at Grace. "We got this new lock system . . . long story, but I have to help install it. So Pangborn and Madison will be dealing with all your Hotbox needs today. You know, in case you wondered where I was."

"Because we're always thinking about you," Grace says sarcastically.

"I know you are, Gracie," he replies, giving her a wink. He leans a little closer, hanging on my locker, and speaks to me in a lower voice. "So anyway, I was wondering what you're doing after work."

Heart. Exploding.

"What's that?" Grace says.

Porter playfully shoves her head away. "I think I hear someone calling you, Gracie. Is that Cadaver? He said you're fired for listening in on other people's private conversations."

"This is private?" she says. "It looks like a public break room to me, and we were talking before you sauntered up, if you do recall."

He ignores her and give me an expectant look. "Well?"

"I'm not busy," I tell him.

"Oh, good. Maybe want to get something to eat later?"

Be cool, Rydell. This sounds like it could be a date. "Yeah, why not?"

"Excellent. Umm, so . . . maybe we should swap numbers. We can leave from here, but, you know, just in case we need to call each other."

"Yeah, that makes sense." I notice Grace when I'm digging out my phone. She's standing next to me with eyes like two full moons. I think she might be temporarily stunned into silence. Which only makes me more nervous. And that's no good, because I can barely handle the basic exchange of a few single numbers, and I still almost mess that up.

"Okay, well . . . ," Porter says, tucking a curly lock of hair behind one ear. How can he be adorable and sexy at the same time? If he doesn't vacate the break room soon, I might swoon to death. "Go sell some tickets."

"Go lock some locks," I tell him.

He flashes me a smile and after he leaves the break room, I

quietly bang my head against the lockers. Lock some locks. *Who says that? What a dork. He's broken my brain.*

I look up and see Grace. She's still staring at me, all wide-eyed.

"Mmm—" she starts.

"Argh! Don't you say it," I warn her.

She keeps quiet until we get to cash-out. "I knew that lad was asking too many questions about you."

The only good thing about our shift is that it's insanely busy, so it passes quickly. I don't even see Porter once. Mr. Cavadini, either. Guess that lock business is time-consuming. So is being nervous, and by the time six o'clock rolls around, I'm wired and ready to get out of there. I count down my cash drawer, inform Grace that if she follows me out to the parking lot, I will slash her tires, and that, yes, I will tell her everything tomorrow, duh, and then I look around for Porter. Nada. No surfer boy in sight. But I do get a text from him: *Almost done. Meet you outside in five?*

Okay, cool. That gives me time to head out to Baby and swap my work shoes for some slinkier sandals, which I've got stashed under the helmet in my seat. I grab my purse from my locker and dash outside. The sky's looking dark. Overcast and grumpy. It hasn't rained since I've moved here, but it looks like that might change today. Driving Baby in the rain isn't my idea of a fun time, so I'm actually relieved Porter invited me out.

I . . .

Look around. To the left. To the right.

Where's Baby?

I parked her right here. I always do.

I double-check. I must be confused. Third aisle from the back door . . .

I spin around, looking for her turquoise frame and leopard-print seat. There's got to be an explanation. Maybe someone moved her for some reason, though. . . . I don't know how they would. . . . She was locked up. I always lock her up. Always. I go through exactly what I did when I arrived that afternoon, making sure I did—and yes, I know I did. I'm positive.

"Anything the matter, dear?"

It's Pangborn, strolling out from the employee entrance.

"My scooter's gone," I say.

"What? Gone?"

"I parked it right here at the start of my shift."

"You're absolutely certain? What color is it? Let me help you look," he says, putting a calming hand on my shoulder. "Don't panic just yet, now. Let's be sure first, okay?"

I blow out a breath and describe it. There are several scooters back here, but none of them are Vespas, none are vintage, none are turquoise, and, really, the employee lot isn't that big. I'm starting to feel dizzy. I think it's finally time to face facts.

Baby's been stolen.

"Aren't there cameras back here?" I say.

"Just over the building exits and the delivery door." Pangborn tells me. "Not on the lots and roads."

202 • JENN BENNETT

"That's the dumbest thing I've ever heard," I say. What kind of hick place is this? Don't they care if a truck pulls up and tries to rob the place?

I'm panicking now. What am I going to do? Should I call the police? Dad and Wanda drove to San Jose today to go dancing, or something. It's her only day off work this week. Now I've got to ruin their day? And how am I going to get to work for the rest of my scheduled shifts? And who's got my bike? Are they taking it around town for a joyride, with all my personal stuff in the seat? I think I'm going to be sick.

"What's going on?" Porter says, out of breath as he runs up to meet us.

"Her scooter's missing," Pangborn tells him in a quiet voice. He's still squeezing my shoulder. God, the old man's so nice, and that makes me want to cry.

"Missing, as in stolen?"

"Looks like it. Didn't notice anything unusual on the door cams, but you know how hard it is to spot anything coming and going way out here."

"It's impossible," Porter agrees, and he starts asking me the same questions all over again—when did I get there, where did I park, did I lock it? I snap at him a little and then apologize. I'm on edge and trying not to bawl my eyes out like a two-year-old kid in front of everyone, because—of course—now there are several other employees out here. And everyone's looking around the lots, making sure they don't see it abandoned in the regular parking area.

Just when I'm about to give up and call my dad, Pangborn says to Porter, "By the way, did your friend catch up with you?"

"Who?"

"The one with the bum leg."

Porter stills. "Davy?"

"That's the one. He was looking for you."

"Here?" Porter's confused.

Pangborn nods. "He was skulking around by the employee entrance when I was coming back from my . . . uh, afternoon medicine break." Pangborn's eyes dart to some nearby employees. "Anyway, he didn't recognize me at first, but I remembered him from when he worked here last summer for a few days. I asked him if he wanted me to page you, but he said he'd just text you."

"No, he didn't," Porter says. "What time was this?"

"Couple of hours ago?"

Porter's face goes as dark as the overcast sky. "Listen to me, Bailey. Does Davy know what your scooter looks like?"

"I . . ." It takes me a second to remember. "Yeah, at the posole truck. He saw me with it when I was with my dad and Wanda. Asked me if it had been restored."

Porter's head drops back. He squeezes his eyes shut. "I think I know who stole your bike. Get in my van. He's a couple of hours ahead of us, but I know where we can start looking."

I'm too stunned to talk until we're speeding away from the museum and headed south on Gold Avenue. I've never been this far on this side of town, and everything looks strange. That's when it hits me that I should probably ask where we're going.

"Is this the way to Davy's house?"

"No." Porter's angry. Really angry. The muscles in his arms are flexing as he holds the steering wheel in a death grip. "He'll try to sell it. He wants cash for drugs."

"Oh my God. Why me? Why my scooter?"

He doesn't answer right away. "Because he's pissed at me. Because he's mad about the party going to shit last night. Because he knows it was his fault. Because deep down he knows he's a screwup, but he hasn't hit rock bottom yet, so he's going to keep going until he's either dead or in jail."

I wait for several seconds, trying to figure exactly how to ask this, and then I just give up and come right out and say it. "What does any of that have to do with me and my bike?"

"Aghhh," Porter says, almost a sigh, somewhere between exasperated and guilty. "Because I went over to see him before work today, and we got into a huge fight. Somehow he's gotten it into his thick, stupid skull that you are . . ." He sighs now—a real sigh, low and long. "Okay, think of it like this. He's got the mind of a toddler, and because he thinks that I have a shiny new toy, you being that toy—not that you are a toy! God, I knew this was a bad analogy."

"Whoa, you are digging yourself in real deep, buddy."

"Look, he thinks I like you, therefore he wants you. And today I told him if he harasses you again or brings a gun anywhere near you, I will burn his goddamn house down."

Well. That's not something you hear every day. A foreign, uneasy feeling ping-pongs inside my gut.

"And because he's a brat, what he's doing right now is retaliation. If he can't have you, he's going to do dumbass, destructive things—like steal your shit and sell it for money, so he can get wasted and forget he's a total screwup. Because he's a maniac, and that's what he does."

"Jesus."

"Yeah," he says in a softer voice, one that's suddenly all out of rage. "So, basically, this is my fault, and I'm sorry, Bailey."

I glance down at my feet and line up the toes of my flats with the floor mat. "Davy *thinks* you like me, or you really do like me?" Last night in the yard seems like a million years ago.

Porter gives me a sideways glance. There's a wariness behind his eyes; he's not sure if I'm teasing. But the corner of his mouth lifts, just a little. "Both?"

"Both," I repeat softly, more than satisfied with that answer. "I think I understand now."

"So . . . ," he says, "I guess the real question is, how badly do you want to choke me right now for what's happened? (A) A little, or (B) a lot?"

I shake my head, both dismissing his question and unable to answer. I'm not mad at him. How could I be? It's not his fault that he's got crappy friends.

"Hey, Bailey? I'm going to get your bike back," he says, face turning stony and serious. "I meant what I said before. Davy will pay for this."

God help me, but at this moment, there is nothing I want more.

After another mile, the van slows, and I see where we're headed. On the left-hand side of the highway, just off the beach, a giant paved lot is banded by a sign that reads: MOTO PARADISE. There must be a hundred used scooters for sale here. Porter pulls up next to a fenced-in trailer that sits on the back of the lot and tells me to wait in the van. "This is the long shot, but it's the closest to the museum, so let's rule it out first. Just sit here and text if you see Davy. He drives a bright yellow pickup truck with blue lightning bolts airbrushed on the side."

Of course he does.

Porter's not even inside the trailer five minutes. My heart sinks. And it sinks again twice more, because we drive to other lots that look similar to this one, just farther out of town and smaller. Now I'm getting worried. What if it wasn't Davy? What if it was one of those two Richie Rich punk kids who tried to steal the Maltese falcon statue? Maybe they stalked me at work and were trying to get revenge. But Porter doesn't buy this. He says Davy has stolen stuff before, and that he never comes by the museum. It's too coincidental. I guess he's probably right, but I'm starting to freak out again, and I'm having a hard time thinking straight.

Porter is tapping the van's steering wheel. He snaps his fingers, and then tugs his phone out of his pocket and looks something up. A couple of minutes later, he's calling someone. That's a bust, but he calls someone else, dropping his family name—I hear him say "Pennywise"—and then a third person. That's the call that sticks, because he's suddenly all relaxed and loose-limbed, one hand atop the wheel, as he tells the person he's looking for Davy. After several grunts, he hangs up, and then five minutes later, someone calls him back.

"I think I may have a lead," is all he says after it's over.

So why doesn't he sound more hopeful?

A soft rain begins to fall. Porter turns on his windshield wipers as we pass a sign telling us that we're exiting Coronado Cove and another identifying some tiny township that has four thousand residents. Everything here seems to be about state parks and camping and hiking. Oh, and car repair—lots and lots of car repair. Auto body, auto detailing . . . auto restoration. There's a small industry built up out here, people who are into muscle cars and racing, and I wonder if this is where my dad bought his car.

But Porter's headed past the nicer places. He's going down a dirt road into the woods, to a cinder-block garage with a number six spray-painted on a door to the left of three closed bays. Carcasses of rusted motorcycles lay in heaps near the building, discarded with other metal scraps. This is some kind of motorcycle chop shop, a place good bikes come to die. I'm suddenly very scared for Baby. A little scared for us, too.

Porter parks the van several yards away, under the fanning branches of some pines. "Stay in the van."

"You must be kidding," I say.

"If he's inside, I don't want you to see what might go down."

He's scaring me a little, but I don't want him to know this. "No way. This area reminds me of *Deliverance* territory. We stick together."

He snorts, hand on his door. "That takes place in the backwoods of Georgia, but I'm not even going to ask how you know about that movie, because we don't have time. So just . . . come on."

Rain dots the dirt road in front of our steps as we make our way to the door with the red six. It's eerily quiet, no one leaving or coming, no signs that the place is even in business. But as we get closer, I hear the faint sounds of a radio and voices, and I get nervous.

As Porter lifts his hand to knock, the door cracks open. A goateed African-American man in a tight-fitting red T-shirt pokes his head out. He looks Porter over, eyes zeroing in on Porter's scars. "Roth?"

"Yeah. You Fast Mike?"

The man's face softens. "You look like your mama."

"Thank God. Everyone usually says that about my sister."

"Never seen her, but my cousin painted that old Thunderbird your mama had."

"Yeah? She sold that a couple of years ago," Porter says. "Hated to. She loved that bike."

Fast Mike looks past Porter and notices me.

"This is Bailey," Porter says. "The Vespa we're looking for belongs to her."

The man blows out a hard breath through his nostrils. He opens the door wider. "Better come inside, then. Got a feeling this isn't gonna be pretty."

We follow him through a small office with two tidy desks, a counter, and an old register. No one's there. Past an old couch and a coffeemaker, another door leads into the garage. Burnt engine oil and old paint fumes hit me as we step onto stained concrete. Seventies rock music plays on a radio on a work bench. Rows of fluorescent lights hum over three drive-in bays, the closest of which is occupied by two motorcycles. The middle bay is empty but for three people, sitting around in folding chairs, talking. But it's what's in the far bay that snatches 100 percent of my attention.

One mustard-yellow pickup truck, blue lightning on the side, passenger window covered in a black garbage bag.

And behind the truck: one turquoise Vespa with a leopard-print seat.

I feel like I might pass out. And maybe that's why it takes my brain a couple of extra seconds to realize that one of the people lounging around in the chairs is Davy. In a way that's good, because I suddenly feel like committing a wild and vicious attack on him. But in another way, it's really, really bad, because Porter isn't dazed like me. Just the opposite, in fact. He's a laser beam, and he's headed straight for his former best friend.

The two other seated people scatter. Davy now sees Porter coming and the look on his face is absolute panic. He rushes to leap up, but his foot slips, and he can't quite stand. Porter lunges with both arms, shoving him with so much unhinged violence that Davy flies backward. Boy and metal both slam against a con-crete pylon and slide across the floor.

"You piece of shit," Porter says, stalking Davy to where he's now crumpled in a heap by the tire of his truck. "Too much of a coward to steal from me, so you jacked her stuff?"

Davy's groaning and holding his head in his hand. I'm worried he's got a concussion, but when he opens his eyes and looks up at Porter, there's nothing but rage. "I hate you."

"That makes two of us, junkie."

Davy cries out, a horrible battle cry that tears through the air and bounces around the garage. In quick succession, he leverages onto his good leg, grabs the folding chair, and swings upward. I scream. The chair bashes into Porter's face. His head jerks sideways. Blood spatters. The chair leg slips out of Davy's hands and sails through the air, clanging into his truck.

Porter's doubled over.

I try to run to him, but strong hands clamp around my arms. "Whoa," Fast Mike says in my ear. "He's okay. Let those boys work it out themselves."

But he's wrong. Porter's not okay. When he pulls his hand away from his face, there's blood all over it. A big gash crosses his cheek. Dumb boy that he is, he just shakes his head like a wet dog and refocuses.

"That's it," he growls and slams his fist into Davy's face. Hard.

After that, the whole thing is a mess. They're on top of each other, both throwing punches that land God knows where. It's not like a well-staged boxing match or a movie, it's just chaotic and weird, and more grappling than anything else. They're shouting and grunting and slugging each other in the ribs so hard, something's going to break or get punctured.

This is a nightmare.

I'm terrified they're actually going to kill each other. These aren't wimpy kids on the playground, giving each other bloody noses. They're rabid wolves, straining with muscle, teeth bared. And someone's going down.

"Let me go," I tell Fast Mike. I can't let Porter do this. If he gets seriously hurt, I don't know what I'll do. But I can help somehow . . . can't I? I look around for something to break up the fight. Maybe I can hit Davy on the head with something—

I can hardly believe what I'm seeing. Davy's grabbing Porter's hair—his hair! He has a fistful of Porter's dark curls, and he's wrenching his head back . . . is he going to bite his face? WHAT THE HELL IS HAPPENING?

Porter's lower body twists. He gives a powerful back kick to Davy's bad knee.

A sickening *crunch!* echoes around the garage.

Davy drops to the floor.

He doesn't get up. He's clutching his knee, mouth open. Silent tears begin falling.

Porter's chest heaves. All the veins stand out on his arms. A thick line of blood flows down his cheek and neck, disappearing into the black of his security guard uniform. "I'm calling your grandma, and I'm gonna tell her what you did today," Porter says as he stands over his friend, looking down at him. "I'm also telling my folks. I've given you so many chances, and you've thrown them all in my face. I can't ever trust you again. We're done."

"Love is the only thing that can save this poor creature."
—Gene Wilder, *Young Frankenstein* (1974)

16

We load Baby in the back of Porter's van. Except for the seat lock being popped, she seems to be in one piece. We found my helmet and all my stuff scattered behind the seat of Davy's truck. We also found my scooter lock hanging off his tailgate; he'd removed it with industrial bolt cutters.

Turns out that one of the two people sitting with Davy when we first walked into the garage was a friend of Davy's. Seeing how he was planning on helping Davy sell my scooter, I didn't say anything to the guy, but Porter told him to drive Davy to the hospital. When they left, Davy could walk—barely—but he was going to need X-rays. And probably some pain medication, which was just lovely, considering what I now know about Davy's history with drugs.

But after all that, Davy didn't say one word to me. He wouldn't even look me in the eye or acknowledge I was in the same room. Truth was, I couldn't really face him, either. It was humiliating for both of us, I guess. And I'm pretty much in such a state of shock over the whole fight that I can barely speak.

When we're ready to leave, Porter thanks Fast Mike, who advises me on a better-quality scooter lock. Turns out that his motorcycle garage isn't a chop shop at all; he was seconds away from kicking Davy out before he got the phone call about Porter looking for my Vespa. So once again, my assumptions and I are completely off the mark. He says to Porter, "Tell your mama next time she wants to sell a bike like that, to come to me first. I'll give her a good deal."

"You got it," Porter says, "We owe you big-time. You know anyone that needs a board, come by the shop."

Fast Mike gives us a wave. We race through the rain and hop inside the van, and then we drive away. The windows are all fogging up, and I'm trying to help, looking for the switch to turn on the defrost, but my hands are shaking. I'm still freaked out. I can't calm down. "The black button," Porter says, and I finally find it. I turn the fan all the way up and try to concentrate on making the windshield clear instead of the fact that he's still bleeding. It works until we come to the end of the dirt road.

"I think we should go see a doctor."

"It's fine."

"You're being ridiculous. Pull over at the first store you see and I'll get something to clean your wound."

He cranes his neck and appraises the damage in the rearview mirror. Yep. Listen to the smart person in the vehicle. Instead of turning right on the paved road to head back home, he turns left. Should he even be driving? Davy did punch him in the head a few times. Or maybe he knows something I don't. Now the road is going uphill. We're winding up some coastal cliffs, and the rain's coming down. And I see a sign that says SCENIC OVERLOOK. He slows the van and turns into one of those pull-over areas for tourists to park. It's got a couple of Monterey cypress trees and a redwood sign with a carving of the central coast of California and all the points of interest marked. It's also got a jaw-dropping view of the Pacific, which we might enjoy if it weren't overcast and drizzling, and he weren't bleeding all over the seat.

"This doesn't look like a store to me," I say anxiously when he opens up his door.

"We don't need no stinking store," he says in a way that almost reminds me of a line from a Mel Brooks movie, *Blazing Saddles*. I never liked that one as much as Brooks's other comedy classic *Young Frankenstein*, which I've watched online with Alex a couple of times. But it makes me a little guilty to think about that when I'm here with Porter.

Porter the animal. I'm still rattled over the insane amount of raw violence I just witnessed. And I'm not sure how I feel about it.

He jumps out, groaning, and heads around the van to a sliding side door, where he retrieves a small box. Then he comes back and slips back into the front seat and opens the treasure he's collected: a plastic first-aid kit covered in stickers.

"Surfers always carry supplies," he explains, rooting around the box with one finger. "We get banged up all the time."

After several seconds of watching him struggle, I realize his other hand is too busted up to use, and pity overrides whatever lingering shock I'm still experiencing. I snatch the kit away from him. "Let me see that. You can't nurse yourself, dummy."

"Oh, good. I did all this as an excuse for you to put your hands on me."

"Not funny."

"A little funny."

I find some alcohol swabs and a bunch of butterfly bandages, along with a couple of condoms, which I try not to think about too hard. "You scared the bejesus out of me. Look, here's a packet of Tylenol. It's been expired for a few months, but better than nothing. You have something to drink it with?"

"You need to work on your bedside manner, Nurse Bailey," he says, groaning as he leans to pick up a half-empty bottle of water wedged in the seat. He pretends to be irritated with me when I pretend to be mad at him as I hand him the pills. He swallows them and grunts.

I kneel on the seat and tear open a swab. The sharp scent of alcohol fills the van. We both make faces. He swings his door open, and the fresh air feels good. The sound of waves crashing against the rocks below is calming. Sort of.

Too chicken to start on his face, I tentatively pull back the collar of his shirt and swipe the cool swab over the dried blood on his neck. He shudders. "Cold."

"Sorry," I murmur. I make quick work of the trail of blood, but it's harder when I get to all his scruff. I unfold the swab, rearrange the first-aid kit in my lap, and get serious about cleaning him up. If I focus on this, then my mind will stop jumping back to frightening images of him ripping Davy apart like a wild beast. He leans his head back against the seat and closes his eyes.

"Porter?"

"Mmm?"

"Remember that time you saw Davy talking to me outside the vintage clothing store on the boardwalk?"

"Yeah."

"He didn't know I was listening, but I saw him come in the store and ask the girl at the counter, Julie, to help him out because he was going down to Monterey and needed something."

Porter's eyes fly open. "What? That's not what he told me."

"He was lying. And when he was talking to her inside the store, she said, 'I thought you were chipping.' And he told her that he was, but he just needed something for today, and that he promised it was only once, and she said she'd try to help him."

"I knew it." Porter hits the steering wheel.

I put a hand on his arm. He's going to reopen the gash on his cheek if he's not careful, and I haven't even gotten to clean it yet. "What's chipping?"

"He's such an embarrassment."

"Yeah, get that. Just tell me. Girl with the alcohol, remember? If you don't tell me, I will make you burn."

A sigh gusts out of his chest as he sinks into the seat, lazily propping one knee against the dash between us, making my knees press against his leg. I absently wonder if he did that on purpose—he's always closer than I'm comfortable being—but he's baring his cheek for me now, so I get back to work while he talks.

"Davy jacked up his leg surfing somewhere he shouldn't have been surfing three years ago. He wasn't watching the weather, and he took a risk. He had two surgeries. When the oxycodone prescriptions ran out, he started buying it from a kid at school. And when that ran out, he started looking for anything else—vodka, coke . . . but nothing kills the pain quite like opiates. And what's a better opiate than heroin?"

My hand stills. "Please tell me you're joking."

"It's surfing's dirty little secret."

"Like, shooting up?"

"As far as I know, he smokes it, but I'm not really around when he's doing it. I'm just going by what I've heard, and I've never seen any needle marks. That really, really stings, Bailey."

"I'm sorry. You probably need stitches. It's bleeding a little again." I push his hair back and see a nasty bump on his temple. He's lucky that chair didn't smash any bones in his face. I'm not entirely convinced it didn't, actually.

He winces. "Keep cleaning it, just be kind. Anyway, 'chipping' is something people do when they think they can outsmart heroin. They do just enough to get high for a weekend, or whatever, but don't allow themselves to have any more until the next weekend—cold turkey all week, so they don't go through withdrawals. If they aren't addicted, they're in charge, right?"

"That doesn't sound like it would work so well," I say.

"It doesn't. Because there's always that one holiday weekend that turns into three days, or they're having a bad week and need to blow off steam on a Wednesday. And before they know it, they're backsliding, and their conservative plan is busted. They're lying to themselves, thinking that they've got it under control. Like Philip Seymour Hoffman. People say that's what killed him."

I'm stunned. I know Wanda said Davy was into serious narcotics, but heroin? That sounds like something out of a movie. It doesn't happen in real life. Not to people my age, anyway. "Does this hurt?" I ask, lightly dabbing antibiotic ointment on his wound. It looks like a crevice in a dry desert, red and angry, cracked open.

"Nothing hurts when you're touching me," he says in a faraway voice.

I have to stop myself from smiling because I'm afraid he might open his eyes and catch me. And I don't want his eyes open, because I can look at him up close now. The sharp lift of his cheekbones. The way his wild curls, damp with misty rain, are honey where the sun has burnished them, darker beneath. The gentle upturn of the outer corners of his eyes, and the prominent jut of his nose.

"Is he going to be okay?" I ask.

"Davy? I really don't know," Porter says, sucking in a hard

breath as I fix a butterfly bandage to his cut. Three should do it, and that's all we have, so I guess it will have to. "I'm less worried about him right now, and more worried that you're sorry you ever gave me your number and will never go out on a date with me, because now you're thinking all my friends are trash and we really have nothing in common."

"Is that so?" I peel off the paper backing for the second butterfly bandage. "And why do you even like me if we have nothing in common?"

"Well, you're a knockout, obviously."

No one's ever called me this. I feel my chest getting fluttery and warm.

"And you laugh at my jokes."

A laugh bursts out—I can't help it. That's . . . so very Porter. It's self-absorbed and kind of endearing at the same time.

"Don't get me wrong, you're pretty witty yourself," he adds, cracking one eye open.

"Oh, am I? That's awfully generous of you."

He gives me a sheepish smile, chuckling, and shoves at my hands, because I'm playfully slapping him on the shoulder. "You're welcome. And, and—listen, now! Oww! I'm injured. Stop laughing, damn you, and listen to me. You have to admit, if you think about it, we get along really, really well when we're not fighting."

Is he right? Do we?

I think we just might.

Porter makes a growling noise. "See, but that's the other thing.

I talk too much when I'm around you. You make me feel way too comfortable, and that drives me bananas."

I laugh one final time and blow my hair out of my eyes. "You drive me bananas too."

There it is, that stupid, sexy smile of his. He reaches for my hand and stops halfway, groaning. "That is not a good way to move my arm."

Now I'm concerned again. I ball up the bandage papers and close the first-aid kit. "Davy didn't injure anything serious, did he? Ribs?"

"If you want me to take my shirt off, all you have to do is ask, Rydell."

"I'm serious."

He sighs. "I don't think so, but I'm not gonna lie—starting to feel a little achy-breaky in the riblet region. Think I'd better take a peek, so you might want to look away if you're sensitive to dynamite male bodies. I don't want you swooning at the sight of raw surfer."

"Lord knows I've been forced to stare at Davy's naked chest a hundred times, so I'm pretty sure I can handle yours. Come on, let's see the damage."

But as he unbuttons his Cave guard shirt, it's the least sexy thing in the world, because all I'm preoccupied with is how I'm going to drive this van if he's got a broken rib. And it only gets worse when his shirttails flap open.

If I thought Davy was built, I was wrong. Davy is a twig. Porter is a cliff. He's what happens when people use all their muscles at once to balance on a tiny plank of wet wood on massive, monster waves every day for years. All at once, I'm amazed at the beauty of the human body, ashamed at myself for using mine to do nothing but walk around the block and watch movies on Dad's couch, and, most of all, I'm completely and wholeheartedly shocked by what Davy has done to him.

When people say black and blue, they mean later, after the bruises have had time to settle. But right now, his torso is mottled with big red welts, some of them slightly bloodied, some of them radiating jagged, crystalline lines of dark pink. It's a hideous map of bruises to come. The welt across his ribs looks like South America, it's so big.

His chin is tucked to his sternum as he holds his shirt open and inspects the damage, and I can tell by his groan that even he's startled. It hits me all at once. I'm freaked out that he's so hurt and didn't say anything, and I'm frustrated that he had to resort to testosterone-fueled rage to solve all this. I'm disturbed by all the violence I witnessed. I'm mad that he has a friend like Davy, and I'm still enraged beyond understanding that Davy stole my scooter.

But despite all that . . . look what he did. Look what he did. For me? And he's sitting here, in pain, falling apart, and all he's worried about is that I'm sorry I gave him my number and don't want to go out on a date with him?

It's just too much. I fall to pieces.

"Hey, hey," he says, alarmed, sitting up quickly, and then groaning a little. And that only makes me sob harder. He buttons his shirt halfway, covering up some of the evidence. "It's okay. I've had broken bones before. I'm not broken today, promise. I'm just sore."

"It's just awful," I say, choking back tears. "I'm so sorry you had to do that."

"He had it coming. You don't know everything he's done to me. This is just the last straw. Hey, whoa, shush." His hands stroke over my upper arms.

I calm down. Turn my head and wipe my nose on my shoulder. Brush away tears.

"There." He swipes a thumb over my cheek, going back over what I've missed. Traces the arch of my eyebrows. Chases a flyaway tendril of hair at my temple. "And you know what?" he says in a low, intense voice. "I'd do it again in a heartbeat, because you didn't deserve what he did to you. I will be your revenge."

My breath catches, and I am overcome. Before I even know what I'm doing, I lean forward and kiss him.

Not a polite kiss.

Not a gracious kiss.

And he definitely doesn't kiss me. O-oh, no. I'm the kisser, which is the first time in my life that's happened—not the kissing, I mean, the initiating. I mean, hello. Evader! Initiating is not my style. But here I am, mouth firmly pressed against his. I'm not ashamed to say that I'm desperate about it and more than a little insistent, and if he doesn't kiss me back soon . . .

But he does. Je-sus, he does. It's as if a switch flipped in his brain—by Jove, I think he's got it! And I nearly start crying again, I'm so relieved, so happy. But then his mouth opens over mine, and a switch flips on in my brain (ding!), and then his tongue rolls against mine, and a switch flips on in my body (ding! ding!), and holymotherofgod that feels good. We're kissing, and it's amazing, and his hand is stroking down my back, and chills are racing everywhere, and DEAR GOD HE'S GOOD AT THIS.

A massive shudder goes through me and I freak out a little. My head's suddenly filled with all the things he's said about being eighteen and sexual freedom, and there is no doubt in my mind that he's exercised his rights with other girls—which is fine, whatever. No judgment. It's just that I have . . . not, and all this super-filthy kissing makes me more than aware of the experience gap between us. Which worries me. And thrills me. And worries me.

(And thrills me.)

Dear God: Save me from myself.

He breaks the kiss—probably because he can sense all the internal freaking out I'm doing. And yeah, sure enough, he says, "Bailey?"

"Yeah?" I say, but now I'm done with the freak-out. Now that I see his face, I can't stop smiling. Because his eyes are like slits and he looks all dazed and confused, and that's how I feel: as if my body is a toy top, spinning so fast that I can't see anything outside the van. All I can see is beautiful banged-up Porter, and all I can feel is this delicious whirling, twirling, buzzing, and I don't want it to ever stop.

Now Porter's grinning too, and I'm sure we both look like raving lunatics. Thank goodness we're sitting in the rain in the middle of nowhere. "Hey," he says, all raspy and deep. "Am I crazy, or was that the best kiss you've ever had?" His smile is acres wide and miles deep.

He knows it is.

"Surprising thing is, it's the best you've ever had too," I shoot back.

Both brows raise, and then he laughs, eyes closed. "You win. Want to do it again? Maybe it was just a fluke. We should test it out."

We do. It was no fluke. I'm going to melt right through the car seat. It's ridiculous. This is how teen pregnancies happen, I'm fairly certain. I finally push him away, and we're both breathing heavy. "See, told you," I say. "Best you've ever had."

"Wanna know a secret? I knew if we ever would shut up and stop arguing, it would be. Come here. Don't get all shy now. I just want to hold you."

"You're injured."

"And you're soft. No more kissing, I promise. Please, Bailey. Let me hold you, no manhandling. Just for a little while. Until it stops raining. I like the rain."

He beckons me into the shelter of his arm, and since I'm on the side that didn't get too beat up, I gently curl against him.

He's warm and solid, and I try to be as weightless and small as possible, try not to cause more pain, but he pulls me against him more firmly, and I give in. He sighs deeply, and we sit like that together, watching the rain fall over the ocean. Not talking. Just us. Just quiet.

But in that quiet, images of his bloody fight with Davy race back. This body that's holding me right now so protectively . . . it was violently tearing another human being apart. How can he be both things—tender and brutal? Is this what boys are? Or is this what Porter is? He's so complicated. I swear, the more I learn about him, the less I understand who he really is.

His ferocity unnerved me today, so why did I kiss him?

And why do I trust someone who can shake me up like that?

I think of our heated arguments. If I'm being honest with myself, I'm not exactly an innocent bystander. He provokes me, but do I allow myself to be provoked? Do I want it? And what about my ruthless takedown of that kid who stole the Maltese falcon? Grace keeps teasing me that I've got secret strength, and it's starting to make me think more and more about my stupid therapist back in New Jersey and all his talk about me paying the price for my avoidance techniques. Shake up a bottle of soda long enough, when you take off the top, it's going to explode.

Am I more afraid of Porter . . . or the person he's unleashing inside me?

LUMIÈRE FILM FANATICS COMMUNITY
PRIVATE MESSAGES>ALEX>NEW!

@mink: Hey, sorry we haven't talked much recently.

@alex: MINK. I'm so glad you messaged me. I've been meaning to talk to you. You haven't made a firm decision about flying out here yet, have you?

@mink: No, why would you ask that?

@alex: God, it took you so long to reply, for a second I thought I'd lost you there. Anyway, that's actually a good thing. Things are crazy at work for me right now. So before you get your dad to buy a plane ticket, just check with me beforehand, okay? Since it's so busy here.

@mink: Yeah, okay. I've been busy too, actually.

@alex: Then you understand. So just let me know? In case my situation changes?

@mink: Okay. Sure. You know I never rush into anything.

"Fight back, you coward! Fight back!"
—Daniel Radcliffe, *Harry Potter and the Half-Blood Prince* (2009)

17

A couple of hours before my shift the next morning, sunlight is already breaking through the gray sky as I pull Baby into a narrow alley behind Penny Boards Surf Shop. Porter's supposed to meet me here. He says his dad can fix the wonky lock on my seat, since it appears that Davy took a crowbar to it and screwed up the lock. I'm nervous about meeting his dad. Really nervous.

This is a mistake. That's all I can think. I'm not sure how he talked me into coming here right now, but I didn't really know what else to do about my bike.

My own dad was none too happy when he got home last night from San Jose and I told him the story of the stolen scooter. If he only knew the entire story, he'd have a heart attack—so really, he's lucky to have a daughter who cares enough about the state of his ticker to make sure that he only got the bare details he actually needed. And those details were as follows: The bike was stolen from the Cave's parking lot, but one heroic security guard, a Mr. Porter Roth, chased the unruly teens off the museum property, sustaining injuries in the process, and got my bike back. A shame that Porter couldn't identify the boys who took it, otherwise he would have filed a police report.

"It all happened so fast," I told him. "I'm glad he was there."

"He didn't see the thieves' faces?"

Err . . . "It was raining. They hit him and took off running."

"I still think we should tell Wanda."

"The museum security is taking care of it, Dad. Let them do their jobs, okay?"

My dad raised his hands. "All right, Mink. I'm just glad you're okay. And Grace knows someone in town who's going to help you get the seat fixed?"

Another lie. But it's necessary, because as great as my dad is in a lot of ways, he's not handy. So he's fine with letting this mystery person handle it; he's even happy to lend me money for a new wheel lock. I don't deserve him.

So that's what started the stress train. What kept the train chugging along the track was knowing I had to face Xander Roth, son of Pennywise, survivor of the great white shark, father to the boy I made out with . . . and then went home last night and before I went to sleep did unspeakable things to myself under the covers while thinking about all that making out with said boy. Which is how teen pregnancies *don't* happen, I'm fairly certain.

Then, what sped the stress train up to full speed was getting those stupid messages from Alex this morning. Because it sounded like he doesn't want me to fly out here. I mean, of course I'm already out here, but he doesn't know that. What if I'd already bought a plane ticket? And why did he suddenly get so freaking busy, anyway? Did he meet another girl? Because it sure sounds that way to me.

I don't know why this bothers me so much. It's not like I'm not doing the same thing (hello, double standard). And we never promised to save ourselves for each other. We might not even get along in real life. Isn't that why I was being so cautious in the first place, drawing out my elaborate map legend of the boardwalk and carefully tracking him down, just in case we weren't compatible?

It's just that nothing is working out like I'd planned. Alex and I have a connection—at least, we're simpatico on paper, but who knows about reality? On the other hand, Porter and I are simpatico in reality, yet we're also opposites. His life is pretty messy, and I don't like messy. Been there, done that. It's why I left my mom and Nate LLC in the first place. And then there's the small, eensie-meensie detail that I'm not even supposed to be anywhere near him, thanks to Wanda's police warnings, ugh. But that's part of the whole appeal, isn't it? Because being with Porter is crazy and exciting. And much like a great thriller film, I'm not sure who's going to end up dead by the closing credits.

A dark blue van pulls up behind me and parks in a space marked for the surf shop. But it's not Porter's van. And it's not Porter driving—or riding, for that matter. Two people jump out, both eying me with great curiosity. The first is Mr. Roth, wearing a lightweight yellow Windbreaker, one sleeve sewed up, and the second is someone I recognize from photographs as Porter's sister, Lana. They are both slightly damp, and, I assume from the droplets of water on the boards strapped to the van, have just come from the beach.

"Hi," Lana says, chewing gum, super friendly and open. "You're Porter's girl."

Am I? This makes my chest feel funny. "I work with Porter," I say as she saunters around the van. God, she moves just like him, slinky, like a cat. And she's wearing skintight long sleeves and shorts—whatever she's put on after getting out of her wet suit, I guess, but she's built like Porter too. Not model-thin, but muscular. Solid and shapely.

"Lana," she says, joyfully chew-chewing her gum.

"Bailey," I answer.

"Bai-ley. Yeah, I remember now," she says, slowly grinning. She's young and pretty, no makeup, long curly hair. Very laidback. Open, like Porter. "He's yapped and yapped about you. Hey, Pops, this is the scooter Davy jacked."

Mr. Roth, who has completely ignored me up to this point, already has his hand on the back door to the shop. He looks at the scooter, then gives me a critical once-over. "You messing around with Davy?" he says brusquely. Not Porter. Davy.

Shock washes over me. "N-no. God no."

"Because the last one was, and why did Davy steal this if there isn't something going on?" He gives me a look like I think he's an idiot. "You expect me to believe my son comes home with his face banged up for no reason? Like he's just some hoodlum, fighting in the streets? I raised him better than that."

"Dad," Lana says, sounding almost as humiliated as I feel. "He was defending her honor."

"Why did it need defending?" Now Mr. Roth is waving his arm at me, angry. "Why did Davy steal this?"

"I don't know," I bark back at him, surprised at myself. "Maybe because he's a scumbag who thought he could make some quick cash. But I didn't encourage it. I don't even know him."

The door to the shop swings open. Porter rushes out, breathless. He looks . . . awful. The cut on his cheek is dark red and swollen. The bump on his temple is now an ugly shade of blue and brown. His usually perfectly groomed scruff is darker and thicker.

"Pops," he says. "This is Bailey Rydell. Remember, I told you about fixing the scooter seat last night? Like that one you fixed before, Mr. Stanley's."

Right now I'm wondering how a one-armed man is going to fix anything—and frankly, with his crummy attitude, I don't think I want him to bother.

His father doesn't say anything for several seconds. Then he looks at me. "I don't know any Rydells. Who're your parents?"

Before I can answer, Porter says, "I told you already. Her dad lives in the old McAffee place. He's an accountant. He's seeing Wanda Mendoza. Bailey moved here in May, from the East Coast."

"Oh, yeah. Sergeant Mendoza. She's all right," his dad says, still gruff, but a little softer, like he only half believes Porter, but maybe he's thinking about considering believing him one day soon. And—poof!—just like that, the interrogation is over. "Get inside and help your mom," he tells Lana before turning to Porter. "Go get the green toolbox out of the van. I'll also need the keys to her seat."

Mr. Roth isn't addressing me. I am dismissed. I'm not sure how I feel about this. Pretty lousy, I think. Porter used to think I was too fancy for him, but now his dad thinks I'm not good enough to date his son? And what was all that business about him assuming I was seeing Davy because "the last one" did? Is this the Chloe girl Porter and Davy were arguing about outside the vintage clothing shop on the boardwalk? Man. This guy is a piece of work. When Porter described him as a drill sergeant, he wasn't kidding. I think Porter dropping Wanda's name was the only thing that gave me a pass.

Coming here was definitely a huge mistake. I'm regretting it so hard and wishing I could leave somehow, but I can't see a way out of it.

When I give Porter my scooter keys, he mouths, *Sorry,* to me and squeezes my hand, and just this tiny bit of skin-on-skin contact feels like when you wake up on the weekend and smell breakfast cooking: completely unexpected and delightful. One crummy kiss (okay, two—okay, AMAZING KISSES), and my body doesn't even care that Porter's dad hates my guts and I'm seconds away from a panic attack; it's too busy enjoying all the actual, real, live tingles being generated by surfer-boy touch. Not good. I'm so terrified his dad will see me react, all I do is drop his hand like a hot potato.

Coward that I am, I'm about five seconds away from turning heel and running down the alley, never to return again, so when Lana nods her head toward the shop, I'm already in such a state of confusion, I just follow her inside. Better than staying outside with the drill sergeant. Or Porter—who I might swoon over in front of his dad. I can't trust myself anymore. WHAT IS HAP-PENING TO ME?

"Pops doesn't mean to come off like that," Lana says as we head through a storeroom filled with shelves of boxes. "He's just grumpy. I think he's in pain twenty-four-seven, but he'll die before he admits it. You ever hear about the whole phantom-limb thing?"

"Yeah," I say. Vaguely. Amputees come back from war and still feel their missing limbs.

"I've heard him tell Mom that he still feels pain in the arm, even though it's not there. He has a lot of nightmares and stuff. He won't take pills or go see a doctor because he's scared of get-ting addicted. Our grandpa was an alcoholic. Pops doesn't want to turn into him."

I don't have time to process any of this before she pushes open another door and we're blinking into the sunlit windows of the surf shop. Redwood and brightly colored boards surround the walls; music plays from speakers hanging from the ceiling. It's not busy, but a few people mingle, looking at boards and wet suits, chatting around displays of gear.

Funny, but this is one of the places that was closed for lunch every time I came by to mark it off my Alex map; either that or I got distracted, because my favorite churro cart is outside—I can see it from here, along with the waves slamming against the pier—and it's that churro cinnamon scent I smell now, mixed with Porter's coconut wax. It's a heavenly combination, almost erotic. Definitely not something I want to think about when I'm meeting his family.

Lana serpentines around the displays, cheerfully greeting customers, and heads to the back of the store. She leans over the counter and tugs on the arm of a bronze-skinned middle-aged woman with generous curves and a massive cloud of frizzy ebony hair. Lana pulls her away from a conversation, whispering in her ear. The woman is definitely Polynesian, and definitely their mother. Like, whoa, crazy familial resemblance. Mother and daughter look in my direction. Both of them smile.

"Hello," the mother calls out, coming around the counter to meet me. She's dressed in jeans and a loose top. Unlike the rest of the family, she's not muscular and fit, but more on the soft and plump side. Her big cloud of hair is pulled behind one ear and hangs to her hips. "I'm Porter and Lana's mom. You can call me Mrs. Roth or just Meli. Everyone does."

God, she's so pretty . . . so nice. Smiling so wide. It feels like a trap.

"Bailey," I tell her.

"Bailey Rydell," she says, surprising me. "Porter tells me you work with him at the Cave."

"Yes, ma'am."

"Pops was super mean to her," Lana reports.

Mrs. Roth scrunches up her face. "I'm so sorry. He gets like that sometimes. The trick is to either play his junkyard dog game and show your teeth"—she imitates a snapping dog, which is kind of adorable—"or you do what I do and just ignore him."

"And don't let his big talk fool you," Lana says. "My mom totally wears the pants in this family."

"That's right, baby." Mrs. Roth wraps her arms around her daughter. "How'd you do this morning? Find anything good to surf?"

"Nah, just paddled. Porter was right, as usual. Onshore winds were crumbling the waves." Lana looks at me and brightens. "You should come out with us one morning, watch us surf. Porter likes it when someone's there to cheer him on instead of Pops yelling at him."

Mrs. Roth nods, smiling. "And boy oh boy, would he show off for you, my dear. You tell him you want to come see him surf one morning when the waves are fine. He'd love that. Just say the word, and he'll be texting you weather reports at the butt crack of dawn."

"He's obsessed with weather," Lana tells me.

"I know," I say too quickly, unable to stop myself.

They both grin back at me like I've solved some big family secret code.

Mrs. Roth glances over Lana's head and raises a hand to a customer. "Hey, baby?" she says to Lana. "Can you do me a favor and help Mr. Dennis?"

Lana makes a gagging noise. "Maybe when you start paying me an actual salary."

Mrs. Roth gives me a sheepish look. "Don't spread that around, okay? We're not forcing them into child labor; it's—"

"Technically, you sort of are," Lana mutters, giggling when her mom pinches her waist.

"—just that times are tight right now," Mrs. Roth finishes explaining.

"And Porter and I are the only suckers in town who'll work for free," Lana adds. "I'll go help Mr. Dennis, but only if you let me stay out an extra hour tonight."

"Half an hour, and go, go, go. He's got that pissy look on his face." Mrs. Roth swivels toward the front door and makes an exasperated noise; someone's unloading a stack of boxes by the front door. "Deliveries go through the back. How many times do I have to tell that guy? Oh, Bailey, I have to take care of this, I'm sorry. I wanted to do girl talk with you. Stay here."

As she races away to redirect the delivery man, I watch Lana struggling to pull down a surfboard from a high-up rack, where it's stacked in the middle of several others. She's all muscle—no eyelash-batting doll—but it's hard work, and she's breathing heavy, shaking out her arm and joking that she nearly smashed her hand getting the board out. It strikes me that there's no one else working here. It's just the four of them, running this place? And with Mr. Roth's limitations, that leaves all the physical stuff dumped on the mom and two kids, neither of whom are getting paid. And then Porter has to turn around and work full-time at the Cave.

This really, really sucks.

And what about when school starts in the fall, and when Lana and her dad go on the surfing tour? Is Mrs. Roth going to run the store by herself? How will Porter keep his grades up and help her and hold down his job at the Cave?

My phone buzzes with a text. Surprisingly, it's from Patrick, as in, Patrick of Killian's Whale Tours and my broken gaydar: *Hey. You free? Wanna get coffee at the Shack? I've got new stuff from the film festival.*

Well, what do you know? He doesn't think I'm a total loser after our "date" fail in the video store. Before I can text back, the back door swings open and Porter breezes in, a huge smile on his face. Delight rushes through me until I see his father behind him . . . then I freeze up. "Pops fixed the seat. You're good to go."

Mr. Roth hands me my keys without looking me in the eyes. I think. I'm not looking him in the eyes either. This might work if we both keep avoiding each other. "Still dented," he mumbles, "and it might stick when you unlock it, but there's nothing I can do about that."

"You'll just have to wiggle the key some and knock it with your palm," Porter volunteers cheerily.

"Or take it somewhere to get it fixed professionally," Mr. Roth says. "But the worst problem you'll have is locking yourself out, so you might want to carry your helmet inside with you until you're more sure about it. And get a better wheel lock."

"I'm headed to buy one right now," I tell him. I scratch my hand, uncomfortable. "Thank you for doing this."

Looking away, he grunts and shrugs the shoulder that doesn't have an arm. After a few seconds of awkward silence, just when I think he might turn and leave without another word, he pins me with a hard stare and points a finger in my face. "You really want to thank me? Next time you see Davy Truand, you call me day or night and I'll finish what Porter started. That boy is stupid and dangerous, and he's obviously got you in his sights, so I'll tell you what I tell my own daughter: You stay away from him as best you can, but if he comes anywhere near you, get your phone out and start dialing my number—hear me?"

Um . . . ?

I feel the rattle of the weird, low note that escapes the back of my throat. He's sort of yelling at me again, but it's in a concerned-parent way, and I'm not sure, but I think he's offering to kick Davy's ass for me now. I look at Porter for confirmation and he's grinning.

So very confused.

All I can do is nod. So I do, several times. This seems to meet

Mr. Roth's approval. He nods back at me, also several times. And then he tells Porter to quit standing around like a lump and help his mom with the delivery that's now coming around to the back door. I watch him head toward Mrs. Roth, and I'm stunned.

"He likes you," Porter whispers near my ear, sending a small cascade of shivers over my scalp. It freaks me out that he has that effect on me in public, especially when his family is halfway across the store.

I find my voice and ask, "How can you tell?"

"For my dad, that was practically hugging and welcoming you into the family. He said you have grit."

Artful Dodgers don't have grit. Is this because I snapped at him outside? It's hard for me to think too hard about it, because Porter is linking his index finger with mine.

"Hey, Porter," a voice calls out.

I drop his finger and look up to see Mrs. Roth smiling sweetly from the door to the back room, her dark storm cloud of hair haloed around her shoulders. "Aw, I'm sorry, kids," she says.

"You ladies met?" Porter asks.

"We did," she answers, "And Bailey's going to come watch you do your thing one morning."

Porter raises both brows and has a look on his face that's hard to decipher, like maybe he's embarrassed, but kind of happy, too. "Yeah?"

"If you want," I say.

"Yeah, maybe," he says. "You should come see Lana, for sure. If you can get up that early."

"Yeah, maybe," I say, mimicking him. "I mean, I know nothing about tides and waves, and all that, so you'll have to alert me when and where it's going down."

Mrs. Roth gives me an enthusiastic thumbs-up sign from the door and then quickly lowers her arm before Porter can see it. "Sounds like a plan to me," she says. "And I'm sorry to break this up, but I really need some help back here—Porter?"

"Sorry, duty calls," he tells me.

I shake my head, dismissive. I've got to buy that new wheel lock before work. There's plenty of time for that, but he's clearly got stuff to do here, so I don't say that. I just tell him I'm busy too, thank him again, and ask him to thank his dad again, who has disappeared with Lana. Mrs. Roth waves good-bye over the top of a stack of boxes when I leave through the back door.

I still have a couple of hours to kill before work, plenty of time to buy my new wheel lock, so I text Patrick back and make plans to meet up with him at the Pancake Shack as I test out my newly repaired seat lock. As I'm doing this, high up on the gutter of the roof, I catch a glimpse of white fur: a cat. Two cats, actually. It's my tabby from the churro cart, Señor Don Gato, and she's stalking a big, fluffy white feline. I laugh out loud—I can't help it—because it's just like that children's song. My Don Gato has found her true love.

"Don't jump," I call out to Don Gato. Both cats look down at me quizzically. "Trust me on this one, you'll only break your leg and die. That stupid white cat is not worth it. But if you do jump, remember that during your funeral, the scent of fish will bring you back to life—or probably, in your case, the smell of churros."

Don Gato plops down inside the gutter and starts licking his paw. She couldn't care less about my warning. Well, I tried. Somewhere on this boardwalk, I silently hope that Sam-I-Am is living a smarter life than these two love cats, risking bodily harm on the roof . . . and then I remember Alex blowing me off.

"You know what? Screw it. You've both got nine freaking lives," I call back up to the cats as I strap on my leopard-print helmet. "Live them a little."

LUMIÈRE FILM FANATICS COMMUNITY
PRIVATE MESSAGES>ALEX>NEW!

@alex: Hey, Mink? You're not mad at me, are you?

@mink: And what would make you think that?

@alex: I don't know. I was just worried that you might be mad when I asked you to check with me before buying a plane ticket to come out here. You haven't messaged since then.

@mink: I'm not mad. I would have thought you knew me better than that.

@alex: Err . . . Is that a joke? I can't tell.

@mink: Sometimes it's hard to tell someone's tone online. Anyway, too busy to talk now. Catch you later.

18

You'd think that two people who maybe, just might like each other (sometimes) and who definitely, usually (almost always) work together would find some time—or any time, really—to be alone. If not for kissing, then at least for talking. But an entire week passed, and all I got from Porter after the visit to his family's surf shop was a daily greeting, a lot of smiling, and enough desperate across-the-lobby stares to fill up the entire cavern.

Every day, I watched the bruises on his face lighten and his wound heal, but as they disappear, so does the memory of what happened between us, and I am feeling something akin to physical withdrawals. Sure, I received some texts from him during work hours. They included the following:

On a scale from 1 to Hades, how humid is the Hotbox today?

You should wear sandals to work more often. Your feet are sexy. Maybe I'm the one with the foot fetish.

I thought about sneaking out to your house last night, but I didn't want to risk getting you in trouble with your dad if I got caught.

I'm tired. Let's go take a nap together in the big teepee.

And when he texted me, *I think I need medical care. Will you come nurse me again?* I nearly fell off my stool in the ticket booth. But when I texted him back that I would be right there, his reply was: *Sigh. I wish. Pangborn is sitting next to me. Awkward.*

The boy is killing me. K-i-l-l-i-n-g.

Things were much simpler when we were archenemies.

"Sometime I feel like Porter is Pangborn's nurse," I mutter under my breath.

Grace hands tickets through the window and mutes the microphone. "Know what I heard? That all that weed Pangborn vapes might actually really be medicinal. The old goat might have the big *C*."

I frown. "What? Cancer? Who told you that?"

"It's just a rumor going around. Don't know if it's true. You know how people talk. That girl Renee up in the café says she heard that he's been in remission for years, and that he just uses it as an excuse to get high. So who knows? He doesn't look sick to me."

Me either, but can you really tell? And it's not like I'm going to walk up and flat-out ask him. I hate rumors. It makes me sad that people are talking about Pangborn behind his back.

"What the hell is going on between you two, anyway?" Grace asks me as she adjusts the portable fan.

"Pangborn and me?"

She gives me a classic Grace eyeroll that clearly communicates: *You know what I'm asking about; don't play dumb.* "Porter and you."

"Beats me," I say, thoroughly grumpy. I'd already told her about the kissing. No details. Well . . . some details. Grace has a way of dragging things out of me. "Maybe he's dating someone else, and he's trying to juggle two girls at once."

Grace shakes her head. "No other girlfriend. He works at the surf shop after he leaves here every day. It's open until nine. Then he turns back around and works there every morning—and that's if he hasn't been surfing. When has he got time for another girl?"

Good point. I feel guilty for even joking about it.

"I saw him arguing with Mr. Cavadini about the schedule that just got posted," she notes as her phone buzzes. She checks the message, texts something back, and smiles to herself.

"And?"

She shrugs as she passes tickets through the window.

Now my phone buzzes with a text. It's Porter. *We both have tomorrow off. If you're not busy, would you like to go on a date? Time: tomorrow afternoon until ? Chance of being caught by your dad: very low. (Please say yes.)*

I look up at Grace. "Did you know about this?"

"About what?" she says, the picture of innocence. "And, yes, I'll cover for you. You can tell your dad you're spending the day with me. But my parents want to actually meet you, so you're coming round for dinner on Tuesday. We don't play nerdy board games, but my dad cooks and will force you to help in the kitchen while he tells stupid jokes, so fair warning there."

"I owe you big-time, Grace." I can't type *Yes* fast enough.

The next day at noon, I park Baby in the alley behind the surf shop, neatly wedging her into a small nook between the building and Mr. Roth's van. Mrs. Roth says she'll keep an eye on it but assures me that no one in their right mind would steal anything from them. One look at Porter's scary-ass dad and I believe her. But I'm not really all that concerned about Davy rejacking Baby, I'm just relieved to stow the scooter back here, where my dad won't be likely to see it if he's out and about.

I slide into the passenger side of Porter's van and smooth the hem of my vintage-patterned skirt as he speeds out of the alley, making all the rubber sea monsters on his dash bobble comically. It's sunny and clear, a beautiful summer day, and we haven't said all that much to each other. We're both nervous. At least, I know I am, and I'm pretty sure he is too, because he's exhaling deeply an awful lot and not his usual chatty self. He hasn't told me where we're going yet, only that I should be prepared to do some strolling. "It's air-conditioned, don't worry. I wouldn't subject you to Hotbox temperatures on your day off," he told me yesterday in the parking lot after work. I've been in the dark about everything else.

"You really aren't going to ask where we're going?" he finally says when we're headed south on Pacific Coast Highway, following the ocean past the boardwalk and the Cave.

"I like a good mystery." I have a couple of flashbacks of our last trip this way, when we were looking for my lost scooter, but I'm not going to bring that up. Instead, I've been trying to solve the puzzle on my own, deducing things from the direction we're headed and the time we're leaving—not exactly primo romantic date time—and what he's wearing, which is a pair of jeans with an untucked wine-colored shirt that fits obscenely well across his chest. I can't stop sneaking glances at his arms. Because, let's face it, they are great arms. Great arms that lead to great hands . . . and I wish those hands were touching me right now.

Once you've had an amazing kiss, can you die if you don't get another one? Because I feel like that's what's happening to me. Maybe I like him way more than he likes me. God, that thought makes me feel off balance and a little queasy. Or maybe I don't like him at all. Maybe our relationship is being held together by the thrill of a good quarrel and raw sexual attraction, and my initial instincts about him were right. I hope this date wasn't a mistake.

"I'm glad you trust me," he says, relaxing for the first time today and showing me a hint of that beautiful smile of his. "Since we've got some miles ahead of us, let's test your musical tastes."

"Oh, brother." We both break out our phones, and he lets me scroll through his music library, finding we have little in common there—big surprise. But, and I'm not sure why this is, I'm almost glad about it. Because we spend the next half hour debating the merits of the last few eras of music history—disagreeing about almost everything—and it's . . . fun.

Really fun.

"This is going to sound weird," I say after some thought, "but I think we're compatible arguers."

He considers this for a moment. "You enjoy hating me."

"I don't hate you. If I hated you, things would be much simpler, believe me. I just think we're good at arguing with each other. Maybe it's because we respect each other's point of view, even if we don't agree."

"Maybe it's because we like the other person so much, we're trying our best to convince them to come around to our way of thinking."

I snort. "You think I like you that much, huh?"

He holds his palms upward on the steering wheel, gesturing toward the open road in front of us. "I've planned this for an entire week like a complete loser. Who's the one who's whipped here?"

Warmth spreads up my neck and cheeks. I quickly stare out the passenger window and hope my hair shields the rest as I listen to him exhale heavily again. I'm happy and embarrassed at the same time when I think about how much trouble he went to arranging this. He argued with Cavadini for both of us to get the day off. And I wonder who's covering for him at the surf shop—his sister?

"I was beginning to worry you'd changed your mind about me this week," I say to the window.

I feel a tug on my sleeve. Porter pulls my hand across the seat and offers me a tentative, unsteady smile that I return. It feels so good to finally touch him again, and now I'm the one exhaling deeply. I'm still nervous, but it's a different kind of jitters. Before, my anxiety was singing solo. Now all this weird anticipation and jumbled excitement has added some strange harmonies into the mix. I'm a barbershop quartet basket case.

It takes us almost an hour to get to our destination, which is the closest nearby city, Monterey. It's about the same size as Coronado Cove, but it has a different feel. Fewer surfers, more boats and bicycles. Porter points out a few things, shows me Cannery Row, which was made famous by local legend John Steinbeck, in the book of the same name. We didn't read that in school—it was *The Grapes of Wrath*—but Porter's read everything by Steinbeck, which surprises me, until he starts talking about tidal pools and a marine biologist named Ed Ricketts who was immortalized in Steinbeck's book as a character named Doc. Then it starts to make sense.

We park a few blocks from the beach near a Spanish-style building with a terra-cotta roof and a stone whale sculpture out front. The sign on the wall reads: PACIFIC GROVE MUSEUM OF NAT-URAL HISTORY.

Porter clips his keys onto a leather strap that dangles from his belt against his hip as we stand across the street. He's examining the blank look on my face, which I quickly try to disguise. "I know this may seem strange. You're thinking, *Hey, we work in a museum all day long. Why would we want to come here?*"

"I wasn't thinking that." Maybe just a tiny bit. "I like museums."

And I really, really do.

"That morning on the Lifts you told me you wanted to work in a real museum one day," he says softly, shoving his hands in his pockets.

I nod, suddenly more than a little embarrassed and wishing I hadn't shared so much of myself with him—yet, at the same time, touched that he remembered.

"Anyway, this isn't really part of the date. We have an appointment."

"An appointment," I repeat, confused.

"Just . . . come on."

The building doesn't look all that big from the outside, and when we head past Sandy the Whale through the front doors and Porter pays the optional meager entrance fee, it doesn't pull a Doctor Who trick and look any bigger on the inside, either. But it's two stories and brightly lit. And it's packed full of natural specimens collected in glass cases—stuffed birds and animals, artifacts, dried plants, rocks—all from central California. And even though natural history really isn't my thing, it has an old-school museum vibe that immediately makes me fall in love with it.

Yeah, totally digging this.

"My parents used to take Lana and me here when we were kids," Porter tells me as we stroll into the main room and pause in front of an eight-foot-tall brown bear that stands into the second story.

"It's fantastic," I say, craning my neck to glance at the bear's face. And before I realize how geeky I sound, I add, "The lighting is excellent."

He's pleased. "Unlike the Cave, all this stuff is the real deal. And the docents are cool. They know their stuff." He glances at his surf watch. "We're a little early. We've got half an hour, which is almost enough time to do a quickie tour of the whole museum, if you're interested, that is."

"Half an hour until our appointment with . . . ?" I ask.

"You'll see." He tucks his wild curls behinds his ears, looking devious and excited, and for a brief moment I panic, wondering if I'm being led into some kind of *Carrie* situation—any second now, prom will be ruined by a big bucket of pig's blood being dumped on my head. I start to ask him about this, just to double-check, but he interrupts my horror-movie thoughts.

"No sense sitting around while we wait when there's so much cool stuff in here. There's a jumbo squid that Ed 'Doc' Ricketts donated and a preserved baleen whale eyeball," he says with the enthusiasm of someone who just scored two tickets to a red-carpet premier of the next Marvel blockbuster movie.

"Okay, I'm game." I'm still nervous about this appointment thing, but eager to see the museum at the same time, so I follow him.

Case by case, he guides me through the galleries of butterflies, mollusks, abalone, fossils. There's a garden out back, and a million taxidermied birds—California condors, ahoy! And when he finally points out the preserved baleen whale eye, I think it might haunt me forever. Especially when, as I'm leaning over to inspect it, Porter gooses my sides. I squeal so loud, a group of small children are startled. He can't stop laughing. I think we're in danger of getting kicked out, so I pretend to slug him in the shoulder a few times, and that alarms the children even more.

"It's always the quiet ones who are the most violent," he tells one of the wide-eyed toddlers as I drag him away.

"You're a menace to society," I whisper.

"And you've got terrible taste in boys. It's time for our appointment."

I follow him back through the galleries to a small gift shop, where we meet a jolly, brown-haired security guard named Ms. Tish. "You look just like your dad," she says, shaking his hand heartily. For the love of surfing, does everyone in California know the Roths? And do they all have an opinion on which parent Porter favors the most? It's ridiculous. Then it hits me that Ms. Tish is a museum security guard . . . and Porter's a museum security guard. Is there some secret guard network I don't know about?

Porter introduces me and says, "So, yeah, like I said on the phone, Bailey maybe wants to be future curator in an actual real museum—not a schlocky tourist attraction like the Cavern Palace—so I was hoping maybe you could give us a peek behind the curtain."

"Not a problem," she says, nodding toward a door marked STAFF. "Follow me."

I'm in a daze as she leads us through the back hallways. First she gives us a tour of the archives and storerooms, where a guy and girl are quietly tagging fossil samples at a big table, listening to music. They are nice enough when we're introduced, but you can tell that they're relieved we're heading back out. I don't blame them one bit; the solidarity I'm feeling is total and complete. Swap out those fossils with old movie stills, and this would be my dream job: peace and quiet, nothing to do but concentrate on what you love. Absolute bliss.

Then we're on to the museum offices, which look a lot different than the Cave's. It's smaller, sure. But people are actually working on stuff that matters back here. Real museum things—not making sales quotas and driving more customers. There are desks and clutter and flurry, and people are discussing exhibits and education programs and outreach.

Ms. Tish stops in front of an office marked with a sign that says EXHIBIT CURATOR. She knocks on the doorjamb and a handsomely dressed woman looks up from her desk.

"Mrs. Watts?" the guard says. "These kids are from Coronado Cove. They work at Cavern Palace. This one here says she wants to steal your job one day, so I thought you might to see what she looks like and prepare yourself."

I'm momentarily appalled until Mrs. Watts grins and stands behind her desk, gesturing for us to come inside. "A future curator? I'm delighted. Have a seat, why don't you?"

Everything's a big blur after that. She's friendly and asks a lot of questions that I'm not prepared to answer. When she realizes that I'm not really all that into natural history, I think she's disappointed, but Porter picks up my slack and starts talking about kelp forests and limpets and she's back on board. Then it gets better because she's doing all the talking, telling us what she does, and it's actually really interesting. And she's super laid-back and cool, and I do want her job—I mean, in a theoretical kind of way.

While she's talking, I sneak a look at Porter, and I'm overwhelmed. This is not technically a romantic date, but it's the most romantic thing anyone's ever done for me. All he had to do was take me to the movies. Heck, I would have been content to park at the end of the alley. Who does this kind of thing? No boy I've ever known, that's for sure.

I'm not certain how long we're in there—a minute or two?—but she gives me her business card, and before we leave she shakes my hand and tells me, "We'd never turn down a good intern. If you'd ever want to put in some time on the weekends, I'm sure something could be arranged. Shoot me an e-mail."

"Thank you," I manage to say.

Ms. Tish and Porter make small talk about surfing as we leave the museum, and I think he gives her someone's phone number to get free tickets to some sort of surfing competition event, I'm not sure. She seems happy. We both thank her and jog down the stairs in tandem, passing Sandy the Whale on our way back to the van.

"Porter."

"Bailey." Lazy smile.

"Porter."

"Bailey." Lazier smile.

"That was so . . . Ugh. I don't know what to say."

"You didn't think it was stupid?"

I bump his arm with my shoulder as we cross the street. "Shut up." I'm full-on lost for words now, completely thunderstruck. Could he be any nicer? Doing this today was beyond thoughtful. . . . It's almost too much.

I exhale hard several times. I'm unable to express how I feel. My words come out fast and crude. "Jesus, Porter. I mean, what the hell?"

He grins. "So I did good?"

It takes me several strides to answer. I swallow hard and finally say, "Today was great—thank you."

"Don't make it sound like it's over—it's not even two o'clock yet. Strap yourself in, Rydell; we're headed to stop number two."

I don't mean to laugh. I sound like a demented person. I think I'm nervous again. I also feel a little drugged. Porter Roth has that effect on me. "Where to now?" I somehow manage to get out of my mouth.

"If this place was a slice of my childhood, then I'm about to give you a front-row seat to my nightmares."

Porter's family has an annual membership to the Monterey Bay Aquarium, and it comes with a guest pass, so he gets us both in for free. This is no Podunk attraction. Porter tells me it draws two million visitors a year, and I believe that. It's huge and beautiful and more professional than anything in Coronado Cove.

Today the crowds are sporadic, and Porter weaves around them. He's clearly been here a hundred times, and at first I think it might be a repeat of the museum: He's going to be giving me a tour, pointing out all manner of marine life. But after we stop to watch a little kid nearly fall headfirst into the stingray pool, things . . . get so much better.

We start holding hands in the middle of the darkened kelp forest exhibit. Unlike the natural history museum, this place is completely romantic, and I hope Porter doesn't hear the little happy sigh that escapes my lips when his fingers slip through mine. I don't even care that his knuckles are making my fingers ache a little, I'm not willing to let go.

The next dark place is the jellyfish room. They are gorgeous, all lacy and ethereal, shockingly red and orange floating up and down in tubes of bright blue water. Porter's thumb follows their fanciful movements, skimming my palm in dreamy circles. A hundred shivers scatter over the surface of my skin. Who can concentrate on jellyfish when I'm getting all this hand action? (Who knew this kind of hand action could be so exciting?)

I would've been perfectly content to stay with the jellies, but a tour group is making things much too crowded, so we seek another place where it's less populated. We didn't exactly verbalize this to each other, but I'm almost positive we're on the same page.

"Where?" I ask.

He weighs our options. We try a few places, but the only thing that seems to be empty right now is the place he doesn't really want to go. Or the place that he does.

The open sea room.

And I think I know why.

"This is what I wanted to show you," he says in a gravel-rough voice, and I'm both excited and a little worried as we step inside.

It's almost like a theater. The room is vast and dark, and the focus is an enormous single-pane window into blue water and a single shaft of light beaming through. There's no coral, no rocks, no fancy staged fish environment. The point is to see what's like to look into the deep ocean, where there's nothing but dark water. It's effective, because it certainly doesn't look like a tank. It's endless, no perception of depth or height. I'm a little awestruck.

A few people mingle in front of the enormous viewing window, their black shapes silhouetted against the glass as they point at schools of bluefin tuna and silvery sardines gliding around giant sea turtles. We step up to the glass, finding a spot away from everyone else. At first, all I can see are the bubbles rising and the hundreds of tiny fish—they're busy, busy, always on the move—and then I see something bigger and brighter moving in the dark water behind the smaller fish.

Porter's hand tightens around mine.

My pulse quickens.

I squint, trying to watch the bigger, brighter thing, but it slips away, into the black deep. I think I catch sight of it again and move closer to the window, so close that I feel the cool glass against my nose. With no warning, bright silver fills up my vision, blocking out the dark water. I jerk my head away from the glass and find myself inches away from a ginormous shark gliding past.

"Shit!" I start to chuckle at myself for jumping, and then realize that my hand is being squeezed to mincemeat and that Porter hasn't moved. He's locked in place, frozen as if by Medusa's stare, forehead pressed against the glass.

"Porter?"

He doesn't respond.

"You're hurting my hand," I whisper.

It's like he doesn't even know I'm there. Now I'm getting freaked out. I forcibly pry my fingers out of his, and it's beyond difficult: It's impossible. He's got me in a deadlock, and he's crazy strong.

For a brief moment, I panic, looking around, wondering what I should do. Wondering if anyone else notices what's going on. But it's dark, and there's barely anyone in here. He's suffering in silence.

What do I do? Should I slap him? Shout at him? That would only draw attention to us. I can't imagine that helping.

"Hey," I say urgently, still working on loosening his fingers. "Hey, hey. Uh, what kind of shark is that? Is that the same shark that bit you?" I know it wasn't, but I'm not sure what else to do.

"What?" he asks, sounding bewildered.

"Is that your shark?"

"No," he says, blinking. "No, mine's a great white. That's a

Galapagos. They rarely attack humans." I finally break our hands apart. He looks down between us for the first time and seems to notice something's wrong. "Oh, Jesus."

"It's fine," I assure him, resisting the urge to shake out my throbbing fingers.

"Fuck." His face goes cloudy. He turns away from me and faces the tank.

Now I'm worried our beautiful, perfect date is ruined.

I have to summon all my willpower to push back the wave of chaotic emotion that threatens to take me under, because the truth is this: I've never been on a date before. Not a real one. Not one that someone planned. I've been on a couple of double dates, I guess you'd call them, and some spur-of-the-moment things, like, *Hey, do you want to go study at Starbucks after class?* But no real dates. This is all new territory. I need this to be okay. I need this to be normal.

Do not panic, Bailey Rydell.

I keep my voice light and tug on the leather key strap that dangles at his hip until he turns to face me again. "Hey, remember how freaked I got at the bonfire? Please. You aren't half as screwed up as me."

"You don't know that."

"Sorry, I do. This time you're going to have to trust me."

"Bailey . . ."

The shark swims by again, a little higher. I jiggle his keys in my palm. "I will admit, though, despite what I've been through,

Greg Grumbacher looks like a dandelion compared to that beast. Now tell me how big your shark was compared to the Galapagos."

His shoulders drop, his Adam's apple rises and falls, and the way he's looking at me now, suddenly clear-eyed and sharp, satisfied—as if he's just made an important decision—makes me feel all funny inside. But I'm not worried anymore—not about him, and not that our date is ruined. The danger has passed.

We both face the window, and he begins to tell me in a low, steady voice about the Galapagos and another impressive shark that swims by, a hammerhead, telling me sizes and shapes and diets and endangered status. And as he talks, he moves behind me and wraps his arms around my waist—questioningly at first, but when I pull him in tighter, he relaxes and rests his chin on my shoulder, nestling into the crook of my neck.

He knows all about these sharks. This place is therapy for him. And sure, he got stuck there for a second, but look at these things. Who wouldn't? Not for the first time, I'm amazed at what he went through. I'm amazed by him.

"In Hawaiian mythology," he says into my hair, his voice vibrating through me, "people believe spirits of their ancestors continue to live inside animals and rocks and plants. They call an ancestral spirit an *aumakua*—like a guardian spirit, you know? My mom says the shark that attacked us is our *aumakua*. That if it had wanted to kill us, it would have. But it was just warning us to take a good, hard look at our lives and reassess things. So we're supposed to honor that."

"How do you honor it?" I ask.

"Pops says he's honoring it by admitting that he's too old to be on a board and that he's better off serving his family by staying on dry land. Lana says she's honoring it by being the best surfer she can be and not fearing the water."

I trace the scars on his arm with my index finger. "And what about you?"

"When I figure that out, I'll let you know."

As the silver of the hammerhead shark glides past, Porter slowly turns me around in his arms. I'm vaguely aware of the silhouettes of the people who stand farther along the viewing window, but I don't care. In our little corner of peaceful darkness, it feels like we're alone. With my arms circling him, I dare to dip my fingers under the loose hem of his untucked shirt, reaching upward until I touch the solid, bare skin of his back. Right over the same place on me where one of my own scars is, though I'm not sure if I subconsciously mean to do that or if it's an accident.

He shivers violently, and it's the sweetest victory.

A pleasant warmth spreads through my chest. The water's reflection shimmers on the sharp lines of his cheekbones as he holds my face in both hands and bends his head to kiss me, softly, delicately, like I'm something special that deserves to be honored.

But the thing he doesn't know, the thing that shocks even me, is that I'm not the gentle guardian spirit; I'm the hungry shark. And I fear his arm won't be enough. I want all of him.

"You're sweet, and sexy, and completely hot for me."
—Heath Ledger, *10 Things I Hate About You* (1999)

19

If I was worried about dying from not kissing before, now the pendulum has swung in the opposite direction. We definitely overdid it. I got home well before curfew, at eleven, but by then, Porter and I had time to eat dinner in Monterey at a cool restaurant that served a raw ahi tuna salad from Hawaii called *poke*—so good—and lots more time to park at Lovers Point Park and watch the sunset behind the cypress trees as the waves crashed over the beach.

Or, in our case, not watch the sunset. Which is what we ended up doing. A lot.

And now my dress is covered in grass stains, and because of Porter's stupid sexy scruff, my face looks red and swollen, as if I got attacked by a swarm of angry bees. And did he really give me three hickeys on my neck? THREE? He swore it was an accident, and that I'm "too white" and bruise too easily. At first I got a little offended by this, but maybe it could be true, because I don't remember any Hoover-like suction happening during the proceedings. And he did apologize a million times. . . .

Then again, I was pretty distracted, because we were lying in the grass on an elevated area above the beach, and he was pressed against me and it was delightful. I mean, nothing serious happened, really. Mostly just a lot of touching that didn't stray to any untoward areas, unless my hips and side boobs count. (They don't, in my opinion, but it was nice. Very nice.) But there was a lot of heavy breathing, and we both agreed once again that we are compatible arguers and kissers. And when he dropped me off at the surf shop, he tapped his temple and told me, "Today is moving up in the brain bank as best day in recent memory."

In my own brain bank, my Artful Dodger eyes turned into cartoon hearts that pinwheeled.

But things got a little tricky after that.

"What in the name of planet Earth happened to you?" my dad said when I walked in the door, looking at my unholy, bedraggled state.

"Grace and I were goofing around outside in the grass," I said. "Just wrestling and stuff with some other people from work. No big deal."

He made a face. "Wrestling?"

Yeah. That sounded like me, all right. I mentally cringed.

"What happened to your mouth?" he asked. He looked appalled and concerned, like I was contagious, and held the sides of my head while he inspected me, lest he catch it too. "Did you get into poison oak or something?"

"Uh, maybe?"

"Should I get some oatmeal? I don't have any calamine lotion. Should I go to the twenty-four-hour drugstore?"

I was pretty much horrified at this point. "I'm sure I'll be fine. Just a mild burn or something."

My dad narrowed his eyes at me. His gaze wandered lower. Don't look at my neck, don't look at my neck, don't—

Uh-oh.

Now we were both horrified. He released my head. "Okay. If you're sure."

"Yep-yep-yep, so sure," I said.

"Did you find your film-fanatic guy? What's his name, Alex?"

I made a face, because just the mention of his name stings. "I'm not speaking to him at the moment. I think he's got a girlfriend now, because he blew me off. And no, I haven't found him yet."

"Bailey—"

"Dad, just . . . please don't."

"Let me say this, okay?" he said, suddenly irritated, which is really unlike him, so it took me aback. And it took him a moment to calm down enough to finish. But when he spoke again, he was serious and eerily fatherly. "You have grown into a beautiful young lady, and people are going to take notice of that, which I don't particularly relish."

Oh, brother.

He raised a hand. "But I accept it. However, what I want to

talk about is you. Because the thing is, Mink, sometimes when traumatic things happen to people, they retreat until they feel comfortable. Which is okay. But when they're finally ready to step back into the world, they can be overconfident and make mistakes. Which is not okay. Do you understand what I'm saying?"

"Not exactly."

"Do you remember when your mom had just won that big divorce case for that state senator and was driving too fast on that icy road in Newark on the way to Mr. Katter's party and the car slid, and then, instead of easing us back on the road, she yanked the wheel and oversteered in the other direction, and we overturned into the ditch?"

"Yeah," I said. We all nearly died. It was a nightmare. Hard to forget.

"Think about that."

Cryptic, but I got what he was saying. He thought I was whoring myself out with some stranger just for kicks. For a brief moment, I wanted to break down and tell him everything about Porter, that I wasn't oversteering and throwing caution to the wind. And for the love of guns, it had been four years! How long did I have to be in "trauma" mode? Wasn't I allowed to make some decisions for myself and enjoy life? I appreciated his heartfelt concern, but I knew what I was doing . . .

Mostly.

Anyway, that's all he said about it. Still, my dad may be the nicest guy in the world, but he's no dummy. The day before I was scheduled to eat dinner at Grace's house, he suggested driving me over there so he could personally meet Grace's parents. What could possibly go wrong? When I told her, she laughed so hard and long, I worried she was having a stroke.

In the meantime, though my kiss-stung face has returned to normal, my heart and all working body parts are absolutely not normal. Because every time Porter so much as even walks within ten feet of me at work, I have the same reaction. Four knocks on Hotbox door? I flush. Scent of coconut in the break room? I flush. Sound of Porter cracking jokes with Pangborn in the hall-way? I flush.

And every time this happens, Grace is there like some taunting Greek chorus, making a little *mmm-hmm* noise of confirmation.

Even Pangborn notices. "Are you ill, Miss Rydell?"

"Yes," I tell him in the break room one day before work. "I'm apparently very ill in the worst way. And I want you to know that I didn't plan for this to happen. This was not part of my plan at all. If you want to know the truth, I had other plans for the sum-mer!" I think of my boardwalk map, lying folded and abandoned in my purse.

Pangborn nods slowly. "I have no idea what you mean, but I support it completely."

"Thank you," I tell him as he walks away, whistling.

Half a minute later, Porter pulls me into a dark corner of the hallway, checks around the corner, and kisses the bejesus out of me. "That's me, destroying all your other plans," he says wickedly.

And if I didn't know any better, I'd think he sounds jealous. Then he walks away, leaving me all hot and bothered.

I'm going to have a nervous breakdown.

Tuesday night at the Achebe house comes. Grace's family lives in a swank part of town, in an adobe-style house with a perfectly manicured lawn. When my dad and I ring the doorbell, my pulse rockets. Why oh why have I been using Grace as a cover for my time with Porter? That was so stupid, and now that everyone is meeting, I feel like we're going to get caught—which is the last thing I want to happen, for obvious reasons. And because I don't want to mess up what I have going with Grace. She's the first decent friend I've had in a while.

Footfalls sound on the other side of the door. I think I might vomit.

The door swings open to reveal a willowy woman with long ebony curls and dark skin. Her smile is warm and inviting. "You must be Bailey." Not Grace's tiny voice, but definitely her British accent.

I say hello and start to introduce my dad when a broad-shouldered man appears behind her, wiping his hands on a dish towel. "This is her?" he says in a big, booming voice full of cheer. He smiles big and wide. "Hello, Bailey girl. Look at that hair of yours. It's like an old-fashioned Hollywood star. Which one? Not Marilyn Monroe."

"Lana Turner," I provide.

He makes an impressed face. "Lana Turner," he says slowly,

with a cool African sway to his words. "Well, well, Miss Turner. I am Hakeem Achebe. And this is my wife, Rita."

"Pete Rydell," my dad says, shaking his hand. "We're both fond of Grace."

I see Grace poke her head down the stairs in the distance, smiling but gritting her teeth at the same time. She's nervous we're going to get caught in a lie too. *Crap!*

"We're fond of Grace as well," Mr. Achebe says jovially. "We think we'll keep her."

My dad laughs. I can already see him planning to hit up Mr. Achebe for board game night—but I really want this conversation to be as short as possible, so I hope he doesn't.

"She's gone on a lot about working with Bailey in that dreadful Hotbox," her mom says with a smile.

"I hear complaints about that too," my dad says. "But I'm glad they've been spending more time together outside work."

Double crap! Please don't bring up the fake story I concocted about Grace and me "wrestling" in the grass, Dad. Would he do that? Surely not. I glance at Grace. She backs up one step on the stairs. *Don't you dare abandon me!* Just in case, I prepare to flee the scene. Where I'll run, I don't know. Maybe I could pretend to faint.

"Well, tonight, it's work before play," Grace's father says, pointing the dish towel in my direction. "We have much preparation to do in the kitchen before dinner. Miss Turner, are you up for the task?"

Oh, thank God. Mr. Achebe: my new hero.

Grace's mom asks my dad to stay for dinner, but he declines, and when he tells me to have a good time, I cannot get inside the Achebe house fast enough.

Grace's dad makes a Nigerian rice dish called Jollof for dinner—it's pretty delicious—along with steak and grilled vegetables. He puts me and Grace in charge of skewering the vegetables. She was totally right: He tells the worst jokes. But he tells them with so much glee, it's hard not to laugh a little. She gives me a look like *I told you so.*

We spend the rest of the night listening to music out by their backyard pool. It's mostly 1970s and '80s bands, I think, her parents' music collection. Grace takes off her shoes and tries to get me to dance. When I refuse, her dad won't take no for an answer. So we dance to a ska song by The Specials, "A Message to You Rudy." And it's silly and fun, and I'm a terrible dancer. Grace laughs at me and then joins in with her mom.

When everyone's exhausted, her parents go back inside to clean up, and Grace and I end the night cooling our heels in the shallow end of the pool, trading stories about growing up on opposite sides of the country and her childhood in England. She then tells me about Taran, her boyfriend, who is in Mumbai visiting his aunt and uncle for the summer. Grace and Taran have been seeing each other for an entire year and are already planning to apply to the same colleges in the fall. I'm a little surprised, because she doesn't really talk about him all that much at work. I want to ask her more about their relationship, but I'm afraid.

Maybe things aren't as good as she claims they are. I wish I could see this Taran guy in person and judge for myself.

"When is Taran supposed to come back to California?" I ask, lying next to her by the edge of the pool with my legs dangling from the knees down in the chlorine-laced water.

Her tiny voice answers, "I'm not sure."

That doesn't sound good. I don't want to have to figure out a way to inflict deadly force against a boy on another continent, but if push comes to shove, for Grace, I will. I scooch a little closer and we lean our heads together, staring up at the stars, until my dad comes to pick me up.

I underestimated just how much wrangling had to go into my one true date with Porter, because over a week goes by and we can't manage another. Turns out that when you combine my sneaking-out requirement with our job schedules, Porter's surf shop obligations, and any other time spent on family duties, you get very little to work with.

And sometimes when you least expect it, you're just walking along, minding your own business, and the universe leaves you a winning lottery ticket right in the middle of the sidewalk. . . .

Friday and Saturday nights in the middle of the summer, the Cave closes at its usual time, six p.m., and then reopens from eight until ten p.m. for people to purchase tickets to the ghost tour. It's basically three groups of people who pay twice the normal ticket price to tour the museum afterhours with cheap flashlights while listening to fake ghost stories. It's a total rip-off. And I know this because the ghost tour guides are Pangborn and Porter, and they're the ones who wrote most of the ghost tour script last summer.

It was mostly Pangborn, Porter admits. He was extremely stoned when he wrote it. He's also extremely stoned when he's giving the tours, and everyone loves him camping it up, especially with his shocking white hair that practically glows in the dark. I work the Hotbox alone, since it's a limited ticket engagement. Once we sell out, I get to put up the AT SPOOK CAPACITY sign in the window and go inside the break room to read magazines until ten, waiting for the tours to finish.

Last night was my first ghost tour, and Porter had to rush home afterward, which sucked, because we never got to spend any time alone.

Tonight's a different story.

It's Saturday, and my dad and Wanda are spending the night in San Francisco. They're coming back first thing in the morning, Dad informed me a hundred times, like I was worried he was going to hop a train and never be seen again. But I think now that he's met Grace's parents, he feels better about those stupid hickeys that neither of us has ever, ever acknowledged again. So after the ghost tour winds up, Porter and I plan to do the unthinkable: We might go on a—wait for it—second date, and on that date, we may be going out to catch a movie.

A MOVIE.

Sure, it will probably be whatever current blockbuster is playing at the local Cineplex, and that's fine. I don't expect him to appreciate my supreme good taste in film. At least, not right away. He can be educated, and I'm happy to oblige. But all I'm thinking about now is that it's a movie and it's Porter—together.

I'm trying not to get too giddy. After all, he's got to get up early and work in the surf shop, so we can't stay out all night, but a couple of hours sounds like heaven. Heaven that might even still get me home by curfew, or thereabouts. See? I'm not even really cheating. Good daughter, right here.

Sometime around ten fifteen p.m., I stop checking for updates from Alex on my phone in the break room (there are none, as usual, and I'm not sure why I even bother caring) and stretch my legs. We're supposed to get to leave around ten thirty. Even though we close at ten, it takes Porter and Pangborn that long to shoo the last tour group out, lock up, put away the flashlights, and make a final sweep of the place to ensure there aren't any dopey kids hiding out or people having heart attacks in the restrooms. After the guests are gone, I'm supposed to help with the flashlights—there are a hundred of them—so when the only other two employees who were working tonight clock out and leave through the employee exit, I head out to the lobby to take care of that. On my way there, I bump into Pangborn.

"How did it go?"

"Excellent," he tells me. He's wearing bright orange socks with little black ghosts on them, which are easy to see because his pants are riding so high, thanks to the matching suspenders. He changed just for the ghost tour. God, I love him. "One woman gave me a twenty-dollar tip."

"How about that," I say, actually impressed.

"I didn't keep it, of course. But it was still a nice gesture." He smiles and pats me on the shoulder in that comforting way he always does. "Your boyfriend is making the final sweep on Jay's corridor. The doors are locked and the system's backed up. Except for the flashlights, we're done for the night."

I know he just said a bunch of words, but all I heard was "your boyfriend." Did Porter tell Pangborn we went out? Or has he noticed anything going on between us at work? I'm too chicken to ask, especially when Pangborn's eyes crinkle up sweetly in the corners.

"I'll get the flashlights," I offer.

"I was hoping you'd say that," he says. "I'm feeling more exhausted than usual tonight, and I've got to open in the morning, so I'm going to head home a few minutes early. Don't want to nod off on the road."

"Hey, not funny." Now that I'm looking at him, he really does look tired. Like, insanely tired. For the first time since Grace told me, I suddenly remember the rumors about him being sick. They may not be true, who knows, but I know one thing for sure: He's too old to be working this late. And Cavadini is an asshole to schedule him opening tomorrow morning.

"I'll stay alert, don't worry," he assures me. "But your concern is much appreciated. I just need a good night's rest. Daisy Dog and I need our beauty sleep. Tell Porter I'm locking the two of you in with the new master code. He'll have to punch in the override to get out. He'll know what I'm talking about."

"Got it." At least he has a dog to go home to. I tell him to be careful driving and when he's gone, I head out to find Porter. It's weird being alone in the museum. It's dark and eerily quiet: Only the after-hours lights are on—just enough to illuminate the hallways and stop you from tripping over your own feet—and the background music that normally plays all the time is shut off.

I quickly organize the flashlights and check their batteries, and when I don't hear Porter walking around, I stare at the phone sitting at the information desk. How many chances come along like this? I pick up the receiver, press the little red button next to the word ALL, and speak into the phone in a low voice. "Paging Porter Roth to the information desk," I say formally, my voice crackling through the entire lobby and echoing down the corridors. Then I press the button again and add, "While you're at it, check your shoes to make sure they're a match, you bastard. By the way, I still haven't quite forgiven you for humiliating me. It's going to take a lot more than a kiss and a cookie to make me forget both that and the time you provoked me in the Hotbox."

I'm only teasing, which I hope he knows. I feel a little drunk on all my megaphone power, so I page one more thing:

"PS—You look totally hot in those tight-fitting security guard pants tonight, and I plan to get very handsy with you at the movies, so we better sit in the back row."

I hang up the phone and cover my mouth, silently laughing at myself. Two seconds later, Porter's footfalls pound down Jay's corridor—*Boom! Boom! Boom! Boom!* He sounds like a T. rex running from Godzilla. He races into the lobby and slides in front of the information desk, grabbing onto the edge to stop himself, wild curls flying everywhere. His grin is enormous.

"Whadidya say 'bout where you want to be puttin' your hands on me?" he asks breathlessly.

"I think you have me confused with someone else," I tease.

His head sags against the desk. I push his hair away from one of his eyes. He looks up at me and asks, "You really still haven't forgiven me?"

"Maybe if you put your hands on *me*, I might."

"Don't go getting my hopes up like that."

"Oh, your hopes should be up. Way up."

"Dear God, woman," he murmurs. "And here I was, thinking you were a classy dame."

"Pfft. You don't know me at all."

"I aim to find out. What are we still doing here? Let's blow this place and get to the theater, fast."

We race each other through the lobby and grab our stuff out of our lockers. When we get to the back door, Porter pauses by the security system panel and tilts his head quizzically.

"Oh," I say, snapping my fingers. "Pangborn said to tell you that he was using the new master code to lock us in, and that you'll have to punch in the override code to get out."

Porter sort of shakes his head, mumbling to himself, and then appears to dismiss it. He unhooks his leather key fob thingy from his belt. I recognize his van keys on it, because there's a tiny shark on the key ring. But when he swings it into his palm he pauses again.

"O-o-oh, s-h-h-i-i-i-t," he drawls. His head drops. He's silently swearing to the floor, eyes squeezed shut.

"What?" I say.

"Pangborn took my key earlier," he says in a small voice. "Right before the tour. He left his at home during the break between the regular shift and the ghost tours, and he had to open the back door. I was about to start a tour, and I forgot to get it back from him. That son of a bitch."

"But you can just use the master code to let us out, right?"

Porter snorts and throws up his hand toward the panel. "If he'd used the master code, yes. But he didn't. See this here, this number? That code indicates that the system is on lockdown."

"And that means . . . ?"

"It means," Porter says, "that you and I are now locked up alone together inside the museum for the rest of the night."

20

That can't be true. I mean, not really. There's always a way out of a place this big, right?

"Remember that day when I had to reinstall all the locks on the doors?" Porter asks.

I do.

"And you know I had to do that because we lost live off-site monitoring of our security system, and that instead of switching to one of a hundred other companies, management just decided to buy this cheap-ass system you see before you now?"

"Uh-huh?" I say, but I'm not totally following, and he's getting really angry. Steam is practically pouring out of his nostrils.

He takes a deep breath and calms down. "What this means is that Pangborn vaped too much weed again, left his manual keys at home, took mine, punched in a code that locks all the doors for eight hours, and drove off."

I stare at Porter.

He stares back.

"But you can deactivate this code, right?"

He shakes his head. "Pangborn is the lead security officer. I don't have clearance for a lockdown code." Oh, the irony. "He lives fifteen minutes from here. So we will have to wait until he gets home, and then—and this is where it gets really funny—we will try to call him."

"Why is that funny?"

"He usually turns his home phone off at night. He doesn't like to be woken up. 'Bad news can wait until morning' is his policy. And if we can't get him on the phone . . . well, I'm not really sure what to do. I guess we could try to call one of the other guards at home, but it's ten thirty on a Saturday night. And not only will they be pissed, but Pangborn could get fired for this. And pretty much everyone is looking for a reason for that to happen. In case you haven't noticed, he's kind of a mess."

That makes my heart twist.

"Mr. Cavadini? One of the shift managers?" I suggest and immediately realize the fault in that plan. Pangborn could get fired, and maybe Porter, too, for letting him go home early.

We both shake our heads.

I sniffle and scratch my nose with the side of my hand. "So basically what you're telling me is that unless we can get Pangborn on the phone, we're stuck here?"

"Let's take one thing at a time," Porter says, but I can tell by his grim expression that he doesn't have much hope. He leads me back to the security room, and I'm so panicked, I barely have time to register that I'm finally inside the inner sanctum: "Heaven." It's weird to be back here. Dozens of tiny black-and-white monitors cross two walls, all numbered, and an L-shaped desk with four computers, two of which appear to be a decade or more old.

We plop down at the desk in two rolling chairs. A swing-arm lamp casts a light over an old phone, where Porter proceeds to speed dial Pangborn's home number a zillion times. Of course the old man doesn't have a cell. Or he used to, Porter says, but he never charged it, and it sat in the glove box of his car for several years; it may still be there.

"Porter?"

"Yeah," he says, completely miserable, head in his hands.

"Is Pangborn sick?"

He doesn't answer right away. "You've heard rumors?"

"Yeah."

"He had colon cancer two years ago. He's in remission. But he went to the doctor last week, and he won't tell me what happened, and that worries me. He's always bragging about his appointments, because he's got a crush on his doctor. So I'm kind of thinking maybe it's back and he's going to have to go through chemo or something. I don't know."

"Oh, no." Grace's intel was right.

"Yeah, it sucks. And that's why he can't get fired, because the last thing he needs is to be screwing around with changing up his doctors and health benefits right now."

My chest aches. Why do bad things happen to good people? And if he does have cancer, and he's still showing up here for these stupid ghost tours, dressing up in his little suspenders and ghost socks, turning down tips from guests . . . it shatters my heart into a million pieces.

After half an hour of calling, we give up. It's not happening.

Deep breath. Time to evaluate the situation: (1) A cancer-stricken, nice old man has accidently locked us inside the Cave overnight. It's hard for me to get too mad at him about that. (2) It's not like we're going to run out of air or food or water. (3) We're not going to freeze or die of heat stroke. (4) We're not in danger of being eaten by bears or tigers. (5) This isn't our fault.

"Look on the bright side," Porter says, obviously having similar thoughts. "The lockdown will release at six thirty in the morning, so you'll still be able to beat your dad home from San Francisco. And if I call my parents and explain what happened, they'll totally understand. They both know Pangborn. And I spent the night on the couch here once before when we were resetting the security system last summer."

I glance over at the beat-up couch in the corner and my heart speeds up. "But what about me? I mean, will you tell them I'm here too? My dad would freak the hell out if he knew we were locked in here together alone all night."

The tension falls out of Porter's face, and the corners of his mouth slowly curl upward.

Oh, boy.

"Well, well, well," he says, leaning back in his chair in front of a bank of security monitors. He temples his fingers together over his chest. "This is an interesting situation, isn't it? Here we were, ready to run off to some crowded theater, but now we have the entire museum to ourselves. For the whole night. A boy prays and prays and prays, and is on his very best behavior, but he never dreams that something like this will just fall into his lap—so to speak."

"So to speak," I say weakly.

"Lots of room to spread out in this big place." The side of his knee bumps mine. A question.

All my earlier boldness has fled the building along with my courage. Now I just feel trapped. I withdraw both my legs and hide them under the desk. "What about all the cameras? I mean, won't this show up on the video footage? If someone reviews it later, or whatever?"

He chuckles. "You think the Cave pays for data storage? Think again. If we want to record something, we have to do it manually. Nothing is automatically recorded."

I glance up at the monitors and search for the Hotbox. There it is. It's empty now, of course, and dark, so I can't see much, but it's surreal to imagine Porter watching me from here. I make a mental note not to wear gaping tops to work, because that is a primo cleavage camera angle.

"However," Porter says, "if you're still worried, I know all the spots that the cameras miss. You know, if that would make you more comfortable."

I give him a dirty look. "Who says I want to get comfortable? We went on one date."

"Whoa." He holds up both hands in surrender. "Now you're making me feel like some sort of criminal sex pervert. Jesus, Bailey. An hour ago, you were talking about putting your hands on me in the back of a theater. I was just teasing you."

I blow out a hard breath. "I'm sorry. I'm just nervous and weirded out. I've just . . ."

"Just what?"

"I've just never . . . spent the night in a museum with anyone before."

Porter's brows lift. "Oh?"

I grimace. "Can you turn around or something? I can't look at you and talk about this."

"What?"

I make twisting movements with my hand. "Face the wall."

He looks at me like I'm nuts, and then gives in and slowly swivels around in his chair, keeping his head facing me, squinting, until the last possible moment. When he's facing the wall, I sigh and start talking to his back.

"Like I said before, we just went on one date." I'm a coward, yes, but having this conversation is so much easier when I don't have to look in his eyes. "And it was a great date. I mean, wow. I don't have much to compare it to, but I think it had to be up there in the history books. And even though you gave me those hickeys and ruined my favorite skirt, I would do it all over again."

"I'm still sorry about the hickeys, but for the record, I got grass stains on my clothes too. And every time I leave the house now, my mom teases me about going out for a roll in the hay and Pops has started calling me Grasshopper."

"Oh, God," I whisper.

"Totally worth it," he says. "But please continue."

"Anyway," I say, trying to gather my thoughts. "We went from enemies to a first date to now having the possibility of spending the night together in a museum, and not that I haven't thought about spending the night in a museum with you, because believe me, I've thought about that a lot."

His head turns sideways, but he still doesn't look at me. "A lot?"

"You have no idea."

"O-oh, that's where you're very wrong, my friend." His knee starts bouncing a nervous rhythm.

I smile to myself as a little thrill zips through me. "Well, what I'm saying is that I'm not opposed to such a thing. But I'm guessing you've spent many a night in many a museum, and you know, whatever. Good for you. But that intimidates me. And when it comes to this, I need you to let me give the green signal."

"First," he says, holding up a finger over his shoulder, "I want to say that I'm insulted that you'd think that I wouldn't. So thanks for making me feel like a sex criminal, again."

"Oh, God," I mumble.

"Second"—another finger joins the first—"I've been with two

girls, and one of those was a long-term girlfriend who, I might add, cheated on me with Davy, so it's not like I spend all my weekends in museums, to use your terminology. So there's no need for all the slut shaming."

I'm glad he can't see my face right now, because I'm pretty sure it's the exact shade of a broiled lobster. Is he mad? I can't tell by the tone of his voice. Ugh. Why did I make him face the wall? I scoot my chair closer and lay my cheek on his head, burrowing my face into his curls.

"I'm an idiot," I mumble into the back of his neck. "I don't know what I'm doing, and I'm so, so sorry."

His hand reaches around the chair, grasping blindly, patting around until he grabs my shirt and hangs on. "I accept your apology, but only because I'm trapped in here with you all night, and it would be awkward if we spent the entire time fighting."

"We're not fighting."

"We're always fighting. That's part of our charm," he says.

"Porter?"

"Yes?"

"Is the girlfriend you were just mentioning . . . Is that the girl you were arguing about with Davy outside the vintage clothing shop? Chloe?"

"Yeah. Chloe Carter. Her dad makes custom surfboards. They were really close with my family. She's friends with my sister, so the whole thing was kind of a big mess."

"Were you in love with her?"

He pauses a little too long for my comfort. "No, but it still hurt when she cheated on me. We were friends for a long time before we started dating, so that should have meant something, you know?"

Plus, it was with Davy, someone who was supposed to be his best friend, so it was a double betrayal, but I don't say this.

Several seconds tick by. I sigh.

"Porter?"

"Yes?"

"This sofa is kind of small, but we have to sleep somewhere. And I do like the idea of sleeping next to you."

"Me too."

After a long pause, I add, "In addition to sleeping, what if I do want to see some of the places in the museum that the cameras don't go . . . just from a distance? Maybe. Possibly. Theoretically. I mean, does everything have to be all or nothing?"

Heavy sigh. "You're driving me crazy, you know that, right?"

"I know."

"Bailey, I spend most of my days looking at you through that tiny square screen up there. I'm just grateful to be in the same room. And the fact that you'll even let me touch you at all is the freaking miracle of the century. So whatever you want or don't want from me, all you have to do is ask. Okay?"

"Okay," I whisper, mentally floating away on fluffy white clouds.

"Okay," he repeats firmly, like that's all decided, and pushes away from the wall. "Now let me call my folks."

He makes the call on his cell, explaining everything to his mom, who, from the sound of things, is completely sympathetic about the situation. But then he waits for her to tell his dad, and suddenly he's gesturing for me to duck under the desk because his dad is making him switch to a video call—like he doesn't believe his story. I hear Mr. Roth's sullen voice demanding that Porter repeat everything all over again, and Porter is showing him the computer screen, which clearly says LOCKDOWN and has a timer showing the remaining time left until the doors unlock and, thankfully, even shows the first few letters of Pangborn's last name as being the person who initiated the command. By now, it's eleven forty-five, and even grumpy-puss Mr. Roth admits that Porter's options are few and getting Pangborn fired isn't one of them.

"I could drive down the beach to his house and wake him up," Mr. Roth suggests.

Mrs. Roth's voice interrupts. "It's a quarter till midnight, and the man may be sick for all we know. Let him be. Porter, baby, is there a blanket there? Can you sleep okay on that sofa?"

He assures her that he'll find something, and she says that Lana will cover for him in the surf shop tomorrow morning if he can't get any sleep. And while they're winding things up, I text my dad and tell him I'm safe—that's not a lie, right?—and that I hope they're having fun in San Francisco. His reply is immediate and includes a geeky Settlers of Catan joke, so I assume he's in a genuinely good mood: *Having a blast. We bought you a surprise today. Love you more than sheep.*

I text him an equally geeky reply: *Love you more than wheat.*

• • •

I have no idea where Porter's taking me that is off camera.

First he digs up a weird old-fashioned key out of a desk drawer in the security room. Then we gather up our stuff and head to the lost and found, where we score a baby blanket. Sure, it's gross to think about using some stranger's blanket, but whatever. It smells fine. Then he takes me all the way down to the end of Vivian's wing. There's a door here that's been painted the same dark green color as the wall, and because of the lighting, it's hard to see. I also know from memorizing the employee map that it's not supposed to be there—as in, it shouldn't exist.

"What is this?" I ask.

"Room one-zero-zero-one," he says, showing me the old key, which has a tag attached to it. "Like, *One Thousand and One Nights*, *Arabian Nights*, Ali Baba, and all that."

"There's another room? Why isn't this open to the public?"

He hoists his backpack higher on his shoulder and flattens his palm against the door. "Now, look. This is a huge Cavern Palace secret. You have to solemnly swear that you'll never tell anyone what I'm about to show you on the other side of this door. Not even Gracie. *Especially* Gracie, because I love her, but she knows everyone, and it will fly around faster than the chicken pox virus. Swear to me, Bailey. Hold up your hand and swear."

I hold up my hand. "I swear."

"Okay, this is the Cave's dirtiest secret." He unlocks the door, flips on the lights, which take a second to flicker on, and we step inside a perfectly round room lit in soft oranges and golds. It smells a little musty, like a library that hasn't seen a lot of action. And as Porter closes the door behind us, I look around in amazement.

Thick, star-scattered indigo curtains cover the walls. A cluster of arabesque pendant lamps hang in various lengths from the domed ceiling over a low, velvet cushion about the size of a large bed. It's tufted and comes up to my knees, and crowning one side of it, like a half-moon, it's surrounded by hundreds of small pillows with geometric designs that look like they came straight out of a palace in Istanbul.

"It's beautiful," I say. "Like a dream. I don't understand why it's not open. Are these pillows from the 1930s? They should be preserved."

Porter dumps his stuff on the floor next to the velvet cushion. "Don't you remember your Cave history? Vivian hated Jay. When their marriage fell apart, he wouldn't give her a divorce, so she had this room constructed as big middle finger to him. Come feast your eyes on her revenge. But don't say I didn't warn you."

He steps up to one of the starry blue curtains on the wall and lifts a golden cord to reveal a mural on the wall beneath. It's a life-size art deco painting of Vivian Davenport dressed up as a Middle Eastern princess, with bells on her fingers and flowers in her long hair, a sheer gown flowing over her buxom, naked body. Throngs of men in suits bow down at her feet.

"Oh . . . my . . . God," I murmur.

There are several big-eyed smiling cartoon animals looking on, like even they can't look away from the glory that is naked Vivian.

"Is that . . . Groucho Marx?" I say, squinting to look at one of the kneeling men.

"Vivian made history come alive," Porter answers, grinning.

"Make it stop," I say, laughing, and he closes the curtain.

I'm scarred for life, but it was worth it. We fall on the velvet cushion together, and a small cloud of dust motes flies up. I guess the janitorial service doesn't come back here much. Porter fake coughs and brushes off the rest of the cushion.

That's when it hits me that this is a bed we're sitting on. "You don't think Vivian had crazy sex parties right here, do you?" I ask, moving my hand off the velvet. "More revenge against her husband?"

"Doubtful. But if she did, it was a hundred years ago," he says, squinting his eyes merrily at me. "And it all ended so tragically for the both of them, what with her shooting him and killing herself, you almost hope she had some fun before it all went sideways, you know? Like maybe she actually modeled for that portrait."

"Yeah."

After a few moments of silence, a heavy awkwardness blooms in the space between us. Porter finally sighs, sits up, and begins stripping the radio equipment from his shoulder. My heart hammers.

He slides a sideways glance in my direction. "Look, I'm not getting naked or anything—cool your jets. How could I compete with all that wackiness on the walls, anyway? I just can't sleep with a bunch of wires and crap attached to me. Or shoes. I'm leaving the shirt and pants on. You can leave on whatever you want. Ladies' choice." He winks.

His good humor puts me somewhat at ease, and I slip off my shoes next to his. He shuts off his radio and sets a timer on his phone for six thirty a.m. But when he takes off his belt, all the blood in my brain swooshes so loud, I worry I might be having an aneurism.

The belt buckle hits the Turkish-patterned rug with a dull *thump*. "You're a great mystery to me, Bailey Rydell."

"I am?"

"I can never tell if you're scared of me, or if you're about to jump me."

I chuckle nervously. "I'm not sure of that myself."

He pulls me closer and we lie down, facing each other, hands clasped between us. I can feel his heart racing against my fist. I wonder if he can feel mine.

"I'm scared," I tell him, "of what I feel when I'm around you. I'm scared of what I want from you, and I don't know how to ask for it." I'm also scared that if I do, it might be terrible or not live up to my expectations, but I don't say this, because I'm afraid it will hurt his feelings.

He kisses my forehead. "Know what I'm scared of?"

"What?"

"That I like you way too much, and I'm afraid once you get to know me, you're going to realize that you can do lots better, and you're going to break my heart and leave me for someone classier."

I breathe him in deeply. "When I first came to town, there was someone else. Not Patrick," I say, as if either of us needs that reminder.

"Your so-called other plans?" he asks.

"Yeah," I say. "I guess you could say he's classy, I don't know. But just when you think you understand someone, it turns out that you didn't really know them at all. Or maybe the real problem was that you didn't understand something about yourself."

"I don't follow."

I blow out a long breath. "It doesn't matter. What I'm trying to say is that before I moved out here, I didn't know I liked churros and moon muffins and Hawaiian *poke* and Jollof rice, and I didn't know I would fall for you. But I did. And who wants classy when you can eat posole out of a food truck on the beach? I had no idea what I was missing."

He slowly traces a wavy tendril near my temple with one finger. "You've fallen for me, huh?"

"Maybe." I hold up my fingers and measure a small amount. "This much."

"That's it? Guess I'm going to have to try harder, then," he says in a low voice against my lips, almost kissing me, but not quite. Then again. Little almost-kisses. Teasing me.

My breath quickens.

"Let's take a quick quiz, why don't we?" he murmurs. "If I put my hand here—"

His fingers slide under my shirt over my belly. It's delicious . . . for all of two seconds. Then he's too close to the off-limits area of my scar. And—no! He's actually touching my scar. No way am I stopping this to explain that. I just . . . can't. No.

He feels me tense up and immediately withdraws. "Hey. I—"

"No, no, no," I quickly whisper. "It's not you. It's something else. Don't take it personally, I . . . just, um." I move his hand to the middle of my bare thigh, under my skirt. Talk about dangerous waters.

"Bailey," he says. A warning.

"Quiz me," I challenge.

He mumbles a filthy little curse, but his hand begins to climb upward, oh-so-slowly. "Okay, Rydell. If you're locked in a museum all night with a guy you're falling for, and he's cool enough to show you the Cave's dirtiest secret—God, your skin is so soft."

"Mmphrm?" I murmur, moving around to give him better access.

"Oh," he murmurs back cheerfully.

Hand firmly gripping my upper thigh, he kisses me, and I kiss him back, and it's desperate and wonderful.

"Okay," he says, sounding drugged. "Now, where was I? Oh yes, here." Much to my delight, his hand continues its roaming ascent. Only, there's not much farther it can go. He hesitates, chuckling to himself, and switches legs, repeating the same pattern on the other thigh.

Then stops.

I whimper. I'm genuinely frustrated.

Until he shifts a little, and I feel him pressed against my hip. No mistaking that.

"I'm having some trouble concentrating on this quiz," he admits, smiling against my neck.

"Whatever you do, don't you dare give me another hickey."

He pretends to bite me, and then he shows me other things besides moon muffins and posole that I didn't know I was missing, things two people locked in a museum overnight can do with their hands and fingers and a whole lot of ingenuity. The boy has every right to be wearing that HOT STUFF cartoon devil patch on his jacket.

Unlike our previous roll in the grass, this touching definitely is not rated PG, and when Porter offers to do the thing to me that I normally do for myself, who am I to look a gift horse in the mouth? It's possibly the most amazing thing that's ever, ever happened to me. I even return the favor—still pretty amazing, though much more so for him, for obvious reasons.

But wow.

All of that touching wears me out, and it's two in the morning, which is too late for my blood. I'm wound up in him, arms and legs, and he's the big spoon to my little spoon, and as I'm dozing off, in and out of consciousness, lights flicker. I hear voices. Not alarming voices. No one's in the museum; we're still alone. But he's reached over me and wedged his laptop out of his backpack, and it's sitting on the velvet cushion above our heads. There's something playing on the screen.

"What's going on?" I say, my voice sounding thick to my own ears as I tilt my head upward. I can't quite open my eyes all the way, but I can make out shapes and moving light through my eyelids.

"Sorry, sorry," he says in a bone-weary voice. "Is it bothering you? I can't get to sleep without a movie or TV on."

"S'fine," I slur, snuggling back against him. A few seconds later, I say. "Is that *Roman Holiday*?"

His deep voice vibrates through my back. "It's an indie film. They're quoting it. Wait, you know *Roman Holiday*?"

"Pfft," I say sloppily, too tired to explain my love of film. "Question is, how do *you* know *Roman Holiday*?"

"My grandma—my mom's mother—lived with us before she died. She'd stay up late watching movies in the den, and when I was a kid, I'd fall asleep in her lap on the couch."

How funny. That's how he knew about *Breakfast at Tiffany's*, too. "Maybe you and I have more in common than you think," I say before I drift into dreams.

"Life does not stop and start at your convenience."
—John Goodman, *The Big Lebowski* (1998)

21

Porter was right. I get out of the museum in plenty of time to beat dad home from his trip. I'm so tired, I even go back to sleep for a few more hours. When I wake a second time, it's almost time for me to get ready for another shift at the Cave, which is crazy. I might as well just move in there. But it's hard to be too sour about it, because I spent the night with a boy.

SPENT.

NIGHT.

BOY.

That's right. I did that. I did some other things too, and they were all excellent. It's a beautiful day, the sun is shining, and I don't even care that I have to spend four hours in the Hotbox. At least I don't have to work a full shift today.

I shower and dress before bounding downstairs just in time to run into Dad and Wanda returning from San Francisco. Talk about two exhausted people. They look happy, though. I don't really want to know what they did all night, so I don't pry. But they dig around in the trunk of my dad's muscle car until they find the gifts they bought for me: a leopard-print scarf and a pair of matching sunglasses.

"To go with Baby," my dad says, looking hopeful but unsure.

"The scarf is to cover up any future hickeys," Wanda adds, one side of her mouth tilting up.

Oh, God. Her, too? Does everyone know? My dad tries to repress a smile. "I'm sorry, kiddo. It's sort of funny, you have to admit."

Wanda crosses her arms over her chest. "Own it, I say. If your dad gave me a hickey and anyone at the station gave me grief, I'd tell them where they could go. I picked out the sunglasses, by the way."

I sigh deeply and slide them on. The lenses are dark and huge, brand-new, but very Italian retro cool. "They're fantastic, thank you. And I hate both of you for the scarf, but it's still awesome. Stop looking at my neck, Dad. There are no new hickeys." I checked just to be sure.

After they give me a briefing of their day in the Bay Area, I race out the door and drive back to the Cave. I know Porter's working, and I'm zipping and floating, high as a kite, eager to see him again. I want to know if he feels as good as I feel after last night. I also want to see Grace and tell her how crazy things were. Though this time, I don't think I'll be sharing so many details. Some things are meant to be private. What happens in Room 1001 stays in Room 1001.

But when I park Baby in my normal spot, I see Porter standing outside his van, which is weird. He's typically inside the building long before I get there. It's not just that. Something's wrong: He's holding his head in his hands.

I slam on the brakes and jump off the scooter, race over to him. He doesn't acknowledge me. When I pull his hands away from his face, tears are streaming down his cheeks.

"What's wrong?" I ask.

His voice is hoarse and barely there. "Pangborn."

"What?" I demand, my stomach dropping.

"He didn't show up for work this morning," he says. "It happened sometime last night in his home. There wasn't anything we could've done. He lied to me about where the cancer was. It was pancreatic this time, not colon."

"I don't understand what you're saying." I'm starting to shake all over.

"He's dead, Bailey. Pangborn's dead."

He gasps for a single shaky breath, and curls up against me, sobbing for a second along with me, and then goes quiet and limp in my arms.

The funeral is four days later. I think half of Coronado Cove shows up, and it doesn't surprise me. He was probably the nicest man in town.

I sort of fell apart the first couple of days. The thought of Porter and me doing what we were doing while Pangborn was dying was a pretty heavy burden. Porter was right: There was nothing we could have done. Pangborn's cancer was advanced. His younger sister tells Grace and me at the funeral that the doctor had given him anywhere from a few days to a few weeks. She says when it's at that stage, some people get diagnosed and die that week. He didn't know when it would happen, so he kept living his life normally.

"He was stubborn that way," she says in a feminine voice that sounds strangely familiar to his. She lives a couple of hours down the coast with her husband, in a small town near Big Sur. I'm relieved to learn that she's adopting Daisy, Pangborn's dog.

We leave the church and drive to the cemetery. I can't find Grace at the graveside service, so I stand with my dad and Wanda. It's really crowded. They've just played "Me and Julio Down by the School Yard" to end the service, which, it turns out, was Pangborn's favorite song. This makes me fall apart all over again, so I'm in a weakened state, sniffling on my dad's shoulder, when the Roths walk up: all four of them.

Well.

I'm too tired to keep this charade up, and it seems like a shame to dishonor Pangborn's memory. So I throw caution to the wind and my arms around Porter's torso.

Not in a casual *we're friends* way either.

He hesitates for a second, and then wraps me in a tight embrace, holding me for an amount of time that's longer than appropriate, but I just don't care. Before he lets me go, he whispers in my ear, "You sure about this?"

I whisper back, "It's time."

When we pull apart, Mrs. Roth hugs my neck briefly—she's wearing a fragrant, fresh flower tucked over one ear that tickles my cheek—and Mr. Roth surprises me by squeezing the back of my neck, which almost makes me cry again, and then I finally face my dad. I can tell by the funny look on his face that he's tallying things up and wondering how in the hell I know this family. His gaze darts to Mr. Roth's arm and a moment of clarity dawns.

"Dad, this is Mr. and Mrs. Roth, and Porter and his sister, Lana."

My dad extends his hand and greets the Roths, and Wanda already knows them, so they're saying hello to her, too. And then Porter steps forward and faces my dad. I'm suddenly nervous. My dad's never really met any boys who were interested in me, and he's definitely never met any boys whom he specifically forbid me to see . . . and I specifically went behind his back and saw anyway. And though, in my eyes, Porter has never looked more hand-some, dressed up in a black suit and tie, he's still sporting that mane of unruly curls that kisses the tops of his shoulders and all that scruff on his jaw. On Mr. Roth, tattoos peek out around the collar of his shirt on his neck. So no, the Roths aren't exactly prim and proper. If my mom were standing here doing the judging, she would be looking down her nose. I mentally cross my fingers and hope my dad won't be that way.

After an uncomfortable pause, Dad says, "You're the boy from work who recovered my daughter's scooter when it was stolen."

My heart stops.

"Yes, sir," Porter answers after a long moment, not blinking. Defensive. Bullish.

My dad sticks his hand out. "Thank you for that," he says, pumping Porter's arm heartily, using his other hand to cover Porter's in one of those extra-good handshakes—making it seem as if Porter saved my life and not a measly bike.

My heart starts again.

"Yes, sir," Porter says, this time visibly relieved. "Not a problem."

That was it? No snotty comments about the hickeys? No accusations? No fifty questions or awkwardness? God, I couldn't love my dad more than I do right now. I don't deserve him.

"You really didn't get a look at who stole it, huh?" Wanda says, narrowing her eyes at Porter. "Because I'd really like to know if you have any information."

Crap.

"Uh . . ." Porter scratches the back of his head.

Lana smacks her gum. "What do you mean? It was—"

"Shut it, Lana," Porter mumbles.

Wanda turns her narrowed eyes on me now. "I remember someone eyeing your scooter at the posole truck a few days before it got jacked."

Oh, crud. She really doesn't miss anything, does she? Guess that's why she's a cop.

Mr. Roth puts a hand up. "Sergeant Mendoza, Porter and I

have had a long talk about this, and I think we all want the same thing. Hell, we probably want it even more than you do." Mr. Roth suspiciously eyes my dad, who is probably the only person here who hasn't put two and two together that Davy is the one who stole my scooter—or maybe he has. I can't tell. Regardless, Mr. Roth clears his throat and says, "What with my kid getting pummeled that day, driving out to Timbuktu to get her bike back."

Too much information in front of my dad, ugh.

"I wouldn't say 'pummeled,'" Porter argues good-humoredly. "You should've seen the other guy."

Mr. Roth ignores him and continues. "What I'm trying to say is that no one wants to punish that joker more than I do. But Porter handled things the best way he knew how at the time, and I support that."

"Hey, I got a kid," Wanda says. "And off the record, I don't disagree with you. But that 'joker' is still out there, and mark my words, he's going to strike again. Next time, you may not be so lucky. He may hurt himself or someone else."

Mr. Roth nods. "I hear you loud and clear. I worry about it all the time. In fact, I saw him hobbling around on the boardwalk last week and it was all I could do not to put him in the hospital again."

A knot in my gut tightens. Last I'd heard, Porter had found out through the rumor mill that Davy had been laid up at home for the last couple of weeks due to Porter reinjuring his knee during the fight at Fast Mike's garage. Guess he's back on his feet again.

Wanda points a finger around our group. "Make me a promise, all of you. Next time Davy Truand does anything, or even starts to do anything, you call nine-one-one and tell them to send me. Let's not meet again at another funeral, okay?"

After the service, my dad doesn't give me any grief about Porter. He doesn't even give me any grief about Davy being the one who stole my scooter. So when we're alone, I just tell him that I'm sorry I kept it all from him, and I explain why I did, and that I won't do it again. Ever, ever, ever.

"It hurts me that you felt the need to lie, Mink," he says.

And that makes me cry all over again.

And because he's the nicest guy in the world, he just holds me until I'm all dried out. And when I'm no longer in danger of drowning the entire cemetery in my misery, à la Alice in Wonderland, he straightens me up and lets me go home with Porter for the rest of the afternoon.

The Roths live in an old house a block away from the beach on the outskirts of town in a neighborhood that probably was halfway nice ten years ago. Now it's starting to get a little run-down, and half the homes have FOR SALE signs in the sandy yards. Their clapboard fence is sagging, the cedar paneling is starting to buckle, and the brutal ocean wind has beaten up the wind chimes that line the gutters. But when I walk inside, it smells like surf wax and wood, and it's stuffed from ceiling to floor with trophies and driftwood and dried starfish and family photos and a bright red Hawaiian hibiscus tablecloth on the kitchen table.

"I'm starving," Lana says. "Funerals make me hungry."

"Me too," Mrs. Roth says. "We need comfort food. P&P?"

"What's P&P?" I ask.

"Popcorn and peanuts," Porter informs me.

She looks around for approval, and everyone nods. I guess this is a Roth family tradition. Sounds a little strange, but I'm on a winning streak with food around this town, so who am I to argue? And when she pops the popcorn in a giant pan on the stove with real kernels, it smells so good, I actually salivate.

While she's salting the popcorn, Porter goes to his room and changes out of his suit, and I help Mrs. Roth dig out bowls in the kitchen. It's weird being alone with her, and I secretly wish Porter would hurry up. Now that he's not here as a buffer, I feel like an actor shooting a scene who's blanking on all her lines. What am I supposed to be saying? Maybe I need cue cards.

"How's your mom feel about you being out here in California?" she asks out of the blue.

"I don't know," I say. "I haven't heard from her."

"Are you not close?"

I shrug. "I thought so. This is the first time I've been away from h-home." *Man. Seriously? I can't cry again. Funerals are the worst.* I swipe away tears before they have a chance to fall, and shake it off.

"I'm sorry, sweetie," Mrs. Roth says in a kind voice. "I didn't mean to dredge up bad stuff."

"It's just that she hasn't even e-mailed or texted. I've been gone for weeks. You'd think she'd want to know if I'm okay. I could be dead, and she wouldn't even know."

"Have you tried calling her?"

I shake my head.

"Does your dad talk to her?"

"I don't know."

"Maybe you should ask him. At least talk to him about it. She could be going through something in her marriage or at work—you never know. She might need to hear from you first. Sometimes parents aren't very good at being grown-ups."

She pats my shoulder, and it reminds me of Pangborn.

We head to a sofa in the den under a giant wooden surfboard suspended from exposed rafters; the board is engraved in pretty cursive with the word PENNYWISE. I sit in the middle of Porter and Lana, holding a big plastic bowl of popcorn with just the right amount of salt and roasted peanuts. The peanuts are heavy and fall to the bottom of the bowl, so we're forced to constantly shake it up and hunt for them, making the popcorn spill all over our laps, which they argue is half the fun. The Roths sit nearby in a pair of recliners, though Mr. Roth's recliner looks like it was manufactured in 1979.

"It's his favorite chair, Bailey, and he won't give it up," Mrs. Roth says, stretching her arm out to touch Mr. Roth's face. "Don't look at it too long or it will grow legs and walk out of here."

Lana giggles. Mr. Roth just grunts and almost smiles. Out of the corner of my eye, I see him kiss his wife's hand before she takes it away.

While eating our feast, we watch *The Big Lebowski*, which is sort of bizarre, because Alex was trying to get me to watch this a couple of months ago. And the Roths have it on DVD, so they are all amazed I've never seen it. Turns out, it's really good. And what's even better, in addition to Porter preparing me for the sound of gunshots in the movie—so I won't be caught off guard—and quoting lines along with the actors, which makes me smile despite the dreary events of the day, is when he leans close and whispers into my ear, "You belong here with me."

And for that moment, I believe that I do.

22

I don't really know how long it takes for people to start feeling normal again after someone dies. But I think I expected Porter to bounce back faster because he's so confident. I have to remind myself that he's already emotionally scarred, and that some of his cockiness is just for show. So when I see him sinking into what I fear is depression after Pangborn's funeral, I wonder if I should say or do something to help him. I just don't know what, exactly.

He tells me he'll be okay, that he just needs time to get over it. When I ask if he wants to grab something to eat after work, he says he might be too tired. He does look tired. He apologizes a lot. That doesn't seem like him—at all, frankly.

Dad tells me not to push him too hard. I'm not exactly a pushy kind of person. But after what seems like an endless stretch of Porter's melancholy, I'm starting to wonder if I need to start nudging. But Grace echoes my dad's advice, telling me to give Porter some space. And what's even weirder is that for once, I'm the one who doesn't want to be alone. I guess Grace can sense this, or something, because she's been asking me to hang out a lot. Our prework breakfast dates at the Pancake Shack are now becoming routine. A definite bright spot of my day. It's helped to get my mind off Pangborn—and stopped me from worrying so much about Porter. Sort of. It doesn't soothe the funny ache in my heart when I think about him dealing with all of this on his own. I wish he'd let me help. I wish he'd talk to me. At this point, I'd give my right pinky toe for one of our good, old-fashioned arguments. Can you miss someone you see almost every day?

A couple of weeks after Pangborn's funeral, at six forty-five a.m., I'm awakened by a series of buzzes. It's my phone. Who's texting me this early? My first reaction is panic, because, let's face it, life has been a shit sandwich lately.

Porter: *Wake up.*

Porter: *Waaaake uuuuup.*

Porter: *How late do you sleep, anyway? You need an alarm clock. (I'd like to be that alarm clock, actually.) (God, please don't let your dad pick up your phone.)*

Porter: *Come on, sleepyhead. If you don't wake up soon, I'm leaving without you.*

I type a quick reply: *What's going on?*

Porter: *Good surfing, that's what.*

Me: *You mean, surfing for you?*

Porter: *That was the idea. So, are you coming to watch me surf?*

Me: *Try and stop me.*

I'm so excited, I throw off the covers and leap out of bed. Okay, so maybe this isn't a romantic invitation, because a few more texts tell me where I'll be meeting his family, but I don't care. I'm just relieved that he sounds cheerful. My only problem is Grace, my breakfast date this morning. She's already up, and when I text her to ask for a rain check, she asks if she can tag along. When I don't answer right away, two more texts follow—

Grace: *Pretty please?*

Grace: *I really need a chin-wag.*

Me: *???*

Grace: *A chat. Girl talk. Yeah?*

Normally, I'd say sure, but I haven't spent time with Porter since the *Big Lebowski* viewing after the funeral. What if he doesn't want a big audience? I consider the best way to handle it as I get dressed, but my mind keeps wandering to Porter.

When I head out, the fog hasn't cleared. The place I'm meeting the Roths is a spot a couple of miles north of town, just up the beach from the Bone Garden. It's pretty out here, all wild and pebble-strewn. And though it's not crowded like the beach at the boardwalk, I'm surprised to see anyone at all this early in the morning. Apparently, it's a popular surf spot, because a dozen other vans are parked along the road and several other onlookers gather, including a couple of people walking along the beach with their dogs as the waves roll and crash.

Clearly, this wasn't a private affair. I even see Sharonda, the president of Brightsea's drama club, who Grace introduced me to at the bonfire party. For a moment, I remember Grace, and tell myself I need to text her back, but Mrs. Roth waves me down, and she's brought doughnuts. I don't want to be rude, and she's in a great mood, so I put Grace out of my mind for the time being and silence my phone.

While I make small talk with Mrs. Roth, I catch sight of the rest of the family. Mr. Roth is in training mode, unloading a board with Lana, and barking commands. But I'm having trouble paying attention to anything but Porter. If there are any traces of melancholy left on him, he's packed them away. It's a new day, and I can see the change in the way he walks across the sand, the way he holds his head high. He's ready to move on.

He's donned a sleeveless black-and-aqua wet suit, and it's clinging in all the right places. Standing next to Mrs. Roth, I'm afraid to look too closely all at once, but hot damn. I catch his eyes once when his mom's busy chatting with Sharonda, who is apparently friends with Lana. I can't wink, so I just look him up and down and mouth, *Wow.* He gives me a spectacular grin in return. He's so cocky; the boy knows how good he looks. I roll my eyes, but I can't stop smiling, and he loves the attention. He could build sand castles on the beach and never even surf one wave for all I care. Mission accomplished.

After that exchange, his focus shifts. I notice the moment it happens. He's stretching, both him and Lana, legs and arms, normal stretches and some weird jumping. They're both super limber. And the entire time, his eyes are on the water. He's calculating the big waves. Timing them, or something. He checks his watch occasionally, but mostly he's watching the water and checking the sky. He's very intense. I like him this way.

There's some sort of surfing etiquette I don't understand, but I can tell Porter and Lana are waiting their turn. And I can also tell that the other surfers aren't very good, and some of them are giving up and clearing out. After a minute, Mr. Roth gives his wife a head signal.

"Okay, girls," she says to me and Sharonda. "We're going up there."

"Up there" is a short hike up a massive sand dune that gives us a great view of the ocean. From here, we can see the waves rolling in much more clearly and all the other surfers who are either surfing on the smaller waves closer to shore (not impressive), or trying to ride the bigger waves farther out and not lasting very long. The ocean is eating them alive. Now I'm a little worried.

"They're not surfing those, are they?" I ask. The big waves looked smaller and flatter from the beach.

"You bet your sweet patootie they are," she says, all fierce mom pride. And from the looks of the crowd gathering behind us to watch, she isn't the only one interested in the show.

I hope this is a shark-free zone.

Lana's in yellow and black, and she goes first. She lies flat on her board and paddles out, and that takes longer than you'd think. Porter gives her some distance, but he's paddling now too. The farther out they go, the scarier it gets. They sometimes disappear under the smaller rolling waves, like speed bumps in a road, then reappear on the other side.

"Have you seen them surf before?" I ask Sharonda, taking a bite of doughnut. I hate to break it to Mrs. Roth, but this is no churro or vanilla moon muffin.

"Yeah, I live down the road, so I see Lana surf a couple of times a week. Sometimes I go watch events, if they aren't too far. I once rode down to Huntington Beach with the Roths. Remember that?"

"Sure do, honey," Mrs. Roth says, watching the water.

"What about Porter?" I ask.

Sharonda nods. "I've been watching Porter compete locally since he was, like, thirteen. He used to have hair down to here," she says, putting her hand halfway down her back. "Nothing but curls. All the girls in our class had a crush on him."

Mrs. Roth sticks out her bottom lip, looking sentimental. "He was such a sweet boy. My little grommet."

"Oh, and we'll be watching all of Lana's surfing heats together on TV," Sharonda says excitedly, reaching around me to tap Mrs. Roth's arm. "Maybe we can have viewing parties?"

This surprises me. It hadn't even crossed my mind that Lana will be that professional. Now that I know her, she just seems like a good-natured kid who chews a lot of gum and drools when she falls asleep on the couch, which is what happened that afternoon at their house.

Lana and Porter are both floating on their boards, bobbing in the rolling waves. I'm not sure what they're waiting for, but everyone is tense. Before I can ask what's happening, Lana's yellow-and-black suit pops onto her board. She's standing, crouched on her board, and cutting through a massive wave I didn't even realize was there.

There she goes!

She's like a beautiful black-and-yellow bee, zipping through the water, making tight zigzag motions that seem to go on forever. I can't believe she can ride the wave for so long. It's crazy. How is this possible? Seems like it goes against nature.

"Yeah, Lana," Mrs. Roth calls out to the ocean, clapping in time with all of Lana's zigzagging. "Go, baby, go!"

By the time Lana finishes, she's so far on the other side of the dune, it's going to take her five minutes to walk back to us. No wonder these kids are in shape. This surfing gig is exhausting.

The crowd on the sand dune explodes into applause and whistles, and I clap along, too. Mrs. Roth rotates her hand in the air, egging them on. "That little peanut is going to win it all," she tells everyone around us, and some of them high-five her.

She's so proud. Everyone's smiling. It's all exciting, but now I'm watching Porter, because he's paddled out just a little farther, and that makes my stomach drop.

Mr. Roth comes bounding up the sand dune, eyes on the water. How long has it been since Porter's surfed like this? I'm suddenly nervous. If he crashes, or whatever it's called, I don't want him to do it in front of me and be embarrassed later. I can't handle that. I want to look away, maybe make some excuse, like

I got sick from the doughnut and had to leave. I can hear about it later.

Then he pops up on his board.

Too late. Can't look away now.

His wave is bigger than Lana's. His stance is different from Lana's. He rides the board up the curling water, up, up, up . . . (please don't fall!) and at the top, he's— Holy Mother of Sheep, he's flying up in the air, board and body! Impossibly, on a dime, he turns the board one hundred and eighty degrees, sharply. Then he rides the wave right back down, smooth as glass, white foam kicking out from the tail of his board like the train of a wedding dress.

"YES!" Mr. Roth bellows, holding up his arm.

The crowd behind me shouts along with Mrs. Roth.

It's happening so fast. That was just one move, and though Porter doesn't take the board up in the air again, he's already made turn number two (crouching low at base of wave, wait, wait . . . rides up again), and whoosh! Turn three! Now he's riding back down, still going, arms out for balance, like fins.

Lana's style was fast and quick, full of spunk; Porter is slower and his moves are grander. Poetic. Beautiful. He's cutting through the water as if he's painting a picture with his body.

I didn't know surfing looked like this.

I didn't know Porter could do this.

He makes the last turn at the end of the wave, a baby turn, because there isn't much wave left to ride, and then neatly comes to a stop where the sand rises toward the beach, the wave washing all around him, as if the ocean found him shipwrecked and is delivering him safely to shore.

The crowd roars.

I crush my doughnut in my hand. "Holy shit," I say in amazement, then apologize, then say it again several times, but no one is listening or cares.

Mr. Roth turns around, grins at the crowd—grins!—and kisses his wife before running down the other side of the dune to greet his son. Mrs. Roth picks me up in a bear hug. For a woman who isn't an athlete, she sure is strong. When she puts me back down, she cups my face in her hands and, shockingly, kisses me straight on the lips. "Thank you, thank you, thank you. I knew you could get him out here."

"I didn't do anything," I say, flushing with excitement and a little embarrassment.

"Oh baby, yes you did," she says, her eyes shining. "He hasn't surfed like that since the shark."

Porter surfs nearly a dozen more big waves. He screws up once, falling off his board pretty hard trying to pull an aerial "alleyoop." Mrs. Roth blames the wipeout on the wind. But otherwise, he's pretty much a demon. He and Lana engage in a friendly sibling competition, and it's awesome. After a couple of hours, word has spread, and a hundred people or so line the beach. My throat goes hoarse from cheering.

When it seems as though they're slowing down—both the waves and the surfers—Mrs. Roth tells her husband to call her "babies" back to shore soon. She doesn't want Porter overdoing it and injuring himself. Mr. Roth grunts and seems dismissive, but he slowly makes his way back down the dune. I guess Lana was right when she said her mom wears the pants in their family.

Someone taps me on the shoulder. "How are they doing?"

I turn around to find Grace, dressed in a magenta jacket and oversize gold sunglasses. Her mouth is arrow-straight, matching the tense line of her shoulders. She is not a happy camper.

"Grace," Mrs. Roth says cheerfully. "You should have come earlier. Porter was on fire."

Grace smiles at her, and it's almost genuine. "Is that so? I'm sorry I missed it. Took me a bit to find out where they were surfing."

"You could have called me," Mrs. Roth says absently, only halfway paying attention.

Grace aims two bladelike eyes on me. "It's fine. I texted Porter and he was more than happy to let me know."

Oh, God. "Grace," I whisper. "I totally forgot to text you back."

"No big deal. I'm not exciting enough, I suppose," she says, and walks away.

My heart sinks. The Artful Dodger in me whispers to let Grace go, but another part of my brain is panicking. I get Mrs. Roth's attention. "Sorry, but I need to talk to Grace."

Mrs. Roth makes a shooing motion. "Go on, baby. They're just about done. I'll send Porter to find you after he's back to shore."

Quickly, I follow Grace away from the small crowd on the beach, down the sand dune, calling her name. She stops near a rock with a clump of yellow lupine scrub growing out of it. My throat is tight, and I can't look her in the eyes. She's so agitated, I can almost feel the emotion radiating off her like heat from a furnace. And she's never been upset at me. Ever.

"Why do you want to talk to me now?" Grace says. "You didn't bother to answer my texts this morning."

"I'm sorry!" I blurt out. "I was going to text you back, but—"

"I called two times"—she angrily claps along with her words to drive her point home—"after the texts. It went straight to voice mail."

I wince. My fingers itch to dive into my pocket and check my abandoned phone, but I resist. "It's just—"

"Easy to forget about your friend when your boyfriend is suddenly back in the picture. When he was moping, you had all the time in the world for me. But the second he calls, you throw me away faster than yesterday's news."

Shame and regret roll through me. "That's not true. I just got distracted. I didn't throw you away."

"Well, that's what it feels like. Don't think I haven't been here before with other friends. The second they fall for someone, they forget all about me. Well, I'll tell you what, Bailey Rydell. I'm tired of being the placeholder. If you don't want a real friendship with me, then find someone else who doesn't mind being disposable."

I don't know what to say. Don't know how to make this better.

I'm a surfer, wiping out and drowning under one of those monster waves. Only, I don't think I'm skilled enough to get back up again.

After a long, awkward silence I say, "I'm not good at this."

"At what?"

"Being close to people." I gesture at her, then me. "I screw it up. A lot. It's easier for me to avoid things than deal with confrontation."

"That's your excuse?" she says.

"It's not an excuse. It's the truth."

Why did I do this? If I could wind the clock back to this morning, I'd text her back and everything would be fine. Whether I actively or passively avoided Grace's texts, forgot them on purpose or unintentionally, none of it matters. I failed her. And maybe in doing so, I failed myself a little too.

I don't want to lose Grace. Somehow, while Porter barged in my front door, she sneaked in the back. I try the only thing I have left: the truth.

"You're right," I tell her, words tumbling out. "I took you for granted. I forgot about you this morning because I assumed that you'd always be there, because you always are. I can count on you, because you're dependable. And I'm not. I wish . . . I wish you could count on me like I can count on you. I want to be more like you. You're not a placeholder for me, Grace."

She doesn't say anything, but I can hear her breathing pick up.

"I guess I told myself you wouldn't miss me," I say, picking at the yellow lupine shrub. "That's how I justified it."

"Well, I did miss you. You picked a fine day not to show.

Because I really could have used a shoulder today," she says, still somewhat upset, but now moving into another emotion I can't quite put my finger on. It's hard to decode people when they're wearing big sunglasses and their arms are crossed over their chest.

A wind whips through my hair. I wait until it passes, then ask, "Did something happen?"

"Yes, something happened," she complains. But now I can hear the distress in her voice, and when she lifts her sunglasses to rest them atop her head, I see it mirrored in her eyes. "Taran's not coming back. He's staying in India for the rest of the summer. Maybe for good."

"Oh, God. Grace." My chest constricts painfully.

Slow, silent tears roll down her cheeks. "We've been together for a year. We were going to attend the same college. This isn't how life is supposed to work."

Tentatively, I reach for her, not sure if she'll accept me. But there's not even a heartbeat of hesitation, and she's throwing her arms around me, crying softly as she clings. Her sunglasses fall off her head and land in the sand.

"I'm sorry," I choke out, surprised to find that I'm crying along with her. "For everything."

My old therapist warned me that avoidance is a dysfunctional way to interact with people you care about, but now I'm starting to understand what he meant when he said it could hurt them, too. Maybe it's time I figure out a better way to deal with my problems. Maybe Artful Dodger isn't working so well for me anymore.

"I've never been alone with a man before, even with my dress on.
With my dress off, it's most unusual."
—Audrey Hepburn, *Roman Holiday* (1953)

23

In the middle of July, Porter and I have another day off together. He tells me we can do whatever I want with it, that he's my genie and will grant me one wish. I tell him that I don't want to see another soul for an entire afternoon. I have something I'm ready to share.

He picks me up in the camper van at noon, two hours after my standing breakfast date with Grace.

"Where are we going?" I say, folding down the visor to block the sun as I hop into the passenger side. I'm wearing my white vintage Annette Funicello shorts and the leopard sunglasses Wanda and Dad brought me back from San Francisco. My Lana Turner 'do looks especially perfect.

Porter glances at my sandals (they're the ones he likes), and then my shorts (which he continues to stare at while he talks to me). "You have two choices, beach or woods. The woods have a stream, which is cool, but the beach has an arch made of rock, which is likewise cool. God, those shorts are hot."

"Thank you. No people at either location?"

"If we see anyone, I will act crazy and chase them off with a stick. But no, these places are both usually deserted."

After some thought, which included taking deep-woods insects into consideration, there's really no choice for the purpose I have in mind, so I gather my gumption and say, "Take me to the beach."

The drive is about fifteen minutes. He has to squeeze through a narrow, rocky road through the woods to get to the beach, pine branches brushing against the top of the van. But when we emerge from the trees, it's glorious: sand, gray pebbles, tide pools, and rising up from the edge of the shore, an arch of mudstone rock. It's covered with birds and barnacles and the waves crash through it.

The beach is small.

The beach isn't sexy.

The beach is ours.

Porter parks the van near the woods. He slides open the side door, and we take off our shoes and toss them in the back. I see he's got his board and wet suit neatly stowed; he's been surfing almost every day.

We splash around in the tide pools for a while. They're teeming with starfish, which I've only ever seen dried on a shelf in a souvenir store. He points out some other critters, but I have more than coastal California wonders on my mind. "Hey, where's the nude beach?"

"What?"

"There's supposed to be a nude beach in Coronado Cove."

Porter laughs. "It's up by the Beacon Resort. It's not even fifty feet wide. There's privacy fencing on both sides. You can't see inside, nor would you want to, I promise."

"Why?"

"It's a swingers' club for retirees. Our parents are too young to get in."

"No way."

"Yes way. Ask Wanda. They get busted for violating after-hours noise ordinances with all their swingers' drinking parties. That's why they had to put up the fencing. People complained."

"Gross."

"You say that now, but when you're eighty and just want to get nude and be served a fruity umbrella drink on the beach by another eighty-year-old nude person, you'll be thankful it's here."

"I suppose you're right."

He squints at me. "Why are you asking me about this?"

I shrug. "Just curious."

"About getting naked on a beach?"

I don't say anything.

His eyes go big. "Holy shit, that's what you're thinking, isn't it?" He points at me and shakes his head. "Something's not adding up here. This isn't you. Now, me, I'm a fan of all things naked. And if you asked me to strip right now, I will. I'm not ashamed. I spent the first few years of my life on this planet naked in the ocean."

I believe that. I really do.

"But you?" He squints at me. "What's this all about?"

Hesitating, I chew the inside of my mouth. "You remember when we were making out that night in the museum?"

"Like every waking minute of my day," he says with a slow smile.

I chuckle. "Me too," I admit before refocusing. "You remember when you started to touch my stomach, and I stopped you?"

His smile fades. "Yeah. I've been wondering when you were going to tell me about that."

"I think I'm ready now."

He nods several times. "Cool. I'm glad."

Of course, now that I've said this, fear overtakes me. I hesitate, gritting my teeth. "Thing is, I need to show you, not tell you. I think this is one of the reasons I've hated beaches for so long . . . the bikini issue. So I think I should just do this, you know?" I'm not sure if I'm talking to him or myself, but it doesn't matter. "Yeah. I'm going to do it."

He looks confused.

"I'm about to get naked on this beach," I tell him.

"Oh, shit," he says, looking truly stunned. "Okay. Um, all right. Yeah, okay."

"But I've never been naked on a beach with anyone, so this is weird for me."

He points at me and grins. "Not a problem. Would you like some company? I'm fond of being naked. It's easier when the playing field's even."

I consider his proposition. "Yeah, okay. That actually would make it easier."

"I just want you to know that there are so many jokes I could make right now," he says.

We both laugh, me a little nervously, and then decide upon a strip-poker method to the clothing removal. Porter volunteers to go first. He scans the beach to make sure we're still alone, and without further ado, peels off his T-shirt. Nice, but it's not really fair, because (A) I've seen it before, and (B) he's not really exposing anything he can't expose in public. He signals for me to go next.

Carefully considering all my options (I'm smartly wearing good matching undergarments), I take off my shorts. He's surprised. He also can't take his eyes off me. I like that . . . I think. I haven't decided yet. I just tell myself that it's the same amount of fabric as wearing a bathing suit, so what's the difference?

"You play dirty, Rydell," he says, unbuttoning his shorts. Before I can open my mouth to argue, he's in nothing but a pair of olive-colored boxer shorts.

Whew. He's got great legs.

Okay, my turn again, as he helpfully reminds me with *get on with it* hand gestures. *Guess it's the shirt,* I think as I pull it over my head and toss it to the sand. A bra is the same amount of fabric as a bathing suit, and it's a good bra. I hear him suck in a quick breath, so I think that's good? My boobs aren't great, but they aren't bad, either, and—

His fingers trace the bottom of my scar. "Is this it? This is what I felt?"

I look down at my ribs and cover his hand, pressing it against my stomach. Then I uncover them and we look together. It's bright and sunny, and we're both halfway naked. And if there's anyone I feel safe with . . . if there's anyone I trust, oddly enough, it's Porter.

"Yes, this is it," I say.

He looks at it. Glances at my face. Waits.

"That's where the bullet went in," I tell him, fingering the puckered ridge of scarring that's never completely healed right. I turn to the side and show him my back. "Here's where it exited."

"I don't understand."

"Greg Grumbacher. That's where he shot me."

"You told me . . . I mean, I thought he shot your mom?"

I shake my head slowly. "My mom wasn't supposed to be home. He followed me home that day because his plan was to kill me. He had a note to leave with my body. His reasoning was that my mom took away his kid in the divorce, so he was taking away hers."

Porter stares at me.

"Mom lunged for the gun, so he missed most of my vital organs. I bled a lot. They had to sew up some stuff. My lung collapsed. I was in the hospital for a couple of weeks."

His shoulders sag. "I'm so sorry. I didn't know."

"You're the first person I've told. My classmates heard, but my mom put me in another school after it happened. Anyway, there you go. Told you I was screwed up," I say, giving him a small smile.

He curls his hand around my waist, rubbing from the front scar to the back. "Thank you for telling me. For showing me."

"Thanks for not making it weird. I don't want it to be a big deal anymore, you know? That's why I wanted to show you. Out here in the sun."

"I get it," he says. "I totally get it."

I lean forward and press my lips against the sweet dip where his collarbones meet. He pushes back my hair with his palm and kisses me in the middle of my forehead, both eyelids, on the tip of my nose. Then he pulls me tight against him and folds me up in his arms. I breathe him into my lungs as deeply as I can, all his sun-burnished, warm goodness. *Thank you, thank you, thank you,* I try to tell him with my body. And from the way he's holding me— like I'm a whole person, not a broken toy—I think he understands.

"Does this mean you want to stop our game now?" he murmurs after a time.

I tilt my head back to see his face. "Are you chickening out on me?"

He grins that slow and cocky grin of his and pushes me back until I'm an arm's length away. "Both at the same time, on the count of three."

"Not fair! I've got two pieces of clothing left."

"I'll close my eyes until you say I can open them. One, two . . ."

With a euphoric cry, I fumble with my bra strap and strip off my underwear. I did it!

"Holy shit, you're beautiful," he murmurs.

"Cheater." I'm 100 percent naked. On a public beach. And more important, I don't care, because Porter's taken off his clothes too, and that's far more interesting than any fleeting sense of modesty I have. Because he's naked. And he's gorgeous.

And he's very excited about our mutual sans-clothing situation.

"Oh," I say, looking down between us.

"I'm pretty proud of that," he admits with a smile, urging my hand forward. When I touch him, he stands on tiptoes for a moment and looks like he might pass out, which makes *me* very excited about our mutual sans-clothing situation.

"Now I'm thinking about the back of the camper van," I say.

He blows out a hard breath and pushes my hand away. "I think that's a dicey idea. Maybe we should get dressed first. God, you're so beautiful."

"You mentioned that."

"Let me look at you some more first. I need to memorize all of you for later. In case I never get to see this again. Shit. I can't believe you talked me into . . ." His eyes are heavy-lidded. "This is either the best or worst idea I've ever agreed to. You're killing me, Bailey Rydell."

"I know you've got condoms in that first-aid kit."

A wave crashes again the rock bridge.

"Bailey . . ."

"Porter."

"It might be terrible. Trust me, I have experience in these matters."

"It might not, though, right?"

Seagulls circle overhead, squawking.

"Are you sure?"

"I'm sure," I say. I've been thinking about it a lot over the last few weeks. And I've made up my mind. "If you want to, with me, that is. I'm not trying to pressure you."

He swears softly. "It'll be a miracle if I can make it all the way back to the van. But if you change your mind, you can, you know? At any point. Even in the middle of it."

But I don't change my mind.

Not on the way to the van, or when we're dumping his surfboard out to make room. And not when he's asking me a dozen times if I'm sure, and trying to convince me otherwise by doing the fabulous thing he did to me in the museum with his fingers, which only makes me want him more. Not when we start, and he's being careful and slow and deliberate, and I can't bear to look at his face, but I don't know where to look, so I'm looking between us, because I'm worried it will be messy, and that it's going to hurt, and it does, but the pain is over fast, and then it's just . . . so much more intense than I expected. But he's going so slow, and then he says—

"Are you still okay?" in a husky, breathless voice.

Yes, I still am.

And I don't change my mind in the middle of it, when it's

overwhelming, and he stops, because he's afraid I want him to stop, but I'm okay—I'm so okay—and convince him to keep going.

And not after, when we're clinging to each other like the world just fell apart and is slowly clicking back together, piece by piece, breath by breath . . . heartbeat by beautiful heartbeat.

I do not regret a single moment.

"What is this?" I ask some time later, tugging on something white that's wedged in a crevice as we lie tangled together on an old blanket in the back of the van. In the back of my mind, I'm thinking that I know for sure I saw another condom in the first-aid kit, and I'm wondering how long I have to wait to bring this up without looking too eager. But I'm propped up on my elbows and Porter's lazily running his fingers across my back, meandering down my butt and the back of my leg, and this feels pretty freaking good, so I guess I'm in no hurry.

The jagged object I shimmy out of the crevice is about an inch long and triangular, and it's got a piece of silver fitted on one side, through which a silver jump ring is attached.

"Huh. I thought I lost that," he says, pausing my sensual back scratch to take it from me. "That came out of my arm. Genuine great white tooth. It's a lucky charm. Or a curse, whichever way you want to look at it. I had it on my key chain, but I was switching keys out and set it down. Must have rolled off the seat or something."

"It's huge," I say.

"No way, that's just a baby tooth. You saw the sharks at the aquarium. Great white was twice their size. And he was a teenager."

I try to imagine the tooth implanted in Porter's arm. "I know it's a bad memory, but the tooth itself should be survivor's pride, or something. A badge of honor."

"You want to borrow it?"

"Me?"

"For your scooter keys. Might match your whole animal-print vibe." He pauses. "I mean, if it's too much, no big deal. I'm not trying to brand you, like you're my girl or anything."

Because if people see this, they'll definitely know we're dating each other. "Am I? Your girl, I mean."

"I don't know. Are you?" He offers the shark tooth in his open palm, hesitates, and closes his fingers around it. "If you are, you have to promise me something first."

"What's that?"

"You've got to start opening up to me." He glances toward my back. "Look, I totally understand why you didn't tell me the whole story about the gunshot wound until now, but you can't be that way around me anymore. I already had a girlfriend who kept things from me, and I spent weeks walking around oblivious while she was screwing Davy behind my back."

"First, ew, I have better taste than that, and second, I would never do that to you."

He kisses my ear. "I believe you."

"So, yeah, speaking of Chloe . . . Were you and Davy having sex with Chloe at the same time?"

"Together?" He sounds appalled.

I smile. "You know what I mean."

"No," he says, sounding sheepish. "Chloe and I were going through a dry spell at the time. There was no cross-contamination, if that's what you're worried about."

I sort of was.

"And we always used condoms. Every time."

"Good to know," I mumble. *Very good.*

"Anyway, back to you," he says. "What I'm trying to say is that you're sort of bad about bottling things up. And I'm not saying you've got to turn into Grace. I like you just the way you are. But in order for this to work, you've got to tell me stuff. I need you to trust me—"

"Of course I do." *Hello. Did we not just have sex?*

"—and I need to be able to trust you," he finishes.

I start to argue, but I'm embarrassed that he's even brought this up.

He nudges my chin with his, forcing me to face him, and speaks quietly against my mouth. "Listen to me, okay? What's between us? This is the best thing that's ever happened to me in my entire life, and I don't want it to end. Sometimes you feel so tricky, like fog over the ocean—like you just showed up at the beginning of the summer, and one day the sun will come out and you'll disappear and go back to your mom. And that scares the hell out of me. So that's why I tell you things about me, because I figure if I weigh you down with my baggage, then you'll be less likely to run."

My heart twists.

I press my brow against his. "Artful Dodger."

"Huh?"

"That's me. Or it used to be." That morning on the beach when Grace was mad at me ghosts through my thoughts. I need to do better. "I'm trying, Porter. I really am. I want you to trust me."

"That's all I ask." He leans back to look at me, smiles softly, and opens up his fingers to reveal the shark tooth again. "So . . . do you want it? People might talk."

I snatch it up with a grin. "Maybe they'll say that you're mine."

"Bailey, I've *been* yours. I've just been waiting for you to make up your mind."

Later that night, after Porter brings me back home, I'm too blissed out to be around people, especially my dad. So I put on my leopard scarf and sunglasses and take Baby out for a drive around the neighborhood. When I get to the big hill at the end of our street, I throw my hands up in the air, shouting, "I'm in love!" to the redwood trees.

> "Pay no attention to that man behind the curtain."
> —Frank Morgan, *The Wizard of Oz* (1939)

24

My dad's no cook, but the CPA in him can follow a recipe like no one's business. Together, however, we managed to ruin a roasted chicken, which was still raw two hours into cooking. That's when we figured out that something was wrong with one of our oven's elements. We dumped the chicken, gave it last rites over the garbage can—RIP—and called for pizza. And even though we were a little upset by the failure, our guests—Wanda, Grace, and Porter—didn't seem to mind.

It's been a week since Nude Beach, and it's the first time Porter's been invited inside my house, so I'm nervous anyway. I'm not sure why. Maybe it's because I've hung out at Porter's house several times, and it's so comfortable over there, and now I'm worried it won't be the same here. He already cracked a joke about hanging out with a cop, so there's that, too. Even though I don't think about Wanda as being some kind of intimidating authority figure, I can understand why Porter might feel that way. Now I feel defensive about her and want him to like both her and my dad, and that feels . . . stressful.

But when the pizza's delivered and Porter's thumbing through my dad's DVD collection, things start looking up. Turns out my dad and Porter like a lot of the same sci-fi movies. Porter has no idea what a huge mistake he's just made, because Dad is thrilled out of his ever-loving mind and will not shut up with the nerdery talk: Have you seen this space-pirate gem from 1977? What about this long-lost 1982 flick? If they start talking *Star Wars*, I'm going to have to shut it all down.

The entire time they're talking, I can't tear my eyes away from Porter. What I'm feeling for him now is like drowning and floating at the same time. When he gives me a quick glance, I'm overwhelmed. Does he feel like this too? This epic connection between us? It's thrilling and frightening. Like the rest of my life was just a series of bad B movies and we just walked onto the set of *Citizen Kane*.

"Lord, you've got it bad," Grace whispers near my ear. "Must have been good, huh?"

Ugh, I should never have told her what happened on the beach. I didn't give her any details, but maybe that's the problem. She's filling them in with her dirty little mind. I bat her arm away, and our discreet, playful slap-fest devolves into immature giggling. When my dad and Porter notice, something near hysteria rises up in me, and I herd Grace toward the sofa, ducking out of sight.

I'm trying so hard to be more open with him, to talk about . . . all of this. These chaotic feelings. About what happened in the back of the camper van. We haven't been together again, not like that. Haven't had time. We've had some lovely deep kisses in the front of the van after work and a lot of midnight phone calls about nothing much at all, really—we just needed to hear each other's voices. But every time I try to tell him how I really feel, how *much* I really feel, my chest feels like a hundred-pound fiery fist is squeezing my heart.

Sheer panic.

Once a coward, always a coward.

What if I can't change? If I can't be as honest and open as he needs me to be? As reliable a friend as Grace wants me to be? What if Greg Grumbacher ruined me forever? That's what scares me the most.

After all the male-on-male sci-fi talk, we all retire to the porch and sit around the patio table near the redwood tree that grows through the roof. Dad brings out the holy worn game box.

"Okay," he says very seriously. "What Bailey and I are choosing to share with you tonight is a Rydell family tradition. By taking part in this game—nay, this cherished and sacred ceremony—"

I snort a little laugh while he continues his speech.

"—you are agreeing to honor our proud family heritage, which extends as far back as . . . well, I think the price sticker on the box is from around 2001, so it's pretty ancient."

Wanda rolls her eyes. "I'll give it my attention for fifteen minutes, Pete."

"No, Sergeant Mendoza," he says dramatically, slicing his hand through the air as if he's some stern politician at a podium, commanding attention. "You will give Settlers of Catan your attention for a full hour or two, because the colonies deserve it."

"And because it will take you at least that long to build up your settlements," I tell her.

"Is there a dungeon master?" Porter asks.

Dad and I both chuckle.

"What?" Porter says, grinning.

"We have so much to teach you," I say, putting my hand on his. "And there's no dungeon master. Wrong kind of game nerd."

"Is this more or less boring than Monopoly?" Grace asks.

"Less," Dad and I say together.

"Monopoly is for losers," Dad informs her.

Porter frowns. "I love Monopoly."

"We have an entire chest full of old board games," I whisper loudly to him.

"I'm not going to like this, am I?" Wanda says on a heavy sigh.

"Now might be a good time to break out that expensive bottle of wine you guys brought back from San Francisco," I suggest.

Porter grins at me and rubs his hands together excitedly. "This looks super weird. I'm *so* in. Let's play."

God, I love him. I don't even know why I was so worried before. This is all fine now.

Dad unpacks the game and explains all the rules, confusing everyone in the process. We finally just start playing and teach as we go. They get the hang of it. I'm not sure if they like it as much as Dad and I do, but everyone seems to be having fun. We're laughing and goofing around a lot, anyway. Everything's going great, until about an hour into the game.

The pizza made me thirsty. I excuse myself to get some iced tea from the kitchen and ask if anyone else needs a refill. My dad does, so I leave to fetch tea for both of us. While I'm headed away from the table, my dad says, "Thanks, Mink."

Behind me, I hear Porter ask my dad, "What did you call her?"

"Huh? Oh, 'Mink'? That's just a childhood nickname," my dad says through the open doorway.

"I hear you call her that all the time," Wanda remarks, "but you never told me why."

"It's actually a funny story," Dad says.

I groan as I pour our tea, but my dad is already in storytelling mode, and I can hear him from the kitchen.

"This is how it came about. When Bailey was younger, fourteen years old, she was in the hospital for a couple of weeks." I glance back briefly to see him giving Wanda a lift of his brows that tells me they've had this conversation, so she knows about the shooting. "The entire time she was there, the TV was stuck on the classic movie station. You know, with all the old movie stars—Humphrey Bogart and Cary Grant, Katharine Hepburn. Night and day, that's all that was on. We were so worried about her, that by the time any-one thought to change the channel, she'd already started to actually like some of the movies and wouldn't let us change it."

I sigh dramatically as I walk back through the doorway onto the porch and set down our glasses of tea.

"Anyway, for a few days, after surgery, it was a little touch and go. And being a dad, I was worried, of course. I told her if she healed up and made it out of the hospital, I'd buy her whatever she wanted. Most girls her age would probably say, I don't know—a car? A pony? A trip to Florida with her friends? Not Bailey. She saw those glamorous actresses wearing all those fur coats before it wasn't PC to do so anymore, and she said, 'Daddy, I want a mink coat.'"

Wanda guffaws. "Did you get her one?"

"A fake fur," Dad says. "It was just the attitude I never forgot. And she still loves those old movies. Is everything all right, Porter?"

As I'm scooting my chair back under the table, I glance up and see that Porter has a peculiar look on his face. He looks like someone just told him his dog died.

"What's wrong?" I ask.

He's staring at the table and won't look at me. He was just laughing and clowning around a minute ago, now all of a sudden he's clammed up and his jaw looks as if it's made of stone and might break off.

Everyone's staring at him. He shuffles around in his seat and brings his hand up with his phone. "I got a text from my mom. Gotta go, sorry."

No way. The old *I got a text* trick? That's an Artful Dodger maneuver. He just pulled my own con on me?

"What's wrong?" I say again, standing up from the table with him.

"Nothing, nothing," he mutters. "It's no big deal. She just needs my help and it can't wait. Sorry." He seems agitated and distracted. "Thanks for dinner and stuff."

"Anytime," my dad says, worry creasing a line through his brow as he shares a look with Wanda. "You're always welcome here."

"See you, Grace," Porter mumbles.

I can barely keep up with Porter as he strides toward the front door, and when we're outside, he bounds down the steps without looking at me. Now I'm freaking. Maybe he really did get a text, but it wasn't from his mom. Because there's only one person that makes him this intense, and if he's avoiding my dad and Wanda, I'm worried it might have something to do with Davy.

"Porter," I call as he heads down the driveway.

"Gotta go," he says.

That just makes me mad. He can avoid my dad all he wants, but me? "Hey! What the hell is wrong with you?"

He spins around, and his face is suddenly livid with anger. "Was this some sick game?"

"Huh?" I'm completely confused. He's not making any sense, and his gaze is shifting all over my face. "You're scaring me. Did something happen?" I ask. "Is this about Davy? Did he do something again? Please talk to me."

"What?" Bewilderment clouds his face. He squeezes his eyes

closed and shakes his head, mumbling, "This is so screwed up. I can't . . . I gotta go home."

"Porter!" I shout to his back, but he doesn't turn around. Doesn't look my way again. I just stand helplessly, cradling my elbows in the driveway, watching as his van rumbles to life and disappears down the street around the redwood trees.

"The time to make up your mind about people is never."
—Katharine Hepburn, *The Philadelphia Story* (1940)

25

I text.

I call.

I text.

I call.

He doesn't respond.

Grace tries, too, but he doesn't answer her, either. "I'm sure it's some stupid misunderstanding," she assures me. But I'm pretty positive she doesn't believe that.

After Grace goes home, I continue to replay the entire porch conversation in my head, looking for clues, trying to remember exactly when I noticed something was wrong. I ask my dad, but he's no help. I'm so anguished, I even ask Wanda, and when I can tell by the expression on her face that even she feels pity for my desperate state, I nearly start sobbing in front of her, and that's when I know things have gone to hell in a handbasket.

"He claimed he got a text sometime during or after your dad was telling that story," Wanda says.

I rub the sockets of my eyes with the heel of my palms; my head's throbbing. On top of this, I think I'm getting sick. "But why wouldn't he tell me about it?"

"I hate to ask this," my dad says in a gentle voice, "but did you do anything that may have wounded his feelings? Lie to him in some way that he may have found out about?"

"No!" I say. "Like cheat on him or something?"

Dad raises both hands. "I didn't mean to imply that. Does he know about your online friend?"

"Alex?" I shake my head. "I haven't spoken to Alex online in weeks. And I never met him in person—or even found him. He blew me off because he found a girlfriend or something, I don't know. It doesn't matter. We never even really flirted. He was a sweet guy. We were just friends, honest."

"No sexting or dirty photos that could have been leaked online?" Wanda asks.

"God no," I say, and my dad practically wilts, he's so relieved. *Way to have faith, jeez.*

"Just checking," Wanda says. She's in total cop-interrogation mode. "And Porter was the hickey giver, right?"

"Yes," I snap. I don't mean to, but I can't help it.

I don't like where this conversation is going. Before long, she's going to ask me to submit to STD testing. And meanwhile, my dad, who's staring absently at his sci-fi movies, makes a choking noise, like he just realized something, but when I ask him what it is, he waves it away.

"It's nothing," he says, looking dazed and almost . . . amused. "Whatever's going on, I'm sure you'll figure it out, sweetie."

That just makes me even more frustrated, and a little angry, to be honest. None of this is really helping, so what's the point? I sneeze twice, and when Dad asks me if I'm coming down with a cold, I ignore him and go to my room. Then I plug in my phone and watch it as if the fate of the entire planet depends on one small, melodic chime emanating from its tiny speaker.

I wait until two a.m., and when that chime doesn't come, I turn on my side and stare at the wall, heart shattering, until I drift into restless sleep.

By the time my shift at the Cave rolls around the next day, I've made myself so sick with worry, I can't tell whether I want to see Porter or not. I've been trying so hard not to use Artful Dodger tactics lately, but I hesitate in the parking lot when I see his van, and take the long way around to the employee door. This must be how alcoholics feel when they fall off the wagon.

When I finally do see him, it's in the cash-out room at the exact same moment that Grace strolls in to count her drawer. My body tenses so hard at the sight of him, I'm in physical pain. Grace has taken on the role of peacemaker as she greets us, lightly complaining about how they've scheduled our lunch breaks, but neither Porter nor I say anything. It's awkward. Everyone knows it.

I can't do this. I've had no sleep. My mind is the consistency of wet sand. I'm pretty sure I'm running a fever, I've got chills, my nose won't stop running, and my eyeballs hurt. I'm not the only one; half the staff is out with some weird, mutant summer virus that Grace is calling "the lurgy." But I ignore how I feel physically, because I need to know what's going on with Porter. I have to!

"No," I tell Porter, blocking his way out of the room. "This isn't fair. I stayed up all night worrying. You need to tell me what's going on right now."

"Can we not do this right here?" Porter says, eyeing Grace.

"Where, then? I texted and called. How can I fix this if you won't tell me what I did wrong?"

"I needed to think." Now that I'm looking him directly in the eyes for the first time, I can see that he looks as bad as I feel. Dark circles band the undersides of his lower lashes, and his scruff looks unkempt. He looks exhausted. Good. "Maybe you need to do some thinking too."

"Think about what?" I ask, completely perplexed.

He glances at Grace again. "Look," he says in a lower voice, "I just . . . I'm really overwhelmed right now. I need a little space, okay?"

His words sting like a thousand hornets.

"Porter," I whisper.

The door to cash-out swings open, and Mr. Cavadini strolls inside with his clipboard. He opens his mouth to greet us, but whatever he starts to say is drowned out by my sneezing. Not polite sneezing either; I have to lunge for the box of tissues by the empty cash drawers afterward, and turn around while I clean myself up. I'm a disgusting mess.

"You've got it too?" Cavadini says, sounding horrified. When I turn around, he backs away and shakes his head. "Absolutely not. Grace, disinfect everything in cash-out that she's touched. Bailey, go home."

"Wha? I'm fine!" I say through a tissue.

"You're Typhoid Mary. Go home. Call in tomorrow and let me know how you are. We'll put you back on the schedule when you're not infectious."

No matter how I try, he won't let me argue. And when Porter and Grace are whisked away to the Hotbox, so are my chances of discovering why Porter needs "space." Miserable and feverish, I retreat home with no answers and crawl back into bed.

I will say one thing: Cavadini was probably right to boot me out of the Cave. A couple of hours later, I wake up and my entire body aches. I cannot stay warm. I call Dad at work after I take my temperature, and it's 101 F. He immediately rushes home and drives me to an urgent care facility, where I see a doctor who gives me something to reduce my fever, basically telling me what I already knew—*You've got the lurgy!*—and prescribes me a bunch of cold medicine.

The second day of my mutant illness, my dad changes the sheets on my bed, because I sweated through them all night like a beast. But at least my fever's broken. Which is good, because now I'm hacking up my lungs. He goes to work in the morning, but takes a half day, coming home at noon to feed me a lunch of soup and crackers. He also tries to lure me downstairs, but I'm content to stay in my narrow flight path of bathroom to bedroom. I have a paid online streaming account and a DVD player in my room. That's all I need to get me through this. I start watching a movie that reminds me of Alex, strangely enough, which makes me feel even worse than I already do.

Grace has checked in on me via text several times. The Cave is down to a skeleton crew, but she's managed to escape getting sick so far. I don't ask about Porter. She volunteers anyway: It's his day off, so she doesn't know if he's sick too—but would I like her to text him and ask? No, I would not. He wants space? Have the plains of Serengeti, for all I care. I'm beyond wounded now. I'm angry. At least, I think I am. It's hard to tell. I started taking cough syrup with codeine today, and it's giving me a little bit of a buzz.

Another kind of buzz lights up my phone midafternoon. I hit pause on the movie I'm watching. It's an alert from Lumière Film Fanatics. I have a new message? Maybe this syrup is making me hallucinate. But no. I click on the app, and there it is:

@alex: Hey. Mink, you there? Long time, no talk.

I stare at it for a minute, then type a reply.

@mink: I'm still here. Laid up sick in bed. Oddly enough, I was just thinking about you, so it's kind of freaking me out that you messaged me.

@alex: You were? Why? *is curious* (Sorry you're sick.)

@mink: I'm watching Key Largo. (Thanks. Me too. It's gross, trust me.)

@alex: Whoa. Bogie and Bacall Key Largo? I thought you said you couldn't stomach that? What about all the being-held-at-gunpoint?

@mink: It wasn't as bad as I thought it would be. I'm almost finished. It's so good. You were right.

@alex: Color me shocked. (I always am.) So . . . anything new happening? We haven't talked in so long. Fill me in on what's going on in the world of Mink. I've missed you.

I pause, unsure what to type. It would be weird to say *I've missed you too*, even though I have, because that feels like I'm betraying Porter. I'm so confused. Maybe he doesn't even mean it that way. Maybe he never did. Lord knows I'm not good at reading people.

@mink: The world of Mink has imploded. Do you have all day?

@alex: Funny, but I do.

I'm not sure whether it's the codeine streaming in my blood or the virus decimating my brain cells, but I settle back against my pillow and type the most straightforward message I've ever sent to Alex.

@mink: Actually, I'm sort of seeing someone—well, we kind of broke up. I think. I'm not sure. He won't talk to me. But I'm not over him. I just didn't want you to get the wrong idea. And maybe you wouldn't anyway, I don't know. But I used to think that there was something between us—you and me—or that there could be. And then this guy sort of just happened. I didn't expect it. So, anyway, I'm sounding like a complete idiot now, especially if you didn't feel that way about me. But I'm trying to turn over a new leaf and be more honest lately, so I just wanted you to know. In case you were still holding out hope for anything. I just can't. Not right now.

@alex: Wow. That's a lot to take in at once.

@mink: I know. I'm sorry.

@alex: No, I'm glad you said it. Truly. You have no idea how relieved I am to get things out in the open, actually.

@mink: Really?

@alex: Cross my heart. So . . . what's this guy like?

@mink: Honestly, he's kind of an ass. Cocky. Super opinionated. Always picking fights.

@alex: ??? And you like him why, again?

@mink: I'm trying to remember . . . Okay, he's also sweet and smart, and he makes me laugh. He's a surfer, actually. Like, stupid talented. And he geeks out about weather, which is sort of cute.

@alex: I see. But he makes you laugh?

I suddenly feel horrible. Here I am, spilling my guts about Porter, but I don't really know how Alex feels about it. About me. About this whole situation I just laid at his feet.

@mink: No one makes me laugh like you do.

@alex: That's all I ever wanted.

I laugh a little, then begin to cry.

@mink: I miss you too. I miss watching movies with you. And I'm sorry everything changed. I didn't know things were going to turn out this way. But I hope we can still be friends, because my life was better with you in it. And that's the truth.

@alex: I hope we can still be friends too. I need to go, though.

When the app tells me he's logged off, my soft crying turns into full-on sobbing. I'm not sure why, but I feel as though I've lost something important. Maybe it's because he didn't agree that absolutely, we should and will be friends—he said he hopes we can still be friends. Meaning what? He's not sure? Have I damaged not one, but two relationships?

My state of illness doesn't allow me to cry for long before my entire upper respiratory system clogs up and threatens to shut down. It's probably for the best. I force myself to calm down, try to blow my nose, and finish watching the last few minutes of *Key Largo*. At least I can count on Humphrey Bogart coming back for Lauren Bacall, though for a second there, it was touch and go.

When the credits roll, I hear noise in the stairwell, and then my dad appears in the doorway. "You— Hey . . . have you been crying?" he says in a hushed voice. "Are you okay? What's wrong?"

I wave a hand. "Nothing. It's fine."

His brow furrows for a second, but he seems to believe me. "You have a visitor, Mink. You feeling up for it?" He gives me a warning look, though how I'm supposed to interpret that look is beyond me.

I sit up straighter in my bed. Visitor? Grace is at work. "I . . . guess?"

Dad moves out of the way and motions for someone to come inside my room.

Porter.

"Hey," he says, gritting his teeth when he sees me. "Wow, you weren't faking, were you? Should I don one of those surgical masks?"

My dad chuckles. "I haven't caught it yet. But you might want to keep your distance and wash your hands on the way out."

Porter gives my dad a casual salute, and before I know it, we're alone. Just me and Porter. In my bedroom. A week ago, that would have been a fantasy. Now I'm stuffed into unflattering booty shorts and a faded T-shirt with an embarrassing, uncool band on it that I don't listen to anymore. My unwashed hair is shoved into one of those messy buns that's actually messy, not sexy messy. And I can't think straight because I'm high on cough syrup.

"So, this is your secret garden?" he says, strolling around as I stealthily try to shovel wads of used tissues off my bedcovers into a wastebasket. He stops in front of my dresser to inspect all the printouts I've taped around the mirror: vintage pin-curl instructions, retro nail-painting guides, and several close-up photos showcasing Lana Turner's hair. "Ah. I get it now."

I'm sort of wishing he didn't. I feel very exposed, as if he's peeking behind the Wizard of Oz's curtain. Why didn't I close my closet door? I hope there's nothing embarrassing in there.

He's made it to my stack of boxes. "What's all this? Going somewhere?"

"No, I just haven't unpacked everything yet."

"You've been in California for how long now?"

"I know, I know," I mumble. "I just haven't had the time."

He gives me an askance look before moving on to my shelves of DVDs. "But you had time to unpack fifty million movies? God, you are just like your dad, aren't you? Total film fanatic, and super organized. Are these alphabetical?"

"By genre, then alphabetical by title," I say weakly, feeling foolish.

He whistles. "We need you over at Casa Roth to reorganize the madhouse that is our DVD library, stat. Lana keeps forgetting to put the discs back in the cases after she watches something."

"I hate that," I say.

"I know, right? Criminal offense."

"Porter?"

"Yeah?"

"Why are you here?"

He turns around, hands in the pockets of his shorts. "I'm done with needing space. That was stupid. Just forget about it."

"Wait, what? How can I forget about it? What is 'it'? I need to know what I did."

"You didn't do anything. It was just a misunderstanding."

Still confused. "About me?" My cough-syrup-addled brain goes back to that night again, like it has a hundred times before, and all I can latch on to is . . . "You got a text from someone? You said it wasn't Davy, but were you lying? What does this have to do with me?"

He squints. "Are you drunk, or is this just how you are when you're sick?"

"Errmm," I moan, waving my hand at the bottle on my night-stand. "Codeine."

"Holy . . . You're on the purp? Glad Davy's not here, or he'd have stolen that and downed the whole thing in one gulp. Are you taking the right dose?"

I stick out my tongue and make an *ahh* sound. When both of Porter's brows slowly rise, I take that as a sign that my answer wasn't appropriate, and sigh deeply, pulling the bedspread higher over my chest. "Yes, I took the right dose," I say grumpily. "And if you're just trying to avoid answering my questions, I'd like you to leave."

He stares at me for entirely too long, like he's thinking things over, or hatching some sort of devious plan—I can't tell which. The keys that hang on the leather strap from his belt loop rock against his hip as he jangles his pocket change. Then, abruptly, he turns around and heads to my DVD shelves, runs his fingers along the cases, and plucks one out.

"What are you doing?" I ask.

"Where's your player? Here? Let's see, what do we have . . . *Key Largo*? Is that any good? Let me just put it back in the case. I don't want to pull a Lana. Is everything—"

"Porter!"

"—set, or do I have to switch the input? Where's your remote? If you've gotten your diseased crud on it, I'm not touching it. Scoot over. And don't cough on me." He's peeling off his HOT STUFF jacket and motioning to let him sit next to me in the double bed.

I'm suddenly well aware that my father is right downstairs. And wait—why do I care? I'm sick. And gross. And we're not even together.

Are we?

"Porter—"

"Scooch."

I scooch. He plops down next to me, long legs stretched out and ankles crossed on top of the covers. When he sees one of my snotty tissues next to his elbow, he makes a sour face.

I angrily toss the tissue onto the floor. "I'm not watching a movie with you until you tell me why you stormed out of my house that night."

"I'm being completely real with you when I say it was the mis-understanding of the century. And it's nothing you did wrong. I realize that now. Like I told you before, I needed some time to think about things, because it was . . . well, it doesn't matter. But"—he crosses his arms over his chest when I start to protest, like he's not budging—"let's drop the whole thing."

"What? That's—"

"Look, it's really nothing. It was stupid. I'm sorry for making you worry over nothing. Let's just forget it. Hit play, will you?"

I stare at him, flabbergasted. "No."

"No, what?"

"I can't accept that. I need to know what happened."

He leans back against the headboard and looks at me for a long time. A really long time. Now I'm uncomfortable, because he's smiling at me—this strange, slow smile that's hiding a secret. It makes me want to hide or hit him.

"Maybe I'll feel like talking after the movie starts," he says. "What's this flick about, anyway? I just picked something random."

Momentarily distracted, I glance at the menu on the screen. "*The Philadelphia Story*? You've never seen this?"

He shakes his head slowly, still smiling that funny smile. "Tell me about it."

That's weird, because it looked like he was choosing something particular on the shelf, but whatever. "It's one of my favorite movies. Katharine Hepburn is a society woman, an heiress, you see, who learns to love the right man—that's her pompous ex, Cary Grant, who she bickers with constantly—by kissing the wrong man, who's Jimmy Stewart."

"Is that so?"

"Your grandmother never watched it?" I ask.

"Don't remember this one. Do you think I'll like it? Or should I pick out something else?" He throws a leg over the side of the bed. "Because if you want, I could go ask your dad for suggestions—"

I clamp a hand around his arm. "Oh wait, it's wonderful. So funny. Like, brilliantly funny. Let's watch it."

"Hit play," he says, sinking back into my pillows. "You can fill me in on trivia as it goes."

"And then you'll tell me?" I insist.

"Hit play, Mink."

I narrow my eyes at his use of my nickname, unsure if he's

making fun of me, but I'll give him a pass. Because, hello! *The Philadelphia Story*. I could watch this a thousand times and never get weary of it. Watching with someone else who's never seen it is so much better. With Porter? I can't believe my luck. I hope he likes it.

We start the movie, and for the moment, I'm not caring that I'm sick anymore. I'm just happy that Porter's here with me, and that he's laughing warmly at the right lines. It would be perfect, really, if he wouldn't stop staring at me. He's watching my face more than the screen, and every time I look at him quizzically, he doesn't even glance away. He just smiles that same knowing smile. And that's creeping me out.

"What?" I finally whisper hotly.

"This is . . . amazing," he says.

"Oh," I say, brightening. "Just wait. The movie gets even better."

Slow smile.

I pull the covers up to my chin.

A quarter of the way through the movie, my dad comes up to remind me to take all my various cold medicines, at which point several jokes are made at my expense between the males in the room. They both think they're comedians. We'll see who's laughing when Porter gets the lurgy after lounging on my bed.

Halfway through, Porter suddenly asks, "What were your plans this summer?"

"Huh?" I glance at him out of the corner of my eyes.

"That time at work, you were telling Pangborn that you had

other plans this summer, and that I wasn't part of those plans. What were those plans?"

My heart pounds as I try to think up some plausible excuse, but the cough syrup is slowing down my thought process. "I don't remember."

His jaw tightens. "If you come clean about that, I'll tell you the reason I left your house on game night. Deal?"

Crap. No way am I confessing that I've been scoping out another guy half the summer—an anonymous guy who I've been chatting with online for months. That sounds . . . unstable. Psychotic. Porter would never understand. And it's not like Alex and I acted on any feelings. We never proclaimed our love for each other or sent heart-filled, dirty poetry.

"I have no idea what you're talking about," I tell Porter.

Even through my buzzy haze, I can sense his disappointment, but I can't make myself divulge my secrets about Alex.

"Think hard," Porter says in a quiet voice. Almost a plea. "You can tell me anything. You can trust me."

There it is again. The *T* word. My mind drifts back to our conversation in the back of the camper van. *I need to be able to trust you.*

I know he wants me to tell him. I just . . . can't.

I'm not sure when it happened, but the last thing I remember is Jimmy Stewart kissing Katharine Hepburn. The next thing I know, I'm waking up dopey several hours later.

Porter is long gone.

• • •

Two days later, Cavadini puts me back on the schedule, and I head into work. I don't see Porter in cash-out. It's just Grace and the new guard who replaced Pangborn. Porter is here today—I know, because I checked the schedule—so I search for him as we head out to the floor. That's where I spot him, handling the changing of the guard. He's letting the morning ticket takers out of the Hotbox—two stupid boys, Scott and Kenny. I step up to the back door before they can all walk away and hand Grace my cash drawer, motioning for her to go inside without me.

"You left my house without saying good-bye," I tell Porter.

"You were pretty sick. I'm kind of busy right now, so—"

"You also left without telling me about game night."

He glances at Scott and Kenny. "Maybe later," he says.

"That's what you said before."

"And my offer still stands." He leans closer and whispers, "Quid pro quo, Clarice."

Not that again. He's not *Silence of the Lambs*–ing me into confessing about Alex. No way, no how. I try another tactic. "You go first, then I'll consider telling you."

"Bailey," he says again, like it's some kind of coded warning I should understand. "You really don't want to do this here." He glances at the two boys.

It hits me like a physical blow that he's using evasion techniques against me. From the moment all of this happened on game night with the fake text message—because it was fake, wasn't it?—to the distraction of *The Philadelphia Story*, until right now, when conveniently he is surrounded by people and therefore cannot discuss the matter.

Is this what it feels like to be Artful Dodgered? Because it sucks, big-time.

Porter clears his throat. "I've, uh, got to get them to cash-out, but—"

"No," I say, cutting him off. I realize I sound unreasonable now, and I'm mildly embarrassed that I'm raising my voice in front of Tweedledee and Tweedledum—but I just can't stop myself. "I need to know what happened on game night."

"Hey. We'll talk later. Trust me, okay?"

"Oh, are we on your schedule now? If Porter deigns to dole out a crumb? I'm just supposed to wait around for you like some well-behaved puppy dog?"

His face darkens. "I never said that. I just asked you to trust me."

"Give me a reason to."

His head jerks back as if I've slapped him, and then his face turns stony. "I thought I already had."

My chest tightens, and I suddenly wish I could take it all back. I don't want to fight with him. I just want things to go back to how they were before that night, when everything changed. As he walks off with the idiots, I hear Kenny say, "Damn, Roth. You've always got hot girls chasing after you. I need to start surfing."

"Yeah, but they're always whiners, and who needs that drama?" Scott says. "Bitches are crazy."

Porter chuckles. Chuckles!

Suddenly, I'm Alice in Wonderland, falling through a rabbit hole, watching the beautiful memories from the last couple of months pass me by as I descend into madness. And walking away from me is the old Porter Roth, the stupid surfer boy that I loathed. The one who humiliated me.

I'm devastated.

I pound on the Hotbox door. Grace swings it open, her face pinched with concern. I don't have time to explain; the line is long, and she's inserted my cash drawer, readying everything for me to start.

Ugh. It's already a million degrees in here. My chest is swelling with confusion and hurt, emotions rising with each passing second.

"Two tickets." Some stoner boy with shaggy blond hair is standing outside my window with some girl, giving me an *I don't have all day* look. I stare back at him. I think I've forgotten how to use the computer. I'm beginning to go numb.

"What the hell is going on?" Grace whispers, tapping me on the arm. "Are you still sick? Are you okay?"

No, I'm not okay. I'm not okay at all. I can't get enough air though my nostrils. Part of me blames Porter for making me feel this way. But once the shock of him laughing at that sexist comment wears off, I'm still left with the sinking feeling that the root of our fight is actually my fault, and I can't figure out why.

What did I do wrong on game night? He said it was just a misunderstanding, but that feels like a cover-up. Because something upset him, badly, and he blamed me for it that night. And now

I feel so completely stupid, because I don't know what I did, and he won't tell me.

It's like I'm staring at a giant jigsaw puzzle and there's one piece missing, and I'm scrambling to find it—looking in all the sofa cushions, under the table, under the rug, checking the empty box. WHERE IS THAT PUZZLE PIECE?!

"Yo, I said two tickets," the boy at the window enunciates, like I'm stupid. Is that a surf company logo on his T-shirt? Is this . . . one of the trashy creeps who was hanging out with Davy at the posole truck? Who was being all disgusting, harassing those girls in front of my dad and Wanda? Oh, wonderful. Just freaking terrific. "Anyone home in there? I'm not standing here for my health, babe."

Camel's back, meet straw.

I'm not quite sure what happens next.

A strange heat rushes through my head—some sort of stress-induced overload, brought about through trying to determine what happened with Porter . . . heart hurting over our fight, over his reaction to Scott's sexist comment. And all of it is topped off with the rotting cherry that is this jerk standing here now.

Or maybe, just maybe, after a long summer, the Hotbox finally gets the better of me.

All I know is that something breaks inside my brain.

I switch on my microphone. "You want tickets? Here you go."

In a manic fit, I pop open the printer, rip out the folded pack of blank ticket paper, and begin feeding it through the slot—

shove, shove, shove, shove! It waterfalls from the other side like the guy just won a million Skee-Ball tickets at an arcade.

"Have all the tickets you want," I say into the microphone. "Bitches are crazy."

Creeper dude looks stunned. But not as stunned as Mr. Cavadini, whose face appears next to his. Cavadini is holding his clipboard, doing his rounds. His gaze shifts from the pile of bent-up tickets on the ground to me, and he's horrified. Customer service nightmare.

To Davy's friend, he says: "Let me take care of this, and comp your attendance today." And he gestures for someone to let the guy's party through and clean up the pile of blank tickets.

To me, he says: "What in blazes is the matter with you, young lady? Have you lost your mind?" His nose is pressed against the Hotbox's glass. His face is so red, his Cave tie looks like it might cut off circulation and strangle him.

"I'm really sorry," I whisper into the microphone, gripping it with both hands as ugly tears stream down my cheeks, "but I sort of *have* lost my mind."

"Well," Mr. Cavadini says, unmoved by my pitiful display of emotion, "you'll have plenty of time to find it in your free time, because you're fired."

"I hate to shatter your ego, but this is not the first time I've had a gun pointed at me."
—Samuel L. Jackson, *Pulp Fiction* (1994)

26

I don't make a scene. I just clean out my locker, clock out, and leave while everyone gawks at me in silence. When Porter calls my name across the parking lot, I refuse to turn around. Helmet on. Kickstand up. Keys in ignition. I'm gone. The Cavern Palace is now a "was." I no longer have a summer job.

I consider not telling my dad about getting fired for about five minutes, but I'm tired of being a coward. Besides, he'd find out sooner or later. I wonder if the Pancake Shack is hiring.

Grace comes over to my house after her shift and I tell her the whole thing, every bit of it and more. Before I know what I'm saying, I'm telling her about Greg Grumbacher and the CliffsNotes version of how I got shot. How Porter was the first person I really told, and now look—just *look!*—where that trust got me. And sure, I was talking to some guy online before I moved here, and yes, I had planned to meet him, but we don't talk anymore, and NOTHING HAPPENED, and that's none of Porter's business. It's no one's business but mine.

For a brief moment, I'm worried that I've freaked her out.

But she says very seriously, "It's a shame that I'm going to be forced to commit severe testicular trauma upon that boy."

After this, our shared appetite for vengeance quickly spirals out of control. She calls Porter a *C* word, which is apparently okay to do if you're English. She then asks if I want her to talk to him (I don't) or spread horrible rumors about him at work (I sort of do). When she starts getting creative about the rumor spreading, it just makes me sad, and I start crying again. My dad comes home from work in the middle of my sob session, and Grace gives him the lowdown. She should be a TV commentator. By the time she's finished explaining, I'm done with the tears.

My dad looks shell-shocked.

"Bet you're sorry you signed up for your teenage daughter to move in with you now, huh?" I say miserably. "Maybe this is why mom hasn't called all summer. She's probably thinking, *Good riddance.*"

He looks momentarily confused, but quickly disregards that last remark, comes up behind me, wraps his arms around my shoulders, and squeezes. "Are you kidding? I wouldn't miss any of this for one single second. And if there's one thing I know about, it's how to get over breakups. Or potential ones. Whatever this is. Get your stuff, girls. We're going out for lobster and laser tag."

Porter starts texting me the next day. Nothing substantial, just several short texts.

Text 1: *Hey.*

Text 2: *I'm so sorry about work. I feel awful.*

Text 3: *We need to talk.*

Text 4: *Please, Bailey.*

Dad advises me to ignore all of those texts and let him simmer. After all, Porter did the same thing to me. Time apart is healthy. Dad also quizzes me, asking me if I've realized why Porter walked out on game night. "You're a good detective, Mink. You can figure this out on your own."

Maybe I don't want to anymore. I've pretty much given up trying.

Besides, I have other things to think about, like looking for another job, one that doesn't mind that I've been sacked from my last place of employment. Dad offers to ask around at the CPA office. I politely decline.

When I'm looking through the classifieds in the local free paper we picked up during our million-dollar lobster feast the night before, Dad says, "What did you mean when you said your mother hasn't called all summer?"

"Just that. She hasn't called. All summer. Or texted. Or e-mailed."

A long moment drags by. "Why haven't you said anything?"

"I thought you knew. Has she called you?"

He rubs his hand over head. "Not since June. She said she'd be in touch with me later to see how we were doing, but she told me she'd mainly be communicating through you. I'm such an idiot. I should have checked in with you. I guess I was too busy being selfish about having you here with me that I let it slip. This is my fault, Bailey."

After a moment I say, "What if something's wrong?"

"I'm subscribed to her firm's newsletter. She's fine. She won a big court case last week."

"So . . ."

He sighs. "You know how long it's taking you to get over Greg Grumbacher? Well, it's taking her just as long. Because it may have hurt and scared you, but not only did it do those things to her, too, she's also living with the guilt that the whole thing is her fault. And she still hasn't forgiven herself. I'm not sure she ever will completely. But the difference between the two of you is that you're ready to try to move on, and she still isn't."

I think about this. "Is she going to be okay?"

"I don't know," he says, rubbing a gentle hand over my cheek. "But you are."

The following day, I decide I am finished letting Porter simmer. No more games. This whole thing has spun so far out of control. I am just . . . done.

At eight in the morning, I text Porter and tell him I want to meet and talk. He suggests the surf shop. He says his family is at the beach, watching Lana surf, and he is there alone opening the shop. It hurts my heart that he's not out there with them, but I don't say that, of course. Our texting is all very civil. And meeting in a public place sounds like a reasonable plan.

It takes me a little while to stoke up my courage. I cruise down Gold Avenue. Circle the boardwalk parking lots. Idle for a minute watching the fog-covered top of the Bumblebee Lifts. Speed down the alley to make sure Mr. Roth's van isn't parked out back.

Since I'm unsure where our relationship stands, I decide to park Baby in front of the shop, like a lot of the other scooters do along the boardwalk storefronts. No special privileges: I can walk through the entrance like any other Mary, Jane, or Sue.

Ignoring the compelling scent of the first churros being fried that morning, I spy movement in the shop and wait for Porter to let me inside. Surf wax wafts when the door swings open. But it's the sight of his handsome face that makes my throat tighten painfully.

"Hi," I say stoically.

"Hi," he answers gruffly.

I stand there for a second, and then he gestures for me to come inside. When I do, that big white fluffy cat I saw on the roof with Don Gato tries to sneak in the door with me. He shoos it away with his foot and says, "Scram."

He locks the door behind me before glancing at his red surf watch, changing his mind, and unlocking it again. "One minute until nine," he explains. "Time to open."

"Oh," I say. Doesn't really look like there's a line of people itching to get inside, so I guess we still have plenty of privacy. Then again, I don't know when his family's coming back. Better make this quick.

Ooaf. Why am I so nervous?

Porter looks in turns hopeful and worried and wary. He shoves his hands into his pockets and heads toward the back of the shop. I follow. When he gets to the counter, he walks around it and faces me like I'm a customer.

Okay, then.

"So . . . ," he says. "You mentioned that you were ready to talk."

Nodding, I reach inside my pocket and pull out the shark tooth. I've already removed my keys. I set it down on the counter and slide it toward him. "You gave this to me on the condition that I be more honest and open with you because you need to trust me. However, I've clearly done something that has hurt you, and must assume that I have broken your trust. Therefore, I am returning your tooth, and dissolving our . . . whatever it is we are—"

"Bailey—"

"Please let me finish. My mom's a lawyer. I know how important verbal contracts are."

"Dammit, Bailey."

The shop door opens behind me. Great. Can't people wait five stinking minutes for Mr. Zog's Sex Wax? I mean, come on.

Just when I'm ready to move aside and let Porter deal with the customer walking up behind me, Porter's expression transforms into something very close to rage. And it's at this exact moment that I recognize the pattern I'm hearing on the wooden floor. It's not the sound of someone walking: it's the sound of someone limping.

"Get the fuck out of here," Porter shouts.

I swing around, heart pounding, and see Davy heading toward me. He looks much rougher than the last time I saw him at Fast Mike's motorcycle garage, which is saying a lot. He's not only wearing a shirt, miracle of miracles, he's wearing a sand-colored trench coat, and it looks like he's still on at least one crutch, partially hidden behind the coat.

"Hello, cowgirl," he says in an emotionless, lazy voice that sounds like it got flattened by an eighteen-wheeler. He's high as hell—on what, I don't know. But his eyes are just as dead as his words, and his head's moving a little funny, bobbing and weaving.

Out of the corner of my eye, I see movement from Porter.

"Nuh-uh." Davy lifts his crutch and points it in Porter's direction.

Only, it's not a crutch. It's the shotgun from the bonfire.

I freeze. So does Porter; he was in the middle of bounding over the counter.

"Saw you riding around in the parking lot earlier," Davy says to me. "Thought maybe you were coming over to apologize. But you drove right past me."

Shit! How could I have not noticed Davy's big yellow truck?

"Put the gun down, Davy," Porter says in a casual voice that sounds a little forced. "Come on, man. That's insane. Where did you even get that thing? If someone saw you walking around with that, you could end up in jail. Don't be stupid."

"Who's going to see me?"

"Anyone who walks in here," Porter says. "Dude, we're open. My folks are on their way back from the beach. They just called. They'll be here in two minutes. And you know Mr. Kramer comes in here every morning. He'll call the cops, man."

Davy thinks about this a second and waves the gun toward me.

Breathe, I tell myself.

"Cowgirl here can go lock the door. I want a private conversation, just the three of us. I've got a beef with the two of you. An apology is owed, and maybe a little cash out of the register while you're at it. Payback for pain and misery suffered. What you did to my knee."

I don't move.

"My parents are just down the street," Porter repeats, this time sounding angry.

Davy shrugs. "Guess you better hurry with the register, then. Go lock the door, cowgirl."

I flick a glance at Porter. He's breathing heavy. I can't read his face all that well, but what I do know is that he's absolutely miserable and conflicted. Funny thing is, for the first time in forever, I'm not. I'm scared and worried, yes. And I hate the sight of that goddamn gun with an unholy passion I can't measure.

But I am not afraid of Davy.

I am furious.

I just don't know what to do about him.

Eyes guarded, I plod to the front door and lock it. The windows are enormous; I can see his reflection in the glass, so I watch him the entire way there. Watch him watching Porter, because that's where he's pointing the shotgun now. And why wouldn't he? Porter's the one who kicked his ass. Porter's the one who nearly jumped the counter. Porter's an athlete, nothing but muscle. Even a rational, sober person would consider Porter the bigger threat.

Davy's not sober.

I take my time strolling back to them, and I think about my dad's warnings about oversteering, and about how I exploded in the Hotbox—twice. I think about all my Artful Dodger skills and how they're partly inherited from my CPA dad, and his love of details and numbers, and partly inherited from my attorney mom, and her love of finding loopholes. I think about how my dad said I'm going to be okay because I'm willing to try to get better.

But mainly I think about that day last month when those two punks tried to steal the Maltese falcon from the Cave. They underestimated me too.

Davy gives me a brief look, enough to see that I'm approaching but giving him a wide berth, head down. "Locked up tight?"

"Yep," I say.

"All right," he says, pointing the shotgun at Porter. "Register. Empty it."

Lowest of lows. Robbing your best friend's family. I know Porter's thinking it, but he says nothing. His jaw is tight as he presses a few buttons on the computer screen. "Haven't started it up yet," he explains. "Can't open the drawer until the program's running. Hold on a sec."

Bullshit. He must have put the drawer in himself, so the computer's on. He probably has a key to the drawer. But Davy's too stoned to realize this, so he waits. And while he does, Porter's eyes dart toward mine. And in that beautiful, singular moment, I know we're both linked up.

Trust is a golden gift, and this time, I'm not wasting it.

I shift my focus to Davy. The counter is in front of him, and behind him is a rack with some short, squat bodyboards on it—a third the size of a surfboard, but "way lamer," as Porter once joked.

I wait. *Come on, Porter. Give me an opening.*

As if he's read my mind, he suddenly says, "Oh, lookie here. The computer is finally waking up, Davy."

Davy's head turns toward Porter.

I step back, slip around, and slide one of the bodyboards off the stand. As I do, it makes a sound. *Crap!* It's also a lot lighter than I hoped. *Oh, well.* Too late now, because Davy's turning around, cognizant that I'm closer than he expected. I don't have a choice.

Right as his gaze connects with mine, I grip the board in both hands, rear back, and smack him in the side of the face.

He cries out as his head whips sideways. His step falters, and he stumbles.

The shotgun swings around wildly and clips me in the shoulder. I grab it and try to wrestle it out of his hand. It suddenly breaks free, and I fly backward with the gun—but that's because Porter has hurdled over the counter.

Porter slams Davy to the floor as my back hits the rack of

bodyboards, knocking them over. I scramble to stay on my feet and hold on to the shotgun, but fail.

I fall on my face.

"Porter!" I'm swimming in a sea of foam bodyboards. The boys are struggling on the floor, and all I can see is Porter's arm pounding like a piston and Davy's trench coat flapping and tangling around his legs.

And then—

A loud whimper.

Heart knocking against my rib cage, I shove the bodyboards aside and jump to my feet.

Porter is lying on the floor.

Davy is below him, facedown. One cheek is turned against the wood. One eye blinking away tears.

"I'm sorry," Davy says hoarsely.

"Me too," Porter says, pinning Davy's arms to the floor. "I tried, man. Someone else is going to have to save you now."

Porter looks up at me and nods. I set the gun on the floor and kick it out of the way. Then I dig my phone out of my pocket and dial 911.

"Uh, yeah," I say into the phone, out of breath, swallowing hard. "I'm at Penny Boards Surf Shop on the boardwalk. There's been an attempted armed robbery. We're okay. But you need to send someone to come arrest the guy. And you also need to call Sergeant Wanda Mendoza immediately and tell her to come to the scene right now."

27

Turns out, Davy's shotgun was stolen. He also had a hella bunch of heroin and other narcotics in his coat. Wanda says since he's a month from turning eighteen and he's been arrested before, he might be tried as an adult and serve some time in prison. Right now, he's being detoxed in a jail cell. Wanda says his attorney will try to persuade the judge to put him a state-run rehab facility for a couple of weeks while he awaits trial. No guarantee that will happen, though.

I get all this information the day after the events in the surf shop, so I relay it by text to Porter and let him know. We haven't really had any time to talk, what with all the chaos. His family showed up a few minutes after the cops and were understandably freaked. Mr. Roth was so angry at Davy, he had to be restrained until Mrs. Roth could talk him down. Wanda called my dad, who immediately left work and rushed over to the surf shop to make sure I was okay. It was a whole fiasco.

By the time we'd given statements and everyone cleared out, Porter had to go to work at the Cave, so I followed my dad home. It wasn't until he was ordering us lunch that I realized Porter had, at some point when I wasn't paying attention, slipped the shark tooth back into my pocket. I got a text from him a few minutes later.

All it said was: *We're not done talking.*

The next day after dinner, out of the blue, my dad asks to see my old map of the boardwalk. I'd almost thrown it away in a fit when Alex blew me off weeks ago. I have to dig it out from my desk drawer in my bedroom. Dad spreads it out on the patio table near our redwood tree and studies it, nodding slowly.

"What?" I say.

Dad sits back in his chair and smiles at me. "You know, you're tenacious and stubborn. You got that from your mom. It's what makes her a great lawyer. I love tenacious women. That's what attracted me to Wanda. It's what makes her a good cop."

I give him the side eye. *Where's he going with this?*

"However, this tenacity thing also has its downside, because it's all forward movement with blinders on. Like a horse, you know?" He holds his hands up on either side of his eyes. "You plow ahead, and you make a lot of progress that other people wouldn't make, but you can't see what's happening on either side of the road. You have blind spots. You ignore things that are right next to you. Your mom did that all the time."

"Is that why you got divorced?"

He thinks about this for a long moment. "It was one reason.

But this isn't about your mom and me. I'm talking about you. And your blind spots. Don't be too tenacious. Sometimes you've got to stop and look around."

"Why don't you ever just come out and tell me what you're trying to say, Master Yoda?"

"Because I'm trying to raise you to think for yourself, young Jedi. I can offer advice, but you've got to do the work. The whole goal of parenting is for you to become an independent young woman and come up with your own answers. Not for me to provide them for you."

"It sounds like you read that in a parenting book."

He holds back a smile. "Maybe I did."

"What a dork," I tease. "Okay, what's your advice, then? Lay it on me."

"Have you told Porter that you were talking to Alex before you moved out here?"

"Um, no."

"Maybe you should. People can sense when you're holding things back from them. I knew your mom was cheating on me with Nate for months before she told me. I had no proof, but I could sense something was wrong."

I'm so floored by this, I don't know what to say. Dad has never talked much about Nate—or that he knew Mom was cheating with Nate. It makes me uncomfortable. What's weird is that he's so blasé. But it's sort of weirder that we can talk about this together now. And wait just one stinking second—

"I wasn't cheating on Porter with Alex," I tell him. "Or cheating on Alex with Porter."

"What you actually did or didn't do doesn't matter," Dad says. "It's the secrecy that eats away at you. Just tell Porter. And maybe be honest with Alex while you're at it. You'll feel better, I promise."

"I don't know about that," I mutter.

"Like I said, it's not my job to do the work for you." He folds up the map in neat squares. "But my advice, dearest daughter, is that you settle up your boy problems in order, one at a time."

It takes me an entire day to think about everything Dad said, but I think I finally see the logic. Alex was a big part of my daily life for a long time. And, sure, he blew me off. But I should have told him I'd moved across the country. Maybe if I tell him now, he won't even care anymore, especially now that I've broken the ice about Porter in that last heart-to-heart messaging we had. I guess I won't know until I try.

@mink: Hey. Me again. Are you still out there?

His reply comes two hours later:

@alex: I'm here. What's up?

@mink: Since we were being all super honest in our last talk, I thought I'd do some more bean spilling. This one is a little bigger. Are you ready?

@alex: Should I be sitting? *is afraid*

@mink: Probably.

@alex: Sitting.

@mink: Okay, so here's the deal. I'm in town, living with my dad, and have been here for a while. Sorry I didn't say anything. Long story, but I was worried it might be weird, and I have a tendency to avoid confrontation. But better late than never? I was wondering if you wanted to get together and have lunch. Anyways . . . this is getting awkward, so I'll shut up. I just wanted you to know that I'm sorry I never said anything about being here, and I thought maybe I could apologize in person, since we're both in the same town and used to be friends. (And hopefully still are?) What do you say?

I wait and wait and wait for his reply. This is a mistake. I should probably delete my message. If he hasn't read it yet, I might still be able to . . .

@alex: What about your boyfriend?

@mink: This would be a nonromantic lunch. I'm sorry, nothing's changed since our last conversation. I'm still not over him.

@alex: Why don't we go with our original plan? Meet me Sunday night on the beach under the California flag, half an hour before the film festival's showing of North by Northwest.

Oh, crap. I wasn't prepared for that! I tear my room apart searching for the film festival guide that Patrick gave me and look up the schedule for the free films they're showing on the beach. *North by Northwest* doesn't start until nine p.m. It will be dark by then. Should I meet a strange boy after dark? That doesn't seem advisable. Then again, it's a public place, and when I browse the film guide, there are photos from last year; all the concessions areas appear well lit. Surely the flag is somewhere around there.

Should I do this? The Artful Dodger definitely would not. But am I that person anymore?

@mink: Okay. I'll meet you there.

That's one boy problem taken care of. Now for the next. This one seems harder. I shoot off a quick text.

Me: *Hey, you busy? I was hoping we could meet somewhere and talk. I'm willing to do the quid pro quo thing now. You win.*

Porter: *Actually, I'm sort of booked until after Sunday. How about after that?*

Me: *Okay, it's a deal. Will text you then.*

Actually, I'm relieved. *North by Northwest* is on Sunday, so that gives me time to meet Alex and mend things with him before I talk to Porter. Who knew two boys could be so much trouble?

•   •   •

In *North by Northwest*, Cary Grant plays an advertising executive who's mistaken for a CIA agent named Kaplan. The thing is, Kaplan doesn't really exist. So throughout the film, Cary Grant is constantly being forced to pretend he's someone he's not—a fake of a fake. Nothing is what it seems, which is what makes the story so fun to watch. Alex and I have discussed the film's merits online, but it's strange to think about those conversations now. I definitely wish I could be seeing it under happier circumstances.

By the time Sunday night rolls around, I'm strangely calm. Maybe it's because this has been a long time coming, me meeting Alex. Or maybe it's because I don't feel the same way about him as I once did, now that Porter's in my life. I think back to the beginning of the summer, when I was so worried and nervous about everything Alex could or could not be—tall or short, bald or hairy, shy or chatty—and none of those things matter anymore.

He is who he is.

I am who I am.

Exactly who those people are couldn't really be identified in an online profile or captured correctly in all our written communication, no matter how honest we tried to be. We were only showing one side of ourselves, a side that was carefully trimmed and curated. He didn't see all my hang-ups and screwy problems, or how long it takes me to pluck my eyebrows every night. He doesn't know I tried to pick up a gay whale-tour host because I thought it might be him. Or that I can't tell the difference between a male and a female cat . . . Or about all the dirty GIFs I've laughed at with Grace, or the number of churros I can put away in one sitting before it starts to get embarrassing for the churro cart vendor, because he knows I'm really not buying them for "a friend." (Five.)

God only knows what I haven't seen of him.

So, you know, whatever. If he's nice, great. If not, no big deal. In my head, I'm holding my head high and wearing a Grace-inspired T-shirt that says I'M JUST HERE FOR THE CLOSURE in big, bedazzled letters.

I arrive at the beach a little more than half an hour before the film starts. They're showing it, ironically enough, near one of the first places I remember when I came into town: the surfers' cross-walk. Only, the whole area is transformed tonight, with one of those huge rotating double spotlights that's pointed toward the sky, announcing to the world, *Hey, movie over here!* They've also lit up the palm trees along Gold Avenue and hung film festival banners in the parking lot across the street, which is jammed with cars. I manage to squeeze Baby into a space alongside another scooter before following a line of people who are swinging picnic baskets and coolers, heading toward the giant white screen set up in the sand.

Alex was right all those months ago when he first told me about this: It looks really fun. The sun's setting over the water. Families and couples are chilling on blankets, and closer to the road, a row of tents and food trucks are selling burgers and fish tacos and film festival merchandise. I head for those, looking for flagpoles. All the palms are lit up, so I figure a flagpole must be spotlighted too, right? But when I've walked the entire row of vendors, I can't find it. No flags near the movie screen either. It's a pretty big screen, so I check around back, just to make sure. Nope. Nada.

This is weird. I mean, Alex lives here, so he knows the place. He wouldn't just tell me to meet him somewhere so specific if it wasn't there. I check my film messages to make sure there isn't anything new from him, and when I don't see anything I head back the way I came, all the way back down to the end of the concession row to the back of the seating area. That's when I spot it.

The flagpole is all the way up a set of steps, on a wide natural stone platform—a lookout over the ocean, where the surfer's crosswalk ends.

Right in front of the memorial statue of Pennywise Roth.

I sigh, and then snort at myself, because really, no matter what I do, I can't escape him. And if Alex is the nice guy I'm hoping he is, we can both have a laugh about it later.

Weaving around blankets, I make my way to the lookout and climb the stone steps. I'm getting a little nervous now. Not much, but this is surreal. The lookout is fairly spacious. It's banded in a wood railing with some built-in benches around the ocean side, where one older couple is gazing out at the sunset. Not him, for sure. I gaze up at the Pennywise statue. I've seen the photo of this online, of course, and driven past it, but it's weird to see it up close in person. Someone's put a Hawaiian lei around his neck; I wonder if it was Mrs. Roth.

Someone's sitting on a bench behind the statue. I blow out a long breath, straighten my shoulders, and lumber around ol' Pennywise. Time to face the music.

"Hello, Mink."

My brain sees who's in front of me, hears the words, but doesn't believe. It recalculates and recalculates, over and over, but I'm still stuck. And then it all comes rolling back to me, out of order.

The video store.

Breakfast at Tiffany's.

Him caring about the Maltese falcon being stolen.

Roman Holiday.

White cat at the surf shop.

Churro cart.

Is it wrong to hate someone who used to be your best friend?

Cheating girlfriend.

The Big Lebowski.

Watching movies at work.

My coworker, the human blunt.

The Philadelphia Story.

Mr. Roth . . . Xander Roth.

Alexander.

Alex.

My knees buckle. I'm falling. Porter leaps up from the bench and grabs me around the waist before I hit the ground. I kick at the stone below my feet, like I'm swimming in place, trying to get traction. Trying to get control of my legs. I finally manage it.

When I do, I go a little crazy. It's that stupid coconut scent of his. I shove him away from me, beat him—hard—landing blows on his arms until he lets me go in order to shield his face. And then I just fall to pieces.

I sob.

And sob.

I curl up into a ball on the bench and sob some more.

I don't even know why I'm crying so hard. I just feel so stupid. And shocked. And overwhelmed. Sort of betrayed, too, but that's ridiculous, because how could that be? Then I stop crying and gasp a little, because I realize that's exactly how Porter must have felt when he found out.

He sits down on the bench and lifts my head onto his lap, sighing heavily. "Where are you at in the screwed-up-ness of it all? Because there are all kinds of layers."

"We basically cheated on each other with each other," I say.

"Yeah," he says. "That's pretty messed up. When I told my mom, she said we pulled a reverse 'Piña Colada,' which is some cheesy 1970s song about this couple who write personal ads looking for hookups, and end up meeting each other."

"Oh, God," I groan. "You told your mom?"

"Hey, this is some crazy shit. I had to tell someone," he argues. "But look at it this way. We ended up liking the real us better than the online us. That's something, right?"

"I guess."

I think about it some more. *Ugh.* My dad knew. He was trying to tell me with all that talk about blinders and horses. Another wave of YOU ARE THE WORLD'S BIGGEST IDIOT hits me, and this time, I let the wave wash over me, not fighting it. The older couple that was hanging around on the lookout has left—guess a bawling teenage girl was ruining their peaceful sunset view—so we have the area to ourselves for the moment, and for that, I'm grateful. Below the lookout, hundreds of people throng the beach, but it's far enough away that I don't mind.

"You didn't know until game night at my house, right?" I ask.

"No."

That makes me feel somewhat better, I suppose. At least we were both stupid about this until he heard my nickname. *Oh, God.* He watched *The Philadelphia Story* with me on purpose. He knew then, and he didn't tell me. My humiliation cannot be measured. "Why?" I ask in a small voice. "Why didn't you tell me?"

"I was bewildered. I didn't know what to do. I couldn't believe you'd been living out here the entire time. Couldn't believe you . . . were *her*—Mink. At first, I thought you'd been screwing with me, but the more I thought about it, I knew that didn't fit. I just freaked for a while. And then . . . I guess I wanted to hold on to it. And I wanted you to discover it on your own. I thought you would. If I dropped enough hints, I thought you would, Bailey—I swear. But then I started thinking about why you didn't tell me—Alex—you moved out here, and how it felt as though you'd been lying to me . . . and I wanted you to come clean."

"Quid pro quo." I close my eyes, fully aware of the irony now.

"I didn't mean for things to go sideways," he insists. "When you got fired . . . Grace told me what happened in the Hotbox. For the record, she also made some threats to my manhood that gave me a few nightmares."

I groan. "I don't blame you for what I did in the Hotbox. I was upset at the time, but I've moved past it."

"I just want you to know that what Scott and Kenny were saying that day . . . I didn't think it was funny. I'm not even sure why I laughed. I think it was just a nervous reaction. I felt awful afterward. I tried to text you and tell you, but you weren't speaking to me. And then Davy happened . . ."

I sigh shakily, completely overwhelmed. "God, what a mess."

After a second, he says, "You know, what I haven't been able to figure out is why you lied about where you lived before you moved out here."

"I didn't. My mom and her husband moved from New Jersey to DC a few months before. I just never told Alex. You. Alex You. Ugh. That's not a random screenname, is it?"

"Alex is my middle name."

"Alexander. Like your father?"

"Yeah. It was my grandfather's, too." He pushes a curled lock of hair behind my ear. "You do realize this whole mishegas could have been avoided if Mink You would have just told me from the beginning that you were moving out here . . . right?"

I use his hand to cover my face. And then I uncover it and sit up, facing him, wiping away tears. "You know what? Maybe not.

Let's say I'd arranged to meet up with Alex You at the Pancake Shack when I first moved here, and that I hadn't gotten that job at the Cave. Would we have hit it off? I don't know. You don't know that either. Maybe it was just the situation we were in at the Cave."

Porter shakes his head and winds his fingers through mine. "Nope. I don't believe that, and I don't think you do either. Two people who lived in two different places and found each other, not once but twice? You could stick one of us in Haiti and the other in a rocket headed to the moon and we'd still eventually be doing this right now."

I sniffle. "You really think so?"

"You know how I said you were tricky like the fog, and that I was afraid of you running back to your mom at the end of the summer? I'm not afraid anymore."

"You're not?"

He looks toward the ocean, dark purple with the last rays of light. "My mom says we're all connected—people and plants and animals. We all know one another on the inside. It's what's on the outside that distracts. Our clothes, our words, our actions. Shark attacks. Gunshots. We spend our lives trying to find other people. Sometimes we get confused and turned around by the distractions." He smiles at me. "But we didn't."

I smile back, eyes shining with happy tears. "No, we didn't."

"I love you, Bailey 'Mink' Rydell."

I choke out a single sobbed laugh. "I love you too, Porter 'Alex' Roth."

We reach for each other and meet in the middle, half kissing, half murmuring how much we've missed each other. It's sloppy and wonderful, and I've never been hugged so tightly. I kiss him all over his neck beneath his wild curls, and he cups my head in both hands and kisses me all over my face, then wipes away my cried-out makeup drips with the edge of his T-shirt.

Applause and cheers startle both of us. I'd nearly forgotten all about the movie. Porter pulls me up with him, and we lean over the railing together to peer into the dark. Flickering light fills the beach, and the old MGM logo appears with the roaring lion. The music starts. The opening titles dart over the screen. CARY GRANT. EVA MARIE SAINT. Chills zip up and down my back.

And then I realize: I get to share all of this with Porter. All of me. All of us.

I glance up at him, and he's emotional too.

"Hi," he says, forehead pressed to mine.

"Hi."

"Should we head down to the beach?" he asks, slinging an arm over my shoulder.

"I seem to remember hating the beach at some point or another."

"That's because you'd never been to a real one. East Coast beaches are trash beaches."

I laugh, my heart singing with joy. "Oh yeah, that's right. Show me a real beach, why don't you, surfer boy. Let's go watch a movie."

"I wanted it to be you. I wanted it to be you so badly."
—Meg Ryan, *You've Got Mail* (1998)

28

I blow out two quick breaths and stash my purse in the borrowed locker. Behind me, through a narrow passageway onto the main floor, I can see the crowds in the stands and the bright lights of the auditorium. Almost time to start. I twist my head to either side and crack my neck before checking my phone one more time.

Some people thrive in the spotlight; others prefer to work behind the scenes. You can't make a movie with nothing but actors. You need writers and makeup artists, costume designers and talent agents. All of them are equally important.

I'm not a spotlight kind of girl, and I've made my peace with that.

These days, I've pretty much given up my Artful Dodger leanings. Mostly. I relapsed a little when school started a couple of months ago in the fall. But that doesn't mean I'm ready to run for senior class president like Grace. It *does* mean that ever since our girl talk on the beach after I let her down, I've tried to make good on being a dependable friend, so I helped her with all her campaigning. She won, but that was no surprise. Everyone loves Grace. I just love her a little more.

After school, I work at Video Ray-Gun, which is much less pressure than the Hotbox—not to mention less sweaty. Plus, I get first pick of the used DVDs that come through. And since Porter's shifts at the Cave are only on the weekends now that school's in session, I get to see him on my work breaks, because the surf shop is only a five-minute walk down the boardwalk from the video store. Win-win.

And I have to see him whenever I get the chance, because next week, he's flying out to Hawaii with his mom. They're meeting up with Mr. Roth to watch Lana compete in Oahu for some special surfing competition. And to talk to someone in the World League about Porter surfing in a qualifying event in January in Southern California. He's already registered, and he's been practicing every chance he gets. There's crazy buzz online in the surfing community that the Roth siblings could be the next big thing; a reporter from Australia called the surf shop last week and interviewed his dad for a magazine.

It's all exciting, and I'm thrilled to pieces that Porter finally wants to surf. He was born to do it. At the same time, I'm glad he's not giving up on the idea of going to college. He says he can do both. I don't think he realized that before, but I can understand why. His family's been through a lot. It's hard to think about next week when you're not sure if you'll even make it through today.

But I don't worry about him now. And I don't worry about him going pro like Lana, and whether he'll be traveling all over the world for a week here and there, Australia and France, South Africa and Hawaii. Maybe sometimes I'll get to fly out with him. Maybe not. But it doesn't matter. Because he's right. Surfing the Pipeline or rocket to the moon, we'll find each other.

"Five minutes," my captain calls out to the team.

Several of the girls around me rush to finish last-minute adjustments to their makeup and pull up their black tights, kneepads, and shiny gold shorts. One girl is running late and just getting her skates on. If the team captain, LuAnn Wong, finds out, she'll have to sit out the first period. LuAnn doesn't take any crap.

I joined the local Roller Derby team, the Coronado Cavegirls, two months ago. We're part of a regional Rollergirls league, so we compete against three other teams in the area, including one from Monterey. That works out well for me, because I also volunteer every other Saturday at the Pacific Grove Natural History Museum. It's mainly cataloging shells in the stockroom, and I don't get paid or anything, but I love it.

At first, I was a little scared to join the derby. It seemed too "spotlight" for me, and most of the girls are a couple of years older. One skater is even in her late thirties. But Grace encouraged me, the uniforms were totally cool, and the more I thought about it, the more I liked the idea. When I'm out there skating, it's not about me, it's about the team. We work together as a group. I'm a jammer, which means I get to wear the helmet with the star on it, and my goal is to skate past the opposing team's blockers as fast as I can. My Artful Dodger skills are put to better use on the derby track than in my daily life.

Plus, it helps me blow off steam. When I was working the Hotbox, I overheated, figuratively and literally. Skating gives me an outlet for my frustrations. I don't have to jump punk kids who steal falcons from museums, throw tickets at customers, or wrestle shotguns away from junkies. I can knock around girls bigger than me and it's not only legal, it's encouraged.

I peek out through the passage and scan the stands for familiar faces, spotting them almost immediately. My dad is sitting with Wanda; they never miss my Roller Derby bouts. In front of them are Grace and Taran—who returned from India at the end of the summer, thankfully, so I didn't have to fly over there and kick his ass—and Patrick with his boyfriend, and then Mrs. Roth and Porter. He's wearing his HOT STUFF devil jacket, which makes me smile. (Note to self: Tear that jacket off later in the back of his van.)

"Three minutes, ladies," LuAnn calls out behind me. "Get ready to line up."

As my teammates zip around me, I whip out my phone and ask one of the girls to take a photo of me smiling over my shoulder with the crowd in the background. My skate name is printed in bold letters on the back of my jersey: MINK.

I text the photo, with the time, date, and precise geolocation, to my mother. I don't wait for a reply; I know it won't come. But

I haven't given up hope that one day she'll be ready to forgive herself. To forgive me for leaving her and moving out here. And when she is ready? She can come and visit me and Dad. Maybe we'll even take her out for posole, who knows.

After the last call, I stash my phone in the locker and line up with my teammates. Everyone's buzzing. It's always like this before we go out. It's such a rush. I shake out my arms and adjust the strap on my helmet. Everything's in place. I can hear the announcer riling up the crowd. They're cheering. It's almost time to go.

"Are you ready, girls?" LuAnn asks, skating down the line, making eye contact with each one of us.

She touches my shoulder, reminding me of how Pangborn used to, and I give her a little nod.

I'm so ready.

I am Mink. Hear me roar.

ACKNOWLEDGMENTS

Megaton thank-yous to:

10. My extraordinary agent, Laura Bradford, for the extremes she endured to deliver good news, which put the US Postal Service's "rain nor heat nor gloom of night" motto to shame.

9. My badass editor, Nicole Ellul, for being the best I've ever had, hands down.

8. My awesome US team at Simon Pulse—Mara Anastas, Liesa Abrams, Tara Grieco, Carolyn Swerdloff, Regina Flath, and all the names and faces I don't know yet—for championing this book and believing in its potential.

7. My amazing UK team at Simon & Schuster UK—Rachel Mann, Becky Peacock, Liz Binks, and everyone else who works tirelessly behind the scenes—for your infectious enthusiasm.

6. My foreign editors, Barbara König and Leonel Teti, for continuing to have faith in my books, and to Christina at LOVE-BOOKS for taking a chance on me.

5. My beta readers, Veronica Buck and Stacey Kalani, for their honesty and kindness.

4. My foreign rights agent, Taryn Fagerness, for tolerating my dumb questions.

3. My personal support team—Karen and Ron and Gregg and Heidi and Hank and Patsy and Don and Gina and Shane and Seph—for all their endless cheerleading. I don't deserve any of you.

2. My husband, for continuing to endure my Writing Madness. I don't deserve you most of all. Love you.

1. And to my readers, thank you for giving me a reason to believe in myself. I hope I can return the favor through the words in this book, even in a small way.

Starry
Eyes

*To my brother and sister-in-law, who married
after getting lost in the wilderness on an overnight camping trip.
Nothing like a little fear of dying to spark a great romance.*

Part 1

I

Spontaneity is overrated. Movies and television shows would like us to believe that life is better for partygoers who dare to jump into pools with their clothes on. But behind the scenes, it's all carefully scripted. The water is the right temperature. Lighting and angles are carefully considered. Dialogue is memorized. And that's why it looks so appealing—because someone carefully planned it all. Once you realize this, life gets a whole lot simpler. Mine did.

I am a hard-core planner, and I don't care who knows it.

I believe in schedules, routines, *washi*-tape-covered calendars, bulleted lists in graph-paper journals, and best-laid plans. The kind of plans that don't go awry, because they're made with careful consideration of all possibilities and outcomes. No winging it, no playing things by ear. That's how disasters happen.

But not for me. I make blueprints for my life and stick to them. Take, for instance, summer break. School starts back in three weeks, and before I turn eighteen and embark on my senior year, this is my blueprint for the rest of the summer:

Plan one: Two mornings each week, work at my parents' business, Everhart Wellness Clinic. I fill in at the front desk for their normal receptionist, who's taking a summer course at UC Cal in Berkeley. My mom's an acupuncturist and my father is a massage therapist, and they own the clinic together. This means that instead of flipping burgers and being yelled at by random strangers outside a drive-through window, I get to work in a Zen-like reception area, where I can keep everything perfectly organized and know exactly which clients are scheduled to walk through the door. No surprises, no drama. Predictable, just the way I like it.

Plan two: Take photos of the upcoming Perseid meteor shower with my astronomy club. Astronomy is my holy grail. Stars, planets, moons, and all things space. Future NASA astrophysicist, right here.

Plan three: Avoid any and all contact with our neighbors, the Mackenzie family.

These three things all seemed perfectly possible until five minutes ago. Now my summer plans are standing on shaky ground, because my mom is trying to talk me into going camping.

Camping. Me.

Look, I know nothing about the Great Outdoors. I'm not even sure I like being outside. Seems to me, society has progressed far enough that we should be able to avoid things like fresh air and sunlight. If I want to see wild animals, I'll watch a documentary on TV.

Mom knows this. But right now she's trying *really* hard to sell me on some sort of Henry David Thoreau nature-is-good idealism while I'm sitting behind our wellness clinic's front desk. And sure, she's always preaching about the benefits of natural health and vegetarianism, but now she's waxing poetic about the majestic beauty of the great state of California, and what a "singular opportunity" it would be for me to experience the wilderness before school starts.

"Be honest. Can you really picture me camping?" I ask her, tucking dark corkscrew curls behind my ears.

"Not camping, Zorie," she says. "Mrs. Reid is inviting you to go *glamping.*" Dressed in gray tunic scrubs embroidered with the clinic's logo, she leans across the front desk and talks in an excited, hushed voice about the wealthy client who's currently relaxing on an acupuncture table in the back rooms, enjoying the dated yet healing sounds of Enya, patron saint of alternative health clinics around the world.

"Glamping," I repeat, skeptical.

"Mrs. Reid says they have reservations for these luxury tents in the High Sierras, somewhere between Yosemite and King's Forest National Park," Mom explains. "Glamorous camping. Get it? Glamping."

"You keep saying that, but I still don't know what it means," I tell her. "How can a tent be luxurious? Aren't you sleeping on rocks?"

Mom leans closer to explain. "Mrs. Reid and her husband got a last-minute invitation to a colleague's chalet in Switzerland, so they have to cancel their camping trip. They have a reservation for a fancy tent. This glamping compound—"

"This isn't some weird hippie cult, is it?"

Mom groans dramatically. "Listen. They have a chef who prepares gourmet meals, an outdoor fire pit, hot showers—the works."

"Hot showers," I say with no small amount of sarcasm. "Thrill me, baby."

She ignores this. "The point is, you aren't actually roughing it, but you feel like it. The compound is so popular that they do a lottery for the tents a year in advance. Everything's already paid for, meals and lodging. Mrs. Reid said it would be shame to let it go to waste, which is why they are letting Reagan take some of her friends there for the week—a last-hurrah trip with the girls before senior year starts."

Mrs. Reid is the mother of Reagan Reid, star athlete, queen bee of my class, and my kind of, sort of friend. Actually, Reagan and I used to be good friends when we were younger. Then her parents came into money, and she started hanging out with other people. Plus, she was training constantly for the Olympics. Before I knew it, we just . . . grew apart.

Until last fall, when we started talking again during lunchtime at school.

"Would be good for you to spend some time outside," Mom says, fiddling with her dark hair as she continues to persuade me to go on this crazy camping trip.

"The Perseid meteor shower is happening next week," I remind her.

She knows I am a strict planner. Unexpected twists and surprises throw me off my game, and everything about this camping—sorry, *glamping*—trip is making me very, *very* anxious.

Mom makes a thoughtful noise. "You could bring your telescope to the glamping compound. Stars at night, hiking trails in the day."

Hiking sounds like something Reagan could be into. She has rock-hard thighs and washboard abs. I practically get winded walking two blocks to the coffee shop, a fact of which I'd like to remind Mom, but she switches gears and plays the guilt card.

"Mrs. Reid says Reagan's been having a really tough time this summer," she says. "She's worried about her. I think she's hoping this trip will help cheer her up after what happened at the trials in June."

Reagan fell (I'm talking *splat*, face-plant) and didn't place in the Olympic track trials. It was her big shot for moving forward. She basically has no chance at the next summer Olympics and will have to wait four more years. Her family was heartbroken. Even so, it surprises me to hear that her mother is worried about her.

Another thought crosses my mind. "Did Mrs. Reid ask me to go on this trip, or did you hustle her into inviting me?"

A sheepish smile lifts my mom's lips. "A little from column A, little from column B."

I quietly drop my head against the front desk.

"Come on," she says, shaking my shoulder slowly until I lift my head again. "She was surprised Reagan hadn't asked you already, so clearly they've discussed you coming along. And maybe you and Reagan both need this. She's struggling to get her mojo back. And you're always saying you feel like an outsider in her pack of friends, so here's your chance to spend some time with them out of school. You should be falling down at my feet," Mom teases. "How about a little, *Thank you, coolest mom ever, for schmoozing me into the event of the summer. You're my hero, Joy Everhart?*" She clasps her hands to her heart dramatically.

"You're so weird," I mumble, pretending to be apathetic.

She grins. "Aren't you lucky I am?"

Actually, yes. I know that she genuinely wants me to be happy and would do just about anything for me. Joy is actually my step-mom. My birth mother died unexpectedly of an aneurysm when I was eight, back when we lived across the Bay in San Francisco. Then my dad suddenly decided he wanted to be a massage thera-pist and spent all the life insurance money on getting licensed. He's impulsive like that. Anyway, he met Joy at an alternative medicine convention. They got hitched a few months later, and we all moved here to Melita Hills, where they rented out space for this clinic and an apartment next door.

Sure, at the ripe age of thirty-eight, Joy is several years younger than my father, and because she's Korean-American, I've had to deal with genius observations from bigoted people, pointing out the obvious: that she's not my real mom. As if I weren't aware that she's Asian and I'm so Western and pale, I'm rocking an actual vitamin D deficiency. To be honest, in my mind, Joy *is* my mom now. My memories of Life Before Joy are slippery. Over the years, I've grown far closer to her than I am to my dad. She's supportive and encouraging. I just wish she were a touch less granola and chipper.

But this time, as much as I hate to admit it, her enthusiasm about the glamping trip might be warranted. Spending quality time outside of school with Reagan's inner circle would definitely strengthen my social standing, which always feels as if it's in danger of collapsing when I'm hanging around people who have more money or popularity. I'd like to feel more comfortable around them. Around Reagan, too. I just wish she'd asked me to go camping herself, instead of her mother.

The clinic's front door swings open and my father breezes into the waiting room, freshly shaved and dark hair neatly slicked back. "Zorie, did Mr. Wiley call?"

"He canceled today's massage appointment," I inform him. "But he rescheduled for a half session on Thursday."

A half session is half an hour, and half an hour equals half the money, but my father quickly masks his disappointment. You could tell him his best friend just died, and he'd pivot toward a meet-up at the racquetball club without breaking a sweat. Diamond Dan, people call him. All sparkle and glitz.

"Did Mr. Wiley say why he couldn't make it?" he asks.

"An emergency at one of his restaurants," I report. "A TV chef is stopping by to film a segment."

Mr. Wiley is one my dad's best clients. Like most of the

people who come here, he has money burning a hole in his wallet and can afford above-average prices for massage or acupuncture. Our wellness clinic is the best in Melita Hills, and my mom has even been written up in the *San Francisco Chronicle* as one of the Bay Area's top acupuncturists—"well worth a trip across the Bay Bridge." My parents charge clients accordingly.

It's just that the number of those clients has been slowly but surely dwindling over the last year. The primary cause of that dwindling, and the object of my dad's anger, is the business that set up shop in the adjoining space. To our shared mortification, we are now located next to a store that sells adult toys.

Yep, *those* kind of toys.

Kind of hard to ignore the giant vaginal-shaped sign out front. Our well-heeled customers sure haven't. Classy people usually don't want to park in front of a sex shop when they are heading to a massage therapy appointment. My parents found this out pretty quickly when longtime clients started canceling their weekly sessions. Those who haven't fled our desirable location near all the upscale boutique shops on Mission Street are too important to lose, as Dad reminds me every chance he gets.

And that's why I know he's upset by Mr. Wiley's cancellation—it was his only appointment today—but when he leaves the reception area and heads to his office so that he can stew about it in private, Mom remains calm.

"So," she says. "Should I tell Mrs. Reid you'll go glamping with Reagan?"

Like I'm going to give her a definitive answer on the spot without considering all the factors. At the same time, I hate to be the wet blanket on her sunny enthusiasm.

"Don't be cautious. Be careful," she reminds me. Cautious people are afraid of the unknown and avoid it. Careful people plan so that they're more confident when they face the unknown. She tells me this every time I'm resistant to a change in plans. "We'll research everything together."

"I'll consider it," I tell her diplomatically. "I guess you can tell Mrs. Reid that I'll text Reagan for the details and make up my mind later. But you did well, Dr. Pokenstein."

Her smile is victorious. "Speaking of, I better get back to her and take out the needles before she falls asleep on the slab. Oh, I almost forgot. Did FedEx come?"

"Nope. Just the regular mail."

She frowns. "I got an email notification that a package was delivered."

Crap on toast. I know what this means. We have a problem with misdelivered mail. Our mail carrier is constantly delivering our packages to the sex shop next door. And the sex shop next door is directly connected with item number three in my blueprint for a perfect summer: avoid any and all contact with the Mackenzies.

My mom sticks out her lower lip and makes her eyes big. "Pretty please," she pleads sweetly. "Can you run next door and ask them if they got my delivery?"

I groan.

"I would do it, but, you know. I've got Mrs. Reid full of needles," she argues, tugging her thumb toward the back rooms. "I'm balancing her life force, not torturing the woman. Can't leave her back there forever."

"Can't you go get it on your lunch break?" I've already made the trek into dildo land once this week, and that's my limit.

"I leave in an hour to meet your grandmother for lunch, remember?"

Right. Her mother, she means. Grandma Esther loathes tardiness, a sentiment I fully support. But that still doesn't change the fact that I'd rather have a tooth pulled than walk next door. "What's so important in this package anyway?"

"That's the thing," Mom says, winding her long, straight hair into a tight knot at the crown of her head. "The notification was sent by someone else. 'Catherine Beatty.' I don't know anyone by that name, and I haven't ordered anything. But the notification came to my work email, and our address is listed."

"A mystery package."

Her eyes twinkle. "Surprises are fun."

"Unless someone sent you a package full of spiders or a severed hand. Maybe you jabbed someone a little too hard."

"Or maybe I jabbed someone just right, and they are sending me chocolate." She steals a pen from the desk and stabs it into her hair to secure her new knot. "Please, Zorie. While your father is occupied."

She says this last bit in a hushed voice. My dad would throw a fit if he saw me next door.

"Fine. I'll go," I say, but I'm not happy.

Summer plans, how I knew and loved you.

Sticking a handmade AWAY FROM THE DESK. BE BACK IN A JIFF! sign on the counter, I drag myself through the front door into bright morning sunshine and brace for doom.

2

Sitting on the corner of Mission Street, Toys in the Attic, or T&A as my mom jokingly refers to it—until my dad gives her his *not funny, Joy* ultradry look—is a boutique sex shop that markets itself toward women. It's well lit and clean. Not skuzzy and filled with creepers, like Love Rocket across town, which has painted-over windows and is open twenty-four hours. You know, just in case you need fuzzy handcuffs at three a.m.

It also has a themed display window that the owners change every month. This month it's a forest, and like toadstools, a curated collection of bright rubber dildos rise from fake grass. One even has a squirrel molded into its side. This might be funny, except for the fact that plenty of people I know see this window regularly, and I have to endure lurid, snickering commentary about it from certain people at school.

Our dueling businesses—and nearby homes—sit together at the tail end of a tree-lined shopping promenade filled with local boutiques, organic restaurants, and art studios. Most of our cul-de-sac contains old Victorian houses like ours that have been sectioned up and converted into apartment units. Not exactly the place you'd expect to find sex for sale.

My dad says a place that sells "marital aids" is "no place for a young girl." The two women who own the sex shop darken his dazzling smile on a regular basis. They are the Hatfields to his McCoy. The Hamilton to his Burr. Our neighbors are the Enemy, and we do not fraternize with the Mackenzies. Oh *no*, we do not.

My mom used to be on friendly terms with the Mackenzies, so she only half agrees with my dad on this. And me? I'm caught in the middle. The whole situation just stresses me out. It's complicated. Very, *very* complicated.

Pink walls and the synthetic scent of silicone envelop me as I duck inside the sex shop. It's not quite noon, and only a couple of customers are browsing—a relief. I divert my eyes from a display of leather riding crops as I make a beeline toward a counter in the middle of the store, behind which two women in their early forties are chatting. I'm behind enemy lines now. Let's hope I don't get shot.

"It wasn't Alice Cooper," a woman with dark shoulder-length hair says as she lifts a small cardboard package on the counter. "It was the guy married to the redheaded talk show host. What's-her-name. Osbourne."

The woman standing next to her, green-eyed and fair-skinned, leans against the counter and scratches a heavily freckled nose.

"Ozzy?" she says in an accent that's a soft blend of American and Scottish. "I don't think so."

"I'll bet you a cupcake." Brown eyes dart over the counter to meet mine. Her oblong face lifts into a smile. "Zorie! Long time, no see."

"Hello, Sunny," I say, and then greet her freckled wife: "Mac."

"Sweet glasses," Sunny says, giving a thumbs-up to the retro blue cat-eye rims I'm wearing.

I have a dozen other pairs, all different styles and colors. I buy them dirt cheap from an online store, and I match them to my outfits. Along with crazy bright lipstick and a love for all things plaid, cool glasses are my thing. I may be a geek, but I am chic.

"Thanks," I tell her, meaning it. Not for the first time, I regret that my dad is fighting with these women. It wasn't that long ago that they felt like my second family.

The entire time I've known Sunny and Jane "Mac" Mackenzie, who have lived directly across the cul-de-sac since we moved into the neighborhood, they've insisted that I call them Sunny and Mac. Period. Not Mrs. or Ms., or any other titles. They don't like formalities, not in names or clothes. They are both quintessential Californians. You know, just your average former *riot grrrl* lesbian sex-shop owners.

"Help us out. We're playing Rock Star Urban Legend Game," Mac says to me, pushing fiery hair shot through with silver away from her face. "Which heavy metal star bit the head off a bat onstage? Back in the sixties."

"The seventies," Sunny corrects.

Mac rolls her eyes humorously. "Whatever. Listen, Zorie. We think it's either Ozzy Osbourne or Alice Cooper. Which one?"

"Um, I really don't know," I answer, hoping they'll give this up so I can get what I came for and leave. They're both acting like nothing has changed, that I still come over for Sunday dinner every week. Like my father didn't threaten to bust up their shop with a baseball bat for driving away his clients and they didn't tell him to go screw himself while dozens of people looked on from across the street with cell phones recording. The footage was uploaded to YouTube within the hour.

Yeah. Fun times. Dad has always disliked the Mackenzies, when they were just the "weirdo" neighbors across the street. But after their sex shop opened last fall and our clinic started tanking, that dislike turned into something stronger.

But okay, if Sunny and Mac want to pretend as though everything is still normal, fine. I'll play that game, as long as it gets me out of here faster. "Alice Cooper, maybe?" I answer.

"No way. It was Ozzy Osbourne," Sunny says confidently, slicing open the package on the counter with a box cutter. "Look it up, Mac."

"My phone's dead."

Sunny makes a clucking sound with her tongue. "Likely story. You just don't want to lose the bet."

"Lennon will know."

My stomach tightens. There are plenty of reasons for me not

to want to come over here. The dildo forest. The fear of being seen by someone I know. My dad's ongoing feud with the two women bantering behind the counter. But it's the seventeen-year-old boy casually strolling out of the stockroom who makes me wish I could turn invisible.

Lennon Mackenzie.

Monster T-shirt. Black jeans. Black boots laced to his knees. Black, fringed hair that's all swept to the side, somehow messy and perfectly spiked at the same time.

If an evil anime character sprang to life with a mission to lurk in dark corners while plotting world destruction, he would look a lot like Lennon. He's a poster boy for all things weird and macabre. He's also the main reason I don't want to eat lunch in the school cafeteria with the rest of the hoi polloi.

Carrying a zombie-splattered graphic novel in one hand and something small and unidentifiable tucked under his other arm, he glances at my blue plaid skirt, then his gaze skims upward to settle on my face. Any looseness in his posture immediately becomes tight and ridged. And when his dark eyes meet mine, they clearly reinforce what I already know: We are *not* friends.

Thing is, we used to be. Good friends. Okay, *best* friends. We had a lot of classes together, and because we live across the street from each other, we hung out after school. When we were younger, we'd ride bikes to a city park. In high school, that daily bike ride morphed into a daily walk down Mission Street to our local coffee shop—the Jitterbug—with my white husky, Andromeda, in tow.

And *that* turned into late-night walks around the Bay. He called me Medusa (because of my dark, unruly curls), and I called him Grim (because of the goth). We were always together. Inseparable friends.

Until everything changed last year.

Gathering my courage, I adjust my glasses, paste on a civil smile, and say, "Hi."

He tugs his chin upward in response. That's all I get. I used to be trusted with his secrets, and now I'm not even worthy of a spoken greeting. I thought at some point this would stop hurting me, but the pain is as sharp as it's ever been.

New plan: Don't say another word to him. Don't acknowledge his presence.

"Babe," Sunny says to Lennon, unpacking what appears to be some sort of sex lube. "Which rock star bit the head off a bat? Your other, less-hip mom thinks it's Alice Cooper."

Mac pretends to be affronted and points to me. "Hey, Zorie thinks so too!"

"She's wrong," Lennon says in a dismissive voice that's so scratchy and deep, it sounds as though he's speaking from inside a deep, dark well. That's the other thing about Lennon that drives me nuts. He doesn't just have a good voice; he has an *attractive* voice. It's big and confident and rich, and entirely too sexy for comfort. He sounds like a villainous voice-over actor or some kind of satanic radio announcer. It makes goose bumps race over my skin, and I resent that he still has that effect on me.

"It's Ozzy Osbourne," he informs us.

"Ha! Told you," Sunny says victoriously to Mac.

"I just picked one," I tell Lennon, a little angrier than I intend.

"Well, you picked wrong," he says, sounding bored.

I'm insulted. "Since when am I supposed to be an expert on the abuse of bats in rock music?"

That's more his speed.

"It's not arcane knowledge," he says, sweeping artfully mussed-up hair away from one eye with a knuckle. "It's pop culture."

"Right. Vital information I'll need to know in order to get into the university of my choice. I think I remember that question on the SAT exams."

"Life is more than SAT exams."

"At least I have friends," I say.

"If you think Reagan and the rest of her clique are real friends, you're sadly mistaken."

"Jeez, you two," Sunny mumbles. "Get a room."

Heat washes over my face.

Um, no. This is not an *I secretly like you* fight. This is *I secretly hate you*. Sure, he's all lips and hair and baritone voice, and I'm not blind: He's attractive. But the only time our former friendship dared to risk one pinky toe over the line—a period of time we referred to as the Great Experiment—I ended up sobbing my eyes out at homecoming, wondering what went wrong.

I never found out. But I have a pretty good guess.

He gives his mom a long-suffering look, as if to say, *You done now?* and then turns to address Mac. "Ozzy's bat story was exaggerated. Someone in the audience threw a dead bat onstage, and Ozzy thought it was plastic. When he bit the head off, he was completely shocked. Had to be taken to the hospital for a rabies shot after the show."

Sunny bumps her hip against Mac. "Doesn't matter. I'm still right, and you still owe me a cupcake. Coconut. Since we skipped breakfast this morning, I'll take it now. Brunch."

"That actually does sound good," Mac says. "Zorie, you want one?"

I shake my head.

Mac turns to Lennon. "Baby, my baby," she says in a coaxing, jovial voice. "Can you make a bakery run? Pretty please?"

"Mother, my mother. I have to be at work in thirty minutes," he argues, and I hate how he can be so cold to me one second and warm to his parents the next. When he sets the book he's carrying on the counter, I see what he's cradling in the crook of his elbow: a red bearded dragon lizard about the length of my forearm. It's on a leash connected to a black leather harness that wraps around its tiny front arms. "Got to put Ryuk back in his habitat before I go."

Lennon is obsessed with reptiles, because *of course*. He has an entire wall of them in his room—snakes, lizards, and his only nonreptile pet, a tarantula. He works part-time at a Mission Street reptile store, where he can be creepy with other likeminded snake lovers.

Mac reaches over the counter to scratch the lizard on top of its scaly head and coos in a childlike voice, "Fine. Guess you win, Ryuk. Oh dear, you're coming out of your harness."

Lennon sets the bearded dragon atop his manga book. Ryuk tries to get away, nearly falling off the counter. "That's an inefficient way to go," Lennon dourly informs the lizard. "If you're going to off yourself, better to overdose on reptile vitamins than jump."

"Lennon," Sunny scolds lightly.

A dark smile barely curls the corners of his full lips. "Sorry, Mama," he says.

When we were younger, people used to taunt him mercilessly at school—*How do you know which mom is which?* To him, Sunny is Mama, Mac is Mum. And even though Mac gave birth to him, neither woman is more or less in his eyes.

Sunny twists her mouth and then smiles back. He's forgiven. His parents forgive him for everything. He doesn't deserve them.

"So, Zorie. What brings you by, love?" Mac says to me as Lennon adjusts his lizard's tiny harness.

I'm forced to step to the side of Lennon in order to have a conversation that doesn't involve me speaking at his back. When did he get so freakishly tall? "My mom's looking for a FedEx package."

Mac's eyes shift toward Sunny's. A subtle but sharp reaction is communicated between the two women.

"Something wrong?" I ask, suspicious.

Sunny clears her throat. "Nothing, sweetie." She hesitates, indecisive for a moment. "We did get something, yes," she says, reaching under the counter to pull out a manila mailing envelope, which she hands to me, apologetic. "I may have accidentally opened it by mistake. I didn't read your mom's mail, though. I noticed the address after I slit it open."

"That's fine," I say. It's happened before, which sends my dad's blood pressure through the roof, but Mom won't care. It's just that Mac is now looking extremely uncomfortable. Even Lennon feels more distant than usual, his energy shifting from mildly chilly to arctic. Warning bells ding inside my head.

"Okay, well, gotta get back," I say, pretending I don't notice anything amiss.

"Give Joy our best," Mac says. "If your mum ever wants to get coffee . . ." She trails off and gives me a tight smile. "Well, she knows where to find us."

Sunny nods. "You too. Don't be a stranger."

Now *I'm* uncomfortable. I mean, more than usual, having to endure the humiliation that is this shop.

"Sure. Thanks for this." I hold up the package in acknowledgment as I'm turning to leave and nearly knock over a display model of a giant blue vibrator sitting next to the register. I instinctively reach out to steady the wobbling piece of plastic before I'm fully aware of what I'm touching. *Dear God.*

Under a fan of black lashes, Lennon's eyes shift to the floor, and he doesn't lift his face.

Must get out. Now.

Nearly tripping over my own feet, I stride out of the shop and exhale a long breath when I'm back in the sunshine. I can't get back into the clinic fast enough.

But when I'm settled behind the shield of the front desk, my eyes fix on the envelope the Mackenzies gave me. It's from a PO Box in San Francisco and is, indeed, clearly addressed to Joy Everhart. Not sure how they missed that, but whatever.

After checking the back hallway and finding it clear, I peek into the envelope.

It's a piece of paper with a handwritten note and a small book of personal photos. I recognize the photo book's brand from online ads: upload your photos, and they send you a printed book a few days later. This one says *Our Bahamas Trip* on the cover in a frilly font.

I open the book to find a million sunny vacation photos. The ocean. The beach. My dad snorkeling. My dad with his arm around some woman in a bikini.

Wait.

What?

Flipping faster, I stare at glossy pages printed with more of the same. Dinner and tropical drinks. My dad smiling that dazzling smile of his. Only he's not smiling at my mom but some stranger. A stranger with a gold ankle bracelet and long lash extensions. He's got his arms wrapped around her, and—in one photo—is even kissing her neck.

What is all this? Some fling after my mother died? Someone before Joy? I pull out the letter.

Joy,

You don't know me, but I thought you'd want

to see this, woman to woman. Photos from our

vacation last summer.

Good luck,

One of many

My fingers go numb. Last summer? He was here, working at the clinic, last summer. No, wait. There was a week he went to Los Angeles for a massage therapy conference. And came back with a shockingly dark tan . . . that he said he'd gotten after lying out by the hotel pool every afternoon.

"Oh, shit," I whisper to myself.

My dad is having an affair.

3

It's all I can think about. That evening, after Mom returns from
seeing Grandma Esther in Oakland and lets me borrow her car,
I'm sitting inside the Melita Hills Observatory's dark auditorium
for my monthly astronomy club meeting. Sometimes we head up
to the roof with our telescopes, but this month, it's an info-only
gathering. And thanks to that Bahamas photo book, I'm paying
zero attention to Dr. Viramontes, the retired Berkeley teacher
who's president of our local chapter. He's addressing the group—a
couple dozen people, mostly other retirees and a handful of stu-
dents my age—while standing at a podium near the controls that
turn the ceiling into a light show of the night sky. I lost what he
was saying a quarter of an hour back, something about where we
were going to be watching the Perseid meteor shower.

Instead, my mind is stuck on that photo of my dad kissing
that woman.

He lied to my mom. He lied to me.

And he forced *me* to lie, telling my mom that the Mackenzies hadn't received any of our mail, because no way was I handing over that ticking-bomb package of agony over to my mom. Not right now, when she's full of cheer and sunshine, encouraging me to go on the camping trip with Reagan. Maybe not ever. I don't know. This will tear our family apart.

I've never been in this kind of position, being forced to decide where I should hide photos of my dad two-timing my mom. Or three-timing. Four-timing? What did that woman mean by "one of many"? The photos are from last summer, and I doubt this woman would want to call him out to his wife if she were still seeing him. So when did the affair end, and how many others were there? *Are* there?

Does he just pick up random acupuncturists from alternative health conventions?

Are they all locals?

Do I know any of them?

Ugh. Considering all the possibilities hurts my brain. And what's even weirder about the whole thing is that the strange woman in the photos looks a *lot* like my birth mother. I mean, clearly it's not her, and this stranger is younger than my mother was when she died, but there's an uncanny resemblance. And that just freaks me out.

My dad is having an affair with someone who looks like his dead first wife. That's not normal.

What am I saying? None of this normal, no matter what she looks like. I think of Mom smiling this morning, completely oblivious to the fact that Dad's cheated on her, and it makes my stomach hurt all over again.

Thank God the normal clinic receptionist came in to take over for me at lunch, because no way could I handle looking my dad in the eye.

My stomach is sick. My heart is sick. Everything about this is wrong, wrong, wrong.

And the cherry on top of this shit sundae is that *the Mackenzies know*. Sunny and Mac saw what was inside the envelope. They had to. I mean, judging from the awkward way they acted, and all that business about meeting for coffee if we ever needed to talk? It's hard for me to blame them for looking at the photo book. If they really did open it by accident, I'm sure curiosity got the better of them. It did for me.

Huge mistake.

Oh, God. Does Lennon know too?

"What's wrong?"

I snap out of my thoughts and realize the meeting has ended. The person speaking to me is a brown-haired girl sitting at my side. I've known Avani Desai as long as Lennon and Reagan, when we first bonded over astronomy in seventh-grade science class, both acing a quiz about the planets. Avani and I used to carpool to Reagan's house for sleepovers, staying up late to listen to music and gossip while her parents were asleep. But when I followed Reagan to the elite courtyard at school, Avani stayed behind, secure with her social status. I always envied her confidence. Now the only time I really talk with Avani is during astronomy club.

"Nothing's wrong," I tell her. No way am I bringing up the humiliation that is my father's affair. "I'm just thinking about something."

"Yeah, sort of figured," she says with a brief smile, crossing her arms over a T-shirt silk-screened with Neil deGrasse Tyson's face and the words NEIL BEFORE ME. "You've been 'thinking' all the way through Viramontes's meteor shower plans."

Most of the club members are filing out of the auditorium now, but a few hover around Dr. Viramontes's podium. Avani is waiting for me to explain my mood, so I say the first thing that comes to mind to placate her curiosity.

"I've been invited to go on a camping trip with Reagan," I tell her.

To my surprise, she brightens. "Oooh, I heard about that."

Wait, she knew, but I didn't? And since when had she started talking to Reagan again?

"I overheard Brett Seager talking about it," she explains excitedly, twisting sideways to face me in the auditorium chairs while she sits cross-legged. "He was at the drugstore with his older sister earlier today."

"What?" Now I'm interested. *Very* interested.

She nods quickly. "I was behind him in the checkout line. He was talking to someone on his phone, saying that he was going camping near King's Forest with some other people from school. I didn't catch any names but Reagan's. He was trying to convince whoever he was talking to on the phone to go with him."

Brett Seager is a minor celebrity in our school. His parents don't have a ton of money, but somehow he's always doing things like skydiving, or going backstage at cool concerts, or jumping off the roof of some rich friend's house into their million-dollar pool. But he's not just a party-boy daredevil. He reads Jack Kerouac and Allen Ginsberg . . . all the American Beat Poets. Most guys I know don't even know what a bookstore is.

So yes, he's pretty and popular, but he's more than that. And I've been nursing a crush on him since elementary school. A crush that turned into a small obsession ever since he kissed me at a party over spring break. Sure, he got back with his on-again, off-again girlfriend the next day, which was humiliating and upsetting for me at the time. Reagan tried to cheer me up by playing matchmaker, introducing me to a couple of boys. Guess it wasn't meant to be for any of us, because I never clicked with those boys, and then Brett and his girlfriend broke up over the summer.

The important thing here is that if what Avani overheard is true, it sounds like Brett could be going on Reagan's camping trip. And that makes the great outdoors a *lot* more enticing.

More panic-inducing, too, because Brett was not a factor in my mental plan for this trip. Reagan's mom had said it would be all girls. No way would my parents let me go on a weeklong unsupervised camping trip with boys. My father would flip the hell out.

Guess this information is under the table.

"Are you *sure* Brett said he was actually going?" I ask Avani.

"Yep." She hikes up her shoulders to make herself look muscular and pretends to be Brett. "'Bruh, you've to go with me. I *need* to jump off that wicked waterfall. We can Instagram the whole thing.'"

I snort at her bad imitation.

She shrugs. "I'm just telling you what I heard."

"Who was he talking to on the phone?" I ask.

"No idea. Probably his latest bromance. He's always changing friends, usually to whoever's parents are out of town and have a house big enough for one of his legendary blowouts."

"That's just an act," I argue. "He's not really that way."

Her face softens. "I'm sorry. I know you like him, especially after that party . . ."

I wish I'd never told her about the kiss. It feels like a weakness.

"Anyway, I guess he's been expanding his friend list this summer. Katy even said she thought she saw him in the passenger seat of Lennon's car a couple weeks ago."

Wait, what? Lennon and Brett, friends? Surely that's a sign of the apocalypse. "I seriously doubt it."

"Maybe not. Lennon seems way out of Brett's league, if you ask me."

"I think you have that turned around," I say with a snort.

"And *I* think whatever happened between you and Lennon is—"

"Avani," I protest. I don't like to talk about Lennon. Avani doesn't know about the Great Experiment. All Avani knows is that we were supposed to meet up with her for homecoming. She doesn't know why that never happened. No one does. Not even me, really. But I stopped trying to figure out Lennon's motivations a long time ago.

It's easier not to think about him at all.

"Never mind," she says. "I'm sorry I brought it up. It's none of my business."

After I'm quiet for a few seconds, she elbows me. "So . . . camping. Alone in the woods. Maybe this is your chance with Brett. When is this trip?"

I texted Reagan earlier, but she only confirmed that the trip was happening and said she'd get back to me later with details. Normally, that would drive me nuts, but I was busy freaking out about hiding the photo book of my dad's affair. Now I wish I had pressed Reagan for more information. All of these Unknowns and Possibilities are stressing me out.

"I think it's in a couple of days?" I say. "Pretty sure she's planning on staying a week."

Avani's face falls. "That's during the meteor shower. I was kind of hoping you were going on the weekend trip with the group."

"What group?"

"*Our* group. East Bay Planetary Society," she says, brow wrinkling. "Weren't you listening at all?"

I wasn't.

She fills me in. "Instead of gathering here at the observatory, Dr. Viramontes is taking the club on a road trip to the dark-sky area on Condor Peak to watch the meteor shower there."

Condor Peak State Park. They host the annual North California Star Party.

"All the other astronomy clubs in the area will be going," Avani adds.

Apart from Death Valley, Condor Peak is the closest dark-sky preserve. That means it's protected from artificial light pollution, which enables people to see more stars. Astronomers take amazing photos in dark-sky areas, especially during star parties—which are basically nighttime gatherings of amateur astronomers to watch celestial events. And though we've hosted a few minor star parties here at the observatory, I've never been to one this big with other astronomy clubs. That's kind of huge.

I weigh my options. On one hand, the geek in me really wants to attend this star party. I mean, hello. The Perseid meteor shower happens only once a year. But on the other hand, Brett Seager.

Rolling a two-wheeled laptop case behind him, Dr. Viramontes ascends the aisle and stops when he sees us. I like the way his eyes crinkle in the corner when he smiles. "Ladies, are you joining us on our pilgrimage to Condor Peak? We'll get some amazing photos. Great thing to add to your college applications, and there'll be other astrophysics professors there, along with many important members of the Night Sky Program. And I didn't want to say this to the group, because I'm not entirely certain, but I've got intel that Sandra Faber could make an appearance."

Sandra Faber teaches astrophysics at UC Santa Cruz. She won the National Medal of Science. She's a big deal. Meeting someone like her could help me get into Stanford, which is where I want to study astronomy after I graduate.

Avani draws in an excited breath and pokes my shoulder. "You have to come now."

"I'm supposed to be camping with a friend in the High Sierras," I tell the professor, suddenly filled with doubt. Why can't anything be easy?

Dr. Viramontes shifts the long silver braid that hangs over his shoulder, bound at the tail by a beaded clasp made by someone in his local Ohlone Indian tribe. "That's a shame. Where?"

I relay the details that my mom shared with me about the glamping compound.

Dr. Viramontes scratches his chin. "I think I know which one you're talking about, and it's not far from Condor Peak." He slips a piece of paper out of the front pocket of his rolling case and hands it to me. It's an information sheet on the trip. He points to the map and shows me the general area of the glamping compound in relation to King's Forest and Condor Peak. "Probably a couple hours' drive on the highway. Maybe you could stop by. We'll be there three nights."

"You can meet me there," Avani says encouragingly.

"I'm not sure what the transportation situation will be like, but I'll definitely check into it," I tell him, folding up the paper.

"We'd love to have you. Let me know what you decide." He raises two fingers to his forehead and gives me a loose salute before reminding us to be safe getting home tonight.

"You're going, right?" Avani whispers excitedly as he walks away.

My mind is aflutter. So is my stomach. "God, I *really* want to."

"Then come," she says. "Meet me at Condor Peak. Promise me, Zorie."

"I'll try," I say, not completely sure, but hopeful.

"Star party, here we come," she tells me, and for a moment, it feels like old times between us.

But after we leave the auditorium and she walks me to the parking lot, I remember what awaits me at home.

I push away the dread and concentrate on enjoying the drive as I leave the hilltop observatory and descend into town. It's a perfect summer night, and stars blanket the sky. My stars. Every winking point of white light belongs to me. They are wonderful, the town is quiet and dark, and I'm just fine.

Only I'm not.

Normally, I love driving my mom's car, even though it's several years old and smells faintly of patchouli. The stereo speakers are bass-heavy, and I relish taking the long way home, cruising the road between the freeway and the dark blue water, with San Francisco twinkling in the distance. Except for the occasional run to the grocery store, this is the only time I really drive. But, hey. At least my mom trusts me with her sedan, unlike my dad, who won't let me near his vintage sports car. It's worth too much.

But now I can't stop thinking about that whole "one of many" line in that letter, and I wonder if my dad has driven other women around in his stupid car. Just how many others have there been? I've always thought my dad was a decent person, if not a little plastic and fake when he's in full-on Diamond Dan mode, but now I'm picturing him dressed like Hugh Hefner with two curvy women on his arms.

It makes me want to vomit.

Dark silhouettes of skinny palm trees greet me as I turn into our cul-de-sac and park the car behind my dad's Corvette in the narrow driveway next to our building. The clinic is dark, so no one's working late. Hesitantly, I hike the steps of the connecting house and warily open the front door of our apartment.

A ball of white fur pads across the open living area to greet me. Andromeda is getting old, but she's still sweet and pretty. No one can resist her dual-colored brown and blue husky eyes. I stick my fingers under her collar and give her a good scratch while kissing the top of her head.

"Hey, sweet thing," my mom says. She's stretched out on the couch under a blanket, reading a magazine under a dim lamp while the mute TV flashes a commercial in background. "How was astronomy club?"

"Fine." I hand her the car keys. "Where's Dad?"

She nods toward the balcony off the kitchen, where I spot a dark shape. "On the phone."

My gut twists when I hear his voice, too low for me to make out what he's saying. He's always on the phone, and those phone calls usually are taken behind closed doors after he steps away. I assumed he was just being polite; my mom is old-school about people talking on cell phones in public.

Now I wonder who's on the other end of the line.

Hoping she doesn't notice my anxiety, I briefly tell Mom about Dr. Viramontes's invitation to the star party while she's flipping magazine pages. She's *mmm-hmm*-ing me, completely distracted. I see her glance toward the balcony door, and a little line appears in the middle of her forehead.

Or maybe that's my imagination.

All I know is that I can't fake a convincing smile around my father, so after feigning weariness, I kiss Joy good night and make an escape upstairs, Andromeda at my heels.

My bedroom is in a converted attic space. My parents' master bedroom is downstairs, so I have the entire upstairs to myself. Just me, an ancient bathroom without a shower, and a storage room filled with overflow supplies from the clinic.

Embarrassingly, my room hasn't changed a lot since I was a kid. The ceiling is still covered with glow-in-the-dark stars—the "glow" ran out years ago—painstakingly arranged to match constellations. Pegasus lost the stars that make up his leg during a minor earthquake. The only decorative room additions from the last couple of years are my oversize handmade wall calendars, or "blueprints"—I have one for each season of the year, and they are all systematically color-coded—and my galaxy photos. I've had my best ones printed and framed. My Orion Nebula is particularly beautiful. I took it at the observatory with a special equatorial mount borrowed from

Dr. Viramontes, and tweaked its purple luminance with stacking software.

After locking my door, I move past framed star charts and duck beneath a mobile of the solar system that hangs over my desk. I stashed the photo book in a deep desk drawer earlier, and when I double-check, it's still there, under a neat stack of graph-lined planning journals and a rainbow bin of highlighters, gel pens, and rolls of *washi* tape. My parents don't touch my stuff—it's all carefully organized—so I'm not sure why I'm so worried. I guess I just feel guilty.

Best not to think about it. "Until I can figure out what to do, it's our little secret," I tell Andromeda. She jumps up on my bed and curls into a ball. She's an excellent secret keeper.

The only window in my room has a Juliet balcony that overlooks the cul-de-sac. There's not room enough for me to stand outside, but it's wide enough for my telescope, Nancy Grace Roman— named after the first woman to hold an executive position at NASA. I open the balcony doors and take the telescope from its black carrying case to set it up. I actually have two telescopes—this one, and a smaller portable model. I haven't really used the portable one much, but now I'm daydreaming about taking it to that star party on Condor Peak.

I wonder if I can really do the camping *and* the meteor shower.

It would take a lot of planning.

I dash off a quick text to Reagan: So, about this glamping trip. Who's going? Are you driving? What day are you leaving?

She responds almost immediately: Slow your roll. I'm in bed. Super tired. Want to go pick up camping gear with me tomorrow afternoon? We can talk about it then.

I'm both relieved and disappointed. Relieved, because I guess it's cool with her that I tag along. And disappointed, because though I need to plan things well in advance, Reagan does everything by the seat of her pants. She's always telling me I need to lighten up and embrace spontaneity.

Spontaneity gives me hives.

Literally.

I have chronic urticaria. That's a fancy name for chronic hives. They're idiopathic, which means doctors can't pinpoint an exact cause for why, when, and how long they flare. Sometimes when I eat certain foods, touch an allergen, or—especially—get super anxious, itchy pale-red bumps appear on the inside of my elbows and on my stomach. If I don't calm down and take an antihistamine, they'll spread into huge welts off and on for days, or even weeks. It's been several months since I've had a breakout, but between Reagan and this thing with my dad, I can already feel the itch coming on.

I answer Reagan's text, asking for details about meeting her tomorrow. Then I assemble my telescope and set up the tripod in the middle of the balcony's open doors.

As I'm adjusting the mount, I look over the balcony railing to scan the cul-de-sac. Viewed from up here, our street looks like a fat raindrop, its center filled with a dozen public parking spaces. At night, they're mostly empty, so I have a pretty clear view of the other side of the street, where I spot Lennon's car. It's hard to miss. He drives this hulking black 1950s Chevy that looks like a hearse, with pointy tailfins cradling a hatchback door that lifts up to carry the coffins, or whatever dastardly thing he hauls back there. And right now, it's parked in front of a pale blue duplex house directly across the street from us: the Mackenzies' apartment unit.

I can't pinpoint the exact moment Lennon morphed from the boy-next-door comic geek to the boy-in-black horrorphile, but I guess he's always been a little odd. Some of that may be due to how he grew up. His biological dad—Adam Ahmed, who used to date Mac—is the former guitarist for a radical San Francisco punk band that was popular during the Bay Area's '90s punk revival explosion. His moms took three-year-old Lennon on tour when his dad's band opened for Green Day.

So yeah, he hasn't always led a so-called normal life, but he always *seemed* normal.

Until junior year, that is. After the night of the homecoming dance, we didn't speak for days. No more hiking down to the Jitterbug to get coffee after school. No more night walks. Weeks passed. I'd see him occasionally at school, but our brief interactions were tense. He started hanging around other people.

Golden light shines from a window on the corner of the Mackenzies' house. Lennon's room. I know it well. We used to signal each other from our windows before sneaking out late at night to meet up for walks around the neighborhood with Andromeda.

We made a game of creating and naming detailed routes.

Lennon would draw them all out, streets labeled with his neat handwriting and tiny sketches. He's drawn maps since we were kids. Some were fantasy maps based on books he read; he redrew Middle Earth about twenty times. And some were of Melita Hills. That's how our friendship started, actually. I'd just moved to Melita Hills and didn't know my way around, so he made me a neighborhood map of the Mission Street area. He gave me a larger, updated one for my birthday last year—one that included our favorite late-night walking route, which extended out along a bicycling path curving around the Bay. It had funny little drawings, all the points of interest we considered important, and a legend of symbols he'd made up.

It's currently upside down at the bottom of the same drawer where I've hidden my dad's stupid photo book. I wanted to throw it away after we stopped speaking, but I couldn't make myself do it, because that walking route he drew? It's where the Great Experiment started.

Who knew walking could lead to heartbreak?

Out of curiosity, I screw on a low-power eyepiece and hesitantly aim my assembled telescope toward the Mackenzies' duplex. Just for a quick look. It's not as if I usually spy on all the neighbors. I quickly focus on Lennon's room. It's empty. Thank God. After an adjustment, I can see an unmade bed and, right beyond it, his reptile terrariums. The last time I was in his room, there were only two, but now there are at least six sitting on shelves and one big floor model. It's a freaking jungle up in there.

I scan the rest of his room. He has a TV and a million DVDs stacked precariously, out of their cases. Probably all horror movies. An enormous map hangs over his desk. A map of what, I'm not sure, but it's professional, not one that's he's drawn himself— definitely not one of our late-night walking routes. Silly even to think it could be.

A shadow catches my eye as the door to his room swings open and closes. Lennon walks into view. One by one, I watch him turn off lights and heat lamps inside the terrariums. Then he sits on the edge of his bed and begins unlacing his boots.

That's my cue to bail.

Only, I don't.

I watch him take off both boots and chuck them in the middle of his floor. Then he tugs up his shirt and pulls it off. Now he's bare-chested, wearing only black jeans. I should definitely look away before this turns X-rated. But holy mother of God, when did he get all . . . *built*? I mean, it's no soccer-player physique, or anything. He's too lean to be buff. But he flops on his bed, lying on his back with his arms spread, and stares at the ceiling while I keep staring at him.

And staring . . .

There are now muscles where there weren't before, and his chest is a lot bigger. Is he lifting weights? No way. That is not him *at all*. He hates sports. He'd rather hole up with a comic book in the dark.

At least, I think he would. I suddenly feel like I don't know him anymore.

"Of course you don't," I whisper to myself. He's changed.

I've changed. Only, I haven't, or I wouldn't still be looking at something that should be off-limits.

When I sharpen the focus, I home in on a stack of muscles rippling down his stomach as he sits up again. And—

I pan to his face. He's staring this way.

Not in my general location, but RIGHT AT ME.

Heart racing, I jerk back from the telescope and lurch to the floor. Smooth move. Like he didn't see me do that. If I had just kept a level head and shifted the telescope to the sky, I could have played it cool and pretended I wasn't really spying on him. But now? My humiliation is total and complete.

Good job, Zorie.

I lie on the floor, dying. Wishing I could take back the last few minutes.

Guess I can add that to the list of everything that's gone wrong today. Andromeda jumps off the bed and licks my nose in concern.

New plan: I *am* going on that glamping trip—and to the star party on Condor Peak—if it kills me. I have to get away from this place. Away from my cheating dad. Away from the daily mortification of living next door to a sex shop. And far, *far* away from Lennon.

4

"Oh, check out this one. It will look great on you," Reagan says in a loud, raspy voice as she pulls a Barbie-pink backpack off a hook. We've been inside this specialty outdoor gear store for all of ten minutes, and she's already filled up a shopping cart with enough hiking gear to outfit the Donner Party. The store's owner is probably counting up the total in his head and putting a down payment on a new house. Reagan's mom gave her a credit card and told her to go wild.

Must be nice.

"Jesus! Look at the price tag. It's too expensive," I tell her. It's one of those structured backpacks that covers your entire back from head to butt and holds whatever it is that backpackers need when they're hiking—sleeping bags and tent poles, things like that.

"Mom said we could buy anything, as long as it's in this store," Reagan argues, giving me a mischievous look as she swings a light brown ponytail over one shoulder. "She will regret that. Besides, my dad just made a shitload of money on the stock market. Why do you think my parents suddenly decided to fly to Switzerland? They can afford a couple of backpacks."

"There're four in the cart already," I point out.

Four backpacks. Three tents. Hiking sticks. Sleeping bags. Headlamps. And a set of enamel cookware, because it was "cute."

"We'll be needing it," she says casually.

"I thought this was glamping," I argue. "Your mom told my mom that the tents are already set up and that all the meals were provided."

Reagan pushes the shopping cart into an outdoor clothing area. "Yeah, I stayed there last year for my sixteenth birthday. The compound has really nice yurts."

"Yogurt?"

"Yurt," she enunciates, pretending to snap at my nose with her teeth. "They're giant round tents. You could host a huge party inside one. Anyway, the tents we're buying today are for the back-country trip we're taking."

I don't like the sound of that. "No one mentioned this."

"It's just walking, Zorie. Anyone can do it."

I snort. "Says the athlete who gets up every morning at the butt crack of dawn to exercise."

A tortured look clouds her eyes. Is she thinking about her Olympic failure? I think of what Mom said about Reagan strug-gling, and I immediately regret teasing her.

"I suppose you're right," I say quickly. "It's just walking."

Reagan glances down at my plaid skirt and surveys my bare legs. "Hiking will do you good."

I'm not sure what she means by this, but I choose to ignore it, and instead route the conversation in a different direction. "You're planning on pitching tents in the wilderness? Like, with wild animals and stuff?"

Reagan smacks her gum and wheels up to a display of hiking boots. On the nearby wall is a giant poster of pretty models dressed in flannel, grinning with perfect teeth as they brave the wilds of their photo shoot, pretending to be roughing it. "There are a zillion campgrounds in King's Forest. I'm sure we'll be sleeping in one of them," she assures me. "At least, I think so. I don't know. All I've been told is that the place we're going is a couple hours' walk from the main compound. Your average Silicon Valley wannabe hikers don't know about it. We're talking totally *off trail*, baby."

Off trail sounds awful. Unlike Reagan, I don't have boundless natural energy and calves of steel. I need to be where there's caffeine in walking distance, not fighting off bears and mosquitoes. I make a face at Reagan.

"We can be as loud as we want and no ranger will be there to shush us," Reagan says in her big, raspy voice. "The people who run the glamping compound are nice, but they know my parents. We can't really let loose around them, you know? I don't need them giving my mom a report card on our activities."

Now I'm wondering what kinds of activities she has in mind.

Reagan points to the poster of the hiking models. "In the

backcountry . . . that's where things will get good. There's a hidden waterfall inside King's Forest to die for, and it's not far from the glamping compound. I'm talking bucket list. Do you know how many people get internet famous just for having the guts to travel to cool locations and take photos?"

Avani's story about overhearing Brett talking on the phone pops into my mind. My pulse quickens. "You still haven't told me who's going."

"I thought I did," she says absently. "Summer."

One of Reagan's troop. Summer sometimes eats lunch with us in the courtyard at school.

"And?" I coax. "Who else?"

"Kendrick Taylor." Goes to the private school across town, Alameda Academy. Which is where Reagan would be going if they had a decent athletics department; they don't, and that's why a lot of rich kids who play sports go to public school with the rest of us riffraff.

"Summer started seeing Kendrick a few weeks ago," she explains before I can ask, and then mutters, "Why are hiking boots so ugly?"

"Because no one cares what you look like when you're sweating your way up a mountain?"

"Look, if you don't think you can handle a little hiking, don't come."

Her words feel like a slap to the face. And could she have said that any louder? Her booming voice carries through the store, and another customer has turned to look quizzically at us. Public shame is the best.

"I'm sorry," she says, mouth pulling tight to one side. "I didn't mean it to come out that way."

I pretend I'm not upset. Ever since the Olympic trials, Reagan has had the shitty tendency to lash out at people to make herself feel better, so whatever is bothering her probably has nothing to do with me. But now I'm wondering whether I *can* handle this trip.

"Quit scratching your arm," Reagan chastises.

I hadn't realized I was doing that. Stupid hives. I'm going to need to take medication.

Exhaling a long sigh, I calm myself and try to focus on what's important. "Who else is going?" I press. "It can't be just Summer and Kendrick."

She shrugs. "Brett Seager and some dude he's bringing."

Bingo. "Oh, really?"

"Yes, really. Don't faint on me."

"I won't," I say.

"I just know how you are about him," she says. "You get obsessed and freaky, and I don't want things getting weird."

"Why would they get weird? You think I'm going to attack him in the woods?"

She chuckles. "You never know. What happens in the woods stays in the woods."

I clear my throat and try to sound breezy. "I did hear he's single again."

Reagan makes a noncommittal noise. "I thought you were over him?"

"I am." Mostly.

"Okay, good. But seriously. This is supposed to be a drama-free trip. I don't want it to be awkward."

"It won't be awkward."

"Excellent." After a nod, she wheels the cart toward a wall of paddles. Colorful kayaks are suspended alongside them, greens and reds and purples.

"So this waterfall we're hiking to is only a couple hours away from the glamping compound?" I ask.

"That's what Brett says. He's trying to convince the guy who told him about it to lead us there. Oh, that reminds me. Bikinis. We'll be swimming. Do they sell those here?" She cranes her neck to peer around the store.

No way am I getting in a bikini in front of Brett. Forget it. My stress meter goes up, but I mentally push it back down and try to focus on what I was going to say. "I'm just wondering exactly where the waterfall is, because there are some people I know doing a meet-up on Condor Peak, and I thought about trying to find a ride out there one night."

Reagan's nose wrinkles. "Who do *you* know who'd be meeting on Condor Peak? Oh, hold on. Is this an astronomy club thing?"

"Meteor shower," I confirm. "There's a big star party."

She considers this. "That's not far from where we'll be, and you can definitely find a ride out there. The High Sierra bus line has a stop near the compound. I'll bet even Uber picks up there, if you throw enough cash at them."

That sounds promising, but I need firmer details. I don't want to scramble at the last minute. "I guess I could email the compound and ask for advice."

"Is Avani going to be there?" she asks. "At Condor Peak?"

I nod. Sometimes I think Reagan might be jealous of the astronomy connection Avani and I share. This is ridiculous, because I only spend time with Avani during our club meetings. Before summer started, I saw Reagan every day.

Trying not to scratch my itchy arm, I pretend to browse a display of wide-mouthed water bottles. An idea suddenly hits me. "You could come with me to the star party. I know Avani would like to see you."

Reagan's quiet. Just for a second. Then she shakes her head. "I can't invite people camping and then abandon them."

I chuckle, slightly embarrassed. "Of course not. Duh."

A heavy awkwardness fills the space between us, and I don't know why. Maybe she's remembering how we used to all be better friends. Maybe she actually wants to go with me to Condor Peak but needs a little push. Sometimes if I prod her, she'll let down her guard and show me the other Reagan—the girl she used to be when we were younger. Before all of the pressure of the Olympic training. Before her parents got rich.

She slaps my shoulder, startling me. Sometimes Reagan doesn't know her own strength. "Don't be such a worrywart. It's all good," she says, voice bouncing with positivity. "I think everything will work out for both us. You can spend a little time glamping with my group and then head to your astronomy thing with Avani."

"Might take some coordinating," I say, still unsure.

"Nah, it'll work out fine," she insists, bugging her eyes out at me comically and then sticking her tongue out briefly. "Just roll with it, Zorie. Let life happen."

I'm not sure if she realizes, but that's Brett's motto. He says it all the time.

Maybe it's time I take this advice.

The next morning, I'm letting life happen in the only way I know how, which is me going over my extremely detailed fifty-five-bullet-point list for the camping trip while sitting behind the clinic's front desk. We leave tomorrow, which doesn't give me a lot of time to ensure that I have everything I'll need. I'm a little worried I might forget something.

What that is, I'm not sure. I've never been camping. But I'm poking around the glamping compound's website, and it's mostly magazine-worthy photographs of the surrounding land-scape. The only information I find is a glowing write-up of their chef and wine collection. That and a list of their prices, which are insane. You'd think we were staying at a four-star hotel instead of in a tent.

Avani and I talked on the phone for almost an hour last night. We firmed up plans to meet up at the star party, and she helped me research the bus lines that run out there in the Sierras—which are not frequent. Seems as though I have two chances each day to catch a bus heading toward Condor Peak. At least I now have a plan, which is all I ever wanted.

The clinic's door opens, and I look up from the front desk's computer, expecting to see my mom's next acupuncture appointment. My dad doesn't have anything booked until after lunch, so he left a few minutes ago to run errands around town. Fine by me. I've still barely spoken two words to him. I'm not sure what to say. *How's it going? Any new mistresses this week?* Or perhaps, *What's there to do in the Bahamas besides betraying your marriage vows and destroying our family?*

I shove all of that into the back of my mind and slip on my polite dealing-with-the-public face. But the smile I'm conjuring quickly fades when I see who's walking toward the desk.

The Lord of Darkness himself, Lennon Mackenzie.

My first thought: *What the hell is he doing in here?*

He never comes in the clinic. Ever, ever, ever. It's probably been a year since he's stepped foot inside this waiting room.

My second thought: *OH SWEET LORD, HE SAW ME SPYING ON HIM IN HIS BEDROOM.*

If there's a God above, please let him or her grant me the power of time travel, so that I can rewind the clock and completely avoid this nightmare of a situation. I blink slowly, hoping Lennon will disappear when I reopen my eyes, but no. He and his too-tall body—*don't you dare think about his bare chest*—are still taking up too much room on the other side of the clinic's desk.

"Hello," he says. It almost sounds like a question.

I think about lifting my chin without saying anything, like he did to me the other day, but quickly decide I'm classier than that. "Good morning," I say formally. No smile. He's not worth the effort.

His eyes drop. He balls his hand into a fist and slowly, gently taps it on top of the desk a couple of times while sucking in a long breath between gritted teeth . . . as though he doesn't know what to say. Or he does, but he *really* doesn't want to say it.

"So . . . ," he finally says.

"So," I agree. Is he avoiding my eyes? It feels as if he might throw dynamite over the desk and race out the door. Now I understand why people say you can cut tension with a knife.

Is he not going to say anything else?

Is he here to confront me?

What do I do?

"I wasn't spying on you," I blurt out defensively. "I was just making adjustments to my telescope. It was repaired. Recently. Recently repaired. I was checking it."

Oh, *now* he's looking at me. Something akin to horror is dawning over his face. Or shock. Or he thinks I'm an idiot. *Why can't I read him?* And why is he not saying anything?

"I didn't even see much," I insist.

He nods slowly.

"Anything, really," I amend. "I was testing my telescope."

"You mentioned that," he says, squinting at me through tight eyes.

"Sorry. I mean, I don't have anything to be sorry about, because I didn't do anything."

"Right."

"It was an accident."

"Got it."

My eyes flick to his arms. He's wearing short sleeves, so now I'm staring at muscle. *Look away! Look away!* Too late. He caught me. Again.

WHAT IS WRONG WITH ME?

"So anyway," he says, setting down a pile of envelopes on the desk, as if nothing is amiss. "I was told to come here and drop off your mail. It got delivered to our shop this morning."

Oh.

I can barely control the low groan of misery that's burring from the back of my throat. If I'd just kept my mouth shut . . .

"Uh, thanks." I shift the letters toward me with one finger and try to recover what little of my pride is left. "These seemed to be sealed, so I guess you guys didn't open them by mistake this time."

He tugs his ear. Chipped black fingernail polish glints under the light. "She really didn't mean to open it. I was there when it happened."

Crap on toast. *He knows.* Of course he does. It's not as if I didn't wonder or consider that possibility. But this doesn't stop embarrassment from washing over me now. I busy myself neatly stacking the letters and avoiding his judgmental eyes.

"Hey," he says in an unexpectedly gentle voice.

I look up and he has a strange expression on his face. I can't tell if it's pity or tenderness, or maybe something else entirely. But it *feels* like he knows something I don't know, and that only increases my panic-fueled pulse.

The door to the clinic swings open. My dad rushes inside. "Forgot my . . ." He spots Lennon and halts. His brows narrow to a dark point. "What the hell are you doing in here?"

Lennon raises both hands in surrender, but the look on his face is baldly defiant. "Just delivering mail, man."

"I'm not your 'man,'" my dad says, voice thick with displeasure.

"Thank God for small favors."

"Show some respect."

"I'll show you mine when you show me yours," Lennon quips, and then adds, "Sir." But he sounds anything but polite.

I'm not sure what to do. Why did Lennon come over here in the first place? He knows how my dad is. To stop things from escalating, I pipe up and say, "Lennon was bringing over mis-delivered mail."

It's as if my dad doesn't even hear me. He just points to the floor and says, "You aren't supposed to step foot on my property."

Lennon shrugs. "*Your* property? Last I checked, you rent this place like the rest of us."

"Don't be a smart-ass."

"Better a smart-ass than a dumb-ass."

Oh, that was a bad thing to say. My dad's expression goes from angry to furious. "Get out."

Lennon gives him a dark smile. "On my way."

"Damn right, you are," my dad mumbles.

Footsteps pound in the hallway behind the desk, and my mom emerges, breathless, head swiveling in every direction as she surveys the scene. "What is going on?" she whispers loudly. "I've got a client on the table!"

"Mrs. Everhart." Lennon nods politely. "Your husband was just throwing me out."

"Dan!" my mom chastises.

My dad ignores her. "Don't come back," he tells Lennon.

"See you, Zorie," Lennon tells me as he pushes the front door open.

"You talk to my daughter again, I'll call the cops," my dad calls out.

Oh, for the love of Pete.

Lennon turns in the doorway and stares at my dad for several long seconds before shaking his head. "Always a pleasure, Mr. Everhart. You're a beacon of civility and chivalry. An absolute *gem*."

Now my dad is livid, and for a second, I'm worried he might punch Lennon. Worse, I'm concerned that Lennon will bring up the Bahamas photo book.

But Lennon's gaze flicks to my mom's, then mine. Without another word, he leaves. The door shuts behind him, and I watch his dark form disappear down the sidewalk.

"Dan," my mother says again, this time in quiet exasperation. In defeat.

Silence fills the waiting room. My father reins in his anger, and just like that, all of his tumultuous energy dissipates into a slant of sunlight that beams through the front windows. He turns to me and calmly says, "Why was he in here? I thought you weren't speaking."

I wave the envelopes Lennon brought. "We aren't. He was telling the truth."

Does he understand how humiliated I am by what just happened? Whatever issues Lennon and I have are ours alone, and I'm sick of being stuck in the middle of my dad's squabbles. All of it: his beef with the Mackenzies, and what he's done to my mom. If he only knew what I was hiding in my bedroom desk . . .

Maybe I should show him the photo book privately and see what he says.

Would he try to talk his way out of it? Or would he come clean? I don't think I have the guts to find out.

Dad stares at me, seemingly expressionless, but I can tell that gears are turning inside his head. Does he have some inkling about what I'm thinking? I relax my features to match his.

After a moment, he sniffles softly and jingles the car keys in his hand. "If that boy bothers you again, Zorie, please tell me. Immediately."

He can hold his breath, but I don't think I'll be confiding anything to him any time soon.

Maybe ever.

5

That was all my dad and I said to each other before he apologized to Mom for making a scene at work. Then he made a pit stop in his office and jogged out the door again. Like nothing had happened. A couple hours later, he's still gone, phoning to tell us to eat lunch without him. He claims he's playing racquetball with a client. Only, I'm not sure I believe that's what he's really doing.

I may not believe *anything* he says anymore.

Mom closed the clinic for lunch, and after nibbling on farm-to-table veggie tacos at her favorite vegetarian restaurant, we are strolling back home through the main Mission Street shopping district.

Apart from food and coffee, the sycamore-lined promenade has nothing anyone really needs, but everything you want. Specialty shops selling Swedish toothbrushes, craft sake, exotic hand puppets, and toys made from recycled wood are tucked between a handful of national chain stores. And all along the sidewalks in front of these shops, moms and tattooed street punks share benches as they listen to a student jazz ensemble that plays for donations outside the Jitterbug coffee shop.

"You barely said anything in the restaurant," Mom points out, carting the leftovers from our meal in a white plastic bag. "I know it was busy and loud in there, but you usually get in at least *one* joke about vegetarians."

It's easy to do. Tacos should have meat. That place goes against nature. Half of the people who eat there are in need of a good iron supplement.

"Just thinking about the trip," I lie.

"The trip . . . or your dad making an idiot of himself in front of Lennon?"

"Maybe both," I admit, slanting my eyes toward hers. "Diamond Dan went a little nuts."

"Diamond Dan can get carried away by his emotions sometimes." She sighs deeply, tugging on the diagonal seam of her tunic scrub top. "I've never agreed with how he's treated Lennon. If the Mackenzies ever treated you that way—"

"But they don't."

She nods. "I know. And it's not much of an excuse, but your father is really stressed out right now about the business. He's lost so many massage clients. We're bleeding fairly profusely now, and I'm not sure how to stanch the wound until the business bounces back."

I consider this for a moment. "You could call Grandpa Sam. He'd loan you money."

Grandpa Sam is my mom's dad. He's the nicest guy in the world. Her parents came to the US when she was a baby, and they own a shipping company, Moon Imports and Exports—Moon is their Korean family name—that ships machinery from South Korea. The Moons aren't wealthy, but they're doing all right. Grandpa Sam's the one who bought me Nancy Grace Roman and all my other astronomy gear. I text him my best constellation photos every month, and he texts me back in nothing but repeated, enthusiastic emojis. He used to send only smiley faces, but lately he's been branching out to thumbs-up signs and stars.

"No, we're not asking my parents for any more money," Mom says firmly. "They've already done enough."

We walk in silence for a few steps, and then I think about something she said. "Why aren't you losing acupuncture clients?"

"Hmm?"

"If the Mackenzies' sex shop is pushing away Dad's massage clients, then why are most of your clients still around?"

She shrugs. "Who knows? Maybe because there are more massage therapists in Melita Hills than acupuncturists. I'm a rare commodity."

"Maybe Dad should take up acupuncture too."

"Believe me, your father and I have considered a dozen options. We've analyzed the business to pieces over the last few months."

When we get to the end of the block, a woman dripping with beaded jewelry wants to tell us about the benefits of psychoneuroimmunology while a man in a shabby suit across the sidewalk tries to hand us a pamphlet about salvation. I wave both of them away. "Can I ask you a question?" I say after we cross the street. "Are you happy with Dad?"

Mom's head turns toward me. "Why would you ask that?"

"I don't know." But now I wish that I hadn't.

"Of course I am," she assures me.

I don't know how to feel about this. How can she be happy while my dad is gallivanting around the globe with other women? Shouldn't she realize that something is wrong? I think I'd know something was awry if my partner was cheating on me. At least, I'd hope so. My only personal experience with relationships is Andre Smith. I started seeing him after homecoming, but right before our second date, his mom got a job in Chicago, and they moved. Our third date was at his farewell party, and because we were never going to see each other again, we got a little . . . carried away with the goodbyes. Bad choices were made. Apart from my taking three pregnancy tests after he left—just to be triple certain—and then confessing what we did to my mom for health advice to be *quadruple* certain, the whole experience was a letdown. For me, anyway. Andre emailed for weeks, trying to keep things going, until I was left with no choice but to flag his email address as spam.

This is what happens when I don't stick to a plan. Complete and utter disaster. Never again.

Mom runs a hand over the top of my head. "Money problems are a strain on any couple. But we'll get through it. Bad times don't last. You just have to hang on until they pass."

But she doesn't know how bad they really are. And the thing that's bothering me, other than Dad's unhinged fit of anger this morning, is the worry that I'm not the only one keeping secrets about Dad's extracurricular activities. The Mackenzies know. Lennon knows. How long before that knowledge leaks and my mom finds out?

I can't let that happen.

"Are those hives?" my mom asks, stopping to look at my arm. "Jesus, Zorie. You're covered in them. Have you had shrimp?"

"No." Sometimes shellfish causes them, but mostly it's stress and the occasional random allergen. It's unpredictable. My body is a mystery.

She frowns at me, worry tightening her face. "You have to get back on daily antihistamines. And we need to get some more of that homeopathic cream from Angela's shop."

The cream gives me a headache, but I don't say this. Mom is telling me that we can stop and pick it up on our way back if we hurry, but something across the street catches my attention. Lennon's big, black satanic hearse is parked at the curb. We're half a block or so away from his place of employment, so he must be working. And thinking about his fight with my dad this morning makes me realize something: I will be gone for a week, while Lennon will be here. All it would take is one more standoff with my dad and Lennon might say something about the photo book.

I need to make him promise that he'll keep his mouth shut.

"Look, you don't need to be late for your next appointment," I tell Mom. "I can walk down to Angela's and pick up the hive cream."

She hesitates before digging inside her scrubs pocket and handing me some money. "All right. Ask her if she'll give it to you for a free cupping session in exchange. Sometimes she'll barter."

"Honor among healers?"

"Something like that. Take an antihistamine when you get home, and let me check on you later, okay?"

"Will do."

"I mean it. Don't make me have to take you to Sacred Heart."

"Not *those* monsters," I say dramatically. "Conventional medicine is for chumps."

She pokes a tickling finger into my side, making me laugh. "Watch your hives, young lady."

I assure her that I will.

After we part ways, I backtrack down the sidewalk to cross the street, passing Lennon's car. Then I head toward the business on the corner.

Reptile Isle is one of the oldest reptile shops in California. The brick shop front is covered in an enormous rainforest mural, complete with lizards and turtles and snakes, oh my. I walk past giant pieces of driftwood and tropical plants flanking its recessed entrance and push open the door.

Inside, my eyes adjust to diffuse light as the thick, musky scent of substrate and snake fills my nostrils. Hundreds of tanks and terrariums line the walls, their UV lights and heat lamps creating a warm atmosphere. Most of the reptiles here are for sale, but the people who own the shop also have a breeding program in the back, and they do a lot of educational outreach.

A large checkout counter sits near the entrance, but Lennon's not running the register, so I glance around the expansive shop and try to spot him. Under wooden beams that crisscross a large, open ceiling, I wind around aisles stacked with plastic caves, plant replicas, and endless reptilian supplies: tank thermostats, feeding dishes, lizard hammocks. In the center of the store, inside a massive habitat cage, the skeleton of an old tree stands, its bare branches decked with tiny wooden platforms. Tropical plants hang from the cage's ceiling and flowering vines creep up its screened walls.

This is where I spot Lennon.

He's standing inside the cage with a giant green iguana draped around his shoulders.

"Her name is Maria," Lennon is telling a child standing on the outside of the cage with her nose pressed to the screen. "She's from Costa Rica."

"How old is she?" the girl asks.

"She's five years old," Lennon says.

"That's how old you are," the mother reminds her.

The girl seems suitably impressed. "This is where she lives?"

"She has the entire cage to herself," Lennon confirms. "She's almost four feet long, so she needs a lot of space to roam around. Want to see her tail?"

He ducks low on the other side of the screen to give her a peek.

Eyes wide, the little girl is both fascinated and wary. "Will she bite?"

"If she's scared," Lennon says, coaxing the big lizard from his shoulders to a platform above, where it crawls beneath a potted tropical plant. "She only likes to be handled by a few special friends. It takes her a long time to trust people enough to let them get close to her. But she doesn't mind if you admire her from out there."

"Can I have her for a pet?"

Lennon pretends to think about this. "She needs a lot of space, and we'd be sad if we couldn't see her every day. If you like lizards, a better pet would a green anole or a leopard gecko. They are pretty easy to take care of, if your mom is willing to buy live insects. . . ." He glances at the mother, who shakes her head firmly. Lennon quickly says, "*Or*, you could just come here to visit Maria."

The girl considers this thoughtfully while the mother gives Lennon an enthusiastic thumbs-up. His face relaxes into a warm smile. I haven't seen him smile like that in a long time. It's sweet and boyish. Unexpectedly, a hollow ache wells up inside my chest.

Stop being ridiculous, I tell myself.

I wrestle unwanted emotions down, packing them away as the mother thanks him and leads her daughter toward the turtle area of the store. When Lennon is alone, I approach the cage with trepidation.

"Hey," I say.

He swings around and spots me. His head jerks back in surprise, and he glances around, as if hidden cameras might appear, more wary than the little girl was about the possibility of an iguana bite. "What's up?"

"I was on my way back from lunch and saw your car," I say, as if this is a totally normal thing, me stopping by. As though I haven't refused to walk on this side of the street for months to avoid accidentally bumping into him.

He shifts into a defensive stance, arms crossing chest. "Sure you aren't here to serve me with an arrest warrant for trespassing?"

I wince inwardly. "My dad is—"

"A dick?"

"Anxious."

Lennon snorts. "So *that's* what we're calling it."

"Look, you'd be stressed too, if the business you built was going to hell because all your clients were scurrying away faster than rats on a sinking ship."

He makes a low, thoughtful noise, and the sound rumbles through the screen, scattering my thoughts and doing strange, unwanted things to the inside of my chest. It's the feeling you get when a large truck trundles down the road. You can't see it, but you can feel it, and that makes you leery for no logical reason.

"That's wrong, actually," he points out. "The original phrase was, 'When a building is about to fall down, all the mice desert it.'"

"Yeah? Well, you better *actually* hope that doesn't happen, seeing how we're all stuck in the same building," I say, suddenly irritated with his know-it-all factoids. "If we fall down, the rubble might bury your shop. And then where would all the neighborhood perverts buy their butt plugs?"

"Gee, I don't know." He braces his hands on the wooden frame of the habitat and leans down until his face is at my level, pressing his forehead against the screen between us. A clean, sunny scent wafts from his clothes, one that's painfully familiar. The scent of Lennon. "Maybe they'll go to the same store where your dad buys the sticks that are stuck up his ass. I think it's next to Adulterers Are Us."

Fury bubble ups. "You . . . ," I start, and then realize how loud I'm being. I lean closer to the screen and lower my voice. "You cannot tell anyone about that photo book."

"I think anyone with a working bullshit meter already knows he's a scumbag."

"My mom doesn't!" I shout-whisper at his stupid face.

Sharp eyes lock with mine. He makes a small noise. "You didn't give her the package."

"Because it will break up their marriage," I whisper. "I can't do that to my mom. It would kill her."

Lennon doesn't respond. Just studies my eyes.

"You cannot say anything to my mom," I plead. "And until I figure out what to do, you need to tell your moms to keep quiet about it too."

"I can't control what they say to your mom. If you recall, they were once all friends. Come to think of it, so were the two of us, before you decided moving up the social ladder was more important."

"What?" That's not how things went down. *He* ditched me.

"Frankly, I'm surprised you'd risk being seen in public talking to me," he says. "Every second you're near me, your hit points drop. Better watch it, or your life meter's going to drop to zero."

"I don't even know what that means."

"That's because you've been hanging around with Reagan effing Reid for too long."

"Says the boy who sits home alone with a bunch of snakes."

"Hey, you would know, spymaster general."

I press my forehead again the screen. "I already told you, that was a mistake."

His dark eyes are centimeters from mine. "Was it?"

"Huge."

"If you say so."

"Enormous."

"I'm flattered."

"I . . ." *Wait. What are we talking about?*

His smile is slow and cocky.

I pull back from the screen. My ears suddenly feel like someone's holding a blowtorch up to my head. Tugging the curling ends of my bob, I try to cover the telltale redness, wishing it away before the blush spreads down my neck.

"Screw this," I say. "I was going to apologize for my dad's behavior, but now I might be glad he bit your head off. I hope you have to get a rabies shot."

"Am I the bat or Ozzy? Because if your dad was doing the biting, technically he'd have to get the rabies shot."

"I hate you so much."

"You know," he says after huffing out a single, sarcastic chuckle, "I genuinely felt bad for you. I really did, for all of two seconds. Guess I was an idiot, because I can see now that nothing's changed. You're still the same cold-as-ice girl. You're just like him. You know that, right? More concerned with appearances than anything real. Maybe lying runs in your blood."

Chaotic emotions bubble up. Embarrassment. Pain. And something else I can't identify. Anger. That must be what it is, because without warning, my eyes sting with unshed tears.

Don't you dare cry in front of him, I tell myself.

"Zorie," he says, voice low and rough. "I . . ."

He doesn't finish, and it doesn't matter. I don't care what Lennon Mackenzie thinks. Not now, and not ever.

"I thought I could come in here and talk reasonably with you," I say, using the calmest, most professional voice I can muster as I step farther away from the cage. "But I guess I was wrong. All I ask is that if you and your parents have any respect for my mother—"

"Zorie—"

I raise my voice to talk over him. "—that you'll stay out of her business and let me handle it. If anyone's going to destroy her life, it should be me, not some stranger who doesn't care about her."

And with that, I walk out of the store.

Tomorrow can't come soon enough.

6

"You have everything?" Mom asks, testing the weight of my backpack. It's almost ten in the morning, and Reagan's supposed to pick me up in a few minutes. I stopped by the clinic to tell my parents goodbye. "Good lord, this is heavy."

"That's my portable telescope and camera." Who knew ten pounds could be so heavy? It takes up a lot of space in the pack, so I've got one of the tents Reagan bought stuffed in the bottom, a compressed sleeping bag, clothes neatly rolled to save space, a couple of energy bars, peanut butter cups, and some chocolate-covered espresso beans—you know, all the major food groups.

I also *may* have brought a grid-lined journal. Just a small one. And a few gel pens.

"You have the emergency cash I gave you?"

I pat the pocket of my purple plaid shorts. They match my purple Converse, which match my purple eyeglass frames. Did I mention the glittery purple nail polish? I'm killing it. Someone should pay me to look this sharp. One modeling contract, pronto.

"Portable cell phone charger?"

"In my pack," I lie. It's an older model that weighs a ton, and in the battle of heavy versus heavy, my telescope and camera won. Besides, they'll have electricity at the glamping compound. I can just plug my phone in.

Mom inspects my arms. "Hive cream?"

"Yes, I've got the stinky homeopathic cream. Where's Dad? I need to leave soon."

"Dan!" she calls out to the back rooms, cupping her hands around her mouth. Then she turns back to me. "He's rushing to head out to the bank. I tried to get an increase on the clinic's credit card, and they say our credit score is too low because we're overextended. Which is crazy, because that's our only credit account, and I paid off your father's car loan last year. There must be some mistake. He'll get it sorted out. Oh, there you are," she says as he jogs into the reception area, keys in hand.

And toward the front door.

"I'll be back in a jiff," he says, keys in hand.

"Dan, Zorie's leaving for her camping trip," Mom says, sounding as exasperated as I feel.

He turns around and blinks at me, and apparently is just now noticing my backpack. "Of course," he says, smoothly covering up his faux pas with a charming smile. "Excited to spend time with the Reid daughter?"

"Reagan," I say.

"Reagan," he repeats. More smiling. He turns to my mom and says, "Everything checked out at the campsite, right? The girls will be safe there?"

"They have security and everything," Mom says. "I told you, remember? Mrs. Reid talked to the owner, and they're going to pay special attention to their group."

"Right, right," Dad murmurs, nodding enthusiastically. Then he smiles at me, starts to extend his arms as if he might hug me—which is weird, because we don't normally do that anymore—and then changes his mind and pats me on the head. "Have a great time, kiddo. Stay in touch with Joy and take your pepper spray in case there are any boys with roaming hands."

There will be boys, and I certainly *hope* there will be roaming hands. But no way am I telling him that, so I just laugh, and it sounds as hollow as his smile looks.

He nods stiffly, and it's awkward. "Gotta get to the bank. See you when you get back," he says, and before I can answer, he's jogging out the front door.

When he's gone, I vent at Mom. "Hello! I'm leaving for an entire week. Does he realize this?"

She holds up a hand in shared exasperation. "He knows. I told him I could take care of the bank on my lunch break, but he insisted it had to be now. He's just—"

"Stressed," I say, resigned. "Yeah."

And what's up with this credit thing at the bank? That sounds fishy. Or maybe I'm just suspicious of everything my dad touches.

"Hey, forget him. I'm right here," she says, holding my face in her hands. "And I'm going to miss you like crazy. I will also worry every day, so please call or text to check in when you can."

"Spotty cell service," I remind her. We read warnings about it on the glamping compound's website.

She nods. "If I don't hear from you, I won't alert state troopers. Not unless you aren't standing here in front of me at noon next Friday. In one piece, I might add."

"Don't know about one piece, but I'll be here. Reagan's got to be back for some presemester orientation thing for her cross-country team," I remind her. "Speaking of, I'd better get outside. Need to stay on schedule."

She grasps my arm to peer at my watch and winces at the time. "Crap. I need to get the room ready for my first appointment."

Good, because I really want to get out there alone before Joy decides to walk me outside and greet Reagan. Like my father, she's still under the illusion that this is a girls-only trip, and I'd like to keep it that way.

"I changed my mind. Don't go." She hugs me extra hard and then clings dramatically.

"Mom," I say, laughing. "You're unbalancing my life force."

"Have I told you how much I love you?"

"Not today. But you *did* buy me turkey jerky, and if that's not a token of affection, I don't know what is."

"I love you, sweet thing."

"Love you back," I tell her.

When she finally lets me go, I lift my heavy backpack onto one arm and salute her goodbye.

"Don't forget to feed Andromeda at dinner," I remind her. That's usually my job; Mom feeds her in the morning.

"I won't," she assures me as I'm opening the door. "You don't pee on your shoes and try not to provoke any bears."

"If I see a bear, I'll pass out from fear, so he'll just think I'm dead."

"That seems reasonable. And, Zorie?"

"Yes?"

"Don't be cautious, be careful. Have a good time, okay?"

I give her a confident nod and head outside.

It's a perfect summer day. Not too hot, not too cool. Pretty blue sky. I'm feeling a weird mix of anxiety and anticipation as I lug my backpack toward a striped no-parking space in front of the curb.

No sign of Reagan yet, so I decide to do one last practice run on my backpack. I tried it on when it was empty, but now that it's full, I'm forced to squat in order to lift it and am struggling to get it on both shoulders. When I finally manage it, I wobble clumsily and nearly topple over backward. How am I supposed to hike a dirt trail with this thing? Feels like an overweight sloth is clinging to my neck. Maybe if I secure the strap that buckles around my waist . . .

"You've got it packed wrong," someone calls out.

I turn around slowly, in case I actually *do* fall over—which is a real possibility, not kidding—and it takes me exactly one second to spot the voice's owner: black Converse high-tops, black jeans with artfully ripped holes in both knees, and a T-shirt with a heart inside an X-ray skeletal chest.

Lennon is sitting on the hood of his hearse, which is parked a few yards away in one of the public spaces in the middle of our cul-de-sac. "You're supposed to pack the heavy stuff in the center, near your back. Let your hips carry the weight, not your shoulders. When it's packed right, you won't be the Leaning Tower of Pisa."

"I'm not . . ." I shift my feet and lean forward slightly, barely preventing a bodily avalanche. *Dammit.*

Lennon's smile is slow and annoying. He's wearing jet-black sunglasses, so I can't see his eyes. Double annoying. Why is he even talking to me? Didn't I tell him I hated him yesterday?

"What do you have in there?" he asks. "Gold bricks?"

"My telescope."

"You fit Nancy Grace Roman inside that pack?"

I'm shocked he remembers. "No, the portable one."

"Ah. Well, it's packed wrong."

"And I should trust you because you're *such* an expert on back-packing," I say irritably.

He leans back on both hands and lifts his face to the sun. "Actually, I kind of am."

"Since when?"

"Since forever. I backpacked with my moms in Europe when I was thirteen—"

Oh, yeah. I forgot about that. "But that was in hostels."

"And campgrounds."

Right.

"And three times this year. Three? Wait, maybe four," he says, more to himself than me. He shrugs a shoulder lightly. "One of them doesn't count, but anyway."

"You went to Europe this year?" I say, surprised.

"No, I backpacked here in California. My parents gave me a national park pass for Christmas and took me camping in Death Valley over spring break. I even took a wilderness survival course."

Does not compute. This isn't Lennon at all. The boy I knew didn't spend time outdoors. I mean, sure, we technically spent most of our time together outside on all those walks, but that was here in the city. Before I can make sense of this new development in Lennon, Man of Mystery, he speaks up again.

"I can help you repack if you want," he says, still looking up at the sky, where misty trails of morning fog are drifting back out to the Bay, silver streaks against bright blue.

Lennon Mackenzie with his hands on my private stuff? *I don't think so, buddy.*

"No, thanks." I let the pack's straps slide down my arms until it's back on the ground. And then, in an attempt to shut him up, I add, "My ride should be here any second."

"Yeah, I just got a text."

Huh? Wait just one stinking second.

Backpack advice. Camping in Death Valley. Spotted hanging out with Brett . . .

Oh, no. Oh *no, no, no.*

This is not Brett's new bromance. This is not the "guy" who's leading us to a secret off-trail waterfall in the Sierras. It can't be! Reagan knows I avoid him. She doesn't know *why*, exactly, but she should have told me. Why didn't she tell me? There must be some mistake.

Panic fires through my limbs as a dark blue SUV whips into the parking lot. Lennon casually jumps from the hood of his car, landing lightly on his feet. He bends to pick up something out of sight, near the front wheel. When he stands back up, he's pulling a red backpack onto one shoulder. The top outer pocket is covered with vintage punk-rock buttons and retro national parks patches. A foam bedroll is neatly secured to its bottom.

Holy hell.

Blaring electronic dance music, the blue SUV skids as it brakes between us, and then Reagan's light brown head pops up from the driver's door. "Glamping time, bitches!" she shouts merrily over the stereo. "Packs go up top in the cargo container. Let's hustle."

My mind can't form a coherent thought. I know I'm staring stupidly as Brett lurches out of the SUV to clap Lennon soundly on the shoulder. "Lennon, my boy," he says, voice full of joy. "That shirt is sick! I love it. Come on, I'll help you get the cargo box open. The latch is screwed up." Brett notices me for the first time.

My stomach flips over.

You know how people say they are blinded by love? That's what happens to me when I see Brett. He looks like a celebrity, all tanned legs and sandy brown curls, a face too perfect for a mortal high school boy. And don't get me started on his teeth. They are insanely perfect. I never knew teeth could be so attractive.

He flashes me those million-dollar teeth in a dazzling grin. "Zorie. Still rocking that sexy scientist vibe," he says, pointing finger guns at my glasses while making a zinging noise. Then he waves me closer for a hug. "Bring it on in, girl. Haven't seen you in forever."

Oh, wow. I'm overwhelmed by the spicy scent of aftershave. He smells a little like my dad, which is a weird thing to think. *Shut up, brain!* This is all Lennon's fault for surprising me. His presence is throwing me off my game. And now Brett lets me go, so I wasted the entire two-second hug with the boy of my dreams thinking about (A) my dad and (B) the boy of my nightmares. Terrific.

"What you been up to this summer?" Brett asks lightly.

Say something. Do not blow this. "You know, working."

Working? That's the best I could come up with? I work twice a week at the clinic for a few hours, so why am I making it sound like I'm slaving over a paycheck at a real job? I want a do-over, but Brett's attention has shifted to the task of opening the big plastic cargo carrier attached to the SUV's roof rack. Meanwhile, Lennon is looking back at me—nay, full-on staring—and I can't tell what he's thinking because of those stupid sunglasses, but it *feels* judgmental.

Is this really happening? Lennon is coming with us?

Brett pops open the cargo carrier and helps Lennon lift his pack inside, nestling it in among several others. Lennon gestures silently with one hand and a tilt of his head, offering to help me lift my pack. I try to do it myself, and end up having to let Lennon and Brett boost it up. Which is humiliating.

"Hey," I say in greeting to Kendrick Taylor, closing the door as I get settled in my seat.

Kendrick's family owns a successful winery that's lauded in the press for being one of the best vineyards in Sonoma County. Since he goes to private school in Melita, I've only met him once, when Reagan hauled me to a party.

"Zorie, right?" he says, squinting one eye closed. In a chambray button-down and khaki shorts that contrast pleasantly with his dark brown skin, he's better-looking than I remembered, and has a friendly, confident demeanor.

A tall girl with long, sun-streaked hair leans around the front passenger seat. Summer Valentino. If you crave gossip about anyone in school, she knows it. And even though her grades were so bad that technically she should have had to repeat eleventh grade, she's on the yearbook committee *and* the online school newspaper—which apparently saved her.

"Zorie's into astrology," Summer tells Kendrick.

"Astronomy," I correct.

"D'oh!" she says, smiling. "I always get those mixed up. Which one is the horoscopes?"

"*Astrology*," Kendrick enunciates, pretending to give her a slap on the head, which she ducks with a silly grin.

Brett speaks up from behind me and introduces Kendrick to Lennon.

"This is my boy," Brett tells Kendrick, roughly shaking Lennon's shoulder. "This kid is *wild*. Right, John Lennon?"

Lennon's sitting behind Kendrick, so I can see him better than Brett. "If you say so," Lennon deadpans.

"Is that really your name?" Kendrick asks.

"Minus the John," Lennon says. "But Brett never lets that stop him."

If I didn't know better, I might wonder if this is a jab. But Brett just laughs as if it's the funniest joke in the world.

Um, okay. What is going on here?

"Lennon's father is Adam Ahmed from Orphans of the State," Summer supplies. "They opened for Green Day a million years ago. His dad was that Egyptian-American drummer dude."

"Guitarist," Lennon corrects quietly, but I don't think anyone hears him except me.

"Didn't one of your moms crash at Billie Joe Armstrong's house for a few weeks?" Reagan asks, programming a route into the SUV's navigation system. "Doesn't she know his wife, or something?"

Before he can answer, Summer pipes in with: "Is it true that your moms were, like, together with your dad all at the same time?" She pauses, and says in a lower voice, "I mean, the three of them?"

"I got your meaning," Lennon says.

"That's just what I heard around school," Summer tells him apologetically. But not so apologetic that she's shutting the question down.

"I've heard that around school myself," Lennon says.

"Well?" Summer prompts.

"My parents did a lot of things," Lennon says enigmatically.

The intrigue inside the car is high. Scandal! Gasp! Thing is, Sunny and Mac are one of the most in-love, devoted couples I've ever known. Whatever they've done or haven't done is none of anyone's business. I start to say this, then wonder why the hell I should defend Lennon if he's not even bothering to defend himself. I know it used to bother him, all the rumors people at school spread behind his back. Everyone loves to discuss his family life. Even my dad has accused Sunny and Mac of being heathens.

Maybe Lennon doesn't care anymore. Maybe he's just embracing it.

"One hundred percent rock-and-roll," Brett says. "Kerouac would have *so* approved of that. Did you know he and his best friend Neal Cassady both slept with Carolyn Cassady, Neal's wife? Wild, huh? I bet you have crazy stories growing up in a punk-rock household."

"So crazy," Lennon says flatly.

Brett claps his hands together and tells us all, "This dude right here has legendary blood in his veins. San Francisco punks were the Beat Poets of the eighties and nineties."

Huh. Now I'm connecting the dots. Brett thinks Lennon has pedigree. That's why he's decided Lennon is a "wild man."

Lennon looks wild, all right. About as wild as a depressed corpse.

"Okay, we're all here and everyone's acquainted," Reagan says. "Are we ready to roll?"

"We're gonna have some crazy-ass fun this week," Brett says, throwing his arm over Lennon's shoulder so that he can snap a quick selfie. Lennon's expression remains dour while Brett sticks out his tongue toward the screen. "Right?"

Lennon leans back in his seat and echoes his previous words. "If you say so."

"Right, Reagan?" Brett calls out to the front.

"Let's do this," she confirms, shifting the SUV into drive. "Sierras, here we come."

As Reagan drives down Mission Street, she informs us that the drive to the glamping compound is more than four hours. And for the first few minutes, the car is loud and chaotic, everyone trying to talk at once. Reagan is telling Kendrick about the camp's amenities while Summer adds her own commentary about a glamping site in Colorado that her parents visited for their anniversary. Brett is trying to tell Reagan about nearby places mentioned in Jack Kerouac's *On the Road*. And surprisingly, Reagan seems interested. This is news to me, because she usually tunes out whenever Brett goes all rhapsodic about the Beat Poets at school. He's always trying to get people to drive across the Bay Bridge into San Francisco for afternoon excursions to Beat-friendly City Lights Bookstore—"It's a historic landmark." And Reagan is always complaining that poetry is boring.

And throughout all of this, Lennon stays quiet.

Maybe it will be easy to ignore him.

I glance around the car, and it really hits me that, minus Lennon, I'm going on a weeklong trip with some of the most popular people at school. Mom was right. I needed to do this to feel less like an outsider. I'm going to have fun. Everything's going to be fine.

Lennon's unwanted presence can't ruin this.

And I am *definitely* not scratching my arm. If anything was going to make my hives worse, it would be Lennon. So I can't let him. Deep breaths. I'm okay. I'm totally okay.

After we head out of the East Bay, conversation becomes as monotonous as the valley scenery. Outside my window, I spy flat farmland, fruit trees, wide blue skies, and the occasional small town. Long stretches of highway are punctuated with truck stops and roadside fruit stands, and people turn to their phones for entertainment. A little over halfway through the trip, Kendrick points out Bullion's Bluff, a tiny historical mining town just off the highway. "They've got a fairly big winery," he says. "My parents brought me once. The downtown is totally nineteenth-century Gold Rush era. I'm talking Old West saloon and general store. Gold Rush museum. The works. It's schlocky, but it's fun."

Since Summer complains that she needs to use a public restroom after drinking an enormous soda, Reagan decides to pull off the highway. After passing a run-down gas station, we spot the downtown area easily enough. Kendrick was right: It looks like a set from an old Western movie. A sign even brags that one was filmed here in the 1980s.

The Gold Rush museum looks pretty shabby and has an entrance fee. We agree to forgo that and head to the Bullion General Store instead, parking alongside a line of travel trailers in front of a wooden hitching post—no horses, alas—and a water trough filled with planted cacti.

Inside, the spacious store is bustling with tourists, jammed from floor to ceiling with goods for sale—everything from old-fashioned candy and brown bottles of sarsaparilla, to gold-nugget jewelry and a mining cart filled with polished stones. It also smells like peanut butter fudge, which makes me hungry. Peanut butter is my weakness.

The candy counter has a line, so while Summer looks for a restroom with Reagan, and the boys are magnetically drawn to a display of mining pickaxes—complete with a cardboard standee of a cartoon old-timey prospector—I meander around the aisles until I'm in an outdoor gear section. A sign advertising "bear vaults" catches my attention. Or maybe it's the gigantic stuffed bear that's standing on two legs with its arms raised. A sign hanging around its neck reads KINGSLY THE BEAR.

"Gross," I whisper, seeing that part of its dusty fur is ripped. It also smells funky. But honestly, I'd take all the motley smells in this place 100 percent over the SUV, where Brett's aftershave was starting to give me a headache.

"You have one, right?" a deep voice says.

Lennon steps next to me like a ghost from the shadows.

"Jesus, sneak up on people much?" I complain under my breath. "Have one what?"

He points to the canisters lining a wooden cubby on the wall. A pleasant scent wafts from his clothes. "Bear vault."

"Not planning on capturing any bears, so no."

"They're for storing food, foolish human."

I give him a sidelong glance. He's holding a square of candy inside wax paper. When he takes a bite, I realize why he smells so nice. Peanut butter fudge.

"So good," he mumbles. He knows I'm a PB addict. At least, he used to know. Maybe he forgot and is completely oblivious that me watching him eat this is total food porn.

I ignore his little moan of ecstasy. "I still don't know what you're talking about."

Juggling his fudge, he grabs a black barrel-shaped canister off the shelf and flips open a hinged lid. "Bear vault, to store your food. Bears can smell food from a couple miles away. Not even kidding. They will tear down cabin doors and break car windows to get their grub on. You have to keep everything inside one of these babies. Food. Toiletries. Anything with a strong scent, like Brett's cologne."

I give Lennon a dirty look. Brett's wearing aftershave, not cologne. At least, I think. Who wears cologne? I mean, other than my cranky grandpa John. That's my dad's homophobic and slightly racist father, who thinks everyone should "speak English." My grandpa Sam doesn't speak English, but he sure as hell doesn't wear cologne.

"I'm sure the glamping compound knows how to keep bears out of food," I tell Lennon.

"They do, which is why no food is allowed in the tents, unless it's in a bear vault," he says, crinkling the wax paper as he peels it back for another bite of candy.

I hold up an invisible phone and pretend to talk into it. "Hey, Siri, is Lennon full of shit? What's that? Oh, he is. Great. Thank you."

"Hey, Siri? Is everything I just said true?" he says, playing along. He pretends to wait for a response and then talks into the bear canister. "Why, yes, Lennon. It most certainly is. You're in a Bear Zone. It's against federal law to store unprotected food."

"That law sounds completely made-up," I tell him.

"Didn't you read the rules?"

What rules?

Lennon rolls his eyes toward the ceiling. "I also emailed Brett a list of things we'll need on the trail. He said he was going to share it with the group."

What list? I'm suddenly worried that I was left out of the loop. Forgotten. And this just reignites my anxieties about whether my presence is wanted on this trip. But I'm not telling Lennon this.

"Reagan bought a lot of stuff for this week," I report. "But I don't remember any bear containers. She's been camping here before, so maybe she knows something you don't. Maybe we don't need them."

Lennon mumbles an unintelligible curse under his breath. "We'll definitely need them when we go backpacking." He holds the canister behind his neck to demonstrate. It's about the same size as his head—too big. "You can strap it to the top of your pack like this, or down at the bottom, which might be better for people prone to balance problems." He smirks at me with his eyes.

I fantasize about bashing his big head with the stupid bear vault. "Why are you here?"

"Why are any of us here, Zorie? Life is a mystery."

I groan. "On this trip."

"Oh," he says innocently. He's not smiling, but there's a fraction of humor behind his eyes. "The cologne bandit invited me. I'm 'the coolest,' apparently," he says making air quotes with one hand while he takes another bite of fudge.

Again with the snark. Why is he hanging out with Brett if he hates him so much?

"But you knew I was coming?" I probe.

"I did."

"Why didn't you say something?"

He shrugs. "I only recently decided to go."

Is that true? I remember back to when Reagan first told me about off-trail backpacking and her not being sure if Brett's "friend" who told him about this bucket-list hidden waterfall was committed to coming.

"Why?" I ask.

"I have my reasons."

"Which are . . . ?"

Lennon stares at his fudge for a long moment. Then he seems to change his mind about what he was going to say and hands me the open canister. "Get this. And maybe a bear bell," he says, pointing to a display of big silver bells designed to be clipped to a backpack. "It gives bears a gentle warning that you're in the area, so that you don't surprise them. A surprised bear is a defensive bear, and a defensive bear kills."

Is he serious? I *think* he is, but I'm not totally sure. And before I can ask for clarification or point out that he's avoiding my question, he retrieves something from his pocket and dumps it inside the open canister. Then he walks away.

I look inside the canister. Sitting at the bottom is a square of peanut butter fudge wrapped in wax paper.

What am I supposed to think about this?

I retrieve the fudge and return the canister to the display shelf, abandoning Kingsly the Bear to catch up with the others. Just because Lennon cries bear vault, doesn't mean I really need it. It's insanely expensive. Besides, Lennon has a penchant for being super technical and obsessive about details. I think he's exaggerating the urgency of bear protection.

Probably.

At the last second, I double back and grab a silver bear bell off the rack.

Better safe than sorry.

Part II

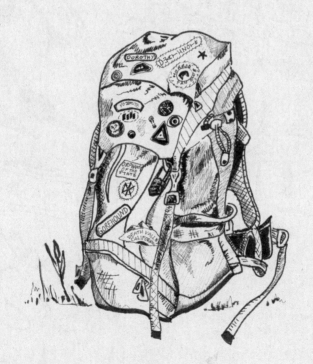

7

The monotonous fruit fields change to rugged foothills covered in lodgepole pine trees as we head west. When we turn off the highway, gray granite cliffs flank the twisting uphill road toward the national forest. Carved wooden signs with painted white lettering point the way to a variety of sights, each marked with distance and pertinent details:

CANYON WALK, 6KM. 3.5 HOUR RETURN.

SCEPTER PASS, 4KM. WEAPONS PROHIBITED.

BLACKWOOD LAKE, 10K. NO PETS. NO FIRES. OVERNIGHT STAY REQUIRES WILDERNESS PERMIT.

And then finally, our destination:

MUIR CAMPING COMPOUND: 2K. 1 HOUR RETURN. WHEELED VEHICLES PROHIBITED PAST PARKING AREA.

Wait, what?

"This is us," Reagan reports, turning. I make a mental note of a High Sierra bus stop here and wonder if this is the route I'll need to use to get to the star party on Condor Peak.

A small, paved parking area sits at the end of a rocky driveway. A dozen or so cars are parked here, most of them luxury vehicles. We find an open space near some wooden steps that lead into thick forest. Another sign sits near the steps, stating that the trail is private property and only for guests of the compound. People using the trail must fill out a form and deposit it inside a locked box.

There is no road past the parking lot.

"Get everything you'll need," Reagan reports. "Unless you want to spend all your time hiking back and forth to the car. The walk back is fine, but it's all uphill to the compound."

"We're hiking to the compound?" I say, staring at the sign. "Two kilometers?"

Reagan gives me a labored look. "Don't start, Everhart. I warned you about hiking."

I'm not even that upset about the hike. It's just unexpected, is all. "I didn't—"

"How long is two kilometers?" Brett asks.

"It's nothing," Reagan tells him brightly.

"A little over a mile," I elaborate.

"Oh, cool," he answers, but he's smiling at Reagan.

And Reagan is smiling back at him. "Easy-peasy, lemon squeezy."

Why are they smiling so big? Did I miss a joke? And now they're high-fiving each other—hard enough to hear the *smack* of palm-on-palm. It's so . . . goofy. Lennon's head turns toward mine, and even though a fringe of black hair obscures one eye, a single dark brow rises in shared judgment of the stupid high five.

Or maybe he's judging *me*.

We all fill out the trail registration cards at the information sign—in case anyone goes missing or gets murdered along the way, they'll know your name and next of kin. And after Brett and Lennon haul down everyone's stuff from the rooftop travel carrier, I'm soon reminded that I'm a human Weeble toy, barely able to stand under the misaligned weight of my backpack. But it's not as if I can repack everything in the middle of the parking lot. So I do my best to strap it on and adjust my stance.

"Saddle up, team," Reagan says loudly to the group. "Luxury awaits us at the end of the trail."

It's just two kilometers, I tell myself. And the woods are pretty amazing, all shady and smelling of pine needles. Birds are chirping, and it's not too warm. I can do this. About five minutes up the first steep hill, I begin to have doubts. Ten minutes up an even steeper incline, I'm picturing Reagan with one of those prospector axes from the general store lodged in her skull. By the time we reach the final stretch toward the compound, I'm just wishing I could drop into a fetal position.

The sign for Muir Camping Compound appears, and I nearly weep when I spot a big building inside a break in the trees. My head is sweating, and I've been walking uphill in a hunched-up position for so long, I'm a hundred-year-old woman with osteoporosis.

But it doesn't matter. The promised land is in front of me, and by God, it may have been worth all that misery, because the compound is *gorgeous*. A modern cedar lodge sits at the forefront: walls of enormous windows, fat timber beams, stacked-stone fireplaces jutting from the roof. Lush forest surrounds it. Jagged mountains in the distance. The whole scene looks like something out of a dream. We head inside.

Warm sunlight streams through double-high windows as we tread across floors of polished river rock and stop at the registration desk. It smells so nice in here, like cedar and fresh-cut flowers. And they have expensive candy sitting in a bowl for the guests. I resist the urge to fill my pockets; Brett does not. He holds a finger up to his mouth and winks at me, stealthily emptying imported chocolate into a pocket on his backpack, while Reagan informs the middle-aged woman working the desk who her mother is.

The woman's name tag reads CANDY. For a second, my oxygen-starved brain reads this as some sort of sign that Brett's been busted, then I realize it's actually her name. "You're Belinda's daughter?" she says to Reagan. "I barely recognize you. Didn't you stay with us last year?"

"I did," Reagan reports cheerfully. "Mom called you about the change in guests, right?"

Candy looks us over. "I was under the impression that your group would be girls. . . ."

You and me both, Candy. I sense a kindred planner spirit in her as she's double-checking her computer screen and an old-fashioned paper registry. Reagan assures Candy that nothing is amiss with our guest list and begins providing her with everyone's names. I meander around the room, and Brett joins me while I examine a wall of framed scenic photos. "Lennon said you take crazy-good photos of stars. I thought you just looked at them."

The jittery feeling I get whenever Brett is nearby returns. Why can't I just feel normal around him? "I . . . do both. Look and take pictures. Of stars. With my camera."

Ugh. Zorie sound like cavewoman.

Brett just laughs, easy and warmly. "Not with your mind?"

"No," I say, hoping my cheeks aren't red.

"Do you just stick a camera on a telescope and zoom in?"

"Sort of. Not exactly? It's . . . There are a lot of fiddly, techy parts. Hard to explain."

His smile is gentle. "Maybe you can teach me how? Because I'd love to take photos of the night sky. Especially the moon. That would be *so* badass."

Is he serious? He's interested in astrophotography? I want to scream, *I WILL TEACH YOU! I WILL TEACH YOU SO HARD*. But Kendrick calls his name, and Brett ducks around me to answer. Before I can open my mouth, he's gone, laughing with Kendrick about a carved wooden statue that looks like two squirrels having sex.

Dammit.

I can't shake the feeling that I'm being watched. It's the same prickly feeling I had in the car, and it makes me anxious. I glance around, and my eyes immediately meet Lennon's. The intensity of his stare is startling.

For the love of Pete, what do you want? It's as if he's accusing me of something. I haven't said a word to him since the Gold Rush store, so I'm not sure what his problem is. I used to be able to read his expressions, but now he's like the mediocre mime who performs outside the Jitterbug on Mission Street, and I can't tell if he's trying to get out of a glass box or signal a taxi. Does Lennon expect a thank-you for the peanut butter fudge? Or is he just trying to unsettle me?

If so, it's working.

But I'll never let him know that. I quickly turn away and head toward Brett and Kendrick and the mating squirrels.

After we're registered, Candy leads us to our cabin tents, giving us an abbreviated tour and answering questions along the way. The main lodge has several lounge areas and connects to a screened-in dining pavilion where dinner will be served later. Outside, winding paths lead to dozens of canvas cabin tents nestled in the woods. Some are rectangular, some round—the yurts—but all are the color of unbleached muslin. They're grouped into areas named after birds, each area a short walk from the next. It takes us about ten minutes to get to our area, Camp Owl, where two of the rectangular tents sitting near a dense forest are reserved for us.

Reagan isn't happy about this. "We're supposed to have a yurt," she argues, "with a view of the valley."

"Sorry, but Camp Falcon was accidentally overbooked. I put a family of six in my last one earlier this morning."

"Not cool," Reagan says grumpily. "We've had the reservation since last summer. My mom isn't going to be happy."

"If you'd like, I'll call her and explain," Candy says. "But this might work out better for you. Girls can take one tent, and the boys can take another."

The implication is obvious. Candy will call Mrs. Reid and inform her that her daughter has brought along three boys. Reagan fumes quietly, but acquiesces. We really don't have a choice.

"Just let life happen," I tell Reagan.

"Yeah," Brett says cheerfully. "That's right, Zorie. You're preaching my word, and I dig it."

The look Reagan gives me could slice through steel.

The tents are both exactly alike: sealed cement floors, canvas walls fixed to a wooden frame, a screen door, slatted windows that can be opened to take advantage of the breeze during the day and closed at night to keep the cabin warm, along with a glass-front tent stove. A small seating area surrounds the stove, with a real sofa and brightly patterned Navajo rugs. Two sets of bunk beds stretch across the back of the tent, all with feather-top mattresses, luxury linens, and down pillows.

Behind the bunks, past a canvas divider, is an en suite toilet and sink. No showers. Those are in the bathhouse down the hill, shared with six other cabins in Camp Owl, Candy reports.

Candy reports a few other things, as well. "You're in bear country, and yes, they've gotten through the national park fence and come into the compound. For everyone's safety, all food must be stored in the food locker when it's not in the process of being served or eaten," she says, pointing outside the tent's door to a green metal box that sits beneath a canopy with two rocking chairs. "Either there, or inside a portable food locker, meaning a bear-resistant food container that's approved by Yosemite and King's Forest."

Lennon's head slowly turns toward mine.

Why, oh, *why* does he have to be right? That peanut butter fudge is not sitting well in my stomach right now.

Candy ticks off a list on her fingers of what we need to store in the locker. "Unopened food, even in cans. Snacks, drink mixes, vacuum-sealed pouches. Every bit of it. All toiletries with a scent. Lotion, makeup, deodorant."

"Cologne, too?" Lennon asks.

"Yes," she says.

"I'm talking *strong* cologne. Like, some kind of extreme body spray."

"Most definitely," the woman answers, perplexed.

Lennon flicks his eyes toward Brett. But Brett is completely oblivious, as he's currently trying to restack water bottles into a pyramid on a console table behind the sofa.

Candy points to the bathroom. "If you need extras of anything—water, razor, towels—just ask at the front desk. You can call, of course, but cell phone service is hit-and-miss up here. If you ever need to make an emergency call, we'll let you use the landline. If it's after ten p.m., Bundy and I stay in the log cabin to the right of the lodge."

"What about backcountry permits for King's Forest?" Lennon asks. "Your website said you can arrange it and have one delivered to our tent."

"For a fee," she says. "We have to drive to a park station to pick them up."

"Put it on my credit card," Reagan says breezily.

Candy gives Reagan a withering look. "You can stop by the desk at your convenience and fill out the form."

Yikes.

"No music is allowed in the tent cabins," Candy says to all of us. "No loud talking after sunset when you're inside your camp. Other guests may be trying to sleep, and these walls aren't sound-proof. Quiet hours start at ten p.m. and last until seven a.m."

"Geez," Summer mumbles under her breath near my ear. "This place is a dictatorship."

Candy points in the general direction of the lodge. "We have a small store that sells sweatshirts and rain gear. You can also rent bear canisters and camp stoves. It's run on the honor system, so you'll need to put cash in the bin or write your tent number and name on the sheet to have it added to your final bill. Also—"

Brett's water-bottle pyramid crashes. Bottles roll across the floor. "Oops, sorry," he says.

Candy pauses, and her inner struggle with patience is showing in the slant of her brows, but, clearing her throat, she finishes her speech. "Evening social time starts at six. We serve drinks, then a four-course dinner. We encourage you to mingle with other guests at the nightly bonfire afterward. The pavilion closes at nine. Any questions, come see us at the registration desk."

What if I have questions now? No one else is paying attention to Candy, but I wish they'd listed all of this stuff on the website or given us a printout so I could review it and memorize everything. I'm itching to ask her to repeat everything so that I can write it all down. Actually, I'm literally itching and resist the urge to scratch. Lennon's gaze flicks to my arms, and I feel as if he knows, which only makes the itch worsen.

If I make it through this week without having a nervous breakdown, I'll consider it a win.

8

Since it's already late in the afternoon, there's no time to do anything before dinner. So the boys retreat to their tent, and we all unpack. I stash all my food and toiletries in the food locker outside and check my telescope for visual damage; it seems to have survived the bumpy trip on top of the SUV and arrived intact. Then I try to call Mom to let her know *I* arrived intact. But there's no service in the tent cabin. There's Wi-Fi at the lodge, so I go ahead and text—both to her and to Avani—and trust that my messages will go through when I get a signal.

Reagan disappears, so Summer and I set out and explore the Camp Owl section of the compound on our own. There's a picnic table between our tent and the boys', and a small trailhead behind us, with a sign warning that the trail feeds into the national forest; Muir Camping Compound absolves itself of responsibility should hikers choose to leave their property. A group of wild, unsupervised kids is running into the woods here, so it can't be all that scary.

We avoid the screaming kids and follow a fastidiously land-scaped trail: cream-colored rocks banded by the occasional flowering shrub and a steady line of path lights. The trail leads to a cedar-shingled bathhouse.

"Whoa," Summer whispers appreciatively when we peek inside, and I'm feeling the same way. It's practically a spa, one that's themed to match our beautiful surroundings, and even nicer in person than it was in the online photos: stained wood countertops, stone benches, pretty lanterns hanging from iron hooks near the mirrors. Unlike our tents, there's electricity here, and a woman is charging her cell phone while she blow-dries her hair. There's even a small sauna in the back.

"I'm getting naked with Kendrick in that sauna later," Summer tells me as we step back outside.

"Too much information," I say.

She laughs. "If you want to get naked with someone, I wouldn't care. Are you still hung up on Brett?"

"Umm . . ."

"He told me you guys hooked up."

What? "We didn't—not like *that*." It was just a kiss, for the love of Pete.

"You're so easy to embarrass," she says, grinning. "Did you know your ears turn red? That's so cute."

Jesus.

"Hey, I was just teasing," she says, slapping my arm playfully. "Brett's sweet. And I like how he's so cool with everyone. Like,

I never would have hung out with Lennon in a million years because I didn't know how cool he was."

I'm not sure how to take this. I think I understand what she's trying to say, and maybe there's a core of earnestness in there somewhere. But I think she's also implying that Lennon wasn't okay until Brett decided he was.

"You and Lennon used to be a thing, huh?"

My body stills. "Who told you that?"

"I just remember seeing you together at school all the time."

"We were just friends," I insist. "Nothing else."

Lie.

One that Summer seems to buy. With a shrug, she says, "I think you guys would make a good couple."

"No," I say, and it sounds like a dog barking. "Absolutely not. We aren't even friends anymore."

She holds up both hands in surrender. "Hey, I only call 'em like I see 'em. Think about it, Miss Astrology."

I won't. And I don't bother to correct her again—not about her word mix-up or Lennon. It's true that people at school used to tease us about being best friends—which was often said with a wink and air quotations—and rumors were spread that we were more. That's precisely one of the reasons we decided to conduct the Great Experiment privately. To avoid gossip at school. Mainly, though, to avoid my dad finding out. Because no way in *hell* would Diamond Dan allow his daughter to date the son of two heathen women.

Anyway, I don't know why I care that Summer assumed something was going on between Lennon and me. I think I should be more concerned that Brett told Summer we hooked up. Maybe Summer heard it wrong or made assumptions. She's making it sound like he was bragging, but I shouldn't assume the worst. He could have been telling her that he liked me, for all I know.

Anything's possible. But now I'm self-conscious about my ears flaming up, which makes me want to avoid the entire topic. I discreetly make sure my bob covers the telltale redness and don't say anything further.

By the time we've finished walking the path around our area of the camp, we spot Reagan and the boys lounging at the picnic table between our tents. I'm a little worried Summer might try to tease me about Brett in front of the group, but she just runs to Kendrick, throwing her arms around him and begging for a piggy-back ride. As though the whole conversation about Brett and Lennon is forgotten.

Good.

It's nearly time for dinner service, so we all decide to trek back up to the lodge. We aren't the only ones. Small groups of campers are headed in the same direction, and once the pavilion is in sight, we join dozens of other guests. Wineglasses in hand, they mingle on rattan-and–carved wood outdoor furniture overflowing with plush pillows on a massive wraparound deck that overlooks a beautiful rocky valley. Everything is suffused with golden light from the setting sun. It's photographic. Literally. Brett is breaking out his phone to take pictures as a waiter circulates with a tray of hors d'oeuvres.

Brett whistles. "They must make a killing here."

"Maybe not," Kendrick says, eyeing a bar that's been set up outside the dining area on a side deck, away from the stunning views. "That wine they're serving isn't cheap."

"Think they'll serve us?" Brett asks with a devious smile.

"That's the same bartender from last year," Reagan says, shaking her head. "He's a dick. I think he's Candy's cousin, or something. He'll probably remember me."

"I'll try," Summer says. "He won't know me, and I look legal."

She casually strides to the bar and flashes the bartender a smile. After several seconds of small talk, she turns around and returns empty-handed.

"No way," Brett says, disappointed. "He wouldn't do it?"

"You were right, Reagan. He's a dick," Summer reports. "Says he was warned by Candy that a group of underage teens had just checked in, and we're not to be served alcohol."

"We'll see about that," Brett says, and turns to Lennon. "We need a plan to get that wine."

"I'll get right on that," Lennon deadpans.

Brett laughs, either unbothered by Lennon's sarcasm or not noticing it. Nothing ever seems to bother Brett. He's always so happy-go-lucky and at ease with his life. I wish I could be more like that.

We trail a group of retirees and investment bankers in

catalog-perfect outdoor clothes. Reagan spots a place for us to sit inside the pavilion, and we follow her lead to a large, round table. It's set with modern-rustic china, and the confusing number of glasses and utensils intimidates me. I'm also sitting between Brett and Lennon, which makes me nervous. It's exciting to have Brett so close, and he's pretending to stab my hand with a fork, his mood fun and playful. But I'm self-conscious and trying to play it cool.

And then there's Lennon. I wish I could just block him out. While Brett's presence feels light and capricious—he's moved on to fake-stabbing Reagan, and she's laughing in that husky voice of hers—Lennon's feels . . . solid. Weighty. Like I can't forget that his leg is a few inches from mine. If Brett is Sirius, brighter than anything else in the night sky, Lennon is the moon: often dark and hidden, but closer than any star. Always there.

One after the other, each table is served the first of four courses, which is some sort of zucchini-and-basil soup. Once it's on the table, I realize how sorry I am that I've only had Lennon's gifted fudge to eat today, and forget all about the silly tableware and practically inhale the soup. I don't even care if I'm using the correct spoon. The second course is grilled scallops with some sort of fancy sauce and a tiny salad. The scallops smell amazing. I'm all in.

"Someone's feeling plucky," Lennon notes, gesturing toward my plate with his knife. "Hive-wise."

"Scallops are a shellfish with which I'm compatible," I tell him stoically. Shrimp and crab are iffy, but anything in the mollusk family is low-risk.

"Oh yeah, that's right," he says, nodding slowly.

We both eat in silence for several seconds.

Then he asks, "Remember when we had that shrimp scampi?"

"You never forget a trip to the ER."

I was fifteen, and at the time, Sunday dinner with the Mackenzies was a regular event. It was just takeout, typically, and a movie in the living room. Sunny is the chef of the Mackenzie family; Mac, not so much. So it was a big deal when Mac decided she'd make something from scratch. It turned out pretty good, but for some reason, I had a major allergic reaction. Face swelling up, throat closing, trouble breathing—the works. Mac freaked out and took all the blame. My parents were out to dinner, so Sunny rushed me to the hospital emergency room in her car.

"Bad shrimp! Bad shrimp!" Lennon says, mocking Sunny in a high-pitched voice.

Sunny had yelled that at the nurse in front of the entire ER waiting room. Loudly. We repeated it for months out of context. It was our inside joke. Anything that went wrong, we blamed it on "bad shrimp." It never got old.

It's still funny. I chuckle softly with a mouthful of scallop and nearly choke.

Lennon's eyes slide toward mine. The corners of his mouth turn up as he struggles with a smile.

Okay, hell has officially frozen over. Pigs flying. Lightning strikes. It's all happening. Because we are both smiling at each other. Actual smiles!

What's going on here? First peanut butter fudge, now this?

Just stay calm, I tell myself. It doesn't mean anything. Enemies share a laugh now and then. I keep my eyes on my plate and try to act normal. But when the third course comes, some kind of braised meat—leg of lamb, I think—and Brett has the rest of the group focused on tracking the location of the bartender, I pick up the next fork in my place setting and accidentally bump his hand. He's left-handed, so his right hand is propped on the edge of the table. And it stays there, even when I snatch my own hand back.

"Sorry," I mumble.

He shakes his head dismissively. "So many forks. And why do we need two spoons? I already used one for the soup. Are they backup spoons?"

"One pair of fancy chopsticks would have saved them some major dishwashing," I say.

"Amen to that."

My mom taught him how use chopsticks. The Korean kind, made of stainless steel.

"What's that quote from that martial arts movie *Once Upon a Time in China*?" I ask. "Jet Li says it when he sees the Western place setting."

"'Why so many swords and daggers on the table?'" Lennon quotes.

"That's it. God, you were obsessed with martial arts movies."

"Jet Li is the king," he says before taking a sip of water from his glass.

"I thought it was Bruce Lee."

"Bruce Lee was a god."

"Oh, that's right," I say. "You made me watch so many of those movies."

"And you liked most of them."

I did.

Lennon picks at his braised lamb. "I also seem to remember watching an awful lot of old *Star Trek* episodes, and not even the good ones. All because someone had a crush on a certain Klingon."

It's true. Worf was my everything. I still follow the actor who played him, Michael Dorn, online. And I've probably seen every Worf meme on the internet. "I'm not ashamed."

Before I can say anything else, Brett's arm shoots out in front of me. I'm forced to lean back while he taps Lennon's shoulder.

"Dude, are you seeing this?" Brett says.

"You know she's sitting here, right?" Lennon says, slipping back into glum-and-dour mode.

Brett glances at me. "Oh sorry, Zorie." He chuckles and flashes me a sheepish smile before focusing on Lennon again. "But check it out. The bartender leaves the bar unattended. All of those bottles are just sitting there."

Lennon's disinterested stare doesn't seem to have any effect on Brett.

"For the taking," Brett elaborates.

"There are a hundred people sitting here," Lennon says.

Brett groans and lets his head loll backward for a moment. "Not now. Later. After dinner. People can't sit here forever."

"Everyone heads to the bonfire below the Sunset Deck," Reagan confirms.

"The bartender's walking back to the bar," Lennon points out.

"So we find a way to divert him," Brett says. "We just need people's attention on the bonfire while we figure out a way to get him to leave the bar. Then, boom! We plunder his stash."

I don't like this plan. We're surrounded by people. This isn't like playing pranks on teachers, like that time Mr. Soniak exited English class to go to the restroom and left his phone unlocked on his desk, and Brett jumped out of his chair and used it to take photos of his ass before Mr. Soniak returned . . . which Brett later claimed was worth the detention he got.

Kendrick gives Brett a distrustful look. "Call me crazy, but isn't that stealing?"

"It's the very definition," Lennon mumbles.

"You would know," Brett says, waggling his brows.

I glance at Lennon, and he looks . . . embarrassed. I wonder what that's all about.

"Look, people. They aren't selling the wine," Brett argues. "It's free to all the guests. If I asked for a second helping of this braised sheep—"

"Lamb," Lennon corrects in a weary voice.

"—they would bring it to me. It's all built into the cost. We're just getting our money's worth."

"My *mom's* money, you mean," Reagan says.

Brett grins. "Your mom is hot."

"Gross," Reagan says, smacking his shoulder with the backs of her fingers. And it *is* gross, but she doesn't seem all that upset about it. Not about that, and not about Brett's dicey proposal. Even Kendrick, who I would consider sensible, is convinced by Brett's arguments. So maybe my bad feelings about it are unwarranted.

After Reagan informs us that we're all going horseback riding tomorrow, Brett continues to hatch a wine-thieving plan throughout the rest of dinner. Dessert is served—some sort of weird strawberry sorbet with balsamic vinegar that I skip, because strawberries are on the "no" list when I'm having hive issues. And when guests begin filing outside to the Sunset Deck, lured by the scent of wood smoke and the sounds of acoustic guitar, opportunities to divert the bartender dwindle.

"I'll figure something out," Brett assures us. "The night is young."

Reagan tugs him by the arm. "Come on. Let's walk around."

He flashes his dazzling grin at her and allows himself to be dragged from the table, briefly linking elbows with her as he makes some joke that I can't hear. They're so easy together, so touchy and lighthearted. I wish I could be as bold as Reagan. I wish he were linking arms with me.

But more than anything, I wish I didn't feel Lennon's gaze on my face. All that memory dredging we did over dinner is overlapping in my brain with Summer's earlier assumptions about my relationship with Lennon. And a troublesome thought suddenly balloons.

Bogus gossip about my so-called hookup with Brett reached Summer's ears.

Did it reach Lennon's, too?

It bothers me that it might have, and it bothers me that I care. Then again, my caring about Lennon was never the problem. It was his caring about me. And a little peanut butter fudge and fond memories of bad shrimp aren't enough to convince me that anything has changed.

9

Following Brett and Reagan, we all head outside to a deck studded with tin lanterns. It's beautiful out here, actually. The sun still hasn't completely fallen, but it's getting close, and the mountains are limned in orange and pink behind darkening silhouettes of pine trees. Everything's in that middle stage between day and night, which somehow seems more exciting out here in the wilderness than it does in the city. As though something's on the verge of happening.

The deck quickly swells with people, some of them standing against the railing to watch the sunset, others claiming seats on the sprawling patio furniture to listen to folksy guitar music. Waiters begin circulating after-dinner coffee and tea. We stroll past Candy, who is chatting with some of her guests, and when she spots us, she calls Reagan over to meet them. The rest of us jog down the wide deck steps to a clearing and head toward the compound's fire pit.

It's a gorgeous bonfire, with rustic split-log benches circling it. A few guests are toasting marshmallows over the flames, and there's some sort of make-your-own-s'mores station on a table. Nearby, white lights are strung on a cedar pergola, beneath which three lanes of horseshoes are set up on sandy ground.

"Want to play?" Kendrick asks Lennon. "I have to warn you, I'm pretty much a horseshoes genius, so I'll probably beat you."

"Is that right?"

"Legendary," Kendrick confirms. "At least, I was when I was ten, which is the last—and, well, *only* time I've ever played."

Lennon chuckles. "If it's like ring toss at the fair, I kill at that. Let's do this." He glances at me. "You in?"

"Hand-eye coordination is not my strong suit," I tell him. Every time I've ever played games where you have to get up in front of others and do something in a spotlight—like bowling or charades—I generally am too concerned about onlookers watching me and end up looking awkward. "Maybe I'll watch a game and see how it's played first."

"Throw a horseshoe, try to hit the stake," Lennon says.

"You make it sound easy."

"No, I think *you're* making it harder than it really is," he says, one side of his mouth tilting. "Sometimes you just have to say screw it and go for it."

Summer chimes in that she wants to play, and it's only now I notice that Brett is missing. Maybe he hung back with Reagan to talk to Candy. Or maybe he's staking out the bartender. Who knows. But I wish he were here so that we could revisit his earlier interest in taking photos of the moon—and maybe so that he could be a natural buffer between me and Lennon.

While we've been talking, all the horseshoe lanes have filled with teams. So we stand at the edge of the pergola and wait for a free stake, watching the games in progress. That's when I feel a gentle tap on my shoulder.

I look up to see a woman about my mom's age, with pale brown skin and her hair pulled tightly back in a smooth ponytail. "Aren't you Dan Everhart's daughter?"

"Yes." My shoulders tighten. Then I recognize the woman. Razan Abdullah. I've seen her in the clinic. She runs a video production company. She used to be one of my dad's patients.

"I thought I recognized you," she says with a smile. "Is your family here?"

"No, I'm just vacationing with some friends." I glance toward Lennon and Kendrick. Lennon nods in greeting.

"Ah," she says. "Beautiful place, isn't it? I've been here the last few days filming a promo video with a small crew."

"That's really cool."

She nods. "It's been a great shoot. We leave tomorrow morning. How's your dad doing? I haven't seen him since he worked on my back this spring."

"He's okay." I feel like I should say something more positive than that, but honestly, it's hard for me to muster the words.

"Oh, I'm sorry." She makes a face, gritting her teeth. "Is your mom still with your dad?"

I'm baffled. "Of course. Why wouldn't she be?"

"I must be . . . confusing them with another couple." Rapidly blinking eyes dart sideways as she seems to be thinking about something, hesitating. "You know how it is. I meet so many people for work. . . . They all blur together sometimes."

"Right," I say. But now a strange, quiet panic is rising inside me. Did she really confuse my dad with someone else, or has she heard a rumor? Please, please, *please* don't let her be someone my dad's had an affair with. I think she's married, but I'm not sure.

Before I can press her for more information, her phone lights up and she excuses herself.

I watch her walk away, head muddled, and realize that if she's getting phone service, we should be in Wi-Fi range. I check my phone, and sure enough, I've got a signal. I also have several texts. Two are from my mom, and as I meander away to answer them, I can't help but think about Razan's question. It doesn't take long for thinking to become obsessing, and now I'm picturing my parents splitting up.

But not for long. Pulling me out of my thoughts, Brett jogs toward me, Reagan in tow. "It's happening," he says excitedly, urging me to follow them while Reagan gets the rest of the group's attention. "We have to go—now."

"I don't understand," I say.

Lennon dusts his hands off. "What's happening?"

"The bar," Brett says. "I convinced one of the guests to order three mixed drinks."

"Okay . . . ?"

"*Which means,*" he says, "the bartender will head back to the kitchen to fetch them. The bar will be unguarded. Now is our chance. Are you going to sit around throwing scraps of iron with old geezers, or do you want to have fun?"

"Fun!" Summer says.

"Come on, then," Brett says, grinning wildly. He winks at me. "Let's go, Everhart."

He takes off, and I follow, slipping around the backside of the pavilion. Summer and Reagan are racing ahead across the darkening lawn, and when they make it to a short set of stairs that lead up to the smaller side deck, they pause for several seconds until Summer flashes us a thumbs-up sign.

We all climb three steps cautiously onto the narrow strip of deck circling the pavilion, staying hidden. The bar is only a few yards away, bathed in a strong cone of light. Like Brett predicted, the bartender seems to be headed toward the kitchen, and stops to talk to a pair of the serving crew, who are sweeping the floor and turning chairs upside down on top of the tables.

"That guest you convinced to order the drinks went to the Sunset Deck with her friends," Summer reports in a loud whisper. "I think she was telling the bartender to bring the drinks out there."

"Excellent," Brett says with a grin, waving Reagan and Summer behind him. "Where's my wingman?"

I realize he's talking about Lennon, and glance around. He's nowhere to be found.

"No time to wait," Brett says. "Zorie, you're taking his place. Stay here at the steps and keep a lookout in the shadows.

Everyone else, follow me when Zorie gives the word."

Keep a lookout? Why me? I frantically glance around while the others clamor onto the side deck. What am I supposed to be looking for? I check the lawn. I don't have a decent view of the bonfire from here. And the people mingling on the Sunset Deck don't seem to be paying attention to us. The only person who has a sightline on the bar is the acoustic guitar player. Can he see us? I can't tell.

"Is it clear?" Brett whispers.

This is too much pressure. I do one last survey of the inner pavilion and wait until a server turns his back. "Okay, now!"

Brett crests over the top step and takes three strides toward the bar, slipping behind it. He punches the air with a victory fist and then ducks out of view. When he pops back up, he has two wine bottles. He hands them to Summer. She tries to pass them to Kendrick, and he waves them away—at least, at first. She says something to him that I can't hear and shoves one of the bottles against his stomach. He caves and accepts it.

More bottles emerge. The clink of heavy glass echoes across the bar. It's taking them forever. Why are they giggling? Someone's going to hear. And just how many bottles of wine do they need? Summer's already holding three.

I suddenly smell roasted marshmallow.

"Stuck on lookout duty?" a deep voice rumbles at my ear.

A small yelp escapes my mouth. I punch Lennon in the arm.

"Ow," he complains, rubbing his sleeve.

"Stop creeping up on me like that," I whisper. "You'll give me a heart attack."

His white teeth flash in the dusk. "Sounds like a challenge."

"Glad you're so gung ho for my early demise."

"You used to like when I sneaked up in the dark."

Memories from last fall flitter through my head. Tiptoeing out of the house to find him waiting behind the palm tree at the bottom of the steps. His hand over my mouth to stop me from laughing. Feeling like my heart would burst out my chest with wanting his arms around me.

Don't think about it. Don't answer him. Just pretend he didn't say anything. Act casual.

"Where were you just now, anyway?" I manage.

"Not doing this stupid shit. And I also"—he holds up a flattened s'more—"found this. Never turn down toasted marshmallow. That's a sin."

"Oh, is it really?" I whisper, irritated that my heart is still racing. Because he startled me. Not because of what he said. Or that he's standing so close that I can smell wood smoke on his shirt. But why *is* he standing so close?

"Pretty sure that's what the preacher said last Sunday at church."

"You still go to church with Mac?" The New Walden Chapel. They have service outside in a small amphitheater, and people from different faiths go there. I think they mainly exist to feed the homeless and do other charity-work-type things around the Bay Area; Mac used to be homeless when she was our age, and she often got her meals from their soup kitchen. My dad says it's not a real church, but what would he know about divinity?

"I don't have a choice. She claims I wear too much black."

I snort. "Okay, so let me get this straight. Mac believes that God forgives her for selling things like . . ."

"Cock rings?" he provides.

That wasn't my first choice. His nonchalance frazzles me, and I get a little defensive. "Yet God doesn't forgive you reading all that gruesome horror manga? All those gory zombie movies?"

"Personally, I'd like to think so. Being prepared for the zombie apocalypse is just common sense."

"Yeah, pretty sure I remember that being mentioned in the Bible," I say sarcastically.

"It's an amendment to the commandments," he says. "Amendment number thirteen. Thou shall arm yourself with machete and shotgun, and remember to aim for the head."

I turn away to keep my eye on Brett.

Lennon reaches around my shoulder, holding up half of a marshmallow. "Want some?"

His voice is dark and velvety, so close to my ear that a thousand goose bumps race down my neck. An unwanted shiver chases them, and I pray he doesn't see it. "No."

"Are you sure?" he asks, voice even lower. Deeper. Seductive.

No. Not seductive. What I'm hearing is the equivalent of a mirage. See, this is where I went wrong before. Just because one person's feeling something doesn't mean the other person intended it. Just because my body wants to slowly turn around, to find him gazing down at me, and our eyes would lock, and—

What's the matter with me? I have to stop. *For the love of God, have some pride, Everhart.*

"No, thank you," I say more resolutely.

"Your loss," he says, sounding bored. His arm disappears.

And now I do turn to look at him. Slowly. But not because I expect anything. I just want to see if he really *is* bored, or if . . .

His eyes aren't on mine. Of course not. He's gazing off in the distance.

"Oh, look," he says casually. "Jack Kerouac is about to get busted."

What?

I swing around and spot the bartender in the pavilion, headed straight toward them. Crap, crap, crap.

"Brett!" I whisper loudly.

He doesn't hear me.

"Guys!" I say louder, panicked.

Summer glances around as if she possibly heard me, but isn't *quite* sure. What do I do? If I take a step into the light, the bartender will see me. But if I can't get Brett's attention—

Lennon whistles.

Brett looks up.

I wave frantically and point toward the pavilion.

He understands now. There's a short scuffle with the wine bottles, and then they're racing toward us. Problem is, when they get to the steps, the bartender can—

Son of a sea cook!

They've been spotted.

"Run!" Brett tells us.

He tears across the lawn, juggling four bottles of wine. Instinct for self-preservation has me running after him. The scent of damp grass and pine needles rise from my feet as my shoes slap the ground. We're all racing as if our lives depend upon it, a panic-fueled herd of buffaloes driven into shadow. I'm completely turned around. Where are the campgrounds? I don't remember all these trees and bushes.

Brett veers left just as I spot the main walkway. It's lit up by tiny gold path lights. Brett and Reagan leap over some flowering shrubs to get to the path. Something crashes.

"Oh, God!" Summer yells.

Glass crushes under my shoes. The scent of wine floods my nose.

"Keep going," Brett says, chest heaving. "Don't stop."

I glance back at the pavilion. It doesn't look like anyone's running after us. We leave the broken bottle behind and continue along the main path until we crest the top of a steep hill. The first camp of tents comes into view. Brett slows to a stop, and we all catch our breath and look down into the valley.

This camp is nothing but yurts, all of them the shape of circus tents. They're eerily lovely, glowing with warm, marigold light— sanctuaries in the darkening forest, one that parts to reveal a black sky. And everywhere—*everywhere*—in that sky, there are stars.

My stars.

It's as if they appeared from nowhere. As if this is a completely different night sky than the one back home. We have a pretty clear view at the Melita Hills observatory, but the cities clustered in the Bay Area collectively produce a lot of light pollution.

No cities out here.

Oh, the photos I could take with my telescope!

"Zorie!" Lennon calls.

Crap. The group is on the move again, and everyone but the two of us has already made it halfway down the hill.

"Sorry," I say. I get my butt in motion and explain, "I spaced out." I chuckle and catch my breath. "Literally."

What a dorky joke. All this physical activity is rotting my brain.

"The stars, you mean?" he says, glancing up briefly. "It's amazing, right? I knew you would love them out here."

He jogs faster to catch up with the group, and I race to follow, his surprising confession tumbling around inside my head. But not for long, because when we're a few yards from the camp, Reagan comes to a stop.

"What's going on?" Kendrick asks.

"On the path, near the third yurt," she says.

I scan ahead and spot the problem. A large man in a dark jacket stands with his back to us, chatting with a couple of campers. On the back of the jacket, the word MUIR is printed in white.

"Mr. Randall," Reagan says. "The compound's security ranger. If you think the bartender was a jerk, he's Santa Claus compared to Mr. Randall. We can't be seen with all this wine. He'll probably have us arrested."

Summer glances around. "What do we do? Should we go back?"

"To the place that's filled with people who saw us run?" Lennon says. "Yes, let's return to the scene of the crime."

"I don't know!" Summer says, eyes bright with panic. "Maybe we can hide until this Mr. Randall dude passes us?"

I gesture toward the yurts. "He's not the only roadblock. Look at all the tents. People are walking around."

"Guests are returning from the bonfire too," Lennon says, glancing behind us, where laugher and chatter carry from a short distance.

"We're trapped," Summer moans. "This sucks so hard. My legs are covered in wine splatter, and now we're going to jail."

"Or we could stash the bottles somewhere," Lennon says calmly. "And, you know, maybe not go to jail. But your plan works too."

Kendrick points to a waste disposal box. It's a metal bear-resistant one, cemented to the ground, with a funny latch. "I doubt they'd clean these out tonight. We can stash the wine inside now and come back later, when people are sleeping."

"My boys!" Brett praises, helping Kendrick unlatch the garbage bin. "Pure genius. Lennon, I was thinking you failed me back at the bar when you weren't there to watch my back, but your position as wingman is now restored."

"All my dreams are realized," Lennon says, voice thick with sarcasm.

While Reagan fusses about stashing the bottles near food scraps, they manage to clear out a space inside the bin for a dozen bottles. The last one doesn't fit, so Brett sticks it inside his pants. Crude jokes are made. I ignore them, mainly because I'm watching the ranger.

"Guys," I say. "Shut the bin. He's coming this way."

I don't think he can see us all that well, but then again, I can see him. And when Lennon points out that we look obvious, hanging out by the garbage bin, we leave it and begin walking down the path. Calmly. Slowly. No getting around the ranger. I steel myself as we approach him.

"Evenin'," Mr. Randall says, giving us all a once-over. "You kids lost?"

"No, sir," Brett assures him. "Just heading back to our camp."

"Which is . . . ?"

"Camp Owl," Reagan says.

He squints at her. "You look familiar."

"My parents stay here a lot," she says.

"If that's true, then I don't need to remind you that quiet hours will be starting soon. Plan accordingly."

"Thank you," Reagan says.

Mr. Randall nods, stepping aside to let us pass. I'm not sure if it's my imagination, but he seems to sniff the air. So now I'm paranoid that he smells wine on us. I mean, we *did* trample a broken bottle into the ground.

But if he suspects anything, he doesn't stop us. And after I sneak a glance back at him, I breathe out a sigh of relief when he passes the garbage bin and continues up the hill toward the lodge.

"I think we're in the clear," I tell the group as we make our way down the dark path through the yurt camp.

"Lucky us," Lennon says without conviction.

For once, I don't disagree with him.

10

Turns out that "quiet hours" really do mean quiet. Even though the tent cabins in Camp Owl are spread apart, when it's pitch-black outside and the usual white noise of city life—traffic, air conditioners, TV—is replaced by crickets, you can hear everything.

And I do mean *e-v-e-r-y-t-h-i-n-g.*

The flush of toilets. Distant laughter. The crunch of gravel as a stranger walks. Even the smallest noise is amplified. So when all six of us converge in the girls' tent cabin to talk about how we are going to retrieve the hidden wine, it isn't long before we decide that Brett and Lennon will get up early and cart the wine back in their packs. Actually, Brett *volunteers* Lennon, and Lennon just says drily, "I've always dreamed of being a rumrunner."

The boys retreat to their tent, and we get ready for bed. It's been a while since I've slept in a bunk bed—and *never* since I slept in a tent. But after logging the events of the day in my mini-journal and a couple of hours spent lying wide-awake in bed, cataloging all the nocturnal noises in camp, I manage to fall into a restless and unsettled sleep, waking periodically.

When dawn pushes away the darkness, I give up on sleep and climb out of my bunk.

It feels strange to be up so early. But Reagan is a morning person, and when I shimmy to the floor, I find her facedown, sprawled on top of a still-made bed. She never got under the covers? It's insanely chilly in here. I'm a little worried something is wrong, so I shake her shoulder.

"Go away," she says in rough, muffled voice into her pillow. She sounds awful. And pissed off. So I leave her alone and gather my clothes as quietly as possible. Summer is still asleep, and I fear I'll wake both of them up if I use the en suite bathroom, so I head out to the camp bathhouse.

It's far brisker outside the tent than inside, but I see lights in some of the other tents and silhouettes moving around, so I'm not the only person up this early. But I'm able to snag a free shower stall in the bathhouse, and I don't hurry shaving and washing my hair so that my phone has time to charge. When I'm finished drying my hair, I hike back through the camp, feeling a lot more civilized. The boys' tent is dark and both of the girls in my tent are *still* asleep. Unless I want to sit here and listen to Reagan snoring, my best bet is to head up to the lodge for early breakfast.

Blue-gray light filters through pine trees as I hike up the main path. The compound looks different out here in this light, so I have trouble spotting the garbage bin where we left the wine. Maybe Brett and Lennon have already retrieved all the bottles. I mentally cross my fingers and continue along the path toward the lodge.

When I enter the pavilion where we ate dinner, I find an expansive breakfast bar set up on a couple of tables. Eggs, bacon, pastries. Also, an oatmeal station with a dozen topping choices, which one guest is browsing. Why anyone would want that over sausage is a mystery to me. Grabbing a plate, I lift up the lid of a silver chafing dish, and through the warm sausage steam, I get a hazy look at the person hovering over the oatmeal station. He's tall, dark, and hot, and—

OH MY GOD, I'm ogling Lennon.

It's like the telescope spying, only worse, because he's three feet away from me, and I can't duck to the floor and hide. At least he's not half-naked.

"Must be the end-times if you're up before dawn," he says, lips curling at the corners.

"I couldn't sleep. Roosters were crowing."

He laughs. "You're thinking of a farm."

"Look, all I know is it sounded like a bird, and it was irritatingly loud." I slide a quick smile in his direction. "So it was whatever you call mountain roosters."

"I think they probably call them hawks," he says, amused.

"Same difference." I load up my plate with sausage and bacon. "So, oatmeal. Really? Can't you eat that at home?"

"I love oatmeal. Oatmeal is life." He sprinkles a spoonful of almonds on his oatmeal. "You know, I believe Samuel Johnson in his infamous eighteenth-century dictionary described oats as something that the English feed to horses but the Scots feed to people."

I shake my head, smiling to myself. "You and the crazy factoids."

"And you're just desperate for meat because you live with Joy," he says, gesturing toward my plate.

True. It's not as if she cares that I'm a carnivore, but if she's cooking, it's a vegan freezer meal. "Last night was the first meat I've had this week," I admit. "So I'm going full-on cavewoman here. Just meat and coffee. Maybe some sugar," I say, adding a giant cinnamon roll to the top of my sausage stack. I spot some brown sugar among the oatmeal toppings and briefly consider sprinkling some on my bacon.

"Ah, the ol' Paleo Diabetes diet."

"I'm the picture of modern nutrition," I say.

"It gives your cheeks a healthy glow." Eyes merry, he looks me in the face for the first time this morning, *really* looks at me, and I feel my ears warming.

"That's just good old-fashioned fear," I tell him as I focus on the breakfast table, reopening a chafing dish I've already inspected once. "I had trouble sleeping last night. Too many things going bump in the night."

"It's different, isn't it? Even sleeping inside tent cabins. It's still . . . wild."

Indeed, it is.

Lennon hands me some silverware wrapped in a cloth napkin. "Want to eat on the deck and watch the sunrise? They've got patio heaters set up, and it looks like they're bringing around coffee."

"Say no more," I answer, hoping I sound casual and not as though I'm inexplicably happy to be eating breakfast with him.

We carry our plates outside and find a place away from the other early risers, near a patio heater. The juxtaposition of gently billowing heat and nippy morning breeze mirrors my feelings about being alone with him. He's both familiar and foreign, and I'm in a constant state of being on edge when we're together.

"Your plaid game is strong today," he comments, sliding a fleeting glance in my direction.

I smooth a hand over red-and-black plaid pants. They're tight, and a little punk rock—pretty daring, at least for me. I don't *think* he's teasing. It's hard to tell sometimes. "Thanks?"

He nods, and I relax.

"So," I say, digging into my mountain of food. "Did you and Brett retrieve the wine?"

"*I* didn't," he says. "He wanted Kendrick and me to go with him last night after we got back to our tent cabin. We both refused. Brett said he'd go himself, but I'm not sure how he planned to carry a dozen bottles, because he left without his pack. But he reeked like a French restaurant when I got up this morning—which is, frankly, better than that disgusting ax-murderer body spray he's been wearing."

"He got drunk by himself?"

"Or maybe he pulled a Summer and dropped another bottle," Lennon says, shrugging lightly. "But when I came up here this morning, I checked the garbage bin and the bottles were gone, so I assume he managed to rescue them."

We eat in silence for a while. I'm not sure I want to discuss Brett any further with him, and he doesn't offer any other information. He finally pats his pocket and says, "I picked up the backcountry permit at the front desk from Candy's husband, so we're good to go with that. I also checked out the store in the lodge. They've got bear canisters for rent. If you're caught with food and you don't have one, you get fined. It's on the King's Forest information sheet that comes with the permit, if you want to see it."

He starts to dig it out from his pocket, but I wave it away. "I believe you."

"But . . . ?"

"It's just . . . I don't know," I say, snapping off a piece of crisp bacon. "I joked with my mom about seeing wild animals on hikes, but it never truly struck me that they'd pose that much of a threat."

Lennon chuckles. "There's danger lurking everywhere. I'm talking deadly."

"Terrific," I mumble.

"Not just wild animals, either. Out in the Sierras, people have been killed by rock slides, drowning, falling off cliffs, heart attacks from hiking tough trails, being crushed by falling trees—"

"Jesus."

"—heat stroke, hypothermia, boiled to death in hot springs, killed by crazy serial killers, poisoned by plants, contracting hantavirus."

"Hanta what?"

"Transmitted through deer mouse droppings."

"Um, hello. Trying to eat, here," I complain.

"I'm just saying, there's a lot of lethal stuff out there. But that's half the fun."

"Not surprised you'd think that."

"I don't mean in a thrill-seeking way. I mean learning how to spot danger and avoid it in a responsible, careful way. You have to understand your environment. Respect it. Do you think my parents would let me go backpacking if they didn't believe I knew how to handle myself out there? They trust me because I treat it seriously. And that's why they wanted me to come. I mean, you know they wouldn't just agree to take care of my reptiles for a week unless it was important."

True.

"Wait," I say. "Your moms *wanted* you to come?"

One shoulder lifts briefly and falls. "I was worried Brett would go derping off to look for the hidden waterfall himself if I didn't help. And we both know what a moron he is. No offense. I know you used to be into him. Or maybe you still are. . . ." Eyes down, his gaze briefly flicks to mine.

I don't know what to say. I'm not even sure how I feel. The last twenty-four hours have been strange. I guess I thought it would be more thrilling to be around Brett outside of school, but we're barely ever alone together. Maybe if we spent any time away from the group, he'd let the whole super-bro personality drop. I know he does it for attention and that there's a different side to him. But then, we just got here.

There's also been Lennon. I hadn't planned on him. And when I wasn't getting spooked about animal noises in the woods last night, I spent my tossing-and-turning moments replaying all of our conversations in my head, trying to figure out if we're friends again, or if he wants to be—if *I* want to be. I haven't come to any conclusion.

Something clicks inside my head now, though.

"Your parents encouraged you to come on this trip," I say, "because of Brett? They know he's here?"

Lennon shrugs. "Yeah."

"Do Sunny and Mac know that *I'm* here?"

A brisk wind blows as he scrapes his spoon on the inside of his bowl, gathering a last bite of oatmeal. "That's why they wanted me to come. To . . . make sure you're safe."

A hundred emotions pummel me at once. I can't even begin to sort through them, so I lash out with the first thing I can wrap my mind around. "I'm not an idiot, you know. I can take care of myself. I may not be in Olympic shape like Reagan, but I can handle a stupid hike."

"Of course you can."

"I can identify thousands of stars, so I'm pretty sure I can read a map."

"Never said you couldn't. You're the smartest person here by a long shot."

"Then why are you making it sound like I'm incompetent?"

He groans. "You're competent. More than competent. I trust you a million times more than anyone else in this compound."

He does? After months of not talking? This does something funny to my heart.

"Think of it this way," he says. "If I needed to know whether Pluto was a real planet—"

"It's not."

"—then I would ask you. But if I needed to know how to build a bong, I would ask Brett. We all have our areas of expertise. Mine is wilderness backpacking."

"But I never knew that!" I say, exasperated. "Your expertise is supposed to be how to survive a night in a haunted house."

"In a way, they aren't that different."

I'm frustrated, and he's cracking jokes. I can't figure him out. "Is this about that photo book?" I ask, suddenly self-conscious.

"What?"

"Is that why you came? Why your parents forced you to come? If you and your moms are just feeling sorry for me about my dad cheating, you can keep your sympathy. I don't need it. I'm fine."

"I don't feel sorry for you. I'm *angry* for you. I want to cut off your dad's arms with rusty hedge clippers. I want to chainsaw his feet off. I want to—"

"Okay! I get it, I get it." Jeez. It's my dad, after all. Though, admittedly, I'm secretly pleased he's indignant. "If anyone's going to *Texas Chainsaw Massacre* him, it will be Joy." And I think she'd be going for something other than his feet.

He's quiet for a moment. "No one forced me to come on this trip. I wanted to. I was hoping . . ." He stops suddenly, groans, and shakes his head.

"What?" I say. "You were hoping what?"

He hesitates. "Don't you ever miss us?"

His words are a jab to my ribs. I'm surprised I don't fall out of my chair.

I want to scream, *YES*. I also just want to scream. How many nights did I lie awake in tears over Lennon? I wasn't the one who caused our downfall. The Zorie and Lennon show was going strong until the stupid homecoming dance, and its ending can be easily outlined in four steps. Trust me. I've literally outlined it hundreds of times in my planner.

(1) On the final week of summer vacation, Lennon and I accidentally kissed on one of our late-night walks. And before you ask how a kiss can be accidental, let me just confirm that it can. Laughter plus wrestling over a book can lead to unexpected results. (2) We decide to conduct the Great Experiment, in which we tried to incorporate intense make-out sessions into our normal relationship without telling anyone, in case it didn't work out,

so that we could still salvage our friendship and save ourselves from gossip and meddling parents. Mainly one parent: my dad, who has always hated the Mackenzies. (3) A few weeks later, the experiment seemingly going great, we agreed to come out of the nonplatonic friendship closet and make our first public appearance as an actual boyfriend-girlfriend couple at homecoming. (4) He never showed. Never gave a reason. Didn't answer my texts. Didn't show up at school for several days. And that's where we ended. Years of friendship. Weeks of *more* than friendship. Gone.

He ended us.

And next to my birth mother's death, losing him was the hardest thing I've ever had to endure. Now he wants . . . what? What exactly does he want from me?

I stumble over my answer several times, starting and stopping, unsure of what to say, and end up sounding like a fool. "I—"

A cheerful server walks up to us holding a tray filled with coffee in insulated cups. Lennon and I each accept one while the server makes small talk. I'm grateful for the intrusion, but it doesn't allow me enough time to formulate a response to Lennon's question.

Of course I miss us. You don't care about someone for years and then just decide to quit. Those feelings don't disappear on command. Believe me, I've tried. But other intense emotions are tangled up with our old friendship. At least, on my end. And that makes it complicated and confusing.

I like things that make sense. Things that follow identifiable patterns. Problems with solutions. Nothing I feel about Lennon fits any of that. But how do I tell him this without a repeat of the homecoming dance happening? I don't. That's how. I already had my heart broken once. Never again.

And yet . . .

Hope is a terrible thing.

"No worries," he says and stands. "I shouldn't have said anything."

"Wait!" I tell him, jumping up to stop him as he's walking away.

He swings around, and suddenly we're closer than I intended.

I blow out a hard breath and stare between us. "Do you . . . um, maybe want to walk with me to the lodge store so I can get a bear-proof food storage thingy?"

A long moment stretches, and my pulse is going crazy. I scratch my arm through the sleeve of my jacket.

"All right," he finally says, and I let out a sigh of relief.

All right, I repeat inside my head.

If I can't have what I want, then maybe we can find a way back to when things were simpler. When we were just friends.

I end up getting a few things from the store: a bear canister, a pocket water filter, and a multitool gadget that has a tiny shovel. Lennon says I'll need it for digging fire pits and cat holes. I'm not exactly sure what a cat hole is, though I have a bad feeling about it.

The walk back to the camp is mostly quiet but not entirely awkward. It's still nippy, but the sun is burning away the fog, and according to Lennon, it should be a nice a day. I was too fixated on our breakfast conversation to utilize the Wi-Fi.

When we round a curve and enter our camp, Lennon says, "Hold up."

My eyes follow his and spot the problem. Candy and the ranger we ran into last night are heading down the steps that lead into the girls' tent. They turn and walk north, headed in the opposite direction. We wait for them to disappear into the trees before continuing.

"What do you think that's about?" I ask.

"Don't know, but it doesn't sound good. Listen."

That's when I hear Reagan. Her raspy voice carries, and she's angry. We jog toward the tent cabin and rush into the middle of an argument.

"No, I won't calm down," Reagan's telling Summer. "Do you understand how much trouble I'm going to be in when my mom finds out?"

Kendrick and Brett aren't doing anything, so Lennon gets between the two girls. "What the hell is going on?"

"Everything's ruined," Reagan says, backing away from Summer to drop onto the sofa, head in her hands. "That's what's going on."

"They found the wine," Kendrick elaborates while Brett paces behind the sofa. "We're being kicked out."

"I thought you were going to go back for the wine last night," I tell Brett.

A look of distress passes over Brett's face. Instead of answering me, he groans and pounds a fist on the console table. "This is so ridiculous. They have their wine back. No harm, no foul. I don't understand why they're being such hard-asses."

"Because you pissed on a yurt," Reagan yells at him.

Umm . . . what?

"For the love of Christ," Lennon mumbles, shaking his head slowly.

"I was drunk, okay?" Brett says before pleading to Reagan, "We both were."

"You were out together last night?" I say, alarmed.

Reagan rubs her head roughly. "We drank the bottle Brett smuggled back."

The one he stuck in his pants, I suppose.

"And we were going to go back together and get the other bottles, but . . ."

"But we were buzzed," Brett says defensively to the group. "We forgot to take an empty backpack with us to carry the bottles. So we just took two and—"

"We planned to come back for the rest," Reagan says. "We just . . . got distracted."

This is not like Reagan. She's not a big drinker. I've been to parties with her, including *the* party—when Brett kissed me—and she never drank. It affected her cross-country running times, and she was always training for the Olympics.

Guess things are different now.

"Were all of you out drinking?" I ask, wondering now if this could explain some of the noises last night that kept me up. I'm also irritated and hurt that I was left out. But I guess Lennon was, too.

"Don't look at me," Summer says. "Kendrick and I went to the sauna, and then I came back here and fell asleep."

"Same," Kendrick says.

"Does it matter?" Brett gripes, throwing his hands in the air. "We're on vacation, and Reagan and I were just unwinding. It's not like we're criminals."

"Technically, since you're both underage . . . ," Lennon says.

"And the destruction of property," Kendrick adds, not bothering to hide his disgust. "You know, with the pissing on the tent."

Brett sighs heavily. "Not my proudest moment, for sure. But what's done is done." He plops next to Reagan on the sofa and rubs his head. "This is all so stupid."

"*Oh*, I'll agree with that," Lennon says, voice dripping with contempt. He turns to Kendrick. "What exactly did Candy say?"

"That the compound could lose its license to serve alcohol if they knowingly let this kind of thing happen and didn't take action. She said if it had just been the janitorial crew who found the bottles stashed in the garbage, they might have let it slide. But another camper reported it—I suppose it was the family inside the yurt."

Oh. My. God. There was a family inside the yurt when Brett . . . ?

"It could have been the other campers that complained about noise in the woods at two in the morning," Summer adds.

Reagan groans and rubs her temples.

"So, yeah. It looks bad for the compound," Kendrick finishes. "And we have until noon to vacate the tents, or they're calling the police."

"My mom is going to murder me," Reagan says.

"Maybe Candy won't tell her," Summer says, putting on an encouraging face.

"Don't you get it?" Reagan says. "My parents don't leave for Switzerland until tomorrow. That means if I come home tonight with my tail between my legs, I'm going to have to tell them why I'm back so early."

No one says anything. A sense of doom falls over the tent. At least I wasn't involved, so my mom won't be mad. But I'm honestly devastated that all of this is suddenly over. I revised my summer blueprint to accommodate this trip. I don't want to go home and face my dad and his cheating. And what about the star party? It's not for four more days, so I can't just take a bus to Condor Peak this afternoon. No one will be there.

If that weren't enough, I'm also freaking that Reagan was out with Brett last night. Isn't it kind of weird? They aren't saying that anything happened between them, and maybe it didn't. I try to remind myself that they've always been friends— just friends. And Reagan knows how I feel about him.

So why I am filled with unease?

Maybe it's because Lennon and I were "just friends" once too, until we started sneaking out at night together.

"So it's over?" Summer says. "We have to leave? No horseback riding or hiking?"

"You and I could pick up my car and drive out to my family's cabin in Napa Valley," Kendrick tells Summer quietly. "No one's using it right now. At least we can salvage some of this vacation." When he sees Reagan's head turn, he says to her in apology, "I'd invite everyone, but it's just a one-room cabin. It's my parents' getaway house. There's not even room for people to sleep on the floor, sorry."

"You guys! We're being stupid," Brett says, suddenly reinvigorated. "Why should we go home? Our plan was to hike to that hidden waterfall in King's Forest, so let's just do that. We'll spend the rest of the week there."

"Our *plan* was to spend a couple of nights at the waterfall," Lennon points out. "That's a lot different from six nights. We'd need more supplies if we were staying that long. Triple the food. And there aren't showers and flush toilets out there. Do any of you even have the most basic of things, like toilet paper? I gave you a list of stuff we'd need, and you ignored it."

"I didn't!" Brett insists. "I passed it along to Reagan."

"Then why don't any of you have bear canisters or water filters? You think there's a sink out there? You have to filter water from the river to drink."

"I have a water filter," Reagan says. "I didn't think we'd need a million of them. And I bought those campers' freeze-dried meal packets." She looks at me for confirmation. I have four of them in my pack. "And Brett said we could just hang our food in the trees."

"That's ineffective," Lennon says.

"Dude, it's worked for centuries," Brett argues. "You're being paranoid."

"Park rules clearly say no bear canister, no backcountry camping."

"Whatever," Brett says. "Stop sweating the details. It will be *stupid* fun!"

"You're half right about that," Lennon says.

Brett's forehead wrinkles. "Huh?"

"There are canisters for rent in the lodge store," I say quickly, before Brett and Lennon get in a fight. "And more freeze-dried food."

"Are we even allowed up there now?" Summer asks. "Are we banned from the lodge?"

Reagan pushes up from the sofa. "Screw it. They gave us until noon. Let's load up on supplies. Brett's right. So our plans changed. Big deal. We'll adapt. It will be way cooler out on our own anyway."

"So we're doing this?" Lennon says. "You want to spend a week in the backcountry?"

"Why not?" she says. "Better than going home. If Candy tells my parents, I'm grounded anyway. Might as well have fun while I can. I say let's go for it. Who's with me?"

One by one, everyone agrees. Even Lennon, though I don't think he's happy about it.

New plan: Don't panic. Everything will be fine. It's the same as it was, just a few extra days at the waterfall. I can just hike back here and catch my bus to Condor Peak when it's time to leave. Right?

Reagan looks at me. "Zorie? You're in, right? Because I don't need you going home early to tattle, and for all of this to get back to my mom."

I sort of want to punch her in the boobs.

Anxious thoughts bloom. Of camping in the woods. Of Reagan and Brett spending last night drinking together. Of my conversation with Lennon this morning. All of these things are giant question marks bouncing around in my head.

But when it comes down to it, I'm still left with one indisputable factor.

Luckily for Reagan, I don't want to my face my parents right now either.

"I'm in," I confirm.

Reagan smiles for the first time since we walked in here. "All right. We're going camping in the backcountry. But first I'm going to take a shower and get breakfast. I need grease and yeast. I've got a wicked hangover."

II

"Which way, my man?" Brett says to Lennon, adjusting his backpack at a crossroad. "There's no sign."

"That's the literal definition of an unmarked trail," Lennon says.

Brett laughs. "Oh, yeah. I guess you're right. How did you even find this hidden waterfall, if the trail isn't marked?"

"I read about it. The waterfall isn't officially listed on park publications because there are bigger falls that are easier for the public to access from the main trails," Lennon explains. "This one is inconvenient for the casual day-tripper. And when I originally found it, I was hiking from the opposite direction, so give me a second to find the southbound trail."

It's midafternoon. We waited until the last possible moment to leave, all of us loading up on sandwiches at the pavilion for lunch and filling up sport bottles with water. Then we had to hike back to Reagan's car and drive a couple hours on scary, twisting mountain roads to get to a national park parking lot. From there, we began hiking marked trails toward the waterfall.

And hiking . . .

We've spent three hours on the trail now. I've never walked so much in my life. But that's not my biggest worry. I'm starting to wonder how I'll manage to hike back on my own to catch a bus for the star party later this week.

"This trail isn't supposed to fork east," Lennon mutters to himself, examining a GPS map on his phone.

"How are you even getting a signal?" I ask. I've checked my phone several times along the way to make sure my mom got my last text explaining not to worry if she didn't hear from me for a few days. But nope. I might as well be holding a brick for all the good it's doing me.

"GPS runs independently of cell service," Lennon explains. "All my digital maps are saved on my phone. But this one is glitchy. Sometimes you can't trust technology. Luckily, I have a backup." He puts away his phone and digs out a small leather journal, its black cover bulging. Where my journals are neat and slim, meticulously kept, his is . . . not. Removing an elastic band that keeps the pages closed, he opens it, and I spy a collection of things: folded paper maps, park brochures, and pages filled with Lennon's distinctive block-letter handwriting and the occasional drawing—trees, wildflowers, trail signs, squirrels. I even catch a glimpse of what appears to be a rough anime-style sketch of Sunny and Mac.

I think of all the maps he drew when we were kids. And the map he made for me, sitting in the bottom of my drawer at home. And I feel a hard pang of nostalgia.

He's changed in so many ways. But not in this.

This is the Lennon I used to know.

Lennon catches me looking at his journal and quickly removes a folded-up paper map before shutting the cover with a forceful *slap*.

Silly to feel insulted. What's in there is none of my business. Not anymore.

He spreads the map over a large rock. Deciphering a tangle of topographic lines, he traces invisible paths with one finger. "Oh, wait. I understand now. Left. We go left."

"How can you even make heads or tails of that?" Brett says. "Are you sure?"

"As sure as you were that a yurt was a urinal, Mr. I. P. Freely," Lennon says, folding up the map and refiling it inside his journal.

"Low blow, man," Brett says.

"I'm just saying, if you piss on my tent, there will be disembowelment."

Brett grins. "I love how gruesome you are."

"Turn left," Lennon tells him in a calm voice, but his gaze is hard as steel. "We'll be there in an hour."

"We're headed left, team," Brett calls out cheerfully to the group, hands cupped around his mouth. He takes the lead with Reagan. Summer and Kendrick follow, and I lag behind with Lennon.

Even with the weight correctly distributed, my pack is heavy and keeps slipping farther down my back. It's a killer on legs, a killer on feet. I'm so glad I didn't get hiking boots like Reagan, because she's already complaining about new-shoe blisters. Besides, I notice that Lennon is still wearing his black high-tops beneath ripped black jeans, so I'm thinking hiking boots are overkill.

"You need to tighten the hip belt," Lennon says when I try to shrug my pack higher.

"I thought I already had." I halt and struggle with the straps. Somehow, I think one of them is stuck.

"May I?" he says, offering a hand.

"Um, okay."

He steps closer. I inhale his sunny, freshly laundered scent. Long, graceful fingers tinker with the fastener around my waist. His hands are more sinewy than I remember. They used to be friend hands, and now they're boy hands. It's strange to have him touching me again. Not bad strange. And it's not as if his hands are all over me—not that I'd want them to be. It's just not every day that a guy is touching me, busy concentrating on a task that falls right below my breasts. He's not even looking at them—not that I'd want him to. At least, I shouldn't. Damn these overactive ovaries!

Calm down, Everhart, I tell myself. I can't afford to let my imagination run wild around him. The last time that happened, I ended up in his lap on a park bench with his hands up my shirt.

The strap loosens. "Got it," he says. "How did you manage to get it knotted like that?"

"I've got all kinds of talents," I say.

He makes an amused noise. "You can be in charge of tying all the tent knots, then."

"No need. The tents Reagan bought are knot-free. They practically pitch themselves. Or so the guy at the outdoor store said. I think he may have been hitting on Reagan, though. Maybe he was just excited because she was spending so much money."

"I believe that. Some of your gear is primo. I'd almost be impressed, if I thought for a second that Reagan knew what she was doing."

With a sharp tug, he tightens the strap on my hip belt, and I gasp.

"Too tight?" he asks.

"Just unexpected. I think it's okay."

"It should be snug, but not uncomfortable." He inspects my shoulder harness. "Okay, now these need tightening. Shouldn't be a gap here, see?" Warm fingers slip between my shoulder blade and the strap. He wiggles them around to demonstrate, and a wave of shivers rushes down my arm.

"Tighten away," I tell him. In a weird way, all this methodical touching feels like getting a haircut at the salon. It's almost sensual, but not quite. Or at least you don't want it to be. The Norwegian man who cuts my hair is older than my dad and wears a lot of rings that clink together in a disconcerting, yet strangely pleasing way when he's using scissors. I really don't want to enjoy sexy feelings around Einar, and I *definitely* don't want to enjoy them around Lennon. Best to stop thinking about it.

"So, hey," I say, forcing my mind to concentrate on other things. "Now that I know some of the crazy noises I heard last night were probably Reagan and Brett trampling through the campground, I feel a little better about our earlier talk. You know, about all the wild animals. I mean, I know it will be different out here, but—"

"Oh, it will be completely different," he says, moving on to my other shoulder strap.

"But it can't be that bad if you're not worried."

"Actually, I was scared out of my ever-loving mind the first night I camped alone in the backcountry. I was so convinced wolves were coming after me, I nearly wet my sleeping bag."

I huff out a surprised laugh. "And how did you get over that fear, pray tell?"

"Knowledge is a beautiful thing. I found out that there aren't wolves in California."

"There aren't?"

"Apart from a few stray gray wolves that occasionally pass through, there's only one known pack—the Shasta pack. They're near the Oregon border." He tests both shoulders. "How's that feel now? Better?"

Yes, it actually does. Way better. The backpack feels more like an extension of me rather than a punishment. It's still heavy, but I can handle it.

"Anyway," he says. "We're completely safe here, wolf-wise. Better chance of spotting a werewolf."

"Oh, you'd like that, wouldn't you, Bram Stoker?"

"He wrote about vampires."

"Same difference."

"Do you enjoy being wrong?" he asks.

"I enjoy your sanctimonious defense of fictional creatures."

He chuckles. "I will gladly defend all woodland-bound fictional creatures. Werewolves, bigfoots, and definitely any wendigos. But, hey. You'll be happy to know that wendigos aren't native to California either. So you don't have to worry about a cannibalistic monster eating you for dinner in the middle of the night."

"This has been a great talk," I say. "Thanks so much for alleviating my fears."

He smiles down at me—the warm, boyish smile I used to know and love so well—and my stomach flutters wildly. "I live to give you nightmares, Zorie."

"Hey," I complain good-naturedly. "Not nice."

"Not at all," he says, still smiling.

And I can still feel the warmth of that smile long after he turns around to catch up with the group.

A few minutes into the next leg of our hike, the unmarked trail bends upward, and we're now battling an uphill climb. One that's rocky and dry and uncomfortably warm as the temperature rises with the elevation. But halfway up, we enter a forest of red firs. Their branches are heavy with pinecones, and they help with shade . . . just not with the incline. Hiking on flat ground isn't so bad; hiking on an incline with rocks poking the bottoms of your shoes is torment of the damned. I concentrate on Lennon's bear bell. Its jingle, along with my own bell's answering jangle, is strangely soothing, and this reassuring rhythm helps me put one foot in front of the other.

It could be worse. At least I'm not hungover like Reagan, who is complaining about her head and already had to stop and lie down for fear of being sick. She's also irritated at Brett, who claims to be feeling fine and won't stop teasing her. I watch them chatting from a distance and try to judge whether they appear to be any different after partying together last night. It's hard to tell.

I check the time on my phone. Lennon's "it's only three hours" hike is now becoming closer to four. The trail has leveled off, which is good. No more climbing uphill. But my upper thighs are on fire, and I'm going to have to pee soon. Just when I don't think I can hike another step, Lennon's head lifts.

"Stop," he says to the group. "Listen."

We listen.

"Do you hear that?" he asks.

We all look at each other. And then I *do* hear it. "Water," I say.

"Water*fall*," he corrects, a victorious smile breaking over his face.

We follow him through a grove of trees that seems to be getting thicker—so thick that I'd have trouble believing there's water here somewhere if it weren't so loud. But then the grove parts, and we step onto the green bank of a river. And there it is.

Lennon's waterfall.

Misty white water drops from gray, rocky tiers and collects in a blue-green pool. Enormous round rocks frame the pool and dot the small river that flows away from it, creating a natural stepping-stone bridge that leads to the other bank. Sturdy ferns gather around tree trunks and bright green moss creeps up the sides of stones.

It's not a big waterfall, but it's private and lush and lovely.

"Whoa," Brett says, looking around appreciatively. "It's even better than I hoped."

"It's beautiful," Summer says. "Look at the water. It's so clear."

"Our own private piece of paradise," Reagan agrees. "Screw you, Muir Camping Compound."

Kendrick points to a narrow path that leads up the left side of the falls. "Looks like you can go to the top and dive off. That's so cool."

"What do you think?" Lennon asks near my shoulder.

"I think it's like a dream," I tell him honestly.

"Yeah," he says, sounding satisfied. "That's exactly what I thought."

We're all exhausted and relieved to shuck off our packs while Lennon explains the lay of the land. Since he's camped here before, he's scoped out all the nooks and crannies. Across the stepping-stone bridge on the northern side of the river is the best place to gather firewood. Where we're standing is a good area to set up our tents, and the campfire can be built inside a granite shelter, where massive boulders form a natural barrier.

"Look," Lennon says, almost excited—almost. He pretty much operates on one even frequency. He kicks away debris on the floor of the granite shelter to reveal ashes. "No digging a pit. It's already here. We just load it up with kindling and wood, and voilà. Instant kitchen."

"Sweet," Brett says.

And the grove of trees behind us that we just passed through is our designated toilet area. It's downhill from the water supply, semiprivate, and has plenty of soft ground for digging cat holes, which are exactly what I suspected. You dig, do your business, bury it. This is part of a backcountry agreement among hikers called Leave No Trace. You're supposed to leave a campsite in the same condition it was when you arrived. This means not destroying anything, no cutting down trees, always putting out fires, and no trash. As in zero. Technically, we're supposed to carry around used toilet paper in a zip-top bag until we leave the park or find a designated trash bin. This is referred to as "packing it out." When Reagan balks at this, Lennon points out that it's illegal to leave trash out here. But I'm with Reagan. I'm not carrying around dirty toilet paper in a bag, and I'm certainly not going to go *au naturel* and wipe with leaves. I'm not a barbarian. Lennon admits that, though it's not strictly legal, the alternative is to use biodegradable paper, bury it deep, and cover it well. Good enough for me.

Brett is walking around with his phone, recording video of the waterfall as he narrates. When Brett finishes, Lennon suggests we get busy setting up the base camp. But no one is interested in doing this. Reagan just wants to rest, Brett wants to swim, while Summer and Kendrick are dying to explore the top of the waterfall. It's like herding cats, and when Lennon gives up trying and heads off on his own to claim a spot for his tent, I feel as if I'm stuck in the middle. I know he's probably right, that it's already past five, and we only have a few hours of sunlight to get everything done. But at the same time, I'm exhausted and ache all over. And it's hot. So hot, Brett is already stripping down to his shorts and wading into the edge of the river.

"It feels amazing, guys," he reports, pushing wavy brown hair away from his forehead.

I watch him splash through water that covers his ankles. It's not as though I'm staring. I've seen it before. Despite getting kicked off the soccer team, he still has a beautiful soccer body— one that he's comfortable displaying to the world. Literally. His Instagram is 75 percent Shirtless Brett Seager selfies. But he's now informing us that he's ditching the shorts to swim in his boxers.

"We're all friends here, right?" he says, grinning at me as he hops around on one leg and tries to remove his shorts without getting them wet. "You coming in, Zorie?"

"I don't know," I say. I brought a bathing suit, but where am I going to change into it—the woods?

"I am," Reagan calls out, sitting down to unlace her boots. Then she says to me, "I saw you getting close and comfortable with Lennon on the hike. Maybe you should go keep him company."

Her tone is playful. Confusingly so. She knows Lennon and I don't talk. She *doesn't* know about the Great Experiment. And Lennon and I were only talking on the hike. Not flirting. All he did was adjust my pack! So why is Reagan's comment making me feel so guilty? I double-check that Lennon is out of hearing range. I think he is. He's already found a flat piece of land for his tent and is unloading his pack.

"Don't you agree, Brett?" Reagan says louder.

He cups his ear. "About what?"

"That Zorie should help Lennon," she says louder.

Oh. My. God. Please shut up!

"If Lennon wants to play good little Boy Scout, let him. There's plenty of time for that later. Right now, I'm thinking about a line Kerouac wrote in *The Dharma Bums:* 'Happy. Just in my swim shorts, barefooted, wild-haired, in the red fire dark, singing, swigging wine, spitting, jumping, running—that's the way to live.'" Brett wads up his shorts and gestures toward me. "Catch!"

I lunge awkwardly to snag them midair. Brett cheers, and then swivels around and wades into the waterfall pool.

"For the love of God, put your eyes back in your head," Reagan tells me.

My attention snaps to her. "I'm not—"

"You are." She takes off her hiking boots, and then says in a lower voice, "I told you before we came on this trip that I didn't want it getting awkward. You promised it wouldn't."

"I didn't ask him to throw his shorts at me!" I whisper back.

"Just watch yourself."

I'm irritated now. And suspicious. What exactly did the two of them do last night when they were gallivanting around the campsite like teenage winos? I want to ask this, but I settle on, "Why do you care?"

She pulls off her T-shirt. She's wearing a bikini top beneath it. Her sigh is long and weary. I think she's still hungover. "You're taking this the wrong way. I've had a shitty morning, and an even shittier summer."

I blow out a hard breath. "I know you have, Reagan. And I'm sorry about the Olympic trials."

Her cheeks darken. "I don't want your pity." Almost immediately, she seems to realize that she's snapped at me and closes her eyes briefly before speaking in a lighter tone. "I just want everyone to enjoy this, okay?"

"Me too," I say, confused. "What does that have to do with Brett?"

"Look, you aren't the only person to take a bite out of him. Summer's been with Brett too."

"What?" This is . . . news to me. My awkward conversation with Summer about Brett and Lennon pops into my head, and now I'm wondering why she didn't mention this.

"I just don't want you to be territorial and get your feelings crushed like you did this spring after that party."

Is she trying to save my feelings or hurt them? Because she's doing a pretty good job at the latter. And how was I being territorial, for the love of Pete?

Reagan is already jogging toward the waterfall. And I'm left confused and stinging, guilty about something I didn't even do . . . and irrationally jealous over that Summer tidbit.

I glance back at Lennon, who is busy clearing away rocks to make a place for his tent, while Brett is whooping loudly beneath the mist of the waterfall, begging for Reagan to take his picture.

All this time, I've been freaking out about wild animals. Maybe I should have been concentrating on the bigger threat: trying to figure out where I fit into civilization.

12

"Tell us a ghost story," Summer says to Lennon from across the campfire.

The sun's been falling for a half hour or more, and we're gathered around the fire inside the granite shelter, watching Lennon carefully feed another stick of wood to the flames. He was right about the boulders: They make good benches. We've all been sitting here for the last hour, drying out from swimming in the waterfall pool, eating our rehydrated pouches of food. I'm still hungry and could eat another one. But then we'd have to boil more water, and it's so dark, I can barely make out the edge of the river. Definitely not worth the trouble.

"Why do you think I know a ghost story?" Lennon says.

A chorus of noises echo around the rocks as everyone encourages him.

"You *totally* know one, dude," Brett says. "Stop playing."

Lennon looks up from the fire. "Maybe I do."

"Ha!" Summer says. "I knew it. Tell us one about killer hillbillies in the woods."

"Please don't," I say.

"Not any about a boogeyman with a hooked hand who attacks people making out in parked cars either," Kendrick says. "I don't like hooks."

Summer laughs and tries to tickle him.

Everyone's in a good mood, relatively speaking. Reagan, in her own way, has sort of tried to make up for what she said to me earlier. She brought along a small hammer—one of her many purchases from the outdoor gear store—so she helped me stake down the poles for a tarp at my tent's entrance. She asked me if I was okay, and I lied and said that I was. Then she gave me one of her extrahard back pats, and that was that. We're good. I guess. She's been sitting on the same rock with me, and Brett just slid between us. Which should be exciting—his side pressing against mine—but I can't enjoy it. I'm too busy thinking about her earlier "territorial" speech and how it seems like she's trying to steer me away from Brett.

Why?

"Come on," Reagan begs Lennon. "You and your freaky goth fetish . . . We know you've got a good ghost story."

"You have the perfect voice for spooky tales," Summer adds. "You sound like one of those old horror movie actors from black-and-white movies. The Wolfman. Dracula. All of that."

"Vincent Price," Kendrick guesses.

"No, the other one. Dracula. He was in *Lord of the Rings*."

"Christopher Lee," Lennon supplies.

"Yes!" Summer says. "Thrill us, Christopher Lee."

Lennon pushes up from a squat and brushes off his hands. "All right," he says. "I heard something a few months ago. But it's not fiction. It's what someone actually told me. You sure you want to hear it?"

No, I do not want to hear, thank you. I don't like being scared. And now that it's getting dark, I'm starting to worry again about sleeping on the ground. The tents I picked out with Reagan are actually pretty cool, I suppose, as far as tents go. They're small, but made for two people, which means that there's some wiggle room inside with just one person occupying. But they're still not tall enough to stand inside, and knowing that I'll be stuck in that tiny space later with little more than a thin scrap of nylon between me and all the nocturnal animals that use the waterfall for a watering hole is starting to freak me out.

But everyone else is apparently a million times braver, and they all want Lennon to frighten them.

"I'm so ready," Summer says.

"Don't say I didn't warn you." Long legs bent, Lennon sits on the edge of a boulder and leans forward, settling his forearms on his thighs. "Okay, so back before school ended, I was taking weekend wilderness survival classes on the other side of Mount Diablo. It's run by ex-military people along with this retired search-and-rescue ranger who used to work in Yellowstone. His name was Varg."

"Varg?" Summer repeats.

"It's Swedish," Lennon says. "And this guy was no one to fuck around with. Six five, big as a barn, scars everywhere. He's rescued people from landslides and cave-ins. Fires. And he's found a lot of dead bodies. People go missing in the wilderness all the time, and if they're lost, they sometimes run out of food and starve to death, or they are attacked by animals or crushed by falling rocks. Fall into hot geysers."

"Jesus," Reagan complains.

"In winter, they freeze. Varg said he found an entire family frozen in the mountains. Amateur mountain climbers. They'd been there a week, trapped on a ledge. An animal had eaten the husband's leg."

"Ew!" Summer says.

I make a mental note to never, *ever* go camping in winter.

Lennon twines his fingers together loosely. "But Varg said even though he'd found dozens of corpses throughout his career—which is a lot of dead bodies—he never once believed in the possibility of ghosts. Not until he traveled to Venezuela."

"What's in Venezuela?" Brett asks, holding his phone up.

"Are you videoing this?" Lennon asks.

"Of course. Now I'll have to edit that part out."

As the waterfall cascades steadily behind him, Lennon gives Brett a long, unnerving look.

Brett shuts off his phone and pockets it.

Then Lennon continues.

"When Varg was outside Caracas, doing some kind of search-and-rescue seminar with local rangers, they spent the night in the mountains during a full moon. Nothing extraordinary happened. They built a fire. Ate. Talked. A lot like this, I suppose," Lennon says. "But when it got late and everyone had turned in for the night, he stayed at the campfire, making sure the embers were out. And as he was sitting there, the hairs on the back of his neck rose. He had the distinct feeling someone was watching him."

"Uh-oh," Kendrick murmurs.

Lennon points to the tree branch hanging above the granite shelter. "Varg looked up at a nearby tree and saw a boy about our age sitting on a branch. He was high up, and the trunk of the tree didn't have any low-hanging branches, so Varg couldn't figure how he'd gotten up there. He called up to the boy, but the boy didn't answer. And because it was dark, Varg couldn't see him well, but his mind tried to rationalize his presence, and—I guess because of the nature of his job—he was worried that the boy was stuck. In trouble, you know. Needed help."

"I don't like where this is going," Summer says, curling up against Kendrick's side.

Lennon continues. "When he got closer and stood beneath the branch, the light from the moon gave him a better view of the boy. He was wearing strange clothes. It took Varg a few moments to realize that they were a soldier's uniform . . . from, like, the eighteen hundreds."

"Oh, shit," Reagan murmurs.

Brett slings his arm around her shoulders. She leans into him. When Brett notices I'm watching, he says, "Come on, girl. I got enough for everyone." And he puts his arm around my shoulders too, and pulls me closer.

I'm not sure how I feel about this. Uncomfortable. I think that's how I feel. Really, *really* uncomfortable. Especially when Reagan's judgmental eyes slide toward mine. And Lennon has paused his story, so I glance in his direction. Murder. That's what his face looks like. Not toward me, but Brett. Flickering shadows cast by the campfire's flames deepen the hollows of his cheeks and outline the sharp planes of his face.

Don't you ever miss us?

Oh, God. Before I can think about it, I pretend to cough and pull out of Brett's arm, slapping a hand against my chest for added effect.

"You okay?" Brett asks, genuinely concerned.

I nod vigorously and cough once more before stealthily scooting an inch away. He doesn't try to put his arm around me again, and I've never been so relieved. My brain is telling me how backward this is—didn't I come out here for this exact reason? For a chance to spend time with him? But my body is telling me to move a little farther away.

What's wrong with me, anyway? Is what Reagan said earlier messing with my head?

"Is that the end of the story?" Summer asks Lennon.

He flicks an unreadable glance toward me before answering her. "Do you really want to hear the rest?"

"Yes!" Summer and Kendrick say.

Lennon complies. "So, Varg was alarmed to find a boy dressed in this manner, but he tried to be rational about it. He called out to him again, but the boy still wouldn't answer. Varg wondered if he couldn't understand English, so he ran a couple of yards away to the tents and woke one of the local men to help translate. When they returned to the tree, the boy was gone."

"Oooh," Summer says.

Goose bumps dimple my arms. I pull down the sleeves of my hoodie and cross my arms over my stomach.

"Varg was badly shaken up by this, naturally," Lennon says. "He didn't know if it was a ghost, or his imagination. Maybe he'd fallen asleep at the fire and dreamed it. He told himself all kinds of things. But that was his last night in the mountains there, so the next day, they drove to the city, and he got on a flight back to the States. When he returned to Wyoming, it was night before he made it into Yellowstone. He lived inside the park, in dormitory-style housing with other rangers. And when he got up to his room, which was on the second story, he opened his window to let in some air, and just outside, on an impossibly high branch, was the silent soldier boy. *He'd followed him home.*"

My eyes water. Not gonna lie: I am 100 percent scared.

"Wicked," Brett whispers.

"No way," Summer says. "Oh my God. What did he do?"

Lennon hunches lower over his legs, leaning closer to the fire. "Well, he—"

"He what? He what?" Summer says.

Lennon's head tilts. "Did you hear that?"

"Shut the hell up," Reagan whispers, visibly frightened. "Stop it, Lennon."

"Are you scared?" Brett asks Reagan, hugging her closer. "Oh my God. You totally are!"

"Hey!" Lennon shouts. "I'm serious. Listen."

The campfire is quiet. All I can hear is the steady cascade of the waterfall. And—

Oh.

"What the hell?" Brett whispers.

It's coming from the tents, and it sounds like—

Like someone's going through our stuff.

Lennon signals for everyone to stay where they are, and then he straps a small headlamp onto his head, flipping on the light as he jumps off the rock and heads out of the granite shelter.

A dozen scenarios race through my mind, and none of them are good. I'm terrified, but I not staying here while Lennon marches away to his death. I jump up and chase him into darkness, tracking the bouncing light of his headlamp until I catch up to him.

"Stay behind me," he whispers.

I can hear the rest of the group debating whether to follow, and they are soon behind us, making as much noise as the mystery interloper.

The sound of our footsteps creeping toward the tents is overloud in my ears. Twigs break. Leaves crunch. We head around a tree that marks the outer edge of the campsite. Our tents are all spread apart, some of them closer to the river, some closer to the woods. The first one is Lennon's. Mine is just to the left, near a big boulder. We creep between the two tents, watching each step. I hear noise, but the dull roar of the waterfall is confusing my brain. I frantically look around, trying to spot danger, when Lennon blindly reaches back a hand to halt me.

My heart slams against my rib cage. Then I spot it near the river.

Several yards ahead, the navy-blue silhouettes of Reagan and Brett's tents stand in the moonlight, their dome shapes like igloos rising from the dark riverbank. One of those tents doesn't look right. It's misshapen. A giant, half-deflated soccer ball. And when Lennon's headlamp shines over it, an enormous dark shape turns around to face the light.

13

Black bear.

Big black bear.

Big black bear tearing up Brett's tent.

The group catches up to us as shock winds through me. Reagan runs into my back, and I nearly topple over. Summer makes a terrified sound.

"Oh, Jesus," Brett whispers, spotting the bear. "Oh Jesus, oh Jesus!"

My mind empties. Every nerve in my body sings.

As if he can hear my panicked thoughts, the bear lifts his head to sniff the air. His small eyes glow chartreuse in Lennon's headlamp, reflecting the light.

"Don't move," Lennon says over his shoulder. "Don't run. He might chase you."

What the hell are we supposed to do, then? The wind blows the bear's musky scent in our direction, and my feet want to flee, despite Lennon's warning.

We all stand silently. Staring. The bear stares back. He sniffs the air again, and a huge pink tongue licks the side of his muzzle. He's curious about us, and completely unafraid. In fact, whatever he smells in the air has made him brave. He steps out of Brett's tent, paw ripping the fabric as his leg swings around.

He's going to charge us.

We're going to die. If I was scared during Lennon's story, I'm petrified now. I inhale a shaky breath. I *really* wish Andromeda were here. She would bark this bear into submission.

Or she'd tuck tail and run, which is exactly what I want to do.

"Hey!" Lennon shouts in a booming voice that makes me jump. "Get the hell out of here! Get out!" He's waving his hands over his head as if he's dressed up like a vampire on Halloween and trying to scare little kids. Only, he sounds absolutely furious. And because his big voice is so deep, it carries over the river and bounces back in a thundering echo.

The bear is now paying attention. He pauses midstep, one enormous paw in the air, and his head stills.

Lennon lunges forward—just one long stride. But he bellows once more as he does it, and images of him stupidly throwing himself at the bear flash behind my eyes. Blood. Screaming. Horror. I see it all unfolding, and I'm too terrified to do anything to stop it.

"I said, get out!" Lennon shouts, clapping his hands loudly several times. He quickly scoops something off the ground and throws it at the bear. A rock? I can't tell. But it hits the bear on the nose.

WHY WOULD YOU DO THAT?

The bear shakes off the projectile. My body prepares to flee. And then—

His big, furry body slowly turns around. The bear shambles away, crushing the tent beneath him in two steps.

Lennon claps again and starts walking toward it, slowly, casually. Shouting as if he's trying to get a horse to gallop. And then the bear picks up speed and runs into the dark woods.

Gone.

I stare at the edge of the forest until my eyes sting. Is it really gone? Or is he faking us out, only to turn around and race toward us on his hind legs? Wait, do black bears stand on their hind legs? Or is it just grizzly bears? I don't know. *Why don't I know?*

"It's okay now," Lennon is saying. His hand is shockingly warm and firm on my neck. "Hey, it's okay. He's gone."

I glance at him, dazed. It takes me several moments to find my voice, and when I do, my tongue is thick in my mouth. "Are you sure?"

"Pretty sure," Lennon says, glancing over his shoulder at the woods. "Listen. You can hear it retreating. Those are pinecones making all the noise under his feet."

I barely hear anything. Which is good. I don't want to hear bear feet making noise.

"Holy shit, that was intense," Kendrick says. "He's really gone?"

"For now," Lennon says.

"What do you mean?" Reagan asks. "Will he come back?"

Lennon shines his headlamp on the destroyed tent. "If he's after something, maybe. Whose tent is that?"

"Pretty sure it's Brett's," Summer says, flicking on a handheld flashlight.

She's right. Reagan and Brett both chose tent spots that were next to the river.

Lennon grumbles under his breath and cautiously walks toward the fallen tent as we follow to inspect the damage. I suspect it's pretty bad, but when Lennon picks up one side of the nylon, I now see that it's irreparable. This is no tear. A gaping hole extends down the length of the one-man tent. Lennon crouches and peers beneath the flap of fabric. "Are you kidding me?"

"What's wrong?" I say.

Lennon holds up the remains of a package of store-bought chocolate chip cookies. Crumbs fall. The whole thing's ripped wide open. It's not the only thing. When Summer shines her flashlight on the tent's floor, she illuminates pouches of tuna. Candy. Pretzels.

Brett's entire food stash.

It's spilling out from an open bear canister—one that Lennon forced him to get. The lid is several feet away, buried under the food rubble.

"The canisters aren't even supposed to be inside our tents," Lennon says. "At the campfire—that's where they need to be stored. And why is this open?"

"Maybe the bear opened it?" Summer says.

"They can't be opened by a bear," Lennon says. "That's the whole point!"

I look around. "Um, where is Brett?"

"I'm here," a voice says. Brett's curly head peeks out from behind a tree, and he puts up a hand to shield his eyes from the dueling lights of Lennon's headlamp and Summer's flashlight.

"Did you not put the lid on your food?" Lennon says, suddenly livid.

"Of course I did," Brett says, surveying the damage with his phone. He's videoing everything. "Holy crap. That bear really went to town, didn't he?"

"This isn't funny," Lennon says. "And you didn't put the lid on, or the bear wouldn't have smelled the food."

Brett's eyes tighten. "I said I put it on, dude. The canister was defective."

"Hmm," Kendrick says, squinting at the tent. "I don't know. I mean, it's a lid and it screws on. How could it be defective?"

"It's not. He forgot to put it on," Lennon says.

Brett bristles. "Are you calling me a liar?"

"I don't know," Lennon replies. "Are you?"

"Whoa," Reagan says. "Everyone calm down. Lennon, if Brett says it was defective, it was."

Lennon stands and gets in Brett's face. "Where were you?"

"Hey, stop shining that damn headlamp in my eyes," Brett complains.

"Just now. You weren't with the group. Where were you? Did you run from the bear?"

"Um, no."

Lennon gestures dramatically. "I told you not to run. They see you as prey, and they'll chase you. Black bears can run faster than humans."

"Not Reagan," Brett says, attempting to lighten the mood.

"Yes, even Reagan," Lennon insists. "Even freaking Usain Bolt, if the bear was angry and charging at full speed. That one there was easily three hundred pounds. It could have killed any one of us."

"Dude, you need to chill," Brett says, getting annoyed. "Your holier-than-thou shit is starting to stink."

"Yeah, well, I'll stop preaching when you pay attention and quit treating this like a game."

"I haven't done anything."

"*You* neglected to put the lid on your canister," Lennon says, stabbing a finger in the air accusingly. "Then *you* ran from the bear after I said not to."

Brett roughly pushes Lennon. "Guess what? You aren't in charge, dude."

Lennon shoves Brett's shoulder. "*You* put us all in danger, *dude*."

"Whoa, whoa, whoa," Kendrick says, getting between the two boys and forcing them apart. "We're not gonna do this. Let's all relax and figure it out."

"There's nothing to figure out," Lennon says.

Reagan steps into the circle. "Hey! Maybe you need to consider that Brett's telling the truth."

"Thank you, Reagan," Brett says, still angry. "I'm glad someone here trusts me."

Everyone tries to talk at once. Kendrick wants people to settle down. Lennon wants Brett to admit that he's wrong. Reagan wants Lennon to leave Brett alone. Summer wants to know if the bear is going to come back—which is something I think we all need to consider. So with her help, I start packing Brett's food remnants inside the now-empty bear canister, sweeping up cookie crumbs into my palm. My eyes fall on the canister lid, poking out from the rubble.

It crosses my mind that all I'd need to do is pick it up and test it out on the canister to see if Brett was lying about it being faulty. Do I *want* to know? If Brett was lying, he'll look like an idiot. Or Lennon might kill him. Conflicting emotions swirl inside my chest, so I continue cleaning up, avoiding the lid.

"This is a wreck," Summer says when the arguing dies down, lifting up a piece of shredded tent. "I know we talked about wild animals, but I swear, in a million years, I never really believed we'd see one. Like, maybe some squirrels or rabbits. But not this."

That makes two of us.

Sullen, Lennon kneels at my side and picks up a dented can.

"Did you see any bears when you were out here before?" Summer asks Lennon. "Is that how you knew what to do?"

He shakes his head. "I've seen them alongside bigger trails in other parts of the park, but they always kept their distance. This one is way too comfortable around people. I think I need to report it, so that the rangers can keep an eye on this area. But right now, we need to make sure the food is contained so that it doesn't come back."

"And figure out what to do about this tent," I say, glancing at Brett. "I don't think you can sleep here."

Summer shrugs at Brett. "You can just sleep in Reagan's tent. I mean, you'd end up there, anyway, right? No biggie."

My body goes rigid.

"Uh-oh," Summer murmurs. "Sorry, guys. I know I wasn't supposed to say anything."

I glance from Summer to Reagan and Brett. "Are you two . . . together?"

Brett turns around and mumbles something to Reagan that I can't hear as he takes a couple of steps toward the river.

"Reagan?" I say. "Is it true?"

"Zorie . . ." She squeezes her eyes shut.

Oh, God. It *is* true.

"You two are together? Why didn't you tell me?"

She lifts a hand to gesture and then lets it fall back down to her side and shakes her head. "I don't know. Because."

"Because why?"

"I knew you'd flip out, okay?" she says, suddenly defensive.

"I'm not—"

"You are doing it right now. Don't you see? You always get freaked out when things don't go exactly the way you've planned, with all your stupid blueprints and checklists, and maybe I just didn't want to deal with that."

I'm humiliated. And confused. If she was seeing Brett, why did she encourage me to go after him back after the kiss at that party? "How long have . . . ? I mean, since when?"

"Does it matter?"

"Yeah, maybe."

"Why?" she says, exasperated. "Don't you get it? I was trying to spare your feelings. That's why I made Brett invite Lennon along."

"What are you taking about?"

"I know you guys dated last fall. One of Summer's friends saw you guys mauling each other's faces near the skate park. Everyone knows!"

Oh, God. I want to die. I can't even look at Lennon. I'm utterly humiliated.

"And the thing is," she continues, "you insisted that the two of you were just friends, even when I asked you point-blank if you were seeing each other. I even asked Avani—because God knows you tell her more secrets than you've ever told me—but she covered for you and said nothing was going on."

This is impossible. Avani never knew, so there was no reason for her to "cover" for anything.

Reagan crosses her arms. "Apparently, I'm not part of the inner circle anymore. I'm just someone you use when it's convenient, like when you need a place to sit at lunch."

"That's not true!" Right? I'm not using Reagan—at least not more than she uses me. *She* cheats off my tests in class. *She* calls to ask for help with homework. Do I not help her?

"Clearly you don't trust me with your secrets," she says. "So why should I trust you with mine?"

I want to respond, but I'm stuck in place, dumbly staring.

"Reagan . . . ," Summer says in a tentative voice.

"You just couldn't keep quiet, could you?" Reagan says, turning on Summer. "A couple more days, and she would be gone on her stupid astronomy club meet-up. All I asked was that you not say anything about Brett and me until after she'd left, but you couldn't help yourself, could you?"

"I—"

"I just wanted one nice thing this summer. Just one!" Reagan's eyes gloss over with tears. "None of you has any idea what I'm going through. You have no idea what's it like to train every single day for years—years! Then my foot slips for a fraction of a second and I have to give up on my dreams."

"You aren't the only person here with dreams," I tell her.

"But I'm the only person here with the talent to back them up."

"Christ," Kendrick says. "Listen to yourself, Reagan."

"I don't care what you think of me," Reagan says, giving him a defiant shrug as she swipes away tears. "Your family has money— big deal. So does mine. But I don't see you trying to do something big with your life. I was headed to the Olympics, okay? The god-damn Olympics!"

"We know you were," Summer says, sympathetic. "And we're sorry."

"I don't need your pity," Reagan tells her. "The only reason Kendrick is interested in you is because you piss off his parents."

"Hey!" Kendrick says, agitated.

"This is *my* trip," she says, thumping her chest. "I paid for all this stuff and I arranged everything. This was supposed to make me feel better. It wasn't about any of you."

"You're being a huge asshole, you know that?" Lennon tells Reagan.

"I'm being real," she says. "And while we're getting everything out in the open, let me just say what a complete and utter dick you've been to Brett on this trip. He wanted you to come."

"Did he? Because he wants to glom onto my dad's fame? Or to distract Zorie from the fact you and Brett are seeing each other because you knew she'd be hurt by this? Either reason is shitty."

"Really uncool, man," Brett says. "I was just trying to help Reagan play Cupid. Everyone knows you're carrying a massive torch for Zorie, so why are you complaining?"

What? No way is that true.

Reagan points at Lennon. "See? Brett likes you, and you've been nothing but a prick to him since we left Melita Hills. You should be grateful he's impressed by your has-been punk-rock father."

Lennon's lips thin into a straight line. "Keep my father's name out of your mouth."

"No one cares! No one even remembers him."

I've seen Lennon angry plenty of times. But right now, he's

furious. He never used to be so defensive about his father. His moms, yes, but every time someone has brought up his dad, a storm cloud drops over his head.

"Everyone, please calm down," Summer begs.

Brett steps forward. "Look, we're all saying things we don't really mean. Zorie, I'm sorry we didn't tell you about us. But that doesn't mean we can't all enjoy each other's company. Reagan and I both want the same thing—for everyone to have a good time. Is that so wrong?"

"A good time?" Lennon repeats. "You could have gotten us killed tonight."

"You'd like to make everyone believe that, wouldn't you? Maybe the problem is that *you* led us out into bear country. Maybe you're a shitty wilderness guide."

This is the tipping point for me. All the revelations that have surfaced in the last few minutes line up in my head like coordinates on a map:

Reagan not only failed to tell me about her relationship with Brett, but she also tried to con me into starting something up with Lennon—just so that she could have Brett for herself.

She's been holding a grudge against me because I'm friends with Avani.

Summer has spread gossip all around school about me and Lennon.

Brett is definitely not interested in me.

I'm definitely not interested in Brett. Not anymore. The thrill is *so* gone.

All of these things stack on top of each other, incremental scraps of trash, piling up on the heap of garbage that is my life right now. Because back at home, I still have to face my cheating father. My unaware mother. The embarrassment of the Mackenzies knowing about our sordid family problems.

And Lennon. Being around him has awakened a dormant hope inside me, and to know that my interactions with him were manipulated is the worst kind of betrayal. I thought I was starting to enjoy his company again, but was I? Or were we both just being scripted to talk to each other inside Reagan's puppet show? Looking back now, I can't tell what was real and what's been forced.

Something snaps inside my head.

I pick up the lid and slam it onto the canister, twirling it into place until the safety mechanism double clicks. Then I walk the container over to Brett, shoving it into his hands. "Not faulty."

Brett blinks at the canister, then at me. No one says anything for a long moment. It's Reagan's voice that breaks the silence.

"You want to be petty?" she says. "Fine. You can forget about sitting with me when school starts back next week. We're done. Go back to Avani."

I turn around and face her, angry tears welling. "Avani never abandoned you. Avani still likes you, for some stupid reason! *You're* the one who started hanging out with private school kids after your parents got rich. *You're* the one who thought training for the Olympics was more important than hanging out with your friends. And what did that get you? A bunch of friends who only hang with you out of pity or social obligation. Wake up, Reagan. No one even cares that you failed the stupid Olympic trials. Running isn't even a talent—it's just moving your legs!"

"Zorie," Lennon says quietly.

I look around and everyone is staring at me as though I've just insulted them. It takes me a second to realize that maybe I did. And you know what? I don't think I care. Maybe it was unfair to drag Kendrick into this, but the rest of them can go to hell. Right now, I hate Brett for ever kissing me, filling me with hope. I hate Summer for trying to manipulate me. And I *definitely* hate Reagan for ruining my summer.

Until I look at her.

For one glimmering moment, she looks as though she might cry. And that makes me feel . . . horrible. I'm not this person. I don't get in nasty fights with people. Arguing gives me hives.

I want to tell her I'm sorry.

I want her to tell me *she's* sorry.

I want to rewind back to the morning my mom told me about this awful trip and tell her no.

Just when I open my mouth to apologize, Reagan says, "Thanks for destroying this trip." She gestures toward Lennon. "You can both go and screw yourselves." She pivots, about to turn around, but then stops. "Oh, and by the way, your skeevy dad tried to sleep with Michelle Johnson's mom after the Olympic fund-raiser in Berkeley this spring. I never told my mom, because she'd stop patronizing your parents' stupid clinic, but you can bet I'm telling her now."

Time stops. I don't move, don't breathe, don't even blink. It's not until I feel hot tears sliding down my cheeks that I realize I'm crying. And for a second, I'm still frozen in place, trying to summon a response. But I can't.

My head is empty. I just want it all to go away. Reagan. Brett. Lennon. This disaster of a camping trip.

My father.

All of it sticks painfully in my throat, unable to escape. I feel as if I'm drowning while tiny piranhas nip at my skin, eating off chunks of my pride. And because we're out here in the middle of nowhere, in the dead of night, with a hungry bear and God only knows what else nearby, I do the only thing I can do, which is to retreat to my tent.

I barely can find my way in the moonlight. It seems far darker out here than it does in the city. And after I nearly break my neck, stumbling over dead wood and rocks, I somehow manage to get inside and zip myself away from the rest of the group. It's an ineffective substitute for a door slamming, *take that!* moment, especially when I realize that I can still hear voices in the distance. I can't make out what they're saying, but it really kills the illusion of privacy.

If my hives were bad before, they're going to rage now. I forage around in my pack for antihistamines and take two, swallowing them dry with no water. Exhaling a ragged breath, I lie back on my sleeping bag and stare into nothing. The ground is hard and cold beneath me, and I can feel a sharp rock poking into my hip.

The fight tumbles around in my mind, and I'm wounded all over again by everything that just happened. And then there's my dad. Does everyone in Melita Hills know about him? Are Mom and I the only ones who've been in the dark? Jesus. How stupid are we? An empty pang stabs my chest, and I wish Mom were here now, so I could talk to her. Or maybe so she could talk to me.

Wind rustles the side of my tent as I take off my glasses and wiggle into my sleeping bag. Everything inside here smells strongly synthetic, like nylon and plastic. Maybe I have it zipped up too tightly. Should I open a vent flap? What if the bear comes back and smells me in here, like he smelled Brett's cookies?

I decide that it doesn't matter. I'm suddenly overwhelmingly tired. No sleep last night. Getting up early. All that hiking. The antihistamines. I feel myself teetering on the edge of sleep, and after a while, I stop fighting. I just let it take me under.

When I wake, the inside of the tent is pale gray and chilly. My fingers and nose are Popsicles, and when I try to move, I realize I fell asleep in my clothes. I also never did anything about that rock beneath the tent, and now my hip feels as if I've broken something.

On top of all that, I had weird dreams about Lennon. Very screwed up, very erotic dreams. He was killing that bear, and *dear God*, why is my brain so messed up? It must have something to do with Brett's comment last night about Lennon carrying a torch for me. Which is stupid, because Lennon's not carrying any sort of torch for me. And how could he be, really, because I'm the one with the unrequited feelings. I'm the torch carrier. Lennon left me.

I'd like nothing more than to stay cocooned in my sleeping bag and go back to sleep so that I can maybe redo those dreams in a different, nonerotic direction. But I sit up to check my hives—present, but under control—and soon realize I have to pee. Badly. There's room enough for me to get into a crouching position, but I can't really stand in here, so after rummaging through my pack for supplies and a pair of glasses, I crawl my way across the sleeping bag and unzip my way to freedom.

All is quiet. It's gray outside, but a marigold light shines through the eastern trees. Everything is damp, and the subtle scent of pine fills my nostrils when I walk. I've never been more awake in my life. I'm on edge, thinking of the bear, eyes flicking to every bird call, every rustling leaf. I don't see anyone. No bear, no people. Just the flattened husk of Brett's destroyed tent next to Reagan's.

After a trek into the forest to relieve my aching bladder, I trudge back to the base camp and spot movement across the river. Anxiety over last night's fight seizes me, and I dread seeing Reagan or Brett. It takes me several panicked heartbeats to clear away the antihistamine fog and recognize Lennon in a black hoodie. He's crossing the rocks from the opposite bank, a hatchet holstered to his hip and an armful of firewood. When he spots me, he lifts his head briefly, and I'm surprised how relieved I feel to see him.

Don't think about the erotic bear dreams.

He's headed for the granite shelter area, and I catch up with him there. He dumps the pile of gathered firewood near the pit. When his back is to me, my eyes roam the denim vest he's wearing over his hoodie. It's studded with horror-movie patches and enamel pins shaped like tombstones and severed body parts. Some things never change.

"Hey," I say. "Guess we're the only people up, huh?"

"Yes and no." He squats near the pit to arrange tinder in the center, bark and dead leaves.

"What do you mean, yes and no?"

"Are you hungover?" he asks, squinting. "You sound slow."

"Antihistamines."

"Ah. Hard drugs. Are your hives acting up?"

"Sort of. What do you mean, yes and no?" I repeat, looking around the camp.

He sighs. "Over there, on the bear canisters."

They're stacked in a row near the boulders we were using for seats, along with some camp cookware. Then I spot a strip of toilet paper sitting under a rock. Something's been written on it, a message in what appears to be eyeliner. It's Reagan's handwriting. I remove the rock and read the note:

Find your own way home.

14

I reread Reagan's note again and again, but it's still not making sense. Did they . . . ? I mean, are we . . . ?

"They left us," Lennon finally says.

"All of them?"

"All of them."

"I don't understand," I say. "Where did they go?"

He carefully arranges sticks in the shape of a teepee around the pile of tinder. "Back to the glamping compound."

"They told you that?"

"Reagan and Brett had a fight after you went to your tent last night." Lennon keeps his eyes glued to his task, but his body posture looks . . . uncomfortable. "Long story short, he said this trip was too much drama for him. Reagan agreed. They decided to go back home."

Is this a joke? It must be. Right?

Gingerly, he props up larger branches over the sticks. "Reagan was going to leave last night, which was nuts. Kendrick and I had to convince her to stay until there was light to hike, and that we'd go back together. Earlier this morning, I thought I heard noise, but it wasn't loud, so I fell back asleep. By the time I'd woken up again and gotten dressed, they were gone."

He's serious. This isn't a joke.

I feel dizzy, so I sit on a boulder. "They left us? Summer and Kendrick too?"

"The last thing Kendrick and I talked about last night before I turned in was trying to estimate how much it would cost to hire a car at the glamping compound to drive him and Summer to his parents' vacation home in Napa Valley." He brushes off his hands and digs a lighter out of his jeans pocket. "But I didn't think they'd just take off like that."

"Without us?"

"Brett left me a note on the inside of that pack of cookies the bear ate. He basically said it was best we all parted ways to avoid further drama, and that he knew I could find my way back. Then I found the other note Reagan wrote outside your tent."

Find your own way home.

He gestures toward the riverbank. "They left Brett's destroyed tent and a bunch of the supplies. Guess Reagan is officially over camping. Nice of her to just leave a huge mess behind for us to clean up."

"How long have they been gone? Can we catch up to them?" Why is he just calmly building a fire?

"Zorie," he says, "if what I heard the first time I woke was the sound of them leaving, then they've been gone a couple hours. We'll never catch up."

"You could have woken me! We could have hustled!"

"I've only been awake for fifteen or twenty minutes. Don't you get it? It was too late an hour ago. By the time we hike to the parking lot . . ."

They'll have driven away already.

Okay. No need to panic. Just think. Make a new plan. What do we do now? It took us four hours to hike here from the parking lot. Another hour or so to drive back to the glamping compound, where we could catch a taxi or bus home. But we don't have a car. "How long a hike on foot is it from the parking lot back to the glamping compound?"

"There aren't shoulders on some of those mountain roads we drove. They aren't made for hiking. Christ, they're barely made for vehicles. You remember the drive here on that twisty main road."

We nearly hit a couple of other vehicles coming in the opposite direction when rounding switchbacks. It was sort of scary, and I definitely wouldn't want to be on that road in the rain or fog. Especially not on foot.

He shakes his head. "We'd be better off taking an actual walking trail the other way around the mountains, but that could take . . . a lot longer."

"How much longer?"

"A day."

"All day?"

"And night. We'd have to camp along the way. There's no straight shot back to the compound from the parking lot out here."

Holy crap. Is he serious?

"This can't be happening," I tell him as I pace across the shelter, trying to figure out what to do next. I'm absolutely panicking now and not even bothering to hide it. "They abandoned us in the middle of nowhere? It was just an argument!"

"Reagan was pretty upset."

"Reagan? *I'm* the one who was humiliated."

"There was a lot of humiliation handed out last night in all directions. Everyone was upset. After you left, Reagan cried . . . a lot. And yelled a lot. I think her Olympic failure is affecting her more than she lets on."

I stare at him. "You're taking her side?"

He holds up his hands. "Not taking her side. I don't even like Reagan and, frankly, don't understand why you and Avani were ever friends with her in the first place. You know how I've felt about her. That hasn't improved over time, especially seeing how she's given Avani the cold shoulder. I'm just saying that Reagan only pretends to be okay, but clearly she's not. As stupid as Brett can be, even he knew it. Reagan's been reaching out for anything to make her feel better, including him. After things calmed down last night, he told me that they'd been talking since spring break, while he was getting back together with his old girlfriend. But I guess they started officially hooking up after the Olympic trials fiasco."

Jesus. Wait. Since spring break . . . ? That party—where Brett and I kissed—was during spring break.

"Did you know they were a couple before last night?" I ask. "Brett and Reagan?"

He shakes his head. "They kept it from me, too. If you haven't noticed, Reagan has control issues. I guess when you and Brett got together at that party—"

OH, GOD. HE KNOWS.

"We weren't *together*," I say. "Not like that."

"It's none of my business."

How does Lennon know about the kiss? Did Brett tell him? Of course he did. I don't know why this upsets me so much, but I feel . . . exposed. "What exactly did Brett tell you?"

He averts his eyes and doesn't respond.

"Oh, terrific," I mutter. "Could this get any worse? It was just one kiss! And believe me when I say that I'm regretting it now."

"I didn't put a lot of stock in most things he told me," Lennon says. "I know his mouth is bigger than his brain. And it's not as if I didn't know you were dating people over the last year. Life goes on, right? I dated someone too."

He did? I had no idea. I want to ask who it was—when it was. Are they still dating? He said "dated," right? Past tense?

"Not that one thing has to do with the other," he says quickly. "Apples and oranges."

"Right," I say quietly. "Apples and oranges."

He shakes his head. "My point is, Reagan has issues. She's wounded and embarrassed, and she's not thinking straight. People do stupid things when they're acting on emotions."

"But I didn't do anything wrong!"

One brow lifts.

"Not wrong enough to get abandoned," I amend.

"Neither of us did. Well, I knew better than to agree to this trip, but I came anyway. So in a way, I was wrong. But, hey, all the agitators are gone, and I'm right where I want to be, so maybe it all worked out."

"Are you insane? This is a complete disaster. What are we going to do? Maybe there's another way to get back that doesn't involve hiking all day. A bus that stops near the parking lot? The Sierras public transportation here has to connect to other nearby towns. Surely, there's somewhere we can catch a Greyhound or something back to Melita Hills."

"Already thought of that. I have a map of the bus routes. The closest one is a grueling eight-hour hike back through the mountains. That's without breaks. And for someone who's not accustomed to hiking—"

He means me.

"—count on it taking ten, eleven hours. Up and down extraordinarily steep inclines. A hike for experienced hikers who want to challenge their bodies. It's labeled on the map as 'difficult.'"

Are you kidding me?

"I don't think they realized what they were doing by leaving us here," Lennon continues. "Reagan's an asshole, but she's not inhumane. Brett just operates on the belief that everything will turn out fine, and he probably convinced Kendrick and Summer of this. At least, that's what I hope."

I hold Reagan's note in my hands, staring at it blankly while Lennon gets the fire going, blowing the tinder and rearranging sticks. I think I'm in shock. Maybe I should put my head between my knees or blow into a paper bag.

"I'm going to miss the star party," I say, more to myself than to him. I know it's the last thing I should be worried about, but I'm having trouble focusing. My brain is moving too quickly, flashing through minor details as it searches for a solution to our predicament.

Lennon looks up from the fire. "Is that the meet-up Reagan mentioned last night?"

"Yeah," I say. "I was supposed to catch a bus to Condor Peak in a couple of days. My astronomy club—Dr. Viramontes, you know?" Lennon's moms occasionally used to drive me to the observatory for my meetings, so of course he knows. When he nods, I briefly explain the star party. "I was supposed to meet Avani there."

And now I know why Reagan was so eager for me to go. I would be out of her hair, and she could enjoy Brett's company in the open. God, what an idiot I've been.

"Suppose I can just text Avani when we get to a place where there's service," I say absently. There's definitely no service out here. "Avani needs to know not to expect me."

"Or you could just go to the star party like you originally planned," Lennon says, something devilish sparking behind his eyes.

A bird trills loudly on a distant branch. "It's too early to catch a bus," I explain. "No one will be at Condor Peak yet. I can't just sit around there twiddling my thumbs for a couple of days and wait for people to show up."

"I'm not talking about taking a bus. Condor Peak isn't all that far from here."

"It's not?"

He reaches into his jacket vest and pulls out his notebook. After a few moments of shuffling things around, he finds a map and unfolds it. "See," he says, laying the map down on a boulder and pointing. "This is where we are. And this is Condor Peak." He measures something and does a quick calculation, mumbling numbers under his breath as he counts them out. "A couple of days' hike through King's Forest. Maybe three."

I snort. "Okay, that's insanely far."

"Not really. The trails would be a hell of a lot easier than the one leading to the nearest bus stop, and we wouldn't hike the entire time, you know. We'd take breaks. Camp at night."

"We?"

"You and me, yes," he says matter-of-factly. "I'd take you there."

"The two of us hiking to Condor Peak? Alone?"

"I wasn't planning on inviting the bear along, but if you think we need a chaperone . . ."

I chuckle nervously and look at the map. "Are you serious?"

"Completely."

"Why would you do this?"

He shrugs. "I don't want to go back home yet. If you do, then I can walk you back to the bus stop. Maybe you'd be able to catch a bus tomorrow. Maybe there would be service and you could call your mom to come get you. Maybe you can hitchhike."

That's a whole lot of maybes. Definitely do not like.

"On the other hand," he says, "if you want to go to Condor Peak, I can plan a less dangerous and much easier hiking route into the national park."

"I don't know," I say, trying to think of a way to turn him down without sounding like a jerk. I mean, I can't do this. It's Lennon. My enemy. My former enemy. And also my former best friend. I have no idea what we are to each other now. We just started talking again, and my body is so stupid that it's already having erotic dreams about him, which is what got me into trouble with him in the first place. I don't want to get my hopes up. I don't even want to have hopes!

"How were you planning on getting home once you got to Condor Peak?" he asks.

"Avani," I say. "She's driving—following Dr. Viramontes and a few other people up there. The star party is for three nights, I think? So she's heading back when it's over. We were supposed to leave Friday morning to be back home by noon."

"Then I can catch a ride back to Melita Hills with you guys," he says, as if it's the most logical thing in the world. "Avani's cool. I'm sure she wouldn't mind."

No, she wouldn't. She likes Lennon. My brain flips back to the stuff she said about Brett not being in Lennon's league. God, she'd love to know what a total screwup Brett was during this trip. She'd probably gloat and say she told me so.

Or she wouldn't, because she's too nice.

This is not what I planned. Then again, none of it is. Nothing has gone the way it was supposed to go. At all.

How did it all go so wrong?

"Look," he says. "The way I see it, if you go back home, Reagan wins. Because now that she's humiliated herself and lost control of her perfect vacation, she wants everyone to be miserable along with her. When school starts, she'll tell her tribe in the courtyard a version of the story that makes her look the best. Like it or not, you will be the antagonist of that story. Don't you think she'd just *love* it if she could tell everyone that you had to take a bunch of connecting rural buses to get back home? Or pay a gazillion dollars to hire a car—or worse, call your mom to come get you?"

"Your knack for making me feel like a failure is extraordinary."

"*Or*," he says, holding up a finger, "*you* could tell everyone that *she* ran home like a spoiled brat who didn't get her way while you had a great time hiking with the coolest guy in school."

I push my glasses up.

"And you can tell them that you went to a star party," he continues. "People will say, *Ooh, what's that?* And you'll be able to say,

No big deal, I just hiked across a national park and met up with some of my fellow astronomers to view— Wait, what is it again?"

"The Perseid meteor shower."

"The Perseid meteor shower, which probably doesn't happen that often."

"Every year."

"Once every three hundred sixty-five days," Lennon says in a mystical voice, wiping his hand through the air dramatically.

"Shut up," I say, smiling a little, despite the dire situation.

"Hey, I know you didn't lug that telescope up here for your health."

I glance in the direction of my tent. I haven't even had a chance to use it.

"Do what you love. Don't let Reagan stop you. Screw her. Screw Brett, too, and his pretentious Kerouac worship. Kerouac drank himself to death. Neal Cassady screwed anything that moved and was a total misogynist—like most of the Beats, who were a bunch of immature dicks. Then he died of barbiturate abuse. So yeah, neither one of them lived past their forties. National treasures, my ass."

Yikes. Someone has strong feelings. "Didn't know you were so knowledgeable about literature," I say.

"I might surprise you yet, Zora May Everhart."

He already has.

"I'm sorry about Brett," he says in a gentler tone. "I really am. Especially if you liked him."

"Funny thing is, I'm not sure that I did. I mean, I thought I did, until . . ."

"You actually got to spend time with him?"

"Maybe."

"Me too. When he first started wanting to hang with me, I was like—I don't know. He's Brett Seager. Everyone loves him. But, Jesus Christ on a pogo stick, I couldn't spend an hour alone with him without praying for a nuclear bomb to hit, because at least I wouldn't have to endure another second of him quoting lines from 'Howl' or *On the Road*."

I think about Brett telling me he'd like to learn how to take photos of stars, and now I wonder if he really meant it, or if he was just preemptively placating my feelings.

"But," he says, "despite everything that's happened between us, believe it or not, I just . . . really want you to be happy. And if Brett is the guy to do that for you—"

"He's not," I say quickly.

"I'm glad," he says in a quiet voice. "I'm so, *so* glad to hear that."

I meet Lennon's eyes with my own. His gaze is unwavering. Too serious. I'm having trouble holding it, so I look at the fire instead.

A long silence stretches between us. Lennon uses a stick to poke the new flames, adjusting his kindling. Last night, I watched him construct this same pyramid-shaped campfire, and eventually the surrounding sticks burn and collapse into the middle. It's amazing, actually. I had no idea there was an art to building a fire.

I had no idea about a lot of things.

"I dare you," he murmurs.

I stop rubbing the cold out of my thighs and glance up at him. "You what?"

"I dare you to go to Condor Peak. Let me take you there. I can do it. I know I can. You used to trust me."

"You used to give me reasons to."

"I never stopped. You just quit paying attention."

Are we fighting? I don't *think* so, but the energy between us feels fierce. As flammable as his artful pile of sticks.

What do I want to do? Maybe he's right, and returning home would be a quiet sort of surrender. And really, didn't I come out here to get away from my family problems? Do I want to walk straight back into them, sitting behind the clinic's front desk, pretending to be okay while my father walks around in a cloud of lies?

But what's the alternative? Hiking in the boonies with my greatest enemy?

Former enemy?

God, I'm so confused.

Lennon squats by the fire and assembles a portable grill. Like everything else we're carrying, it's lightweight and compact, all the pieces fitting inside a single metal tube. When he's finished clicking all the pieces together, it stands on four legs. He gingerly settles it over the campfire, and then sets a pan of filtered stream water atop it. Flames lick the sides of the pan.

We both watch the water heating as if it's the most interesting thing in the world.

"Let's think this through logically, okay?" he says.

"Yes, please." Logical is good. Logical is safe. And I can tell by the look on his face that he's about to use logic against me, because he knows me oh-too-well. But I'm so stressed right now, I don't even care. I just need for things to line up in my brain.

He pushes dark hair out of his eyes and counts off a list of things on his fingers. "One, the group left us. Whether they thought through that clearly and realized what they were doing is inconsequential now. We're stranded. Two, we can hike all day on brutal trails and hope either a bus or a nonmurderous Good Samaritan willing to pick up two hitchhiking teens can take us out of the Sierras—"

"Oh, God."

"—*or* we can hike all day on easy trails and be halfway toward Condor Peak tomorrow. Three, you shouldn't cancel your plans with Avani, because she's a *way* better friend than Reagan ever was. Four, you have a perfectly capable guide who can take you where you want to go, and enough time to get there. Five, what do you have to lose?"

"Plenty."

"Like what? You afraid Joy will forget to feed Andromeda?"

Smart-ass.

"*No*," I say.

"Need to get back and press all your plaid skirts before school starts? Or maybe you're expecting a big order of imported *washi* tape to be delivered and need to spend all day organizing it by color and pattern?"

"Oh, ha-ha. You're a regular Bill Murray."

"What, then?"

"I don't know, that my dad would kill us both if he knew you were part of Reagan's group. I can't imagine what he'd do if he knew I was contemplating spending several days alone with you."

"Good point. Alone." He whistles softly and opens a bear canister. "We'll have trouble keeping our hands to ourselves."

"I didn't mean *that*." I sound like a Victorian schoolteacher, shocked by the very idea of impropriety—all *Heavens to Betsy!* and *How dare you, sir!*

"No?" he says, feigning disappointment.

Is he flirting with me? That can't be right. I think I'm losing my mind. "N-no," I stutter, and then say more firmly, "No."

"Let me take you to Condor Peak. Give your dad a big middle finger. Zorie and Lennon exploring the world. Like old times."

"Like old times," I mumble. "Hey, Lennon?"

"Yeah?"

"We don't really have a choice, do we? I mean, hiking to the bus stop . . . it was never an option."

He gives me a tight smile, and then shakes his head. "It will be okay. I promise. I'll get you to Avani in one piece. And if you change your mind, at the very least I can get you to a ranger station inside the park by tomorrow."

The water is boiling. He carefully tilts the pan's contents into his steel carafe before settling a mesh plunger on top. Then he sets a timer on his phone.

"What's that?" I ask.

"French press."

"For coffee?"

"Yep."

"Real coffee? Not instant?"

"We're camping, Zorie, not living in a dystopian nightmare."

"I'll try to remember that when I'm digging cat holes."

He holds up two blue enamel coffee cups. "It could be worse. It could be winter."

Or I could be stuck in the wilderness, miles away from civilization, with the boy who crushed my heart in the palm of his hand.

Oh, wait.

I am.

Part III

15

Over coffee and a couple of rehydrated gourmet breakfast pouches that Reagan left behind, Lennon breaks out his big topographic map of the area and a black metal compass that unfolds to reveal several dials, a clock, and a ruler. He makes several measurements and jots down numbers with a mechanical pencil, and it all looks complicated.

"How are you?" Lennon says, nodding toward my arm, which I'm scratching.

"A little itchy," I confess. Last night's bear attack and fight sent me back into Hive Overload. "I've got some stuff to put on it, but—"

"But what?"

"It's that stuff from Miss Angela."

He makes a face. "Oh, *God*. The miracle weed lotion that smells like a scented candle factory got hit by a bomb?"

I point at him. "That's the stuff. And not only does it make my eyes water, I'm sort of afraid to use it out here after last night. I don't want to attract bears."

"Hmm," he says. "Your worry is valid. I'll try to think of a solution. In the meantime, here's the route I have in mind."

He turns his map around to show me and opens up his journal, laying it on top. Across two of the journal's pages, he's drawn a not-to-scale map of our planned route, complete with a few tiny symbols sketched at various stopping points. I spot a notation for a waterfall near the bottom and point.

"This is us?"

"This is us," he confirms.

"And these tents are—"

"Camping spots. We have to pass over two chains of mountains to get to Condor Peak."

"Rock climbing?" I say, suddenly freaked out.

"No. Patience, grasshopper. If we go this way," he says, tracing a dotted line with his finger, "we can hike through a network of caves that passes under the mountains. The caves have four exits, and one of them is on the south side of the mountain. Once we make it through, there's an excellent valley where we can camp tonight."

"Hold on. Back up. Spelunking?"

"Walking through a cave is not spelunking. It's walking."

"In the dark."

"We'll have headlamps." He holds up his phone. "I saved a PDF of a hiking book that covers backcountry trails. It says there are several big caves along these foothills, but this one is the longest. And once we get to the other side of the mountain, we'll be able to pick up a bigger trail."

I look at where he's pointing on his homemade map. "I see three sets of tent symbols. Three nights?"

He nods. "To make it to Condor Peak without killing ourselves. And if you change your mind, this is the nearest ranger station. It's on the way, and we'll be passing by it tomorrow. Whatever happens, I won't leave you stranded. If you're thinking that I've abandoned you before—"

"I wasn't." I totally was.

He presses his lips together, then adds, "We can do this, I promise. As long as we follow the rules, we shouldn't have any more bear problems. This will be safer than spending three days in civilization. You're more likely to die in a car accident than in a national park."

"There you go, bringing up the possibility of death," I say drily. "I had forgotten about it, but now it's fresh in my mind, thanks."

"You're welcome," he says, grinning. "Now, let's pack up and hit the trail. Miles to go before we sleep."

Okay, I can do this. It's not the plan I wanted, but it is a plan. One that's been calculated and drawn on paper. I like that. It makes me feel less panicky. I just wish it were my plan and not Lennon's.

Getting ready to leave takes longer than I imagined. The group didn't leave just the corpse of Brett's mutilated tent behind. They left Reagan's and Summer's tents too, along with a bunch of camping supplies Reagan purchased for this trip. Guess she doesn't intend to use them again, but holy moly, what a frivolous waste of money. Lennon is mad, because all of this mess completely violates the leave-no-trace policy of the backcountry. And we can't physically take it with us: That would be impossible. All we can do is pack some of the food inside our bear canisters and scavenge a few items we may need. A single-burner camp stove. An additional Nalgene bottle. A backup lighter. Eco-friendly wet wipes. Reagan's water filter. Because of my telescope, I can't hold much of anything else in my pack, so Lennon carries most of it, attaching things to the outside of his pack with carabiner clips. What we don't need, he stacks in a single pile inside Reagan's tent.

"We can report this stuff when we get to the ranger station," he tells me. "They'll send a ranger to pick it up."

"If the bear doesn't come back and destroy it all first."

"Or that," he says with a sigh.

After all of this is finished, it's late morning. I change into fresh clothes, brush my teeth, and try to tame my frizzy curls. When I'm finished getting ready, I take down my dome tent. It's harder to pack than it was to unpack. And after watching from the sidelines, saying, "Nope," and "Wrong way," Lennon finally takes pity on me and helps. Then it's just a matter of getting it inside my backpack, and I'm ready to go.

As ready as I'll ever be, anyway.

We climb to the top of the waterfall, where Kendrick and Brett took turns diving the day before. I still can't believe they're gone. Or that I'm alone with Lennon. This is crazy. And it's also physically demanding. Climbing a hilly trail, as we did yesterday, is far different from pulling yourself up tiers of rocks with a giant back-pack. It takes me longer than Lennon, but halfway up, I begin to get the hang of it. There's a sort of rhythm to climbing, one that's careful and patient. Looking for the right handhold, taking time to push up with my legs, leaning into it. By the time we get to the top, I'm breathing heavy but feeling exhilarated.

"Goodbye, Mackenzie Falls," I say, peering down into the waterfall's pool below.

Lennon laughs. "The book I found it in called it 'Unnamed Waterfall #2,' otherwise known as 'Greaves River Falls.'"

"Those are terrible names."

"Mackenzie Falls sounds way better," he agrees. "When I write my backpacking book, that's what I'll name it."

"Oh, you're a writer now? And when can we expect to see *Grim's Super-Gothy Guide to the Dark Wilderness* on the shelves?"

"You remembered my code name," he says, smiling.

"Of course I do. I'm the one who came up with it."

He makes a satisfied noise, and we smile at each other for what I'm now realizing is a little too long, so I break the connection and look away. You know, before things get weird.

Weird*er*.

"Come on," he says. "The trail I originally used to find this place is just beyond that boulder."

We make our way through the brush and spy Lennon's trail. Much like the one we used to get here, it's narrow and barely there. It could even be confused as a deer trail, or some sort of animal path. That makes me a little nervous, but Lennon assures me that it's a real trail for real people. And at least it's mostly under the trees, because the closer it gets to noon, the hotter it gets. I was prepared for this; I strip off my long-sleeved T-shirt to reveal a short-sleeved one beneath. It's all about layers.

After a half hour or so of hiking in silence, I feel more comfortable with both the trail and being alone with Lennon. He's intense and quiet, walking steadily alongside me with his eyes constantly scanning the distance. And despite the zombies, chainsaws, and anarchy signs covering his denim jacket, he looks . . . not out of place, oddly enough.

"When did your zeal for camping start?" I ask.

He pushes a dark slash of hair away from one eye. "Last year, I guess. I was . . . going through some stuff, and Mac suggested the family trip to Death Valley. It just clicked for me. I loved everything about it."

"Sleeping on rocks?" My hip still hurts from the rock poking into it last night.

"No, but that's better with a bedroll beneath your bag," he says, reaching back to pat the rolled-up pad attached to the bottom of his pack.

Wish I had known that.

"I just thought wilderness camping was exhilarating," he explains. "You're alone out here with your thoughts. No stress or pressure. No timetable. You could read all day, if you wanted to. Just set up your camp and do whatever. And I liked doing it all myself. At home, everything is provided for you. School is scheduled, dinner is served. You turn on the TV and everything's programmed. But out here, nothing happens unless I do it myself. And that may sound weird, but I feel like I'm doing something real when I build a fire and cook over it. Like, yeah, if the end of the world came, I could actually survive. Most of the people at school would die in the wilderness after a week or two, struggling to stay warm or forage for edible food, or getting attacked by wild animals."

"You were pretty impressive with the bear last night," I admit. "If you hadn't told me, I would've run and probably ended up as bear dinner."

"Bear attacks aren't common, but if you follow a few basic rules, you're fine. If you were aggressive to a mama bear around her babies, then the chances of you being mauled are higher. It's basically just common sense."

"Still. You knew what to do."

"The trick is avoiding them altogether," he says. "But when you can't, and the people you're camping with are blockheads—"

"Not all of us," I say.

"No," he agrees, a hint of a smile in the corners of his mouth. "But when you can't avoid animals, you just have to treat them as a real threat and respect that they have the upper hand."

That makes sense. "So you got into camping because you like making fires and outwitting bears?"

"I feel like I've accomplished something that's measurable. I can feed myself—"

He figured out how to make coffee out here, which is pretty much the pinnacle of cooking in my eyes.

"—and find my way without a computerized voice telling me which way to turn. I know first aid basics. I know how to collect water if there's no river in sight. I know how to build a lean-to in the woods. And that's . . ."

"Not nothing."

"Yeah," he says. "It's being a capable human being, which is something I think a lot of people have forgotten how to do."

"So you come out here to feel like a manly man," I say.

"Right," he says sarcastically. "Big, burly lumberjack. That's me."

Well, he has the big part down. When I walk by his side, his tall frame keeps the sun out of my face.

"I come out here because of all that, and because look at this place," he says, gesturing toward the trees. "It's serene. When Ansel Adams said, 'I believe in beauty,' he was here, in the Sierras. Maybe even walking this same path."

I have a weird sense of déjà vu, because this sounds like the Lennon I know, rattling off obscure quotes and talking about the city lights over San Francisco Bay as if they were magic. So maybe I *do* understand why he'd be attracted to hiking.

He becomes self-conscious now, and laughs a little. "Besides all that, you never know what can happen out here. And that's the thrilling part. A million things can go wrong."

I groan. "No, that's what I don't want to hear. I like all my things to go right."

"That's not how the world works."

"It's how it should work," I say. "I like plans that go smoothly. That's the beauty I believe in. Nothing is better than when things go exactly how I expect."

"I know that's what you like," he says, eyes squinting out the sun to peer down at me. "And there's comfort in that, sure. But there's comfort in knowing that when your plans fall apart, you can survive. That the worst thing imaginable can happen, but you can get through it. That's why I like to read horror fiction. It's not about the monsters. It's about the hero surviving them and living to tell the tale."

"It's nice that you feel that way," I tell him. "But I'm not sure I have that same level of comfort. Some of us weren't meant to survive."

"You survived the group abandoning us."

"For the time being. It's only been a few hours. I'm weak. I may not make it through the night."

He chuckles. "That's why I'm here. If you can't survive on your own, hire help."

"I hope you know that the Everharts are broke as a joke and you will get no reward for bringing me back alive."

"Alive *or* dead, then. Excellent. That actually takes a lot of pressure off me," he says with a devilish smile. "Oh, look. Here's the trail that leads to the caves. Am I good or what?"

A wooden post with several vertical symbols carved into it sits where our trail crosses with a wider one. It appears that the caves are a mere five-hour walk. In the midday sun. Uphill. Fantastic. It all looked so much simpler and kinder on Lennon's homemade map.

We walk until early afternoon, chatting occasionally about landmarks in the surrounding area and the places Lennon's hiked previously. But when I fail to answer a question because I'm staring too hard at the rocky path, worried I might be close to passing out, Lennon makes us stop for lunch.

We take off our jackets and sit on them, and after draining half my water supply, I break out my mom's gifted turkey jerky while he pulls out roasted peanuts and dried fruit. We decide to share. He informs me that high-calorie, high-salt foods are the best things to eat when you're hiking. These are pretty much my favorite foods, so maybe hiking and me will work out, after all.

After lunch, we fill up our Nalgene bottles with filtered water from a nearby creek and hit the trail again. The land here is rockier, which sucks, because an hour into the hike, I'm getting tired already, and my feet keep stumbling over loose pebbles that slide over the sandy ground. It's like trying to avoid thousands of land mines. I'm thinking the hiking boots might be better in this situation.

"Not much longer now," Lennon tells me after I slide and nearly fall.

I don't think I can make it. I really don't. The sun is low in the sky, and we've easily been hiking for hours. I'm one slippery pebble away from casting aside my pride and begging him to stop again, when we crest a hill and find a small trail breaking away from the main one. I look up, breathing heavy, and am surprised to see a massive granite mountain across a field. One second it was in the distance, and now it's right here.

"This is it," Lennon says excitedly, pointing toward the smaller path. "One of the cave entrances should be at the end of this trail."

"Oh sweet God, I thought we'd never get here," I say, finding a renewed burst of energy to head down the new path. It doesn't hurt that it's level ground. "I can't feel my feet. Should I be worried?"

"No. You should enjoy the numbness," Lennon says. "Later, when they hurt so badly and you're begging me to cut them off, then you'll look back on these moments with nostalgia. Oh, look. Do you see it?"

I do. It's a black mouth leading inside the gray mountain. And as we cross the field and approach it, I'm startled by how big it is. The path just ends. No warning. No posted sign.

"I thought you said this cavern has been explored," I say. "Shouldn't there be a park sign announcing it, or something?"

"That's only on the commercialized caves. A few around here have lights strung through them for tourists. This one gets a lot of cavers."

"Cavers."

"People who explore caves."

"I thought that was a spelunker."

"Spelunkers are the idiots who get lost in caves and have to be rescued by the cavers." Lennon slides a glance down at my face. "Brett would make a great spelunker."

I roll my eyes, but secretly I'm thinking he's probably right.

"So what's the plan?" I ask as we pause in front of the cavern's entrance to unhook our packs and retrieve our headlamps. I decided to snag the one Reagan left behind, since Lennon pointed out that it cost several hundred dollars more than my basic model and would be a shame to waste.

"It's only about two miles from here to the exit on the other side," he tells me as he straps on his headlamp. "It's completely safe, so don't worry. Thousands of people have been here before us."

"Okay," I say, feeling cool air emanating from the darkness inside. It's like natural air-conditioning. Feels nice. "What's the catch? Is there a cave troll we have to conquer?"

"This isn't Moria, Zorie. We aren't crossing the Misty Mountains."

"Evil armies of miner dwarves?"

"You mean orcs. The dwarves weren't evil. Did we not do an annual Christmas viewing of *The Lord of the Rings* trilogy during Sunday dinners every December?"

"Unfortunately, yes."

"You loved them."

I did. "Okay, Gandalf. What's the catch about this cave?"

"No Balrog to fight. No catch. That I know of. I mean, I've never been inside this cave."

"But you've been in others, right?"

"Just the Melita Hills Caverns and Zip Lines," he says, the corners of his mouth lifting.

"On that school field trip?"

"When Barry Smith vomited on the bus after the zip lines."

"Those are the only caves I've been inside too," I say, alarmed. And it was basically just an excuse for them to build a gift shop and charge everyone a million dollars for Cokes. "Maybe we shouldn't do this."

"We'll be fine," he assures me. "The book says the tricky part is that the tunnels are all connected. It's one big maze. There are supposed to be a pair of ropes that lead up to a higher level of tunnels, and that's what we're looking for."

"We're climbing ropes?" This is gym-class horror all over again.

"No."

"Oh, thank God," I mumble.

"The ropes are just our visual landmark. There are several exits, and the one we need to find is near the ropes. It will take us out to the northern side, where there's a big trail that leads to that valley I told you about." He slips on his hoodie. "You might want to put a jacket on. It's going to be chilly inside. And it should take us about an hour to make our way through. Then there's an easy path down into the valley on the other side, where we can make camp by a creek and have dinner."

An hour. I can do that. Better than climbing up that rocky path behind us. And at least it's out of the sun. I should have brought a hat like my mom suggested. I think the part in my hair is sunburned. Pretty sure my cheeks are too. But who's got a vitamin D deficiency now, huh?

I flick on Reagan's headlamp as we step into the mouth of the cave. The entrance is a big, round room. Scattered rocks lay in heaps, as well as a couple of empty water bottles and what looks to be a pile of toilet paper. So much for "leave no trace."

A fat tunnel at the back of the room leads farther into the mountain, and that's where we head. Once we are inside, sunlight wanes at our backs, and our headlamps become our new sun. It's much chillier here, and the air smells damp and musty—like rock, I suppose. I never thought about rock having a strong scent. It's not an unpleasant one, though, and the cool air feels good in my lungs. Clean. Uncomplicated. Much like our path. The tunnel is wide enough for the two of us to walk side by side, and the ceiling is several feet over our heads. Veins of color thread through the rock walls—marble, Lennon guesses—and though the floor is rock, it's better than walking outside.

"This isn't so bad," I say, letting my headlamp bounce around the walls.

"I told you."

We soon come to another tunnel. Two, actually: one to our left, one to our right. They're both about the same width as the one in which we walk.

"What now?" I ask.

"You don't need to whisper, Zorie."

"Everything echoes in here."

"Echo, echo, echo," Lennon says in his deep voice, cupping his hand around his mouth. "If an echo bounces off the walls of a deserted cave in the middle of the woods, does anyone hear it?"

"Are you finished?"

"For now." Lennon unhooks his black compass from the belt loop of his jeans and flips it open. "We need to head south. Seems like this is the maze part I was telling you about."

"This isn't going to be like the hedge maze in *The Shining*, is it?" I ask.

"God, I hope so. I love that movie," Lennon says. "Did you know that in the book, there's an army of topiary animals that come to life?"

"Please don't talk about that while we're in the middle of a dark cavern in the middle of the wilderness where no one can come to our rescue," I say. "And no ghost stories, for the love of Pete. Did your survivalist teacher really tell you that story? Wait. Never mind. I don't want to know."

"I should tell ghost stories for a living," he says. "That was fun. Until the bear. Well, that was fun too. Until the fight." The bright beam from his headlight shines in my face. "Too soon?"

I hold up a hand to block the light. "Can you not do that?"

He turns his head away to beam light in front of us. "Sorry."

"I'm not sad about Brett, if that's what you're thinking," I tell him.

"Good. He's not worth your tears. Though, for the record, you have terrible taste in guys," Lennon says, shining his light back to the compass in his hands.

"Pardon me?" I say, lightly shoving his compass hand with mine.

He chuckles. "You're pardoned. And forgiven. And absolved

for all your sins. So let's focus and get through here, because I'm starving." He steadies his compass again. "Okay, so as I was saying, all of these tunnels eventually lead into a huge cavern room. If we hit that, we've gone too far west. So I think we can just choose a tunnel and try to walk in a northern direction."

"We go to the right, then?" I say.

"Wrong north. Otherwise known as south. Take a left."

He's awfully merry for someone who has only a vague idea about where we're going. We head left and continue into the cave, walking in silence for several minutes. A noise echoes in distant tunnels, and this raises my pulse. I probably should have asked about bats. Or maybe I'm better off not knowing.

As he navigates a sharp turn in the tunnel, I stew over his words.

"Sins?" I say.

"What?"

"You said I was absolved of all my sins. What did you mean by that?"

"I was just teasing."

I don't think he was.

After a short silence, he says, "I mean, you know how I feel about Brett. But Andre Smith, too? Are you into jocks, or something? What was up with that?"

This conversation is moving into territory that I don't care to relive. "Andre was nice to me when I needed a friend."

"Yeah, I saw him. Being nice to you." He pauses and then says,

"But I didn't know you were seriously seeing each other. Brett caught me up and told me . . . well, more than I needed to know."

I stop walking. "What did Brett tell you?"

"Can we talk about something else?" Lennon says.

"No, we can't. Because if Brett was gossiping about me, I think I have a right to know."

Lennon considers this and continues walking, until I have no choice but to either catch up with him or be left behind in the maze.

"Tell me," I insist.

"All right," he finally agrees. "Brett said you and Andre were, you know . . . exchanging body heat."

That's a funny way to put it. In a way, it makes it seem worse. Like Lennon—someone who sees all kinds of crazy sex toys on a daily basis—can't even bring himself to say what Andre and I did out loud.

"Andre and Brett talk," Lennon adds. "Multiplayer."

"What?"

"Online gaming. One of the sports games, *FIFA* or *Madden*, or something. I don't know. I only play survival horror games. Maybe a little *Minecraft*. Okay, and some *Final Fantasy*, but don't tell anyone about that."

"I don't care."

"Hey, I didn't ask for it," he says. "Brett volunteered it."

"I only saw Andre for a couple of weeks."

"I saw you guys out at Thai Palace once."

"You were spying on us?"

"The restaurant is across the street from my place of employment," he says irritably. "So no, I wasn't spying. I don't own a telescope."

Ugh. I was hoping we could avoid bringing up that mishap. Like, forever.

"And if you want to know the truth," he continues in a crabby voice, "I thought it was sort of shitty of you to flaunt that in my face."

"I didn't even know you saw us! How could I be flaunting?"

"A million restaurants on Mission Street, and you pick *that* one?"

He's actually 100 percent right. I did pick that restaurant on purpose. I was still mourning Lennon at the time, so yeah. I wanted him to see me with someone else. I know it was shallow, but I was in pain.

What's puzzling me now is his complaining about it. Because if I didn't know better, I'd think he sounds as if he's mad about me dating Andre, and why would that be? Could there be some truth in Brett's torch-carrying remark?

Is he having second thoughts about us? Why? What changed?

The path splits again, but this time one of the side tunnels only heads east. Lennon hesitates, checking his compass and glancing down our current tunnel. It looks to curve ahead, and that's back where we came from, so he points us down the eastern tunnel.

It's even wider here, and the walls begin changing. Gone is the smooth rock. Now it's craggy like the fabric of a curtain, and the ceiling is much higher. It also feels as if we're ascending.

"Funny that you heard all about me," I say after several minutes of walking. "Because I didn't even know you were dating someone."

I hear my own voice, and it sounds petty. What is wrong with me? Maybe I'm grumpy because of the dropping temperatures in here. My fingers feel like ice, and I really wish I weren't wearing shorts.

"Maybe you weren't paying attention." He's said this before, and I don't understand why. Am I missing something? Before I can ask, he throws me off guard and says, "I dated Jovana Ramirez."

Oh.

Jovana. She's one of the nouveau-emo girls who hang out at the skate park with the stoner kids. I don't really know much about her. I certainly had no idea she and Lennon were a thing. "When?"

"We started seeing each other a few months ago. We like a lot of the same bands."

Suddenly, all the defenses I've built up over the last year come crashing down like a poorly played Jenga move, and a horrible warmth floods my chest.

What is this strange feeling? Jealousy?

"Are you still dating?" I ask, and immediately regret it. *Take it back, take it back, take it back!* I don't want to know.

And when he doesn't respond immediately, I fear the worst.

That's when it hits me like a kick to the ribs.

I'm not over Lennon.

I tried so hard. I ignored him. I got rid of all the stuff that made me think of him. I stopped going places we used to go. I cried until there were no more tears to stop me from getting angry. And then I moved on.

Only, I didn't.

How did I not realize this before?

Something hits my shoulder. I swing my headlamp up to see Lennon's arm blocking my path. He's staring intently down a branching tunnel. I follow his gaze and squint into the darkness beyond my headlamp's reach. A shadow shifts.

"Someone's in here with us," Lennon whispers.

My pulse picks up speed, though I'm not sure why. This cave is open to the public. It's probably just another hiker. No cause for alarm.

"Hello," Lennon calls out. His big voice reverberates off the rocky walls.

No answer.

Okay, this is starting to worry me. The dark was fine when it was just the two of us. Sort of calming. Peaceful. But now that peace feels threatened.

Lennon gestures for me to move back a step, and then he leans down and whispers in my ear, "I thought I saw a man. But maybe I was imagining it."

"Why are we whispering, then?" Something drips on my arm,

startling me. It's just water from a stalagmite. Or stalactite. I could never get those right. Whichever one grows from the ceiling.

Lennon shakes his head and his chuckle sounds forced. "It just freaked me out a little."

Yup, me too. We listen for a minute. I don't hear anything. It's eerily quiet in here. Images of ax-murdering miners flood my anxious brain.

"Shouldn't we be out of here by now?" I say.

"We've got to be close to the exit."

"Is that the way we're supposed to go?" I ask. "Where you didn't see a creepy shadow troll?"

Lennon studies his compass and looks around. If I squint, I think I can make out two more branching tunnels ahead of us. Possibly a third. This maze is getting complicated.

He sees the tunnels too. "Stay here. I'll go check those out."

I watch his back disappear past my headlamp. I don't like this. At all. I'm beginning to feel a little claustrophobic and have to force myself to calm down when water drops on my shoulder again. I shift positions to get away from the cave drip and accidentally kick a big, loose rock. It clatters against the wall.

I wince and look down. Something's moving. It's a black-and-white striped ball. Only, one end of the ball is unraveling, like yarn. Shiny yarn.

It's a motherfucking snake.

16

I freeze.

The snake is unraveling faster. I've disturbed its hidey-hole, and now it's lifting up its head, looking around for the person who dared to wake it up.

I have no idea what to do. I quickly flick a glance at the tunnel ahead, but I don't see Lennon's headlamp right away, and I'm too scared to take my eyes off the snake.

Maybe I should stay still, as Lennon instructed during the bear incident. Do snakes have good eyesight? It can't smell me, right? Maybe I'm blinding him, and if I stay super still—

My headlamp flickers. This catches the snake's attention.

WHERE IS LENNON?

"Bad shrimp," I call out softly as the snake's head lifts. Its tail shakes, slapping against the rocky floor. That seems . . . not good. "Bad shrimp!"

The snake's head strikes.

I jump away.

My headlamp flickers out.

Panicking, I scramble backward and bump into the wall behind me. My foot feels caught on something. I jerk it, and it doesn't help. It's heavy and . . .

Oh sweet God, I'm dragging the snake! It's wrapped around my ankle, and I can't tell what's going on. I shake my foot around and that's when I realize that the snake is biting me. Its mouth is clamped onto my leg, just above my sock. I can barely feel anything—why can't I feel it? Is that poison, numbing me?

I scream.

Lennon's light bobs into view. He's running toward me, and now I can see the banded snake wrapped around my ankle. It's huge. I'm going to die.

"Whoa, whoa, whoa!" Lennon says, holding up his hands. "It's okay. Calm down. Stop kicking."

I take in a sobbing breath and nearly fall down.

"It's only a kingsnake," he tells me in a calm but firm voice, dropping in front of me. "Only a California kingsnake. Let me get it off. It's okay. He's just scared. I want you to stay still while I get him to release you."

I don't know what any of those words mean. He might as well be speaking in tongues. And maybe he realizes this, because he softly shushes me—or maybe the snake, I'm not sure. But his fingers are digging inside the snake's tightly wrapped coils, searching for the head, which is firmly attached to my leg.

"Shit," Lennon mumbles.

"What?"

"Hold on," he says. "Are you in pain?"

"Maybe. Yes. I don't know," I say. It's sort of pinching me. Smashing me. Like my ankle is being slowly crushed. "Get it off of me. Please, Lennon."

"I'm trying. It won't let go. I'm going to need to—"

"Kill it!"

"I'm not killing it," he says, unbuckling his pack and shrugging it off his shoulders with a grunt. "I can get it off. Just hang on. I need something."

He quickly unstraps the bear canister from the top of his pack and opens it, dumping out some of the contents until he spots a tiny plastic bottle of blue liquid. It isn't until he's got the cap unscrewed that I recognize the bottle's contents. Mouthwash.

Angling the bottle against my leg, Lennon pours a small amount in the side of the snake's mouth. The sharp scent of mint and alcohol fills the air. Nothing happens. Is he trying to freshen its breath? What the hell is going on?

He pours another few drops out. And suddenly, I feel the snake's mouth release me. Its black-and-white stripes shift, and it stiffly uncoils from around my ankle as Lennon holds it behind its head and forcibly helps to unwind it.

I gasp and start breathing faster. A *lot* faster. It sounds like I'm about to give birth, but I don't even care. I'm just so relieved. The second Lennon lifts it away from me, a terrible animal-like sound comes out of my mouth.

"It's okay," he tells me. "I've got it."

I smell blood. I *see* blood. It's dripping down my ankle onto my sock and staining it bright red.

I'm going to pass out.

"You're not," Lennon says.

Did I say that aloud?

"You're just hyperventilating," he says. "Sit down and slow your breathing. I need to take this somewhere and put it down, or I can't help you."

Take it far, far away. Better yet, take me and leave the snake.

"Breathe slower," he says again.

I close my eyes for a moment and try to calm down. I hold my breath until my lungs feel like they're about to burst. Then, after a few unsteady inhalations, I get myself under control.

"Okay?" he says.

I nod.

"What happened to your headlamp?" he asks.

"I don't know. It went out."

"Try to turn it off and back on again," he says.

My fingers fumble for the switch. "It doesn't work," I tell him.

"It's fine. You have a backup."

"It's in my pack," I say. But I really don't care about that. I just want the snake he's holding to stop moving.

"Okay. I'll get it for you as soon as I get back." He adjusts his arm as the snake's tail tries to wind around it. "I'll be gone just a second. Right where that first tunnel veers off to the left. See it?"

I do. But as much as I want that snake out of my sight, I really don't want Lennon to leave again. A fresh wave of panic rushes over me as darkness envelops my section of the tunnel. I can't think about it. Or wonder if that snake was a mama and there's a possibility that other tiny baby snakes are going to swarm in the dark. So I just slowly slide down the wall until my butt hits the cold, rocky floor. And I lean against my pack, watching the moving white light of his headlamp. When he ducks down the branching tunnel, the light disappears.

Total darkness.

Thoughts stutter inside my head, and I'm suddenly remembering being a kid, waking up in a dark house and not knowing where I was. For several seconds, I was panicked, trying to figure out where the door was and how I'd gotten there. But what was worse was the moment I *did* remember. My birth mother had died two days before, and my father had shipped me off to his parents—people I barely knew. Strangers. And I didn't know when my father was coming back to get me, or if he ever would, and in that moment, I'd never felt more alone.

It's okay. You're okay, I tell myself. *You're in a cave, and he's coming back.*

When Lennon turns around and jogs back to me, the light is like the sun, and I couldn't be any more grateful.

"Don't leave me again," I say.

"I'm not going to leave."

"That's what you do, you leave! Without any explanation, you abandon people." I'm crying, and possibly a little delirious. I feel stupid for being such a coward, and mad at him for dragging me into this stupid cave.

"I'm here," he says, holding on to both of my arms. "It's okay. You're just panicking. That's normal, but you're going to be okay. I promise."

"You don't know that."

"I do. Can I look at the bite? Does it hurt?"

"Yes," I say, angry. "I think."

His hand is warm on my leg. How are his fingers not cold like mine are in this icebox of a cave? Why are boys always so warm? My dad always tries to freeze me and Mom out of the apartment, cranking down the air-conditioning to subzero temperatures.

He's pulling up the edge of my sock to wipe away the blood. "Does this hurt?"

A lot less than I would have expected after being mauled by that devil serpent. "It's a little sting-y," I tell him.

"He got you pretty good."

"Am I going to need antivenin?"

Lennon chuckles. "California kingsnakes aren't venomous."

Right. I know this. I think. "Are you sure?"

"It's one of the most popular snakes we sell at Reptile Isle. I've handled a couple hundred of these. Been bitten by several too."

"You have?"

"And much worse. I know exactly what you're feeling now, and I promise it will go away. We need to get it disinfected, but you aren't going to die. I have a first aid kit in my pack." He glances down the tunnel as if he's wary of something. And that's when I remember the shadow troll Lennon thought he spotted in the cavern.

Lennon is clearly thinking the same thing.

"Get me out of here," I say in a shaky voice.

His headlamp shifts back to my face. His stoic features are chiseled and stark under the light shining down from his forehead. "Can you stand?"

I can. And after testing out my foot, I find that I can walk, too. I guess he was right: I'm not dying. But I'm in an intensive state of anxiety, forced to rely on Lennon's light to see. My muscles are so rigid, I'm in physical pain. And I can't see directly in front of my feet, which slows me down.

"I found the way out," he says. "It's just down this tunnel."

"You saw the ropes?" Our landmark near the northern exit.

"No, but there's sunlight. See it?"

I do. Even better than some stupid ropes. A literal light at the end of the tunnel. It quickens my awkward steps. I can do this. We're getting out of this hellhole, with its attacking snakes and lurking, nonexistent shadow trolls.

The exit is a lot smaller than the entrance we used to get in here. Only one person can fit through at a time, and Lennon has to clear away an old spiderweb before we can pass. But when we emerge into late-afternoon sunlight—so warm, so golden—I'm so happy, I could kiss the ground.

However, there isn't a lot to kiss.

"Oh, wow," I say, squinting.

We are standing on a narrow cliff bathed in afternoon light. Only a few meters of land stretch between the wall of mountain we just exited and a fall that would kill any living creature. We are far, far above a sprawling, tree-lined valley. Mountains rise all around us. Some of them are granite; some are green and covered in trees.

It's the most beautiful thing I've ever seen.

I'm awed. Completely and utterly awed.

And then I glance around the cliff, and that awe shifts into wariness. The ground we're standing on is little more than a balcony that stretches around the side of the mountain. A few trees and shrubs are growing, but nothing substantial. No creek. Certainly no easy path down into the valley below that Lennon promised. A giant bird soars above the trees, circling until it disappears into the canopy.

"How do we get down from here?" I ask.

Lennon is silent. That's not good. He walks around the cliff, heading past a lonely pine tree, and scopes out our landscape. Maybe the path into the valley is hidden. But even so, we are really far up.

"Shit," Lennon mumbles.

"What?" I ask.

When his eyes meet mine, I know it's bad. "I think we went the wrong way."

17

There are few worse words to hear right now. All I want to know is (A) How "wrong way" are we, and (B) how do we get back on track?

Lennon whips out his phone to study the book he's saved. His eyes flick over the screen, and then he whimpers softly. "I knew it. This isn't the right exit. We got turned around somehow. I knew it felt like we were going up. I just . . ."

"Where are we?"

"We're at the eastern exit. We need to be south, which is lower in elevation. A lot lower."

Do not panic.

"Is there a map of the cave?" I ask.

"If there were a map of the cave, we wouldn't be standing here, would we?"

Jeez. No need to get snippy. I'm the one with the snake bite. And speaking of snakes, I glance back at the dark, spiderwebbed exit. "I'm not going back in there. Forget it."

"I don't think we have to," he says, flipping to another screen to reread a passage. "This cliff goes all the way around to the exit we should have used. It's just . . ."

"Just what?"

He takes his compass out of his pocket. "It's roundabout. The other exit was a straight shot to the path in the valley. It's about a mile down from here to the northern exit, as a crow flies. But that's more like two or three miles, hiking around this cliff. Then another mile down into the valley."

"So, we're talking, what?"

"Two hours. A little longer. It won't be an easy descent. It's not an actual trail." Lennon looks down at my bloody ankle. It's starting to swell.

I glance around the cliff. How could a place that's so beautiful make me miserable?

"Hey, look," I say, spotting something dark on the mountain wall, several meters away from where we exited. Maybe Lennon's wrong. Maybe we are in the right place. That could be the southern exit there.

But as I hobble toward it, and Lennon shines his headlamp inside, I lose hope. It's another cave entrance, yes, but not to the network of tunnels we were just hiking. It's just a big, wide single cave. As though nature used a melon baller and scooped out a hole in the side of the mountain.

"This isn't an animal cave, is it?" I say, imagining us waking up some hibernating family of bears.

"It looks clear," Lennon reports.

We have to duck to enter the mouth of the cave, but once we're in, the ceiling is high, so we can stand and walk around. It's maybe a dozen feet wide and twice as deep. There are no hibernating animals. No stream. Not much of anything at all, except a dip in the rocky floor near the mouth that cradles the remnants of burned firewood.

"People have camped here," Lennon says, bending down to inspect it. "Not recently, I don't think. But look." He kicks a discarded, empty can of food in the corner. It's covered in dirt and bone-dry, so it's been here a while. "Bastards. What about 'leave no trace' don't people understand?"

I'm having trouble caring about that right now. I turn toward the half-moon mouth of the tiny cave and look toward the valley of trees. It's like gazing into a framed painting.

"Look, it's not what I'd planned, but I think we should camp here," Lennon says. "It's flat and protected. Seems reasonably safe—it's obviously been used as a site by other hikers. There's room enough for us to erect both of our tents inside this cave and build a fire."

"What about water?" I say.

"I've only taken a swig out of my bottle. How much do you have left?"

The entire bottle. I haven't touched it since we filled up at lunch.

"It's enough," he assures me. "I mean, we won't be washing

our hair or anything, but if we're careful, we can make it until we can hike down to the creek. Or, if you feel up to it, we can hike down there now." He checks the time on one of the compass dials. "It's almost six. It will get dark at nine. That should be enough time, but we'll be cutting it close. And this isn't a big trail, so it might be a little rough walking it during dusk. We also need to take care of your ankle."

I debate this. I'd like fresh water. It worries me that all we have is the precious little in our bottles. But I look at my ankle, and suddenly the weight of my backpack seems to double.

I'm tired and hungry and injured.

I want to stop.

"Let's just stay here," Lennon says encouragingly.

"What about your map? This wasn't the plan."

"No, but it's workable. The map was just a general guideline. Things happen out here, and you adapt."

I'm not good at adapting.

"This little cave is pretty sweet," he says. "And I'll bet you can see a thousand stars from this cliff."

He's probably right. I look at the clear sky above the mountains.

"Come on, take off your pack," he tells me. "Let's get you fixed up, okay? One thing at a time."

Maybe he's right.

Following his suggestion, I unbuckle my backpack and plop down on a boulder near the entrance of our little clifftop cave while he digs out the first aid kit. I spy my blue Nalgene bottle, and it makes me realize that I'm dying of thirst, but I resist the urge to drink. *Must save it.* Now I'm wondering if we need to spare water for cleaning my wounds, but Lennon has broken out alcohol swabs, and he squats at my feet to use one.

"Cold," I say, flinching. "Oww!"

"Hold still and let me clean it," he says.

"It stings."

"That's how you know it's working." He cradles my heel in one hand and cleans off the bite. "I once got bitten by an emerald tree boa. Beautiful snakes, but boy, do they have a mean bite." He holds up his hand and twists it around to show me. A U-shaped line of scars arches around his wrist and the heel of his palm.

"Holy crap. When did that happen?"

"About six months ago. She was eight feet long and this big around." He shows me with his hands. "I had to go the emergency room and get a couple stiches. The snake was upset about being moved into a new habitat. She was old and set in her ways. I get a lot of little bites at work, but they usually don't hurt. This one scared me. I was so shaken up by the whole thing, I was scared to pick up another snake for a couple of days."

"I don't ever want to see one again, much less pick one up. If I'd known to expect snakes in those caves, I wouldn't have agreed to go inside."

"Nobody expects the Spanish Inquisition."

"Don't quote Monty Python to me right now. I'm mad at you."

He snorts a laugh. "No, you're not. You're just grouchy because you're in pain."

"I'm grouchy because you led me into an evil serpent's nest!"

"Snakes get a bad rap," he says. "They only attack when they're scared or hungry. We're monsters in their eyes. And that snake that bit you shouldn't have been in that cave. The temperature is too low for a kingsnake. I'm thinking it must have gotten lost in there somehow. I hope it finds its way out."

"As long as it's not through some tiny crack in the walls here. This is our cave, you hear me, snake?" I call out. "I wonder how this cave formed. You know, thousands of years ago, or whatever."

"I don't know, but it reminds me of *The Enigma of Amigara Fault*."

"What's that?"

"Well, Miss Everhart, I'm glad you asked," he says, jolly. "See, it's this Japanese horror manga story—"

"Oh, lord," I grumble.

"—in which thousands of human-shaped holes appear in the side of a mountain after an earthquake. People soon discover that there's a perfect hole for each person, made just for them, and when they find their own hole, they become crazed, trying to climb inside of it."

"That sounds . . . weird. What happens when they get inside?"

"Are you sure you want to know?"

I shake my head. "I really, *really* don't. No more creepy stories. Especially if we have to sleep here tonight."

He chuckles. "My work here is done. And yes, I think we should definitely stay here tonight. So I'm declaring that the official new plan. Agreed?"

"All right." I lean back on my palms as he finishes cleaning my wound. It's pretty swollen, I think. He says it will be fine by tomorrow. He finds a couple of Band-Aids to keep the puncture marks covered, so they won't get infected.

"We're not, by the way," he says quietly, pulling the paper backing off a bandage.

"Excuse me?"

"Jovana and I aren't dating. We broke up before summer break. Well, she broke up with me."

Oh.

This is unexpected, his bringing this back up now. I'm also a little embarrassed about how relieved I am to know it. "I'm sorry," I tell him. "I mean, if you were upset."

What a stupid thing to say. Of course he—

"I wasn't," he says, surprising me. His eyes are on my ankle as he adheres the bandage. "It was cool at first, me and Jovana. But we never really . . . clicked. I tried. I really did. It just felt like something was missing. She said I was distant and distracted, and that I was hung up on someone else."

My heart thumps rapidly inside my chest. "Were you?"

"Yes."

I hold my breath, unsure of what this means. Part of me would like to pass him a note that reads *Do you like me? Check YES or NO.* But I'm too much of a coward to say it aloud. Too afraid that he'll laugh. And then it will be awkward between us for the rest of the trip.

"Were you and Andre serious?" he asks.

It takes me a long time to answer. "I was hung up on someone else."

It takes him an even longer time to say, "Are you still?"

Does he know it's him? Or does he think it's Brett? I can't tell if he's just curious about my personal life, trying to make idle conversation. Being polite. I can't tell anything from his blank expression and monotone rumble. Whether he's talking to me strictly friend to friend, like when he had a crush on Yolanda Harris when we were fourteen, and I had to endure his ramblings about how cool she was, and would I help him talk to her?

But there's that hope again, poking its head up when I don't want it to.

Say something.

But I don't. And he doesn't. He just packs up the remnants of the bandage paper and stands up. "Don't know about you, but I'm starving. Let's make camp."

He spends the next half hour assembling both of our tents inside the cave while I find a place for our bear canisters outside, and farther around the cliff, find a few hidden places behind shrubs appropriate for an outdoor toilet. The cliff is narrow, but it's long—miles long—and now that I see the distance with my own eyes, I'm thankful we're not hiking it, because my ankle is starting to complain.

I find a few pieces of dry wood and carry them back to the

cave. Lennon has set up our tents side by side, and he's pulling out these twist-top LED lights that fit in the palm of his hand. He shows me how to use the light's handle on top to hook it to a loop on the ceiling of my tent. The tiny lanterns thoroughly illuminate the insides of our tents, which makes me feel better about the encroaching darkness as twilight falls.

While I unroll my sleeping bag and dig through my pack, Lennon gathers more wood and kindling. He finds some small rocks and uses them to ring the old fire pit, to ensure that the fire stays contained. Then he teaches me how to set up his pyramid-shaped fire, which seems complex, because he has a million little rules about the tinder and how thick the wood should be. But I like that he's so detailed and precise. I do the honors of lighting the tinder, and after a couple false starts—it needs more oxygen—I finally get the campfire going. Which feels . . . satisfying.

Once the wood settles into place, Lennon sets up his little portable grill and pan over the flames and we carefully measure out the exact amount of water we'll need to rehydrate a couple freeze-dried meals. I've never been so excited about beef Stroganoff. Scratch that, I've never been excited whatsoever about beef Stroganoff, but when we pour the boiling water into the pouches, it smells amazing.

We don't have any big boulders to sit on like we did back at the waterfall, so we spread out the rainflies from our tents on the ground near the fire and utilize our bear barrels as tables. And when we're done eating, we use a wet wipe to clean our sporks in order to conserve water. Lennon adds more wood to the fire and we sit and watch the sunset. Stars are already visible, and I'm so glad Lennon suggested we stay here.

"How does it feel now?" he asks, glancing at my leg, which is stretched out in front of me. It's hard to get comfortable on the ground.

"Still swollen. And sore," I say.

He waves my foot toward his lap. "Put it up here and let me look at it."

Hesitant, I prop the heel of my shoe on his thigh, and he inspects the bandages on my ankle. "I think it's going to be fine. Just leave it here," he says, stopping me from moving away with a gentle hand on my knee. "Keeping it elevated will help with the swelling."

"Or force germy snake saliva to make its way up into my bloodstream."

"That's already happened."

"Oh, good."

"Actually, that's the biggest worry with nonvenomous bites. Bad bacteria. You don't know when his last meal was, and he could have chowed down on something rotten or diseased."

"Are you *trying* to freak me out?"

He smiles. "Sort of. I like watching your face twist into horrified expressions. Everything shows on your face. You know that, right?"

648 • JENN BENNETT

"That's not true."

"It is. I can read you like a book."

This embarrasses me a little, and why is his hand still on my knee? Not that I'm complaining. It feels . . . nice. "Well, I can't read you at all, because you're expressionless."

"That's my poker face."

This makes me laugh. "You're a terrible poker player. Remember when your dad taught us to play? You lost so many Oreos to me that night." I haven't spent a lot of time with Lennon's dad, Adam, because Lennon mostly went to visit him in San Francisco instead of Adam coming to Melita Hills. But every once in a while, his father would come into town to visit, and last summer he brought playing cards and a supersize pack of Oreos to use for bets. We sat around Mac and Sunny's dining room table playing Texas Hold'em until past midnight. My mom had to cross the street and come get me because I'd turned my phone's ringer off and hadn't realized it was so late. Then she'd ended up playing a few poker hands—until my dad called at two a.m., and Mom and I both got in trouble.

Lennon smiles. "That was so fun. I remember laughing so hard, I sprained my side."

"It made us laugh even harder."

"Your mom cleaned up, didn't she? She took the entire pot. Who knew she was such a vicious poker player."

That surprised me, too. She was so loud when she won. Probably woke half the neighborhood with her victory shouts. "Your dad was hilarious, showing up in that casino poker dealer outfit with the green visor. When he does something, he goes all out, doesn't he?"

A wrinkle appears in his forehead. "Yeah," he says softly.

Sunny and Mac have framed photos in their hallway of Lennon and Adam dressed up for Halloween in superdetailed complementary costumes. Milk carton and cookie. Batman and Robin. Mario and Luigi. Surfer and shark. Luke Skywalker and Yoda. This went on from the time Lennon was a baby until the year I moved to Mission Street, actually. Lennon was too old to go trick-or-treating, and Adam went on some punk reunion tour.

"I never figured out where he got that giant package of Oreos. There were hundreds."

"I think he stole it from work. Or 'borrowed,' according to him," Lennon says, one side of his mouth turning up. "Mac gave him hell for it later when she found out. You know how she feels about stealing."

She has zero tolerance for it. I think it has something to do with her being homeless when she was a teen. May God have mercy on anyone who tries to shoplift vibrators from Toys in the Attic, because they will end up getting a tough-love speech from her while she calls the cops.

Now Lennon seems bluesy. I'm not sure what I said that made his mood go downhill, but before I can ask, he shoos away a moth that's flying around our fire, attracted to the light, and grabs my knee harder, shaking my leg to get my attention. "Hey.

I just remembered. I have cards in my backpack. For Solitaire. You want to play poker?"

"With what? We have no cookies. And Joy would kill me if I bet the emergency money she gave me for the trip."

Lennon thinks for a moment. "We could use the M&M's in your trail mix."

We could.

"Just a couple of games before it's black out here," he says. "Then you can break out your telescope and do some stargazing."

I chuckle. "All right. You're on, buddy. Prepare to lose!"

It's getting too dark to see all that well by the fire, and the bear canisters aren't big enough to play on. So we decide to shove both of our packs in Lennon's tent and play cards inside mine—it's the bigger of the two—where we can spread out the cards. The palm-size LED light Lennon loaned me provides illumination, and we open the outer door flap and zip up the mesh screen to allow airflow while keeping away the bugs. It takes a while to pick out all the M&M's from the trail mix, and then takes a couple of hands to remember how to play. I keep getting a straight flush confused with a full house, and Lennon forgets half of the rules. We're probably still playing wrong, but neither of us cares. We're too busy laughing.

And it feels natural and good. Easy.

We play until the moon rises outside and stars dot the black sky. The campfire nearly burns out. I even forget about my snake bite until he accidentally bumps into my ankle, apologizing profusely when I cry out. Then he rubs my leg, asking about my hives. I took a mild antihistamine at dinner, so they aren't bothering me *too badly* at the moment, or maybe it's just that his warm palm gliding over my bare skin is distracting me from the itching. It's *definitely* making me forget about the snake bite all over again. I forget about everything, actually, including my current hand of poker. He wins the entire pot of M&M's.

Despite the leg rub ending, I'm still happy. I smile to myself as I gather up the cards and stack them neatly in a single deck. "This is so not fair, you know." I was distracted.

"Totally fair," he says, carefully bagging all the M&M's to put them back in the bear canister. "Tomorrow you're going to be eating boring nuts-and-fruit trail mix, and you'll think, *Self, why did I go crazy with all those ridiculous bets? Sure wish I had some chocolate.* And I will just laugh like an evil overlord." He demonstrates said laugh in his deep voice.

"Okay, okay," I say, pushing his shoulder. "Your dad will be proud that you lived up to your poker potential. You'll have to tell him that you finally won next time you see him."

Lennon sniffles and rubs his nose, dark eyelashes fluttering. He keeps his eyes on the deck of cards as I'm sliding it over to him. "Yeah, that will be difficult."

"Why is that?"

His eyes lift to meet mine. "Because he's dead."

18

I freeze. "What are you talking about?"

"My father died."

"When?"

"Last fall."

How could this be? Last fall? "But . . ." I can't even talk right. "What do you mean? How?"

"He killed himself."

Without warning, tears flood my eyes. "No. That's impossible."

Lennon slips the cards into their cardboard sleeve. "He attempted once and failed. His girlfriend found him and got him to the hospital in time for doctors to pump his stomach. He said it was just an overdose of pain pills, and that he didn't mean to, but his girlfriend didn't believe him. And she was right. Because a few days later, he did it again. Successfully."

I'm crying now, not making any noise, but stinging tears are tickling my cheeks, plopping onto the nylon floor of the tent. "I didn't know."

Lennon's expression is somber. "I know you didn't. Almost no one at school noticed. I mean, I thought *you* might hear. . . . It was in the paper. It trended online for a few hours." He shakes his head softly.

"I didn't hear," I whisper, lifting my glasses to swipe away tears. "I'm so sorry. I just don't understand why I didn't hear. And I don't understand. . . . Your dad was happy. He was so funny, always laughing. How . . . ?"

"He'd been on antidepressants for years and didn't tell anyone he'd stopped taking them. He started obsessing about his music career being over. He was depressed that no one cared or remembered."

"That's not true! People still buy their records."

"Barely. And he had a skewed idea of his success. I mean, how many people can say they had their songs played on the radio? But he didn't see it that way. He wasn't making much off royalties anymore, and the band was never huge—not like others. I don't know. I guess being forced to work a nine-to-five job was failure to him. He couldn't handle being normal."

"Oh, Lennon."

He nods, eyes downcast.

Did no one in our group know? The way Brett and Summer were talking about his dad when Reagan drove us to the glamping compound—and what was said about him during the big fight last night—I'm almost positive they didn't realize.

I know Lennon didn't see his father every day—or even every month—but Lennon was closer to Adam than I am to my dad.

And now I'm thinking about Sunny and Mac, and how they must have been grieving too. And I never acknowledged it. What kind of monster do they think I am?

"When was the funeral?" I ask.

"Last October."

When everything fell apart between us. The homecoming dance. The sex shop opening. My dad fighting with Sunny and Mac.

Is this the reason why?

It makes no sense. Why would he shut me out? "I should have been at the funeral."

Pained eyes flick to mine. "Yeah."

"Why didn't you tell me?"

His face turns rigid, and he grabs the bag of trail mix. "I don't want to talk about it."

"Well, I do! I should have been there. Didn't you want me there?"

"Yes, I wanted you there!" he shouts, startling me. "My dad died. It was the worst time of my life. Of course I wanted you there, but . . ." He squeezes his eyes shut and lowers his voice. "Look, it's getting late, and we're both tired. I don't want to talk about it."

"Lennon!"

"I *said* I don't want to talk about it right now. Goddammit, Zorie. What don't you understand about that?"

This smarts. I'm shaking now, still fighting tears. And I'm

utterly confused. But Lennon is unzipping the mesh door, and he ducks out of my tent before I can think of the right words to stop him.

Dazed, I try to sort out the events that transpired last year. Try to make sense of them. To understand Lennon's anger. On the final week of summer vacation, Lennon and I kissed. We conducted the Great Experiment in secret. We decided make our first public appearance as a couple at homecoming. Lennon stood me up and stopped talking to me. The Mackenzies' sex shop opened. My dad started fighting with them.

New information: Lennon's dad died. He didn't tell anyone.

Where does this fit into our friends-to-enemies road map?

All this time, I thought he'd freaked before the homecoming dance and decided that he didn't want to go public with our relationship. That our experiment had failed, and he was too much of a coward to tell me to my face.

And yet he just blew up at me about not being there at his dad's funeral. Now I feel like he's bitter about our breakup—that somehow this is my fault.

What am I missing?

I crawl outside my tent, but Lennon isn't around. The light inside his tent shows the dark silhouette of his backpack. He's dumped my pack in front of my tent, as if to signal that we're done talking for the night.

Well, I have news for him. We're not.

I'm too chicken to trample after him in the dark and definitely don't want to catch him heeding the call of nature behind the bushes. So I wait by the fire's glowing embers, hugging myself to keep the chill away. He was right. The stars are amazing out here. I find the constellation Cygnus, and then Lyra right next to it, but I'm too upset to appreciate what normally brings me joy.

Several minutes pass, and Lennon doesn't come back. Now I'm worried, and a little angry. We need some kind of system. He should tell me where he's going so I don't sit around wondering if I should go look for him. What if he's attacked by a bear or falls off the cliff?

Anxious and irritated, I retreat into my tent and roll out my sleeping bag. Take off my shoes. Put them back on. Take them off again, because my ankle feels better with them off, and then decide to change quickly into my loungewear for sleeping. Halfway through, I remember that the light in the tent shows everything, so I turn it off and dress in the dark.

Guess he's getting the last word after all.

I don't hear Lennon until I'm zipped up inside my sleeping bag, wishing that we were sleeping on softer ground instead of the unforgiving rock of the cave floor. I listen to his movements, and hear him doing something to the campfire's embers—putting them out, I suppose—before he enters his tent.

The cave amplifies every sound. Zippers zipping. Plastic crinkling. Rummaging. He clears his throat, and it makes me jump. Then his light goes out, and after some rustling, all the noise stops.

And the silence is oppressive.

This is crazy. I can't sleep while I'm upset. And what's worse, my mind begins pulling up other anxieties. My swollen ankle. Snakes. Shadows moving inside the caves. Lennon's stupid manga story about people-shaped holes in the side of the mountain. And then I can't take it anymore.

"Lennon?" I say quietly.

No answer.

I try again, this time louder. "Lennon?"

"I heard you the first time." His voice is muffled yet close. I imagine where he is in relation to me and wonder if I could stretch my arm out and touch him if the tents weren't there.

"Remember when you thought you saw a shadow move in the caves? What if there really *was* someone creeping around and that someone comes out here?"

"They probably already would have if they were going to."

"Or they could be waiting to murder us in our sleep."

"Or that."

"I'm serious," I tell him.

"What do you want me to do about it, Zorie?"

He doesn't have to be so grumpy. "I'm not sure."

"Well, when you think of something, let me know."

I blow out a long breath.

"Hey, Lennon?"

"Still hearing you," he says.

"Are you sure there aren't any tiny holes in this cave?"

"What are you talking about?"

"Holes snakes can slither through."

I hear him cursing under his breath. "I'm sure. No holes. Go to sleep, Zorie."

Yeah, that's not happening.

"Hey, Lennon?" I whisper.

"Oh my God!"

I wince and grit my teeth in the dark. "So, I was just thinking. Since there's a possibility that shadowy cave trolls may sneak out here to murder us, you should probably keep your hatchet handy. Just in case."

"I sleep with it next to me."

"You do?"

"Just in case."

"That doesn't make me feel better," I argue. "That makes me feel like there really *are* threats out here at night."

"Of course there are. Do you see any door you can lock? We're completely unprotected out here. Anything could happen."

I sit up in my sleeping bag. "Hey, listen."

"I didn't know I had a choice," he mumbles.

I ignore that. "I think you should sleep in here."

Silence. For several seconds. Then he says, "Um, what?"

"This tent is for two people," I tell him. "I'm not trying to exchange body heat, as you so eloquently put it earlier. It's just that I would feel better if you were in here when I get murdered by the cave troll."

He doesn't say anything.

"Lennon?"

"I heard you."

"Well?"

"I'm thinking."

I wait, heart hammering. After some rustling, I hear a zipper, and then a silhouette appears outside my tent door. It zips open, and Lennon's dark head pops inside. "Give me your pack."

I pull it across the tent floor and shove it toward the door. It disappears and *thud*s nearby. I think he stashed it in his tent. Another zipping sound. Then my mesh door parts and something unrolls next to me. Some sort of foam sleeping pad. The one that stays rolled up, strapped to the bottom of his pack. It's followed by a sleeping bag, which he throws on top.

Lennon crawls into the tent and zips the door to close it. And before I know it, he's slipping into his bag, a flash of black boxer shorts below his T-shirt, muscular legs . . .

Then he's lying next to me. The tent is suddenly so much smaller.

"Happy?" he says, sounding vaguely sullen.

I smile to myself. *Yes.* "That depends. Did you bring your hatchet?"

His sigh is epic. "I'll just have to choke the life out of the cave troll. Good enough?"

"Yes, that'll do, pig," I say in my best James Cromwell. "That'll do."

The hood of his sleeping bag looks fluffier than mine is, and he punches it around until it makes a pillow. Then he lies on his back, one arm over his head. Facing him, I curl on my side and stare in the murky light until my eyes adjust to him, my own gaze tracing over the sharp, straight line of his nose and the spiky fringe of hair over his brow.

"I'm sorry I wasn't there," I whisper in the dark.

"I needed you," he whispers back. "It was so terrible, and I needed you."

An image of his father fills my head, and then unexpectedly, I think of my birth mother. Her face. Her laugh. How empty I felt when she died. I know exactly how Lennon feels, and that makes it all so much worse. Because I'd never in a million years want him to hurt that badly.

A strange, stifled noise fills up the space in the tent, and it takes me a moment to realize he's crying. Lennon never cries. Never. Not as a kid, and not when we got older. The sound rips my heart to shreds.

On instinct, I reach out for him. When I lay my hand on his quaking chest, he seizes it with steely fingers. I can't tell if he's about to push me away, and for a brief moment, we're frozen midway between something.

A tense sort of twilight.

He turns toward me, and I'm pulling him closer, and he buries his head against my neck, sobbing quietly. I feel hot tears on my skin, and my arms are circling him. The scent of him fills my nostrils, shampoo and sunniness and wood smoke, the tang of sweat and fragrant pine needles. He's harder, stronger, and far more masculine than he was the last time I hugged him. It's like holding a brick wall.

Gradually, the quiet crying stops, and he goes completely limp in my arms.

We're in a strange cave, slightly lost. Off plan and definitely off trail.

But for the first time since we left home, I am not anxious.

19

We've been walking for several hours now, and we've only just made it past the valley below our cave. My back and legs hurt, despite the ibuprofen Lennon gave me at breakfast. He had it laid out for me on a bear canister when I woke up, along with one of the blue coffee cups. I'm not sure how he got out of the tent without me knowing. All I know is that every time I woke during the night, his arm was still wrapped around me. And then sometime around dawn, I was vaguely aware of being a lot colder. By the time I fully emerged from sleep, he'd already started a fire and was readying everything for our breakfast, last night's roller-coaster emotions exchanged for the promise of hot coffee and a new day.

Not a bad way to wake up. Except that my body feels as if I've been hit by a truck that's backed over me several times out of spite.

Hiking hurts.

It hurts even more when we crest over a steep hill. But it

STARRY EYES • 663

doesn't matter, because I'm eager to see where we're going. Lennon made another map. He drew it inside his journal this morning and recalculated our route while I tried not to stare at the dark stubble growing over his jaw, because it gives me inappropriate feelings about him. After taking that wrong turn yesterday inside the cave, he said we're going to stick to a more established trail that I'll like better: It's marked on the official King's Forest map and leads to not only a ranger station but something scenic along the way—only, he insists on that scenic thing being a surprise.

He knows I hate surprises but talks me into accepting it. I tell myself that I'm relenting because of what he revealed last night, but it's probably the stubble. It's really good stubble.

We are at a crossroads where two trails diverge. A signpost tells us that the larger path in front of us is Emperor Trail. And through a break in the cedar trees, we are now staring at white-capped mountains that glitter in the bright sun.

"Oh, wow," I murmur.

"Right?" Lennon says. "The brown peak on the left is Mount Topaz and the gray jagged one on the right is Thunderbolt Mountain. So many climbers die up there."

It doesn't *look* deadly. In fact, it looks beautiful. Majestic. Yes, I definitely see why people say that about mountains. I stretch out my arms and fill my lungs with clean air. Something stings. I slap my arm.

"Oh, we're entering mosquito territory," Lennon says, turning around and pointing at his pack. "Dig around in the second pocket. There's a small bottle of insect repellent."

I unzip the pocket and slip my fingers inside, finding the bottle in question. We take turns anointing ourselves in citronella-scented oil that makes my eyes water. Once we're slathered up and mosquito-proof, we set out on the trail that cuts through a cedar grove. It doesn't take long for two things to happen: (1) we see other hikers ahead of us, and (2) we see them walking up a towering set of granite stairs that's been carved into the mountain.

"What the hell is that?" I say.

"Emperor's Staircase," Lennon says, waggling his brows. He's wearing a slouchy, black knit cap with a skull on it, and the spiky ends of his hair stick out from beneath it. I wish I had a hat to cover up the disaster that is my mass of frizzy curls. Nature is unforgiving.

"We're going up those rock stairs?" I ask.

"Not just rock stairs, Zorie. It's nature's noble staircase," he says in a grand voice. "More than eight hundred steps carved into the granite cliffs in the late eighteen hundreds. Three men died building them, and nearly every year since then, someone's died on these stairs. Fifteen in the last decade. This is the currently the deadliest trail in all the US national parks."

"*What?*" I say, alarmed.

He grins. "Don't worry. The people who die are generally just idiots who fall over the side trying to do stupid things. You'll understand why when we get farther up. If Brett were here, I'd give him a fifty–fifty chance of surviving, because he wouldn't be able to resist the call of death. Which almost makes me wish he were still with us."

"That's not nice," I complain, though I can't help but smile a little.

"*But*," he insists, "you and I will not be following in any daredevil footsteps."

"Um, I would hope not?"

"It's fine. Thousands of people with basic common sense hike these stairs every year and live to tell the tale. It's one of the park's most popular features. You are going to love it, I promise. There's a huge treat at the top."

"A hot tub and a pizza?"

He chuckles. "Not quite, but you're going to like it. We'll break for lunch halfway up. Let's do this, Everhart!" he says enthusiastically, an infectious smile splitting his face.

And so we begin the ascent.

We have to climb a normal uphill path for about a half hour before we hit the stairs. They're rough and wide, and pretty wildflowers and lacy grasses grow alongside them. They casually snake up the mountainside, and the top steps are hidden from view, around the back of the peak. The steps are steep in parts, and a little wonky, but apart from the strain on my calves, I can't really understand why they'd be dangerous. I hear water that gets louder as we ascend, so I assume there's a nearby river, just out of sight.

Climbing, I realize that I'm feeling better physically. Not

exactly 100 percent, but Lennon says it takes time for the body to get used to hiking. It's a slow and steady endurance, not a race. And the pristine scenery definitely helps to motivate me.

The problem with hiking is that it strips away everything. There's no distraction of checking your online feeds. No TV. No schedule to keep. It's just you and your thoughts and the steady pace of your feet moving over rocky ground. And even when I try to keep my head clear, it's busy working in the background, quietly trying to solve things that I don't want solved.

Like Lennon.

And me.

Us.

We haven't talked about last night. Not about sleeping in the same tent, and definitely not about his dad dying. I have questions upon questions, but I'm waiting for him to give me some sort of indication that he's ready to answer them.

Or maybe I'm not ready to hear those answers.

I hate quandaries.

After we've been hiking up the steps for twenty minutes or so, both my head and legs feel close to exploding. No amount of internal reflection or pretty scenery can distract me from the pain. "I can't go any farther," I tell him, breathless. "Worst StairMaster workout ever. I hate these dumb steps. I hate them, I hate them, I—"

"Take it easy. We're almost to the halfway point. Right up there," he tells me, and I spot a place where the steps break. There have been a few rest areas along the way up the mountain, but this one is a smooth granite plateau with several carved-rock benches. One is occupied by a family of tourists with day packs—two kids and a mom and dad. They're also loud, shouting to each other over the ever-present roar of that unseen river. This is startling after not hearing or seeing another soul all day yesterday.

Lennon dumps his backpack on a shady bench over near the mountainside of the plateau, and I collapse next to him, sitting for a moment perched on the edge of the bench before I unhook the straps on my pack. We're in a semiprivate, protected area, so the noise of the river isn't as bad here.

"I'm sweating," I tell him. "I don't remember the last time I sweated before this trip."

He opens up his bear canister and retrieves the same lunch we ate yesterday. "It's good for you."

"Is hiking how you went from skinny to jacked?"

Squinting eyes fix on mine. "I didn't realize I was."

"Oh, you are," I say as my neck warms. *Smooth, Everhart.* I'm veering too close to the subject of me spying on him in his room with my telescope and decide to quit while I'm ahead and drop it.

"You never got to look at the stars last night," he says after a moment.

Ugh. He was thinking about me spying too. Terrific.

"It's fine," I tell him.

"I promise that you'll get some quality stargazing time

tonight," he says, and after some reflection, clears his throat. "I haven't asked today if you want to keep going all the way to Condor Peak. The ranger station I told you about is on the other side of the mountain. We should get there this afternoon. I mean, I know I just assumed you'd be here tonight to stargaze, but if you want to call a car at the ranger station . . ."

Oh. I actually *hadn't* been thinking of that.

"You don't have to make a decision right now," he says. "Just think about it and let me know. So I can make contingency plans."

I nod, and the subject is dropped. We eat in silence, mostly because I'm too tired to do two things at once. Chewing is all I can handle. But by the time we're packing back up, the tourist family has left, and we're alone on the cliff. That's when I start to notice Lennon's leg bouncing like a jackhammer. He does that when he's concentrating too hard—when he takes tests—and also when he's antsy about something.

When he catches me staring at his leg, he immediately stops bouncing it and sighs. "This is stupid. We should just talk about it."

"Excuse me?"

"Last fall. Look, I told you about my dad. Now I want to know about yours."

"My dad?"

His eyes narrow and flick to mine. "I'd like to know what he told you about me after homecoming. I assume he told you something. I just want to know how much of it was true."

"Not following," I say, shaking my head.

"After homecoming. What he told you."

I stare at him. "Um, he just had a talk with me and told me I'd be better off staying away from you. That it would be best to make a clean break and move on, because it was causing me . . . stress."

"That's it?"

I don't know what he wants me to say. "Pretty much. I didn't tell him about . . . you know. The experiment."

Lennon squints at me. "And he didn't bring it up?"

"Why would he?"

He starts to answer, but then changes his mind. Twice. After biting his lower lip and another rapid leg bounce, he finally says, "I'm trying to figure out why you cut me out of your life and started seeing Andre."

"You ditched me at homecoming!"

"I texted you."

"Once. 'I'm sorry.' That's it. That's all you said. I texted you back a million times and you didn't answer."

"Well, excuse me if I was busy with my father attempting suicide."

My body stills. "That was . . . on homecoming?"

"It was one of many shitty things that happened that day."

"Umm . . . Do you want to share these things with the class?"

He stares at the mountains in the distance as if they might grow legs and walk away. "That's why I was asking about your dad. He didn't say anything about what happened that day? At the hotel?"

"What hotel?"

He closes his eyes and mumbles something to himself, slumping low on the park bench. "Never mind."

"Oh no, you don't," I say, getting irritated. "Absolutely not. You brought this up. You finish it. What hotel?"

He covers his eyes with one hand and groans.

Which totally cranks up my anxiety several notches. If Lennon thinks it's bad, it must be far worse than I ever imagined.

"Just tell me," I plead.

He slaps both hands on his knees, elbows bent, as if he's about to stand, but instead inhales sharply and blows out a hard breath. "Last fall, things had been, well, changing between us. The Great Experiment was undertaken."

"I was there," I remind him.

"I thought it was going well. Well enough that we agreed to tell our parents and go public," he says, leaning back against the bench and slouching lower, arms crossed over his chest. "And I guess I . . . was overenthusiastic about the importance of home-coming. I thought, well, you know. That we had the friend thing down. We were expert friends. And when we . . . I mean, my God. The things we did on that park bench."

"Not everything," I say, feeling my ears grow warm.

"No, but it was good. I mean, really, *really* good. Right?"

It was amazing. Awkward at times, especially at first. It's odd to kiss your best friend. But also not odd. Also very nice. So nice that I can't think about it right now, because it makes me flustered. This entire conversation is making me flustered. I think I'm sweating again.

He relaxes when I hesitantly nod to confirm. "So, yeah. Things were going well. We agreed to go public. It felt right. But then homecoming was approaching, and you were getting a little stressed out about telling your dad—"

My fingers are starting to go a little numb.

"—and I don't blame you. He's not friendly or approachable. And, you know, he's never liked me."

I don't correct him, because it's true. When we were kids, Dad didn't seem to have an opinion about Lennon—until he found out that Lennon had two mothers and a Muslim father. That's when he began to say snarky things about the Mackenzies.

Lennon continues. "I'm just saying that at the time, I understood you not wanting to tell him, but I especially understood after what happened the day of homecoming."

"Which was what, exactly?"

He sighs heavily. "I knew some seniors who were getting hotel rooms for homecoming night."

That happens every year, both at homecoming and prom. Sometimes the rooms are reserved by groups of kids who want to party, and sometimes it's just couples.

"I thought I'd get a hotel room for the two of us. Alone," Lennon says.

I make a strangled noise. This is . . . not what I expected to hear. At all.

"In retrospect," he says, "I'm aware that this sounds as if I was making some pretty big presumptions about where our relationship was headed. And I guess I was. But to be fair, I thought we were on the same page. Or at least, that's what I told myself."

I have no idea what I'm feeling right now. My skin feels like it's on fire and numb at the same time. "You couldn't have asked me about this?" Honestly, at the time, I probably would have been thrilled out of my mind, but it's weird to hear about it now. "Like, consulted me beforehand?"

"I thought I was being romantic by surprising you."

"By renting a room where we could have sex?"

He squints one eye shut. "Well, when you say it like *that*, yeah, it sounds pretty skanky. But I never would have pressured you. You know that. Right?"

"But that wasn't your intention?"

"Like I said, I thought we were simpatico on this subject. At the time."

Okay, maybe we were, that's true. There are only so many extreme, heavy-metal, *where did my bra go?* make-out sessions you can have before you start to lose your mind a little.

"Please do go on and tell me what happened next in your romantic hotel scheme," I say drily.

He sighs again. That's not good. When he sighs a lot, it's because he's about to say something he doesn't want to say. "So anyway, you may not remember this, but the day of homecoming, I wasn't at lunch."

I nod.

"I had sneaked off school grounds to reserve the hotel room. Only, I was worried the hotel wouldn't let me, because I was sixteen, and I knew that other kids getting rooms there were using their parents' credit cards, so . . . I sort of borrowed Mac's credit card."

"You . . ."

"Okay," he admits. "I guess I stole it."

"Oh, God."

"I know. It was stupid. I wasn't thinking straight. I thought I could charge the room, sneak the card back into Mac's purse, snag the bill when it came in, and pay for it before Mac noticed. And Ina Kipling's cousin was working the desk at the Edgemont Hotel—"

"Whoa. That's—"

"Fancy. I know. Ina told a few of us about it in drama class. She claimed her cousin would bend the hotel's minimum age policy, so I sneaked out of school and went to the Edgemont Hotel the day of homecoming. I was at the desk, and it was Ina's cousin, and she asked me what name to put on the reservation, and I didn't want to use our real names. So I panicked and used my dad's name. And as I'm spelling out 'Ahmed' for Ina's cousin, she's asking me if I'm Arabic—which sort of pisses me off, because first, I'm not a language, and second, she's acting like I'm a terrorist or something."

I roll my hand to move Lennon along. Get on with it, man!

"And as we're having this conversation, and I admit that

Ahmed is actually my father's name, she tells me that I have to give real names or she'll get in trouble. So I give her my name and your name, and then, out of nowhere, your dad shoves me."

Hold on. What?

"My dad?"

"Your dad," he repeats in a voice that's heavy with resentment.

"What in the world was he doing there?"

"He was apparently behind me in line and overheard the whole thing. Because he made a huge scene. We're in the middle of this luxury hotel, with bellhops and gold luggage carts, and he's screaming at me that if I so much as look at his daughter again, he will beat the shit out of me."

I cringe, covering my eyes in horror as Lennon continues.

"Then he threatens Ina, saying that she should be fired for giving a hotel room to a minor, and . . ." Lennon sighs loudly. "It was *horrible*. I wanted to die. And then your dad snatched Mac's credit card off the counter and demanded to know if my moms had sanctioned this. He called them . . . something horrible."

"Oh, Jesus Christ."

"Yeah," he says. "That's when I lost it."

"What happened?"

"I slugged him."

WHAT? I stare at Lennon in disbelief.

"Yep," Lennon says, tapping his thigh repeatedly with his knuckles. "Punched him the jaw. Hurt like hell. My knuckles were bruised for days."

My mind flashes back to memories from last year. Dad had a swollen cheek and his jaw was bruised. He told us he'd been hit by falling scaffolding when he was walking past a construction site.

"After I landed the punch," Lennon continues, "he started to go after me, but one of the hotel employees stepped in. And then Ina ran to get the manager. And . . . to make a long story short, your dad hauled me outside the hotel and said he wouldn't call the cops and have me arrested for assault and battery if I stayed away from you. No homecoming dance. No visits at home. No talking at school. No phone calls or texts. He said he'd be monitoring your phone."

"Jesus," I say, shocked. Can he monitor my phone? Has he already? My parents have always given me a fair amount of freedom. I never thought in a million years that they would invade my privacy.

"So that was it, basically," Lennon says. "I planned on telling you anyway. At least, after I drove around town and stopped freaking out. That's when I texted Avani and told her to let you know that I'd meet you at the homecoming dance, because our plan for me to show up at your house and tell your parents we were dating was . . . not happening. So I thought I'd just tell you what happened with your dad at the dance and we could figure out what to do. But then Sunny called and said my dad had tried to commit suicide, and we rushed into the city to wait at the hospital, because they didn't know if he would live or not."

He swallows, and his throat bobs. "Dad made it through the

weekend. And my moms made sure his girlfriend was prepared to handle him at home—bought groceries for them, and stuff. And anyway, it was draining. And I didn't get back into town until Sunday night. I was going to try to talk to you at school the next day, to apologize for homecoming and explain what happened. But then my dad made his second suicide attempt, and that time, no one was there to stop him."

"Oh, Lennon."

"Yeah." He gives me a tight smile that fades. "That's when I texted you the last time."

I'm sorry.

I see the text in my mind as clearly as the day I received it. "I thought . . . you were saying that you didn't want to be in a relationship. That you were chickening out of telling me in person."

"I was afraid your dad was monitoring your texts, and I was in the middle of a nightmare. I couldn't think straight. I just told myself that when I got back after the funeral, we'd sort it out. The last thing I expected was to come back to school and see you with Andre."

Oh, Jesus.

Everything begins to slot together inside my head.

I remember that Monday with perfect clarity. I'd been crying all weekend, thinking he'd decided that being anything more than friends was too weird, and that he'd bailed on me. I didn't want to go back to school. Mom forced me to go after I confessed about the Great Experiment. She said I should talk to him and find out what happened. Give him the benefit of the doubt. And—

"My dad had a long talk with me," I say, too agitated to sit. I jump off the bench and pace around the plateau. "He said Mom told him I was upset and that I'd be better off not talking to you. To let it go, that all relationships change, and it was better to have pride than be the one begging. He . . ." I stop and put my hands on my hips to steady myself. I think I'm going to be sick. "I thought he was being a concerned father. Why would he care what we did or didn't do?"

Lennon throws his hands up. "Right? I never understood it. I mean, I know my parents are way less uptight about sex—"

Dear God. I feel myself flush.

"—but it was so weird to me that he blew up like that."

"Oh, he blows up, all right," I say, pacing again. "He's a keg of dynamite."

"He's petty, too. He kept Mac's credit card—for leverage, he told me. When she went into a tizzy, trying to find it after my dad's funeral, I couldn't stand lying to her. So I confessed to the whole thing. She was furious at me. You know how she is about stealing."

"I know."

"But afterward, she was more furious at your dad. All the shit he said about the sex shop . . . That was the first big screaming match between our families, you know. It was about you and me. Mac went over to your parents' clinic while we were in school and gave him a verbal ass-whipping."

It was about us? All of this mess is what started the bad blood between our families?

He nods his head. "I wanted to talk to you about everything, but after my dad's funeral, I walked into school, and there you were, kissing Andre in front of your locker."

"I thought we were over! I embarrassed myself, crying at homecoming, and he was nice to me. He was there, and you weren't, and I thought you didn't . . . I never would have, if I'd known the truth. I didn't know your dad died—you could have told me!"

"I thought you'd find out. It was on the news. But you didn't say anything, and I wasn't supposed to go near you, or your dad would kill me. The only time I could talk to you without him knowing was at school, but there you were, with Andre. Andre! And you wouldn't so much as look my way. I felt like a disease. You moved to the courtyard at lunch to sit with Reagan and Andre, and then I saw you guys on a date at Thai Palace. . . ."

"I thought you hated me. I thought we were finished."

He lifts his cap to run a hand through his hair and then settles it back down more tightly, tugging it low on his forehead. "I was messed up about my dad. . . . I didn't know what to do. Everything was completely screwed up, and I thought you didn't want anything to do with me anymore. I was shattered, Zorie. Shattered."

I hear the hurt in his voice, and it matches what I'm feeling in my heart.

Overwhelmed, I walk to the edge of the plateau and glance

down the twisting steps. They look otherworldly, like ancient steps of a Tibetan mountain temple. Only, it's just California, and there's nothing holy here. No monks. No shrine.

Just the mountain and the sun and the two of us with all this pain in the middle.

A group of hikers climbs the steps far below. They look like ants. I walk a few steps to the benches circling a short wooden rail and gaze out over the jagged scenery. I wonder if this is one of the spots at which people fall off the mountain. It certainly doesn't seem like a place people should die. It's far too beautiful.

I hear Lennon approaching, but I don't turn around. I don't know what to say. I can't process this. I'm trying, but I'm angry and utterly heartbroken, and everything feels raw.

Is all of this my fault, for crying on Andre's shoulder and assuming the worst about Lennon's motivations?

Is all of this Lennon's fault, for assuming the worst about me?

And then there's my father. . . .

"Everything that happened in the hotel . . . ," I finally manage, talking more to the mountains than to him. "I mean, it's almost blackmail, what my father did to you."

"Actually, it was. See, there was something niggling me. Why was he at that hotel checking in? It was the middle of the day. And who needs a hotel in town when they live twenty minutes away? I didn't really think about it much after everything went to hell. Not until that package was misdelivered to my parents' shop last week."

My body stills, heart racing erratically. "Why?" I ask, almost a whisper. I'm not even sure I want to know.

"Because the woman in those photos . . . I realized I'd seen her before. She was in the hotel lobby, standing near the registration desk. And then I saw her again, looking out the rotating doors when your dad dragged me outside." Lennon pauses, and then says, "When I thought about it later, I wondered if maybe he made such a big scene to distract me from seeing her."

This is the final blow. I want to hold my hands up in surrender. I'm dead now, so you can stop shooting, please and thank you. Nothing can hurt me anymore. I'm beyond pain. I'm just numb.

I stride toward our bench and slide into my pack, hoisting it onto my shoulders.

"What are you doing?" Lennon asks.

"I need to think," I tell him. "I just . . . need to think."

20

And that's exactly what I do. Alone with my thoughts, I ponder everything that's just happened all the way up the last hundred or so steps of the mountain staircase. Wondering if I'll ever stop being angry with my dad. Wondering if I'm angry with Lennon, too. And I'm so busy being lost in my own self-centered thoughts, it doesn't quite register that the water is getting louder. And louder. When the steps begin curving sharply to the right, I suddenly see why.

Waterfalls. Two of them. Not the small, tranquil cascade of Mackenzie Falls. If *that* was a roar, this is God herself speaking. And she is fierce.

Blue water plummets off a sharp-angled cliff many stories down into raging white foam. It's flowing so savagely, a good third of the falls are nothing but gauzy mist. I even can feel mist on my legs—and the base of the falls must be a good quarter mile or more away.

I hike the last few steps to a large lookout area on a plateau twice the size of the one below. No one's up here. How is that possible? I spy another set of stone steps at the end of the lookout leading to the topmost point. There appears to be a trail all the way around the falls, and at the top of the falls is where several tourists are taking photos and looking through viewfinders. If I'm not mistaken, there is a tram and a couple of toilets up there. Guess most people choose to ride up there instead of climbing the world's most dangerous steps.

I walk toward the edge of the lookout, dump my pack on a section of dry rock, and peer across the gap to watch the waterfalls.

"Emperor and Empress Falls," Lennon says loudly from my side, ditching his pack next to mine. "They're actually part of the same river, but that bumpy rock formation that sticks out between them is what splits the flow. Three hundred fifty feet tall."

They are beautiful. I'm truly stunned. By the view, and by the entire conversation we just had. I wonder if I can just keep looking at the falls, just pretend it never happened until I come up with a plan—

"Zorie," he pleads from behind me. "Say something. Please."

I have to speak louder than normal to be heard over the roar of the falls, and it sort of turns into yelling. "If you confessed everything to your parents, then my dad didn't have anything to hold over you as leverage." I swing around to face him, bitterness in my voice. "Why didn't you tell me then?"

"You weren't speaking to me."

"Because I was under the assumption that you hated me!"

"I never hated you. I was angry that you shut me out, and I damn sure was furious about Andre. Seeing you with him in front of your locker was one of the worst days of my life—and believe me, I had a *lot* of bad days last year."

"I was only with Andre because I was trying to get over you." I'm crying now—half in anger, half in grief—and I feel as if my chest is going to explode and I'm going to fall over the edge of the lookout and die in the waterfall mist. Because not only am I thinking about what I did with Andre, but I'm also thinking about Lennon doing the same thing with Jovana Ramirez. And I don't know which image is worse.

"And then," he yells, "I had to listen to Brett—fucking *Brett*, of all people—brag about how close he was to 'hitting that.'"

Ugh! What did I see in him?

"It was just a kiss!" I tell Lennon. "One kiss, and it wasn't even that good. It wasn't good with Andre, and it was less than nothing with Brett. Is that want you want to hear?"

"I don't mind hearing that, honestly," he says, cheeks dark with indignation.

"And what about Jovana? Andre and I had sex one time. Once! You probably screwed Jovana's brains out for months."

"I'm not going to dignify that. She's a nice person."

"Aha!" I say. "You avoided the question."

"There was a question? Because all I heard was an implication. And yeah, we had sex. But I wasn't in love with her."

"Does that make it better?"

"You're not hearing me. *I wasn't in love with her.*"

"I heard you."

"She left me because I was hung up on you."

"Then why didn't you talk to me?" I say.

"Because you made it clear that you didn't want me to. Because you were busy making out with Brett at parties. Because you made new friends and avoided me at school. Because your father was always watching me."

"You should have fought for me!" I shout. "Why didn't you fight for me?"

"You gave up on me!" he yells back. "How can I fight for someone who pretends I don't exist?"

"I was trying to protect myself. You hurt me. My entire world fell apart."

"So. Did. Mine."

I'm shaking now. At least the angry crying has stopped.

"It's not supposed to be like this!" I tell him.

"What isn't?"

I gesture angrily from him to me. "This! If this were meant to be, it would be easier. Maybe the universe is trying to tell us something."

"Oh?" He stalks closer, getting in my face. Towering above me. "Is that so?"

"Yes," I say, less sure.

"I really want to know, Zorie. What do *you* think the universe is trying to tell us?"

"That we . . ." My mouth hangs open, and I can't finish the thought. He's too close. Inches away. My head is empty; the words on my tongue have vanished. I don't know what I'm trying to say. What I'm feeling. I just have the sense that we've come to a decisive moment and something is about to snap. It's as if the energy between us has suddenly spiked and is now vibrating. Like the sign behind me warns: STAY CLEAR OF THE EDGE. ROCKS ARE SLIPPERY.

"You want to know what I think?" Lennon says, head dipping lower as he tries to get level with my eyes. "*I* think that if the universe were trying to keep us apart, it's doing a shitty job. Because otherwise, we wouldn't be out here together."

"I wish we weren't!"

"No, you don't," he says firmly.

"Yes, I do. I wish I'd never come on this trip. I wish I didn't know any of this, and I wish—"

Without warning, his mouth is on mine. He kisses me roughly. Completely unyielding. His hands are on the back of my head, holding me in place. And for a long, suspended moment, I'm frozen, unsure of whether I want to push him away. Then, all at once, heat spreads through me, and I thaw.

I kiss him back.

And, *oh*, it is good.

His hands relax, fingers tangling in my hair, soft tongue rolling against mine. And when I run out of air and have to pull back, he kisses the corner of my mouth. My cheek. My forehead. A trail of kisses on my jaw. All over my neck. My earlobe—and now I'm close to passing out with pleasure. He even tugs back the collar of my shirt to kiss the hidden skin beneath it. His mouth is hot, and his stubble is rough in the best way possible. The kisses are long and slow and deliberate, and they are very, *very* confident. And it feels as if he's drawing a map on my body, following a path of landmarks that he's plotted in his head.

He's relentless with all of his exploration, and I'm making weird groaning noises that are halfway embarrassing. But *I just can't stop*. And now I'm struggling to get my mouth back on his skin, any skin I can reach, and my arms are around him, pulling him closer, and I've found my way back to his mouth, and GOD, IT'S GOOD.

How could I have forgotten?

Did he get better at this? Did I?

Because *my God*.

Waterfall mist covers my legs, and my knees are giving out. My bones don't work anymore. It's as if he's pressed some sort of secret on switch, and I'm at the mercy of my body—which likes his body quite a lot and desperately wants to drop to the ground and let Lennon have his wicked way with me, right here in front of God's Voice. I absolutely would, too. In this moment, I'm a trollop. An unrepentant floozy. I'm a raging wildfire of feelings and sensations, and I can't put them out.

Oh, wow. I seriously can't breathe. I think I need to learn how to pace my trollop-y ways. Or at least learn how to breathe through my nostrils while kissing.

I try to steady myself, and that's when the voices in my head start whispering. *He abandoned you. He hurt you.*

The sound of approaching hikers intensifies my uneasy feelings.

I pull away from Lennon.

He pulls me back.

"People coming," I warn.

"Zorie," Lennon says, his hand roaming down my back. "I want to try again. I don't want to be enemies. Or friends. I want . . . everything. You and me. I don't care about your father anymore. I will fight for us, if that's what it takes. We'll figure something out together. Tell me you want that too."

And for a moment, I almost give in and agree, but then one of the hikers laughs—they are *way* closer than I expected—and it fractures the moment, a proverbial bucket of icy water over all our shared warmth. And with a jolt of clarity, I remember Lennon saying a lot of the same sentiments to me before homecoming, when we decided to take the Great Experiment public.

Can we be together again?

Do I want to?

Has what he's revealed changed how I feel about last fall?

Why can't I make an easy decision?

And finally: *What is wrong with me?*

"I need to think about things," I tell him.

The anguish on his face is unmistakable.

He closes his eyes and then blinks rapidly, gathering himself. Then he nods and steps back, putting distance between us.

"I'm sorry," I say. "I just . . . It's a lot at once, and . . ."

And I can't function like a normal human being.

He nods. "I know. I understand."

"Lennon—"

The approaching hikers surge onto our plateau. It's a group of college-aged boys. Their laughter scatters my thoughts and puts an invisible wall between Lennon and me.

"Come on. Let's get out of here," he says, gesturing toward our backpacks. All the emotion disappears from his voice and posture, and he's back to being unreadable.

I want to scream. I want to beg him to come back. I want to be alone so that I can think through every detail of what just happened. I want to stop thinking.

But I can't do any of those things, so we return to the trail in silence, both of us deep in thought . . . never closer, never further apart.

21

After leaving the falls, we hike Emerald Trail the rest of the afternoon, communicating only when necessary, and occasionally delving into safe subjects. The national park system. The weather. We maintain a polite distance from each other, as if we're just two acquaintances, sharing the trail. As if we didn't just kiss each other's faces off. As if my entire world hasn't flipped onto its back like some stranded, flailing turtle.

Though we pass quite a few hikers, when we get to the end of the trail in the early evening, I'm startled to see not only a ranger station, but also an entire campground bustling with people. A road. Cars. The scent of meat cooking on grills. Music playing in someone's RV.

"Camp Silver," Lennon informs me. "The trailhead is here. You need reservations to hike Silver Trail at this time of year. They try to keep the number of people on it at a certain level, so it's not elbow to elbow."

"It looks pretty elbow to elbow now," I say, scanning the campground.

"Everyone wants to walk where Ansel Adams took photos," he says. "The trail goes up to the Crown, which overlooks the whole park."

I think I've heard about that. It sounds familiar, so it must be a big tourist draw.

"There are campgrounds along the way for people who like a few modern conveniences, but this is probably the biggest one," Lennon says. "And here's the ranger station I told you about."

The station is a small, dark brown log cabin on the edge of the campground. Outside the door stands a board of printed notices—announcements about the weather, the status of each campsite, and which trails are closed. There's even a warning about a mountain lion in the area, several missing people, and another about a small, twin-engine plane that's crashed in the mountains. Hikers are to stay clear of the wreckage until the park can arrange to have it transported.

"What in the world?" I murmur, reading the flyers. I'm not sure which notice is worse.

Lennon doesn't seem worried about the mountain lion, because he taps on the plane-crash announcement and whistles softly. "I've heard about stuff like this. The entire Sierra Nevada mountain chain is a graveyard for lost planes. It's called the Nevada Triangle."

"Like the Bermuda Triangle?"

"Just like that. From Fresno to Las Vegas—basically, a big dead zone over the California-Nevada border where planes go down or disappear entirely." The drama in his voice increases. "Some say it's a combination of rapidly changing weather, strong winds, and hidden peaks. But the whole mountain chain has this spooky Area 51 mythos. More than two thousand planes have gone down here since 1960. Some just fell off the radar, never found."

"Whoa," I say, suitably impressed.

His lips pull into a gentle curve—just for a moment. Then he sobers up and goes quiet.

"So, this Silver Trail . . . ," I ask, trying to recall his map. "Is that where we'd be going to get to Condor Peak?"

He shakes his head. "We don't have hiking reservations, and it's headed south. We'd need to go west from here. There's a smaller trail through the backcountry. I've been on it before, so no surprises like the caves yesterday."

"I see."

He gestures toward the ranger station. "Unless you've decided to go home."

Have I? I've been thinking about that decision the entire afternoon. Along with everything that he told me about homecoming. And about the kiss.

Definitely thinking about the kiss.

I could continue on. (But what if we end up fighting?)

I could call for a ride home. (But what if I regret not staying?)

The energy between us feels heightened, strained, and slightly awkward. But Lennon is patient, not pushing me to decide, and for that, I'm grateful. He glances at his phone. "Still no service. There should be a phone inside the station."

"I should call my mom, at least," I say. "Just to let her know I'm alive."

His gaze intensifies. He's studying my face, trying to figure out what I'm going to do. If I knew that, I'd just tell him.

"Me too," he finally says. "And I need to report the abandoned gear Reagan and Brett left behind. Shall we?"

I nod and take a deep, steadying breath as we head to the door to the ranger station and step inside.

The single-room cabin is dim and cozy. Though the floor plan is small, the high ceiling is crossed with rough wooden beams, which makes it feel larger. There's a small desk at the front and a rack of local wilderness travel books for sale. In the middle of the room, a couple of chairs huddle around an old heating stove, and in the back, near a giant wall map of the park, there's an old pay phone.

"Evenin'," a ranger says with a quiet smile. "We're about to close for the day."

"We'll be quick," Lennon assures him before gesturing me toward the phone, eyes hooded. "You want to go first?"

I make my way past the chairs while Lennon begins telling the ranger about Reagan and Brett's abandoned gear. I'm worried that the national park might get judgmental about a couple of teens backpacking alone. But it seems fine, because Lennon sounds confident and knowledgeable, and the ranger is taking him seriously. They aren't paying attention to me, and that gives me to time to take a deep breath and focus.

Stay or go?

Go or stay?

If I stay, I don't think Lennon and I can just forget about everything that's happened and go back to being just friends. That much I know. There's too much history between us, and that kiss pretty much wiped out an entire year's worth of trying to bury old feelings. Now I'm right back where I was, ribs cracked open and heart exposed.

I wish I could ask Mom for advice, but if she knew I was out here alone with Lennon . . . Well, it's not so much her I worry about as my dad. But he'd find out eventually. I wish I had time to think out exactly what I need to say to her. Maybe write out a script. But the station is about to close, and if I'm going to call her, it's now or never.

It takes me a little while to figure out how to use the ancient pay phone, but after reading the posted instructions, I dig out some quarters and slip them inside. Then I dial my mom's cell phone.

"Joy Everhart," my mom's voice says, crackling over the line.

"Mom?"

"Zorie? Is that you? Are you okay?" She sounds frantic.

"I'm totally fine," I tell her, looking up at the giant map hanging on the wall. "I'm in King's Forest."

Her exhalation is loud. "Dammit, Zorie. I was so worried. You didn't answer my texts."

"No service out here," I say. "We talked about that, remember?"

"We did. You're right," she says. "But it's a relief to hear your voice. Wait, did you say you're in the national park? Why aren't you at the glamping compound?"

"Um . . ." Do I tell her what happened? I hate lying to her. But if I stay here with Lennon, I can't tell her that's what I'm doing. Now that I'm forced to make a decision, I close my eyes and just let whatever comes out of my mouth be my choice.

One, two, three—

"Remember how I told you we might go on that backcountry trail?" I say. "That's where I am. I'm hiking to the star party."

Oh my God, I'm doing this. I'm staying with Lennon?

I am.

Relief rushes through me, unknotting my shoulders and loosening my limbs.

"I can barely hear you. Did you say you're hiking to Condor Peak?" Mom asks, her voice going up an octave. "I thought you were taking the bus. Are you hiking alone?"

"It's not that far and I'm not alone," I assure her. "Dr. Viramontes and Avani will be at the star party to meet me when I get there."

"Okay, but who are you with now?"

Crap on toast. Why didn't I write a script? "We changed our

plans for the week. And I'm with a guide, so you don't have to worry."

"A guide?"

"Someone who really knows the wilderness. Right now we're in a campground at a ranger station."

"Zorie—"

"It's fine, I promise. There are families camping here and a park ranger. I'm completely safe. Please trust me. I need you to trust me, or I can't enjoy this. You told me to be careful, not cautious, remember?"

She sighs. "But you *are* being smart, right?"

"As smart as possible. I swear on my backpack."

"Oh, good. Okay. All right." I can hear the relief in her voice. "Hives?"

"Under control."

"Thank goodness. You have plenty of food?"

"Yep. Still have your emergency money too."

She pauses. "Are you having fun?"

I glance back at Lennon. He's several inches taller than the ranger is, and is now pointing out a location on a laminated map on the desk. He is insanely good-looking. I don't think I allowed myself to think about that too much over the last year, but I'm thinking it now, and it's making my stomach flutter. That voice, those lips, that—

"Zorie?"

Oh, crap. "What? Oh, um, yeah. I'm having fun." A snake

bite, a bear, and the greatest kiss of my life. "I'm sore from hiking, and I need a shower, but it's really pretty out here."

"I'm so glad. That's terrific," she says, sounding happy. I like it when she's happy. She deserves someone better than my shitty father. Lennon's story about the hotel pierces my thoughts, and the weight of this secret affair is becoming heavier and heavier. But I'm still too much of a coward to tell her about my dad. I can't do it on the phone, not like this. I'm scared of hurting her, but I'm even more terrified of losing her. So I just tell her what day I'll be at Condor Peak and assure her once more that everything's fine.

I'm a selfish, selfish person.

"Baby?" she says, her voice taking on a different tone. "Do you have anything else you need to tell me?"

My pulse increases. "What do you mean?"

"I mean, you know I don't like secrets."

"I know."

"And when people keep them, it's usually for a bad reason."

Oh, God. Does she know I'm here with Lennon? Or is she talking about my dad's affair? She couldn't be. I'm paranoid.

"I know that sometimes it seems like . . ." She pauses. "Zorie, I care about you more than you can fathom. But . . ."

"But what?" Why is there a *but*?

"I just want you to know that you can tell me anything," she says more firmly.

"I know that."

"Okay, that's all."

That's all? What is going on? Why is she being so cryptic? Maybe I should tell her about Lennon. But if I do, I'm worried she'll tell my dad, and they'll drive out here and make me come home. I made up my mind already. I know it took me forever, but now that I've decided, I really *don't* want to go back to Melita Hills.

I hate lying to her.

But I want to stay here with Lennon.

Why can't this be easier?

The phone is playing some prerecorded message in the background, telling me to deposit more money. "I don't have any more quarters, so I've got to go," I tell her. "But I just wanted to check in and tell you that I'm safe, and that . . . well, like I said, I have a really good trail guide out here. So you don't have to worry."

"Wait! When will you get to Condor Peak?"

"Day after tomorrow. Late."

"Promise me that you'll text when you get there."

"I promise. And I love you."

"I love you too, sweet thing." She sounds sad. Or disappointed? "And I miss you. Please stay safe."

Ugh. She's breaking my heart. And I don't even get to say anything else, because the pay phone finally realizes I'm not putting more money inside it and cuts me off. I hang up and lay my forehead against the receiver.

"Everything okay?" Lennon says in a low voice near my shoulder.

"I think so. Hope so."

"What did you decide?"

I turn around and absently scratch my arm. "I hope you haven't changed your mind about taking me to Condor Peak, because you're stuck with me now."

He sighs. Twice. On a third sigh, his hand tentatively reaches toward the side of my face, and he gently pushes an errant curl out of my eyes, fingers lingering. "I'm glad. Really glad."

"You are?"

"I am. No presumptions made. I'm not booking us a hotel room, or anything."

I groan softly, a little embarrassed.

"Too soon?" he says with the hint of a smile.

I shake my head and smile back.

His hand drops from my hair, and a moment of awkward silence passes before I speak again, attempting to move the focus away from the heavy topic of *us*. "I'm worried that I should have told Mom about the lady you saw last year at the hotel with my father. And about the photo book. I just couldn't."

"It's probably for the best. Some things you just don't want to say over the phone, believe me. Like, Hey, I'm an idiot who tried to get a hotel room because I have no clue about how to have a relationship, and, oh yeah, I punched your father, and we're not allowed to see each other. You know, things like that."

I chuckle a little.

"I still don't," he whispers.

"Don't what?" I whisper back.

"Know how to have a relationship."

"Oh good, because I don't either."

"We'll figure it out eventually. If you want to, that is."

"I think so," I whisper.

His smile is almost shy, but when he sighs one last time, exhaling sharply through his nostrils, he sounds content. And that makes me feel less anxious about everything.

He clears his throat. "So . . . I rented us a campsite," he says, holding up a small, perforated card with a number printed on it. "Not a presumption, by the way. If you were leaving, I needed a place to sleep tonight, and I really didn't—"

"Calm down. I believe you."

"Okay," he says, and we both smile at each other again.

Focus, Zorie. "Campsite. We're not camping in the wild?"

"The sites make things easier, so I thought why not take advantage of convenience for a night? And we're lucky to get it. They were completely booked until the mountain lion scare we saw posted on the board outside. Apparently one tried to attack a small child at another camp."

I'm suddenly alarmed, but Lennon holds up a calming hand.

"Mountain lions usually steer clear of populated areas, but if they try to attack, small children look like prey in their eyes. We aren't children. We'll be fine, especially with all the other campers around. And besides, that report was miles from here, and the little boy escaped unharmed."

Still not feeling better about this. . . .

"Now skootch," Lennon says, waving me aside. "Let me call the parental units before the ranger kicks us out."

I feel strange about listening in to his phone conversation, so I busy myself outside the station, picking up a free park map from a covered plastic box as the sun begins setting, shining warm orange light through the trees. When Lennon emerges, he's all smiles, poise, and swagger. Whatever was said between him and his moms lifted his mood considerably. But before I can ask about this, he waves the camping permit at me.

"Okay, Medusa. We're looking for an open site somewhere down there. Let's make camp. And bonus, there are toilets and hot showers."

(A) He hasn't called me that nickname in *forever*, and (B) showers. SHOWERS!

"You really know how to win a girl's heart," I say, grinning.

"I'm trying my best," he says, and I feel said heart skip a beat.

We wander down a trail through the camp, nodding at strangers who lift a hand in greeting. It must be a camping thing. I'm not accustomed to so much open friendliness among strangers. Don't these hippies know this is a good way to get mugged? Head down, eyes on the sidewalk—that's my motto. Then again, maybe they're so cheery because they all have cars, either pulled up right next to their tents or out in the nearby parking lot, and Car Camping seems to be a completely different ball game. These people have coolers of actual food—not freeze-dried meals—and portable chairs. Since when did I become jealous of a chair and a package of cheap hot dogs? But, gods above, it looks enticing.

"Bingo," Lennon says, pointing toward a deserted piece of dirt. "Ranger Bob said there were two sites open, and we can choose. I see another one open near the toilets, and I'm gonna suggest we pass on that, because I've camped near restrooms before. It's like sitting near the toilets on an airplane, but worse. So much worse."

"Say no more. This one smells and looks perfect." Well, that's a stretch. It's somewhat barren, and the sites on either side of it are a little closer than I'd like. But on the other hand, it's flat, there are no rocks or twigs to clear away, and it has a private picnic table, a bear locker, and a rusty fire pit ring with a grill. "Score. If only we had some hot dogs."

"We have freeze-dried macaroni and cheese, and if you're nice to me, I'll let you have some of my M&M stash."

"Deal," I say.

There's an awkward moment when we set our packs on the picnic table to fish out our tents. I don't know what he's thinking, but I'm remembering sleeping with him the night before. Only now . . .

Yeah. I look up and see the confirmation in his eyes. He's thinking it too.

Now it's different.

"Uh, should we set the tents up side by side, here?" he says after a few tense seconds.

"Sounds good."

It doesn't take us too long to get the tents in place, and Lennon eyes the forested area near the campsite. "I can probably collect wood out there, but it might take me a little while, especially if other campers regularly hunt for it. You want to take a shower while I'm looking?" He squints and holds up a finger. "That came out wrong. While I'm looking for wood. In the forest."

I snort a little laugh.

"Or the other thing," he says.

"Just get the firewood."

His smile is playful. "If you change your mind, holler."

"Aye, aye, Captain."

Before he heads out into the woods, Lennon informs me that now is a good time to wash out any clothes that need washing, and he digs out a minibottle of biodegradable castile soap. My snake-bitten, bloodied socks definitely need cleaning, as well as my underwear and a couple of tank tops. I gather them up, get my toiletries and a change of clothes, and head to the shower house, which is another rustic log cabin building that looks similar in design to the ranger station. After watching another camper parading through the campground in a bathrobe and flip-flops, I realize that this place truly is hippie-land, and no one's concerned about etiquette.

This is no glamping compound.

A slat-wood partition shields a door marked WOMEN. When I head inside, I find lockers for clothes and big, long sinks in front of mirrors. The water there is cold, and in order to get hot water in one of the three shower stalls, you have to feed money into a little machine. I have enough quarters for five minutes of hot water, and even though I rush to shampoo, wash, and shave, it still runs out when I'm peeling the bandages off my snake bite, making me yelp in surprise when the water turns icy cold. But I manage to endure it long enough to finish up, and after toweling off with a small microfiber camp towel—one of Reagan's purchases—I brush my teeth and wash out my clothes in the sink.

One problem with showering in the wild is the lack of hair dryers, and the temperature outside is starting to fall along with the setting sun. It's not chilly, but with a head full of wet curls, it's not exactly warm, either. Luckily, by the time I walk back to our site, Lennon has gotten a fire going. He's also set up a low-hanging rope between his tent and the picnic table for hanging up wet clothes to dry. I feel a little weird putting up my underwear for all the world to see, but other campers are doing it in their sites, so I guess this is one of those moments where I have to swallow my pride and say screw it. I quickly hang everything up before taking a seat on a bear canister in front of the fire, letting the heat dry my hair while Lennon takes his turn at the shower house.

The camp is really bustling, now that everyone's coming back from day hikes and getting ready for dinner. It's weird to be around so many people. It seems like a lifetime ago when Reagan abandoned us and I was freaking out about being alone with Lennon. I watch all the activity, wondering where all these people came from and why they decided to camp here. They're definitely different from the glampers. I don't know if that's good or bad, or if it just *is*. But at least I'm not on edge, wondering which fork to use at a four-course dinner. Plus, everyone here seems to be in a better mood. And despite a bit of lingering worry over that call to my mom, I think maybe I am too.

After a few minutes of combing my curls out upside down in front of the fire, I hear a soft whistle.

I jerk my head up to find Lennon's long legs walking up to our site. "My oh my. Look at all your unmentionables blowing in the wind. I mean, wow. I'm getting a real French-lingerie vibe here, and, to be honest, I expected plaid."

"Oh my God," I say, kicking his leg. "Stop looking, you perv."

He's hanging up his own underwear next to mine, a towel draped over his shoulders and his black hair damp and sticking up in the most adorable way. "I'll stop looking when you do."

"What's there to look at? Black boxers? I already saw those last night when you were getting in my tent."

"Mmm, that's right. And have you been thinking about me in my skivvies all day?"

"Please stop talking."

"Stop talking altogether, or . . . ?" He laughs and dances out of the way as I try to kick him again. I smell shaving cream and notice that he's gotten rid of his stubble. "Okay, okay. Try to control yourself, and I'll try to do the same. We have more important matters to take care of, like the fact that my stomach is trying to eat itself. Let's get to making with the macaroni and cheese, shall we?"

As he breaks out our cooking gear, I keep my eyes on the other campsites, watching the comings and goings of kids and adults. There's even a site filled with several teens, and one of the guys is unpacking an acoustic guitar. Lennon tells me there's a wannabe guitarist at every campground. It's practically required.

While the water for our dinner is heating up, Lennon checks my snake bite and fixes another bandage over the healing wound, proclaiming it "much better." Then we prepare and eat our not-so-fabulous macaroni meal, which along with a cloying cheese sauce, also has dried beef in it, so we do a whole comical bit together, wistfully pretending it's the same grilled hamburger we're smelling from the campsite next to ours. Halfway through eating, it's dark enough that Lennon needs to switch on our little camp lights—to see my underwear better, he jokes, and I throw my spork at him. When he pretends to be injured, the teen campsite with the guitar-playing dude starts group singing a hymn. Loudly.

"Noooo," I whisper. "Nightmare. They aren't even on key."

"And it's not even a good hymn. What about 'Holy, Holy,

Holy'? Now, *that* would be one you could really go nuts with."

"Aha!" I say. "I just realized why Mac has you going to church. It's not your diabolic ensemble of all-black clothes. It's because you stole her credit card to use for the hotel room."

He looks sheepish. "Busted. Though I *did* turn myself in, so that has to count for something. But yeah, she makes me sit through hymns as penance."

"It's all clear to me now."

"So basically, it's your fault."

"Mine?" I say.

"You're a tempting girl, Zorie. If you hadn't kissed me last year that first time, I would have never wanted to get the hotel room, and—"

"Me kiss you? That was an accident!"

"Kissing is never an accident. Never in the history of kissing has it been an accident."

"I slipped when I sat on the bench."

"And your mouth just happened to land on mine?"

"Andromeda was pulling against the leash, trying to chase a squirrel!"

"Keep lying to yourself. Meanwhile, I've made my peace with my part in it, which is that I was completely innocent."

"If it wasn't an accident, then it was both our faults."

"Not according to evangelicals." He switches to a street preacher voice. "And yea, though I was seduced by the sinful demon female in the garden—"

"Hey! You're the one with the dildo garden in the shop window."

"Dildo *forest*, Zorie. Get it right. I helped put that up, by the way. I took a photo of Ryuk walking around inside the display."

"I'm going to need to see that," I say, but my words are drowned under the hymn-a-thon at the tent across the path. "Ugh, all these people," I complain. "I wish we were camping in the backcountry. I mean, don't get me wrong, the shower is great, and it's much easier to get drinkable water out of a faucet than to scoop it out of a river and wait for it to filter. But jeez, civilization is noisy."

"Well, well, well. Look who's been bitten by the bug," Lennon says, pointing at me.

"What bug?" I frantically glance across my clothes and legs.

"No, the backpacking bug," he says, laughing. "You prefer the peace and quiet. That's how it started for me. I just wanted to get away from people and think."

"Well, I'm not ready to do this on a regular basis, but I'm starting to see the appeal."

He gestures toward the back of the camp. "You know what? When I was gathering firewood, I walked down that big hill there. It's just grassland and meadow, but I bet it has a decent view of the stars. At least it's away from the lights of the camp. Want to take your telescope there before they start singing 'Kumbaya'?"

Yes. Yes, I do. After we clean and put away everything, and

Lennon puts out the fire, we gather the rainfly from my tent and my telescope. After strapping on headlamps—and dumping Reagan's expensive broken headlamp in the trash—we haul all of our supplies out of camp and head toward the hill.

It doesn't take long to find a good spot where the lights from the camp are at our backs. We can still hear people, but it's not as loud. Lennon spreads out the rainfly, and we sit on it picnic-style. I flick off the light on my headlamp. The stars are amazing out here. I don't think I'll ever be used to seeing them this way, without light pollution from the city. Thousands upon thousands of them, glittering points of light. It's as if I'm looking at an entirely different sky.

"Look," I say, pointing up at a wispy white trail. "The Milky Way. You can't see that at home without a telescope. Not even at the observatory."

Lennon takes off his headlamp and leans back on his palms. "It looks unreal. I know it's not, but my mind doesn't want to accept that this isn't some fake, projected light show."

No projection could look like this. We both stare up at the sky for a long moment. "I don't even think I want to use the telescope," I say. "I think I just want to look at them. Is that weird?"

"Not at all. It's not every day you get to see all this."

My phone still has a little charge on it, and I quickly turn on the screen to use it as a flashlight in order to see where to move my telescope. That's when I notice something.

"We have service!"

"Well, what do you know?" Lennon says, taking out his phone. "Oh, look. I've got texts from the Brettster."

"You do?" My only texts are from Mom and Avani.

"He's apologizing for leaving us. Well, it's sort of a non-apology. Oh, wait. He's taking it back. No . . . He's apologizing again. Aren't Reagan's parents in Switzerland, or something?"

"Yeah, why?"

"Because he's not making any sense. Now he's blaming Reagan for ditching us. I think? He's an atrocious speller, by the way."

"How many texts did he send?" I say, glancing at his screen.

"One, two, three, four . . . eight. And the last one is asking if I can get him weed again."

"Again?"

"He's already asked once. He's laboring under the false presumption that because my dad was in a band, I somehow have unlimited access to drugs. I swear, Brett is the absolute worst. I'm not even responding."

Avani's message is just confirming that she's leaving for the star party tomorrow and will see me there. I quickly decide to tell her that I'm with Lennon, backpacking through the park—super casual, no details—and asking if it's okay that he rides home with us. After she confirms, and I tell her when we'll be arriving, I read my mom's message: I'm glad you called today. Please stay safe and text me when you get to Condor

Peak. If you ever want to talk about anything, you know I'm here, right?

Why does she keep saying this? I replay our phone conversation in my head and something starts to bother me. "I left that photo book in my desk at home."

"What?" Lennon says, switching his phone off.

"I'm worried that my mom might have found it. She keeps asking me if there's anything I want to tell her, like she's trying to get me to confess to something. And it's either that photo book, or she knows I'm here with you."

"How would she know?"

"Do your parents know that we're alone right now?"

He hesitates. "Yeah, actually. They're pretty happy about it."

They are?

"Look," he says, "they know your parents don't realize you're here with me, but they wouldn't go run and tell your mom that. They know we're safe, and that's all that matters."

"Then it must be the photo book," I say.

"Was Joy upset?"

"Not particularly. She sounded . . . disappointed."

He doesn't say anything for a while. "Look, if you want my opinion, I'm betting she already suspected something was up with your dad a long time ago. So if she found the photo book, then she found it. But there's nothing you can do about it now."

I know he's right. Worrying won't do me any good. It's just

hard to make myself stop. I don't like feeling unsettled.

But I try not to think about it, shutting off my phone and stuffing it in my pocket. Then I lie on my back and look up at the stars.

Lennon lies down next to me, shoulder to shoulder.

"We're under the same starry sky," I say.

"We always are."

"Not together," I argue.

"I think we've always been together, even when we were apart," he says, slipping his hand around mine.

"I know it's a cliché, but sometimes I would look up at the stars and wonder if you were ever looking at them at the same time," I admit.

"When I looked up at the stars, I saw us. You were the stars, and I was the dark sky behind you."

"Without dark sky, you couldn't see the stars."

"I knew I was useful," he says.

"You're essential."

He makes a happy sound and tucks his arm behind his head. "When we were apart, I would always try to find constellations and imagine you talking about them. Like the Great Cat."

"The Great Cat? You mean the Great Bear . . . or Leo?"

"Which one is Felis Major?"

"There is no Felis Major. There's Ursa Major, and that's the Great Bear. It's the one with the group of stars that make up the Big Dipper."

"I could have sworn there was a big cat constellation. The Great Tomcat."

"Tomcat?" I say, exasperated.

"Could have sworn there was a tomcat constellation with a long tail. Right there."

"Where?"

He points upward. "Standing on the fence."

"You mean Taurus?"

"Is Taurus a cat?" he asks.

"It's a bull!"

"I know," he says, rolling toward me. "I just wanted to hear you get riled up about stars."

"You're a jerk, you know that?" I say with a laugh, poking his ribs repeatedly.

He jumps and tries to grab my finger. "Such a jerk. If I were you, I wouldn't put up with this crap."

"Oh? What should I do about it? Leave you out here to find cat constellations while I go back to camp?"

I pretend to get up, but he grabs my arm and pulls me back down. "Noooo."

"You're going to make me squish my telescope."

He picks it up and moves it behind him. "There. Better?"

"Well, now I can't use it."

"You weren't using it anyway. Unless you had plans to spy on the Bible Camp kids up the hill. But I doubt you're going to see anything sordid, and we both know you like a little skin when you're spying on—Hey!" He shields himself with one arm, laughing. "Ouch! Stop hitting me! I didn't spy on *you* when you were naked. I'm the victim, here."

"You weren't naked."

"Five more seconds and I would've been. Would you have looked away if I hadn't caught you?"

I wait too long to answer.

He grabs me around the waist and pulls me closer. A lot closer. My boobs are pressing against his chest. "Or would you have taken photos?"

"You insult me, sir. I don't use my telescope like some peeping Tom." Usually.

"And I'm supposed to take your word on that? For all I know, you've already secretly photographed me with your spy lens," he says near my lips. "Should I be worried?"

"From what I saw, you don't have anything to worry about."

"You shock me, miss. Have you been watching me do bad things in my room?"

"You always shut the blinds. Spoilsport."

He chuckles in that deep voice of his, and the sound vibrates through his chest and into mine. "Zorie?"

"Yes?"

"God, I've missed you."

"I've missed you too."

"I'm going to accidentally kiss you now."

"Okay."

Softly, slowly, his lips graze over mine. His mouth is soft, and his hand is roaming up my back. I exhale a shaky breath, and he kisses me:

Once, briefly.

Warmth flickers in my chest.

A second time, longer.

Melting heat, uncurling low in my belly.

Three times, and . . .

I'm lost.

Drowning in him. Nothing but goose bumps and buzzing endorphins and pleasure rushing over my skin. Nothing but his mouth, connecting us, and my fingertips slipping up his shirt to dance over the hard planes of his back. Nothing but his arms wrapped around me like a warm blanket.

Nothing but us and the stars above.

It's perfect. As though we've been doing this for years. As if he knows exactly how to make me shiver, and I know exactly how to make him groan. We're brave explorers. The *best* explorers. Lewis and Clark. Ferdinand Magellan and Sir Francis Drake. Neil Armstrong and Sally Ride.

Zorie and Lennon.

We are *so* good at this.

And before I know it, we're rolling around, a tangle of arms and legs, half on the nylon rainfly, half in the night grass. Like we used to do, back during the Great Experiment. My glasses are somewhere, and his hand is up my shirt, and he's saying all these insanely shocking and intimate things he wants to do to me, which should be making my ears turn pink, but right now it all sounds like poetry. And my fingers are headed for his belt buckle, and—

A scream.

Not me. And not Lennon. It's in the woods.

It sounds like a woman. In trouble.

22

Another scream follows. It's from a different location. An answering scream.

Not a human scream. An animal?

"What the shit is that?" I whisper, hand stilling on the hard muscles of his bare stomach. Someone's lifted up his shirt in a completely indecent manner. Oh, that was me.

"It's fine. Just a little mountain lion. No danger," Lennon whispers, guiding my hand lower.

Oh.

Wow.

He's definitely excited about the mountain lion.

This makes me extra excited in return.

Wait. Mountain lion?

"*Mountain lion*?" I whisper hotly.

"Caterwauling. Probably trying to find a mate," Lennon confirms in a drugged voice. "God, your hand feels good."

"Are we about to get attacked?" My voice sounds drugged too. I know I should move my hand away from his jeans, but I'm having trouble relaying the message to my fingers, which *really* want to linger and continue with exploration. My body is saying: *Ahoy! I sailed on a deserted sea for months and have finally spotted land. Fertile land. Land better than I remembered. No way am I turning this ship around now.*

"What?" he whispers.

"Did I say that out loud?"

"Is this some dirty pirate routine? Because I've *really* got a thing for Anne Bonny."

Another scream rips through the night air.

"Jesus!" I say, heart racing, and not in the good way. "That sounds like a human being."

"It also sounds really, really close," he says, voice sobering up. "As much as I would like you to never, ever, ever, *ever* stop . . . I think we should—"

More screaming. Okay, talk about a bucket of ice water. I'm genuinely scared now, imagining something jumping out of the darkness and clawing my face to shreds. Nature is a horror movie. And we're out here in the middle of a field, being stalked by killer animals.

I panic, unable to find my glasses or my headlamp, but Lennon spots them. We can't gather up our stuff fast enough. Then we're jogging back up the hill as the horny wildcats scream behind our backs.

By the time we get up to the camp, several other campers are standing around in long underwear, warily listening to the caterwauling. All eyes turn to us, and—terrific—I'm flushing like a guilty person. Well, technically, I *am* guilty, but now I'm also the camp hussy, so yay?

Lennon, on the other hand, acts calm and collected, breezily talking to the other campers as he lugs the rainfly around, reporting that, yes, it's probably two mountain lions down in the tree line at the bottom of the hill, but no, they likely won't come up here. Someone else, a middle-aged man with a Jamaican accent who introduces himself as Gordon, says he's encountered several mountain lions in this park over the years, and agrees with Lennon. He's telling other campers to make sure their kids aren't wandering around alone, and to be cautious.

Since the camp ranger has left for the night, several people, including Lennon, volunteer to keep an eye out for a little while. And after we get our stuff put away, he digs out an extra camp light from his pack—another one of those palm-size ones—and puts that on our picnic table.

For a while, the camp is buzzing with murmured conversations, and a few campsites are lighting fires in their pits. We eat some of Lennon's M&M stash in a late-night anxiety binge, and when I'm on my second handful, his eyes go big.

"Oh, shit."

"What?" I say, frantically looking around for a wildcat.

"No, no," he says, turning me back around. "Hives."

I look down where he's gently tugging down the collar of my T-shirt. Pink welts all over my neck and chest. I pull up my shirt. They're on my stomach and arms, too.

My first thought is: I'm somehow now allergic to Lennon. And of *course* the universe would punish me for all that rolling around in the proverbial hay with him. Camp hussy, after all. I'm cursed. But Lennon's analysis is slightly less paranoid.

"All the long grass on the hill. Whatever kind it is, your hives don't like it." He inspects my body and asks me if I'm having trouble breathing. I'm not. No loss of vision. No throat swelling up. None of the urgent 911 symptoms.

"You have an EpiPen?" he asks.

"Yeah, but I don't think it's that bad. This has happened before, remember?"

"That day we were hunting for metal out by the abandoned warehouse," he murmurs.

We were fourteen, and someone had given his dad a used metal detector, which he'd passed along to Lennon. We were so positive we were going to get rich, finding hidden pirate gold. Our booty ended up being one vintage metal name tag that looked like it belonged to a waitress, an old quarter with a hole drilled in the middle, and a bent-up veterinarian syringe. All worthless. Lennon kept the name tag—the engraved name on it was "Dorothy"—and I kept the quarter.

Oh yeah, and I developed a superfast case of hives from overgrown dandelions.

"What about Benadryl?" he asks.

I nod. "Got plenty of that."

"Why don't you take the maximum dose," he suggests. "Like, now."

I do that, taking a couple extra pills just to be safe. The hives look ugly. I just had one of the best make-out sessions of my life, and now I'm a monster.

Screw you, universe. Screw you.

My sleeping bag is still rolled up, so I use it as a pillow, lying down on the floor of the tent. I try to concentrate on calming down, because stress will only make this worse. I'm vaguely cognizant of the "may cause drowsiness" effect of the antihistamines, which turns into "you bet your sweet ass these will cause drowsiness" when I double up on them, but the next thing I know, Lennon's waking me up, and I have a horrible neck cramp.

"Izzt morning?" I slur, utterly groggy.

"No, it's just past midnight. You've been snoring for about an hour."

"Good God."

He chuckles. "It was super cute. Not a loud snore. Your mouth was open."

I groan and stretch out my neck. "Stupid antihistamines."

Lennon lifts the hem of my shirt. "They're working, though. Hives are going down. Tired?"

"So tired," I whisper.

"The mountain lions are gone. Let's crash."

One step ahead of you, buddy.

But he doesn't let me fall back down on the tent floor. He gently urges me into the chilly night air, which makes me grumpy, until I see the magic he's working. He's managed to zip our sleeping bags together into one massive bag. They aren't quite the same size, so it's slightly askew and mismatched, but he rolls out his foam mat and arranges the merged super bag on top. He also makes a long pillow out of some of our clothes, covering them up with our now-dry camp towels.

He's a freaking camping genius.

And if I were more conscious and less addled, I'd like to show him how much I appreciate his skills by continuing where we left off before all the cougar screaming. But I can barely keep my eyes open. While he stows our packs in his tent, I climb into the double sleeping bag, shimmying out of my jeans once inside. And then he's slipping inside with me, warm and solid. We gravitate toward each other, and as I curl up against him, head on his chest, his arms around me, random thoughts pass through my head.

First: *This is heavenly.*

Second: *I don't want it to end.*

And the last thought, I say aloud. "The only way my dad will ever let me see you is if I confront him about his affair."

Lennon's response rumbles through my cheek after a long sigh. "I know."

"It's going to break up my parents."

"I would never wish that. Not in a million years. If my parents split up, I'm not sure I could handle it."

"What do we do, then?"

He runs his hand down my arm. "We'll figure something out. I promise. Stop worrying."

And I don't. I'm too tired. But somewhere in the back of my head, I know our time together is dwindling, and that once we get home, there's a chance everything will fall apart. I'll need to come up with a solid plan of action. Create some sort of mental safety bunker in case my world is destroyed.

All this time, I've thought my life would be easier if Lennon wasn't in it. I was half right. Now that he's back, things are a million times harder. I never realized "us" would be so complicated.

The next morning, we leave the camp sooner than expected.

I wake up to a cold sleeping bag and manage to track down Lennon outside, finding him dressed. He's also a ball of nervous energy. At first I fear that we still have a mountain lion problem, but he assures me they are long gone. There's something new to worry about.

A summer storm is coming. A big one. It's been brewing from the remnants of a tropical Pacific front off the coast of Southern California, and now it's gathered strength and is headed north.

If we're going to get to the star party, we need to make it

through Queen's Gap today—a narrow canyon passageway between two mountains. A river runs the length of it, and that river floods during storms. As in, floods the entire canyon.

"I talked to the ranger. He warned me that we can't get trapped in there," Lennon explains. "So we either need to hike through it before evening, or we need to stay here for another night. But there's a chance if we do that, it could be another day before the canyon is cleared for hiking."

"Are you sure we can get through it?"

"If the storm follows the track it's on, we should have no problem. But we need to leave soon. In the hour."

"Oh, wow."

"How are your hives?" He inspects my arms, pulling up my sleeves. "Not as scary, but still there."

"At least they're not itching all that bad at the moment." All I can do is keep an eye on them, manage them. Keep my stress level low and be proactive about medicating. I'm still groggy from the Benadryl, but I'll take a nondrowsy prescription antihistamine with breakfast. And there *is* breakfast, I see, because Lennon already has everything laid out, including the all-important coffee.

"I'm going to need that caffeine as soon as I get back from the restroom," I tell him. "As much as you can spare."

"I'll make it extra strong. It'll taste like burned sludge. Milkshake thick."

"I forgot how much I like you."

One side of his mouth twists up. "You'll like me better if I can get you to the star party without us being drowned in a storm, so hurry it up."

"Hurrying!"

We have to rush to eat and get our camp packed, which involves lining our backpacks with garbage bags in case of rain. Once we're ready, we head out of the campground with a few other wretched souls who are also up at the crack. It's not long before those hikers leave us for the Silver Trail. Our western path is much smaller. Smaller means no fellow hikers—good— but it also means that we're returning to the backcountry.

No posted signs, no bathrooms, no cell service.

We're on our own.

The morning fog wears off as we head toward a small chain of mountains covered in Ponderosa pines. And after a brisk uphill hike, the forest levels off and opens up to a river that snakes through a long canyon: Queen's Gap.

The canyon is fairly narrow and lush with ferns and moss. A slowly inclining trail on the right bank of the river is barely wide enough for two people to walk comfortably, and occasionally I fall behind to avoid running into overgrown brush. But it's worth all the hassle—the rough path, spiderwebs, and occasional low-hanging tree branches that nearly poke my eye out—because it's really spectacularly gorgeous here. The canyon river is babbling, creating a light mist where it dips down small hills of polished river rock, and unworldly ferns that cover the canyon floor seem to be growing larger and more luxuriant the farther we walk. It's an embarrassment of ferns. As if nature said, here, you deserve an extra helping.

We're making great time, and I'm glad to be away from guitar-playing campers and all their tempting grilled meats. I'm also glad to be alone with my thoughts. For once, instead of worrying about my parents or cataloging my plans for the day, I spend my hiking time in the canyon watching Lennon. Thinking about Lennon. In my head, I revisit our make-out session from the night before and throw some additional fantasies into the mix that are 50 percent dirtier.

But by midday, my energy wanes. Not even filthy thoughts can sustain me. I'm sore and tired, and I just want to drop on the ground and sleep. "I need to stop," I tell Lennon.

He glances at me, brows knitting together. "You all right?"

"Just tired."

"Me too, actually. Come here," he says, gesturing for me to come closer. "I want to check on your hives."

"You just want to gawk at my deformity," I tell him as he lifts the hem of my shirt to reveal a sliver of my stomach. The skin there is speckled with raised, pink bumps, but the bigger wheals are breaking up. "So sexy, right?"

"The sexiest," Lennon agrees, running the backs of his fingers over the puffy welts. "Itchy?"

"I'm not sure. It's hard to concentrate on feeling bad when you're feeling me up."

His lips curl at the corners. "Are you saying I've got magic hands, like Jesus?"

"Are you saying I'm a leper?"

He tugs the edge of my shirt back into place. "Totally. That's exactly what I'm saying. Please stay away from me and definitely don't kiss me."

"Got it."

"That was supposed to be reverse psychology."

"I know. I was just realizing something."

"Oh? What, pray tell?"

"You're the only person besides Joy who isn't afraid to touch my hives."

"They aren't contagious. And if you think a few splotches on your skin are going to stop me from touching you with my magic healing hands after what we did last night, think again."

"Good. I mean, uh . . ."

"It *was* pretty good, wasn't it?" he says.

Am I blushing? My ears feel hot. And a few other parts of my body.

We never did a lot of flirting last fall. It wasn't like this. We were friends in the daytime, make-out partners by night, and we managed both the secrecy of our relationship and this strange new world we were exploring together by keeping things separate.

Now there's a different energy. A thrilling kind of tension.

I know I'm not the only one feeling this new energy between

us. I've caught him sneaking glances at me out of the corner of his eyes, as if he's trying to measure me. Study me. It's exciting and maddening, and I feel as if I might have a heart attack if something doesn't give soon.

There's that smile again. "Anyhoo, your hives look a shit-ton better than last night, but you don't need to overtax your body."

"Is that your scientific opinion, Dr. Mackenzie?" Okay, maybe I have a *little* more energy for filthy thoughts. Definitely willing to overtax my body if he's going to help.

"Gordon told me they had to airlift a guy out of here with hives last summer."

"Gordon?" It takes my brain a second to crawl out of the gutter and realize it's the Jamaican man from the camp last night.

"We chatted this morning."

"Look at you, being all non-antisocial."

Lennon rolls his eyes humorously and continues. "Gordon said that apparently this hiker, he'd never even had hives before, or not in a big way. But he was mildly allergic to peanuts, and even though he could have them in small quantities from time to time, he ate a bunch of candy with nuts while climbing. And that, combined with exhaustion . . . His throat swelled up so much, he lost consciousness."

Angioedema. That's when your face swells up like a balloon. A lot of people with chronic hives have it. Luckily, I've managed to avoid it.

And I hear what Lennon's saying, but I'm more concerned

about the source of the airlift story. "You told Gordon about my hives?"

"He camps here a lot, and I was just trying to find out if he knew what kind of grass was on that hill. It's velvet grass and oxeye daisies, by the way."

"Ooh, *yeah*. That oxeye daisy weed is on my no-fly list. High-risk allergen."

He gives me a look that says *there you go*.

"And I'm sorry about that idiot hiker who decided to gorge on Snickers bars while climbing, but I'm not allergic to nuts," I say. "I mean, God. Can you imagine a world without peanuts?"

Lennon's mouth twists humorously. "The horror. You may not be allergic to peanuts, but look at all the other stuff that sets you off." He ticks off a list on his fingers. "Stress, daisies, shrimp that Sunny cooks—"

"Bad shrimp," I murmur cheerfully.

"Bad shrimp," he repeats in Sunny's voice. "Oh, and there was mean old Mr. McCrory's dog. Remember? He licked your hand and five minutes later . . ."

"That was just bizarre. I'm not allergic to Andromeda's kisses. How was I supposed to know his hellhound's saliva was poison?"

"Maybe it had been chomping on daisies."

"Or shrimp."

"You're an anomaly, Zorie Everhart."

"I am nothing if not an original."

"Well, OG, let's feed your hive-ridden body some lunch, so

we can get through this canyon before the storm hits."

After finding a good place to sit, we eat a quick meal out of our bear canisters, and when we hit the trail again, my body isn't hurting like it was earlier. Either the break helped, or the extra meds, or maybe I'm just getting used to hiking. Whatever the case, I'm able to get into a comfortable groove. Just one foot in front of the next, watching my surroundings, and breathing.

Clear head, steady steps. Moving forward.

We take a second break in the afternoon, and that's when I start to feel the change in the air. A different scent. Sweet, almost. It's sharp and fresh, and it's carried on winds that are picking up.

Lennon looks toward the sky. "See those? Cumulus clouds. They'll start stacking up to make cloud towers. That's when the rain's coming."

"Uh-oh."

He checks the GPS on his phone. "We're almost out of the—ah, crap. Phone died. Let me see yours."

I dig out my phone, but the battery's dead too. Crap. I can't text my mom. Surely she'll understand and chalk it up to no cell service.

He stares at the black screen for a long moment before handing it back. "Doesn't matter. I know where we are. We'll be out of the canyon in a half hour or less. Are you okay to keep walking?"

"If it means not getting wet, then hell yeah. Let's march."

We walk briskly for several minutes, but the winds are really whipping through the canyon now. Enough to blow my hair in my face. Lennon keeps looking up. I think it's getting darker. I'm sort of wishing I had asked him for more information about the storm. This isn't like me *at all*, but I'd been concentrating on the knowledge that we needed to get through the canyon without being eaten alive by mosquitoes. I didn't think about what would happen after. And this storm isn't going to give us a pass for winning. Like: *You guys made it through? Great job! I won't rain on you.*

What do we do when it rains?

"Am I good, or am I freaking fantastic?" he says, several paces ahead of me.

When I catch up to him, cresting a hill, I see what he's seeing.

A shady forest filled with giant trees.

23

The canyon's arms open up and deliver us straight into it, the river arrowing down the center.

"Majestic Grove," Lennon says, stopping to look up at the enormous trunks. "Giant sequoias. World's largest trees. Many of these beauties are a thousand years old. The redwoods on the coast can get taller, but these here in the Sierras are bigger."

I've seen coastal redwoods around the observatory at home, but I've never seen an entire forest of giant trees. Some of them here are as big around as a car and they nearly block out the sky. And the canyon ferns we've been walking through have nothing on these. They create a pale green carpet on the forest floor, and their fronds are so large, it's as if they're in competition with the sequoias to see who can grow bigger.

"It looks prehistoric," I murmur.

"Endor Forest scenes with the ewoks in *Return of the Jedi* were filmed in the Bay Area in a forest like this. So cool, right?"

"It's stunning," I say as we enter the ancient forest, craning my neck up at the gargantuan trunks. The ground is spongy, and it smells strange here, like an outdoor library—musty. A good kind of musty. And it's quiet. Which is odd, because the canyon was filled with the sounds of singing birds and the echo of the river off the rocky canyon walls. The water is still flowing here, but it's a softer babble, absorbed by the great trees.

I walk up to a sequoia and run my hand over soft, corrugated bark, marveling, and then stretch out my arms and try to hug it. "How many people would it take to reach all the way around?"

"Too many." Lennon stands near me and stretches his arms around the tree, too. We don't even make it a quarter of the way around together.

"I love this place," I say, and mean it.

"It's my favorite part of the park," he says, eyes sparkling. "My cathedral."

I understand why.

He points to our left. "There's a bigger trail that runs along the northern edge of the sequoias, several miles from here. No one comes down this way. It's secluded. From man and beast. The trees block out the sunlight, so there's less food for animals. Fewer insects for birds, so it's quieter."

"No mosquitoes."

"Fewer mosquitoes," he corrects.

"I'll take it. Any improvement is a good thing," I say, looking around. "This is surreal. I wish we could stay here."

"We can," he says. "This is where we're camping."

"Tonight?"

"Right now. We're stopping early."

"Really?"

"Truly. Reason one being that I love it here. I know it might sound weird, because it's so dark in here, but it's sort of my happy place. And when I first found it, one of the things I thought was that I wished you could be here to share it with me."

I look into his face and my heart melts.

"Now you can," he says, softer.

Thunder booms in the distance.

Lennon points upward. "And that right there is the second reason. That storm is going to be fierce, and we need to find a place to make camp. Let's get a little farther away from the canyon and find a good spot. Hurry."

There's not a trail here, so we have to pick our way around the trees and ferns as we follow the river and make our way deeper into the sequoias. The thunder's getting louder, which scares me, but every time I find a clear spot big enough to accommodate our tents, Lennon glances up and shakes his head.

"Why?" I finally say in frustration after the third rejection. "It's close to the river, but not too close. It's flat, it's—"

"There," he says, pointing to another spot. It looks the same as this one, basically. Maybe a little more room. I'm tired of looking, so I follow him and am relieved to stop and dump my pack on the ground.

He's looking up into the canopy. "Yes, this should be okay. We'll build the tents close to these two trees. They're half the height of the others around us." He's already unzipping his backpack, fishing out his tent as lightning flashes above the trees. He stills, listening.

Thunder booms in the distance.

"Fifteen seconds," he says. "Five seconds per mile. That storm is three miles away."

"Is that bad?"

"These trees will offer protection, but they're also tall, and tall attracts lightning. That's why I wanted to build under shorter ones"—he gestures between the two trees flanking our tents— "so that the taller surrounding trees would absorb any strikes. This isn't like a storm at home. People get hit by lightning out here and die."

"Everyone dies out here," I complain. "It's practically a tragedy."

His lips tilt upward. "I know, right?"

"But—"

"Build tent, talk later," he says, unsheathing his tent pieces.

I rush to get mine out, and by the time I do, he's already got his tent erected. I start to lay out my floor next to his, as we've been doing, but he shakes his head. "Let's build them door to door, facing each other."

I don't ask why, but just trust that he has a plan while he checks something on my tent and measures out space, showing me where to start. Wind is whipping through the forest pretty fast, and the sky is so dark, it's almost as if night's fallen beneath the tree canopy. I get the tent in place and fit all my poles together, but we have the extra step of securing rainflies on top. It seems to take forever, and I'm trying to rush to stake my tent down before it blows away. Lennon finishes his and helps me erect the small vestibule awning that extends over my front door. He's measured accurately, so apart from a tiny crack, it covers the space between the two tents, a tiny covered passageway.

He hauls our packs into his tent, minus our sleeping gear. "I'll get everything set up inside the big tent," he tells me. "You fill up our water bottles. Mine's almost empty, and we'll need it for cooking. Don't leave my line of sight, and hurry."

Thunder rumbles. I grab the water bottles and Lennon's water filter, which is faster than mine. There's a tiny path to the river that snakes between a pair of giant ferns. The water is running swiftly here, and though I could probably cross the river in a dozen steps, it looks deep. I bend by the water, careful that I have decent footing, and begin pumping water through the filter.

As the first Nalgene bottle fills, thunder rumbles. I mentally count the seconds and watch the trees. *One, two, three, four, five—*

Lightning flashes.

Five seconds. That strike was a mile away?

"Hurry!" Lennon's voice calls out from the campsite, making me jump.

"I can't make the water filter any faster," I mumble to myself.

Finally, the first bottle fills. I cap it and get the filter into the second one, then start pumping.

I feel something on my head. Is that a raindrop? I slant my face upward. Definitely a raindrop. Two. Four. Twenty. It seems silly to be so concerned with collecting water when it's about to fall all over us.

Thunder booms so loud, it's deafening. But almost immediately, the sky lights up. And just like that, the rain comes down. Hard. I hear Lennon calling my name, but I'm trying to concentrate. "Shit, shit, shit!" I say, pumping faster.

But not fast enough.

The entire forest lights up with the loudest bang I've ever heard.

I lunge away from the river. The second bottle falls into the rapids, along with the pump filter. I'm disoriented for a moment, unable to hear anything. The bottle bobs and disappears under the foam. I start to run after it, but a stony hand grabs my arm.

"Leave it!" Lennon shouts, dragging me away from the river.

He grabs my hand, and I can tell by how hard he jerks me down the path through the ferns that he's not fooling around. We're in trouble.

My heart hammers as I race after him in the rain, the green scent of sorrel and moss rising up from the soles of my shoes. And I smell something else, too: like Christmas on fire. The lightning. It singed the treetops.

That scent terrifies me.

I scramble across slick, springy ground, and our tents pop into view. Before we can make it there, lightning strikes again. For the first time in my life, I truly get the whole Zeus-throwing-bolts thing, because that's what it looks like. As though an angry god is zapping Earth with a giant laser gun. It sounds like a bomb, and shakes the entire ground. Shrubs, these enormous trees, us— everything.

I think I'm going to wet my pants in fear.

My mind has flipped off. I want to cry, but I'm too scared. I'm nothing but blind terror and am wholeheartedly convinced I'm going to die.

All these giant trees, and yet there's nothing here to protect us. No shelter. No door to close and hide behind. No car in which to outrun the storm. And it makes me feel small and helpless.

Right before we make it to the tents, Lennon pulls me down on the ground and crouches over me.

Boom!

My world goes white.

I'm squatting in something that's neither dirt nor mud, soaked to the bone, and the rain is driving down on us while burning wood fills my nostrils. It feels as if it will never end. *Just kill us*, I think. Go on, get it over with.

Lennon's muscles are steel when the next strike comes. But I feel him jump, too. It's as if we're in the middle of a war zone. Seconds later, another strike hits.

But.

This one isn't as loud. Or as close. The thunder and lightning are separating again. We wait—for seconds or minutes, I don't even know. But at some point, the world doesn't feel like it's falling apart around us, and Lennon's body loosens.

Is it over? I still hear thunder in the distance.

"We're all right," Lennon's voice is saying in my ear. "Told you it was a big storm, didn't I? And listen to that. It's moving more slowly now. I'm still counting thunder. Slow means a lot of rain, but we're out of the lighting zone for now. Come on, let's get up."

He pulls me to my feet, and I can't see. "My glasses," I say.

Lennon looks around. "You lost them somewhere."

"I lost the water bottles, too."

"One's on the riverbank. We'll get it later. And we have another filter. Worse comes to worst, we'll boil water."

And I can live without glasses for a couple of days. I'm too numb to worry.

He lifts up my chin. "It's all good. You okay?"

"Yeah," I say, nodding.

"That was intense."

"That was . . ." I laugh. I can't help it. I'm not sure if it's nervous laughter or just a release, but I'm pushing wet hair out of my face and laughing. "We just nearly got blown out of our shoes. We almost died."

"No, Zorie, we just *lived*." Lennon lifts up both arms and pumps victory fists, yowling. "We're alive! We won!"

He's right. We did live. Survival is a beautiful thing. I laugh again and hold up my dirty hands, letting them fill with rain until the mud washes away. Adrenaline is still coursing through my veins, and I feel invincible.

Lennon shoves dark hair out of his eyes. His clothes stick to him, clinging to his shape. Every sharp plane. Every muscle. It's practically X-rated. Or maybe that's *exactly* what it is, because I blink away rain and see his gaze roaming over me too. And there's nothing polite about the way he's looking at me.

Maybe the storm broke something in both of our brains.

I inhale sharply. He makes a low noise in the back of his throat.

Our gazes lock.

We both pounce on each other at the same time.

He pulls me against him, one arm slung around my shoulders, his other hand cupping the back of my head. His rain-slick clothes are cold, but his mouth is hot on mine. He kisses me hard. It's an impatient, greedy kiss. Ravenous. And when thunder rumbles in the distance, I jump a little, but I don't let go.

My back hits the smooth, wet bark of a sequoia, and he presses himself against the length of me. He's taut and solid, a brick wall of lean muscle, lifting me up until my toes skim the tree's bumpy roots. And when he pushes his hips against mine, I push back, feeling unmistakable hardness between us. A thrill zips through me.

My legs wrap around his hips, and he's holding me in place against the tree, pinning me as he warms my neck with kisses. I smell his hair and the scent of sequoia bark, and the rain is coming down so hard, my grip around his shoulders is slipping. I throw both arms around his neck and cling.

"Tent," he says into my ear. I'm not sure if it's a question or a statement, but I'm telling him yes. And he tells me to hold on, but I think if I hold him any tighter, I'm going to break bones. My back leaves the tree, and he's carrying me several steps. We slide in the mud, and when he sloppily sets me down in front of the tents, I'm clutching so hard, I nearly pull us both down. His head bashes into mine.

"Oww!"

We're both laughing, and I feel a little delirious. "We're drenched," I say.

He pushes wet curls away from my face. "Yeah."

"The sleeping gear's going to get wet."

"Maybe we should just, I don't know"—he shrugs slowly—"get out of these clothes before we go in."

My pulse pounds in my ears.

Naked.

Lennon.

Me.

Us.

"That would be the practical thing to do," I agree, trying to sound casual.

But this is *so* not casual. And we both know it.

We lunge for each other, and he's stripping off my shirt. My arms are tangled, and he's laughing, trying to peel away the wet fabric. It gives, and his arm flies back. My shirt hits the tent with a loud slap.

Lennon pauses for a moment, looking me over, a slow smile lifting his cheeks. "Are we doing this?" He sounds dazed.

I'm a little embarrassed, but not enough to stop. "Oh, we're doing this."

Shoes and socks are dropped in the mud. And then I get his shirt off, and we're both attacking each other's jeans as if they'll self-destruct if we don't get them off fast enough. And oh, okay, wet boxer shorts are *definitely* pornographic. I CAN SEE EVERYTHING, and I can't stop looking—I don't even care that I'm shivering in my bra and panties in the middle of the woods.

"Wait, wait, wait." I put a hand on his chest. My mouth moves faster than my brain. "You can't get me pregnant," I tell him firmly.

Lennon's face contorts as several expressions flash. "That's something a guy never thinks he's going to hear."

"I mean, I'm sure you *could*, which is the problem. I just didn't plan for this. That's what I meant." *Ugh, idiot*, I think, suddenly self-conscious. I was thinking of what happened with Andre, and how stupid we were. And now I'm making assumptions, because we're getting naked. Should I not be making assumptions? I'm completely rattled now.

"Forget it," I say.

When he opens his mouth to respond, he pauses and then says, "Hold on."

He dives under the short canopy connecting the tents and unzips the door to his tent, disappearing. I don't know what to do. I'm standing in the rain, half-naked and humiliated, and—

Lennon emerges. He crawls under the canopy to the big tent, unzips the door, and throws our camp towels inside. Then he holds up a long line of shiny metallic condom packages to show me before tossing them inside the tent, too. "You may not have planned, but I did," he says, smiling. "Boy Scout motto. Be prepared."

"Good God." How many of those are there?

"Call it hopeful thinking. I guess I didn't learn anything after the hotel-room fiasco. And, you know, one good thing about Toys in the Attic is an endless supply of free condoms. Come here."

Heart racing, I duck beneath the canopy, taking his offered hand, and quickly crawl inside the double tent. It's dim inside, and it smells strongly of nylon and rain. I'm acutely aware of how cramped the space is, and how long Lennon's legs are. How much bare skin is on display, both his and mine. Those pornographic boxers—DO NOT LOOK.

Too late. Guess he's not anxious.

But all of the sudden I am. So, *so* anxious. Why?

I glance down at myself and see all my hives on display. That doesn't help. I hope it's dark enough that he can't see them, too, and quickly move my arm to cover my stomach.

"Hey," Lennon says in a soft voice, pulling my hand away from my stomach and threading his fingers through mine. "It's only me."

"*Only?*" I shake my head. "That's the problem. It's you. And me. And I just got you back. We don't even have a plan yet for what's going to happen when we go home. Everything could fall apart. My parents could divorce. I could be forced to move in with my dad—"

"Or things could work out just fine."

"That's the problem, though. Life is unpredictable, which is the worst part about it. I need dependable. I need something I can count on. And if this is terrible or weird, then—"

"Then what? How terrible could it be? I'm pretty sure I understand the basics."

"It's easier for you. You're a guy. Your body isn't a mystery."

He considers this for a moment. "I like mysteries. I'm very good at solving mysteries."

I hesitate. "How good?"

"Very, *very* good. I will not rest until a mystery is solved. I'm Nancy fucking Drew."

My chuckle is breathy. "Oh?"

"Remember Mr. Henry's missing tabby? Who figured out it had been catnapped by the white supremacist at the end of the cul-de-sac?"

"You did. Stop making me laugh."

Eyes merry, he opens a camp towel and crooks a finger. I lean forward and let him dry my hair. "And who discovered that the hair salon was siphoning electricity off of the Jitterbug after the manager kept complaining about her electricity bill?"

"You did," I murmur, head bowed. His hands feel good on my hair, and it's giving me a really good view of his chest and arms. "Wait, we both solved that mystery. I'm the one who first said someone could be stealing their electricity."

"But who looked up online how to do it and traced it back to the salon? Who made you sit in the alley and be my lookout while I checked the meters, and then you yelled at me because I wouldn't let you get coffee until we were finished?"

"I didn't yell at you."

"You totally did," he says, pulling the towel away and quickly rubbing it over his own wet hair until it stands up. "And it made me furious. And *that* was the first time I really wanted to kiss you."

"Wait, no. That couldn't be. We were . . ."

"Fourteen."

"You wanted to kiss me when we were fourteen?"

"I wanted to do lots of things to you when we were fourteen. Fifteen. Sixteen. By the time you kissed me, I'd built a Zorie vault of sexual fantasies bigger than Fort Knox. I thought you'd never catch up to me."

My voice fails. I'm stunned, trying to fit all of these confessions into my memories of what we were.

What we are now.

"And I know you hate my parents' shop, and sometimes I do too," he says, tossing the towel into the corner of the tent. "But other times, it has its advantages."

"Besides the free condoms?"

"Besides that," he says, a sly smile lifting his lips. "You'd be surprised what I've learned. Customers are surprisingly specific, and you would not believe the shit they tell you. Anything you can imagine that could go wrong—or right—someone else has probably had that happen to them, too."

"Um . . ."

"What I'm saying is, all bodies are weird. Throw whatever mystery you have at me. Let me help you solve it."

"It's not that I can't solve it by myself. I just want to make that clear."

"This is the best conversation we've ever had, by the way. And I'm definitely adding an image of you solving your own mysteries to the ol' vault for later—"

"Oh my God," I murmur, mildly horrified.

"But right now, wouldn't it be more fun to team up and solve crime together?"

"I'm worried it could be bad or awkward," I say in a small voice.

"I've worried about that too," he says, running the backs of his fingers along my shoulder, down my arm, following the path he's tracing with his eyes. "This isn't nothing. This isn't not serious. It's big. It's epic."

"It's you and me," I say.

He nods. "But after last night out on that hill, and then just now, out there?"

"We're so good together," I agree, opening my hand when he runs his finger over my knuckles. "Right?"

"We are goddamn amazing. We're a rocket ship filled with potential. Either we die in a fiery blaze before we leave the Earth's atmosphere, or we make it through and orbit the moon."

"If you're trying to seduce me with space stuff, it's totally working."

His smile is divine. "Yeah?"

"Yeah."

"Do you want to try?"

I nod slowly. "I think so."

"You sure?"

Yeah. I actually am. "Fly me to the moon."

Rain drums against the tent as he pulls me closer, and we sink into the sleeping bags. Mouth on mouth, hip on hip, heartbeat on heartbeat. We're less desperate than we were outside, more aware of each other. It's a fervent awareness, both nervous and thrilling, and when we remove the last layers of our clothes, he steadily talks to me in a calm, low voice, and I follow it like a lighthouse beacon.

He guides. Assures. Makes sure I don't veer off into dark waters and crash.

Then it's my turn to navigate. He listens. Follows directions. Uses my instructions to create a new path.

It's a brave new world.

And an all-consuming one. I'm ready to chuck everything

I've learned out the window, because he can't find the condoms, and I don't even care, and I definitely *should,* but I'm willing to give up my entire civilized existence and live in this tent like homeless hippies if he will just—

"They were right here!" He's about to have a panic attack.

"Wait, what's this?" I pull something out from under my back.

"Thank you, thank you, thank you," he murmurs.

"Hurry."

"No, don't say that. Believe me, I'm hanging on by a thread here."

"Please?" I whisper.

"You're killing me, Zorie."

Every time he says my name in that rumbling voice of his, I think I might die myself. I'm in pleasure overload, here, on the verge of something great, and I really, *really* don't want him to stop. But then . . . it's happening. It's actually happening. It's good, and a little awkward, and sometimes funny, because wow, human bodies *are* weird. But it's also more than I expected— than I even hoped.

It's all of him and all of me, and most of all, it's us, it's us, *it's us.*

24

"Told you I'd solve that mystery," Lennon says after we've been tangled up in each other's arms for a while, listening to the slowing rain outside. "Twice."

I smile against his chest. "I never doubted. You're Nancy goddamn Drew, after all."

"And you're Sherlock fucking Holmes."

"If we start our own detective agency, I want both of those names painted on the door, just like that."

"My parents should have named their shop 'The Detective Agency.'"

I chuckle and he pretends to bite my neck, and that makes me squeal. He just holds me tighter. Fine by me, because I can't stop touching him. The stubble on his jaw. His heavy eyebrows. The curving ridge of muscle above his hips. I've never been so close to him, and there's so much begging to be explored.

But when my stomach growls, we both realize how late it

is. Not *exactly* how late, because both our phones are dead, and Lennon's fancy compass—our only source of time—is currently sitting inside the pocket of his jeans, buried in mud outside the tent. But we've been at this detectiving for a while now, and I'm in need of things that are stashed in the other tent. Like food. Wet wipes. Dry clothes. Okay, maybe I'm not in a hurry for those, but when Lennon volunteers to crawl beneath the canopy to the smaller tent, I add that to the list, and he bravely extricates himself from our sleeping bag.

The other tent is only a few feet away, and it's silly, but I hate for him to go that far. As I tie back the mesh flaps of our door to open it up, the sight of him crawling naked into the second tent's entrance has my complete attention. "That's an interesting view," I tell him from the open door of our tent.

"I aim to please," he calls back.

He has to make two trips, and between them, ducks outside into the rain for a couple of minutes. Naked Lennon in the woods. Now would be a good time for a photo. But when he comes back, he has one of our water bottles, which he hands to me through the door, shivering, and dives back into the other tent. This time, he emerges wearing boxers and tosses me a T-shirt. He's also raided our food stash, hallelujah!

Lying on our stomachs with our heads sticking outside the door flap, we set up the one-burner camping stove under the canopy. The stove is just a tiny bottle of fuel with four prongs that unfold above it to hold a pan. We heat up water for hot cocoa, which is inside two brown packs of military MREs that Lennon brought. There are also a million other things in each ration bag: a pastry bar, crackers, dried fruit, and holiest of holies, a packet of peanut butter.

"I thought you might like that," Lennon says with a smile as we look through the contents of the meal packs. There are spoons, napkins, matches, and even a tiny bottle of Tabasco and some candy. The entrée gets heated up inside a flameless heater bag that needs to be filled with a little water to activate the heating element. It doesn't taste quite as good as Reagan's gourmet freeze-dried camp meals, but I'm starving, and the peanut butter and crackers make up for everything.

After we've eaten and cleaned up, Lennon breaks out his journal and maps, and I lie on my side, watching him recalculate the last leg of our trip to Condor Peak. "Six hours of walking," he says. "Maybe seven with long breaks."

"That's not too bad."

"Nope."

"Huh. I thought it would be farther." We both look at the map that's unfolded atop his journal. "You sure you want to go to the star party with me?"

"Why wouldn't I?"

"It'll be a lot of people I don't know, and some people I see at club meetings every month."

"And Avani."

"I'll need to use her telescope to take decent photos, and setting them up takes a lot of time. It could be boring for you, just standing around while the rest of us star nerds look through lenses and try to get face time with Sandra Faber."

"I don't know who that is, but I'm assuming from that quiver in your voice that she's someone important."

"She only has an astronomical law named after her and figured out how to estimate the distance between galaxies. No big deal."

He grins. "Impressive."

"Anyway, I'm just saying that you might hate the star party."

"Don't worry, I won't be bored. I'll be with you. Besides, I'm interested in whatever you like."

"Yeah?"

"Meteor showers are cool. You can take lots of cool pictures and talk galaxies," he says. "And whenever you're ready to leave, we head back to civilization. Avani's not our only option for transportation."

"A regular bus runs up there several times a day," I confirm. "I know from my research."

"I've got a park bus schedule in here somewhere," he says, rummaging through a pile of papers stuck between the pages of his journal. "It's from last year, but I doubt much has changed."

As he's looking for it, something catches my eye in his journal, and I stick my fingers on the corner of the page to stop him from flipping. "What's this?"

"Ugh, don't look," he says, covering it with his hand.

"Why?"

"Because it's embarrassing."

"Well, *now* I'm going to just forget it," I tease, tugging his fingertips. "Show me."

He groans, but releases the page. I peer over his arm and see drawings of people. They look like anime characters, a bit stylized, with simple, clean lines and big eyes. It takes me a moment to realize they're all girls. The same girl. Repeated over and over, from different viewpoints. Sitting at a desk, bent over schoolwork. Eating at a picnic table. Reading on the stairs. Drinking coffee at a café. They're mostly drawn from behind her, so there's only a partial view of her face, but . . .

But . . .

She has dark, curly hair and glasses, and she's wearing plaid.

I slowly turn the page to find more drawings. The same girl, drawn dozens of times. Each one is dated in Lennon's careful, neat handwriting. They go back to last fall. Last spring. Early this summer.

The newest one is from last week. The girl is standing on a balcony, looking down with a telescope.

The drawings are flattering. The drawings are sad. The drawings are filled with longing. Lennon's heart on the page.

Tenderness and pain rise to my throat. It's a bittersweet pain, one that's tarnished by how awful this year has been for both of us. I tried so hard and for so long to push all my feelings for him away, to tamp them down into a tiny box and hide it somewhere dark in my mind. I did everything I could to forget.

And Lennon did all he could to remember.

Tears drop off my cheek onto the page, splattering. I try to wipe it away with my finger, but the ink bleeds.

"I'm sorry," I whisper. "They're beautiful and I ruined them."

He shuts the journal and tugs me closer to swipe tears from my cheek with his thumb. "It's okay," he murmurs, kissing my eyelids. "I don't need them anymore. I have you."

The next day, I beg him for one more day in our sequoia cathedral. We'll have plenty of time to get to the star party's final night, which is the best time to see the meteor shower anyway. Our phones are dead, so I can't tell Avani to expect us a day late, but what does it matter? She'll still be there. And likely she'll be so busy enjoying the star party, she won't even notice. The only thing I see as a potential problem is Mom, because I *did* promise I'd text when I arrived at the star party. But I also told her we'd be getting there late tonight, and what difference would one day make? Besides, I'm hiking, not taking a scheduled bus. Surely, she'll understand that this isn't an exact science. I can call her from Avani's phone the minute we get to Condor Peak tomorrow.

I argue all of this to Lennon, but frankly, I didn't need to convince him. He is completely agreeable, and we stay put.

The storm has passed, so we spend the day doing practical things. Washing mud out of our clothes in the river. Collecting firewood and putting it in the sun to dry. Finding my glasses.

We also spend it doing impractical things. Bathing in the river together. (Less bathing, more touching.) Reading the manga book Lennon brought in his backpack. (Less reading, more touching.) Taking a nap. (Less sleeping, more sex that nearly permanently blinds Lennon when a tent pole snaps.)

My hives are still there, but I'm not clawing at my arms as much. Partly because I'm keeping up with medicating, and partly because I caved and let Lennon slather me in Miss Angela's stinky sativa salve. I don't think I've ever been so relaxed—sexlaxation, Lennon dubs it, and says he'll make a fortune marketing it as a cure for allergies and stress.

But all good things must come to an end, and when we run out of condoms, we know it's time to go.

Goodbye, sex camp.

As we're packing everything up, I check to make sure my camera is still working, and it strikes me that I haven't taken one single photo on this trip. It's not just that. I haven't obsessively checked my messages or my social media feeds. I don't know what's trending, and I haven't posted anything. I can't check views or likes or favorites or reblogs. And I have no idea what's going on in the news.

"We disconnected," I tell Lennon.

"I know. Isn't it great?"

It actually is. Maybe I wouldn't want to do it forever, but I didn't die, either.

We've waited as long as we can, leaving well after lunch. My pack feels heavier, somehow, even though there's exactly the same amount of things inside. I think it's as reluctant to leave as I am.

But it's time to go.

We walk through a string of meadows all afternoon and have dinner near a lake that's one of the largest alpine bodies of water in the state. We're well above five thousand feet, so the water's too cold for swimming, but it's a calming view. Not as calming as sexlaxation, I point out. Lennon triple-checks: We're definitely out of condoms.

When we're back on the trail again, my mind starts wheeling. We haven't discussed what we're going to do about my father when we get back home. Or anything about the future. I don't want to think about it. I want to stay here. This is impossible, and I know it, but when I start thinking about what awaits us—parents, school, the so-called friends who abandoned us, the looming threat of my dad's affair . . . all of this creates doubt in my head. Doubt, worry, and a growing sense of dread.

The sun sets during the final stretch of the hike up the foothills. We've connected up to a major trail with official park signs informing distances to several nearby attractions. Condor Peak is outside King's Forest in a state-maintained area. There are several scenic points on and around the mountain, but the one we're headed to, the Northern Viewpoint, is right in front of us, point-five kilometers. The star party is gathered at a small campground below it, just across a road that borders the national park.

An actual road. With actual cars whizzing down it.

I never thought I'd be reluctant to return to civilization.

All my misgivings move to the back of my mind when we spy a big sign for the star party posted at the entrance to a parking lot connected to a small campground. The sign warns the public that they are approaching a protected Dark Sky area, and nothing but red lights are allowed past the campground, to avoid light pollution. The actual viewing area is a quarter mile up a short path that curves around the mountain. Even small amounts of white light are objectionable to astronomers, and many of the cars and RVs here have red tape adhered to their headlights. I'm prepared for this, and have brought along a small red penlight.

"Whoa," Lennon says. "Lots of people. This is a big viewing party, huh?"

Bigger than I expected. "Maybe we should see if Avani is down here before we go up to the viewing area. The meteors won't be fully visible for another half hour, at least, so we still have some time."

We walk through the parking lot, and it's jammed with cars. Overflow is parking on the side of the road. People are hauling telescope cases out of their cars—some professional, some not. Several families are here with small children. I try to spot anyone from my club, but it's dark, and the lot is chaotic.

A cedar split-rail fence divides the parking lot and campground. It's half the size of the one we stayed in three nights ago, and the individual campsites are all crammed together. It seems to be mostly RVs. A sign we pass as we enter says that it's at capacity.

We walk along the main road circling through the campground, and get only halfway around when someone comes barreling toward us, arms waving.

"Zorie!" It's Avani, and she slows just in time to throw her arms around my neck. "You're alive."

"Of course I'm alive," I say. "Sorry we're a day late."

Avani pulls away to blink at Lennon with wide eyes. "Whoa. You're really here. I mean, hey, Lennon. It's just weird to see you together again. But good!"

"It's good to see you too," Lennon says, mouth quirking up. He gives her a quick hug, and I'm reminded that they've spent more time interacting at school over the last year than I have with either one of them.

Avani is breathless, glancing back and forth between us. When she catches her breath, her brow furrows. "Look, I'm so, *so* sorry."

I squint at her. "About what?"

"I didn't have a choice. I never would have said anything, but he insisted."

What is she talking about?

"It's bad," she says, face twisting. "I feel like it's all my fault."

"Slow down and tell us what happened," Lennon says.

Avani glances over her shoulder. "From what I've been told, Reagan's mom called your mom, Zorie. And that's how it all started."

Oh, God. No, no, no . . .

"Reagan's dad got sick," she says, "and they couldn't fly to Switzerland, and then apparently Reagan came home with Brett, and she was supposed to be at that glamping thing with you. But you guys got kicked out?"

My stomach is turning to stone.

"It was Brett's fault," Lennon says.

"Oh," she says, distracted for a moment before shaking her head. "So, anyway, your dad called Dr. Viramontes yesterday, looking for you."

"What?" I say, alarmed.

She nods. "Your dad was really upset, and he said he and your mom had tried to get in touch with you, but you weren't answering texts—"

"Our phones died," I argue, but all I'm thinking about is that phone conversation with Mom at the ranger station three days ago. She knew!

"—and I guess the last time your mom had heard from you, you told her you'd be here at the star party yesterday, so he was freaking out. And Dr. Viramontes asked me if I knew anything, because your dad was going to call the police and file a missing persons report. And so . . ." She squeezes her eyes shut. "I told him what you texted me a couple days ago. That you were hiking here with Lennon. That you were supposed to arrive yesterday."

"Oh, God," I mumble.

"Dr. Viramontes called your dad back and told him. And he assured your dad that we would call when you guys got here. But you didn't show up last night—"

"We were just running late!" I say, exasperated.

She nods, glancing at Lennon, who is biting out filthy curses under his breath.

"What happened?" I ask.

"I just overheard a few things," she says. "Your dad is loud when he's angry. He was saying stuff about the Mackenzies, and how they allowed Lennon to kidnap you."

"What?" I say, pressing my hands against my temples.

"And I tried to butt in and defend you, Lennon," she says, glancing over her shoulder again. "But Mr. Everhart is . . . well, he yelled at me, and accused me of aiding and abetting—"

"Oh, for the love of Pete," I say. "Wait, wait, wait. You said you overheard . . . you said he yelled at you. On the phone?"

Avani bites her lip and shakes her head. "I'm so sorry, Zorie. I texted and called to warn you a couple hours ago, but you didn't answer."

And that's when I look in the direction she's been glancing. The door to an RV swings open, and three people file outside. Dr. Viramontes is the first. And behind him are my parents.

25

"Zorie!" my mom shouts from across the campsite, relief in her voice. She rushes ahead of the men and throws her arms around me. "You're all right."

"Mom . . . ," I say, hoping the right words will come out, but I'm stuck between her concern and the shit storm that's approaching.

She pulls back and holds my face. "You're fine."

"I'm fine."

She moves one of her hands to Lennon's face. "You're okay too?"

He nods. His expression is taut.

"What in God's name is going on?" my father roars over my mother's shoulder. He's not talking to me. He doesn't even give me anything but a cursory look. His eyes are on Lennon, and he pushes my mom aside to get in Lennon's face. "You snatch my daughter away and take her into the woods?"

"I didn't snatch anything," Lennon says, eyes narrowing.

"I asked him to take me," I tell my dad. "Reagan left us. She was our transportation home. And Lennon knows the park—"

"I don't give a damn," my dad says. "Reagan came home five days ago. Five days! You've been alone in the wilderness with my daughter—*my daughter*," he shouts at Lennon.

"Dan," my mom says, trying to pull him away from Lennon.

Dr. Viramontes clears his throat. "Zorie, I'm glad to see you and Mr. Mackenzie are well."

"There was never anything to worry about," I say, giving him a tight smile. "I'm sorry you were dragged into this."

He shakes his head. "I'm just glad you're all right. I invited you here, so I feel responsible."

"Damn right, you're responsible," my dad snaps. "These are underage kids."

"I find that most of our club members are smart, self-aware individuals who don't need a babysitter."

My dad snorts. "Then you're obviously not a parent, because these kids don't know their asses from their faces."

Dr. Viramontes holds up his hands in surrender. "I told you before, I'm not going to fight with you. Since my club member is seemingly unharmed and accounted for, I will leave you to sort this out among yourselves. I just ask that you don't upset the other campers. We're here to witness nature, not disturb it." Dr. Viramontes glances at me, a look of pity on his face, before he turns to walk away.

My mom gently inserts herself between Lennon and my dad. "Let's talk about this civilly."

"The time for being civil has passed," Dad says.

Something snaps inside my head. I glance back, making sure Dr. Viramontes in out of earshot, and then I turn to my father.

"It absolutely has," I tell him. "It passed when you threatened Lennon last fall in that hotel. Yeah, that's right. I know. I know *everything.*"

"What hotel?" Mom says.

Something close to rage passes over my father's features. "Oh, really? Did he tell you that I caught him trying to use a stolen credit card and that he took a swing at me?"

"Yeah, and that's the bruise you told Mom and me that you'd gotten at a construction site," I shout. "You lied about that. You lied about Lennon. Instead of telling his parents, you took it upon yourself to administer justice that you had *no right* doing."

"What in the world are you talking about?" Mom says. "Dan, what's going on?"

"I caught him trying to get a hotel room for the two of them," Dad says.

Mom blinks rapidly. When she opens her mouth, a strangled noise comes out.

"That's right, he did. And my love life is my business alone," I tell my dad. "You took my best friend away from me. You ruined both of our lives just to keep your dirty little secret."

A tense silence follows. I can't believe I just said that. It just . . . came out, and now, as Mom's eyes narrow quizzically, I wish like anything I could take it back. I glance around to see if anyone at the campground can hear us arguing; no one seems to be paying attention but Avani, who looks as if she can't decide whether she should stay or go.

"Zorie," Mom says evenly. "What dirty little secret?"

"Nothing." I can't look at my dad. Why did I open my mouth?

"Zorie," Mom repeats, this time more firmly.

"Lennon was at the hotel because it was homecoming," I tell her, tears sliding down my cheeks. "Dad was at the hotel because . . . he was seeing another woman."

My mom stares at me and then calmly turns to my dad. "Was this Molly?"

He nods once, quickly.

"I see," my mom says.

What?

"That's it?" I look back and forth in disbelief, at her, then him.

"I know about her," she says. "We were going through a rough patch. We're past that now."

Now it's my turn to stare with an open mouth. When I finally speak, I sound like an idiot. "How . . . ? When? You knew? You didn't tell me. You knew?"

My mom glances at Avani, who is still standing nearby, pretending to look at the night sky. "It's not something I'd like to discuss in public. But yes, your father told me about . . . the other woman. He ended it. We worked through our issues."

"He cheated on you," I whisper.

"I'm not discussing this with you now," she says quietly.

"You didn't discuss it with me at all!"

"It wasn't your business," she says, now angry. Her dark eyes shine with intense emotion. "It was mine. Mine alone. And your father's."

"Am I not part of this family?" I ask. "Don't I deserve to know that my father is a piece of shit?"

"Hey!" my mom says.

"You're not going to talk to me like that," Dad says. "Joy's right. It wasn't your business."

Lennon crosses his arms over his chest. "You made it her business when you fucking lied to her."

My dad points a finger at Lennon and stalks toward him. "You listen to me—"

"No, I won't," Lennon says. "You want to punch me? Then do it, old man. I was too stupid to realize it then, but I know now that I didn't need to be afraid of your threats. We have a camp full of witnesses here. You want to hit a minor? My parents will see you in court."

"No one is hitting anyone," my mom shouts, angrily pushing my father back. "This is ridiculous. And everyone's emotions are out of control, so this is not the time or place to discuss this. The only thing I care about tonight is that Zorie and Lennon are safe. We will go home and talk about the rest of it later."

"I'm not taking that punk home," my father says, then peers

over my mom's head to address Lennon, pointing an angry finger in his direction. "You can find your own way. God knows you feel adult enough to trample through the woods with my daughter. Get a taxi, catch a bus, call your own parents. But you're not riding in my car."

"Dan," my mom argues.

"No, it's fine," Lennon says, mouth rigid. "I wouldn't dream of accepting a favor from him. I'll catch my own ride."

"We both can," I agree, clasping Lennon's hand. "Because I'm not getting in the car with you either, Dad. I'm staying here with Lennon."

"Like hell you are," Dad says. "You're going home with us."

New plan.

New plan.

New plan.

I can't think of a new plan! I'm crying, and vaguely aware that half of the campground is now staring at us—and probably some of them are people I know. People I wanted to meet. Sandra Faber! My God, a renowned astronomer could be witnessing all of the ugliness, right along with everyone else in the region who could help me potentially get into Stanford.

But none of it matters now, because my heart is shattering. My family is a sham, and I'm about to lose Lennon again.

"I've never hated you more than I do right now," I tell my father.

Hurt flashes behind his eyes, but instead of talking to me, he points at Lennon. "You did this. I blame you for corrupting my daughter. And guess what, hotshot? Nothing's changed. You're not allowed to see Zorie."

"I don't take orders from you," Lennon says.

"You may not, but she does," he says, nodding toward me. "And if you don't remember, I've got proof of what you did last fall."

Lennon shrugs. "My parents know about the credit card, and they know about the hotel room. They also know I'm here with Zorie, and you don't see them flipping out."

My dad is going to kill him. Straight-up murder. I seriously wonder if I should call for help, and then I see him physically force himself to calm down. Hard breaths. Crack of the jaw. Eyes on the ground. "Zorie, you're coming home with us. And that's final."

He's serious. This is all falling apart.

What am I going to do?

"I won't leave you," I tell Lennon through my tears, turning away from my parents. "I won't let him do this to us. I won't lose you. *I won't lose you*," I repeat, desperate, fisting my hands in his shirt.

Lennon's face is stony, and he's glancing over my shoulder at my father. His head dips low, and he speaks quickly in my ear. "Go home with them. I'll be okay here. And we'll figure something out."

How? How will we figure something out? I can't see how this

can work. But more than that, I can't see my life without him in it. I tried living like that over the last year, and it wasn't living. It was surviving.

Without thinking, I stand on my toes and kiss him. It's quick and hard, and I'm still crying. He kisses me back, and it feels like goodbye.

"Joy," my father says coldly, "talk sense into Zorie before I say something I regret. We're leaving in three minutes."

"I came here to take photos of the meteor shower," I protest weakly. It doesn't even matter anymore, and I'm fighting a battle I've already lost. "I was supposed to meet Sandra Faber."

My dad shakes his head. "You lost that privilege when you lied to us about who you were coming out here with."

"I came to the Sierras with Reagan! She didn't tell me Lennon was coming along, and she definitely didn't tell either one of us that she was going to abandon the glamping trip and take off with her friends. Lennon and I didn't know we were going to be stranded in the middle of the wilderness. We didn't plan this!"

"Life is hard," my dad says, turning away from me sharply, storm clouds behind his eyes. "None of us plan for any of it."

The atmosphere inside the car is silent and oppressive as my father drives out of the camp's parking lot. I turn around in the backseat and see all the red lights of the star party. Lennon is already lost among the masses, so I can't even see his face one last time. All I can see is my freedom slipping away as white meteoroids streak across the black sky. Dust and particles, some no bigger than a grain of sand, disintegrating as they pass through Earth's atmosphere. Something so small can create a brilliant flash of light. It looks like a miracle. Unearthly.

Shooting stars.

No wonder people wish upon them.

And though I know they aren't really stars, and that wishing is pointless, I watch the white streaks zipping over the mountains, and I wish. I wish so hard. *Don't let me lose him again.*

26

My father speeds the entire way home and heads straight for my parents' bedroom without saying a word. It's as if he can't get away from us fast enough. Fine by me. I don't have anything I want to say to him. I don't want to fight. I don't want to make up.

At this point, I never want to see his face again.

With Andromeda on my heels, I hike up the stairs and shut the door to my room so hard, one of my glow-in-the-dark stars falls off the ceiling. It's weird to be back here. This used to be a safe space, but now it feels tainted. Everything smells weird. Dusty and artificial. I think I was out in the wild for too long, because this feels like a prison, not a sanctuary. Andromeda is the only happy thing in this apartment. At least she seems to have missed me.

It's one in the morning, and I'm in that weird state of being exhausted but not tired. I can't even look at my wall calendars. Summer is a disaster, and right now, instead of helping me stay calm, they are a reminder of everything that's gone wrong. So I busy myself with what I can control, steadily unpacking my gear. And I'm in the process of making a pile of dirty clothes to take to the washer when I hear a soft knock on my door.

"It's open," I say flatly.

My mom's face appears in the doorway. "Can I come in for a second?"

"How am I going to stop you?"

She sighs, closes the door behind her, and sits on the bed next to my backpack. "I know you're angry with us right now."

"You have to admit, I have pretty good reasons to be."

Dark circles hang beneath her eyes. "And we've got reasons to be angry with you, too. You lied to me, Zorie. When we talked a couple of days ago, you could have told me you were with Lennon."

"Did you already know?"

She fiddles with a zipper on my backpack. "Reagan's mom called me. Apparently, Reagan came home early with Brett Seager, but she didn't tell her mother that they'd abandoned you and Lennon in the national park. The glamping compound got in touch with Mrs. Reid, and they're the ones who informed her what actually happened. Kicked out for stealing wine?"

"I wasn't a part of that plan," I argue. Mostly. "It was Brett's idea."

Mom sighs and shakes her head. "Regardless, the glamping compound's phone call poked holes in Reagan's story, and that's when Reagan admitted that they left you and Lennon. Mrs. Reid called me in a panic, a couple hours before I heard from you. Your dad wasn't here, so I went next door and talked to the Mackenzies."

I groan quietly.

"Yeaaahh," Mom drawls, and then gives me a tight smile. "It stung to find out that they knew you were on the trip. Lennon had told them, but you hadn't told *me*. It made me feel like a bad parent."

"I didn't know before I left, honestly. I knew . . ." I hesitate, but what's the point of lying anymore? "I knew Brett and the others would be there. But I didn't realize Lennon was coming until we were leaving."

"But you obviously made up with him. That wasn't a friendly kiss."

"No, it wasn't."

She sniffles. "I always knew it would be a matter of time before your friendship changed. The way he looked at you. The way you looked at him . . ."

"What's so wrong about that? You should be happy. You used to like Lennon."

"I still do. Quite a bit, actually."

"Then what's the problem?"

She doesn't answer, just pets Andromeda, who's jumped onto the bed and is trying to insert herself into the conversation.

Fine. She doesn't want to talk. I don't either. I lift my portable telescope out of the backpack and set it on the floor. Check all the pieces. So stupid to think that I lugged it up and down mountains for days and I didn't even use the damn thing.

"Lennon and you spent a lot of time alone," my mom finally says. "I hope you were safe."

"We were."

She makes a small noise and then blows out a hard breath.

I don't want to talk about that right now. I set my camera next to the telescope and steer the conversation in a different direction. "We had plenty of time to talk about all the secrets that everyone's been keeping from me."

"Zorie . . ."

"Did you know his father died last year?" I say angrily.

Mom blinks at me. "Adam . . . ?"

She didn't know either. I think this might be worse, somehow. Were we all so caught up in our own petty issues that we didn't realize our neighbors needed us? It makes me hurt all over again.

"Yes," I tell her. "Adam died. You can say it. He killed himself last October. None of us knew because Dad tore our families apart."

She covers her eyes and makes a low noise, and then pushes up from the bed to pace around the room. "I can't believe it."

"Believe it," I say. "Can you imagine what it must've felt like for Lennon? He was there for me when we first moved here and I was grieving. And all this time, he's been alone, trying to cope. How unfair is it that—" My voice warbles, and I have to stop for a moment. "None of us knew because Dad was too busy trying to cover up the fact that he was banging some side chick."

"Don't talk like that to me," she says sharply.

"Dad can do those things and get away with it, but I can't say it?"

"We went to counseling."

I stop unpacking. "Counseling? *Counseling?* Not only did you fail to mention that my dad was a cheating asshole, but you secretly went to counseling?"

"It was our issue, not yours."

"I thought we were friends."

Her face falls. "We *are* friends. Zorie, I care about you more than anyone else on this planet. More than . . ." She stops. Start again. "I only wanted to keep this family together. I didn't want to poison you against your father."

"Too late. He did that all on his own."

"Relationships are complicated," she says. "You will understand when you're older. Things aren't always black and white. People make mistakes because they're damaged inside, but that doesn't mean they don't deserve forgiveness. It doesn't mean they can't change."

"Dad is damaged all right," I mutter. "And I don't see how his forgiveness is elevated above the respect that you deserve. How is he worth more? He cheated on you with God knows how many women—"

"It was just one, and he was still mourning your mother."

"My mother? She's been dead for years! I never even saw him cry over her death. Never! Not once."

"That's how he coped. He tried to compartmentalize it—to box it away and forget about it. I don't know if he learned this from his jackass of a father, but it's something he does. He thinks if he ignores a problem, it will go away."

She's right. He does do this. All the time.

So do I.

Sighing, Joy looks out my balcony window. "Grief is sneaky. Sometimes you think you're over something, but you've just been lying to yourself. If you don't face up to it, grief will hang around until you do, whittling away small parts of your life. You don't even know it's happening."

This I understand.

My birth mother's death came unexpectedly. One day she was there, and the next, she was gone. It was the worst kind of surprise. My world was upended. I never even got to tell her good-bye. And that sudden loss triggered my anxiety problems . . . and altered how I dealt with change. If I have a plan for something that's stressful, if I've carefully considered all the angles and possibilities, then I'm controlling it. I'm in charge. Nothing can pop up and surprise me, because if I've planned very carefully, then I'm ready for any situation.

Except I'm not. Because you can't control everything. Sometimes, you can be minding your own business, but your father is busy having affairs. Sometimes, you can plan all the details of a trip with friends, but those people weren't really your friends at all. Sometimes, you can follow a well-planned route through the woods and still get stalked by mountain lions.

And sometimes, *sometimes*, you give up on your best friend, but he never gave up on you.

"I never knew Dad was struggling with my mother's death," I tell Joy. "But you know what? When I make bad choices, I have to pay for them. He's a grown man, so he gets a free pass? I think that's shitty. And I think you deserve better than him. We deserve better."

"Zorie," she pleads softly.

"I was so worried about what would happen if you and Dad got divorced, because I couldn't stand the thought of being forced to live with him. I imagined you deciding that you were done raising a kid who wasn't really yours, and then my life would fall apart all over again. I'd lose another mother."

"That will never happen," she says, grabbing my shoulders. "Do you hear me? You're the reason I agreed to make this marriage work. You, not him."

"What?" I say, confused.

"I stayed for you. Because you need me, and I need you." She cups my head in her hands. "I *am* raising my own kid. You are mine. I didn't need to give birth to you to love you, sweet thing."

I'm crying now, and I think she is too. We're apologizing in whispers, and she hugs me as she always does, hard enough to hurt.

And it's a good pain.

When the tears slow, she eases up on the hugging and strokes my back. "I'm sorry about tonight. About the meteor shower and the scene . . . about Lennon."

"I can't believe we left him there. He would never leave me."

"I called Sunny and apologized before I came up here to see you."

"Is she mad?"

"She's not happy. I didn't tell her much, but she sounded like she already knew more than I did about what's been going on." Her eyes catch mine. "Are you in love with Lennon?"

Am I?

Oh, God.

I am.

I'm in love with my best friend.

I blink at her through tear-stung eyes. "I think . . . I may have been for long time."

She nods and sniffles, smiling softly. "I'll talk to your father. He's emotional now, but maybe he'll realize that he's being stubborn. I can't promise he'll change his mind tomorrow, but eventually he'll have to see reason. Okay?"

That's actually not okay. I don't want to live with my hand out like a beggar, asking for my father's permission to see Lennon. But I don't say this. I know she's trying.

"It's late," she tells me. "And you've had an eventful night. Get some rest, and we'll talk tomorrow. Yes?"

I nod, and she gives me a tired smile before leaving my room.

Here I am, selfishly talking about being in love, as if she didn't have any problems of her own in that department. I can only fathom what she's gone through with my father. I think about how she matter-of-factly rattled off the name of Dad's mistress, as if it was just something she'd accepted.

Molly.

That's the name my mom used.

Only, that's not the name that was on the photo book's envelope.

Catherine Beatty.

One of many.

Was it the same woman? Maybe she was using a fake name to send the package. All I know is that Lennon recognized the woman from the photo book because he'd seen her in the hotel with my dad. And then there was Reagan's accusation that my dad tried to sleep with Michelle Johnson's mom after the Olympic fund-raiser. I don't know if that's true, but my mom said they went to counseling this past winter. The Olympic fund-raiser was this spring. Something doesn't add up.

What should I do?

I perch on the edge of my bed and begin analyzing my options. I could give her all this information and risk my parents getting into a fight—or worse. I could confront my dad privately and hope to what? Shame him into telling the truth? Then what? I could keep all of this to myself, and maybe things would go back to normal.

Isn't that the result I want? To avoid pain? To cling to some semblance of normality? Dueling images of my parents together and apart float in my head, and I try to sort them out and solve all the equations, but other things erode my thoughts. Things from the last week. The bear attacking Brett's tent. My snake bite. The mountain lion. Lightning in the sequoias. Falling asleep in Lennon's arms.

Unpredictable outcomes. Some of them bad, some good.

All at once, I realize that I need to let go. Of planning. Trying to control everything. It doesn't work. The best-laid plans of mice and men often turn to shit.

Could I have avoided some hives and a whole lot of nail biting if I'd just handed over the photo book to my mom? Because all that worry got me nowhere. Here I am, still knowing my father's a liar, but unsure what will happen. Still wondering about the fate of my family. Still unable to prevent a disaster.

I can't constantly be on guard, trying to avoid every single catastrophe, measuring and managing every expectation.

Besides, Lennon's right. Nobody expects the Spanish Inquisition.

From now on, no new plans. No trying to control every detail of my life. You can plot a course that will get you to your destination, but you can't predict what you'll find along the way. So I'm just going to let life happen, and whatever that brings, I'll face.

Starting now.

The photo book is still in the drawer where I left it. I take it out, along with the letter. It's not my secret to keep. It never was.

My purse is where I left it in the closet before the camping trip. I stuff clean clothes and my cell phone charger inside it. Then I head downstairs, calling Andromeda to follow and get in her dog bed at the foot of the stairs. All of the lights are off but the one over the kitchen sink, where Mom is drinking a glass of water. My dad is nowhere in sight.

"Here," I tell her in a quiet voice when she looks up at me. "This is the package you asked me to get from the Mackenzies the week before my camping trip. I told you they didn't have it, but they did. They opened it by accident, and when I was carrying it back to the office, I peeked. I hid it from you. I'm sorry."

Hesitantly, she takes it and opens the letter. Her hand shakes. She blinks several times. And then she closes the letter and slips it inside the photo book.

"Dad lied to you. It wasn't just Molly, or this Catherine person. Reagan knows about another incident. I saw Razan Abdullah at the glamping compound, and she asked me if you and Dad were still together."

She stares at me with a shocked look on her face.

"People are talking," I tell her. "That's probably why Dad's been losing clients and you haven't. Because everyone knows he's a scumbag."

We stand there, neither of us looking at each other for a long moment.

"I'm sorry," I tell her. "I love you, and I'm so sorry. For everything."

"I'll see you in the morning," she says quietly, and heads toward my parents' bedroom. A second later, she disappears, shutting the door.

I don't know what's going to happen now, but dread knots my stomach, and I feel the urge to run after her and snatch the photo book away.

But it's too late. Nothing I can do will turn back the clock. *Deep breath*. I scribble a quick note to my mother and leave it on the kitchen counter. And as the sound of my parents' voices arguing gets louder, I quietly head out the front door of the apartment.

It's cool outside. A soft breeze rustles through the fronds of the palm tree outside our house. I jog down the front steps, hiking my purse higher on my shoulder. It's so much lighter than the backpack. I almost miss its weight. Almost.

Half the stars have disappeared out of the sky. Like the universe just swiped a hand and erased them. But as I'm walking, a pale white streak appears, and I hope Lennon is watching it with Avani. Miles away, but the same starry sky.

I head toward the left apartment in the blue duplex across from our house. Lights are still on in the windows. The Mackenzies have always been night owls—another thing my dad points to as proof of their hedonism. But I'm not thinking about him now as I ring the doorbell and wait. In fact, I'm not thinking or planning anything past this moment, and when Sunny's oblong face appears, and she's blinking into the porch light, I say the first thing that comes to mind.

"I'm sorry to bother you so late. Can I spend the night here with you and Mac? My parents are having problems."

She stares at me, surprised, standing in a pair of pajama bottoms printed with tiny cartoon trolls. "Of course you can, baby. Come on inside before you freeze to death."

Then she pulls me over the threshold, past the photos of Lennon and his dad dressed in Halloween costumes. Their house smells just like it always has, like vanilla frosting and old books. And when I see Mac curled up on their worn living room sofa in front of the TV, looking up at me with welcoming eyes, I feel as if I'm finally home.

27

When I wake the next morning, I'm completely disoriented. It takes me several seconds to realize that I'm not in a tent with Lennon; I'm sleeping in his empty bed, and the sheets smell like him, freshly laundered and sunny. So good. For a moment, anyway. Then I spot his dastardly wall of reptiles, including Ryuk, who's staring at me through his lizard habitat.

"Sorry, buddy," I tell the bearded dragon. "Your dark master is not here."

And he won't be for several hours. Mac got a text from Avani last night before I showed up. Apparently, Lennon's phone is still dead, and she informed them that he was safe and would be riding home with her today.

I hope he's okay.

Sitting atop a pile of gruesome graphic novels, the clock on Lennon's beside table says it's half past nine. I smell bacon and coffee, and my stomach leaps with joy. Even though I showered here last night before I dropped dead in Lennon's bed, I didn't eat, and my body is more than aware that the last meal I had was freeze-dried stew yesterday afternoon when Lennon and I were hiking toward Condor Peak.

Part of me wants to hibernate in Lennon's room among the stacks of horror comics and DVDs, but I know I can't linger here forever. So after checking the state of my hives—not great, but not out of control—I dress in the clothes I stuffed in my purse last night and head down a short hall to the Mackenzies' main living area. Sunny and Mac are already dressed and sitting at the dining room table, browsing news headlines on a tablet with a cracked screen.

"Good morning," Sunny says brightly. "How'd you sleep?"

"Like the dead."

"Excellent," she says, getting up to head around the kitchen counter. "How about some sustenance?"

"Yes, please. I'm starving."

Mac squints at me. "You haven't developed any new allergies to eggs or pork, have you?"

"As long as no one's cooking shrimp scampi, I'm all good."

"Ugh," Mac says, pretending to be exasperated. "Will I ever live that down?"

"Bad shrimp," Sunny calls out cheerfully from behind the stove.

I exhale deeply and take a seat next to Mac. "I've missed you guys."

"We've missed you too," she assures me, bumping her shoulder against mine.

Sunny brings me a plate piled with eggs, bacon, and toast, and I help myself to the pot of coffee that's sitting on the table. "Any word from Lennon this morning?" I ask, hopeful. I charged my phone overnight, but there were no messages from him.

Mac lifts her coffee cup. "Avani said she'd text when they were leaving today. I told her to let him know you're here with us."

I'm glad, but I also feel left out and unconnected from him. It's weird to be on the other end of the no-phone-service problem. I liked it better when I was the one without reception.

I'm not sure what it is about civilization, but now that I'm here, the nagging urge to stay connected has returned. If I can't have him in front of me, I need him to be a text away.

Resisting the urge to double-triple-quadruple-check my phone, I instead answer Sunny and Mac's questions about the trip. They're curious, asking questions, and I tell them a lot of things . . . but not everything. I get the feeling they know exactly what Lennon and I have been doing in the woods; they're smiling a lot, and it's making me a little uncomfortable, so I just focus on the life-and-death parts of the trip, not the sexlaxation parts. The doorbell rings as I'm telling them about the lightning storm, and when Sunny answers it, she talks to someone for a moment and then calls me quietly into the hallway.

"It's for you," she whispers.

I glance down the front hall toward their cracked front door. "Is it my mom?"

She shakes her head. "Go on. It'll be fine. And we're steps away if you need us."

With trepidation, I shuffle to the door and open it. The face staring back at me is familiar, yet unexpected: a handsome Korean man in his fifties with short hair that's gray along the temples, black in the back.

"Grandpa Sam?" I say, utterly confused.

"Zorie," he says, enunciating carefully. Then he launches into a string of incomprehensible sentences that sound urgent and decisive.

"You know I don't understand Korean," I tell him. I can say hello (*Annyeong-haseyo*) and please (*juseyo*) and a few choice words that my mom uses when the man who owns Pizza Delight tries to overcharge us for extra toppings. Occasionally, I can figure out what the actors in my mom's favorite K-dramas are saying after we've binged several episodes in a row, but that's about it.

Grandpa Sam, on the other hand, understands most English. He just doesn't speak it well. He says "okay" and "yes" and "no," but he doesn't bother with much of anything else, which is why emojis are his preferred way of communicating with me.

Right now, he lifts his head and mutters to the sky. Then he sighs heavily and motions for me to come with him. "Okay?" he says.

"Okay, hold on." I run back into the house and get my stuff, and when Mac asks what's going on, I tell her, "I have no freaking idea."

They tell me everything will be fine, and I head outside where

Grandpa Sam is waiting. He silently guides me across the cul-de-sac, one gentle hand on my back. He's still talking to me in Korean, but now he sounds less upset. He's trying to assure me of something, but when I see my mom sitting in the backseat of his shiny Audi sedan, parked in front of our apartment, I have a horrible feeling.

"What's going on?" I ask. Mom is looking the other way. Is she avoiding me? What about her promises last night? She said she wouldn't leave.

Grandpa Sam points to our front door and gives me a command in Korean, then says, "Okay?"

"No, I don't want to stay here," I tell him, desperate. "Take me with you."

"Yes," he says, vexation in his voice.

"What do you mean, 'yes'? Yes, I can come? Yes *what*?"

Before he can give me another one of his exasperated rants, the front door of our apartment swings open to a torrent of swear words that I *do* understand. Only, they're coming from the mouth of my tiny Korean grandmother, which makes them sound so much worse—mostly creative combinations involving animals.

Esther Moon never swears. She never yells, either, so I know we're in uncharted territory now. She has Andromeda on her leash, and smoothly transitions from anger to murmuring baby talk at my dog in order to coax her down the front stairs. I'm not sure who's having more trouble navigating them: the old husky, or the woman in stiletto heels and a designer skirt that fits like a glove.

My grandfather calls out to her, and she lifts her head. "Zorie! Thank God. Pack a bag and say goodbye to your fly-covered dog turd of a father."

Like I said, unlike Grandpa Sam, she speaks English just fine.

"Grandma Esther," I say. "What's happening?"

"You and Joy are staying with us for a few days," she says brightly, scratching Andromeda's head while the dog tries to lick her skirt. Grandma Esther is the Korean dog whisperer. She has two Frenchies and a Boston terrier, and they adoringly follow her around the house like her posse. She coos at Andromeda, "And you're going to have so much fun with my girls, aren't you, sweetie?"

My head is trying to process everything. "We're going to Oakland?"

"No, to our vacation home in Bali," she says sarcastically. "Of course, to Oakland. Are you all right?" She tears herself away from the dog and gives me a thorough once-over, smoothing my curls with delicate fingers.

"I don't know," I say truthfully.

"You will be. I'll make you chicken and rice soup."

Admittedly, that's a strong motivator. Grandma Esther is an amazing cook. She does *that* in heels too.

Grandpa Sam pleads with me about . . . something. I can't tell. He talks too fast.

I look back and forth between them. "What?"

Grandma Esther sticks her tongue out my grandfather. "Don't

pay any attention to him. He's trying to rush back to watch the football game. Take your time. We'll be waiting in the car." She clucks at Andromeda, and as she heads toward the sedan, adds sweetly over her shoulder, "If your pig-shit father tries to talk you into staying, tell him he can sue for custody."

Oh, God.

Grandpa Sam chuckles to himself, pats me on the back, and follows her to the car. I'm left alone, and I really wish I weren't. It feels like I'm walking into a haunted house filled with ghouls waiting to jump out at me.

Steeling myself, I step inside our living room. My dad is there, red-eyed and bleary. He looks like he's just been told someone died. Shell-shocked. Blank. Unable to comprehend.

Confident, charming Diamond Dan has left the building.

"Hey," I say warily.

"Oh," he says, sitting down on our sofa. "Zorie."

"What's happening?"

He rubs his head. "That's an excellent question. I'm not quite sure, myself. What did Esther tell you?"

"That I'm staying with them for a few days."

"That's it?"

"That's it."

He nods while placing both hands on his knees as he gathers his thoughts. Then he gives me a reserved smile. "So, your mother and I may be separating. It's not decided yet. I won't go into the details, but you don't want to hear them anyway. Well, you already heard a few things last night, so I'm assuming this isn't a surprise—"

"Dad, the entire last two weeks have been nothing but surprises."

"Ah. Well."

That's it? That's all he's going to say? How about, *Hey, I've been sleeping around and this family is a sham. Oopsie!* I mean, come on. Give me something.

A silence hangs between us.

"Why?" I finally ask.

He shakes his head slowly. "You wouldn't understand."

"I understand more than you think."

After he looks away, I think about what Mom had told me—that my father was still having trouble getting over my birth mother's death after all these years. Last night, that sounded like a convenient excuse, but now I'm thinking about the photo book, and how that woman looked a little like my birth mother.

"You can't bring her back," I tell him. "She's dead, and there was only one of her, and you can't bring her back."

"I know," he says in a broken voice.

"You could have talked to me instead of shutting me out. I was mourning her too, you know? She was my mother."

"I know she was."

"Then why didn't you talk to me? Ever?"

One shoulder lifts slowly, and then falls. "I was unprepared to raise you on my own. I felt like a failure. And then I had to watch while Joy swept in and provided what I couldn't. She was a natural. How could she do better than I could, when I was your own flesh and blood? Her parents spoiled you—"

"Spoiled?" I hardly think so. It's not like Grandpa Sam showers me with gifts constantly. He just buys me practical stuff.

"Christ, even the Mackenzies do a better job raising you than I could," he says. "Your mother would roll over in her grave."

I don't remember my birth mother being homophobic, but maybe I blocked that out.

"You don't need me," my father says in a low voice, despondent.

"Dad—"

"It's true," he says. "I know it. Everyone knows it. You're better off without me."

I'm not sure if this pity party is genuine, or if he's trying to manipulate me into feeling sorry for him—or if he's trying to push me further away. But I give him the benefit of the doubt.

"It's going to take me a long time to forgive you for what you've done," I say. "To Mom, and to me. However . . . you're still my father. I'll always need you. At some point, I think you'll realize that you need *me*, too. And when that day comes, I'll be here."

He looks up at me, face pinched in pain.

"But today," I tell him, turning away, "my mom needs me more."

28

We spend the weekend at my grandparents' house in Oakland. They live in a small house in an upper-middle-class neighborhood, where everyone pays landscapers to maintain their lawns. Which may sound nice, but it's also boring, and it doesn't take long for me to feel unmoored and restless. As though my life is going backward instead of forward.

As though we've been fighting a war and lost.

Grandma Esther feeds us constantly, and that seems to help my mom. She's not completely falling apart like I worried she might, but she's crying a lot, and that makes *me* cry. And all the conversations in Korean between her and Grandpa Sam make me feel ineffectual.

Everything's chaos. I'm homeless. Our family's broken. My entire future is up in the air. And I'm missing Lennon desperately. Even though he made it home from Condor Peak just fine, and we text constantly and occasionally talk on the phone when I can get away from everyone, it's not the same.

I miss him in a way I never have.

I miss his deep voice and his dark sense of humor. I miss his face and the feeling of security I have when he's nearby. I miss the way he holds me, and the thrill of his fingers stroking down my back. I miss him so much, I feel physically ill.

I don't want more food or a nap or to watch a movie. I just want to go home and see Lennon. Only, I don't know where home is anymore. I think about how Lennon and I spent the last year avoiding each other, and what a waste that was. We didn't know how good we had it, living so close. We were both stupid. I wish I could erase the entire year and start all over. Stop him from getting that hotel room. Stop my father from cheating and ruining the business and our credit, because now Grandma Esther is saying that he's the reason my mom was having trouble with the bank before I left on the camping trip. He secretly spent all my parents' savings and credit on his affairs. Trips. Hotel rooms. Expensive restaurants. Gifts. He was living large while my mom was trying to keep the business afloat.

My grandparents say they're going to sue him for all the money they gave him to invest in the business. Grandma Esther is sure the judge will grant my mom full custody if my dad fights it. The good thing is that he won't; the *sad* thing is that he won't. I can't decide how I feel about him, and I'm tired of trying to figure it out and weary of my life being in limbo. Something has to give.

And on Tuesday morning, it does.

Everything changes.

I'm restless and a little depressed, watching Andromeda lounge listlessly in a dog bed that's too small for her while Grandma Esther's energetic dogs unsuccessfully try to coax her into playing. Mom appears in the doorway, and I think it's probably to check my hives again, because she's been monitoring me like a doctor.

But Mom is not interested in my allergies. She has a strange look on her face. It's like happiness, but a little angrier. Happy angry. Hapry.

"Get your stuff," she says. "We're going home."

"To Dad?"

"Your father has moved in with one of his mistresses in San Francisco. You and I are going home, changing the locks, and I'm going to figure out how to keep the clinic running without him."

It sounds too good to be true. "Can you do that?"

"Zorie, I can do anything I damn well want." she says, sounding unexpectedly confident and positive. "And what I want is to go back to Mission Street and be the East Bay's best acupuncturist while raising my future astrophysicist daughter. So that's what I'm going to do, goddammit."

"Maybe sound a little surer of yourself, while you're at it," I mumble, smiling.

And for the first time since all of this chaos exploded, she smiles too. Just for a second.

"I'm not sure," she admits. "Not yet. But I have to have faith that I will be one day. *We* will be. We'll make a plan and take action. And that's how we start."

Her words click into place inside my head, and I realize something.

Planning can't save you from everything. Change is inevitable and uncertainty is a given. And if you plan so much that you can't function without one, life's no fun. All the calendars, journals, and lists in the world won't save you when the sky falls. And maybe, just maybe, I've been using planning less as a coping mechanism and more as an excuse to avoid anything I couldn't control.

But that doesn't mean preparation is altogether bad. Planning can be useful when you've come out on the wrong side of a cave and need to figure out a new way to get back on route.

When all you can do is put one foot in front of the other and push forward.

"We'll be okay," Mom tells me, and I believe her.

"All right," I say. "Let's go make a plan."

All I wanted was to go home and see Lennon. So of *course* the Mackenzies would pick now of all times to leave their assistant manager in charge of Toys in the Attic while they go visit friends in the city—some old punk musicians who knew Lennon's father. I want to scream. I need to see Lennon. It's not optional. *Need.* And I know we spent an entire year apart, so a couple of days should be nothing. But it's not. It's painful.

Lennon briefly considers taking the BART train across the Oakland Bay Bridge to meet up with me. But we decide it's best to wait until he comes back on Thursday, when we can have an actual real, live date. Funny that we've never had one.

Meanwhile, he has tickets for a concert in San Francisco—some band that's dark and despairing—and I'm insanely busy. Grandma Esther is staying with us for a couple of days to help with something she's dubbed the Purge. It's not the horror movie by that name, but it might as well be, because it's endless hours of work that involves getting rid of everything that doesn't help us move forward.

It's as bad as it sounds. And as much as I love Grandma Esther, she's starting to drive me nuts. Apparently, my mom feels the same way.

"I'm going to kill her," she tells me privately.

"Please don't," I say. "Her body would be just one more thing we'd have to carry to the porch. She looks lightweight, but so did that box of shoes I just took downstairs."

"Right. Good thinking. We'll wait until she's outside. You trip her, and I'll push her into oncoming traffic."

"Who will cook for us?"

"Dammit, Zorie. I'm trying to plan a murder!"

"I don't think you can kill her. She has too much energy. It's unnatural."

"Imagine growing up with her," she says. "It's a wonder I'm not in jail."

By the time we're finished with the Purge, we're pretty sure Melita Hills is going to charge us extra for excess garbage pickup, because the curb outside the apartment is overflowing with black plastic bags—and that's not counting the stuff we gave away to a local charity. I never knew we had so much literal baggage. I even take down the old glow-in-the-dark stars from my ceiling, and Mom helps me paint my room a new color, a sunny yellow that contrasts nicely with all my night-sky photos.

All my homemade wall calendars? I threw them in the trash. But I'm not ready to give up on blueprints altogether. Instead of obsessively bulleting every detail of my schedule for every day of the year on multiple calendars, I use star-patterned *washi* tape to map out a single grid on a corkboard, and pin fun paper cutouts on major holidays and planetary events.

Baby steps.

Avani comes by on Wednesday with her mother. They bring hummus, homemade banana bread, and a tray filled with sandwiches. It feels like someone died, and when I point this out, my mom jokes that she should get divorced more often.

In her defense, it's *really* good banana bread.

While our moms chat, Avani tells me in detail what happened after we left Condor Peak—and everything that happened the two days before we arrived. Apparently, I missed both everything and not that much, all that the same time. It's only when she shows me some of her photos of the meteor shower that I feel a little envious. But there will be other meteor showers, other star

STARRY EYES • 797

parties. For the first time, it really hits me that if Lennon and I hadn't stayed in the sequoia grove that second night, no one would have worried that we were missing, and we may not have set off the chain of events that led to all of this.

The important thing is, I don't have any regrets.

When Thursday arrives, Grandma Esther leaves after buying massive amounts of toilet paper and laundry detergent as a house-warming gift "for good luck"—a Korean tradition, she says. I'm sad to see her go, because of all the home cooking, but also glad, because the murder fantasies were starting to get out of control. And I have better things to think about than bumping off nice old ladies.

Like Lennon.

I'm so eager about him coming back into town that I'm shift-ing into anxiety mode. It's been a week since we've seen each other—the longest, weirdest week of my life—and so much has changed. What if all of that alters the way we feel about each other? What if that week we spent in isolation was an anomaly? Sure, we reconnected in the wilderness, but what if we can't make it work in the real world? I worry that the delicate balance of our friendship and our more-than-friendship can't withstand the weight of everyday life.

My parents couldn't make it, and they were married.

How can the two of us fare any better?

The longer I'm away from him, the more a particular thought niggles: What if we were just seduced by nature? The magic of twinkling stars. The scent of redwood. Majestic mountains.

What if this is what influenced Lennon to kiss me that first time at the top of the granite staircase? If we were here at home without the alluring rush of waterfalls in the background, would he have still made that first move?

Would I have been as receptive to it?

Is there a nature-related equivalent to beer googles?

Making out on a blanket under starry skies certainly is more romantic than groping each other on a park bench while Andromeda watches.

The thing is, we had a chance to make this relationship work last year, but neither of us wanted it hard enough to try. I allowed my dad to talk me into shunning Lennon. Instead of wallowing in pain, I could have gotten off my ass and forced Lennon to tell me what happened at homecoming. And Lennon could have come told me what happened. If he was brave enough to confess stealing Mac's credit card for the hotel room to both his moms, he could have faced me.

But he wasn't.

And I wasn't.

And after all that time together in the woods, neither of us came up with a plan for what to do after we got back to civilization. No promises were made. No pacts. No *I love you*s were whispered in the dark. Does he still feel the same way about me, now that we're home?

Can we make it as real couple in the real world? Or are we better off staying friends?

It's easy to think you're falling in love out in the wilderness, where everything is beautiful and a tent full of condoms is just steps away. Did we just have one weeklong one-night stand?

How do I know for sure if what we shared together is fleeting or real?

It probably doesn't help that I haven't heard much from him over the last couple of days—only a few brief texts to make plans for our date when he gets back. I try not to let uncertainty get the best of me and do my best to ignore random thoughts of him meeting someone hipper than me in the city and deciding I'm not worth the trouble. I know that's just my monkey mind, chattering away, restless and distracted. But when he texts me that he needs to delay our date until after dinner, I have flashbacks about homecoming last year.

What if I'm being ditched again?

I know it's not logical, and my mom tells me to relax before I'm covered from head to toe in massive welts. But I'm dressed and ready, wearing my most flattering red-and-black plaid dress, and the sun is setting, and still no Lennon.

It's eight o'clock.

Eight thirty.

Eight forty-five.

The doorbell rings.

I nearly fall on my face, racing to answer it. And then he's there, standing in front of me. Black hair. Black jeans. Boyish smile.

Lennon.

My emotions go haywire, and I'm so happy to see him, my voice dries up and vanishes. We're both standing here stupidly, and I need one of us to say something—anything!

"You're late," I finally manage.

He looks dazed. "I had to arrange some stuff. God, you look beautiful."

Fireworks go off in my chest. I think I might faint if he doesn't touch me.

Just when I can't take it anymore, his arms are around me, and my arms are around him, and he's warm and solid, and he smells good, like freshly laundered clothes hanging in the sun. I'm overwhelmed with relief. Gratitude. Joy.

I know right at that moment that it wasn't just the twinkling stars. I don't want to be Just Friends. But what about him?

"Hi," he murmurs into my hair.

"I missed you," I say, tightening my arms around his back until I can hear his heart thudding inside his chest.

I want to tell him, *I missed you so much, it felt like I was dying.*

I want him to say that to me.

But we're both silent, and I feel his arms stiffen. He pulls back, looking over my shoulder. My mom is standing behind us, arms crossed.

"Hi, Lennon," she says. "It's good to see you."

"You too."

She hands him a bag with something in it. "Here you go."

"Thanks," he says, smiling.

I glance back and forth between them. "What's going on? Is this some sort of drug ring?"

Lennon's brows waggle. "You'll see."

My mom and Lennon in cahoots? That's definitely interesting.

He gives her a shy look. "Are you . . . ? I mean, is it okay that we leave?"

"It's fine. *I'm* fine." She makes a shooing gesture. "You guys go on out. I'm actually looking forward to some peace and quiet. Just come back at a semireasonable hour."

"We will," he tells her, lifting the bag she gave him in thanks.

As we head down the steps, she calls out, "And, Lennon? Keep her safe."

"Don't worry," he calls back. "I always do."

He leads me toward his car, which I haven't been inside since he got it last summer. The heavy door creaks—loudly—and the inside of the car smells like old leather and engine oil. It's not entirely unpleasant.

"No dead bodies in the back, right?" I ask when he slides into driver's seat next to me.

"Not this week." He smiles at me, and I feel like I'm melting into the seat.

For the love of God, get ahold of yourself, Everhart.

"Now, strap in," he instructs me, "so I can make good on my responsibility for your safety."

"Where are we going?"

"That's a secret, Medusa."

A tiny, electric thrill shoots through me when he uses my nickname. "I don't like secrets," I remind him.

"You'll like this one. I think. I hope. Let's find out."

He drives down Mission Street and won't give me any hints as we speed across town. I try to figure it out—a movie? A restaurant? Coffee at the Jitterbug?—but he just says, "Nope," after each guess. Honestly, I'm so happy just to be close enough to reach out and touch him that I genuinely don't care where we go. But when we pass familiar landmarks and the car's engine strains climbing a hill at the edge of town, I think I realize where we're headed.

The observatory.

He pulls into the parking lot, and we're the only car here. Not surprising, because it closed half an hour ago. But Lennon parks, and he pulls me across the parking lot toward a zigzagging cement pathway on the left side of the building, which heads to the public rooftop area. We head up inclines bordered with painted metal railings until we get to a locked gate. Lennon punches in a key code.

"How did you know that?" I ask.

"Guess I got lucky."

"*Lennon*," I say, serious.

"*Zorie*," he says, not serious. "I did not come by the code illegally, nor did I promise to do anything illegal in exchange for it. Now, please, if you would, Miss Everhart . . ." He holds the gate open and gestures.

I squint at him and step through.

Red lights border the low wall around the dark viewing platform. Below us, at the base of the mountain, the city unfurls to the Bay, a grid of white and yellow lights, sparkling like fallen stars on black ground. San Francisco's skyline glitters in the distance, and we can see both the Golden Gate and Bay bridges stretching over dark water. The wind blows, and I smell eucalyptus trees.

It's a beautiful view. A breathtaking view.

And it's our view; we are alone.

When the observatory is operational, a connecting oxidized green dome opens up to allow a large, high-powered professional telescope to scan the skies. That's closed right now, but the two smaller public telescopes that normally are rolled into a small metal shed every night are still sitting out.

"What is this?" I ask.

"I'm not positive," he says, scratching his chin, "but I think it's an observatory."

I slant a hard look at him.

He flashes me a smile. "Avani helped me arrange it with Dr. Viramontes. We talked a lot after you left the meteor shower. I thought he'd hate me after the big scene with your dad—"

I groan. It's still humiliating.

"But Dr. Viramontes was surprisingly cool about everything."

"He's a cool guy," I say.

"He likes you an awful lot," Lennon says. "Which makes two of us. Here. You'll need this."

I accept the bag that my mom gave him and look inside. It's my good camera. "My mom's in on this?"

"I wanted to make sure she was okay about where we were going. Things were weird between us in the past, and I didn't want her to hate me like your dad does."

I shake my head. "She always stood up for you."

"Are you okay? I mean, about your father moving out. I know it's not easy—for you or you mom."

"It's weird," I admit. "I'm not sure it's hit me fully yet."

"I wish things had been different. As much as I've fantasized about horrible things happening to him, I never wanted to see you or Joy hurting."

"I know," I tell him, crinkling the paper bag that holds my camera. "At least something good came out of it."

"What's that?"

"I'm not banned from seeing you," I say, feeling inexplicably shy.

"Not yet," Lennon says, eyes merry. "The night is young."

I set the bag with my camera on a stand next to one of the telescopes. "I can't believe you did all this."

"Pfft. I just got a key code," Lennon says. "Dr. Viramontes said you'd know how to use the camera mount or jig or tripod, or whatever the hell it is you use—it's supposed to be in the shed. We just have to lock everything up before we leave. And if we break anything, we're in huge trouble. I'm talking beheadings. Or lawsuits. I'm not sure which would be worse."

"Probably the lawsuit," I say, looking around. "I've never been up here alone."

"There's a lunar eclipse tonight," he says.

Huh. He's right. There is. I remember now.

He gives me a soft smile. "I know it's not as good as a meteor shower and the view isn't as good as Condor Peak, but I did promise you I'd take you to see the stars. I'm making good on that."

My breath hitches. I struggle for words, and after glancing around the rooftop dumbly, I blink up at Lennon. "I don't know what to say. It's one of the most thoughtful things anyone's ever done for me."

"I don't know . . . I'd argue that rescuing you from an angry bear should get me a few points."

I chuckle. "That's true. But I let you win at poker and gave you most of my M&M's stash. If that's not love, I don't know what is."

I suddenly realize what I've said.

He realizes it too.

Still holding my hand, he slings his other arm around my waist and pulls me closer. "I'm so glad to hear that."

"Are you?" I whisper.

"Yes, I am. Because I love you too."

Goose bumps rush over my arms. "You do?"

"I've always loved you," he murmurs. "And I probably always will. You're my best friend, and you're my family. The year I waited for you was the worst of my life, but it was worth every second. If I had to do it all over again just to hold you in my arms, I would."

"Well, I would not," I say, bleary-eyed. "Because I love you too, and I can't stand to be apart from you for another minute. So stop jinxing it."

"You love me," he says, grinning stupidly. He dips his head lower, until his nose brushes mine.

"Of course I love you. You're mine, and I can't go back to being just friends. So if we have to sleep in the woods or fight with our families, then that's just what we're going to do. I don't want to live a life that doesn't have you in it."

"Tell me again," he says as he kisses my neck right below my ear.

Warmth rushes across my skin. "I can't think straight when you do that."

"I'll stop, then."

"Don't you dare."

"Tell me again," he repeats, kissing my jaw.

"You're mine."

"The other thing."

"I love you."

He pulls back to look at me, pursing his lips as he blows out a hard breath. Then his smile is monumental. "That's the best thing I've ever heard. I'm going to need to hear it a lot. My ego is fragile."

I laugh, pushing away a tear. "Your ego has never been fragile."

"It is around you."

I kiss him under his chin, and he shivers with pleasure. "*I* can't think straight when you do that either."

"Good. Let's not think. It's overrated."

"I know we promised your mom that you'd be home at a decent hour, but that eclipse won't be happening until midnight—"

"You did say there were no bodies in the back of your hearse."

"It's *sooo* body-free back there," he assures me. "And it's no tent in the middle of the forest, but it's pretty private. There may even be a blanket and a pillow. You know I follow the Boy Scout motto. Be prepared."

"It's my favorite thing about you."

"When we were in the tent, you said it was something else," he murmurs, grinning as he pulls me closer.

"I was starving and scared and not in my right mind. I probably said a lot of things. You may have to remind me."

"Yeah? Well, I'm in the mood to solve a mystery. What do you say? Want to do some detecting with the boy you love?"

I do. I absolutely do.

29

"I'm telling you, the members of KISS mixed their own blood into the red ink used to print the first KISS comic book," Sunny says. "Bet you a cupcake I'm right."

It's nearly dark outside, and I'm standing in Toys in the Attic next to Sunny, who is lording over a stack of boxes near the front window display. Her face is animated as she talks to us. "It was in the seventies, and one of the big publishers, Marvel or DC Comics, put out a KISS comic—you know, Gene Simmons and Paul Stanley in makeup, being superheroes, or whatever. And they used the band's blood in the ink. I swear it's true."

Mac rolls her eyes. "Who starts these demented rumors?" she says in her Scottish lilt. "That is *so* not true. And it's disgusting."

My mom crosses her arms, nodding at Mac. "Can you imagine how many STDs those guys had? Who would want their tainted blood in a comic book?"

"Plenty of people, apparently, because it's a fact," Sunny insists. "Ask Lennon."

I tug a belt loop on the back of his black jeans. He's bent over, half of his body inside the back of the shop's window display—a group of carved Halloween pumpkins and a black cauldron overflowing with condoms and bottles of massage gel instead of witch's brew. Halloween was last night, so we're swapping out the jack-o'-lanterns for a Thanksgiving cornucopia.

"Did you hear all that?" I ask.

He emerges from the window display, standing up to full height. "Sunny's right. A nurse drew their blood, and they flew to New York and had pictures taken at Marvel's printing plant, where they dumped vials of their blood into a vat of ink. A notary public witnessed and certified it."

"Eww," we all say in chorus.

Lennon shrugs. "KISS was always doing silly, shocking gimmicks like that to sell their merchandise. They were more interested in making money than music."

"And that's why *you* owe me a cupcake," Sunny tells Mac, her face lifting into a delighted grin.

Mac shakes her fists at the ceiling. "Curse you, Rock Star Urban Legend Game."

I'm not sure why she bothers siding against Sunny. She always loses. Or maybe that's the point. All I know is that a cupcake sounds pretty freaking good about right now, and I'm wishing this window display were filled with actual candy instead of condoms.

I think I've been eating too much junk food lately, which is something I didn't know could happen. But Mom and I have been too busy to go to the grocery store for real food. Our only home-cooked sustenance has been Sunday dinners at the Mackenzies'.

It's been a couple of months since my dad left. He's still in San Francisco, and he's already in full-on Diamond Dan pivot mode, doing something impulsive. He enrolled in a certification course for—I kid you not—equine massage therapy. That's right, he wants to move to Sonoma and give horses back rubs. Hey, it's his life, I suppose. I've talked to him on the phone a couple of times, but I haven't seen him. A good thing, probably. I'm not as angry as I once was, but I don't need any more disruptions in my life.

And Mom doesn't either. She's been busy too. Everhart Wellness Clinic is now Moon Wellness Spa. Yes, she's the one who decided to christen the spa with her maiden name, but I'm the one who suggested she use an actual moon in her new logo. Sunny and Mac found her a new masseuse—a friend of a friend who was moving out here to the East Bay, because she couldn't afford the rent in the city anymore. San Francisco got Dad and exchanged him for Anna, a young Latina who has purple hair and likes dogs. Win-win.

While Mom is busy rebuilding her business, my focus is on school. At first, I was hyperconcerned with college applications, but now Lennon and I are starting to think about taking a year off between high school and college—a so-called gap year. It would allow me to build my astrophotography portfolio and take a Korean language class at the local community college so I can communicate better with Grandpa Sam. Lennon wants to work full-time and save up some money. He wants us to go backpacking in Europe. I'm definitely amenable to this idea.

We're also talking seriously about trying to hike the Pacific Crest Trail. It's more than twenty-five hundred miles long, running through California, Oregon, and Washington—all the way from Mexico to Canada. It takes six months to hike the entire thing. I'm not sure if I'm up for that just yet—or ever, actually—but if we start next June, we can do part of the trail from the High Sierras up through the Cascade Mountains and stop at the Canadian border.

We'll see. Right now, we've been camping every other weekend. Just short two-night trips—nothing majorly off trail. This weekend, we're going up the coast to Redwood National Park in Humboldt County. I won't lie: Half the fun of camping is the potential for sexlaxation. But I'm actually enjoying being outside, away from the city. Lennon is using his mapping skills to get me to nearby areas with clear night skies; I finally started using my portable telescope to take photos, instead of hauling it around for no good reason.

"I hate to break it to you, but you'll have to get your own cupcakes," Lennon tells his moms. "I have a hot date with an astrophysicist at the Jitterbug."

"That's me," I say, waving my hand. "I'm the hot date."

"Isn't it too late for caffeine?" my mom warns.

"Is it ever?" I ask.

"Herbal tea, please," she says.

"I'll think about it."

"We're actually going there to do homework," Lennon admits. "Decent Wi-Fi and an employee discount are a potent combination."

I started working there part-time after school a couple weeks ago. I practically live there now, but that's okay because (1) I've always loved their coffee, and (2) now I get paid to drink it. I also need all the money I can get, because camping is expensive when you're broke.

"Back by ten," my mom says. "It's a school night."

Lennon salutes her as I tug Andromeda's leash. We tell everyone good night and head out of the shop into night air that's starting to get a little chilly. It feels pretty good, actually, and it's not so brisk that Andromeda minds. We've been walking her several nights a week, and she's perked up considerably, as if she has a new lease on life. And maybe she does. I think she missed walking with Lennon over the last year. My mom says pets can get depressed when their owners do. Or maybe it's just that we see a lot more of Grandma Esther's perky dogs, and Andromeda's had to learn to keep up.

Lennon takes her leash and she trots ahead of us, tail swinging as she scouts our trail. He slings an arm around my shoulder as we saunter to the corner and wait for the streetlight to turn green.

"Okay, milady," Lennon says. "We both know we're not doing homework at the coffee shop."

"I finished mine during fifth period," I confirm.

"Finished mine at work earlier while I cleaned out gecko cages. Multitasking to the rescue."

"We are so good," I say, holding up my hand for a fist bump.

"The best." He knocks knuckles with me, his arm still resting on my shoulder.

Juggling school and work and us hasn't been easy. It helps that we get to eat lunch together every day in the school courtyard. We sit with Avani and her boyfriend, and sometimes Brett, unfortunately. Once he begged Lennon for forgiveness in his part of what's now known as the Battle of Mackenzie Falls, we haven't been able to get rid of him. Reagan, on the other hand, transferred to private school. The official word is that she's no longer focused on the Olympics, so she doesn't need the support of our athletic department. Unofficially, Reagan's parents forced her to transfer after she was busted over the glamping incident.

I wish I could say we made up, but that hasn't happened yet. I'm ready to forgive her, but she has to meet me halfway. The days of me kowtowing are over.

"So where are we headed tonight?" Lennon says. "Mission and Western Avenue, or Mission and Euclid Street?"

We now have four different routes we walk. One is our old path, from when we were kids, and one goes through the farmers' market, which is so deserted at night, it's practically romantic— you'd be surprised what two people with dirty minds can do on bales of hay. Two of the routes go in different directions around the edge of the Bay, but my favorite one snakes through a park, where we can climb a hill and look at the city while sitting under a big old oak tree. It's not dark enough for ideal stargazing, but it's private enough for making out.

Oh, the make-out spots we've discovered. They're on all our routes.

"It's too brisk for the Bay routes," I say. "Andromeda will get fussy."

"We could take Wick Boulevard up through the edge of the warehouse district and cut through to the train tracks up on the hill."

"That sounds suspiciously like a fifth route."

"It does, doesn't it?"

For our one-month anniversary, he made me a picture map. It has all the milestones of our intersecting lives. Where we met. The night we played poker with his dad. Our first fight. Our first kiss. The homecoming debacle. The sequoia cathedral. The night we said *I love you* at the observatory.

A map of us.

It's years in the making, and it's messy and convoluted, some of it even tragic. But I wouldn't change the route, because we walked it together, even when we were apart. And the best part about it is that it's unfinished. Uncertainty isn't always a bad thing. Sometimes it can even be filled with extraordinary potential.

"So what will it be?" he asks when the light turns green. "Old route, or new route?"

"Surprise me," I say.

He smiles down at me, and I thread my fingers through his. We put one foot in front of the other. Clear head, steady steps. And we move forward.

Acknowledgments and Thanks-a-Millions

For their hard work:
Laura Bradford, Taryn Fagerness
Nicole Ellul, Lucy Rogers, Sarah Creech
The entire Simon Pulse and Simon UK teams

For cheerleading:
Karen, Ron, Gregg, Heidi, Hank
Brian, Patsy, Don, Gina, Shane, Seph

For feedback:
Aya Sharif

For inspiration:
Yosemite, Sequoia, and Kings Canyon National Parks
City of Berkeley, California
Nancy Grace Roman, Neil DeGrasse Tyson, Carl Sagan
Tsugumi Ohba, Takeshi Obata
Kimberly Saul

For existing:
Every single librarian
Every single bookseller
And you

RIVETED

BY *simon* teen ♥

BELIEVE IN YOUR SHELF

Visit RivetedLit.com & connect with us on social to:

DISCOVER NEW YA READS

READ BOOKS FOR FREE

DISCUSS YOUR FAVORITES

SHARE YOUR IDEAS

ENTER SWEEPSTAKES FOR THE CHANCE TO WIN BOOKS

Follow @SimonTeen on

to stay up to date with all things Riveted!

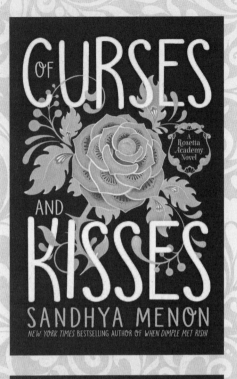
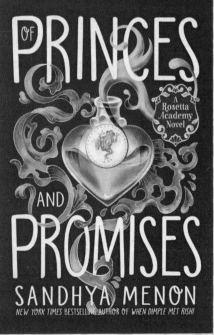

Leap into summer with these

swoon-worthy

reads by *New York Times*
bestselling author Morgan Matson.

"Poignant, timely, and thrilling." —JULIE MURPHY, #1 *New York Times* bestselling author of *Dumplin'*

WE ARE THE
Wildcats

SIOBHAN VIVIAN
NEW YORK TIMES BESTSELLING
AUTHOR OF *THE LIST*

PRINT AND EBOOK EDITIONS AVAILABLE
FROM SIMON & SCHUSTER BFYR
simonandschuster.com/teen